By John Stuart Goldenberg

***Oneiro***
*Book I: Anumen*

***Oneiro***
*Book II: Gauntlet*

***Daughter of Pallas***
*A Tale of Cold War*

John Stuart Goldenberg

# Oneiro II
*Gauntlet*

*To Bill,
With warmest
regards —
JSG
St Paul de Vence
June 2012*

This book is a work of fiction. Many names, characters, places and events are products of the author's imagination, or are used fictitiously.

Copyright © 2010 John Stuart Goldenberg
All rights reserved.

http://www.john-goldenberg.com

ISBN: 1451510675
ISBN-13: 9781451510676

ATSS SA

Cover Photograph Plasma Globe Prototype IV Out Gassing

by Scott Bogard - bogard.110mb.com

For

Sam
Colonel & Paleontologist
Roberta
Teacher & Very Patient



With Sincere Thanks
Mr. Mark Osojnicki (Captain)
Mrs. A. M. Zender

# The *Gauntlet*

<u>Obiter Dictum</u>
<u>Given by</u>
<u>Dr. Chandresh ABHAY, Director</u>
<u>United Nations Extra-Solar Contact-UNESCON</u>
<u>To the</u>
<u>United Nations Security Council-UNSC</u>
<u>In</u>
<u>Extraordinary Secret Session for Heads of State</u>
<u>Venue</u>
<u>Vianden Castle, Luxembourg</u>
<u>Under the Auspices of the</u>
<u>United Nations</u>
<u>And the</u>
<u>Honorable Aoko Itō, United Nations Secretary General-UNSG</u>

# Most Secret

Good morning.

The enclosed excerpt from the germinal QAVL contact message was transmitted eighteen months ago by the QAVL Alpha-Craft in synchronic solar orbit 1,620,000 kilometers distant, specifically directed by a remarkably focused carrier beam to the Proteus Point communications concentrator, coordinates N40 37 43, E25 36 12. Oneiro Island in the **Aegean Archipelago.** Earth.

If you are unfamiliar with this island, that will end today.

As is now well known, the general population of Earth inadvertently, or perhaps vertently gained hitherto restricted knowledge of the events discussed herein and limited familiarity with what we term 'The DOCUMENT'.

This sparked the most widespread outcry in human history. The first truly trans-cultural insurrection. A planet-wide, non-sectarian, non-political, humanist uprising. To date an estimated one-hundred-eighty-seven million people have perished. Property damage is estimated to exceed 69.2 trillion Euros. It is widely held that their wrath, if not their violence, is justified.

Whatever.

This is the most tragic day in human history.

Crusade? Jihad? Lachem-Yamin? Holy War? It is indeed challenging to adequately characterize this extraordinary event. Possibly we must contemplate a new word. For the purpose of this *Obiter Dictum*, I will refer to it as the:

## Ghazi Khan Insurgency

In one respect, the Ghazi Khan Insurgency had a profoundly unifying effect on a major segment of humankind. The final consequence of which will entail decades to fully understand; and may militate to the ultimate benefit of the human race. It is compelling to hope that such horrors may forebear an improved human condition.

Growing pains indeed.

This uprising was not fomented by a charismatic dictator, greed, hate, religion, nationalism, power, or any form of militancy. Instead it was provoked by righteous indignation that a tiny island populated by exceedingly advanced humans, conspired to conceal an historic alien visitation from another world. Moreover, they plotted a mission to the center of our galaxy to meet with representatives of beings representing the pinnacle of cosmic life itself.

That on the one hand.

On the other hand, this body should appreciate the dangerous and complex predicament forced upon Oneiro. Intensive reviews tend to confirm thus far they acted responsibly, and in the best interest of humankind. Their conundrum approached insolubility. If they failed, it is not because they failed to act. They simply failed to act quickly enough. However, even this may not in equity be viewed as negligence, or culpability. In fairness, we have no idea how anybody on this planet could or would react to the same circumstance. We conclude Oneiro deserves our respect and our gratitude. I believe for the first time in human history a worldwide tumult was incited in good faith, for legitimate reasons by all concerned. An ironic tragedy.

There were no malefactors engaged in these extraordinary events. Only two parties keeping faith with their natures, consistent with their beliefs, both confronted by an unprecedented enigma.

The general population's vague awareness of The QAVL DOCUMENT to a large degree prompted commission of this study. The DOCUMENT played a significant role in precipitating events. Therefore The DOCUMENT was brought to the attention of the United Nations Office for Outer Space Affairs (UNOOSA).

Each member has been provided a written pre-briefing prior to this Extraordinary Session and allowed time to submit any questions which may have already arisen.

These will be addressed shortly.

Understandably the highest priority for all member countries is the question of possible threat from the QAVL and the races with which they share common interest. We have received vigorous assurances, in the most detailed and emphatic terms, from all levels of the Oneirion administration attesting the QAVL are benign in the extreme. These arguments are quite compelling. As we are all aware however, this falls far short of the proofs we so urgently require.

Accordingly, Mr. Philip Carr, the Honorable Consul of Oneiro has provided UNOOSA with a set of coordinates. At this locus, Mr. Carr contends we will find (and I quote):

> *Positive, irrefutable and empirical evidence in support of QAVL non-belligerency, proof of their various assertions, and their esteem for humankind.*

Mr. Carr was, and is, totally unaware of what may be found at these coordinates. We dispatched a team of highly qualified expert scientists and engineers. They have carefully excavated at these coordinates with instructions to retrieve this 'evidence' with greatest possible speed, tempered with scientific discipline and rigorously applied paleontological and geological practices. We will present their astonishing discoveries in this afternoon's session.

It is undoubtedly prudent to express concerns about potential alien aggression and to take any precautions available to us. Equally, we risk acting recklessly and quixotically if we fail to realistically recognize QAVLian abilities. We are confronted with immortal, invisible, incorporeal beings that exist upon and control the latent power of the universe. They are a civilization hundreds of millions of years old. They have studied humans since before we could stand truly erect. Theirs is the wisdom of the cosmos; and even if they bear us no ill, they have, they can, and they will stride our Earth with impunity. We are powerless to oppose them and would appear foolish in doing so. Our evaluations indicate an open, welcoming stance is preferable and perhaps the only avenue available to mankind. Perhaps for eons to come. If we as a race survive that long.

Studies of this particular nature are well removed from the charter and the expertise of UNOOSA. Accordingly, a plenary United Nations Agency was authorized, chartered and allocated emergency funding by the UNSC:

## United Nations Extra-Solar Contact (UNESCON)

(a) UNOOSA is now an arm of UNESCON, duly placing this study under their adducement; whereupon UNESCON established an Executive Advisory Commission charged with analyzing the current exigency and formulating strategies for UNSC evaluation. Membership is drawn consistent with the make-up of the Security Council. UNESCON drew upon the expertise of government, educational and private agencies throughout UN membership — far from the least of which were seconded from Oneiro University — during which time we were pleased to welcome Oneiro as the newest member of this community of nations. Oneiro is the only country represented on the UNESCON Advisory Commission, not presently represented on the UNSC. This appointment was made with unanimous sanction of the UNSC

<u>Conclusion:</u> Considering the import and the sensitivity of these and upcoming studies, and the vast long-term implications for mankind; the Committee submits in all deference, the suggestion Oneiro be considered for permanent membership on the UNSC. Moreover, UNESCON nominates the Right Honorable <u>Patron of Oneiro</u> as mankind's first <u>Ambassador Extraordinary and Plenipotentiary</u>, to the QAVL; and further nominates His Honor the <u>Consul of Oneiro</u> as Earth's first <u>Emissary and Special Ambassador</u> to *Kentrikos*.

*Kentrikos,* as we are now aware, is much akin to the UN, drawing its membership from civilizations throughout the Universe. Albeit our mission is to provide aid and promulgate peace on a single planet; theirs is the quest for knowledge throughout the Cosmos. Simply stated, *Kentrikos* is an organization, a planet, a language and a project of vast dimension. *Kentrikos* is to our galaxy what the United Nations represents to our Earth.

(b) The Commission acted to facilitate, collect and compile the results of a massive, highly confidential, worldwide joint project. A complete list of participating agencies is appended to this report.

<u>Conclusion:</u> If man chooses to undertake a true understanding of the DOCUMENT, it would require a human effort dwarfing the Lunar Exploration in the mid second millennium, or the Geo-Fiscal-Reformation initiated in the early third millennium. The complete text of the first message (The DOCUMENT as it has epistemologically evolved to its current state) is appended to this introductory report.

(c) As history reflects, selected passages of the DOCUMENT provoked the Ghazi Khan Insurrection, igniting hundreds of thousands of mujahid. The insurrection erupted first with Muslims in Ghazi Khan, An-Nafūd and SULAWESI. Second with Christians in São Paulo, Belo Horizonte and Corpus Christi. Third with Sikhs in Delhi and finally Hindi in GHUMUSAR UDAYAGIRI. The first purely secular breakout occurred in Tiānjīn, The Peoples Republic of China. With spectacular speed the violence spread worldwide across all religious, political and economic boundaries.

INTERPOL investigations revealed the ignition trigger in these events was unequivocally the ATSILA Missive. The ATSILA Missive will be released to this body in its entirety in the next UNESCON Memorandum scheduled for publication in two months. We believe Aiyana ATSILA was murdered concurrent with circulation of the ATSILA Missive. Although this is as yet, unconfirmed.

Conclusion: UNSC faces no greater risk than the potential mishandling of the DOCUMENT.

(d) Fully cognizant of the appalling nature of this assertion, we nevertheless stipulate our studies ineluctably conclude The DOCUMENT itself harbors the intelligence to self-evolve.

Conclusion: The DOCUMENT should be handled with great care and closely reviewed at frequent intervals to monitor adaptations as they surface. Accordingly, UNESCON produces two hundred hard copies of this DOCUMENT at one hour intervals. Each copy is officially registered, time and date stamped, and physically secured at secret locations.

(e) The team set about to validate this singular assertion. The DOCUMENT was utterly isolated in an appropriate, inactive digital ambiance, equipped with an independent power source and environmental supports. Totally removed from light, sound, radio, vibration, external electricity, radiation, even magnetism. Everything except Earth's gravity and kinetic forces. Lead-lined walls one meter thick, on shock absorbers surrounded by particle wave disrupters, 3.5 kilometers down in the East Rand Mine, South Africa. Total darkness, within and without, in a near perfect vacuum kept as close as possible to a constant Zero Kelvin. The entire configuration was then fully insulated and lowered into 125,500 liters of purified mineral oil. The team carefully monitored for neutrinos, quarks, in fact any sub-atomic particle passage, during the test period. None were recorded during the test period. Which is not to say no particles penetrated the tank. We are capable neither of blocking, nor reliably recording the track of such particles. A lead shield one kilometer in thickness would have negligible effect at best. Therefore results (positive or negative) derived from our tank may be discounted as categorically unreliable. Nonetheless it represents every conceivable effort currently available to our science.

Conclusion: We cannot stipulate the manner in which the DOCUMENT communicates; nor can we stipulate with any assurance the DOCUMENT does in fact communicate. If it does communicate, it does so using astonishing technology. If it does not communicate with any outside source, the implications are truly profound, beggaring any extant science available to mankind.

(f) An elaborate, covert, credible and totally specious, mock invasion of Oneiro was then staged. The objective being to deceive the DOCUMENT into revealing the consecution of the 'invasion' in subsequent versions. Notwithstanding its isolation, the DOCUMENT continued to evolve and did make a minor tongue-in-cheek allusion to human game-playing (Ref: Extract, Paragraph 1. Line 5. "…charades with such colorful constructs." Extant only in release 45.25.1B34 and subsequent.). Previous paper copies remained unchanged. The QAVL have apparently mastered the technology to literally implant sapient entities into an automated document. Sapience with formidable capabilities.

Conclusion: We are unable to isolate The DOCUMENT. We are unable to comprehend The DOCUMENT.

(g) This study spanned months. Some of the most turbulent in human history. This provided fertile ground for analytical comparison of document releases as occurrences transpired. Calamitous events would transpire somewhere on Earth and would be reflected in the DOCUMENT. On occasion, the DOCUMENT would reflect changes _prior_ to such events. Reaction? Provocation? Projection? Prescience? All of the above? None of the above? An impenetrable enigma thus far.

Conclusion: Something totally unknown resides within the DOCUMENT.

(h) It may be centuries before mankind fully understands the mechanism at work here. It appears a profoundly intelligent construct is steganography imbedded in the DOCUMENT itself. This entity is capable of information gathering and formulation of logical and intuitive illative in sophisticated, narrative English prose. The QAVL exhibit what appears to be absolute trust in this entity; evidenced by leaving it to act independently here on Earth. These are chilling accomplishments when compared with our own modest abilities to insert comparatively mindless AI, viral and neural objects into automated media.

Conclusion: An autonomous presence possessing formidable powers undoubtedly resides within the DOCUMENT.

(i) Current studies indicate there exist, on average, 634 digital documents for every human on Earth. Moreover, all significant human historical, scientific, artistic, political, philosophic, administrative, economic, martial and defensive erudition has been invested in digital documentation. We estimate this equates to roughly fifty-five trillion five hundred and eighty-nine billion documents.

Studies further conject the sort of countenance steganographically obscured within the DOCUMENT could easily propagate itself through Earth's digi-verse at astonishing speed. Conceivably more than fifty-five trillion five hundred and eighty-nine billion sentient entities may now reside amongst us. Totally undetectable. Beyond our comprehension. Beyond our control. In possession of all knowledge. Able to manipulate all knowledge. All automated communications. In a real sense, masters of our reality. Our past. Our future. Perhaps these beings are united in a kind of emergence? Perhaps they have a leader? Perhaps they operate in total independence? Are they a permanent element in our world? Or are they here for a finite mission? Do they wish only to know us better? To aid us? To control us? Do they exist at all? Unknown. These conjecture, and far more, are categorically unconfirmed.

One of the dangers of information automation is the potential entrapment of humans into believing whatever is presented by such technology as irrefutable fact. Consider contemporary youth, unable or unwilling to perform mental calculations, accepting results of an adding machine without question. Right or wrong. Unable to even apply credibility evaluation within tolerances. Now expand this problem by a factor of trillions upon trillions. You now have some idea of the potential magnitude of this problem. Human reality itself can be called into question.

Conclusion: The DOCUMENT may saturate and perhaps even control our world. UNESCON sub-Director, Dr. Leyland Harman conjectures The DOCUMENT is attempting to establish a heuristic relationship with mankind. Assuming we are engaged in this sort of interplay with the DOCUMENT; as we err, the DOCUMENT points it out and discourages further actions of such nature. As we advance, the DOCUMENT exhorts us to pursue subject behavior.

(j) Dr. Harman further speculates the DOCUMENT may expand to extraordinary proportions. It would then persistently dwindle as the dialogue evolves—as alternatives are selected—as options are progressively excluded. As a definitive course is established.

Conclusion: One day, perhaps centuries from now, the DOCUMENT may have been distilled down to only one of two words. Two alternatively plausible, entirely disparate conclusions:

Conclusion 1)  *ATTAINMENT*
Conclusion 2)  *ANNIHILATION*

(k) The appended excerpt from the QAVL preliminary contact dossier seems to reflect a genuine affection for humans, as well as honesty, even a degree of playfulness; all couched in an empathetic and ostensibly straightforward candor.

Conclusion: We hope this is truly the case. There appears precious little we can do in any event.

(o) The second and final transmission consists of some 12,000,000 pages in two parts.

Conclusion: Any risks or perplexity currently presented by The DOCUMENT will soon be exponentially compounded. The unmanageable will quickly approach the unimaginable. If we wish to stop this process, we should re-consider our motivations. If we move to block these transmissions, we should ourselves be blocked. The DOCUMENT is only one of the smaller, more trivial wonders forthcoming from the QAVL. Our door is now open; and we neither opened it, nor have the ability to close it.
Scant months ago we lived on Planet Earth in isolation, and this gathering ruled our world.
We now inhabit the cosmos; and we await exordium from the supreme rulers.

(p) Extract (Release 45.25.1B34). I would share this brief extract with you:

*...We suspect your unique propensity for language is one key to your dramatic accession. As our communications of images and concepts is not based*

in propagation of gaseous wave resonance, we greatly enjoy the depth of your linguistic varieties. True art forms. So many languages. Subtle nuances. Exquisite modulation of wave generation. Many ways to say the same thing. Such beauty. Horrific and grotesque as well. You create things that do not exist. Yet you value truth. You love it. You devote your lives pursuing it. It ennobles you and emancipates you. Yet you lie with remarkable alacrity. You produce charades with such colorful constructs.

Love. Hate. Fear. Courage. Cowardice. Greed. Loneliness. Selfishness. Selflessness. Lust. Mercy. Near infinite spectra of emotions and concepts.

From your language flows your art. Literature, music, painting, sculpture and much more of great meaning and great beauty.

And great foulness. Consider the words of your Camir Rouge. Cambodia. A savage war:

To preserve you is no gain.
To destroy you is no loss.
Beware such words. Their bestial hubris can echo for eons.

Words bind you together.
They isolate you.
They fire your imagination. They shackle your mind. They enable your mind and limit your conceptions and understanding.
They make you well and drive you insane.
You cannot live without them. But we fear they may ultimately destroy you. Such enigmatic contraction. Such antonymic polarity leaches into your other arts as well, unfortunately.

Taboo words. The names of those things you most prize describing those things you most execrate. Obscenities. Insults. Racial epithets. "Dirty" words. "Dirty" talk. Vitiation of physical love, gentle pleasures, religious credos, ancestry and Earth fauna into something base and vulgar. Progenitors of shame, guilt and brooding, deeply disturbing anxieties. At times flamboyantly blithe, resplendent in a matrix of ludicrous counterpointal, puritanical infecundity. Amazing. Ironically amusing and perversely tragic.

Man should be proud.
Man should be ashamed
One word singularly attracts us: Gauntlet

This word is rich in meanings for us. A hybrid derivative of your old Norske, Swedish, Old English and Frankish. It conveys a bounty of meanings and interpretations:

- *The Coming Together of Paths*
- *Something that Protects*
- *A Challenge*

- *A Punishment*
- *A Ceremony of Passage*
- *A Trapping of War*

*The word Gauntlet eloquently characterizes our message.*

*There is a roiling darkness on Earth's horizon. Roughly one hundred kilometers distant. To the east. Just at night's ebb. It is there. Man cannot quite penetrate its wraithlike portent.*

*In a watch unchanged in millennia, as man has advanced on a thousand fields of combat, bundled in fear, embracing his weapon, exhaling frosty vapor in the chill half-light, heart pounding out the reassurance his spark still burns....Homo Sapient Habilis warily awaits the dawn.*

*The dawn of death, or life?*

*Is the black terminator between earth and sky fashioned from the smoke of burning flesh, and the stench of decay and blood?*

*Or does it nurture the emerging bloom that flourishes in the abrupt semi-darkness. It intensifies and sharpens as your star's terminator passes over...a mute fire racing at more than 1.3 times the speed of sound...a fleeting heartbeat in advance of a brilliant sunrise? A resplendent, nescient day?*

*Shadows or splendor? Elysium or Perdition?*

*After 2,000,000 solar years, the QAVL wish you to succeed. To survive. To assume your place in cosmic sentience.*

*Our concluding communication will commence in 24.6 hours. Please ensure adequate recording media is active. These communications will approximate 12,000,000 of your pages, involving several months of transmission.*

*Compliments to Oneiro. Greetings to Earth. Greetings from the QAVL.*

*The Gauntlet is extended...in amity.*

*Stand by.*

It is clear how an excerpt of this nature might foster a not altogether unjustified frenzy throughout humanity. We have no more pressing priority than formulation of a tactical and strategic plan for pacifying and subduing this situation. Any questions are welcome. Any suggestions are desperately needed.

We have already received some questions from our members we would like to share and jointly confront in the context of this opening Obiter Dictum:

<u>Question:</u> Can The DOCUMENT be partially or totally disabled or destroyed?

Response: Unknown.

If only one DOCUMENT exists we are extremely loath to tamper with such technology. Although we have carefully run some experiments in this direction. If over six trillion exist. If all human knowledge in digital form has been saturated. Destruction is categorically impossible.

Question: If The DOCUMENT can be destroyed, would this constitute murder, or digi-cide, or whatever term may apply?
Response: Unknown.

There is little doubt it would embody the act of extirpation of a sentient essence. An act much akin to murder. It is entirely possible as well, the QAVL might consider this a hostile act.

Question: Have the QAVL been confronted with these issues?
Response: Yes.

They candidly stipulate this is the universal digi-gnomic medium employed by all *Kentrikos* information retention technology. Our experts from Oneiro inform us very little, if any, information technology is needed by the QAVL. Total, limitless recall being congenital to their race.

Question: Has the UNESCON Commission attempted to methodically dissect the DOCUMENT? Disassemble the DOCUMENT piece-by-piece, down to the most granular, meaningful level.
Response: Yes.

The most granular constituent is comprised of a single alpha, numeric, or symbolic digit. In response to electronic vivisection The DOCUMENT restores itself instantaneously.

Question: Have you attempted to reproduce The DOCUMENT?
Response: Yes.

We have experimented with copying the file to another media and re-indexing. A simple procedure. One of the oldest in runtime information technology. The DOCUMENT will not permit this action. We have attempted this thousands of times. Totally impossible. The duplicated file simply disappears at the moment any part of it is written to its new environment. No trace. No history. No footprint whatsoever.

Question: Can you estimate when you will have achieved a working technical knowledge of The DOCUMENT?
Response: No.

Question: Do you have any further means at your disposal to secure and isolate The DOCUMENT?
Response: No.

Question: Do you have any means of quantifying the probable intelligence resident in The DOCUMENT?
Response: No.

Question: At this time would you recommend generally releasing further elements to, or later releases of The DOCUMENT?
Response: No.

The great risk inherent in withholding should not be discounted. The Ghazi Khan Insurrection has demonstrated relentless pursuit of their not unjustified beliefs; and the Committee perceives no change forthcoming in the foreseeable future. The Ghazi Khan rage was an understandable reaction to exclusion from knowledge relevant to every human on this planet.

Dr. ABHAY looked up. "Speaking personally, I vividly recall the anger I felt when briefed on existence of The DOCUMENT and by association, the QAVL, *Kosmas Antiaô* and it concomitant, nihilistic portrayal of the Universe.

Despite its inherent inequity, we strongly recommend a policy of withholding new releases of the DOCUMENT until fully understood. Conceivably this could delay new releases for an indefinite period.

If ever.

# Wrap Up

The two men left the building through the main entrance, out the portico and down the long circular access drive. Windy and gray. They buttoned up their coats, pulled down their hats and pushed up their collars. They seldom left via the Diplomatic Entrance. Too many tourists and reporters. Far more worrisome though was the intense scrutiny of 'diplomatic delegations'. Innocuous and always present. Hovering at the doors. Probing eyes heedless of nothing.

In fact the men seldom left the building together. Their backgrounds and allegiances prohibitively diverse. Therefore, open affinity was to be avoided. Today however, all their normal, more discrete means of egress were jammed with UN delegates equally anxious to review the mornings events. So they departed, reasonably unnoticed by the 'front door'.

They hurriedly walked. And hurriedly talked. The shorter Ajisaka was slightly pressed to keep up.

"You knew about this. Didn't you Gregory?"

Gregory favored Ajisaka with an enigmatic grin. His expression suffused with something of the owl, and something of the wolf.

"Well?"

"Ajisaka, were you forewarned last April when your navy engaged and sunk the Filipino research vessels *Agbayani* and *Tagalog*? It was a carefully planned and well executed attack. I believe we both happened to attend a reception hosted by the French embassy in Washington that night?"

Ajisaka peered up at his colleague in unconcealed annoyance. After some acerbic rumination, punctuated with sporadic ticks and teeth grinding, he replied.

"Gregory. Both you and I have been delegates to this august body for nearly twenty years.

I hold advanced degrees and commendations from organizations and governments girdling the world. I am well acquainted with nearly every senior delegate on the floor of the UN General Assembly. I am widely published. I have been considered for a Nobel Peace Prize."

"Really? I'm impressed."

Exasperated. "*You* told me about the nomination Gregory."

"Oh. Right."

He continued. "You on the other hand, are famous for marathon drinking, brawling, colorful language, and chasing anything jiggling about in a skirt.

Your temper is the stuff of legend. You grew up on potatoes and Kalashnikovs; and you have the mind-set, manners and education of a coal miner. You quite literally fought and killed your way up to the Dip-Corps.

So why...*why* do many of the most important personages on this planet entrust you with the darkest, most dangerous secrets on Earth, while I fecklessly bumble from meeting to meeting, utterly unaware of impending catastrophe?"

Gregory's lips pursed and un-pursed in a manner Ajisaka found very irritating. Gregory was vainly attempting to simultaneously contain his laughter, and bestow a warm smile on his longtime friend.

They found their way to the warmth of the restaurant. When they were seated and had ordered drinks, Gregory grew serious. "You're not going to like the answer Ajisaka."

"I didn't like the damned *question*." Ajisaka rarely resorted to profanity, so Gregory was mildly surprised.

Gregory took a deep breath. Once seated and ordered, he continued.

"On an interpersonal level, people will confide in anyone they deem trustworthy and sympathetic. When diplomacy, or power, or sometimes great danger are at stake, commitment of trust takes on a profoundly different aspect. Instead of soliciting sympathy, or perhaps even trust, people seek out strength, and...well...tallness."

"*What?*"

"Don't take this personally. It's just human nature. I'm tall. You're short. I'm physically imposing. You are not. Such people do not share confidences looking for advice or commiseration. They want recognition. They want *protection*. Or at least the illusion of protection. Physically, economically, militarily and diplomatically. Whether such protections may be forthcoming, or not. Whether or not such protections are simply illusion. This is not logic. This is emotion. Sadly, the human body politic behaves in exactly the same manner. Do you understand Ajisaka?"

Ajisaka had been leaning over the table perched on elbows, tapping his swizzle stick. He sighed, put down the stick, and lent back in his chair. "Gregory, you are wise beyond your potatoes and anthracite and bullets. Let's move on to something productive."

"Agreed."

"What is the real implication of this Oneiro matter?"

"We are in very, *very* deep trouble. How familiar are you with eschatology?"

"The study of human excrement?"

"No Ajisaka. That would be *scatology*. Eschatology is a philosophical approach to theology dealing with the end of our world. This is close to the nature of our troubles. The 'End of Days' type trouble. Apocalypticism."

"Such esoteric eloquence from a man made of potatoes with coal dust under his nails." Quipped Ajisaka good naturedly.

Gregory's voice raised almost unnoticeably and took on a gnarring quality "I'm serious Ajisaka. We are about to entomb ourselves in carnage that will engulf the world. And we've forfeited our power to influence events."

"And *who* has this power?"

"Forgive my melodrama Ajisaka, but as Mr. William Shakespeare so elegantly described it, power has been seized by the *Jaws of Darkness.*"

# ANUMEN

*...that Man, for example, ceasing imperceptibly to feel himself Man, will at length attain that awfully triumphant epoch...In the meantime bear in mind that all is Life –Life –Life within Life –the less within the greater, and all within the Spirit Divine.*

*<u>Eureka</u>*
*Edgar Allan Poe*

Oneiro is a beautiful, remote island in the Aegean Archipelago. Resplendent reclusion at the confluence of the Mediterranean, Ionian and Aegean Seas.

The rugged island rises dramatically. Straight from the sea. A lofty, water-bound highland, enshrouded by sun-bleached limestone cliffs hundreds of meters high...rimmed by immaculate beaches, culminating in a natural underground harbor of enormous proportion.

Two hundred kilometers to the south lies its nearest neighbor, the Greek island of Lefkada. Amongst the more than 1,400 islands in the archipelago, the vast majority are uninhabited. Standing high and alone in splendid isolation, Oneiro is perfectly suited to its distinctive purpose.

Oneiro was developed specifically to home a lavishly funded University and its laboratories. A University unique in human history. Staffed with exhaustively vetted experts. Drawn from all academic disciplines. United in the single-minded pursuit to actualize human...ANUMEN. 1/

The Founders, Faculty and Students of Oneiro believe the achievement and amelioration of human ANUMEN equates to no less than survival of the human species itself. A species purged of its inherent self-destruction, capable of adaptation and survival on a celestial scale. Their ultimate goal:

A human genus no less immortal
than the heavens themselves.

| *ANUMEN* | | |
|---|---|---|
| *Anomalous* | *(Greek: anómalos)* | *Unexpected Deviation* |
| *Numen* | *(Latin: nūmen)* | *Power, Spirit* |
| *ANUMEN* | *(Concatenation)* | *Unexpected Power* |
| *ANUMINA* | *(Plural Concatenation)* | *Unexpected Powers* |
| *ANUMINOUS* | *(Greek: aithérios)* | *Aethereal NUMEN* |

They began to succeed. They began to exceed.

Oneiro is now an independent Micro-nation. It boasts its own Flag, Constitution, Chief Executive, National Bank, Inter-Nation Recognition, and possibly the most advanced and deadly defensive systems on Earth. Oneiro specializes in the most exotic, world-transforming Exports in human history, having no appreciable Imports. Its current population amounts to roughly 24,000 souls. This population (graduates, undergraduates and cadre) constitute the wealthiest, best educated, physically and mentally gifted population in all of contemporary man's 160,000 years.

In terms of evolution – predicated on inception series – Oneirons are estimated at sixty thousand, to four-hundred and fifty thousand years advanced beyond Earth's anthropic populace.

Phenomenal leaps in evolution have revealed themselves in exceptional manifestations of ANUMINA; and Oneirons are only beginning to plumb their limits. A complex evolution as their native ANUMINA evolves and expands at near geometric rates.

At any given time, roughly half the population of Oneiro lives and works on assignment away from their island home. In fact there is hardly a country or geographic region on Earth not supported by covert or overt representatives of Oneiro. Far from tourists, these envoys hold exceptionally influential positions in industry, government, the military, academia, the arts, sciences… in fact, nearly every consequential aspect of human enterprise.

Not sedition. Not insurgency. Not treachery or subversion. Their commission is strikingly synonymous with the deployment of antibodies to defend their host's body from disease or harm…and from itself.

Food, energy, information, pharmaceuticals, raw materials and a wealth of new products freely introduced to an eager world. Enlightenment spreads as a natural byproduct of food dissemination. Subtle, methodical, gentle, benign. A new order. Hitherto unknown on planet Earth. The dawn of robust, global sapience.

In terms of world awareness: Process unknown. Source unknown. Cause unknown. Objective unknown. No identifiable leader. No histrionic charismatic messiah. A mystifying, benevolent silence. A mute, impalpable reformation. Indefinable and reserved from within.

Disease, overpopulation, hate, war, terror, poverty and the specter of violent, futile death, serenely, relentlessly, imperceptivity ebbs from mankind's tableau.

The overriding problem: Oneiro can assist, even instigate this process. However, Oneiro can take mankind only to the path. Realization demands at some point humans assume ascendancy of this process and commit themselves to its fruition. This may not occur. Or tragically, it may not occur at a rate sufficient to overtake extinction.

Their power and wealth slipping away, leviathans of industry, government and religion erupted in outrage, smoldering ire, and caustic frustration. Of greatest exasperation, there was no distinguishable cause, or identifiable entity to condemn or attack. No defense or offense against a phantom specter. Dressed for the kill and nothing to exterminate.

No sanctioned target. No target at all.

Inevitably they would identify their nemesis. And they would strike out with a murderous vehemence.

Meanwhile, Earth was a happier, safer, more prosperous…somewhat bewildered world. Even some sea creatures were behaving bizarrely. Despite their widespread improved quality of life, many cultures found this new world immensely unsettling. Unable to adjust. A world of staggering contradictions. A fragile time of precarious transition.

Oneiro was founded decades ago by Dr. Craig Webber. A brilliant scientist. He sought an obscure retreat for his studies in human development. He devoted the majority of his energies, personal fortune, and ultimately his life to the project. His plan and his vision were straightforward. Create an environment where his team could freely advance human development through a process he innovated and designated:

## *Compression*

Webber subjected the female blastiocyst to profound evolitive tension through augmentation six days subsequent to manipulated fertilization, and subjecting it to repetitive accretionary washes. This allowed him to compress the years comprising generations into days, ultimately even hours. Moreover he was able to incorporate, with absolute mathematical equity and precision, all extant races of contemporary man. A stunning achievement in congenital eugenics. An absolute abjuration of genetic bigotry. Unequivocal validation of his genius and vision.

It was his hope such an advanced and enriched Homo sapiens would demonstrate superior abilities. The ability to quite literally survive the ages. Abilities he termed ANUMINA.

Indications thus far: He was correct.

The products of compressed inheritance demonstrated talents far in excess of his dreams. Although they were not the powers (as Webber himself often stated) of the "superhero-comic-book-sideshow-freak-variety". No comic-book style flying, levitation, telepaths, or any other costumed frivolity. ANUMEN was far more subtle, useful, creative, and intelligent and – under the rigorous control of Oneirons.

The scientific iterations requisite to developing ANUMEN in humans generated a wealth of byproduct learning and expertise. Knowledge could be passed through the ingestion of food. Art could be produced so compelling it had the power to overwhelm the mind. Even kill. Genetics was discovered as the repository of human language. Actually all language. Language was recognized as the cosmic denominator of sapience. Communications with selected sea creatures became viable. Food and energy could be produced without harmful byproduct or excessive consumption, using simple sea water as it prime ingredient.

With each achievement, each breakthrough in language, art, science, music, food, communications, the Oneirons found themselves immersed evermore profoundly within their deep sub-molecular essence.

Oneirons ultimately suspected such imponderable micro-corporeality held the great common anima mundi, the great anima universitas of the cosmos themselves. The infinite linkage. Creation's awareness. They were right.

Oneiro became the center of the Earth. Earth's Incipient Isle.

Then with a simple radio signal. 1,620,000 kilometers distant. A race who called themselves the QAVL. They had maintained a synchronous solar elliptic relative to planet Earth for some 2,000,000 solar years. Time and location having quite literally no import for the QAVL, they were content to hold their position for an indefinite period, studying Earth life forms, among their other pursuits. This is a service they have maintained at millions of planets for millions of years. Invariably they await one prime event: The achievement by any indigenous life-form of the cosmic language: *Kosmas*

Oneirons succeeded in this as well.

Oneiro, thereby Earth, became the newest constituent of a transcendent consciousness, as boundless as the universe itself.

There was much to learn…much to do. Perhaps danger. Primarily from Earth. A vast journey. An infinite voyage without desuetude.

The ascension of humankind to universal congress.

# 0618 Thursday: The Aegean Sea

The sun burst into the sea and onto the sky. From horizon to horizon, a vast fiery liquid of gleaming red and ochre coalescing with an endless sky of blue and amethyst. Finally a single disc of blinding platinum…greater and higher every moment.

No other boats. No islands. No one on deck. No clouds. Not even birds. Only the sea, the sky, and a warm breeze lightly from the southwest. For the moment Philip Carr was as alone as any human on Earth. And not lonely in the least.

With each succeeding sunrise he yearned more for the solitude beneath the desert sea. His alone for a brief time. He ached to see the sunrise from below. A faithful mirror of the sun's unending movement and ever changing hues filtering down from above.

A smooth jump from the fantail. A booming plunge into the waves encased by frothy bubbles. Into the cool blue shadows below.

Phil descended un-encumbered by air tanks, fins, mask, snorkel, or swim suit. No gear whatsoever. His body could ill afford any area unexposed to the life giving sea. Even his eyes had learned to compensate for water distortions. He required no mask or goggles. Over the years this sea had become his collateral home, above and below. He needed no breathing equipment. Or protection. He could remain down for astounding periods of time. Perhaps indefinitely. He could achieve depths confined only by his current preference for shallower warmer waters, hovering above the cold and gloom of the deep.

He had given some thought to the mechanisms involved. Certain amphibians, some rare frogs in Borneo, a few salamanders and such, literally had no lungs, absorbing oxygen directly through their skin. They survived based on naturally reduced metabolic rates which helped sustain them when oxygen was absorbed through passive respiration. In or out of the water. Phil accomplished this using both his voluntary and autonomic nervous systems to lower his metabolism and to concentrate specialized fats in his dermal areas. This served to insulate him and aid in gas exchanges. How had he learned to do this? He had no idea.

Neither the sea, nor its creatures augured danger for Phil. Nor they of him. A playful nudge, perhaps a meaningful punch, or even just a quick turn, and even the largest predators became docile, or at least disinterested. He couldn't be surprised. Impervious to attack from above, below or behind. Somehow he always knew when there was a hunter about. Some slight change in the water and its creatures perhaps. Perhaps the same way the jungle reacts to a prowling beast.

At the turn of the last century, the Mediterranean had supported the largest population of White Sharks in the world. Human predation had decimated their ranks. Still they remain. Along with rays, many other sharks, octopus, squid, whales and an endless variety of fish. Phil was now a native to a diverse sub-marine community. Had he the time and inclination, he had no doubt he was capable of swimming back to Oneiro by himself, under the sea or on the surface. Not rapidly necessarily. But relentlessly.

This morning his dive was limited to about forty minutes. Disappointingly short. Their commitments demanded they cast off early for Oneiro. Fascinating things were always taking place on Oneiro. According to Mike Auslander (the island's current Patron) something special was in the works. There had been an excitement in Mike's voice last night not even the raspy radio transmissions could conceal.

When their island assumed micro-nation status, Phil was Oneiro's founding Proprietor, some five years ago. Nearly the instant Phil was convinced Oneiro had stabilized to the degree it was self sufficient and capable of defending itself, he turned the Patronship over to Mike Auslander (a island born and educated Oneirion) and literally fled to the sea. He would never admit it, even to himself, but he had already crossed the fine line into an acute stress disorder. The last years had been far more traumatic that Phil recognized. He had become numb and detached. Things (understandably) had become surreal. His phenomenal mind suffered periods of forgetfulness, or he was plagued with flashbacks. Horrible memories that refused his fervent assignment to an inactive file. And he was seriously depressed. Although he refused to admit his disease, he did admit the price. He had to get away. He desperately need time. Then Aliens appeared on Oneiro. But aliens or not, he had to heal before facing this next great challenge.

In point of fact, Phil had found the QAVL rather anticlimactic. He couldn't speak with them. Couldn't see them. As mild and diffident as a schoolmarm. Not the awesome celestial super-beings he might have conjured. The QAVL were the most cerebral of space invaders. No sizzle. No rockets and ray-guns, or even lipid beguiling eyes and graceful, hairless, tapering limbs. Instead there were millions of pages of exceptionally complex data to struggle through, and unrivaled communications to overcome. It would be a long, arduous task before really viable contact was established.

All-in-all, Phil was quietly relieved to escape the island for a time.

In point of fact Phil owned Oneiro. He had inherited the island, and a fortune, from Dr. Craig Webber. Webber's sole heir. Though he never exerted any form of ownership prerogative, he did continue to take great interest in Oneiro's progress and was called back to the island frequently. In the last few months, such calls had been frequent to the degree he seldom ventured too far on his boat, the *Sea Tigress*. Tigress was a state-of-the-art, luxury, commercial fishing vessel. In recent months though, Phil and crew had confined themselves to sea studies and simply roaming the seas and its endless coastline. Shores and bays, dramatic rocky points, and countless ports and islands.

Phil quickly descended to thirty meters and came to a restful stop. Dancing in weightless grace high above the darkness below. With subtle oscillations of hands and feet he maintained station-keeping. His field of vision a slowly rotating 360°.

As he leisurely wheeled in the crystal water, his observable respiration was of course, non-existent. His passive respiration was equally imperceptible. He exchanged gasses internally, autonomously manipulating the air in his lungs and circulatory systems to equalize and optimize oxygen consumption. He even did a bit of re-breathing. Soon he would be filling his lungs with seawater to further expand his oxygen exchange efficiency. After some practice he would learn how to exit the water directly, hand-standing to drain the water from his lungs. He was well along in his amphibiancy. Any cell of every corpus codified to replicate the gnomic of any cell of any other corpus. Essentially a question of interpretation and manipulation. Phil's corpus was learning to respond to that question. With dazzling speed.

Phil was one of about ten percent of humans with accessory spleens. Somehow his normally superfluous organ had adapted itself to the function of *scrubbing* erythrocytes, his red blood cells (removing Nitrogen and $CO_2$). The spleen's normal task is the destruction of spent cells. This was a spectacular departure for this gratuitous bio-structure. His heart and metabolic rates dramatically declined; and subtle variations in his vascular pressure provoked integumentary diffusion of hemoglobin.

His body then initiated a unique process. A novel variation of self-synthesis of ethanol. Normally involving an anaerobic process. His cellular messenger Ribonucleic Acid (mRNA) bonded elements such as carbon-monoxide and hydrogen, producing L-lactate dehydrogenase from Thermoanaerobacterium Saccharolyticum.

This prevented an accumulated oxygen debt, and dangerously high levels of lactic acid in his blood. In return Phil's body rewarded him with a light *cocktail* of acetic acid and ethanol. The acetic acid was eliminated via his sweat glands, imparting him with musky, spicy pheromones for an hour or so after diving. Phil was invariably amused by feminine reactions to his proximity during these periods. The ethanol was processed normally in Phil's blood, lending his mood a slight euphoria. All in all, quite an equitable bio-chemical barter.

This process also provoked production of 2-nonenal and certain lipid peroxides, all of which accelerated oxidation and vascular permeabilization. These had the effect of improving overall process efficiency while generating beneficial Omega-3 oils. Good for the heart, lacing his already rich phernomes with a robust underlying pungency.

Concurrently, his blood commenced accretion of Fatty Acid Ethyl Esters, or FAEEs, at the surface of his skin. Toxic in high concentrations. Often a byproduct of alcohol abuse. In this case, FAEEs actually fostered the interaction between Phil's red blood cells and sea water via his epidermal capillaries. This in turn forwarded the exchange of oxygen-nitrogen molecules with waste carbon dioxide and nitrogen. This process was augmented by his eccrine sweat glands, as well as his Excretory System. Intuitively, Phil always drank generous amounts of water before diving. His entire body was rendered a massive…if comparatively inefficient…gill.

Phil had no idea how his body acquired these anomalous capabilities. At his instigation, Oneiro University had run many tests. Analyzed the bodily processes in detail. Mapped out every step. A Doctor John Marlowe, a gifted biochemist out of Johns Hopkins, headed the analytical team. His unofficial and extemporaneous reaction to their findings and conclusions:

*Such sequences are absolutely ridiculous in their entirety. Nothing remotely related to science, rational biology, or bio-chemistry. Among other divarication, Esters cannot accrete in sufficient concentration to support significant oxygenation. This is processing gobblygook. Bio-babble. The stuff of witchdoctors.*

Nonetheless, there is was. Here he was. Tens of meters submerged. No ancillary breathing support whatsoever. Clearly, further study was required. To conduct such investigations, Oneiro University was the best qualified in the world. Phil had no doubt they, or he, would ultimately understand the mechanisms at work.

As always under the sea, his mind relaxed and he started to mentally drift.

Today was his birthday. Philip Webber-Carr. Phil had added the Webber after Phil had learned of his true heritage and Dr. Webber's savage murder.

Hidden away in the Maryland countryside, in Dr. Craig Webber's private laboratory, forty-five years earlier, June 12th at 11:38 am. Phil was delicately liberated from his embryonic membrane. An Extra-low voltage (ELV) emitter coaxed an insensate aquatic embryo into making the dramatic graduation to air breathing, human, male infant. Aerobic life.

All relevant records reflected Philip entered the world at George Washington University Medical Center. Birth certificate and all. A healthy young baby boy. Philip. 2.94 kilograms. Newborn son to proud parents–lifelong friends of Dr. Webber–Stuart and Diana Carr. Ostensibly a flawless, natural childbirth.

So stipulated the records. Phil himself would unquestionably take this for granted for the next thirty-nine years.

In point of fact, Phil had absolutely no specifically identifiable mother or father. He was conceived as the deftro-type of a bio-genesis experiment conducted by Dr. Webber. The proto-type had been his elder brother Michael.

Emotionally he had two fathers and one mother. All dead now. So in reality he was the purest possible acquittance of orphan. He had no parents. Neither legally, nor emotionally, nor biologically. In human history there never had been an orphan quite as 'orphanized' as Philip Carr.

Phil was well equipped to confront this reality. As were 24,000 of his fellow Oneirion 'orphans'.

His unique ancestry placed him many thousands of years advanced from contemporary humans. Comparative with native Oneirions however, Phil was a genetic primitive. Just touching down to *terra firma,* completing his first prodigious leap from the trees.

Strangely though, he demonstrated strengths unique even on Oneiro. His prowess in water was without peer. His physical powers were beginning to approach those of the Oneirons, albeit somewhat longer to fruition. Far more profound than any other singularity was his…insight. He could recall information to which he had never been exposed. He could instantly understand, analyze and unravel exceedingly complex problems. He could correlate labyrinths of complex variables, detect subtle patterns…unswervingly predict the next action…formulate a plan of action. Make decisions and visualize unfolding scenarios dynamically, with astounding acuity.

He was sure this was nothing paranormal, or even mystical. Supra-natural? *No*. Preter-natural? *He wasn't even sure what these terms meant*. Nonetheless, thus equipped, his command and leadership skills were formidable indeed. Hannibal, Alexander, Cesar, Attila, Napoleon, Rommel. The envy of all.

From whence came such knowledge? The beginning of a solution was forming. An unimaginably vast repository of knowledge. Duplicated one-hundred-trillion times. *Little did he know, or even suspect*. Every cell in his body? Could be. DNA? Something smaller. Much smaller.

Human DNA, by and large, has surprisingly little to do with humans. With what they are. How to build them. Predominantly it consists of the leftovers of billions of years of evolitive life. Well over half the DNA in a human cell. Does it contain knowledge? Anything of value? Probably not much. Perhaps it could be a fascinating paleontological history were it an interpretable chronology. In fact it has been given the ignominious name *Parasitic DNA*. Junk DNA. Even Junk RNA. Purportedly a roadmap to nowhere. Probably a roadmap to the remote past. The future as well?

Phil brought his slow rotation to a stop. He hung perfectly still in the water. DNA …Deoxyribonucleic Acid… RNA…Ribonucleic Acid**…**

He remained in frozen suspension for ten minutes totally lost in concentration. Eyes closed head down. No longer aware of the water. Or any ambience. He could actually *see* the answer. *Not DNA. Not RNA. Smaller. Infinitely smaller. Where is the source? What is the source? The repository for* όλα. Ola. Everything. All?

His time was running out.

He was due to surface soon.

They were waiting for him. Yet he couldn't lose this moment. This insight.

*Think. Concentrate. Make it pass.*

Five minutes. Ten.

The lifting of a great weight. A dark room suddenly alight.

Finally. Illumination. A wraith smile slowly dawning.

*Of course*.

# Quantum Cue Shot

The answer was unsettlingly obvious. It was simply deeper. Much deeper. Smaller. Infinitely tiny. It came to him quickly. It had always been there. Been there longer than he could possibly conceive.

Did it come from the stuff of sub-atomic astrophysics? *W boson, Z boson, Muon, Quark, Gluon, Graviton, Higgs boson?* No. This was new. Unexpected. A door opening with a strangled cry of wonder and surprise. An astrophysical plane populated by particles unknown to man. Smaller particles than science ever imagined. A new discipline altogether. Quantum-quantum? $Q^2$? A googolplex of such particles in a single tear-drop? What inhabited this realm?

Phil already knew that as well. Just a matter of impelling it to consciousness. Exploring the universe that dwells within every cell. Every atom. Phil was getting excited. He gave it a name. SNA. Subatomic Nucleic Apperceptum.

DNA and RNA were the aggregation of random adaptation over 3.5 billion years on Earth. Then again, maybe not so random after all.

SNA was the aggregate consciousness of the Universe. Nearly 14 billion years old. Passed on at inception within the atoms of all existence. Awaiting discovery. Imagine if DNA were a code built of a code. DNA made of SNA. Patterns within patterns. Steganography of the gods. SNA organized in the same general manner, yet unimaginably vast in capacity. Capitalizing on the astoundingly miniscule size of its carrier. Infinitely propagated since the Big Bang itself. DNA and RNA might not be universal. SNA most definitely was. A dazzling spectacle from the primeval birth of the cosmos. The Big Bang. A point in space? A dot? A bubble or bubbles? Strings? Whatever. It is the nascent DNA. The primordial universe. And far more. He was getting there.

He thought about Anthony Leeuwenhoek in the 1600's; developer of the first truly powerful compound microscope. Phil imagined being the first human to witness microbes–dozens of unearthly tiny creatures–swimming about in a single, small drop of water. Animals so small they are invisible… titanic relative to Phil's SNA.

Seconds after creation itself, hydrogen, helium and lithium isotopes fused in this particulate mini-verse, nucleosynthesizing vast spectra of exotic particles. Some known to man. *Tau leptons, gravitons, quarks* and many more. Others, unknown to man. Phil seemed to be christening them himself. Somehow driving their ultramontane natures and idoneous designations. Gestalting their names. *Mavros-pragma morio, mavros-energeia morio, aspros-pragma morio, aspros-energeia morio, safis-pragma morio, safis-energeia morio* and thousands more. He peered down an endless corridor lined with these exotic micro-bits of creation. A number approaching infinity. Each with their supersymmetric heavy counterpointal particle. A cosmic whirling dervish. Dancing and swirling, interacting, glowing and unfolding. Blossoming in sublime substance and meaning. Beyond beauty, beyond measure, beyond comprehension.

He envisioned these micro-miniature swirling universes. His vision was so clear he could actually see them. Infinitely small. Alive. Stunningly beautiful. Swirling bright, glittering crystal chandeliers of creation. Phil stood atop a lofty cliff. Star frosted darkness. Looking out on distant fires stretching beyond an endless horizon.

This realization electrified him. It inspired him. Somehow he had inadvertently happened upon one of the pivotal moments in his life. The primordial elements of existence. Phil was deep under water. Nonetheless he suspected he was doing something akin to weeping.

For this single point in time, Phil was the first and only human in all of history possessed of such wondrous knowledge.

Happy birthday indeed.

SNA permeated the Universe. Everyone. Everything. Humans. Radios. Rabbits. Stones. Water. Chocolate cake. Atoms. Stars. Quasars. Black Holes. Dark Matter. Strings. Novae. Galaxies. Everything.

Philip's great personal human singularity: He could access and interpret the SNA comprising his being.

SNA. Inviolable. Undeviating. As sacrosanct and transcendental as Newton's Laws. Everything in and of the universe since its stygian eruption. Everything that has been. Everything that is. Everything dissipating towards the ultimate entropy. Or compressing towards the ultimate congeries. If this was so, then logically it contained everything that *would be*, as well.

Dr. Webber had suspected as much it seemed. Years ago he declared to Phil "Chaos? Bullshit! God gave no latitude for such folly in his universe."

Perhaps he was right.

Breathtaking and dizzying. Difficult sensations to manage underwater.

What did this say to determinism? He supposed it denied its existence. Could not exist. No randomness. Phil's mind interplayed with itself:

*Forget about Heisenberg. Forget about uncertainty?*
*No. Not forget. Superimpose it.*
*This flies in the face of Quantum Mechanics.*

*No. Uncertainty is an illusion, superimposed on reality, described by Quantum Mechanics.*

*So Quantum Mechanics got it right.*

*No. It is only a layer. There are deeper truths. More profound dimensions. Infinitely smaller particles. Vibrating at unimaginable frequencies. Smooth, non-chaotic, predictable.*

*This from the first primordial matter and antimatter particles exploding outward to infinity. From the first billion-billion-trillionth of a picasecond. No nucleic constituent had ever, or would ever deviate so much as one trillionth of a Nano-millimeter in any direction from its precisely targeted predestination for a million-billion years.*

*Like flies in amber. A triacontatrillion to the hundredth power beings, spanning the cosmos for all time. Marching unswervingly to a cadence drummed out literally since the beginning of existence. A cadence resonating until the end of time.*

*Smacks of a god.*

*Sounds like a plan.*

*An insouciant escapada to hell.*

*Or heaven.*

*Or purgatory.*

*Or oblivion.*

*Or whatever.*

*Life and death passing without control.*

*Without responsibility.*

*So Einstein and General Relativity is right.*

*All that stuff about God and dice.*

*No free will.*

*Could something have raided the game?*

*Free will?*

*No. Not necessarily.* **I think this is very important.** *I believe an entity could...can...**will** free will...can divert the flux, move contrary to the grain.*

*Has this been done?*

*Perhaps. Maybe things are already out of place somehow.*

*Can it be done again?*

*I think so. And I think uncertainty can be exacerbated, or things could be put back into place.*

*Why do that? Why 'put things back in place'?*

*I DO NOT KNOW.*

The physical movement of particles was actually the definition of everything from form, to action, kinetics, to thought, history, science, art, emotions, good, evil, life, death, gold, bananas, televisions, super novae, funny, monstrous, noble, brave, worthy, mundane…everything. If physical movement is predetermined, everything else inexorably follows. Just as billiard balls on a flawless two-dimensional slate plane, every movement, every clash of balls and drop in pockets, all predetermined by the first, single stroke of the Cue. SNA. The blueprint of eternity.

All things predetermined by subatomic particles 14 billion years ago, blazing outward in all directions. A fabulous balloon stretching and expanding. Inflation bearing the sinews of creation faster than light itself. Matter and antimatter in a monumental conflict. Explosively abrogating one another. Matter exceeding antimatter; or antimatter simply finding its own cosmic eddies. Either way, matter prevailed. The titanic opening skirmish of existence itself. Predetermined as well. Perhaps we come by our nature naturally. Not our fault. Conceived in the blistering furnace of sub-atomic violence of mutually assured particulate destruction.

Phil was unprepared to face this or further analyze it. This was inspiring. Or it was devastating. This was wondrous. Or it was infinitely ironic. This was profoundly disturbing and cried out for an intensity of concentration lasting a lifetime. Far more than he had to give now. Instead, as he was taught in Fear Training, *he wrapped the problem.*

Only he carried it incalculably further. Initiating the process at the Medial Prefrontal Cortex, that part of his mind would commence independent analysis. Then he would let his mind or minds, continue the process, sort it out; and he would review conclusions at critical intersections for the rest of his life.

Phil's gifts were not explicitly bred into him as with ensuing generations of Oneirons. His powers were latent. Extant. Awaiting animation. He vivified them through the strength of his own will and the crucible of his ordeals. Genetic annealment from within and without. He was not a product of his genetics. He was the master of his genetics. Arousing them. Compelling them. Goading them into exponential leaps forward. Evolution as a rite of passage. Where would it end? Ever the outlander in his own world. His own body.

What had he accomplished in the forty-five years given him thus far?

Well, he was an extraordinarily skilled attorney. Famous in some circles. He had led and successfully governed his own nation. Managed a major corporation and chancellored an advanced university. He had fought and won small wars. Skirmishes really. Still they were violent and deadly. He had tortured and murdered. He had been close to death. Even craved death. He was wealthy beyond any fantasy of greed. He had saved uncounted lives and materially improved the human condition. He had been contacted by other life. He knew things other humans had yet to dream of.

Thanks to the singular cuisine developed by Oneiro he had acquired vast knowledge through the simple act of consuming food. Phil's body had digested the equivalency of doctoral degrees in Quantum Physics, Cosmology, Organometallic Chemistry, Marine Biology, Astrophysics, Renaissance Art, World History, Philosophy and Electronic Engineering. And he was only warming up.

For reasons unclear to him, he had decided to next undertake studies in Celestial Navigation. His phenomenal mind(s) had lifetimes of remaining capacity. And his remarkable Enteric System (humankind's unplumbed thoracic sapience) extended his neurological network nearly beyond comprehension. He could now draw on his SNA as well. Much to know. To learn. To discover. He had the capacity, the time, the money, the motivation, the tools, the genius and the freedom.

Among other talents he was a highly competent seaman; and knew he had no human equal underwater. He was deeply in love with a wonderful woman, Anne, who returned his love as deeply. Dr. Anne Jones. PhD in Fine Arts. Department Head and Professor of Arts at Oneiro University, until rendered gently redundant by the exceptional prowess of her students. Students who now managed the department, the University and the island itself. Tall, statuesque, sun-streaked chestnut hair, sensitive, lovely features, patient, gifted and brilliant. A perfect partner for Phil and their emprise into the ages.

In terms of family, Dr. Craig Webber, his loving and corporeal father, was dead. Stuart and Diana Carr, his adoptive and loving parents, were dead. His brother Michael was dead. One of his few close friends, Rachael Stone, was dead. All had suffered violent and malevolent deaths. His particular insight was attempting to detect a common linkage to their killings somewhere in the background processes of his complex intellect.

Remaining in his family were Anne, his Uncle Herbert, their first Mate Demetrious and of course, his family on Oneiro. He was not lonely. Never had been. Never would be. He could live in total isolation for years and never feel loneliness.

His health and fitness were essentially perfect; and given the bio-technology of Oneiro, he suspected he might endure for a long time indeed. Phil could easily pass for more than twenty years younger. He had a long, propitious life to look forward to.

The future was bright, healthy, wealthy, long, loving, interesting and even glamorous. Problem was...his particular introspections alerted him the future augured something more. Something deeper. More audacious. He sensed something. Something big. Beyond big.

Time to get to Oneiro.

Time under the sea always helped him sort things out. The familiar strangeness; and the strange familiarity. He flourished in the beauty. The grace. The peace. The music.

***...The... music?***

*Yes...yes music. There was music! Not music from a concert hall. Not whale-song. Not sound from any instrument he had ever heard. Music nonetheless. Beautiful, wistful and haunting. How could he have overlooked it for so long? It had always been there. Just at the margin of his perception. So many new things to understand. The singular beauty of his life grew ceaselessly more intriguing. A haunting violin crescendo rising through the night. Racing towards an end known perhaps only to his deepest, most profound particuverse.*

# 0715 Tuesday: Castoff

Phil savored the majestic, cascading curtains of blue-green light, shafting down into the depths. He lingered a moment longer, then kicked off, smoothly ascending towards Sea Tigress. He noiselessly broke the surface, his forward momentum carrying him to a stern cleat on the fantail. He effortlessly pulled himself up.

Time for their promised 0700 cast off.

It felt good. It all felt good. He hadn't realized it, but he had desperately needed time away from Oneiro. Out of the darkness. Escape into the light. Onto *Tigress. Thank God Anne and Herb bullied me into taking this trip.* He didn't think any power on Earth could drag him away from the QAVL. He had seriously underestimated Anne and Herb.

The past years had left him psychologically exhausted, depressed, and just about half crazy. Even with all his strengths he had severely overextended himself. The things he had seen. The things he had done. They weren't for free. He had been paying the price every minute of every day, awake or asleep. He could never stamp PAID IN FULL on this chapter, but he could live with it now. For awhile.

He emerged, dripping on deck, alone in the early sun. He wrapped himself in a towel, shaking out his sandy hair. He was compact, well-built, deeply tanned and exceptionally healthy. His symmetrical, precisely sculpted face and nearly transparent blue eyes graced him with good looks difficult to associate with any specific ethnicity.

Phil showered, dressed and emerged onto the bridge, just as the huge twin diesels were coming up to full throttle. Blue sky and blue water all about. Phil loved the bass rumbling of power from deep within the ship's bowels. The ubiquitous vibrations. The subtle rise of the deck and the smooth acceleration. Ever invigorating.

"Morning Philly. Happy Birthday!" His Uncle Herbert, Captain of Sea Tigress, was at the helm.

"Morning. Thanks Uncle Herb. Beautiful day uh?"

The First Mate interjected. "Nai pragmatika! Happy birthday Phil."

"Thanks Demetrious." Smiled Phil.

Tigress gracefully lifted her bowsprit above the horizon and they were soon sweeping over the calm sea. Herb and Demetrious had things well in hand. They were about three hours out of Oneiro Harbor. So Phil went below for breakfast.

Anne was in the galley, already dressed for the island. Breakfast was set out. Heady aromas warming the air. Coffee, orange juice, the homey char of toast, marmalade and Oneiro Country Sausage links. Another birthday greeting accompanied by a gentle hug and a warm kiss.

Eyebrows raised, Phil nodded questioningly at the sausages. Anne examined the package and responded to Phil's tacit question.

"Pork, high potency vitamins, fat substrate enzymes, muscle mitosis stimulators, proteins, carcinogen and cholesterol inhibitors, selected carbohydrates, spices, Oneirion Veg-Oil, *Course:* Advanced Diesel Maintenance, *Language Release:* New words and technical terms in English, French, German and Spanish within the last six months. *Current Events:* U.S. News and World Report & Financial Times, extracts, last two months, *Literature:* Plato's Republic, *Science:* Gödel's Incompleteness Theorem."

"The comestible library must be enormous by now." Wondered Phil. "Sounds good though." He said. And it was.

With the exception of restaurants at a few ports of call, the crew generally confined themselves to Oneirion food and the learning it contained, supplemented by fresh caught fish. In the case of foods such as breakfast sausage each package featured a different course of studies, subtly modified spices and attacked different bodily maladies. Often one package would last for two or three days, which entailed eating the same course three times.

Phil sometimes worried this could lead to duplication of information at sites in his brain. However, Dr. Simon Butler, University Resident Chief Cuisenaire, gave him absolute assurance no such redundancy occurred. Repeated testing had confirmed eating the same course multiple times was exactly as reading the same book over again.

The brain selects an algorithm germane to the information packet. It searches for and utilizes extant synaptic connections if they exist. The information is then rewritten *verbatim* across extant engramic sites, while the brain automatically and selectively maintains any discordance. The only effect is reinforcement and perhaps a deeper understanding. In fact Dr. Butler highly recommended eating particularly complex courses at least twice, maybe more often. He assured Phil the result was well worth the culinary investment. Reinforcement conditioning never tasted so good. And matriculation was roughly six times faster after the second seating.

After breakfast, Phil manned the radio.

"Oneiro Harbor this is Oneiro Sea Tigress. Over."

"Oneiro Harbor this is Oneiro Sea Tigress. Harbor access code: OST-999, Oscar-Sierra-Tango-Niner-Niner-Niner. Over."

"Acknowledged Tigress. Harbor Master Moore here. How are you Phil? Over."

"I'm fine Steve. Please engage the Heisenberg Monitor and the scrambler."

After a slight pause "Acknowledged and engaged at this end Phil. Your end?"

"Acknowledged. How's the weather Steve?"

"33° Centigrade. Humidity 42%. Winds 3 knots, south-southeast. Wind Force 2. Clear. Visibility unlimited. Traces of broken Cirrus at 6,000 meters. Seas calm. Barometer high and steady. Chance of rain zero. Beautiful day unless you want to do some serious sailing. We were alerted of your arrival. What's your ETA?"

"We should enter the reef at around 1200. I'll call for clearance when we're in range. Can you put me through to Mike?"

"You got it Phil."

"Thanks Steve. See you soon. Out."

"Hello Mike, Phil here."

"Hi Phil. Happy birthday."

"Thanks."

"What's your 20?"

"We're about two and a half hours out of harbor. Still on for lunch?"

"Absolutely. I appreciate you coming in."

"Sounded urgent last night Mike. What's up?"

"Quite a lot actually. A lot to discuss. I suppose the radio's secure?"

"Yes. Troubles?" Phil's voice betrayed a sudden tension.

"No. No Phil. Just good news. I think you'll be pleased."

"Good. So what's up?"

"Well first, the QAVL are halfway through their transmission. Part I is fascinating. I've prepared a briefing on the high points. Relevant department heads are attending. Part II is a total surprise. I'll brief you on Part II as well. Then I've got a couple of propositions to discuss with you. I think you and I have some decisions to make."

"Interesting Mike. Sounds like a long lunch."

"Understatement. I'd say much longer. I thought we would have lunch today and do a little pre-brief. Then the real briefing commences tomorrow afternoon."

"Whatever it takes Mike. See you in a couple of hours."

After dressing, Phil spent the rest of the morning on the ship's fantail pondering his new underwater revelations staring into wake spreading aft of the ship for hundreds of meters. Little over an hour out of Oneiro Phil broke his reverie to find himself surrounded by a smiling threesome.

Radar confirmed there was nothing around for kilometers, so Herb lashed the wheel and they came back for a quick party. A small cake. Cold Champagne. And something wrapped in gaily-colored paper.

"Happy birthday!"

"Well, thank you very much. What a nice surprise."

Anne handed him the package. "Open first. Champagne second. Cake third."

Phil smiled and tore off the gift wrapping. It covered a small wooden box. Exquisitely crafted in expensive hand rubbed Boxwood.

Whatever was inside must be something special. He carefully slid a small gold latch and slowly opened the box.

Inside was the most beautiful antique pocket sundial Phil had ever seen. Gold, silver and brass. Filigree etching of ancient Greek surrounding its outer boarder.

*Chronos Peto.* Time Flees. He'd never seen anything like it.

"This is lovely. Unique. Thank you all very much."

"Shockproof, waterproof and dustproof. Works above and below the water and on any planet with a sun. Better than a watch." Smiled Anne.

Somehow her playful statement shocked Phil. Strangely it lent more meaning to his newly found term, SNA. "So how about the Champagne and cake?"

The cold Champagne tasted good. Phil was always thirsty for hours after a dive and it was a warm day already. He had the stern to himself again. Anne was below preparing for arrival at Oneiro. Herb and Demetrius were driving the boat. So Phil was sharing the fantail solely with the remaining half of the bottle of cold wine. The bottle would be empty before Phil went below himself.

Phil had passed the most traumatic time in his life. He had done things to himself and others. He had seen things done. Lost friends and loved-ones. Tasted the true horror and base repugnance of torture and murder. And he had submerged himself in a sea of self-pity and alcohol. Within a short march of days he was deeply dependant on alcohol and nearly died from it.

Anne, Herb, the Sea Tigress, his innate strength of will and the sea itself. These forces combined to save him; and Phil lived through the dark period, luckily unscathed. There was little doubt however Phil had all the earmarks of a profoundly addicted alcoholic.

Still he continued to drink. Sometimes heavily. Always with enjoyment. Sometimes morosely reviewing the events of his life. Sometimes in boredom, or celebration, or for fun. Nothing better than a tall, icy Gin & Tonic on the fantail at sunset. He did this knowingly and intentionally. In some way he needed to prove he could continue to drink and control it and survive it. Rationalization? Certainly. A reflection of his weakness? Yes. A proof of his strength? Possibly. Did he survive it? Definitely. He continued in this fashion for well over two years. Then he noticed something interesting. His tolerance to alcohol was increasing commensurate with his prowess underwater. He was aware his body was managing oxygen, nitrogen, carbon dioxide, fats, oils…even producing its own alcohol as a by-product. This was beyond that. This was his body designing and implementing its own defenses using biological means already available. Hugely heightened adaptive response.

One rainy Sunday afternoon with nothing to do he was sitting alone in the ship's salon watching an indifferent movie. For no particular reason, Phil drank a bottle of good Scotch. To his surprise and some dismay, he found he was cold sober.

This so intrigued him he sought out Dr. Craig Simplon the next time he was ashore. Dr. Simplon had conducted the test and attempted to map Phil's meta-bio-chemical processes facilitated his fascinating underwater capabilities. He was part of the medical and teaching staff, second only to Dr. Gold. After a full day, half a bottle of Scotch, three blood samples, a skin scraping, some study and several tests, Dr. Simplon's findings surprised Phil.

"The best I can figure Mr. Carr is you are processing alcohol molecules in much the same manner as ah…" Dr. Gold consulted his computer "…Scendentia Tuparia Palawanensis."

"Say again Doctor?"

"The Southeast Asian Tree Shrew. One of our direct, but ancient ancestors. Related to us through the primates. This little guy draws a great deal of its sustenance from fermented flower nectar. He apparently loves the stuff and drinks it all the time. He would also be drunk most of the time except his metabolic rate combines with his integumentary biochemistry to break down the alcohol, metabolize it and eliminate the left-overs through his hair."

"…and my body has learned how to perform the same process?"

"Yep. It also produces amounts of doxapram derivatives. These negate some of the byproducts when your body metabolizes ethanol. Your increased metabolism also allows you to withstand the extreme cold of the depths; and explains your considerable appetite after a dive. This we already knew from your previous studies."

"Smart body."

"I'd say so Mr. Carr. And it learns to adapt at an imposing speed."

"So what *have* we learned Doctor?"

'Let's see. We've learned you can drink till the cows come home; and it seems it will never harm you in any way I can conceive of. Physically. In fact it seems to act as a well paroled, albeit efficacious palliative.

If you do persist in drinking, understand you have, and will continue, to develop a psychological dependency on alcohol. However I must be candid... and this statement sounds odd, coming from a physician...I find nothing particularly pernicious in a harmless psychological addiction.

In this context, such an addiction effectively amounts to nothing more than a quirk. For example, I personally love the smell of rubber tires."

Phil smiled broadly. "Son of a...I do too Doc...and oil and gasoline."

"There you go." The doctor shrugged amicably.

"I believe you can also *eat* anything you like, in any quantity you like, and never give a thought to weight or nutrition. In my opinion, your adaptations in conjunction with Oneirion nutrition will combine to provide you a long and healthy life. And I do mean long."

"How long?"

"I really have no basis for an accurate prediction Phil. Anything I say would be pure conjecture."

"So. Conject."

The Doctor paused and thought for a few moments.

"Let's just say you'll know the future Phil. As for me, I am sure I will devote years attempting to generalize your unique adaptations to humankind."

"Can it be done?"

"I doubt it. I doubt it very much. Not safely in any event."

# 1218 Thursday: Home Port

Phil found every entrance to Oneiro Harbor as stunningly powerful as his first. He never tired of it. An incredible bubble accreted in sedimentary limestone thousands of millennia ago. Carbon, hydrogen, nitrogen, sulfur, oxygen, methane, carbon isotopes nitrogen and helium. Gaseous migration or volcanism? They had yet to identify either the exact gasses or the precise geologic processes that formed the bubble. The relatively soft limestone was badly weathered by time and turbulent seas. Much of the geologic history written in the stone was destroyed – protection afforded by the huge cave notwithstanding.

They did know its geologic culmination. An out-gassing of titanic proportion as the island was violently lifted from the sea by a massive volcanic event and the bubble's shell was severely stressed on the seaward side. This had formed the entrance to the harbor. The bubble could well have been formed by methane. An explosion audible for 400 kilometers. A flare lit up the sky as far as the North Sea. In all likelihood a respectable tsunami as well. Everything in its proximity dead. Compressive concussion. Gas poisoning. Killing heat. Huge stones and ash falling from the sky. All this compounded by the monstrous volcanic forces already unleashed. A violent day indeed. Eons ago.

The harbor bubble itself described an immense pear shaped sphere. One fifth filled with sea water 50 meters deep. 17,600 square meters of harbor surface. Rising more than 200 meters to its interior apex. Over 548,000 cubic meters. The out-gassing had explosively expelled the harbor entrance; about seventy-five meters in diameter, and the sea had boiled in. All in all, the most astounding geologic feature of Oneiro. An inspiration to Dr. Webber as he incorporated it into his plans for the island. It was a perfect natural harbor seamlessly connecting to his vast underground complexes.

Tigress smartly cleared the entrance. Oneirion flag and zig-zag burgee flying. She quietly motored into her designated slip, the throaty rumble of twin diesels thundering her arrival. Mike Auslander appeared on the dock just as they finished securing her lines and setting out fenders.

"Ahoy Tigress!" hailed Mike.

A chorus of "Hi Mike" followed and they were soon gathered together on the dock around one of the now familiar Oneiro Reception Bars. This was a fully stocked bar. However, the featured drink at the harbor was the crystal blue liquid in a tall chilled, crystal cylinder. Mike filled four Champagne glasses with the blue liquid for each and handed them around. For himself Mike filled a glass with Champagne.

Phil frowned. "I thought we were immunized against your Sentry Plants long ago?"

Sentry Plants were unique Oneirion hybrids. *Vascularis Polypodiophyta Veneficus Oneriois. Oneirion Poisonous Vascular Fern.* Profoundly engineered to detect, alert, immobilize and even kill if necessary. There were tens of thousands of them blanketing the island. Any non-immunized intruder was in serious jeopardy.

"You certainly were Phil, but we've modified their chemistry to the extent we thought boosters were warranted. Considering the degree of coming and going on Oneiro these days, we plan to re-release the plant every thirty-six months as a matter of routine. So we'll be re-releasing the immunizing agent at the same time." Mike raised his glass. "Cheers and welcome!"

They drank. Tasty medicine. The flavor reminiscent of Blue Curacao.

Anne asked "How do you prevent these plants from spreading to other islands, or the mainland for that matter? Don't they produce airborne spores, buoyant seedpods, or flotsam cuttings–something capable of propagating the species?"

"Easiest thing in the world." smiled Mike. "As with any fern, they require a water-rich environment as a prerequisite to reproduction. No water, no spores. We particularly articulated this attribute in Sentry Plants, so they do not naturally reproduce on Oneiro. Too dry here. And we deny them any form of artificial irrigation. Instead, we breed them underground in a lush tropical setting and plant the seedlings as they achieve sufficient maturity. On the surface they flourish for many years without ever producing offspring. They do propagate extensively however, via a vast underground networks of tap roots, as do some conifers. So we are under little pressure to constantly conduct underground breeding.

Someone would need to intentionally transplant a Sentry Plant off-island; and unless you have been immunized, this would not be possible. If you have been immunized, you would be an Oneirion, and we are forced to assume you would never do such a thing. Reinforcing this, these plants have been specifically engineered for Oneiro. Difficult for them to survive elsewhere. So they live, reproduce underground, spread by taproot. No wind or sea borne spore are ever released. Should some spurious spore be germinated and freed to the winds, it would never survive the long voyage over the seas. A given. Another mechanism is birds. Eating sporophytes, traveling with them and transerting them via droppings. First, they would never survive the bird's gut. Second, the birds will have nothing to do with Sentry Plants."

"Transert?"

"Yes. My own word. To transport and insert."

"Been spending some time with Dr. Kahn have we?" smiled Phil.

Ignoring Phil's observation "All in all, we are convinced Sentry Plants will never find their way off Oneiro."

"Would all the world was so reliably managed." mused Phil.

Demetrious elected to remain aboard Tigress and take advantage of their protected slip to do some maintenance out of the weather.

All other bags were collected and routed to their respective quarters.

Herb wandered off to look up old friends. Girl friends.

Ann left for their apartment to see Edward.

Mike and Phil left for lunch.

Mike had arranged for a private table at Oneiro's newest and trendiest restaurant, *Brasserie QAVL*. They served what they termed 'Oneirion and QAVL'ian Specialties'. Qruxin Organic Soup, Twisted Rainbow Trout, Light-Fare, Hundred-Million Year Old Eggs and so on. Phil didn't understand many of the allusions and Mike assured them he soon would. In any event the food was creative and excellently prepared, even by Oneirion high standards.

Over coffee "So what's up Mike? You're actually carrying papers. I even see a pen in your pocket."

Mike smiled, a little self-consciously "Oneirion growing pains I suppose. So I've got a couple of things to discuss. First on the agenda: Our people want to demote me."

Phil raised his eyebrows without comment.

"...not demote me really. Limit my authority. Yours too in a way. They sheepishly came to me a few weeks ago. As you know, we now have diplomatic missions in most countries and our version of a State Department I suppose."

"Yes?"

"Well, what with diplomatic relations and all, they've been getting a lot of questions about the governmental structure of Oneiro. Is it democratic? Elections? Freedom of expression, religion? Human rights? Those sorts of questions. They encountered strange reactions when they said we were a Patronship. Outsiders can't seem to accept a Patronship as a governmental form, so they are convinced this is some sort of oligarchy. Perhaps something even worse.

So they came to me and posed the problem. I told them to make-up anything they thought would satisfy the situation. They reminded me the founding constituents of a national government were normally a matter of written public record. Moreover, many inter-governmental agencies required such papers on file as well. Diplomatic missions will visit the country and expect to see the national constitution in place. Bottom line is we can't just make it up."

"We'd be caught in a lie."

"Exact."

"That would look pretty bad."

"Exact."

"So we need something real."

"Exact."

"A real, tangible, existent governmental apparatus…actually at work."

"Exact."

"Well. Why not?"

"I agree."

"So…whatcha got?"

Mike started arranging papers on their table "They've proposed a Democratic Constitutional Patronship. It's based on a tripartite sharing of power as with many democracies. Difference is the composition of the three branches."

"No legislative, executive, judicial?"

"No, not really. Instead they propose we have a Consul. You."

"A what?"

"A Consul. From the French, or Italian. I believe it roughly translates as 'senior practitioner'.

"And your title?"

"Patron. No change…"

"…and easy to pronounce too…what else?"

"The third body of the triad, the Shareholders. The Consul retains a 51% share. I am given an 11% share; and the Shareholders control 38%. The Patron is appointed by the Consul, subject to Shareholder approval. Shareholders are elected by simple majority. Representatives who won the top 38 shares of the vote. One Shareholder, one vote. In certain cases I cast a vote. I have 11 votes. You have absolute veto, without the ability to introduce legislation, or to vote. Other than that, things run pretty much as they do today. I am reportable to you and the Shareholders. Between us we can act autonomously in most situations. Straightforward really. What do you think?"

Phil peered at Mike. "Do you have any idea how many hundreds of millions you're asking me to just give away?"

"I sure do." Mike smiled. Then his smile faded. "You think you have assets? The way I see it you got nothing but liabilities. You owe. You owe Dr. Webber. You owe every man, woman and child on Oneiro and on the planet Earth; and you owe yourself. Do you seriously believe Dr. Webber ceded you this island, the science and his fortune, not to mention the billions sitting in

Treasury, so you could go fishing? You know better. Your job is to protect and nurture and continue his work wherever it leads. My God Phil, he *bred* you for this work. You know that. So don't give me a bad time about a few bucks. I think you ought to climb down from that boat of yours and get back to work. We need you. I need you."

Phil signaled for another drink and sat lost in thought for long minutes.

Finally "I think this new government charter of yours needs some more fleshing out."

Mike sighed silently and smiled inwardly. "Agreed."

"How about–and it troubles me deeply to bring it up–raising an army, courts, prisons, police, regulatory functions and the whole depressing bureaucratic mélange?"

"I did a preliminary check-off of basic governmental functions against whatever is active on the island today. Surprisingly, we have most bases covered. Security equates to military and police. The Law Department is our Department of Justice. I don't think we need to build a prison. We should be proud we don't need one. We have a State Department of sorts. Culture, History, Museums? Well we have existing departments in the University. Anything left out we can delegate to the Shareholders to figure out if anything further may be needed."

"Sounds reasonable. Need to print up some calling cards and letterhead I suppose." smiled Phil. "How do you feel about it Mike?"

"I like it actually. I improvise many of my duties as I go along. I imagine you did the same. Why not share the joy?"

"Why not indeed."

Phil lent back in his chair and closed his eyes for roughly thirty seconds. Mike could see his eyes darting in all directions under his eyelids. Mike could remember when Phil was fascinated watching the same eye darts in Mike's eyes. Phil's breathing literally stopped. Then he relaxed. Sighed. Took a deep breath.

"We've always thought of Oneiro more as a University than a country. I think those days are done though. I originally devised the Patronship so we could change and react quickly. It is time for a change; so we change. Quickly. This new structure seems to retain the flexibility we need. I like it too. Let's go for it. Next?"

"The opening message from the QAVL."

"What about it?"

"Well, the message keeps changing in small ways. This is partly explained by improvements in their digitalization of English. However, the document seems to grow as well, extrude new text. It's nearly mystical. We assume more than digital information has been transmitted. We theorize some sort of steganographic insertion. We have no idea what activates it, or where its ideas originate. For all we know it may be an intelligent, sapient document. And we haven't generally disseminated it yet...only the barest high level extract."

Phil nodded.

"When you say disseminated Mike, I assume you refer only to Oneiro."

"Absolutely. In any event, there's some pretty rough stuff in there Phil. Some parts could be deemed extremely hurtful and offensive. They could even alienate us to the QAVL. Even more so for Landers when this gets out."

"*If* this gets out." Phil corrected. "Alienation? Such as?"

"Such as the way they suggest we control human population levels. Such as their rather pessimistic prognosis for human survival. The way we treat each other and the world."

Phil became quiet for several minutes. Finally he signaled the waiter "Scotch please...a double. For you?" He peered at Mike.

Mike quietly shook his head.

"Do you ever feel guilt Mike?"

"Guilt?"

"Yes. Things you've done in your life. Maybe things you haven't done. Things you could've done better. Things lost. Perhaps could have been saved. People and things you've hurt and destroyed. Things you've thought, you've wanted. Things you may find unworthy in yourself. Regrets. Like me, you've killed. I trust you haven't done worse."

"No."

"I have."

"Phil, I've not done worse than kill; and I can't say I do feel guilt. Never have. The hurtful things I've done had to be done. As with you. I do not harbor guilt. I've never had any puritanical inhibitions drummed into me, or any other types of hang-ups for that matter. None of the anemically moribund tyranny prigs love inflicting on mankind. I've always been fascinated by the term *original sin*. Hapless humans are supposed to jump right out of the Womb sorry as hell for whatever it is they've done. Peek at a girl. Guilt. Peek at a boy. Guilt. Peek into a mirror. Guilt. Have a thought. Guilt. What a small-minded, hidebound way to manipulate people. Steeped their whole lives in guilt. Poor bastards. No. I do not feel guilt. I've never felt guilt."

"Good on you Mike. You shouldn't. I'm sure you and the QAVL are much alike in this respect. As for me. I have. I do. And I will. Just like every other human on Earth, except Oneirions. Guilt's a special, very painful emotion. It's the spawn of evil, cowardice, cruelty, lust, revenge, ignorance, apathy, greed...a thousand human weaknesses.

Guilt triggers contrition. A redeeming virtue.

It is also an effective prod to evolve. Truly advanced specie should be spared such a pernicious, gnawing presence. Should have grown far beyond it."

Phil paused and moved his chair closer to Mike. He was now speaking softly. "The QAVL message belies their knowledge of our guilt. And our guilt is real. The message *should* be hard. It *should* be upsetting and hurtful. It *should* inspire guilt. I'm convinced every word of the message was skillfully thought out. It seems straightforward. Even simple. I believe over the years we will continue to learn from it. We will continue to find new meanings in it. Maybe even eventually, wisdom.

We've raped the Earth. We've brutalized each other beyond imagining. Hideously ugly acts. We've indulged in thoughtless, ignorant and maudlin, rutting reproduction–at the expense of gentle, loving humans who must ultimately deny themselves progeny. We must now stop and face terrible remedies. We need the guilt; and *the happy few* here on Shangri La should learn all about it and understand it, as sickening as it is."

Phil paused and looked piercingly at Mike. "The message goes out to the island *verbatim*."

# Class in Session

*Education is the transmission of civilization*
*Durant*

The next day at 1200 Phil, Anne and Mike met again at the access to the Board Room. They triple mated PM's (People Movers) for the long ride through the enormous underground access tunnel. As they sped through the huge dramatically painted tunnel, Mike explained their agenda for the next two days.

"We're meeting in the Boardroom primarily for its presentation and computer facilities; and maybe a little nostalgia. I'm going to brief you on the QAVL communications to date. We have about 6,000,000 pages of information. Fortunately the QAVL downloads are exceptionally well organized in a sort of top-down structure. It's easy to develop extracts and analyze huge amounts of material relatively fast. So we have a pretty comprehensive extract for you."

"What sort of 'top down' Mike?"

"Well they start with an introduction to the QAVL. Then they break the material down into forty main headers. Inside each header is another, more detailed introduction in the area, which is further broken down into forty sub-headers. Then each one is also divided into forty. Soon you have roughly 64,000 sub-chapters. You can skate through the high level stuff easily, which will give you a clear picture of the QAVL and their history.

If you want a deeper understanding, particularly of the science involved, it would require decades to completely work down. This information is stored in digital format on our systems, so we can work out an intelligible trickle to propagate the information through ingestion. If we encode two chapters in every meal, three meals a day, we calculate it would take about twenty-nine years to eat it all…much longer to complete matriculation. And we're not sure about the effect on the individual. Of course there's no requirement to consume the whole thing. It could be broken into increments, either laterally or horizontally. Even diagonally if you like. We are forming a team of 64 Oneirons, each assigned to a horizontal specialty. In this way the team will have fully MGL'd everything in little more than a year. We will have functional experts in all facets of QAVL knowledge we can call on at any time."

"MGL?"

"Metrignosiculate. Pronounced met-rhee-goss-cue-laete. MGL for short. Comes from Latin and Greek (l,gr. *Metri*–womb, *gnos*–knowledge, *culate*–metabolize). It's our term referring to the brain's complete ingestion and storage of information in digestible form."

"Interesting. Sounds like a complex process."

"It is."

"Christ! We're going to cover this material in less than two days?"

"As I said Phil, the QAVL did an astounding job of top-downing this stuff. They've perfected it with millions of cultures over millions of years. So they should be pretty good at it. Of course we could simply feed you, literally, the two-day presentation. I thought it would be more productive if we discuss and analyze this, step-by-step, as we proceed."

Anne and Phil both agreed. Their concerns unspoken, ingestion of totally unfamiliar alien information without further study seemed precipitous. Classical methods were more than adequate for the present.

They parked in front the Board Room Center some eighteen minutes later. It was now officially named the Webber Interchange Center, with large brass letters attesting to same. Oneirons now referred to it as the WIC instead of the BOD. Aside from the brass lettering, a large brass plaque and a bust of Dr. Webber in the lobby little had changed.

They proceeded directly to the dining room.

A notice board listing those in attendance for the series of briefings:

Landers:

    Dr. Enoch Wilson – Sciences
    Dr. Emily Johansen – Genetics
    Dr. Simon Butler – Cuisenaire
    Dr. Jackson Gear – Chief of Medicine
    Dr. Sun Kahn – Religion & Philosophy
    Dr. Judy McLean – Languages
    Dr. Eve Dunedin – Psychology
    Dr. Sean Gray – Realization
    Mr. Charlie Stein – Communications
    Mr. Oscar Pearce – Security

Islanders:

    Dr. Mark Gray – Sciences
    Dr. Thomas Rio – Genetics
    Dr. Richard McCloud – Cuisenaire
    Dr. Philip Gold – Medicine
    Dr. Robert Brown – Religion & Philosophy

Dr. Sochi Inchowa – Languages
Dr. Alberto Omani – Psychology
Dr. Michael Dundee – Realization

Panel:

Mr. Philip Carr – Consul of Oneiro
Mr. Mike Auslander – Patron of Oneiro
Dr. Anne Jones – Professor of Fine Arts
Mr. Bob White – Head of Deputation & Diplomatic Corps

With the exception of Communications and Security every department was represented by its original mainlander Head (at the time of Islander Transition) and the current islander Department Head. Phil felt the slightest touch of coolly reserved partisanship delineated by the terms 'Lander' and 'Islander', finally rejecting the suspicion as unworthy of Oneirions.

The group was randomly scattered about the room, aperitifs in hand. When the three entered they all gravitated in their direction with much hugging and shaking of hands. Phil was amused to note with few exceptions, islanders held fruit aperitifs and mainlanders held wine. Phil accepted wine for himself and Anne from a circulating server.

When all had drinks in hand Mike opened the conference. "Welcome all and thank you for coming. As you all know, the QAVL have completed their first incremental communication. A landmark of eminent consequence in the human experience. Oneiro is truly fortunate to be here, now, at this juncture, in human history. We are indeed lucky. We should be proud though. As with most luck, we summoned it. We brought it to Earth. We brought it to Oneiro. Dr. Webber's vision is being realized in many ways.

We are just now starting to get a glimpse of the second part of the communication. The first part was a history of the QAVL and of the Kosmos themselves. Truly incredible. Mankind will devote decades to understanding it. The second half will not disappoint. I assure you. We will be briefing you on both parts insofar as we understand them thus far. We do know the transmission will tax our science and intelligence, perhaps beyond their limits.

I have been in constant dialogue with our QAVL representative, so I'm ahead of Part II in many respects. Much of this briefing is based on those interviews.

Our objective over the next two days is to get everyone in this room up to speed on the QAVL and begin to analyze what we have. A process which must finally include the rest of planet Earth. That's also a topic to which we will devote some time during these sessions. Accordingly we will be calling upon Mr. White during these discussions.

Let's welcome back Phil and Anne (applause), then let's eat and get to work (more applause)."

One hour later in the meeting room. Phil noticed the already formidable conference table had been expanded to accommodate up to thirty positions. Essentially it was now a round table. Plenty of space remaining in the amazing room –seemingly suspended in mid-air. Two hundred meters above the highest point on Oneiro. An unrestricted 360° view of the entire island and the sea surrounding it for 200 kilometers to the horizon.

Another plaque dedicated to Dr. Webber. Beyond the plaque, the Board Room was unchanged.

Mike stood and a large black two dimensional square appeared, floating in the space above him. A bright sunny day poured into the conference room. Despite the brilliant ambience the square seemed to drink all light. The result was precise and easy to read.

# The QAVL

| | |
|---|---|
| Quadrivium | - Crossroads |
| Apud | - Present |
| Vita | - Life |
| Lucis | - Light |
| QAVL | - Crossroads of Living Light |
| Pronounced | - Kav'l |

"The QAVL derived their Earth-name (acronym really) from the ancient indo-European language spoken in the Roman Republic. Latin. They claim this name is accurately descriptive and fairly close to their own name, native to their home-world. In Oneirion we would refer to them in terms something like Kosmosagkelioforos – cosmic couriers – messengers of the gods…couching it in dramatic terms.

For some reason the QAVL have a tendency to intersperse ancient Latin with ancient Greek. They have mastered every ancient language to some degree. The number of languages they quote is three-hundred and twelve. Although there have been more than 10,000 languages over the ages. We refer to written languages, documented and demonstrable. ISO-639-3 only recognizes two-hundred and thirty-two dead languages. So they have a better grasp of ancient and extinct language than we. As well they should. They were there.

Incidentally they have offered to share this knowledge with us. I imagine historians, linguists, anthropologists and archeologists will be thrilled. Clearly modern languages are easier for them with radio, TV and data communications. As I said, for some reason they treat Greek and Latin as an amalgam.

When communications were well under way, we dialogued with the QAVL extensively. They cannot form the sounds of any language. They cannot manipulate gasses to generate sonic vibrations. They manipulate light. They do have a sort of mechanism for voicing digitalized Oneirion, or *Kosmas* as they call it. And they have jointly done the same with English. Encoded actually. They aren't prepared to do the same with any other languages now, as it would apparently entail another race they work closely with who are presently elsewhere. Whatever that means.

We do not actually know if their technology is binary. We only know their transmission to us is binary. This in itself is fortunate. It allows us to produce a rough version of their transmissions in English. Please do not infer from this we can translate Oneirion now. We cannot. We cannot because we cannot digitalize Oneirion. Like trying to digitalize a snake hissing. One can digitalize the sound, not the meaning. Maybe someday the QAVL will aid us in this. As you will find, they are exceedingly accomplished at written English and spoken Oneirion, so we've had some lively and enjoyable discussions.

They have faithfully recorded all of human history. They have a wonderful perspective. They compose poetry. They love fiction. They find humor a wonder. One of the keys to human survival in fact. Everything having to do with human language fascinates them. They are empathetic, and as a species they are likable in the extreme.

Naturally we invited them to join us on Oneiro. Meet face-to-face as it were. The classical human bond. They politely though categorically refused, stipulating it would serve no purpose. This struck us as a little aloof at first. It took us a few sessions to understand the reality of the situation.

Were they to physically visit our Earth, which they have done continuously over the millennia, we could neither see, nor hear, nor in any way be aware of their presence. Our perceptions would record only white light. Nothing else. Perhaps we have some equipment which could detect their presence. I really don't know. I don't believe so. They were correct. It would serve no purpose at this time.

I can see the incredulity on your faces. When you think about it though, we are comprised of matter. They are comprised of energy. If matter can organize itself into animated life, something that has a consistent form, reproduces, takes in energy, expels waste, and attains sapience, why not energy? Why can't energy organize itself with even greater alacrity? Maintain its form longer? Resist the deterioration we call aging?"

Phil. "Well let's see...among other factors matter has a tendency to accrete, to clump together and organize...whereas energy has a propensity to behave in just the opposite manner."

"Good point Phil. I am certain we need to review our definitions of matter and energy. I believe the boundaries are more nebulous than we suspect in many respects and better defined in ways we can't imagine. We are hadronic in nature..."

From the audience "Hadronic?"

"Yes. Our essences consist of particles that are protonic, neuronic and electronic. Hadronic. Whereas the QAVL are essentially electronic and photonic.

Phil "And pure electronic entities are possible?"

Mike "Apparently. Evidence the QAVL."

Phil "How about pure protonic matter and pure neuronic matter?"

Mike "Well, the math simply doesn't work. There are neutron stars. However, protonic matter wouldn't accrete. Of course the same applies to electronic matter. As we understand physics it requires more gravimetric energy than electronic repulsion. This is not possible, by a factor of about twenty. If such energy were applied, the result would be impressively explosive

The QAVL are literally made of energy. Light. They are a totally incorporeal life form." Mike activated the screen. "This table outlines the process in straightforward terms:

| In/Out | Material | Form | Matriculation | Process |
|---|---|---|---|---|
| <u>Input One:</u> Light | Photon | Non-Particulate Wave | Consume | Passive Spectronic Absorption |
| <u>Input Two:</u> Energy | Plasma | Gaseous Isotope | Digest | Dendritic-Electro-Osmotic Depletion |
| <u>Output:</u> Matter | Antiphoton | Aphotonic Depleted Photon Particle | Expel | Electromagnetic Expulsion |

Much as light is specturalized as it passes through a diamond, the QAVL slow Photonic Waves sufficiently to consume it, deplete it and convert its energy directly into a usable, storable state, as Plasma, or Ionized gas. They are quite literally living proof of VSL (Variable Speed of Light). In some cases light can be slowed to an unbelievable 56 kilometers per hour. One hellofa transformation from 300,000 kilometers per second. It may even be suspended in something like a cesium cloud chilled to near absolute zero Kelvin. I suspect somewhere in these spectacular accelerations/decelerations may reside the metamorphosis from wave to particle and back."

"So they essentially eat light and crap depleted photons."

"Well and graphically put Phil. But do not discount energy plasma. Ionized gas is arguably the most common phase, or state of matter in the universe. Staggering amounts drifting about in interstellar space. A valuable and plentiful secondary source of nutrition. Often ingested directly by the QAVL when photonic energy is scarce. I would imagine inter-galactic travel constitutes the only type of voyage requiring they transport supplies, if even then. The same source for sustenance and propulsion. Our galaxy is one big buffet for them. And one big gas station as well.

Mind you, their energy consumption is extremely low by our standards. Nearly immeasurable when they are in repose. They can increase their energy profile at will. They can leverage their utilization using their proto-neuronic 'tools'. And, thanks to a race called the Gammon (I will be briefing you on them.), they can further leverage their profile using hadronic tools."

"Why even bother with light? It just adds another step in the process."

"I asked them the same Phil. They said the light *tastes better*. They also stated it was *fresher*. And they claim they can modulate the *flavor* in nearly infinite variation. These terms may not be fully appropriate to their use."

"I suppose when they stipulate flavor modulation, this refers to some sort of spectral array?"

"I made the same supposition."

"Einstein would've loved these guys." Observed Phil.

"I agree." Said Mike soberly. "And Sagan and Clarke and Hubble and countless other talented genius who will never know the QAVL." We are so incredibly lucky it's humbling. We must remember we cannot withhold this information indefinitely. There are many non-Oneirions who are unambiguously worthy of exposure to the QAVL."

## *DAKHALA* Manu

One of the most dangerous countries on Earth dominates the apex of Central Asia. Iran in the west, Pakistan to the south. Tajikistan, Uzbekistan and Turkmenistan define the northern border, as the colossus of China spawns the eastern sun.

The land of the Afghans. As the Persians designated it: Afghanistan

Before the Greeks. Before the Persians, the Mongols, the Durrani, the British, the Russians. Before the Americans and a procession of others... Afghanistan was already deeply steeped in violence and death. When other countries weren't invading, tribal warlords jealously oppressed and slaughtered the populace throughout the centuries. If warlords weren't infighting, there were diverse *al-Jama'at al-Islamiyyah*: terrorists, militants, insurgents, fundamentalists, Hezb-e-Islami Gulbuddin, Taliban, and Al Qaeda. And as always, assassins, smugglers, mercenaries, thieves, drug runners, slavers and pimps ensured life remained a misery. A dangerous life, often too lamentably brief. Nothing in the topography, climate, flora, or fauna of Afghanistan is remotely as deadly as its indigenous humans.

Afghanistan is a wild country of great contrasts. Sizzling heat to arctic cold. Barren plains to towering mountains. Mountain passes that render the country alternately accessible and inaccessible.

Passes hold a unique place in human history. In human war. There are many famous and infamous passes around the world. The Cilician Gates, the Donner, Cumberland Gap, the Iron Gate of the Danube, the St. Bernard Passes, Simplon Pass, the Gates of Thermopylae. Arguably the most famous of such passes straddles the very top of Afghanistan. The Khyber.

From Alexander of Macedon, the Mughuls, the early silk and spice traders, the Khyber Rifles, the hippies of the '60s, to modern-day troops of occupation, the Khyber Pass is synominus with romance and danger. At the turn of the last century an officer in the British Forces aptly described the pass "Every stone in the Khyber has been soaked in blood." True words.

At the Afghan terminator of the pass lies the Towr Kham Checkpoint, balanced on the border with Pakistan. Not far from there is a Fire Base used by troops of occupation, primarily supporting a modest artillery installation.

\* DAKHALA – Arabic for 'Enter'.

Such fire bases were strategic innovations emanating from the South-East Asian Wars. Fire bases are invariably remote and dangerous. Not a soldier's dream posting. In the case of the Towr Kham Fire Base, it also imposed great physical and mental hardship due to its altitude and exceptionally harsh climate. A skeleton crew. Eschewed by locals. Lonely, threatening, bad food, no women, no alcohol, no entertainment. Hot, cold, dismal and primitive. Hard duty by any standard.

Describing a triangle with the checkpoint and the fire base is the village of Towr Kham, or Torkham. Villagers scratch out a meager subsistence servicing the trucks that ply the Khyber.

Inevitably, villagers are familiar with foreigners, or AJNABI as they refer to them. And they are tolerated of necessity. No difference to the natives if they entered Torkham in tractor trailers carrying livestock, psychedelically painted VW Vans carrying hippies, or M60 tanks bringing death. Although these AJNABI represent a lifeline to Torkham, they are intuitively disliked and mistrusted. Any man found fraternizing with AJNABI is shunned. Women who fraternize face an ominous reprisal, far more stringent than mere shunning...

It was sunny for a change, and she could see far down the gorge. The rugged beauty of this high country was one of her few pleasures. Manu had been walking for some time from her home on the periphery of Torkham – not actually a home, or house. More of a wing. Not a wing really either. It was actually a three-quarter sided shack with a corrugated iron roof and plywood walls leaning precariously against her father's home. Which was not much better. As was their custom, Manu lived with her parents until her father found her a husband. As their small home was crowded, when Manu neared maturity – her first menstrual cycles, budding breasts, a quickening of hormones – the elegant solution was to simply throw up three walls and a door, cover it with a corrugated roof, *et voilà*. Cold in winter. Hot in summer. Spring and fall were times of relief. Ostensibly the same house with her parents. The same strict supervision. Propriety was satisfied. The parents had far more room. And Manu finally had some privacy. The dignity of her own room. Even her own entrance. A quiet spot to grow into old maidenhood, as her family furtively feared she would.

Her wandering had taken her right to the periphery of the towering, windy precipices. She had hardly noticed where it had led her. She was lost in contemplation of her strange life the last few weeks; and where it could be leading...

In addition to her duties at home, Manu was sent to work at a local service station for the Khyber trucks. Aside from fuel, tires and light repairs, the station provided a small café, featuring coffee and simple foods. Owned and operated by a Pakistani who paid rental to the station. Chef as well. As Manu was not married, she was not allowed to work in front, so she was put to work in the back. Hard work, but a welcome excuse to be away from home. Her normal duties consisted mainly of cleaning and keeping the area tidy. She did have one talent, or more precisely stated : <u>a dish</u> A dish she made so well she was given a regular hiatus from her cleaning duties. The truck drivers always asked for it. *Mourgh*. A sort of marinated, smothered chicken. Garlic, yogurt, lemon, salt, pepper and filets of chicken. Manu would discretely add olive oil, a few drops of dark vinegar, turmeric and a generous dollop of Yemen Sahaweg. Somehow this made all the difference; and her chicken was known up and down the Khyber. Even the chef, Malik, an overweight, unshaven, greasy Pakistani, credited her for the dish. Although he allowed her to cook only once a week. He limited Mourgh on the menu partly to sustain demand, and partly just to be mean. When he wasn't harassing, abusing, or sexually assaulting the help, he was just mean. Meaner than blue hell.

Manu worked with two other girls in the back. Uzuri and Narmir. The three greatly enjoyed gossiping and chattering and analyzing the mysteries of the few young boys in the village. Manu had never had any real friends before. She'd never really had the opportunity to meet anyone. So this became an unexpected source of lively happiness in her bleak routine.

Uzuri and Narmir were both younger than Manu and so were surprised when she was unable to satisfy their eager quest for knowledge about sex and boys and their own bodies. Manu was kept ignorant about such things until her mother saw fit to educate her. Ideally until Manu was to be wed. As the years wore on, this seemed less and less likely. Other girls her age were already married. Many with children. Manu was far from the comeliest of the village girls. In one respect this was lucky. Malik had no interest in her.

Beyond that, her appearance had plagued her all her short life. No chin to speak of, much too generous a figure, a conspicuous overbite, unruly hair and eyes that seemed to pop out of her head. Had her intellect evolved consistent with her aspect, she might still have known the happiness of guileless, incognizant bliss. No such luck. She knew she was homely. She was exceptionally intelligent. Far more than her family; and she was just now coming to appreciate this. Nonetheless she knew little of sex aside from revolting glimpses of Malik gratifying himself in the store room, rutting with some hapless trucker girl. Manu knew nothing of boys. Nothing of the outside world. She could neither read, nor write, nor do ciphers, nor any of the skills imparted by an education. Just as her parents deemed entirely proper and acceptable to their neighbors. Her native intelligence was her only defense in this cold and remote crack in the world.

Her only experience relating to sex was a source of shame and bitterness. It brought memories of unbearable pain. She would share none of it with Uzuri and Narmir. No need to frighten them. They would face their own ordeal soon enough.

One day she had finished her work at the service station and walked to their hut. She found her father Zalmai, unexpectedly at home, along with her entire family, grandmother included. They were all drinking strong tea and munching on Khatai biscuits. Their mood was festive. In the center of the gathering, Manu spotted an aged crone, withered and dry, with bright eyes fixed on her. The old woman noisily savored her tea, cookie crumbs clinging to her fuzzy chin, a well worn leather bag in her lap. When he saw Manu her father stood and the room grew quiet. He smiled. "Manu, your day of womanhood has arrived. This is Abagull." Gesturing to the strange women "She will look after you." He smiled again. "Go to your mother." Manu did as she was told.

Her mother rose, tenderly taking her face in her two hands, and pressed her lips to her forehead. "Sit here child." Manu sat. Her mother moved softly behind her and firmly took her arms in an unbreakable hold. Her aunt took Manu's legs and ankles. Her mother whispered in her ear "Relax child. There is no reason to be afraid. This will not hurt. This is good for you. It must be done." The old woman brushed between Manu and her aunt, kneeled between her legs and brusquely exposed her genitals. Mercifully her father had stepped out of the hut. She opened her bag and removed some well worn metal implements. Manu's initial intrigue blossomed into suspicion, then into a nebulous realization, then into a pounding fear. Manu was terrified. She began to struggle in panic, to no avail. For such an elderly woman Abagull was strong. She moved fast with learned strokes. She worked not cruelly, but dispassionately. Oblivious to the torment and inhuman mutilation she was inflicting.

Thus began the most monstrous afternoon of Manu's young life. She screamed, and squirmed and fought and wept and suffered. She witnessed mutilation of her body such as she could never dream in her worst, most odious nightmares...

No antiseptics. No painkillers. No analgesics. No ointments, opiates, sedatives, or tranquilizers. No anesthetics. Cold razored steel. Female Genital Mutilation. FGM: The partial or total removal of the clitoris and the labia minora, with or without excision of the labia majora. The complications of such a procedure range from death to myriad serious and painful maladies and infections, to sterility. The overriding common bond between such sufferers who survive is the lifelong persistent memory of agony, humiliation and terror.

For weeks afterward she would curse her family, hating them, and the horrid old hag that inflicted such butchery, for a meager handful of copper Afghanis.

But most of all her father. He was not the man she had loved and trusted all her life. She would no longer look to his strong arms for protection and comfort. Her loss of love and respect did not suddenly emerge with her circumcision. It was a gradual dawning. She had not been overtly aware of it, but her keen intellect had been penetrating this superficial man years ago. This was the culmination of innumerable lesser incidents...beating her mother for no reason...his cowardly, slavish fealty to the conventions of the village...his clumsy, lumpish mannerisms...his incessant hypocrisy...his fawning approbation of other men...his terror of *losing face*...his dogmatic, pharisaical espousement of religious precepts exceeding both his education and his intellect...his tedious yearning for respect...and finally this ignominious treachery. Manu suspected much of his insecurity was his lack of sons and a large family. He had only her. Her mother was never able to give him more children. Probably as a result of his incessant beatings. The author of his own afflictions.

As yet, she had no inkling her sex-life might now be forever extirpate. She didn't really grasp the concept of a sex life. What effect would it have on her mind, and her perception of her family when she did understand? Small wonder she had no wish to share with Uzuri and Narmir.

For days afterward she endured a high fever, stabbing pain and infections. Her only medicine was a dark brew left by the old woman that smelled of corruption. Manu refused to drink it, or to apply it to any part of her body. She was unable to work for three days and returned only then following a demeaning slap to the back of her neck from her father. "We need the money. You are not sick. Go."

Work was an exhausting hell. Uzuri and Narmir questioned her constantly seeking the cause of her radically changed demeanor. She had no energy, no passion, or interest in life. In many respects she had lost her innocence; and with it her regard for men, and it showed. Compounding her misery, Malik was constantly beating and berating her. "Move girl!...Faster!...You've done this wrong...You've done it wrong again!...Your Mourgh tastes like fermented goat-shit today...What is wrong with you, you stupid girl?...Get out of my kitchen!"

She was finally relegated to garbage duty and truck cleaning, usually assigned the young Chai Wallah, the Chai-boy named Zemar. Malik wanted especially demeaning work for her. Difficult, cold, dirty, smelly. Long days and long hours relegated to garbage and the big trucks as they came rolling through, muddy, wet and frozen. Nor was she hidden away in the back anymore as a maiden should. Truckers and soldiers and workers saw her ghostly countenance regularly. Dirty, raggedy and tired. Cold eyes followed her, seeking opportunity and perverse pleasure.

One freezing night she lurched in from the raw cold to warm herself and find some tea. Hot, strong Chai. The kitchen was closed, so she looked forward to a few moments of merciful solitude and rest. She sat in the darkness warming her hands on her cup wondering where her dreary life would lead. Despite all her ills she was growing stronger. Healing. She saw her life in a profoundly different way now. Perhaps it was time she began to take some control? Who else could she possibly trust? Who else even cared?

Her thoughts were interrupted when she heard a muted choking sound. It seemed to emanate from the pantry. Then nothing. Then a strangled sort of groan. Her curiosity conquered her bodings of danger; and she soundlessly found her way across the restaurant, through the kitchen, to the large pantry, and peered in. She was electrified by what she found. She had never heard of such a thing. She had never seen such a thing. She had never dreamt of such a thing. She was not even sure she understood what she was seeing.

Malik had poor little Zemar, the Chai-boy, by the throat. His panic-stricken eyes looked like luminous dinner plates in the murky light. By the head, the ears? Was he choking him? Trying to kill him? Her eyes grew accustomed to the murky light. She was beginning to make out details. No. No he wasn't trying to kill Zemar. He had his pants down and he was forcing his...his penis!...into the small boys mouth. Now she understood. It was uh, *BADA'A...copulation...in his mouth. How strange. How...grotesque. Poor Zemar.* She sighed sadly.

Malik looked around, suddenly alarmed. *They could behead me for this!* His heart was pounding. His mouth dry with fear. *Manu! I should have known.* He released the frail boy, dropping him to the floor and spun on Manu, exhibiting his fat belly and hairy crotch. Scrabbling with pants and belt "You little bitch. What are you doing here? I'll..."

Manu was already running from the station, into the snow, blindly racing away. After a time she found her hut. Soon she was in her bed, wrapped in cloth, freezing. She shivered and wept all night. The next morning she was so drained she couldn't stand. Zalmai assumed this was simply more of the aftermath of her circumcision. After several sharp hits to her head, and much screaming, to no avail, her father finally concluded she should remain home today.

# Back in Session

Mike returned to his briefing.

"As Phil so colorfully observed in our previous session, the QAVL essentially ingest PHOTONIC WAVES, absorb their plasma as isotopic nutrients and expel depleted APHOTONIC PARTICLES. Various trace elements are useful in establishing and maintaining electromagnetic, gravitonic and other fields devoted to manipulation of light. This bonds their TROICA (their tripartite life-form). It's used in the manipulation of ethereal tools, memory, even specially adapted vehicles and machines. One of which they use for speaking. Basically maintaining their form, moving about and performing the functions of an advanced form of life."

"…so the QAVL actually have tools *per se*?"

"Yes."

"…and these tools are made of tangible, solid matter?"

"Particulate matter and organized energy in various states."

"How is that even remotely possible?"

"That is a long story. Tens of thousands of years long. It even involves alien creatures. I will be going over this soon if it can wait?"

"Certainly."

"Much of this may be mitigated by concepts such as Special Relativity, Proca Theory, Polarization, Quantum Field Theory, Gauge Invariance, and the Wilsonian Effective Field Theory. All this would take quite some time to work through; so I suggest instead you try the *Fettuccini al Carne* at dinner tonight. All will become deliciously clear.

The QAVL themselves consist of clear ionized gasses bonded by photonic electromagnetic energies. They communicate and reproduce through plasma discharge and electrical impulse. Hardly the stuff of god messengers. In point of fact however, they are an inspired choice. They are supremely intelligent, immortal, passive, impartial, unkillable, charming and caring. They have the patience to devote hundreds of thousands of years in observation; and they can conduct their own work and studies anywhere. Their relative position in the universe at any given time is a matter of total irrelevance to them. They can never be detected in their observations. They are familiar with every known advanced race in this galaxy and beyond. They allude to even more advanced races. Although I can tell you I feel primitive in *their* presence, not to mention something more advanced. By the reckoning of our ancestors, they are gods."

"Mike, I am in awe. And I know you do not run to overstatement. So after you've grown to know them, do you believe humans at large are prepared to meet beings of this nature?"

"Humans at large Anne? Are you suggesting we selectively inform mainlanders?"

"That's one approach."

"What would be the selection criteria for such a choice?"

"Well, I suppose representatives should come from a stable, open society. Educated. Free. No fundamentalists. Able to gain from such knowledge and contribute to future joint projects and such."

"Scientist and academics?"

"Essentially yes."

"…and risk the murderous fury of politicians, philosophers, churchmen, ordinary people…and fundamentalist…not to mention the military?"

"It's also a question of which will outrage them more. Informed or uninformed? All the same it's a good point. Maybe we should just keep it to ourselves. After all, had you not evolved the Oneirion language, we would never have known they exist. Have you discussed this with the QAVL? How do they feel about it?"

"They were explicit. In all their contacts they had never encountered a civilization where only a small sub-culture evolved sufficiently to speak Oneirion. They appreciate the risks inherent to both releasing and withholding this information. They also understand the injustice of keeping the general population in ignorance. As a consequence they don't believe it lies within their purview to make a recommendation one way or the other."

"Sounds like it's up to you Mr. Proprietor." grimaced Anne.

"Anne, you know I am not qualified to make such a judgment. I do not believe we can selectively release news of the QAVL. All or nothing in my opinion. If we did a selective release and then the news were leaked, there would be hell's own to pay. I'd like to draw on everyone in this room, and possibly more, if necessary to make an enlightened decision. I would hope a decision is forthcoming within the next few weeks."

"Anyhow, we need to complete these briefings before we can intelligently start to analyze this issue."

"Agreed Anne. The longer the wait, the more dangerous it gets. Let's continue."

# Quo Venīre Tu QAVL?

Mike brought up another slide. An image of a mountainous purple and brown planet.

This is the QAVL home world. About half the mass of Earth. It is the 2$^{nd}$ planet in a ten planet eclipsing binary solar system, 61 Cygni (a binary in the constellation Cygnus, composed of two K class (orange) main sequence stars, 61 Cygni A and 61 Cygni B). Some 10 light years distant from our star Sol. Qruxin has six moons. Considering the make-up of their solar system this alone is incredible. Qruxin is constantly bathed in light by their binary stars which is further intensified by its moons. Qruxin is not tilted on its axis and therefore has no seasons. Although if it did have seasons they would be hellish and more hellish.

Locked with Qruxin in an extremely protracted, synchronous orbit through its binaries is a gas giant. Were it any larger it would be a star itself and Qruxin would not exist. It exists at the limits of gravitational mass. Interior heat sources probably inflate the size of the planet somewhat. So its mass may be appreciably less than its size might suggest. This may be the reason the gas giant has never birthed a star, and why Qruxin exists at all.

These planets and moons are bound in a perfectly balanced embrace, dancing around the two suns. Their common center of mass. Compounding this, Qruxin has no dense liquid seas, of true liquid composition (water, methane, mercury, or whatever). Therefore, the moons do not induce gibbosity of the oceans, seas and major lakes, other than some subsurface magma shift. Therefore, there is no physical and gravitation protrusion on Qruxin to lead and impel these moons to orbit ever faster. A sort of whiplash effect consistent with Qruxin's rotation. Therefore, they do not produce sufficient torque to migrate away from Qruxin. Therefore, the effects of these moons on Qruxin are, to say the least, significant. Enormous gravitational tides, constant storms of incomparable violence, unending tectonic stress and ceaseless thermodynamic calescence. If Qruxin supported an Earth type ocean, it would have tides measured in thousands of meters.

Qruxin's relationship with the gas giant is somewhat comparable to Earth and Jupiter…only much more intense. Closer. More dramatic. Over billions of years literally no rogue astral bodies (asteroids, comets, planets, planetoids) or space junk of any description have slipped past the gas giant through to Qruxin. This has allowed the QAVL to survive in relative tranquility for billions of years–at least insofar as celestial bombardment is concerned. It has also denied Qruxin water in cometary or asteroidal quantities sufficient to propagate carbon based, water dependant life. Several other factors militate against carbon, silicate, or other dense-matter, proton-ameliorated life forms in any event.

The gas giant engulfs Qruxin in a titanic magnetosphere. Its powerful gravitational force fosters continuous volcanism which, with Qruxin's moons and the binary suns, works in concert to constantly pull the planet's crust in all directions. Tidal flexing on a mammoth scale. A living hell of a planet.

I'm no planetologist, although I can hardly understand what keeps the planet from ripping itself apart.

The gas giant emits killing radiation as well. Qruxin's nickel-iron core is never allowed to cool in the least. Hot, molten, generating a formidable magnetosphere of its own. Were darkness ever to descend on Qruxin, the night sky would be a wonder of ionized particles; our own aurora borealis rendered by contrast a flashlight in a blizzard at high noon.

There is no appreciable atmosphere above 47,000 meters. Such atmosphere as does exist is a product of volcanic plumes; and is constantly renewed by gasses emanating from subduction zones in a patchwork of tectonic plates, comprised of carbon dioxide, sulfur and an amalgam of trace gasses. Without these gasses Qruxin's atmosphere would disappear, prey to photonic winds and gravitational, inter-planetary larceny. In this scalding, chemically rich, turbulent atmosphere there is incessant electrical activity. Extremely violent.

This brings us to the evolution of the QAVL.

Roughly eight billion years ago a giant volcano arose on Qruxin's southern hemisphere. Thanks to low planetary mass it rose relatively uninhibited. Incredible subsurface volcanism drove it high and wide. Further coaxed by five moons, close proximity suns and the nearby gas giant, Mount Qrux as it's called, achieved a remarkable summit, even by Qruxin standards. 36,000 meters. Dwarfing Mars' Olympus Mons, *Nix Olympia*.

Its fiery birthing pains covered the entire world in toxic gases for a half million years. The atmosphere, in its own parody of sea level alignment, rose concurrently to 47,000 meters. Well over half the planet was covered in magma. Billions of metric tonnes of Qruxin were ejected into space. Accretion of volcanic ejecta would eventually form Qruxin's sixth and tiniest moon. The foot-print of Mount Qrux is of awesome dimension. Successive eruptions over the millennia spawned the final and ultimate caldera. Cauldron. From the South Pole to beyond the equator it stretches some 8,000 kilometers. From east to west it is a vast, irregular 12,000 kilometers encapsulating the South Polar Region running north to the equator. Remarkably it literally represents an expelled tectonic plate.

400,000 years after its birth, the interior of Mount Qrux finally cooled. Drained and depleted, it collapsed, completing a caldera of 60,000,000 square meters. 35,000 meters deep. 680 trillion cubic meters. Far and away the most astounding geological feature on Qruxin; and its entire solar system for that matter.

So massive is Mount Qrux it challenges the planet's nickel-iron core for gravitational dominion. While the planet is not tilted on its axis *per se*, it does exhibit a detectable wobble in kinetic reaction to Mount Qrux's commanding mass.

Long before the rise of Mount Qrux, the crust of the planet had been geophysically massaged like bread-dough. Magma-dough. The surface sank nadir-ward deep into the interior, then ascending to the surface—repeatedly over the eons—a geologic loop current of pythonic proportions and unimaginable pressures. A massive subduction process in the absence of tectonic plates.

This constant churning, occurring within no less than ten mammoth energy fields, serving to create massive amounts of highly charged Qruxian-lodestone. High yield, vectored magnetite. Neodymium Iron Boron. Permanently hard magnetic material forged and tempered on an igneous and sedimentary geologic anvil under titanic pressures; capable of a formidable magnetosphere in such an extraordinary mass.

The result: Mount Qrux is one of the most phenomenal geophysical peculiarities in the galaxy. A colossal ring-magnet the size of a moon. A magnetosphere larger than Jupiter's. A Qruxian-lodestone, crowning a planet generating a colossal magnetosphere extant within the most ferocious ambience imaginable.

The next step. The birthing of Mount Qrux provoked what may be the most colossal Flood Basalt event in galactic history. Beyond the treacherous ash, gasses and magma, the overtaxed planet split releasing a wave of molten Qruxian more than three thousand meters high, overtaking the entire planet. This volatile combination of forces in turn triggered an absolutely unique pyro-technique planet-wide magnetic eruption event, seeded by the explosive release of static magno-electric energies. Qruxin's luminance bathed its solar system in blinding white light, strobing the galaxy for ten thousand years.

The stage was set for genesis.

The caldera of Mount Qrux aggregated into an intense magno-electro-gravitonic 'sea' of plasma energy. The Qruxian Sea. Currents, tides, whirlpools, even immense tsunamis. Although comprised of highly compressed gasses and magnetically entrapped particles, instead of hadronic liquid, its physical and emulsification properties behaved much like a true liquid. It continued to intensify and grow driven by gravity, heat, incessant lightning discharge and competing magnetospheres. The result: A sea of magnetized, non-neutral, partially ionized, plasma, 23,000 meters deep. In this high-energy matrix, the elements came together at the quantum and even sub-quantum levels to initiate organization of the non-hadronic equivalents to thymines and guanines under the general sub-atomic particulate heading of monomers. These non-hadronic monomers organized themselves seemingly randomly…certainly idiopathically…into intelligible, reproducible linkages of interpretable, stable and sustainable energy within the matrix of Mount Qrux. Once so organized, self assembly, or replication commenced. Mitochondria on Earth. Electrochondria on Qrux."

A question came from the audience. "Mike you appear to emphasize this was an idiopathic event as opposed to a simple spontaneous occurrence."

"We believe this was not an aleatory event. It was an event simply having no known cause – much as life generated here on Earth. Absence of an antecedent cause does not logically exclude a teleological driver. Thanks to the QAVL we may be discovering the existence of true randomness. Real spontaneity is the single driving quest in the universe. A profound task."

After a short pause, Mike continued. "This was the birthplace of Qruxin life and ultimately the QAVL. A breathtaking testament to the infinite diversity of cosmic evolution. At this point however, the QAVL presently station-keeping between Earth and our Sun awaited 2.5 billion years into the future."

Phil quietly stood. "Mike this is the most unimaginable scenario I've ever heard. I need time to think. To digest. I need a break. I need a drink."

Mike smiled. "Tomorrow morning. 0930."

Mike realized his intense preoccupation with the QAVL made it hard to keep up with him. The room quietly emptied. Soon there was a throng of PM's speeding through the mammoth, beautifully decorated tunnel connecting to Oneiro's central complex.

Atypically, no one was of a particular disposition to socialize. Instead they dispersed in all directions to be alone and think. That evening, wherever they dined, they would all unfailingly order *Fettuccini al Carne* as their main course.

"This is excellent." observed Phil. He poured more wine for Anne, Herb and himself. They had decided to dine on Phil's terrace. Herb had decided to forego Special Relativity and Quantum Physics in favor of a thick steak and baked potato as only Oneiro can serve up.

"So where do you think all this is going Phil?" Anne swirled her wine and looked up at the stars. A beautiful clear night. Warm. Somehow expectant.

"I've got some ideas. The QAVL's openness in sharing information indicates to me even more information is forthcoming. Perhaps something on the practical side. Perhaps something important. Damn I wish I spoke Oneirion!"

"What about releasing this news to the world Phil?"

Herb interjected. "Would you like my opinion?"

"Certainly Herb." Responded Anne.

"I only know what I've been overhearing about this. It's all pretty damned unbelievable. If you ask me, non-Oneirion humans would react badly to this. It taxes credulity too much. It's too frustrating. Humans have been waiting for an alien visit for hundreds of years. Then we learn they've been with us since long before our recorded history—before we even existed. Then we learn we can't even see them, or communicate directly with them. On top of that we must become experts in advanced physics to even begin to understand what they are. They're not going to be a damned bit happy. I could see some of them reacting violently. Another aspect to this that will certainly annoy hell out of people is its elitism."

"*Elitism?*"

"You're damned right. Elitism. On the one hand you have a space-faring race that makes us look like comparative lab rats. On the other hand you have an island full of genetically superior humans, mostly university students at that, who are the only ones the QAVL will deign to speak to because the rest of us are too goddamned stupid to learn their language. Dangerous as all hell. Has all the earmarks of a killing scenario."

"You could be right Herb. It brings to mind a famous, or infamous quote out of the history of the Nixon Whitehouse by the then Vice President Spiro Agnew. Wonderful name…sounds like it would be delicious grilled with Saffron Rice and Greek Beans." Phil chortled a moment then refocused his attention. "Anyhow, Agnew, referring to dissenters to the war in Viet Nam – primarily academia – called them 'effete intellectuals'. A nearly whimsical cerebral vesicle for a highly anti-intellectual message. All the same, that term may be germane to world reaction to Oneiro. We are a group of intellectuals making some devastatingly important decisions on the world's behalf. Depending on the second half of the message, I suspect we may need to sit on this for quite some time. Maybe indefinitely."

"Mike's going to resist that." said Anne.

"I know." sighed Phil. "And his reasoning is sound. As is yours. As is Herb's. As is mine. Anne when do you estimate the human race will catch up to Oneiro?"

"I doubt it will ever catch up. They project it will take about two centuries to attain Oneiro's current development at the current rate of food supplementation."

"I wonder if this can be accelerated."

"You know as well as I Phil. These people can damn near do anything."

"Mm. More wine?"

# Qruxin *Camena ab Universum*

"Good morning. I hope you enjoyed your meal last night and now have a clearer understanding of some of the physics surrounding the QAVL."

"Great with a good Cabernet too." said Phil.

Light laughter.

"As I recall we left Mount Qrux having formed a plasma sea in its caldera. The QAVL naturally refer to this as the Qruxian Sea. It's difficult to conceive of the energy concentrated here. 23,000 feet of ionized plasma constantly subjected to external energy and excitation. This is the stuff of magneto-optical phenomenon. Exactly the event that transpired.

Ever heard of the Faraday Effect, or the Faraday Rotation?"

From the audience, "Michael Faraday was a chemist and physicist in the 1800's. The effect has to do with the bending of light I think."

"Correct. Among many other things, he worked on electric motors. He investigated and subsequently proved the relationship between light and electro-magnetism. He discovered there is such a relationship which is termed electromagnetic radiation. Essentially electromagnet fields can bend light. Twisted light. If you submerge such light, warping thousands of meters beneath a sea of energy. An optically transparent dielectric medium beneath the Qruxian Sea. The light is slowed, bent and trapped. Much as it is at the sun's core. Bouncing around like a pool ball for millions of years. Then cook it for a couple of billion years. This twisted energy hybrid learns to maintain its form. A sort of photo-organic-amino-acid. The first key.

Then it learns to replicate electro-magnetically. Not by design, or by any intent. Just physical laws at work, bonding sub-atomic elements in accordance with universal forces. The second key.

Then it demonstrates massive linkages between twists and performs a sort of lensing action. Radiant energy is magnified and it facilitates further twisting replication. Suddenly there is adaptive advantage in replication. The third key.

The fourth key is more complicated. Let's take a break."

Over coffee. "So Mike, have the QAVL revealed how many types of life forms they have encountered?"

"How many types Phil?"

"Yeah. Carbon base, silicon, light, methane and so on."

"I see. I imagine it may be buried deep into one of their top-downs. Apparently it's important we have a working understanding of their nature for some reason. I would imagine that Part II of their communication will make this clear."

"If we're grappling with this, how will the world at large handle it?"

"Good question. Big problem. Unless Part II gives us something to work with."

"So effectively you're saying we must keep this to ourselves at least another six months?"

"Unless they reveal something germane to this problem sooner."

"What's the rush Mike?"

"I have to admit this is a personal and emotional issue for me in many respects."

"Such as?"

"People are dying every minute who will never know we have been visited. The universe truly teams with incredible living diversity and they will die alone. I think it's tragic."

"Continue."

"We do not *own* this knowledge. It rightfully belongs to all mankind. It will change the world, and every minute we wait, delays the leverage which could save man altogether."

"Anything else?"

"Isn't that enough?"

"Go on Mike."

"Okay. Backlash. Were I to discover this news was knowingly withheld from me, I would react with…incendiary…rage."

"Well Mike, you make some good points. Although I'm not at all sure we don't *own* this knowledge. It was entrusted only to those who speak Oneirion. The QAVL are not stupid. They have excellent reasons for withholding their presence until a civilization qualifies itself by speaking Oneirion. You do. The world doesn't."

"Phil, *you* don't speak Oneirion."

"Of that I am painfully aware Mike. I assume I can be entrusted with this information because I helped bring us to the point of contact. I make the same claim regarding the rest of us non-speakers here. I also bring one other item to my argument."

"Which would be…?"

"I *own* Oneiro."

Mike laughed. "Good arguments Phil. I withdraw my comment." He smiled. "That brings me to another point Phil. You free for dinner tonight?"

"Sure, I reckon. Who's invited?"

"Just you, if that's okay Phil."

"Fine. Where?"

"Well I'd be happy to show you my digs."

"I'd be interested to see where you live Mike. On the surface right?"

"Right. I'm still working on it."

"You're doing the work yourself?"

"Ah, most of it. Except for the heavy equipment stuff. I really enjoy it and the design just sort of organically educes as I build it. Been a few years now. I should finish it soon."

"Well I'd love to see it."

"Okay. Just input *Auslander Quarters* in a PM. Say 1930?"

"Fine. Back to it?"

"Yep."

# Qruxin *Camena ab Universum – Persevero*

The reassembled group seemed a bit restive. As though they were anxious for a denouement that would crystallize this mass of arcane concepts. Mike seemed to sense this and quickly moved along."

"As I said before the break, this is where it gets complicated, so I'm going to try to make it fast and as simple as possible."

Phil was amused to see a group of top-of-the-line Oneirions vexed with the difficulty of a subject. He conceded however this group wasn't simply absorbing the facts as presented–they were attempting to understand the science behind the facts.

"These large colonies of twisted light gained such size they became ponderous and began to break up. They grew to great size again, and broke away again. And on and on. Within a few millennia the Qruxian Sea evolved into a rich stew of contorted energy. This fostered energy competition. The fourth key.

Things were getting interesting.

As with any environment in the galaxy, competition applied pressure to evolution. The twisted light creatures developed adaptations to make them more successful. They grew more complex. They developed a memory. They learned to communicate basic ideas.

The QAVL theorize, for the first time in their geologic history, a meteor event impacted the Qruxin Sea. Its angle of attack must have been absolutely perfect to escape the plethora of celestial sentries marching about Qruxin. Nonetheless it made it through and explosively disbursed throughout the Qruxin Sea. This played a unique function in Qruxin history. The meteor was primarily ferrous in composition, so it populated the sea with millions of inert, magnetic obstacles.

This was exactly the boosted evolitive tension required to push the primitive life forms into something special. These obstacles provided a landscape of sorts. A landscape provides many valuable services to life. It serves to store and concentrate energy sources. It hides energy sources. It modifies energy… sometimes releasing potential energy into active energy…magnetic, thermal, kinetic, and so on. If there are predators it provides attack opportunities. If there are predators it provides refuge from predation. It proliferates life forms. It creates diverse ecologies, thereby phylic diversity. It magnifies seasonal shifts. It separates ecological niches.

The list goes on and on, and much of it applied to primordial Qruxin. It provoked an urgent need for communication, advanced thought, exploration, co-operation, conservation of energy, memory and physical adaptation. Bottom line. It pushed them over the top. They learned they could leave the sea, move about magnetically, just as in the sea and they became true sentient creatures, evolving for millions and millions of years.

Primitive QAVL developed from the extant communal beings. Constantly in physical contact, early communications were both instantaneous and language independent. In a critical adaptation they discovered by breaking away from each other they could learn more about their surroundings and absorb energy more freely. This entailed they evolve. He turned to the viewer. "Here's their profile today:

- The QAVL are tri-sexual. The QAVL TROICA. They literally bond for life and they are essentially immortal by our definition.
- They can control/manipulate gravity and magnetism which provides them movement in nearly any environment–including the near absolute zero, hard vacuum of interstellar, even intergalactic space.
- Aside from the ability to manipulate electricity and plasma energy, they can also manipulate magnetic and gravitational fields.
- No QAVL entity is specialized. Within each TROICA, set specialization does exist. One is charged with memory, another movement and manipulation, one reproduction and leadership.
- Food gathering is not a task. They draw energy directly from light. Within their energy manipulation skills they can store a limited amount of sustenance. However, they devote most of this capacity in retention of information, stored and accessed through intensely delineated spectral breakdown of white light. This media has near infinite capacity.
- They reproduce rarely, although they incessantly engage in sex for pleasure. Their current population consists of some two billion beings–most of which are now space-borne. Reproduction is a function of plasma extrusions from each member of the troika resulting in asexual beings which randomly drift, finally finding a match with two others as part of a highly secretive communal rite. Their version of DNA/RNA is stored as light spectra. Some infinitely small genetic drift does occur. Over the eons this has resulted in unimaginably slow evolution. Instead however, they manipulate their own genetic material. If they develop a modification of particular benefit, they communicate it to their race.
- The QAVL suffer no predation. They have never engaged in any type of warfare. They understand violence from observation of other creatures as they rise and fall, never having engaged in it themselves. They

have no need to compete for space or resources. Matter is beyond their ability to mold and has no inherent value to them. Food (energy in light form) is constantly in abundance. Living space is not an object of competition. They find concepts like wealth, war, hatred and crime extremely difficult to assimilate.

- The QAVLs prize information, knowledge, memories, poetry, literature, music and a type of imagery they were unable to adequately describe. These things they share with relish. They share everything. They are totally incapable of dissimulation, or of a lie by omission.
- QAVLs have a sense of humor. They are emotional. They experience some emotions indescribable in any non-Qruxin language. They have a sense of play and enjoy life with a joy unheard of on earth. Incorporeal sex being one of their greatest pleasures.
- They had a religion at one point in their history. It was quite similar to Dr. Kahn's multi-Deism. They had pondered this for eons and concluded they would never know the nature of the creator. They do believe the creator exists–witness creation –and that was the extent of their belief system…with one important exception: The new Language. They then discovered the universe resident in every QAVL and the beginnings of understanding was born.
- QAVL refer to it as the *Song of the Cosmos*. They had visited over 100,000 planets inhabited by sentient beings. Invariably when the indigenes achieved a certain level of intelligence and civilization they evolved the Language. The QAVL were firmly convinced the Language was of the Creator itself and permeated the substance of creation, of the universe, of existence itself. They had to develop a language (An early form of Oneirion.).
- The Psychology Department calculates QAVL intelligence exceeds human, even Oneirion, by factor of roughly 600. Their knowledge spans the universe. Their imagination renders anything possible.
- They represent the ultimate Jungian paradigm of racial memory, back some two billion years. They remember back to the time when they achieved sentience itself, and everything since. Literally they forget nothing–although they do occasionally *purge* extraneous information. This they achieve through dreaming. They do not sleep. They dream incessantly though.
- They are quite literally immortal. They are unkillable. They are incapable of self-destruction. When queried if immortality didn't ultimately represent an endless, inescapable nightmare, they were amused. They responded such questions were invariably a rationalized response of ephemeral species."

"There is literally no way to kill them?"

"Not that they are aware of."

"What if they were encased in a light impermeable material? Wouldn't they starve to death ultimately?"

"I asked pretty much the same question Phil. They responded that in total darkness there still remained copious sources of energy they could use. They also stated the question presupposes they could be enclosed against their will." Mike gave Phil a knowing smile. "They need neither defensive nor offensive capability."

"Okay. What about say…a 100 kiloton nuclear blast in their exact proximity?"

"Phil they classify nuclear weapons as not far removed from the spear, or the stone knife.

I think that's enough for today. You can only take so much in a given sitting. Tomorrow I think will require a full day. We'll talk about the introduction of the QAVL to space-faring life forms. How they acquired tools and machines. How they met the *Kosmos*. Afterward we should discuss when the rest of the world learns of the QAVL. This may take a total of four days to kick this project off on a good footing."

Phil. "What project Mike?"

Mike smiled. "See you at 0930. Thank you."

# Dinner with Mike

Anne was quite happy to leave Phil to his dinner meeting with Mike. She was anxious to visit her friends in the Art Department and catch up on progress. She anticipated many exciting new developments had emerged in her absence.

Herb was off with his girlfriends. Edward was left to his own devices.

A PM reported to Phil's quarters promptly at 1915 and transported him to the surface at the airfield end of the university.

Once above ground the sleek little three wheeled chariot took him cross-country and cross-desert. Wild, rough countryside. The PM then impressively negotiated a long, rugged, potholed, dirt path to Mike's home. Phil stopped briefly to take in the island and the afternoon. The air was still and hot. Small flying insects and motes of dust glowed in the afternoon sun. Drifting down between the trees, much as sediment drifts down undersea. A warm flinty scent emanating from heated dust and stone blended with the pungency of pine and undergrowth. There was a wonderful clean and dry freshness to the semi-desert. Forests were always loamy, laced with the heavy, wet scent of rotting vegetation. Phil much preferred arid desert air.

Phil noticed sentry plants amongst the foliage. He soon realized they were everywhere. They looked surprisingly natural in the setting and they went easily unnoticed, although ferns were a rare desert flora. He stepped down from the PM and inspected one more closely. What looked like a normal fern from a distance was actually pretty bizarre on close inspection. Strange pods at the ends of spiky branches interspersed with fern fronds. Waxy leaves engineered to stand up to drought. Leaves that seemed to move. A rhythmic movement having nothing to do with moving air, or any external force. A sort of awareness about the plant. Formidable flora. It seemed to be inspecting him as much as he inspected it. It was watching him. It was sniffing him. It was testing him. He was sure of it. He backed away and returned to his PM with a decided feeling of relief.

Where did the PM's power come from anyway? Certainly not this rocky dirt path. He made a note to ask Mike.

When the PM did come to a stop he wondered if a mistake had been made. There was no home of any sort in sight.

The PM had delivered him to a wild desert garden. Abundant cactus, wild flowers of every color and description, sentry plants; even some pine and olive trees. Boulders randomly placed throughout artfully framed the enormous rock garden. In the midst of the garden there was a lake enclosing a hilly, rocky island. Shallow. Clear and sparkling. Water lilies in abundance. The lake was fed by a small water fall at one end of the island. Where it drained he couldn't make out.

The island consisted mainly of a small granite mountain covered with huge round boulders of native stone. There was a rough hewn bridge to the island which connected the dirt road to a rocky dead-end on the island. The bridge was relatively large. Clearly lovingly crafted. Sturdy logs beautifully patterned. Strong. Skillfully joined. Not a nail or bolt in the entire construct that Phil could make out. A design he had never seen. It looked capable of supporting heavy transport. *Transport to where?*

The combined effect of the island, the lake, the bridge and the desert garden was quite pleasing. Phil made the logical choice to cross the bridge. He concluded Mike had set him up to figure out this place on his own.

As he approached the far side of the bridge, the face of a large bolder smoothly pivoted outward high above him. Standing in the shadow of the doorway stood Mike smiling broadly looking down from a height of at least thirty meters.

"Am I going to have to do some climbing?" Phil yelled up.

He could hear Mike's quiet laugh as though he were standing close. Apparently there was an intercom cached somewhere in the rocks here.

"Welcome Phil, please come through the break in the rocks in front of you and stand in the middle of the clearing."

Phil found himself standing on a flat rock, enclosed by a natural looking stone balustrade, soundlessly ascending to the summit where Mike awaited. He hydraulic lift smoothly arrived at Mike's door. They shook hands and entered the coolness of the home.

"Mike I'm in awe. This is a wonder. You built that bridge didn't you?"

"Yes I did."

"All by yourself?"

"Yep."

"Ever build a bridge before?"

"Ah no. It was a learning experience. I studied bridge engineering a bit. Then I designed my own."

"The wood?"

"One of our few imports. I traded an oil synthesizer to a logger on Corsica."

"Well done. Are you actually strong enough to do all this work without any help? Sling those logs around?"

"Apparently. I was a little surprised myself. It was a labor of love and I did use some machine assists. I expect that bridge will be there when I've been gone for ages. Solid oak. 76x304 millimeter oak pegs. No nails. No bolts. Those logs were injected, seasoned, kiln dried, then further aged and treated for five years. In this climate the bridge should just get dryer, stronger and tougher. No part of the bridge is footed in water, or even wetland. It is footed in flint and steel hardened concrete and epoxy sealed against moisture. I'm assured no wet or dry-rot, no ant, termite, or anything can attack the wood. Not even a normal fire. Since most of the bark remains intact, I injected under the bark. Then I permanently sealed the entire bridge with three treatments of epoxy resin after the bridge was complete. Given reasonable maintenance it will last for three hundred years. If it lasts for three hundred, I think it's good for a thousand."

"Jesus. You really got into this bridge Mike. Impressive. It looks like your home will last as long."

"Hope so. That's the plan. Come on in. Let me show you the rest of the place."

As Phil had anticipated, the entire top floor of the underground home was a periscope. It felt like walking into a high mountain peak just as the top was suddenly blown off. A wonderful open feeling. An expansive terrace, open to the sky, atop a mountain. The air was fresh and cool with the slightest breeze, laced with a hint of sea and sand and semi-desert. The sun was clear and sharp casting shadows of equal clarity throughout the huge room.

A 360° view from a high rocky summit–surrounded by mountainous boulders–surrounded by the island–surrounded by the lake–surrounded by the garden–surrounded by Oneiro– surrounded by the sea–surrounded by the sky and onto the stars. Infinitely concentric.

A bright, riotous Earth-sphere of form and color and symmetry and movement. Breathtaking.

"Well Mike you've certainly taken best advantage of the natural beauty of the island."

"My first priority. I've always fantasized about a place like this. And unfortunately since security remains a consideration, it's quite practical as well."

"From the air this must look like a park. What can theses boulders take?"

"Anything short of a direct hit. Even then it would have to be pretty powerful. A thousand pounder, or more. Those boulders are enormous, even larger than they look, mainly granite, covering two meters of flint hardened, steel re-enforced concrete."

"Impressive. Do you have direct access from below?"

"I will have. They are tunneling under this complex now. They should be finished this month and there'll be an elevator directly into the lower reception."

"So where's your PM...not to mention jeeps and trucks...maybe a motor cycle?"

"All stowed in ground level area concealed by its own swiveling boulder. Not far from the lift."

"I see. By the way, how is a PM powered out on your dirt road?"

Mike was setting up the bar. "Mmm?"

"The PM I took here clearly passed beyond the limits of the Oneiro power grid. So what powered it?"

"Oh. That's one of our niftier new developments. We are transmitting electricity now. Safely and reliably. 110, 220, 440, whatever's needed. Hellofa lot less expensive than installing below ground radiant power grids as we do today. Much stronger as well. A single transmitter can supply about 80,000 square meters on the surface with megawatts of power. We camouflage them as tall pines. Our engineers can have one up and operating in about three days. We do suffer interference from strong electromagnetic storms. So we are installing backup power storage units in all surface devices and buildings as a matter of routine now."

"Power transmitters aren't dangerous?"

"These apparently are not. I'm told they've been rigorously tested in all conceivable conditions. I'm not clear on the details though."

"Do you transmit power to the transmitters?"

"In fact yes. From Proteus Point."

"So these are actually relay transmitters."

"Yeah. What's your point?"

"What's the maximum range?"

"I'm not sure. We should ask Charlie Stein. His people set this up."

"But why the interest in max range Phil?"

"Not sure Mike. Have to give it some thought..." Phil let his mind wander and looked about his surroundings.

The interior furnishings were in engaging harmony with their surroundings. Rustic. Solid. Comfortable. Durable good looks in Oneirion imperleather and solid, vat-hybridized hard woods. The American Southwest. The floors were covered in valuable, hand woven Pueblo Indian rugs. Phil noted the only fireplace he had seen anywhere on the island. A huge stone affair ascending into an endless clear sky. Crooked live-oak logs neatly stacked to one side. A most imposing living and reception room.

The far end of the room opened onto the most impressive staircase Phil had ever seen. A vast, broad, long staircase with a high arched ceiling descending into the depths of the mountain. Bright sunlight from indirect periscopes lining the entire passage. The ceiling was colorfully frescoed in abstract designs, also American southwest in style, color and motif. Bright, artfully structured, clean lines and pleasing. The overall impression was of an enormous tunnel in an ancient Indian cliff-dwelling. Cool stone and pastel decorations enhanced by dizzying heights and larger than life architecture, assiduously decorated as if by ancient peoples celebrating vanished gods, and lives ended long before history's chronicle. He'd never seen so many symbols. Frogs, bears, lizards, horned toads, turtles, coyotes, wolves, water birds, owls, eagles, snakes, animal tracks, the Navajo Yeii Spirit, Kokopelli, the seed bringer, the Thunderbird, and more. All exquisitely executed in vivid colors. Some in pale pastels.

The staircase opened onto several landings in the course of its long descent. Some landings connected to meeting rooms, offices and guest quarters. Others looked into swimming pools, game rooms, gymnasiums and spas, sitting rooms and libraries. One landing even boasted an art gallery.

"Get a fair amount of exercise on these stairs do you Mike?" Smiled Phil, footsteps echoing in the vast inclined chamber.

"Yes. Yes I do. Normally I run the stairs. Although they're installing a discreet six person lift in a week or so. Clever design. Native stone, just as the stairs. They're mounted and tooled into the kick plates; and the steps seem to magically rise up from their matrix and travel up and down along with their own part of the banister. By actually moving across the landings passengers can easily step off whenever and wherever they wish. Up to six units can travel up and down concurrently. Noiseless, safe and relatively speedy."

*Clearly to accommodate VIP's and heads of state. Not Oneirions for sure.*

They finally arrived into a voluminous area, which was in part the dining room. Simple and beautifully crafted. The walls were an artful blending of logs, huge stones and sand washed slate. Paintings were in abundance, augmenting and reinforcing the motif. Phil guessed they were Mike's work, as he noted a few were covered by dark cloths. Phil assumed this was for his protection. Oneirion art can debilitate or even kill those not genetically adapted. Phil's mind bore lifelong scars in testament of the terrifying power Oneirion paintings can achieve.

Light danced and rippled about the room as though they were undersea. Phil looked up and immediately understood. The high ceiling of the dining room was not a periscope. The entire ceiling consisted of a large, thick clear pane looking directly up into the lake. Phil could see the rippling waves sparkling on the surface of the lake and the occasional silver flash of a fish. From beneath. His favorite perspective on water.

"I'd show you more Phil. Problem is, the rest is just being finished."

"That's okay Mike. I already love this place. Have you given it a name?"

"Yes I have: I brachia–η βράχια–The Rocks. Haven't figured yet out where to post the name though."

"Appropriate. How safe is that window looking up into the lake?"

"That's 355 millimeters of polycarbonate thermoplastic. Few conventional battlefield weapons could penetrate it; and the water reinforces it as an effective buffer from above."

"I thought water was effective at transmitting shock waves?"

"It is. But our lake is wide and shallow, so any such force is disbursed more laterally than horizontally. And with a window such as this, the weight of the water is almost negligible. All the same, should the window be breached somehow, it automatically triggers explosive deployment of 50 millimeter hardened tungsten steel and titanium laminate hatch."

They turned back up the stairs. "How 'bout a drink?"

"Sure. Gin and Tonic?"

"You bet."

"Do you swim the lake?"

"Every morning and evening I do about forty laps. I have a terrace partly obscured by rock providing access to the lake. I do a good deal of rowing as well. I've even experimented some with your underwater skills. No luck so far."

"How do the ladies feel about this place?"

"They like it ... a lot. Especially the lake." grinned Mike.

Soon they were seated back in the reception room. Drinks in hand. They spent some time discussing the day's meeting. Both were similarly amused by the difficulty the material presented to landers and Oneirions alike.

"How about you Phil? This stuff seems too easy for you. You were always quite intuitive, but you're exceeding intuition by one hellofa lot now. I've also heard you've now developed some unexpected new prowess under water. You're getting stronger and faster. You seem to know the answer to questions before they're even asked. You appear to recall information you were never previously exposed to. You can make complex analysis and decisions nearly instantaneously. And you continue to act as some sort of catalyst on events as they unfold around you."

"You've been talking to Anne. What are you getting at?"

"As far as I am aware, you are a perfectly normal lander. You're not the product of the compression of hundreds and thousands of generations. Yet I believe your talents are on a par with, and perhaps well beyond, anyone on this island. This is all part of the proposals I have for you tonight."

"So what do *you* think it is Mike?"

"Dunno. Some kind of ESP?"

"ESP is just another term for *I haven't one damned clue*."

"I guess we'll have to figure it out one of these days."

"Alright. So what's for dinner? I'm starved."

Mike smiled "Meat loaf, macaroni & cheese, baby lima beans, Côte d'Oneiro Rosé and chocolate *cake*."

Phil frowned. "That menu is familiar. Why"

"The meal you served when you gave me this job."

"Ah yes. Still your favorites?"

"You bet."

"And you're serving this because … you have a job for *me* now?"

Mike laughed "Let's eat."

Again they descended the imposing staircase to the dining room. When they were seated, a pretty server entered. Phil recognized her from the restaurant in the Mansion complex. Soon dinner was on the table.

"Actually Phil I could never offer you a job. I can offer you a proposal though. And a choice."

"Tell me about it."

"This is directly related to Part II of the QAVL message. The QAVL were explicit in their introduction to Part II."

"Explicit about what?"

"About the intent of Part II. It's an invitation. An invitation to join them."

"Where? Aboard their invisible ship? We wouldn't survive a second."

"No. Aboard our own."

Phil paused for a few moments, sipping his wine and looking up into the darkening lake. The colors of sunset were filtering down through the water now. Suddenly a bank of underwater spotlights was activated. The ceiling pulsated and glowed with surging blue-red-golds.

Phil turned his scrutiny to Mike, regarding him seriously.

*Have I been spending too much time on Sea Tigress? Are things getting out of hand here? Did I put Mike in this job too soon? Too young. No. Mike is the man for this job. No one could have anticipated what he would face. No leader's ever faced anything like this. Give him time.* All the same, Phil had seen the relief on Mike's face when they arrived Oneiro.

"Tell me about this Mike."

"Okay Phil." Mike frowned in concentration. "But first, there's a word we should discuss. *Kosmas*."

The word awoke something in Phil. As if Mike had struck him a powerful blow. Nearly electric. His brain actually tingled. It shocked him into rapid thought. His eyes darted at near unbelievable speed. His mind literally shot through thoughts and memories. All his thoughts, all his work on SNA, now *Kosmas*, raced through his mind again in its entirety. He felt a slight tremble in his left hand. Less than two seconds later he calmed and looked up at Mike. A sharp intake of breath ending in a slow sigh.

Mike was watching him intently in undisguised fascination.

"Yes. I discovered it three days ago about thirty meters under the Aegean. I was unaware of the term…*Kosmas*." Phil stumbled imperceptibly on the word. "I termed it SNA. Subatomic-Nucleic-Apperceptum. Resident in every cell in our body. Every atom. Extant from the Big Bang itself. Spread across all creation. Every entity in the universe is part of it. It defines all knowledge. It defines time. The past. The present. And I think the future. I have not analyzed it fully. That would take lifetimes I suppose. I suspect all our declarations of free will, of determinism, whatever, may amount to nothing. Only hubris."

"What do you base this on Phil?"

"Exploration? Determinism? Quantum Physics? Cosmology? Mathematics? Empirical evidence? Direct observation? Rejection of Chaos and Randomness? An intuitive leap? Cheap whiskey? Hard work? Clean living? Take your pick."

"My god Phil! There is no keeping up with you. There is no understanding you. How on earth did you discover this? You are describing something millennia beyond human experience. What does this imply for current science.?"

"It bankrupts Quantum Theory. Or maybe it's vastly enhanced. Perhaps it facilitates a Unified Theory."

"Can you explain this? Do you understand it yourself?"

Phil took some moments to organize his thoughts.

Finally, just above a whisper, head down, a faraway look in his eyes "I was questing my own nucleotides. I was exploring my neurons. Using them as a gateway to existence at its smallest, most basic level…assuming there is a finite end…a final granularity. I became a sort of zetetic probe. Alone in my own cellular galaxy. Its beauty…beggars description. Creation itself glowing and swirling towards an infinite horizon. I have penetrated this region before. Under the sea. I had many questions. I still do.

I was attempting to locate. Locate my memory. The memory of things I have never consciously known. I suspected it was comparable to genetic retention. A kind of Jungian racial memory. Upon much deeper observation, I realized the smallest basic granular substance of nucleic acids, or anything really, is actually comprised of what I termed SNA, at the extreme end of the micro-subatomic level. Infinitely small. Then I realized everything was comprised of them. Particles we never dreamt of. Particles we're centuries from physically detecting, or surmising. Infinite capacity. A wonder of the cosmos. In fact, a mirror of the cosmos. An infinitely small mirror faithful in every respect to the infinitely large. A straightforward physical *unified theory of existence*. The blueprint of creation begins with the infinitely small and faithfully echoes forever, to the infinitely large."

But it comes down to this Mike: *If randomness/chaos exist, what we call God does not, or it exists far beyond human relevance, on a plane beyond imagining, alien to this universe, apart from and unknowing of us. Our hopes, dreams, prayers & adulation of God, and God for us…No more than mist at sunrise.*

Mike was clearly incredulous, even repelled by Phil's statements. "Look, this is more than ridiculous. In effect you're saying that the velocity direction and relative position of every single particle in the entire universe is knowable , was predetermined fourteen billion years ago, and is predictable literally forever. Until the end of the universe itself. *I find that categorical, uncontestable NONSENSE!*"

Phil regarded Mike, not unsympathetically. "This is tied to the nature of existence itself Mike. Therefore, pretty incredible. I agree. But, and this is important Mike, look at the corollary."

"The corollary?"

Yes. If non-deterministic, how do you account for the position and trajectory of a particle?"

"How do I *account* for it?"

"Yes. How did it get there? What established its speed? Its direction? Its interaction with other particles? Where is the *causality*? What could possibly intercede to modify its preset odyssey throughout the cosmos?"

"It's impossible to say. There are just too many…"

"…there are too many variables?" Phil smiled. "We simply don't have all the elements to predict such a thing. That does not render it unpredictable by any means. Physicists have constructed machines which they purport to demonstrate chaos. Some very simple…double hinged bits of metal and such; and they claim the action of these machines is totally unpredictable. They simply lack all the elements that define the machine's actions. All the relevant variables."

"Phil I'm getting a headache."

"Okay. Let's cut through it. If chaos, true randomness, does indeed exist. That implies that actions occur without cause. If that is true. What process does that define?"

"What?"

"*MAGIC.*"

Mike softly huffed "Ridiculous."

Phil cocked his head and pursed his lips. "Exactly. So which do you prefer? A universe based on shamanism, or upon absolute predictability consistent with physical laws? Black or white. There is no room for gray Mike."

"Jesus Phil, there is absolutely no way you can empirically prove any of this."

"Exactly Mike. You're not considering *the* fundamental limitation of the scientific method."

"...and that would be?"

"You cannot observe a process from within that process. And we are most definitely within the universe."

"So what's left."

"Metaphysics, logic, ontology. We can *think* our way through this."

"The muse of the gods themselves."

Phil frowned, looking inwardly. "Quite right. The Universe...infinitely small to infinitely large...an eternally infinite regression..."

"Multiverses?"

"That model seems too simplistic. Even naïve in some respects. Indications are, there is a cyclical repetition however, as there must ultimately be in any system lacking infinite constituents...."

"*Lacking* infinite constituents?"

"Yes. Otherwise the Big Bang would be continuing today. Therefore, there are near endless repetitions of every conceivable universe...ours being just one...we therefore repeat. Not a flat universe. I call it ubi-space. Only the size and particle composition differs. Logic demands with respect to our universe, there be multi-gradient-verses, mirror-verses, modi-verses and anti-verses. On and on with every conceivable gradient in between."

"When was this *cosmic trauma* inflicted?"

"Inflicted? Nothing was ever inflicted. Such a thing is not possible, as it introduces an external force. Nothing exists outside this process..."

"You said God did."

"Set that aside for a moment. Instead, every possible particle was dispatched in every possible direction, initiating every possible cosmic chaining at the moment of the big bang. Something akin to beaming a multicolored projector, only with an infinite number of beams. Each beam occupying its own space, its own nature. This is within the context of *Kosmas* I believe. Every particle, movement, action and behavior – is *ordained*. The velocity, even the direction, of a particle governs the nature/properties/definition of the particle. And the concomitant particles govern the nature of their universe"

## *DAKHALA* Private Dunn

Manu was still rambling the high cliff-lands – still savoring the rugged beauty, the freshness and blessed isolation surrounding her – still pondering the dark uncertainties of her future – when she realized it was growing quite late. The sun would soon disappear behind Mount Sikaram and she would be in trouble. She reluctantly turned towards home, nearly running into her father.

Red faced. Sweating in the cold air. Clearly angry. He'd been walking hard and long. Zalmai angrily cuffed the back of her head hard. "It's late. I've been looking everywhere for you." He growled through grinding teeth, clenching her arm in a painful grip. He look about suspiciously. "Out here by yourself...I should beat you silly." He stopped to regain his breath. "Malik came to our home." Manu started at mention of the name. She had yet to face the filthy man after their wretched encounter two nights ago. "He wants you to cook tonight. Some soldiers are having a party at the restaurant. Fifteen men, and they want your Mourgh. Hurry! They will be there in less than an hour." Zalmai pushed her roughly in the direction of the village nearly causing her to stumble and slightly spraining her ankle.

Manu painfully limped the long way to the station, dreading it every second. When she arrived, there was Malik, as though nothing had happened, screaming at her for being late. Berating her for disappearing. What a slow, ugly, unreliable girl she was. She must be stupid *and* half crazy. He yelled even louder so the restaurant and staff could all hear "Don't lie to me! Don't lie to me about where you have been, like you lie about everything else! The others may believe you. I know better. Now get to work. There is little time."

As she gathered pots and pans and ingredients she thought *Now I understand. That fat pig is making me out a liar... in case I tell people what I saw in the pantry. What an evil man. I wish he would die.*

Despite all her problems the Mourgh was ready by the time the soldiers appeared. They were being rotated to another posting. Their replacements would arrive tomorrow, so tonight they would celebrate. There were thirteen men and the restaurant was closed to all save them. They were all foreigners – AJNABI – so she understood nothing they said. They were clearly happy, all drinking some sort of fruit juice mixture they brought themselves. Manu had heard of alcohol and she feared this was what they drank. It made her uneasy. Their bill would be sizable in relation to normal business at the restaurant, and Malik could smell a sizable tip in the offing as well. So he served them himself, laughing, talking and generally doting over them. He even accepted a drink of their fruit juice when offered. After they had finished their Mourgh (without comment or compliment – although they greedily devoured everything) their behavior grew worse. They became louder. Some went outside to be sick. They all were flushed and sloppy. Malik demanded Manu help with clearing the table and in the process noted Malik nod and leer at her, one eyebrow arched, while his eyes were fixed on a young soldier with very bad skin, very drunk. Dinner was over but a great deal of fruit juice remained so the party drank and smoked and laughed and cavorted. Manu hurried through cleaning up and fled as quickly as possible.

It was a great relief to escape into the cold quiet of the night. It was snowing. No one was about. The snow muffled all sound and it was beautiful. Peaceful. Manu stopped for a moment, closed her eyes and took a long, deep breath. *My! That feels better.* His mood much improved, she set out to enjoy the long walk home. *Why rush? It's just as cold at home. Why not enjoy the night?*

Her thoughts returned to earlier that evening walking the high cliffs. What could she do? How to get away? Well, what were her strengths? She was young, healthy and strong. She was not beautiful, but what would beauty do for her anyway? Get her a husband like her father? No...*shurkran jazilan*. She was smart. She knew she was smart. And she could cook and look after a home. She knew children. She'd cared for many neighborhood young ones. Maybe she could find work with a good family, or a nice little restaurant? But that needed a larger town. She would have to find her way to Nangarhar, or even Kabul. Maybe a trucker would give her a...

Something grabbed her and violently threw her to the ground. Her head cracked painfully on a rock and she was dazed and hurt. Then a man was on top of her. The same young soldier with bad skin from the restaurant. His eyes were glazed with a wild feral look. He was drunk. She didn't know drunk. But she was sure, he was drunk. She was nauseated by the smell of garlic, alcohol and tobacco on his breath. Initially she was surprised and confused. But fear was swiftly overtaking and she was losing the capacity to move, or even think. The man tore open her skirt and ripped her underwear apart looking hungrily between her legs, running a hand up her thighs to her small breasts. He smiled at some inner thought and began to unzip and expose himself. Somewhere, slow-motion in her mind, this made her recall Malik in the pantry that terrible night. He grinned down on her and in a strange accent "You a ugly little turd but I bet you fuck like a monkey." Then he laughed drunkenly and clumsily forced himself inside her. Bestial and inept, he hurt her terribly. *Hasan Allah* such pain! Her circumcision was still a raw wound;

and this savage violation compounded her agony. Instinctively she threw her arms above her head to grasp something to help endure the pain. Nothing. Only snow. And...the rock she had fallen on.

Her festering pain, her fear, her bitterness and futility exploded like a ruptured abscess. She could take no more. She grasped the stone and cracked it down on the soldier's head with all her strength. A brief grunt, a short spasm and a dead soldier. For a time she simply lay in the snow, breathing the clean air and trying desperately to withstand the pain. Then she rolled him off and weakly trembled to her feet. What to do? He was an AJNABI and she had.... *lain with him.* They would beat her to death. She cast about in panic trying to find a solution. It began to snow harder.

There was a deep gully ten meters away which eventually found its way down to the Khyber. If she could get him into the gully the snow would cover him and the melts in the spring would carry him into the pass. And that would end it.

The combination of cold, fatigue, a sprain, a head injury, rape and the accumulated damages to her genitals mitigated against her. Dragging the dead soldier was nearly impossible. It took her some thirty minutes to cover a scant ten meters. When she made it though, the body rolled satisfyingly deep into the gully. It was already difficult to see and the snow would conceal him until June. She dropped to her knees and wept. Eventually it occurred to her if she were too late her father would awaken, suspicious and probably beat her. *Allah min fadlik.* The thought of another beating tonight terrified and sickened her. She hurried home and entered her shack without a sound.

Manu made a point of being conspicuously up and about the next day, hiding her pain. At the restaurant, Malik regarded her quizzically as she entered. However, he re-instated her position in the back. Poor Zemar was re-relegated to the garbage and the trucks and the Chai. Uzuri and Narmir were delighted to see her back amongst their ranks. Muni made an efforts to be light and giggly, despite her true feelings.

Mid-afternoon, a half-track carrying Military Police rolled into the station. Apparently a Private Dunn had gone missing after a platoon party at the restaurant last night. They brought an interpreter and interviewed all who had been at the station the previous night, Manu included. Manu had expected as much and thus was prepared. She didn't recall the man during the party (despite an ID photo presented her) and saw nothing of him after the party.

By day's end, the news was all over the village. Speculation as to Private Dunn' condition and whereabouts became the primary entertainment for the village for days to follow. People disappeared regularly in this area, but a soldier drew special attention.

# Dessert with Mike

Mike and Phil sat for a time. Eyes locked. Saying nothing. Hardly breathing. Mike finally stirred.

"So if chaos is non-existent, then the future is as predetermined as the past. Both exist. Both are immutable."

"Yes. That would be the implication."

"So if these are palpable factors, then what…time travel?"

Phil cast a hard look at Mike. "We're talking about the nature of existence Mike. Not a carnival ride."

"Hmm." Mike was clearly embarrassed by his apparently feckless question. Despite his cumbrous duties, a telling example of his comparative youth.

Phil continued. "Even if chaos does not exist, I doubt God gives a tinker's damn about us. But let's get down to tangibles. Suppose you tell me how *you* know of this. How did *you* discover it?"

"Fact is Phil, I didn't. I learned it from parts of the introduction to Part II of the QAVL DOCUMENT."

"Tell me about it."

"They essentially describe *Kosmas* as you do. This is critical to their introduction because once they are assured we understood *Kosmas,* they can then explain the rationale behind their offer."

"Their offer?"

"Yes. They've made us an offer. That's really what I want to discuss this evening. To fully appreciate their offer, we must first have some understanding of the micro-macro-universe model we've both learned about; and a great deal more actually."

"A great deal more. Such as?'

"Such as… Well, how familiar are you with Hubble volume and the Hubble limit?"

"I know it attempts to describe the size, shape and boundary of the universe based essentially upon its age and its temperature, along with its rate of expansion."

"Exactly. How familiar are you with Anthropic Principle?"

"Let's see, Anthropics stipulate cosmic superlaws govern everything from sub-atomic to universal forces. These laws may appear to vary based on the observer, or what they call Anthropic Bias. And…such bias may be elucidated from universe to univ… Oh Christ Mike! We're not getting into this multiverse nonsense with doppelgangers running all about, are we?"

"It's not nonsense Phil. There is solid, responsible, quantum mechanics supporting it now. And when you think about it, it puts our perspective of macro-micro right in perspective. Totally logical. Totally defendable. Results reproducible and demonstrable. Perhaps the more useful term than multi-verse might be Parallel Universes. They each describe a different scenario; and there are a few conceivable scenarios. In one scenario there would be an infinite number of such mirror universes which would constitute mega-SNA in your parlance. If they are truly mirrors, doppelgangers and all as you said, that puts the lid on self determinism altogether. The *Kentrikos* scholars claim we're about half a billion years from physical observation itself. In fact this is close to your earlier description."

Phil grimaced "Close is not much of a criteria Mike."

"Well, other theories and the QAVL don't dispute their possibility, describe universes as non-mirrored and may accommodate free will.

The answer is there. Repeated a hundred, hundred billion times under your thumb nail, or a hundred billion, billion times in units fourteen billion light years across and progressively inflating. Infinitely small. Beyond comprehension. Infinitely large as well. Beyond comprehension as well. And every gradient between. The same question. The same answer. *Two to the $212^{th}$ power times N.*"

Phil stared up at the glittering ceiling. "I think man fails to appreciate perhaps the most powerful forces in the universe…"

Mike squinted at him "…and that would be?"

"Accretion."

"Accretion?"

"Yes accretion. The accumulation of mass of a celestial object by amassing ambient interstellar materials….allegedly through the forces of static electro magnetism and then gravity when sufficient mass has been attained."

"Allegedly? What's *alleged* about gravity and electro magnetism?"

"I believe that at all levels – quantum to cosmic – accretion is fundamentally the force that explains gravity, thermodynamics, even magnetism. Accretion *is* gravity."

"Now that's one hellofa statement Phil. I think we should confirm you're not simply swapping one term for another. Suppose you explain what exactly comprises accretion."

"Okay. But you're going to find it pretty damned uninspired."

"Uninspired?"

"Yes. Mundane."

"I think I can take it."

"Spurs."

"Spurs. You mean like cowboys wear?"

"No. Spurs like fighting cocks use to rip each other apart."

"You're saying it's that simple. Matter has tiny spurs that hook together and comprise most of the interactions and laws of the entire universe."

"Essentially yes. Quantum Entanglement."

"What does this presage for your augury of predestination…particles behaving exactly as directed ever since the big bang?"

"In fact it is totally consistent."

"How do you know all this?"

"I don't know. But I will. I'm convinced of that."

"Can you demonstrate the underlying mathematics? Something observable? Provable? Can you isolate a spur in say…an accelerator?"

"No, no, no. Then again, don't you believe that the existence of *Kosmas* goes a long way in verifying this?"

"I really don't know."

"Neither me, if we make a fine point of it. Are you familiar with what they term Quantum Entanglement?"

"No. But it has the sound of your 'spur' at work."

"That's exactly what I suspect."

"So, what is this entanglement stuff?"

"Mmm. Essentially it is a phenomenon wherein two separate particles take on the attributes of the other – status, spin and so forth – to the degree that neither particle can be described in the absence of the other. The mechanism for this is currently something of a mystery."

Mike pursed his lips and gently rubbed his eyes "I think my question still stands. I do not understand. But let's move along. I assume you're suggesting that this, this…entanglement is a manifestation of your 'spurs'?"

"That's correct."

"And what do you hypothesize these spurs look like?"

"Like a spur. Actually more of a grapnel I suppose. A super tiny particle whose behavior is analogous to say…a Neutron to the power of $-212*N$. That is, it is difficult to describe this particle as matter or as some form of charge. In fact I think of these tiny bits of agglutinative energy as grapnons. These spurs easily link particles, consistent with some fairly rigorous rules. They can stretch, nearly to infinity. And they disengage; disentangle if you will, given sufficient contra-leveraging.

This is the wondrous part: Were you to construct the universe of ultra-tiny colored ball bearings, each with a fuzz of micro-fine little hooked wires attached, then nothing in the universe, at its most fundamental level, would behave counter-intuitively. I believe this is exactly the case."

Mike thought for a time. Eyes half closed.

"How did you arrive at these conclusions Phil?"

"I took a few long, deep swims."

A long silence ensued. Neither spoke, or moved. They could hear the serving girl humming somewhere. Gershwin. Nice voice. Probably in a service kitchen nearby. The light seemed too yellow somehow, the air suddenly stuffy, and it was a strain to focus clearly.

After a time. "You've been busy Mike."

"As have you Phil."

# ...and miles to go before I sleep...

*Stopping by Woods on a Snowy Evening*
*Robert Frost*

Both men were already growing tired. And there remained much to discuss.

"Your art must be suffering."

"My art," smiled Mike "as you put it, is irrelevant. You saw to part of that. The QAVL took care of the rest."

"Sorry Mike."

"Don't be. My perspective and priorities have never been as clear. And frankly, the limits to this new Oneirion art are a little ominous."

Phil stood and walked to the bar. He made himself a large Scotch. "So tell me about the QAVL offer."

Mike cleared his throat blinking to clear his head. "They offered us the plans to build a ship. They will also perform a major part of its construction. A ship capable of carrying two hundred Oneirions to a destination they call *Kentrikos* (Cosmos Central). They term the project *The Kosmas Gauntlet*. When they refer to the full universal project, they term it the *Kosmas Nisus, or Kosmas Antiaô*."

Again Phil felt a thrill at hearing the name. "*Nisus?*"

Mike smiled. "I had to look it up too. Its derivation is Latin. '…striving towards a particular goal…'"

"I see. What is *Kosmas Kentrikos?* Why go? Where is *Kosmas Kentrikos?*"

"Whoa Phil, one question at a time please. Let me catch up.

One. *What is Kosmas Kentrikos?* This is a planet where vast numbers of enlightened specie congregate. To share information. Share cultures and histories. Even goods, entertainment, art, science, mathematics, philosophy, religion and more. Even to have fun. Most importantly *to seek any differences in their Kosmas which may exist.*

They generate random actions, energy waves, matter disruption, migratory patterns, etc. to detect any modification in *Kosmas*. Prove or disprove determinism. They develop a working familiarity with tens of thousands of races and cultures. Learn. A universal confederation, an *omospondia pagkosmios* of life.

And the particle-by-particle drudge work as well. Imagine two seemingly identical planet Earths. Then imagine the only way to detect any difference is to compare and catalogue each grain of sand down to the molecular level on one planet, with its counterpart on the other. Millennia after millennia of painstaking analysis."

"Good grief! Why all the fuss?"

"As you said yourself Phil. You have empirical *experience* of *Kosmas*. They must have empirical *proof*. Proof these extraordinary nebulae of wisdom are unchanged throughout the universe."

"Surely there must be some logical, mathematical way of proving this? Some quantum…"

"They say no. This question has been approached through theoretical means for millennia. Mathematics, cosmology, cathronic implosion, globular astrophysics, entropic dispersion, quantum mechanics, antruzium measurement, cylindrical inversion, gravitational variances and much, much more. Direct empirical preponderance appears to be the sole arbiter. Therefore, to achieve a reasonable certitude *Kosmas* is truly universal, this painstaking analytical correlation is mandatory."

"Quantum Entanglement at a cosmic level…and if it's not?"

"Not what?"

"If *Kosmas* is not cosmically identical …?"

"Then self determinism exists. Uncertainty exists. Randomness exists."

"Of course. I should've seen myself. They are right. The implications are shattering. This must be their most profound question."

"It is. According to the QAVL, for many races it is their *only* question. This is why the QAVL were selected to perform the task of qualification and recruitment of new races. This is one reason they are so forthcoming. They need the largest possible sample size from a population which literally approaches infinity."

Phil smiled. "Well let's see. If I recall correctly, the larger the population size, the smaller percentile sample is required to achieve a reasonable confidence interval. Say +/- 3%."

Mike peered at him. A little piqued. "This is not market research. Proof, not confidence interval. It is the search for god and the nature of existence. I would also add a percentile sample of an infinite population is itself infinite."

"Just having you on a bit." Phil grinned.

Mike smiled back patiently and indulgently. "Next question. Two. *Why go?* I believe the *why* is explained by the *what*."

"Agreed Mike. Where is the end? Is this an endless quest for all time? Or is there some point, some sample size, some definitive result will signal completion of the study? An unequivocal conclusion."

"They stipulate they're hoping for some eventual indirect proof. They freely admit to the inconclusive methodology of top loading specie after specie. Perhaps they will reach the end. Or not.

More likely, or hopefully, sometime in ensuing eons some super-genius may develop a *probamentum posterus*, the ultimate proof one way or the other providing the *logicus dominato*. The inescapable logic that will resolve the great problem of all time."

"What happens then?"

Mike looked thoughtful "That depends on the result I suppose. There are essentially two possibilities. Let's call the first the Alpha Solution. Succinctly put, identical *Kosmas*, truly parallel universes, therefore god, therefore pre-destination. The other is the Beta Solution. Random *Kosmas*, multiverse, chaos, therefore no god. Free will."

"You pack a lot of concepts into few words Mike. I don't see what the concept of multiverse has to do with anything. But okay. What if the Alpha Solution is proven?"

"They will then strive to *know* god."

"The Beta Solution?"

"They will then strive to *find* god."

"So. No matter what, they believe in a god?"

"Perhaps a better way of expressing it is they believe in a creator. The concept of *god* is a human invention. The concept of *creator* is rooted in logic. Consider creation. It exists. It is real. It logically demands the presence of a creator by virtue of its existence. God is essentially an anthropomorphism for a process or object that may not be deific in the least.

Perhaps we should coin the term theopomorphism?

But disregard either solution for a moment. There may still be VOLITION OPTIONS waiting to be discovered."

"And ah…where would you look for them?"

"They may lie in the potentially variable nature of the universe. We have discussed Parallel Universe and Multiverse. There may remain Quantum Branches, Alternate Realities and conceivably much, much more. Only Parallel Universe implies an absolutely fixed, forward reality."

"It is amazing to me a vast alliance of supremely advanced life forms can be so obsessed with a single issue."

"Well Phil I'm not so sure it is a single issue as much as it is *the* issue. Perhaps I am distorting the occupations that engage these beings. Most have conquered death, or any maladies of the corpus. Some have relinquished their corpus altogether. Many never had one. They explore the universe. They are actively seeking other universes. They pursue art, science, games, philosophy, entertainment, something they call Freenuer and something else they call Thun. They are exceptionally social - enjoying the company of creatures abounding in our galaxy and many others. The occupations of food gathering and medicine and survival no longer trouble them. They have a lot of fun and enjoy their lives. Beyond that, these are some busy guys."

"Look. I've experienced some of this for myself, so I appreciate what you're saying. What they claim. Yet have they put any of this to any sort of empirical tests. Any pragmatic application?"

"Oh yes. They can site thousands of examples. They even have one applicable to Earth."

"Yes?"

"They caution mankind must soon start pulling together. There is a tangible event in process as we speak which will, for all intents, destroy Earth beyond any recognition. It will annihilate two moons and one planet from our solar system and replace them with a vast, new asteroid belt in close orbit with the sun, creating havoc amongst the dense inner planets. The end of Earth and of our moon."

"Good grief Mike! What is the cause of such destruction?"

"The rotation and orbit of Mars' outer moon, Photos. It is ejecting it from the Mars gravity well. The break-off will occur at a perfect time and trajectory to drive it into a glancing blow off our moon, then directly into the Earth. Total destruction of all three bodies and a highly disruptive force on the entire solar system. Armageddon for any human inhabitants, anywhere in Sol's influence. The entire human race will have had to evacuate not only our planet, but our star as well."

"Jesus. When?"

"14.561 million Years."

"For Chrissake Mike, a hundred equally catastrophic events could intervene first."

"The QAVL say no. Not a terminal extinction event. They further stipulate this is *Kosmasically* confirmed. They can accurately interpret *Kosmas* respective to massive astrophysical events. They nurture a tiny class of beings they call Verterors."

"Verterors? What does it mean?"

"Not really sure. I believe their word translates to something like *benders*, whatever that means. That's really all I know at this point."

Phil looked off into space with a crooked grin"…amazing how we deliberate events of cosmic importance from an easy chair, over drinks."

The two men were quiet for time. Reviewing things in their minds. Refreshing their drinks.

Phil broke the silence "Do you know who you're dealing with?"

"Who I'm dealing with?" Phil heard the defensiveness in Mike's voice and realized he had misunderstood.

"I mean, who in the QAVL? Are you talking to a specific individual?"

"Oh. Yes. Ambassador Qasi. Nice fellow…if 'fellow' applies. I have a Missive for you from the Ambassador. He knows you are The Consul. He looks forward to a formal introduction with you and many interesting meetings to follow." Mike leaned forward proffering the Missive to Phil. Phil frowned at the document. Mike explained. The Ambassador requested we print this in confidence exclusively for you. We scaled it and marked it Mr. Philip Carr, The Consul of Oneiro, <u>EYES ONLY</u>.

Phil nodded in understanding, took the envelope. Leaning back, drink in hand. He opened it and read:

*The Honorable Philip Carr*
*Consul of Oneiro*

*Esteemed Consul Carr,*

*I look forward with great anticipation to meeting you, to presenting my credentials, to introducing the race known as the QAVL, and to the community of civilizations known as Kentrikos.*

*Thanks in no small respect to your good works; we are most honored and pleased to welcome humans of Earth into the Kentrikos Antiaô.*

*I personally take profound pride and joy in the opportunity allotted me to play some role in these historic events.*

*Until we are afforded the occasion to share these conspicuous times together, I extend herewith Qareen, our council and experiences. I trust you may find these helpful; and aspire, as do I, to enduring, collateral camaraderie.*

*With best personal compliments and respects,*
*Qasi QaQAVdun46*
*Ambassador of the QAVL to Earth QaSol3*

Phil regarded the short, convoluted document for some time. "*QaQAVdun?*"

"This is ancient QAVLian. It means QAVL of the forty-sixth level. We're unsure if 'level' in this context alludes to a lateral positioning. An address? Perhaps The Ambassador's native region on QAVL. They do inhabit a sea. Albeit a sea of ionized gas. Or it may be some sort of rank. If such is the case I would assume a *QaQAV* of the forty-sixth (*dun*) level *very* high ranking."

"*Earth QaSol3?*"

"Earth, the third planet from the star known as Sol."

"I see. You've read this?"

"Good heavens no. We've encountered these terms in many other documents. I have total respect for the QAVL wish for private communiqués."

"Mmm. Here Read it." He passed the document. Mike read it carefully.

*The Honorable Philip Carr*
*Consul of Oneiro*

*Esteemed Mr. Carr,*

*I look forward with great anticipation to meeting you, to presenting my credentials, to introducing the race known as the QAVL, and to the community of civilizations known as Kentrikos.*

*Thanks in no small respect to your good works; we are most honored and pleased to welcome humans of Earth into the Kentrikos Antiaô.*

*I personally take profound pride and joy in the opportunity allotted me to play some role in these cosmically historic events.*

*Until we are afforded the occasion to share these conspicuous times together, I trust you aspire to, as do I, an enduring camaraderie.*

*With best personal compliments and respects,*
*Qasi QaQAVdun*
*Ambassador of the QAVL to Earth QaSol3*

Mike looked up blandly at Phil. "Nice."
Phil frowned "I found it very confusing."
"Really? Why?"
"What the hell was all that foolishness about '*Qareen*'?"
"*Qareen*? What the hell are *you* talking about?"
"Please read the document aloud."
Mike did so.
"Let me see that." Phil snatched the Missive from Mike's hand. He read it over again twice. He withdrew into himself. Deep concentration. His eyes oscillating unsettlingly. "I think the Son-of-a-bitch ran one on me."
"Ran what on you Phil?"
"Goddamned *Qareen*. You know the translation of that term?"
"Generally yes. Although it is quite complex. Let's see…*Qareen*. A reflexive-heuristic learning-mnemonic surrogate. In this context reflexive

implies a subject and object with identical referents. Therefore the heuristic or self-learning surrogate dialogues the learning process with both participants. The *Qareen* and its host."

"Do you know the term 'steganography'?"

"No."

"Never mind." *Mike wouldn't understand, or believe it if I told him. This was incredibly disturbing. Had something alien had been placed in his mind? He could damn near feel its presence. Had he been invaded? Violated?* Suddenly the QAVL did not appear as charmingly benign.

Phil calmed himself. He forced himself to concentrate on the situation at hand. In no way did he wish for Mike to suspect he may have been mentally violated. "I need to take this for a swim. For now though, let's finish the three questions. I believe you had completed number two."

"Yes. So. Three. *Where is Kosmas Kentrikos?* In this we are lucky indeed. The gods have smiled upon us. There are roughly one million *Kosmas Kentrikos*. Our target is about twenty light years away. The star Gilese 581. A surprisingly active, old, red dwarf. Part of our constellation Libra."

"*Only* twenty light years away? Let's see…our fastest spacecraft these days travels through deep space at some 132,000 kilometers per hour. Twenty light years equates to something like …mm…189,214,609,451,616 kilometers. So at such speed it would take ah…327,270 years, round-trip. Quite a jaunt."

Mike had to smile. Phil's mental *ledger-de-main* could be imposing at times. "I'll take your word for it Phil. Clearly we envision a craft of exponentially greater speed."

Phil nodded. His mind was still digesting. "How long have the *Kosmas* analysis been active? My God. One million *Kosmas Kentrikos?* Coordination alone would take thousands of millennia."

"Two point eight billion years so far. A little older than QAVL civilization."

"Any end in sight?"

"Not really. Races continue to join *Kentrikos* which almost infinitely extends the job. Coordination is a huge factor. Realize though, they aren't in any great hurry. They learn an incredible amount and gain in a thousand ways through such rich diversity. They also enjoy it thoroughly. Without exception they find it a supremely worthy enterprise. The old human genome project is a good metaphor for this vast undertaking. The veritable genome of creation."

"I don't get it Mike. SNA, or *Kosmas*, or whatever. It exists in every atom in the Universe. Why do they need the input of various living specie? Matter is matter…animate or inanimate. Am I missing something?"

"Ah, yes you are. Not your fault though. There are some facts you couldn't, or at least shouldn't be able to know, even with your insight."

"Yes?"

"I only partly understand it. In some respects it seems to be something akin to Heisenberg's uncertainty. The closest I can come is animation of matter provokes a process best defined as 'super-vision'. Sentient matter does far more than just observe particles, thereby modifying them in some way, it seems to resist the particle's trajectory. But without any real effect. However, according to Qasi, a minority of beings, so small a percentage they approach non-existence, may actually be capable of materially modifying the particle's advancement. This was discovered only a few hundred thousand years ago. And it now plays an enormous role in their studies. They're called Verterors.

Please understand, even the most advanced Quaestors in this enterprise have yet to fully qualify and finitely delineate the number, size and types of particles which constitute a complete SNA, or *Kosmas* set."

"Quaestors?"

"Uh. That's how they refer to most advanced intellects on *Kosmas*. Quaestor is an honorific of sorts. I believe they also act in some sort of guidance capacity.

Anyhow, they are unable to strictly stipulate if a process of modification is really transpiring. This discovery is important. It is also unproven. If it is true, then perhaps there does exist a quantum mechanism capable of modifying – I should say deviating – the trajectory of a given particle. If this is true, we must re-think the nature of creation. Our place in the universe. The existence of god. Predeterminism itself. Everything."

Phil looked confused. "Deviating the trajectory of a given particle...for Chrissake that's occurred a trillion times squared in this room, during our discussion."

"I'll clarify that. 'Deviating a given particle from its geometrically, precisely predetermined trajectory.' Does that help?"

Phil ignored the question, countering with another question of his own. "You've got to gradient this problem as well."

"Gradient the problem...?"

"Yes. Delineate the boundaries between inert matter, pre-animate matter, animate matter, post-animate matter, back to inert matter; and at what gradient is uncertainty effected, or disaffected?"

"I would conject only animate matter is capable of performing observation."

"I would agree. By the same token, are you prepared to firmly conject it is positively and solely observation that provokes uncertainty? You may be guilty of *non causa pro causa.*" Phil smiled brightly, eyebrows slightly elevated.

"False cause?"

"A false syllogism."

"Do you have some basis for that statement? Some of the finest minds in history, in the universe for that matter, subscribe to this postulate."

"I have no basis whatsoever. Certainly the finest minds have shared in common errors many times in the past."

Mike thought about the problem and had no immediate response. So he continued "They also state the second aspect of their studies to truly confirm whether *Kosmas*, or SNA, or whatever actually cascades downward to infinity. Likewise whether it cascades infinitely upward as well. Or does it simply end? Or does it loop? An infinite circle? You can go crazy trying to sort it out."

"I believe I began to appreciate the import of all this." sighed Phil. "But back to this twenty light year voyage…"

"QAVL vessels attain light speed as a matter of routine. Considering their makeup, not surprising. They can equip *us* with a vessel capable of achieving a sustained .77 light speed for an indefinite period. And we can survive it."

"I don't believe Einstein would agree with you."

"How so Phil?"

"If you recall, relativistic speeds result in time dilation."

"Of course I do…" Mike began to sound a little frustrated.

"Einstein also stipulated that as an object approaches the speed of light, there is a mass dilation as well. It's mass, or weight approaches infinity."

"I see. Certainly you would reasonably assume the QAVL are extraordinarily well versed in this aspect of relativity?"

"Just tell me how I survive a weight of say…twenty million metric tonnes."

"Okay. You're thinking in terms of General R*elativity* as opposed to Special Relativity. But you're overlooking *proportionality*."

"Suppose we go over the difference. Just for fun."

"Okay. Special Relativity deals with velocity. General Relativity addresses mass. GR is Newtonian. SR relates back to Lorentz. They both stipulate the same dilation of relative time. One due to speed. The other due to mass. Effectively they have the same effect."

"Alright. We're on the same page. Continue."

"You may weigh eighty kilos, twenty million tonnes, or twenty billion tonnes and you will never perceive the difference, since mass inflation acts exactly in proportion with inertia, your body, the energy you consume, your strength, your ambience and the ship transporting you.

You will never feel the difference; and it cannot hurt you. Failing that, you would self-destruct into a puddle of goo. Only dissociated hadronics are affected. However that occurs outside your acuity. This must be accounted for in navigation as a matter of routine. For the QAVL even this is not an issue as they do not occupy hadronic mass. In the case of protonic/neuronic/electronic creatures such as ourselves, it can be expressed mathematically. I like to call it *relaportionality*. A variable $y$ is exponentially proportional to a variable $a$, if $y$ is contiguously proportional to the expression $a$ given a real constant. Call it $k$. Therefore the complete expression is:

$$\int E(y=ka^a) = [\int M(y=ka^a) \int C(y=ka^a)]^2$$

"I'll take your word for it. Continue."

"At that velocity the trip would require a one way elapse time of 26.97 solar years, factoring in the time needed to achieve full acceleration."

At that point, Phil's brain kicked in. "Let's see...at .77 of light speed that would attract a dilation factor of....1.5688734646305626...so a one way trip expressed in terms of General Relativity, let's call it GAT, would take..."

"GAT?"

"General Absolute Time. It would take 42.4 years and in SRT it would..."

"SRT?"

"Special Relativity Time. It would take about 27 years. So we're looking at a round trip of some 84.8 years, GAT, plus time spent on *Kosmas*. That's some business trip. I assume we're not paying *per diem*.

I also assume it would have exceptional navigation capabilities. Running into a star, a planet, an asteroid, a micro-meteorite, even dust at relativistic speed. As I understand the QAVL this would have negligible effect on them. Any one of those events could be catastrophic for us."

"True. We will have autonomous control over the ship's bearings. However, the onboard nav systems have highly intelligent DAR systems. At .77 light-speeds these systems constantly probe a spherical safe zone extending out in all directions to nearly a light year from the ship. It can react to anything–dust and micro-meteorites notwithstanding."

"DAR's?"

"Detect-Analyze-Respond."

"I see. So...we're in the constellation Libra. Tell me about *Kosmas Kentrikos.*"

"There is a red dwarf star within that proportional parsec orbited by a barren planet referred to as Kentrikos. It is many times larger than Earth. However, there is apparently an astounding construct on *Kentrikos* extending thousands of kilometers into space. Thousands of ambient levels. Each level supports the gravity any given race requires by accommodating them as an appropriate level. The surface supports *Kentrikos* normal gravity, call it G1. Gravity below the surface is diminished and slightly diffused, call it G1-n/d. At half the depth of G1-n/d gravity reverses. Essentially there are four points. The point of diminishing gravity, deeper the neutral point followed by the inversion and finally the negative point. Above the surface gravity diminishes linearly to the extent of the *Kentrikos* gravity well, say G1 or above the surface of *Kentrikos*. Not addressed here is what they term *gravity clusters*."

"Interesting term."

"It *is* isn't it. And to be honest, the physics and mathematics behind it are advanced well beyond our grasp. Essentially it states that gravity within any well is not linear in the least. It forms 'clumps' of variable strength, or density at certain predictable points within the field. Most notably at G0 and within G1, so..."

"...what does this mean for us?"

"For us? Let's see...it will partly effect the design of *Gauntlet*. It is used extensively in the *Kosmas* ambient domes. It means that a certain amount of energy must be constantly expended to maintain the necessary gravity fields."

"No Mike. What does this imply for *us*? Humans."

"Oh I see. I suppose it's another example of our inability to manage this project, and will continue to be for hundreds of years. Phil, I can quote you verbatim what he said: Man has the concept. You have for decades. And you may learn the fuel, but you need time to learn to manipulate it. To control it and translate it into energy capable of doing work. You have the ability to make intuitive leaps, lucky guesses, serendipitous discoveries and startlingly brilliant insights...it's more plodding now unfortunately. Your science is now by necessity a product of society instead of the solitary genius...too many variables to juggle...so it takes time. I will take time..."

Concern and resignation played across his features. "Mmm. Continue."

"Light, atmosphere, temperature, conventional references. And of course habitable area increases exponentially with each succeeding level. Whatever they need. Each such level, or area within a level, maintain sizable assembly centers. Here multiple species can come together for short periods. Meet face-to-face, or face-to-whatever, using their own life support. There is also a vast *Kentrikos* lab where all inhabitants work. Seek, share, catalogue and compare.

Below ground they house one of more than twenty of the largest library, communications and computational centers in the universe. All *Kentrikos* are in constant communications. It's an impossible task considering the number of sites, the distances involved and the incredible amount of data.

All the same, they attempt to achieve a consistent release of the latest studies at each site."

"I wonder why our SETI people never tapped into this?"

"Simple. They don't normally use carrier wave transmissions."

"This all sounds impossible, even for them. But they do use plain old radio from time to time?"

"Yes."

"So, why haven't we intercepted some of their traffic? It must have been bouncing around the galaxy for eons."

"As I understand it, communicating civilizations identify planets which are disqualified to receive their transmissions. Their term for such planets is cute. It translates to 'Black Balls'. Earth has been Black Balled for millennia. They then divert the carrier wave to exclude such civilizations. "

"My God. So they can literally guide a radio wave to a selective coordinate. Routing and destination. That's how they first contacted us I suppose. How do they do it?"

"A technique termed SWAT/VISL."

"*What*?"

"Ah. Actually that's our own acronym. Based on our translation. SWAT is Skewed-Wave-Alternating-Twists. Pre-routed and controlled by VISL. Variably-Induced-Steganographic-Lensing. It's loosely shares the same technology as the QAVL DOCUMENT. That's all I really know. Or understand for that matter."

"Damn. It's a shame FTL communications are not possible."

Mike sipped his drink without comment.

"What about wormholes, black holes, white holes and such, as a means of overcoming light speed."

"I asked the QAVL pretty much the same question."

"Yes?"

"Digital laughter is very unsettling."

"The question amused them?"

"I got the distinct impression there are some forces in the universe you just don't want to monkey around with."

Phil rose and stretched. He walked about aimlessly. "Do we have the materials and expertise to build this ship according to their specs?"

"We certainly have the materials. The expertise is contained in Part II. The QAVL will provide, install and calibrate drive apparatus, gravity processors, onboard nav systems and spin the hulls. They have offered to leave a QAVL liaison to assist in construction and accompany us to *Kosmas Kentrikos*."

Phil stared up, through the ceiling, at the stars.

He whispered. "It's really beginning isn't it?"

"Is what beginning Phil?" Mike spoke softly as well, cocked his head, a shadow of a frown on his face, his demeanor empathetic.

"Homecoming."

# *DAKHALA* Zalmai

A few weeks later, Manu sat in her shack reviewing the events of the past four months. It was terribly cold now and the pass was temporarily closed for snow and rock slides. The restaurant was therefore quiet and she was not needed.

Several events competed for her attention, but the death of Private Dunn would not leave her in peace. *I killed that man. I guess I murdered him. But he raped me. He would kill me. He hid. Waiting for me. I did right. Allah fahima...*

*My God!* The realization finally dawned on her. She jumped to her feet and began pacing her small room. *It was Malik! That pig Malik. He set that man on me. He was afraid I would tell about him and Zemar. He was going to have me raped and killed. It must have been a terrible surprise to see me the next morning. And then he learned the Private was lost. I'll bet that scared the fat goat. That's why he's changed. That's why he treats me different....*

She grew still. Calm. She sat on her mat and was soon deeply lost in thought.

Two months later, Manu's mother came into her hut. This surprised Manu. Her mother never came here, always calling Manu into the house. They seldom spoke any more. Manu cared little for her since her mutilation. The beginning of her disenchantment. Now she had lost all respect for her, mainly because of her father. Her constant deferral to him. The way she endured beatings uncomplainingly. Her unending forgiveness for his constant bullying transgressions. Her utter lack of self-respect. Her cowardice.

Despite all this, Manu's mother had once been an intelligent, sensitive woman in her youth. Little escaped her insightful regard even now. She sat down beside her daughter.

She smiled and brushed Manu's hair from her face. "How are you?"
"I am fine. Why?"
"Are you certain you're fine?"
"Yes. Of course. What are you talking about?"
She looked at Manu thoughtfully before she continued.
"Manu, you have not flowed for three months."
The words struck Manu like a club. It was true. She was not having menstrual cycles. She had but barely adapted to their routine. So it was perilously

easy to overlook their absence. Something was wrong. An icy uneasiness blossomed in Manu's belly and despite the cold, she began to perspire.

"What does it mean mother?"

"It means you are pregnant."

Manu looked at her mother blankly.

She tried again. "*You are going to have a baby.*"

She couldn't think. She couldn't breathe. She could hardly see. She jumped to her feet and fled from the hut, into the snows, towards the cliffs. She hardly heard her mother calling out behind her.

She didn't stop until she was staring down hundreds of meters into the Khyber. How glibly unfair her life. After all she had suffered, she was pregnant? *Pregnant!?* Like some trucker girl who gives her body for a meal, or a few coins. What was she to do? She knew her mother would tell her father. Her father was stupid. But not so stupid to figure out the timing. He would quickly link her pregnancy to the missing soldier and realize she had been with an *AJNABI*. No telling what he would do then. No telling what she would do then.

She knew nothing of abortion. She could expect no justice from her family or the village. She had no money. She had no options. She had no escape. And then...a plan of sorts began forming in her mind.

That afternoon found her listlessly sitting in her hut. She had no other place to go. Nothing else to do. Just sit and wait.

"Manu." She looked up. He father. Looking stern. "Yes father?"

"We must talk. But not here. Too many ears. Come with me."

She rose and they left the village together. Soon they found themselves among the cliffs where they had talked the evening prior to her rape. Manu felt nauseous and her heart was pounding. What was her father going to say. He seemed calm enough, but she knew he would be angry. He would be terrible to listen to. She dreaded it. She dreaded him.

When they arrived at the cliff, she turned to him. *Might as well get this over with.* "Father I..."

She was lying on the snow, looking up at the darkening sky. Her father stood over her. A stout staff in his hand. He lent down, grabbed her arm and roughly yanked her to her feet. *Where did he get that?* she wondered. When she had regained her balance, the staff came round with a great whack on her head. She was literally knocked silly. She turned to fend the next blow, which took her achingly on the back...then the arm...then the head...the stomach...a thigh...

*Hasan Allah! He's going to kill me. No. Please no. I don't want to die.*

She was on the ground now, blinded by blood, crawling towards the cliff-line. Zalmai was breathing heavily now. Pounding her over and over. An incredible awareness dawned amidst her torment. *Father...is...truly...killing...me....*

Zalmai raised the staff high for the final killing blow. He looked of something out of an abattoir. Something out of a nightmare. In desperation Manu turned and with all her strength wrapped her hands and arms around his ankles. Try to explain. Beg for mercy.

Suddenly he wasn't there. She looked at her arms. They were empty. She looked at her hands. No ankles. It was almost comical. At first Manu just lay on the ground. A creature of only pain and fear. Gradually she quelled her fear. The beating had stopped. At least for now. The pain was another thing altogether. From her knees to her head, every bone and muscle had been mercilessly pummeled. Movement was agony, but her father would be even angrier if she didn't start to quickly show signs of life.

She looked up timidly. *Allah don't let him hit me again.* "No father. Please." She looked all about her. Amazed. She was alone. She spotted the staff balanced on the cliff's edge and a thought occurred to her.

A shadow of a smile...a quickening incredulity. She breathed low uncertain whisper "Nooo..."

She edged forward to the cliff's dizzying margin, and peered down furtively. Far below her lay her father. Broken. Clearly dead. She silently mouthed "SHUKRAN Allah." Thanks God. She wept.

Half an hour later, with pain and great effort, she retrieved the strong staff, drew herself to her feet, and set off for the restaurant. Home was out of the question. It was snowing hard now. It would be a long walk to the station. She closed her eyes and took another of her long deep breaths. She smiled wryly, squinting into the rising wind. *It's okay.* She thought. *I'm alive. I have time.*

# Specs

Phil pressed his analysis with Mike. "Tell me about the ship."

"The ship is pretty much equivalent to living in and navigating a hollow asteroid. It is a perfect sphere two kilometers in diameter. The skin is forty meters thick. Fabricated from hardened, reinforced limestone and granite, blended with metal alloys. The entire sphere is covered in a black, light absorbent matrix of grapheme, polycrystalline ceramic and titanium. The sphere envelops two seas and four hulls. The exterior hull is forty meters thick. The second hull is ten meters thick and inset by forty meters from the exterior hull. The sphere weighs as much as a small mountain. That takes care of the dust and micro-meteorite problem, even meteorites, as well as lethal radiation."

"Not to mention Klingon disruptors." Phil grinned, pleased at his witticism.

Mike acknowledged no familiarity with his allusion. Somewhat abashed, Phil remained silent.

Mike continued "This forms the bio-solate for the outer sea."

"I've never heard the term *bio-solate*."

"It's our own term. A concatenation of bio-sphere and isolation. The outer sea hardly describes a sphere. It's something more akin to an aqueous hull. And that is exactly its purpose if the exterior hull were to be breached. We call it the Oneirion Sea. The water would freeze near instantaneously and automatically form a rock hard seal until we could make a permanent fix. We've thought about draining the outer sea at *Kosmas* to support and sustain the Oneirions who will remain on *Kosmas*. We then replenish the Oneirion Sea with fresh water for the back-haul, unless the *Kosmians* suggest something more interesting. Although the QAVL assure us they can.

Surrounding the power source is the inner sea. Vital, enriched, living seawater. We call it Webber's Pelagikós (Webber's Open Seas)." Mike smiled.

Phil smiled warmly. "Very thoughtful Mike."

Mike returned the smile and continued. "The QAVL like to call it the Ouroboros Ring. Food, oxygen, all the necessities, and luxuries. Everything produced from the sea and recycled back through. It also shields the crew from any potential radiation leak from the power source.

All in all three hulls and two seas. Hull A., the exterior hull forty meters thick. The outer sea is forty meters deep. Hull B. is the deck for Oneiro City. It is twenty meters thick plus four meters of topsoil, stone, sand and underground infrastructure. The airspace above Hull B. is more than 470 meters. There are hundreds of massive struts fixing Hull A. to Hull B. They also provide excellent sanctuary for sea life. The same is true of the inner sea and the drive compartment. The relationship between the inner sea and Hull B. is stabilized by gravity processors; and at the zero-g poles access is extremely easy with a simple jump. There is a transport apparatus which provides some addition stability as well. As you would imagine, it is also effectively invisible.

We will install the largest periscope viewer ever conceived by man. We call it the Spheriscope. The outside of the inner bio-solate of Webber's Pelagikós will be so equipped. Crew living in this enormous area will have the exact feel of life on the surface of Earth. Should be breathtaking on an extravagant scale. We call it Webber's Sky."

Mike drew out a large sheet of paper. "This is a basic schematic of the ship:

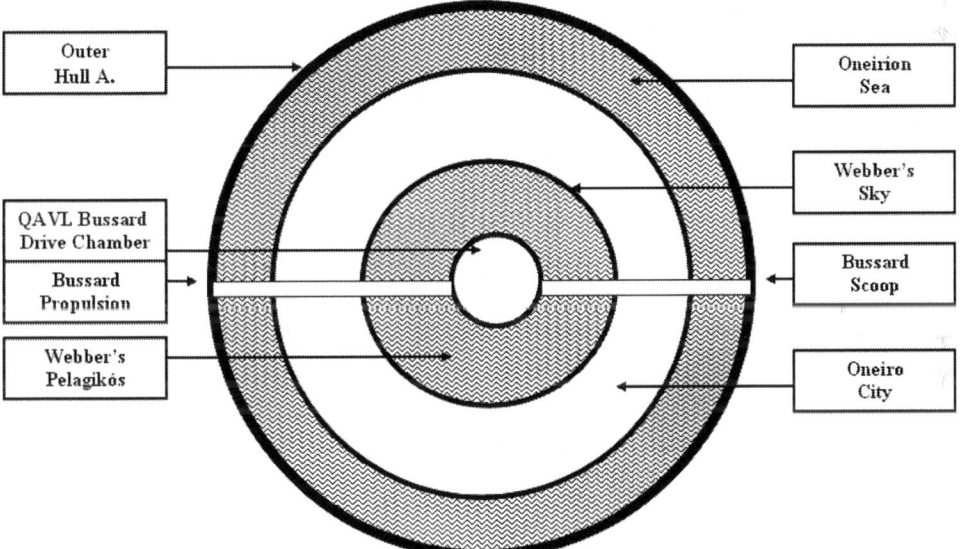

There is a huge bridge engineered specifically for human use. A vast Oneirion food processing facility. Each of the 200 crewmembers will benefit from enormous, comfortable living areas. Each designed, equipped and even decorated according to individual specifications. A small city, six labs, six workshops, a computer center, a cultural center, shopping, meeting rooms, theaters, sports facilities, hospital, restaurants, bars, an endless library, books, and movies. Navigation Center. Communications and Computer Center. Command Bridge, Captain's Residence, Briefing Room and Captain's Mess. Including a Crew Mustering Center for briefings, launch, arrival and course corrections.

Imbedded in the hull, will be one hundred tenders for…"

"Tenders?"

"Yes. Ship's tenders. Escape-craft, shuttles, jigs, run-abouts, whatever. Four-man vessels equipped with gravity drives and energy sources, environment, water, food, coms, hibernation and medical facilities. Even a digital library to help keep you sane. These can be used in case of catastrophic failure, a means of commuting between ships and planets, hull inspection, and so on.

For quality of life, there will be parks, woodland, hills, lakes, a small river, waterfalls, hills, walking paths, even farming. We plan on ultra-lights for sport flying."

"Updrafts?"

"The Womb weather processor will generate surface hot spots on demand. Location and intensity adjustable. This is not just for pleasure flights; it also assists in crop management, air circulation, environmental maintenance and a credible Earth ambience."

"There's really room for all this?"

"Phil, we're talking about 12,560,000 square meters of habitable area."

"Christ!"

"Yeah." Mike smiled.

"If this is a sphere resting on Earth how in hell can you fill a river and lake without it sloshing about in the bottom of the sphere?"

"Phil, as I told you. The QAVL can manipulate gravity. They can place the entire sphere in a type of stasis. A kind of acediadic state. If you were to touch water in its grip, it would have the consistency of the thickest molasses you can imagine. This holds the interior in place while it is being positioned."

"Escape velocity. Something like eleven kilometers per second from Earth if memory, or whatever, serves"

"Eleven-point-two to be precise Phil." Mike smiled. It was nice to be up on him for a change. "And the inertial momentum to escape the Sun is much greater…some forty-two-point-one kilometers per second."

"If I understand correctly, escape velocity is more an exercise in ballistics. It relies on the kinetic energy imparted to the mass of an object allowing it to simply inertially emerge from its gravity well. Much as a bullet achieves its target, without further assisted thrust."

"That's exact. The sphere moves away from the Earth and out of the solar system at a relatively leisurely pace, under constant acceleration from its gravity thrusters. On the Earth, during ascent and in-flight, everything is held safely in place by these localized fields within the ship itself."

"What about detection from Earth tracking stations?"

"A few things. First, their window of opportunity will be small. Despite our independence from escape velocity, we'll still be moving fast. About two kilometers per second. Secondly, we'll be launching from a site literally never monitored. Thirdly, this is a clean, totally trackless propulsion system. There is no heat signature, no contrail, no noise or lights, residual ionized particulates or radiation. The size and contour fit no known profile. In fact its material and form render it close to what used to be termed 'stealth'. In short, undetected, just a blip, or just another unidentified. A damned big one at that.

By the way, as part of the gravity engineering, Webber's Pelagikós and the Oneirion Seas, sealed in their own bio-solates, travel in a gravity stasis until it is safe to activate the QAVL Drive and commence rotation."

"Right. While I'm thinking of it. Sea life?"

"Yes. Both are complete biosphereic seas, each with artificial suns, entirely self contained."

"Sea life can survive extended stasis?"

"Better than we. But there's no need for it. They will pass a normal existence. They'll feed and breed and provide us a normal environment from the marine food chain."

"Artificial sunlight...can any creature survive years under artificial light?"

"I don't know. But in fact this is not artificial light. It is concentrated, focused starlight. The constituent spectral properties of such light do not too greatly differ from our own native white sunlight. Often there is no difference whatsoever. It all depends on the type of stars in a given region. Any significant variances can be filtered, or magnified, as needed. The basic stuff however, will suffice indefinitely. No rickets or scurvy or any such for this crew matey. Arrrr!"

Phil cocked his head and an eyebrow "...Aye and avast ye."

"What the hell does *avast* mean anyway?'

"Essentially it's another form of belay, meaning *stop*, or *disregard*."

Mike frowned. "Hmm. Does your infinite repertoire of knowledge ever get on people's nerves Phil?"

"I suppose it must. There's little I can do about it though. A part of my mind behaves like an over-eager freshman...always throwing a hand up when a question is posed. I must admit though, it is immensely useful. The instant I ponder on anything, most answers spring to mind full blown. A question must be posed however, before I start popping up with answers and all sorts of arcane knowledge."

"So the art-form is to ponder the right questions. Which I suppose could be posed as a question unto itself. *What question shall I pose to learn what I must*?"

Phil remained quiet. The conversation was bordering on areas which made him uneasy. Areas he was not prepared to discuss with anyone yet. He had just begun to explore this aspect of his mind himself. He was learning how to learn from a totally unknown source.

"You know Mike, sea creatures need gravity too I think…"

Mike smiled to himself at Phil's suddenly artlessly feigned uncertainty. *He knows damned well they do.* "Yes they certainly do. That's why the seas rotate in concert with the entire ship. Yet there is nearly no open-air surface *per se*. That's why we place an artificial sun in the center of the Webber's Pelagikós, and at four points in the Oneirion Sea. Neither is far from their large bubble access and ARH Facility."

"ARH?"

"Aeration, Recycle & Harvest Facility. Where we keep the sea alive and it helps keeps us alive. This is where you might take extended dives and we can go talking with the fishies. Marine research will continue in space. It's also where we can monitor and adjust gaseous mixtures in the sea if need be."

"I understand. If there is no open-air surface how are the seas aerated? "

"You're quite right about the air. Most oxygen enters our seas and oceans and lakes by dissolving at the water's surface. It is then distributed by normal current circulation. The purpose of the gas entrée point I was talking about."

"Yes. Of course. Let's talk about the power source for this brute."

"Sure. At the core of the ship is the power source. Based on the QAVL engines. But exponentially larger. The QAVL ships have nearly zero mass to power. On our ship the drives must push a mountain.

Energy intake is at the leading edge of the sphere. Photons, dark matter, and an extremely exotic ionization of subatomic particulates. Exhaust at the back. Something like a titanic energy conversion ramjet. The outward thrust can be adjusted by 180° in any direction. The thrust can also be reversed for slowing and is equally adjustable."

Phil looked over the ships schematic. "So the QAVL Drive is something akin to what we term a Bussard Ramjet?"

"Exactly."

"For a vehicle of this mass a Bussard Scoop would have to be gigantic. A diameter of hundreds and hundreds of meters. I notice the intake scoop on this specification is proportionately tiny."

"It is. Based on the fuel source used by the QAVL and their efficiency at using it, a small amount of intake is needed. In fact both the intake and exhaust can be sealed into the hull when not in use, which is a surprising percentage of the flight duration."

"And the tubes connecting the intake with the exhaust…"

"We call them the Bussard Arteries.""Everything is well thought out Mike. Is this a product of the QAVL, or Oneiro design?"

"Both actually." Mike continued. "The giant Spheriscope applied to the exterior skin of the Webber's Pelagikós bio-solate, it completely covers the sphere, providing a sky that will be indistinguishable from the real thing on Earth. Digital Spheriscopes providing for night, sunrise, sunset, noon. Womb-type acclimatizers provide storms, snow, rain, everything. All the seasons.

The best part Phil will be the nights. No Womb technology. The real thing. And it should be astounding. Doppler red-shift at the leading side, Doppler blue at the following side. At .77 light it should be something to see. A giant, ever changing, night sky at near light speed. It will be a wonder of the ship. Consequently there will be a wealth of the finest, highest powered telescopes currently available disbursed throughout the sphere. Not to mention the formidable capabilities of the Spheriscope itself.

We will maintain a normal 24 hour diurnal cycle. Circadian rhythms should be uninterrupted from point of launch for the entire journey; which should be similar to life on Oneiro today. Not perceptively different from Earth. Crew on shift assignments will maintain their own cycles within living and duty areas. Shifts will be short. Two, to maybe six a day. Lots of overlap with the rest of the crew. No one will feels left out, isolated, or lonely. On-board technology will allow for liberal time for the entire crew to socialize."

Mike stopped to sip his drink and unwind. Phil could feel the excitement building in Mike, and it was contagious.

Mike continued. "Normal gravity. Normal air pressure and $O^2$ mix. Good healthy sunshine. Wind. You can sail. Even fish. We plan on opening the surface of the Oneirion Sea for all sorts of recreation.

The sphere will be roomy in the extreme, natural and luxurious. A wonderful environment. This all may sound somewhat indulgent. Remember they're facing a long, long trip. You can't suffer; you can't rough it and live in depravation for sixty-two years.

By the time it arrives *Kentrikos,* the entire crew will have had enough time to absorb all 12,000,0000 QAVL pages. Well prepared to face the cosmic community and participate in its studies.

The ship's specs go on for millions of pages. I think you get the idea."

"Where in hell would we build such a ship?"

"There is an uninhabited island about two hundred kilometers south of Oneiro which is effectively just a big basalt, limestone and granite mountain. Anastasios Island. Anastasios is roughly ten by sixteen kilometers. Mount Anastasios rises nearly 6,000 meters. The QAVL assure me it is a simple procedure to vaporize a two kilometer sphere in the middle of the mountain, blending and casting the skin and interior spheres at the same time. They effectively spin the interior structure during the same process. Practically the same process as making cotton candy at a carnival except it involves millions of degrees, unimaginable energy and gravity manipulation.

Then it's just a matter of outfitting it. In terms of building it, Shad Alexander in legal says we can purchase the island for about twenty-two million Euros."

"If you take out a two kilometer chunk of a mountain, even on a deserted island, someone's going to notice."

"Actually the processing will take place inside the mountain. The outer shell will remain intact during construction."

"Gravity?"

"The entire ship rotates anti-clockwise so we live on the skin itself, with a QAVL backup system. Naturally we will approach zero gravity as we near the poles. Those areas will be set aside for recreation and special production. If we elect to, at least partially, gravitate these areas, we'll provide PM access."

"PM's?"

"Sure. The habitable interior circumference of the sphere is over six kilometers. A pretty good walk if you're in a hurry. We'll have a fleet of bicycles as well; and we're augmenting the PM's with another innovative people transport system."

"What would that be?"

"Newtonian QAVLGates."

"Nifty name. What does it mean?"

"QAVLGates are based on QAVL materials engineering and good old Newtonian gravitational dynamics. Hence the name."

Phil, with an eyebrow slightly raised made no comment.

"Newton postulated correctly. Were a tunnel somehow drilled directly through the Earth one could jump down the tunnel and drop to the center of the Earth. At Earth's center the rider would continue to the opposite side of the Earth slowing commensurate with gravity inversely proportional from the center.

Imagine a jump from Chicago to Beijing.

He then generalized this mind experiment to say…New York to San Francisco, even New York to Baltimore if you like. The elegant beauty of his discovery was every such trip, regardless of the distance between city-pairs would take exactly forty-two minutes."

"Brilliant."

"It is, isn't it? Anyhow we will be constructing tubes from the surface of Oneiro City, down into the Oneirion Sea, surfacing at another point. We plan on hundreds of tunnels connecting points all over the sphere. The maximum trip is defined by the depth of the Oneirion Sea and reasonable stress on the human body. Newton's tunnels were straight regardless of direction. Ours are curved and cannot penetrate the total depth of the sea without imposing too much G-force."

"Why?"

"Because the sphere is spinning, gravity pulls to the outer crust instead of the inner core. Were you to turn the ship inside-out, the tunnels would be straight. This restricts a trip to about half a kilometer. If the sea were half its depth and we were to travel to the bottom, the same restriction would apply. In the absence of a gravity driver this form of transport is impossible at the two poles. We plan to operate within this restriction. Every QAVLGate will connect to several others at surface transfer points. An optimized network in fact. A traveler can arrive at one point and immediately jump to another point. As with rail systems, we will install duel tunnels for one way only traffic, for obvious reasons.

The crew will travel anywhere on the sphere within minutes, without energy expenditure whatsoever. Free, fast, easy, safe, non-polluting, zero maintenance, and even fun."

"How long will a given trip take?"

"The QAVL can produce a material which is totally frictionless. The interior and exterior of each tunnel will be spun of this material. Riders will zip from point to point in about .65814 minutes."

"Factoring in the lower mass and gravity of the ship?"

"Partly. There is lower mass for sure. Except the gravity's the same. That's why we spin her. They will enter from On-Point in a sitting position, slide down like crazy, and then up to a graceful stop at Off-Point in a standing position. From our perspective up and down are reversed. Gravity controls everything. The exterior of the tubes are frictionless to prevent any build-up of algae, minerals, or any living thing. They are undersea after all. The bonus is the QAVL can produce these tubes totally transparent. Since the sea is lit, recognizing night and day, it should be a beautiful ride, as well as fast and fun. We are going to great pains to populate the sea with a rich biosphere of marine flora and fauna."

"What if one of these SeaGates broke. Any danger of flooding?"

"No. Despite their 'up and exterior' location, they actually reside at sea level. Therefore, the water could not rise beyond its current level. I suppose if the sphere were to cease rotating and a SeaGate broke… Mmm. I'll ensure an emergency port is added at the SeaGate apertures.

# The Main Course

"Where will we draw crew from?"

"We'll ask for volunteers from Oneiro's latest 5,000. The latest iteration. I imagine every one of them will eagerly step up. Then we'll select the brightest and the best, emphasizing those disciplines most needed. Actually they're all needed. I suppose we'll need to concentrate on genetics, particle physics and cosmology. Certainly we will want representation from all our disciplines. However, we will have access to the entire Oneiro food library."

"Womb?"

"No. No reproduction en-route. No such laboratory equipment will be aboard and chemically enforced."

"Why?"

"Birth by a single pairing would upset our compression cycles irreparably. A child born en-route would be onboard without benefit of volunteering. Progeny exposed only to space-faring existence would be a completely unknown and possibly disruptive factor. Not to mention inbreeding. No kids. It's just not fair. There's too much risk. Oneirions have never reproduced. We believe reproduction represents a bio-anachronism best relegated to our past. Weaning relegated to the Womb back on Oneiro."

The Womb is a remarkable structure built for the express purpose of weaning Oneirion infants from birth to early childhood. The Womb is staffed by care giving nannies; and the physical facility itself nourishes the child with an exceptionally enriched environment. Aromas, shapes, lights, forms, sounds, food, water, total freedom in a totally unstructured environment–insulating the child from frustration, confinement, repression and any sort of parochialism.

In the words of Dr. Jackson Gear (former Chief of Medicine & Managing Director of the Nursery) the resultant children:

*"[Sic]...suffer none of the frustrations and phobia and hang-ups of babies. They aren't tightly cocooned in fabrics until they can't move. They aren't strapped into chairs and cars. They aren't imprisoned in bassinets, cribs, perambulators, or any other device of torture. They don't spend their young lives too hot, or too cold, hungry or thirsty. They live on their own schedule. They live without frustration. They are independent. They eat when they want, drink when they want, void themselves when they want, sleep when they want and play when they want.*

*They are given more love by more people than any Lander baby ever dreamt of. They know how to interact with other humans better than any child ever built. Aggression, frustration, inhibition are concepts unknown to them.*

*They are 100% healthy. They are 100% happy. They are 100% neurosis free. Anal retentive or expulsive absurdity is unknown. They are never, never abused physically or verbally, nor are they ever subject to neglect. They are guarded and watched and supervised constantly and unobtrusively. They benefit from the richest ambience humans can devise. Sexual, societal and personal hang-ups never enter into their psyche.*

*The adoring, benign tyranny of the mother and father figures play no part here. Oedipus and Electra are only characters in an Greek ancient play. These children are free of preconceptions, bigotry, bitterness; the entire range of beliefs humankind has hobbled itself with. They have no baggage to suffer. They are simply the happiest and healthiest children on Earth..."*

"How long will it take to construct this *space mountain* Mike?"

"Five months. No coincidence it coincides with the end transmission of Part II. Do you know Nick Farrow?"

"Mmm I think we've met...yes."

"Nick's the Project Director. He confirms we'll make the five month completion date. He knows the ship cold. He knows the plans and he immerses himself in new plans as they are downloaded. He is learning an amazing amount."

"Sounds like they are downloading Part II in case we wish to build other vessels. The first one will be complete before we even have the plans."

"I'd say it's a fair statement. In fact the QAVL seem to support your statement. I've discussed it with them and they state this is the way they've done it for eons. Problem is I'm quite sure we're eons from learning their drive and gravity systems. Not to mention how they spin objects out of granite and nickel-iron alloys. Just because they give us a set of instructions doesn't at all imply we can build it. Like giving a chimp the plans for a bicycle."

"So it's a rather hollow gift then?"

"Could be. I haven't been able to figure out this specific aspect yet... amongst many other aspects I haven't sorted out."

"What do we know about their drive systems?"

"They operate on principles much as the QAVL themselves, but the objective here is to provide thrust, not sustenance. Scoop photonic energy, dark matter, even sub-atomic space loess. Deplete it of its energy. Then immense volumes of depleted particles are explosively exhausted, moving at relativistic speeds, driving the ship. The energy gained will power the vessel. It'll require well over a year of constant acceleration to achieve .77 light. As the ship approaches Kentrikos she'll come about; and it will need nearly another year or so to slow down. Hopefully we'll better understand it all in the near future. For near Earth maneuvers the ship can manipulate gravity wells, and it will break us out of Mount Anastasios."

"I'd like to see this."

"You will Phil. Nick and his people have been working like crazy to set up a tour of the ship as it presently stands. I understand they have some surprises in store. You're invited."

"When?"

"Soon. Couple of weeks, give or take."

"Do you believe we will ever be able to duplicate this technology ourselves?"

"Yes. Absolutely. In just a few thousand years, give or take. Ultimately we have little choice. Move out there or die. Die from atrophy, or asphyxiation, or famine, or drought, or war, or stones from the sky, or heat capable of melting rock, or a thousand other ways to extinct."

"Considering Earth's current leadership that may take a good deal longer."

"Say again Phil?"

"Earth's leadership wantonly squanders time and energy. They pursue their own self-besot, base desires. No country on Earth escapes such men. They are obscenity. Millions die, millions are misdirected, millions starve and suffer, and millions pass their lives in darkness and ignorance. None. *None* may be trusted."

"Yes. I agree Phil, I..."

"*... and you would share these wonders with such creatures?*" Phil's voice was low. Accusing. A threatening growl. To Mike's ears it seemed a bellow.

"Please Phil. I don't know. I need your help."

"You know the solution as well as I."

"… Which is?"

"Evolve. Until then, let the bastards burn in the hells of their own invention. By they own volition their coming and passing means *nothing*. An obscene, cosmic RF."

"And what of the innocent millions. They burn too?"

"If they acquiesce to such scum. Yes. They burn. Oneiro has always done its best for them."

"Jesus Phil…" Mike was literally at a loss for words. *What in hell had made Phil so venomous?*

They both sat lost in a brown study for some time.

"If I understand the QAVL messages correctly Mike, they are saying the same thing."

"Oh really?"

"Look. We evolved intelligence in the same way the tiger developed claws. A survival mechanism. However, there comes a point when natural forces are insufficient to further the evolution of sapience. Just as there comes a point when the tiger's claws are long and strong enough. Therefore, progression stops, or it slows down, or it destroys itself, or it changes direction, or it innovates something so bizarre it extincts. At such a watershed the species must self-evolve. Must further their own intelligence. Must take command of their promise. If they fail? Well there is no promise. There never was. Only fossils."

Mike slowly nodded a tacit, brooding agreement.

Phil roused himself. "This undertaking...dangerous?"

Mike cleared his throat. "They say no. They've done this hundreds of thousands of times in the past." Mike extended a DOCUMENT, consisting of six or eight pages marked CONFIDENTIAL. "This is a summary of my findings to date, based on interviews with the QAVL, the QAVL DOCUMENTs, and as much validation as we've been able to perform thus far on the science involved. We have been through it all with great care, over and over; and we have detected nothing, nothing contradicts their statements."

"What about encountering a belligerent species out there?"

"The QAVL state such a thing is effectively not possible. Economics for one. It simply renders the idea ridiculous. There is absolutely nothing to be gained which offsets the time, technology and tools required to achieve interstellar travel. No commodity is of such value that seizing it by force justifies the investment. The motives of race hatred, illusory territorial boundaries, paranoiac xenophobia, blood-lust, imperialism and so forth are utter nonsense. The distances involved and the sheer number of potentially habitable planets completely nullify any arguments along those lines."

"No commodity. Okay. What about a planet?"

"Say again Phil?"

"Suppose some species wanted the Earth for their own?"

"There are millions of Earth-type worlds throughout the universe. Why pick a fight?"

"Well one good reason is Earth-type planets frequently support life. Life normally doesn't suffer replacement too well."

"It does if it's single-celled. In fact it doesn't give a damn. Now. Consider the near impossibility of mounting a voyage of exploration. Then consider mounting an invasion armada. Ridiculous. Lebensraum exists."

Phil frowned inwardly for a moment.

"Lebensraum. German. Space to develop and live. First came to common usage through – of all people – Adolf Hitler, in his book Mein Kampf. Later it appeared in a musical composition by...Sasha Barth."

"Right as always Phil. Discounting Lebensraum for the moment, there are two and only two real reasons to take on the stars."

"…and they would be?"

"One. Survival. Propagation as a hedge against extinction. A cosmic bolt-hole in case the home planet becomes unlivable."

"…and two?"

"Knowledge. The unadulterated quest to understand existence. In such an endeavor, belligerence has no place. It is to the advantage of any space-faring race to establish friendly relations with any race they may encounter."

"Why?"

"The sharing of knowledge. Experiences. No matter how advanced, encounters with a any alien culture can often vastly advance their studies and their knowledge base."

Yes. I understand Mike. Yet I still can envision warlike races in the stars."

"Phil, any race advancing into space for violent purposes would have to be insane. Insane specie would be totally incapable of the cooperative effort and intelligence needed. The QAVL contend an altruistic, cooperative approach is profoundly intrinsic to such endeavor. They equate it to the ancient Egyptians laboring in concert to produce the great pyramid for Khufu. The QAVL are correct. The $3^{rd}$, $4^{th}$ and $5^{th}$ dynasties – the height of pyramid building – were periods of great domestic tranquility.

Throughout their millions of years in the stars they have never encountered a warlike species capable of interstellar travel. They have never encountered interstellar, or even interplanetary war."

"Interplanetary, as in the same star-system?"

"Correct."

"I see. And they don't deem humans as warlike?"

"Not the ones who speak Oneirion." Mike continued, warming to the subject. "They then laughingly added should protection prove really necessary against a predatory species, we would simply turn our exhaust on them. Absolutely devastating for up to 89,000 kilometers. So virulent in fact, for close proximity planet maneuvering they can only use modulated gravity drives. All interstellar drives must be inactive."

"But still, they're *giving* us interstellar capability. What if we were to prove aggressive after all?"

"I asked them the same question."

"And?"

"They said they would take it away. They perceive no risk whatsoever."

"That simple?"

"That simple."

"Could that be one rationale for providing a QAVL liaison?"

"Maybe. I doubt it. I suspect they could dismantle our drive with a thought. From there we would face a rather ignominious tow back to our solar system... where we would remain for a thousand years...or perhaps they would let us pass a few punitive generations crawling back under gravity power."

"You're discounting human technology in space exploration altogether then?"

"Not at all Phil. And I imagine we will achieve viable, manned interstellar travel ourselves. In a thousand years or so, give or take."

"You toss out a few thousand years before humans achieve this level of technology. And along come the QAVL and just give it to us?"

"Perhaps lend-lease is a better term..."

"Lease? There's a term I can relate to. So what's the price of this lease?"

"Mmm. Sorry Phil. Bad choice of words. There *is* no price. Humans can offer absolutely nothing of interest to them. All we have, and we are is hadronic in nature. And their *Lebensraum* is quite literally infinite. Just lend. No lease."

"Well, that certainly lends some credibility to their..."

Phi's face went entirely blank. He didn't move. He hardly breathed. He became very pale and appeared to be perspiring.

"Phil?"

"Phil?"

"Uh. Damn. I just experienced the strongest waves of discordancy I've ever felt. Everything was suddenly...wrong." He ran hands up both arms as though he'd felt a chill.

"What does it mean Phil?"

"I don't have the first damned clue. Go ahead please."

Mike stared hard at Phil, concern and confusion playing across his features.

"Okay. The QAVL are letting us hitch a ride as it were. We will still be millennia removed from true command of the science and technology involved. Look at it this way: Were we to encounter an enclave of humans somewhere on Earth so removed they had no medicine, would you withhold modern drugs from them because they were centuries from developing such medicine themselves? I doubt it very much.

Because we now speak *Kosmas,* we are now part of the *Kentrikos* cosmic family, which they deem worthy and qualified for any support they can provide. A sort of foreign aid. In reality, more of a loan."

"... any collateral for such a loan?"

"Mastery of *Kosmas*. That simple."

"I see. Seems too easy. Too benign. Even for a race as advanced as the QAVL. You're quite sure you have all the facts?"

"Given that rationale, why not assist us in extricating ourselves from our other deadly propensities, they outline so lucidly in their DOCUMENT?"

"You haven't answered my question Mike."

"I cannot. Only they can; and I believe they would respond that they have limitations. Self-imposed and those established with *Kosmas*. Considering the time and distances involved, each QAVL garrison acts autonomously. They have only two guidelines."

"Yes?"

"The first is called the *Kosmasian Franchise*. Essentially by speaking *Kosmas* a race is entitled to unquestionable membership in the *Kentrikos Community*. No other criteria can, or will be imposed."

"...and the second guideline?"

"They refer to it as the *Kosmasian Ukase.*"

"Now there's one hellofa damned moniker. Ukase..."Phil closed his eyes."...an absolute, often arbitrary proclamation which carries the force of law."

"Correct. The *Kosmasian Ukase* is an inviolate rule which stipulates the QAVL will speak no other language with new races other than *Kosmas*. This admonition constitutes a barrier to dabbling in inter-linguistic, thereby inter-cultural polity. Succinctly stated: Blow yourselves to hell if you like. It's not our problem."

"What's the big deal?"

"Divisiveness."

"Divisiveness?"

"Yes. Cultural divisiveness. They say nearly any race in the galaxy speaks more than one language. Often several. Such as on Earth. Although we are a little excessive. As any language is basic to the culture of its society, were the QAVL to use the language it would automatically constitute a cultural bias on their part. Divisiveness. Therefore they speak only *Kosmas*. Apparently this does not preclude written communications incidentally. But it goes much deeper than that. *Kosmas* is a truly universal language, emanating from the deepest fabric of existence. It requires a specie achieve insight and cognizance sufficient to effer the language from within."

"Okay. So we've mastered *Kosmas*. More correctly *you've* mastered *Kosmas*. We're still a damned primitive specie. What can we contribute?"

"Remember, they're attempting to gather samples from all *Kentrikos* qualified species throughout the universe and incorporate them into the study."

"We are specimen for their *collēctus omnimodus*."

Mike smiled wryly. "In a certain sense, I suppose so. But, by the same token, all members of Kentrikos are specimen as well. All members are also students, teachers and researchers in the Kosmas Antiaô."

"*Antiaô?*"

"Yes. That's another appellation they use. They love the Greco-Roman languages. Although, for some reason they don't seem to differentiate too rigorously. In this case they opted for Greek. It means Quest."

"Yeah. I know. Go ahead."

Mike flashed a baleful glance. "If you're questioning human equality in this endeavor – yes – there are races involved that render us comparative amoebae. Yet I do not believe equality is even considered there.

More importantly, in point of actual fact, a large percentage of races on *Kentrikos* have no native interstellar flight capability."

"Interesting. Why?"

"As the QAVL explain it, they either aren't physically adapted to construction, or their interests take an entirely different direction, or they evolved in an astrophysically deprived environment…"

"Astrophysically deprived?"

"…they couldn't see the stars…in the midst of nebulae and such…as in the early years of the QAVL, for example. Or there was a dearth of requisite heavy elements on their planet respective to the requirements of their physical transport. Yet all these races evolved to speak *Kosmas* and have a great deal to contribute to the project. Our inclusion in the studies is not at all unusual. You can see why mastery of *Kosmas* is so important."

"Okay. Another problem. Most Oneirions would not survive the round trip."

"Why?"

"Old age."

"In fact *Kosmas Kentrikos* has youth rejuvenant technology; and the QAVL have brought it to us. A gift. They've had it for millennia. They always provide it for new short-lived members. Apparently it requires minimal adaptation for use between carbon derivative life forms.

Another gift. They're also providing us a powerful dormancy sedative. Every crew member should sleep a total of about eight years in shifts. Use of both medications should ensure returning Oneirions will have only aged about six years. Naturally many of the crew will remain at *Kosmas Kentrikos*. Probably to be relieved by the next crew."

"And islanders will have aged … let's see …"

"Roughly twelve years. Oneiro will be provided the same medicines. In terms of elapse time dilation however, the Lorentz factor, would apply. The ship would arrive Earth about ninety years after departure, factoring in time spent on *Kosmas*."

"Mike if any part of this were revealed to the world, in all likelihood we would be obliged to reveal everything. Oneiro, the QAVL, the stupefying technology behind it all, *Kosmas Kentrikos,* the rejuvenant. Everything."

"I understand Phil."

"Not one aspect of humanity would remain unchanged. A revolution of unimaginable proportion. Can mankind survive this? Would mankind *allow* us to survive this?"

"That's the first of the two big questions Phil."

"The second?"

"Shall we mount the mission?"

Mike fixed Phil with a penetrating stare. Long moments. Phil evenly returned his stare.

"We can *absolutely* trust the QAVL Mike?"

Mike was suddenly burdened by the degree of trust being exhibited by Phil. "I am convinced. Without reservation of any kind. I have carefully studied the QAVL every day for close to a year. I do not delude myself into believing I am too sophisticated not to recognize duplicity from such an advanced race. Yet, I am unequivocally certain we are dealing with an open hand. Extraordinary good faith. I should make this clear however. Even were I not unequivocally certain, I would be in favor of this mission."

Phil spent some time looking over Mike's report. He brought all his concentration to bear. Mike had included *verbatim* radio dialogues. These Phil found most interesting. Even through a digital interpreter, radio transmission over tens of thousands of miles, transcription to an impersonal report, Phil could perceive the positive feelings of the QAVL, their good faith, their fun and their obvious fondness for humans. This was clear and compelling. Phil didn't believe a non-human could synthesize such quintessence. He believed them. Yes. He agreed with Mike. Phil's unique gifts confirmed this.

Mike had never witnessed Phil protracting a decision. He found it both upsetting and reassuring.

Phil looked up. "My answer is: *Of course.*"

"I expected you'd say that." Breathed Mike.

"And the *first* big question Mike?"

"Tell the world? I don't have the answer. I need help. We need help."

"One more question."

"Yes Phil?"

"What's her name?"

"Her working name is *Gauntlet.*"

# Night Watch

Dinner was long over. The detritus cleared away and the serving girl relaxing to her quarters. They had talked to exhaustion. Probing, questioning, re-probing, analyzing, what-ifing. Back and forth. They moved to the starlit outdoor terrace overlooking the lake. They had emptied a bottle of Oneirion Brandy. And still they continued. Finally, Phil stood and stretched.

"I've had it Mike. I've got to think. We need to talk more. I need to *wrap* this and see what comes out. I think I'll go underwater with this."

"Okay Phil. Shall I postpone tomorrow's session for 24 hours?"

"Great idea Mike. Do it. All the same, I better hit the road. But one last question…"

"Yes?"

"What was your proposal?"

"Damn! What with everything, I actually forgot. Feel up to a few more minutes?"

"Got any coffee?"

"Sure. I need something from the kitchen anyhow." Mike smiled at some personal thought.

A few minutes later they settled in the living room. Coffee in hand. Stars, planets and the moon all round. Coldly, starkly beautiful against the raven sky.

"Okay Mike. What is it?"

"As we discussed earlier you've demonstrated some exceedingly unique mental abilities. Not attributable to advanced genome development as we understand it."

"Yes?"

"I've done some special studies in food processing with Dr. Gold, Dr. Butler, Dr. Rio and his geneticists. We devoted quite some time to develop some singular adaptations of nutritional data absorption…much of it rooted in QAVL biochemistry …just for you."

"For *me*? Why?"

"Oneirion. *Kosmas*. The language. I think you can learn it. You can MGL it. You can eat it. Or you can drink it. It would take a good deal of time to explain it all to you. So here's a small gift" He extended a waxed paper object.

"What's this?"

"That is an exact reproduction of hotdogs sold at O'Hare International Airport in Chicago. Anne tells us you constantly mourn their loss. It also contains a full explanation of the MGL *Kosmas* process...right down to the molecular level. Enjoy."

"I'll be damned." He took a bite (medium catsup, light mustard, fresh soft moist roll and perfect dog – red, overcooked, under-spiced). "That's amazing. The real thing. Delicious. Thanks Mike."

"Edward is now fully stocked with these dogs. You'll understand it all in a few hours. However you elect to ingest it, if it works, and if it doesn't kill you, you'll speak *Kosmas*."

"Mike, that would be...special indeed."

"Dr. Butler and I agree it could also be dangerous as well."

"How so exactly?"

"Brain damage. Insanity. Irreversible loss of memory. Stroke, ischemia from a thrombosis, embolism, or hemorrhage. Paranoia. Blindness. Paralysis. Catatonia."

"Goddamn Mike, you sound like a pharmaceutical ad in the U.S. What are the odds with all this?"

"We have carefully thought this through. We calculate 75:25 in your favor. I must be honest. Even if you get through it unscathed, the odds it actually works are about the same. Either way we are convinced it will be difficult. Hell itself in fact. A real nightmare. Painful as well. It would most certainly kill the normal human. We believe you are strong and adaptive enough."

"If I tried it, I believe I'd attempt it underwater."

"How long can you stay under Phil?"

"I don't know. Indefinitely."

"Anyone else, I'd say they were insane. You? I'd say you probably know best. I would insist however, we could observe you closely and have rapid access if there's trouble."

"Agreed. I'll *wrap* that question as well. Next?"

Mike, among many others, had difficulty keeping up with Phil's near instantaneous decision making. Progressing abruptly to the next issue. Those unfamiliar with Phil often mistook his staccato reactions for flippancy, disinterest, or a lack of serious analysis. Mike knew much better, and resiliently continued.

"Phil let's assume you undergo the language ordeal successfully. One of the primary reasons we've worked so hard on this is to enable you to lead the mission to *Kosmas Kentrikos*. Or as a second choice, I lead the mission and you reassume Proprietorship of Oneiro. Either way you must speak *Kosmas*."

"I see."

"What do you think Phil?"

"Why not you Mike?"

"Lead the mission?" Phil nodded. "I don't have your leadership skills. You do. I'm too close to the troops. Your decision making powers. Your speed. Your situational awareness. Your knowledge of things unknowable. I think these are critical factors."

"Interesting. I would have assumed your first choice would be to lead the mission yourself. The idea of leading an expedition to *Kosmas Kentrikos* excites me more than you can imagine."

"Believe me Phil, I can imagine. If you were unavailable for some reason, nothing could stop me. I *will* take the next one."

"There's two more days, excluding tomorrow, remaining of your seminar. I suggest lunch, you, me, Anne, three days from now and we'll start making some concrete plans. What say?"

"Great. Agreed. I think I've had it for the night too."

"Agreed Mike. Let's pack it in."

"Thanks for taking the time to come out Phil."

They walked to the door as the boulder face slid smoothly open. Now he had more of the facts, Phil was reassured. His faith in Mike was well placed.

"Thanks for *your* time Mike, and for dinner. Forgot how much I like meatloaf. See you 0930 day after tomorrow at the Webber Center."

"Goodnight Phil."

The lift carried him soundlessly down. The lake was still brightly lit from beneath, so Phil could easily find his way across the bridge to his waiting PM. He enjoyed the breezy moonlit ride back to the university. He peered up at the stars all the way to the university. Stars he might soon be joining.

To his surprise, Phil immediately developed a splitting headache. He couldn't remember the last time he'd experienced one; and this one was a beaut. Bringing his PM to a halt, he held his forehead. As quickly as it came upon him, it was gone. Phil sighed with relief and continued his journey.

It occurred to him his time roving the sea on Sea Tigress had not been wasted. He hadn't realized he was in preparation for a great challenge. *There is magnificence here. What is the source? This was beyond luck. Beyond serendipity. This was beneficence.*

The sun was just ascending from the eastern sea as Phil entered his bedroom to join Anne.

# Chip and Dip

Phil slept soundly until noon. Mike had efficiently put out the word on their meeting's postponement so Anne was there to join him for brunch on the terrace. Sunny. A few high clouds. No appreciable wind.

Edward was *en forme* today. A huge *café au lait*, fresh chilled mango, creamed chipped beef on toast and hashed brown potatoes. An iced-cold Tequila Sunrise to finish it off.

"You and Mike must have had quite a time last night. Fun?"

"Yes. I enjoyed it. You've got to see his home. He's really quite talented. I made a lunch appointment with him on Friday for the three of us. Maybe we should dine there? Let you see it for yourself."

"Sure. Sounds fun. Are you really going to eat that chipped beef stuff?"

"You bet. I learned to love it during a short stint in the ROTC at the U-of-M before I went to Johns Hopkins."

"What do you call it again?'

"SOS."

"Right. SOS. Meaning?"

"Shit-on-a-Shingle."

"Right. I remember why I forgot the name now. So what did you do last night?"

"Last night was deadly serious business. Amazing actually. Let me tell you about it. I need your opinion."

They spent the next three hours on the terrace going over the previous night. They covered everything in exhaustive detail and re-tracked the same analysis Mike and Phil had worked through the previous night. Anne found it nerve-wracking and grew understandably weary. A long, complex, emotional session.

Nap time.

While Anne slept, Phil took an elevator down to the sea.

He swam out a few kilometers passing huge schools of squid, rays, sharks and whales, even a few sea lion. Apparently Oneiro continued unabated with marine communications research.

He dove down to about twenty meters. The water here was clear. Cool. Crystal. He was suspended in air. He triggered his mind to commence its peculiar wandering. Unwrapping and processing active enigma.

*I do trust the QAVL. Just as they had responded to Mike's query about warlike spacefarers–there was no conceivable reason the QAVL would represent themselves as anything other than they were.*

*They could easily take anything they wanted. Kill anything they wished. Dominate. Destroy. Exterminate. Nothing was beyond their grasp. Mercifully there was nothing they wanted or needed. No one they needed to kill. Earth domination for the QAVL would be tantamount to a human standing on a termite mound and declaring himself emperor.*

*If this is so, we should logically regard them to be as adept as they appear. The 12,000,000 pages, the ships design, Kosmas Antiaô, Kosmas Kentrikos, the QAVL liaison, .77 light-speeds, and the whole story. Everything true. Reliable. I can confirm elements of this myself. I can corroborate.*

*Okay. Given that. I must lead the expedition. I must.*

*I wonder if Mike really wants me to lead, or is doing what he thinks best? Irrelevant. This is my trip.*

*Given that. I must speak Oneirion. Next Tuesday. Mike, Dr. Butler, Anne and myself. Mike's going to want Dr. Rio and Anne's going to want Dr Gear there as well. Can't hurt. Probably can't help either. On Monday I'll meet with Mike and Butler. Get a more in-depth understanding of this procedure. Mike didn't say it. He did know. There had to be more at work here than smart food. The language exists with humans at the genealogical level. Therefore, there must be some form of genetic modification involved. Explains the many dangers*

He remained underwater well after dark. As he kicked off towards the surface, he suddenly stopped. He froze. There it was again. *Music.*

He listened and slowly rotated for some time. He savored the strange beauty and he attempted to identify its source – at least its direction. It came from everywhere. And nowhere. Animal? Fish? Had the Oneirion language experiments catalyzed something? Currents? It was definitely the same music he heard three hours from here three days ago. So apparently it was fairly wide spread, if not altogether pervasive. Lovely. Peaceful. Maybe the word was sublime? A wistful quality too. Phil determined to bring recording equipment on his next dive.

When he returned Anne was up and dinner was being set out.

"How was your dive?"

Phil smiled. "Good. I'm thinking I should undergo the *Kosmas* language treatment."

Anne turned to Phil, eyebrow raised, favoring him with an enigmatic, piercing look. "Taking a trip?"

"Yes. I'm taking the mission to *Kentrikos*."

Anne sat down and looked out to sea. Then up at the stars. She could see their destination from here. She couldn't see the potentially monstrous perils they might encounter.

He gathered her lightly into his arms. "Coming along?"

"*Kentrikos*? The jury's still out. I don't know. I'm not going for a swim with the fishics, and I'm not going to drink some damned joy juice laced with RNA transmogrifiers. I was certain this would be your decision. So I've been thinking about it."

Phil release her. "More than fair. You'd have years to ponder *Kosmas Antiaô*."

"How do you feel about the whole thing? Frightened about learning *Kosmas*? About the voyage? Excited? How about *Kentrikos*? I can't describe it. Something so utterly alien. Benign or not, still terrifying, intoxicating, inspiring. I suppose excited is the best word.

I never told you how my mother died."

"No."

Anne sat down and lifted a glass of wine. "My father was a bright man. He was a commodities broker. Made his money exceptionally young. So he bought a custom-built, twenty meter motor-sailor. A Bristol. One of the most beautiful boats in the world. Canoe stern, wood work and bright work so beautifully crafted you don't want to put it in the water. A yar and seaworthy boat. When he had mastered the boat he decided to sail around the world. I think he retired far too young and was desperately looking for some worthy endeavor. Money was all the meaning he gleaned from life before retiring, so I imagine his life was a pretty empty vessel. Maybe that's why I embraced art. Anyhow, he became obsessed with the idea and badgered my mother incessantly to join him. She didn't even know how to sail. The idea terrified her."

"Did she go?"

"They vanished off the Baja coast. A white squall was suspected. Must have been horrific. They couldn't find a trace of the boat, or them. Ever."

"I'm sorry Anne."

"Me too."

"Are you drawing an analogy?"

Quiet pause.

"Dinner's almost ready Phil ..."

"I'll be right there. I need to make a quick call."


"Hi Charlie.

Phil here.

I'm fine.
You?
Good.
Say Charlie. Do you have anything like small, lightweight, sensitive, underwater recording device?
Oh…no more than twenty or thirty meters down.
I'm trying to record a soft, sort of subtle sound. This will sound a little crazy. I'm not at all sure anyone or anything else can actually hear it.
Beats me why not. It seems a little mystical actually.
Music.
Music. It's music.
Yes. Underwater.
I'm sober as a judge Charlie.
You got anything?
Great.
Tomorrow morning's fine.
Thanks Charlie."

The next morning a technician appeared at Phil's door with a tiny wrist mounted recorder and straightforward instructions.

"Morning Mr. Carr. I'm Paul from communications. Mr. Stein sent me over. This is your digital recorder. Strap it on like a watch. The battery lasts for about seventy hours. Push this button for ON and again for OFF. Turn this button to the right for HIGH VOLUME. To the left for LOW. It's good for a depth of fifty meters. When you've finished recording, give me a call on x1879. I'll pick it up and transcribe it to disc for you."

"Thanks much Paul. I'll give you a call."

# The Neon Rainbow

Mike was seated at the head of the table. "Good morning. I'm sure we all benefited from a day away from this difficult briefing. So assuming we're all in fine fettle, so let's get started."

"What is *fettle*?"

"Mm. It's a horse thing I think. Something to do with their fetlocks?"

"What are *fetlocks*?"

The morning was not beginning well for Mike.

Phil joined in. "Actually the term *fetelede* derives from middle English. About eight hundred years ago. Verb. To shape or to shore up, as in old hearths. It now indicates a state of good form, or readiness."

Mike looked a little weary. "Let's get started." *So much for the bright young chief executive persona.*

"Today we're going to cover how the QAVL acquired tools, how they communed with another species, and how they became crucial space-faring members of the *Kentrikos* civilization.

The QAVL led a happy, rich, solitary existence on Qruxin for roughly seventy million years. Over time their intellect, their culture, their arts and sciences blossomed. This period marked the beginning of their racial memory. Despite their advanced civilization, space travel had never occurred to them, nor had they any conception of astronomy, cosmology, or physics germane to anything but the ambience of Qruxin. They couldn't see the stars. Their sun was a nebulous red glow travelling quickly across their sky towards the galactic center. The moons, the gas giants, everything else unknown to them. They couldn't see out. Nothing could see in. Any other sort of scrutiny, short of physical exploration was equally impractical. Alone in the vastness of space.

One stormy morning their world, their universe, everything, was transformed for all time.

An enormous interstellar craft softly touched down. High above the shores of the Qruxian Sea. It was soon securely moored atop the massive shoulders of the Mount Qruxian caldera.

They were spotted instantly by the QAVL. The QAVL of this era had achieved exceptional cognizance. They were remarkably aware of any change in their ambience. And they had explored their world exhaustively. Therefore they were regaled with delight and wonder by the immediate realization this huge object was not of their world. Aliens! They had no word for it. They called them nav-QAVL. Their innate logic and intelligence convinced them this object was not the product of natural forces. So it came from…somewhere…something…someone… else. Their joy was indescribable. Their curiosity was insatiable.

This observation was quickly authenticated by the first appearance of alien life on Qruxin, ponderously disembarking their mammoth craft. The single most galvanizing event in all QAVLian history.

The Gammons had arrived.

Gammon are large quadrupeds. Space-faring for roughly ten million years. One of the more advanced creatures in the galaxy. By human standards, not attractive. Four massive legs. Thirty finely attenuated tentacles. A product of a marine evolution in their remote ancestry. Several eyes. No auditory senses whatsoever, sensing only massive shock waves with their primordial aquatic ears. Though they communicate using language, independent of sound.

Far from telepathy. Whatever that is, or is not. Yet outwardly, it appeared as such. In fact they had evolved the ability to generate and acquire low frequency, long carrier wave signals. Radio of sorts. In their early evolution in a successful adaptation to their water world, they developed a muscular membrane capable of vibrating in water. Useful in mating rituals, danger alerts, locating each other in the murky depths and indicating food sources.

When the ancient ancestors of the Gammon made the revolutionary departure from the sea, they brought their vibrators in their heads with them. Of course they didn't work. Even if they did, they had no ears sufficiently sensitive to distinguish none but the most intense sound waves travelling through their atmosphere. All the same, they continued to vibrate and their reciprocal organs continued to "listen". Nature finally developed an extremely low voltage generator by accumulating and crystallizing minerals in their diet. An organic default much as the human appendix. The default receptacle for such accretion: Their ancient aquatic vibrator.

After the march of a few million years, the tentative beginnings of send/receive. Primitive. Yet useful. In paleontological time, the Gammon quickly developed what amounted to crystal radios in their heads powered by the micro-electrical impulses of their own bodies.

An important event. It provided the Gammon with an exceptional adaptive advantage. Their world was populated by a diverse number of species, many were formidable predators. It also precluded the prevalent means of communication in the universe. The interrogation and manipulation of atmospheric gasses, or liquids. Audio acuity. Sound. Speech. Hearing.

The QAVL were deaf as well. Difference was they could detect the Gammon. The Gammon had no idea the QAVL existed, nor any means, or method for seeking them out.

The Gammon's closest terran equivalents would be reptilian herbivores. Something akin to the Cretaceous Hadrosaur, descendant from Jurassic Iguanodons. Most specifically Gryposaurus momumentesis, the duckbilled dinosaur. A rugged integument covering all, save eyes, tentacles, ingestion, excretion, reproduction and respiration cavities, and trans-ception organs. Their primary diet consisted of tough, giant marine kelp. As a consequence they developed rows of huge rugged grinding teeth capable of masticating the enormous kelp stalks. In a shark-like adaptation these rows regenerate themselves, row-by-row indefinitely.

Adaptive intelligence also evolved in response to exceptionally skilled predation, rounding out their survival inventory.

Strong creatures. Old. Very gentle. Very intelligent.

Unlike the QAVL, the Gammon were not immortal. They were quite long lived however. They could comfortably and contentedly pass their long lives aboard their geo-ship. Something on the magnitude of twelve hundred solar centuries. Consequently they shared the QAVL near geologic patience. They settled down on their huge geo-ship to study Mount Qruxin. This planetary oddity was a rarity throughout the galaxy. Initial and ongoing results were sent to their home world; and the Gammon awaited centuries for an analytical response. A tedious dialogue by other than cosmic measure.

The QAVL devoted nearly twelve solar centuries trying to communicate with the Gammons. Strangely, the breakthrough finally came when the Gammon implemented neon light technology. The Qruxin atmosphere rendered visual movement inefficient; and the Gammon highly valued their time walking about on all fours. An integral element in their constitutional, social and even sexual practices. So they installed long bright, flexible yellow neon tubes, lining their extensive complex of walkways.

Because of their organic transceivers, the Gammon had no interest in proximity voice or higher frequency electronic carrier wave transmissions. Else it would have been ridiculously simple to establish communications.

However, neon was particularly useful, because the QAVL could easily slip into these gas filled tubes and easily interrupt the electron flux at given points. They used the flux to flicker a codified message. Problem was, since long distance communications were not part of their thinking, they had no Morse code or its equivalent. They didn't even have a written language. All Gammon knowledge was embodied in Saga.

After much effort, they hit upon the idea of talking to them in their own language, only visually. Similar to the way in which an oscilloscope can visually represent human speech. The QAVL used the neon tubes to talk to the Gammons. They tried for a long time. It wasn't until all QAVL infested all neon tubes, and commenced speech at the same time. When their communal attention was engaged, their combined intelligence brought to bear, they finally figured out the problem. The Gammon discovered the QAVL. True communications were initiated and joint development became a permanent bond between the two cultures. The *Neon Language* of the Gammons was in fact *Kosmas*. The radiographic language of the Gammon was *Kosmas*. Just as Oneirion is *Kosmas* as well.

Although the QAVL seldom referred to it, they could be visible if they so wished. Other ahydronic creatures did share their world. Younger, primitive and often dangerous. Spectral manipulation of the light comprise and nourished them. Dazzling multicolor displays date back eons to their earliest memories, millions of years ago. Exhibited with trepidation, lest it attract QAVLian predators. Contemporary QAVL suffer no predation. Only their trepidation remains.

These beautiful, gracefully spirally, twined rainbows are mating displays. In a ritual of rare beauty, in a liturgy almost older than life on Earth, The Mating, QAVL mate and breed for life. A QAVL engages in this only once in their immortal lives. They mate for eternity. The QAVL TRIAD. An immortal, indestructible bond.

They then reproduce. Subsequent to propagation the single progeny seeks out its own triad. The incredible spectral gradient is absolutely unique to each QAVL and is the sole source defining the common affinity, even love, of each QAVL to its TRIAD. To engage in this in the sight of non-QAVL, or na-QAVL is unthinkable. Impossible. Hence they had great difficulty in establishing communications with the Gammon in the absence of some type of intermediary. In this case tubes filled with neon gas and trace elements were the ultimate mediator.

QAVL spectral displays range from the simple primary prismic colors of a rainbow to infinitely fine gradients, from most wavelengths (invisible to humans), to black (invisible to humans) to white (invisible to humans) and every conceivable hue in between, to pulsating designs – helixes, circles, bows, eights and more – rhythmically glowing and evolving. Rippling throughout millions of sources, the effect and beauty must be breathtaking. Although no creature that ever drew breath had ever witnessed such phantasma."

"How did you learn this about them?" asked Phil.

"Oh. They're quite open about discussing it. It's even described in their documentation. They simply will not display in front of a non-QAVL. After eons they finally consented to a single bright flash of white light alerting other beings of their presence."

Dr. Omani (Psychology). "So as incredibly advanced as these beings are, they suffer from plain old human-type inhibitions."

"Interesting point. If you think back to our Fear Training, one of the elements beaten out of us early on was inhibition. All sorts of inhibitions. Essentially sexual inhibitions.

Remember the primary method? Repetition. They ripped off our clothes and forced us into all manner of humiliating kink in front of audience after audience. Until we finally just didn't give a damn. The QAVL have sex constantly without a qualm. However, they mate only once in an eon."

"Good counter-point."

"Although, as you said, they are supremely advanced. With such beings we should probably differentiate inhibition from discretion. Perhaps they simply do not wish to share such experience with other beings. Any other questions?"

"More than you know." Responded Anne. "But I suppose we're trying to avoid too much detail."

"Quite right Anne. We've covered a lot. I think that's enough for today. Tomorrow I'll have about a three hour briefing on Part II and we're done with this part. After lunch tomorrow I'd like to initiate discussion regarding our release of these events to the outside world. I imagine debate will continue long after these briefings are over.

Thank you. See you in the morning."

"For those interested, you are welcome to stay. I'm conducting a short security briefing for Mr. Carr."

Phil looked slightly irked. "That was on the schedule?"

"Phil, I believe this is important."

Phil grimaced "Okay. Let's get this done."

Mike switched on a chart, Phil sighed, and they began.

"I'll make this fast.:

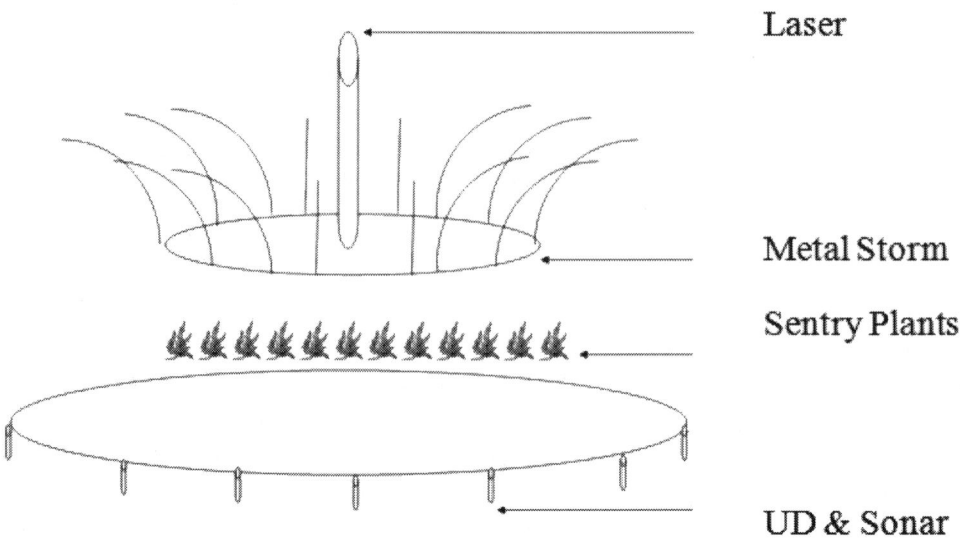

- 1st Sentry Plants.
- 'First we've doubled the height and capacity of Proteus Point, and it now has a totally redundant back-up concealed in something akin to an underground missile silo. The second concentrator can be raised and fully deployed within three minutes. Although it's not interactive to our Board Room. And yes, we still use that extraordinary room extensively.
- Either concentrator can see *anything* within hundreds of miles at around 240°. That covers any threats from marine or air surface incursion, as well as airborne, in fact any sort of incoming. Our only blind spot is below our cliff lines and we've now covered that as well, interactive to Proteus. We have also greatly improved our underwater surveillance capabilities (we even have some marine life sort of "standing watch", audio interactive to Proteus), so we're pretty damned hard to penetrate by stealth.
- Our primary system for remote targets is a completely new derivative of the old solid state laser systems developed for the U.S. Military. We can take out *anything*, hundreds of miles away, at literally the speed of light, and retarget instantly with a near 100% reliability rate, and an absolute 100% accuracy rate. That system can be elevated to roughly two hundred meters. Dependant on weather, we can go higher, but that entails constant retargeting and should we need to go higher, the implication is we have a greater targeting window in any event.
- Secondary to that, should a threat or threats somehow come within range, we have installed a formidable back-up: The latest models Metal Storm ADWS (MS227/B's I think).'
- Phil frowned 'Metal Storm? ADWS?'
- 'Metal Storm is an incredible system wherein something in the magnitude of *one million* 40mm shells can be fired in *less* than one minute. Anything within range no longer exists, period. It is quite literally vaporized. ADWS is an acronym for Area Denial Weapons System, which is the version of Metal Storm most appropriate for our use. We are strictly defensive. Simply stated, anything that achieves position above or in the vicinity surrounding Oneiro won't survive for a minute. Guaranteed. We are installing forty such units, blanketing the island.
- We will retain the conventional defense systems already in place to fend off any undersea assault. Although about twenty of our MS's have an automated 270° pivotal targeting prowess. They are positioned at the various apogees of our cliff-lines, so we can take out about anything down to a depth of a few meters.'

Further to all this, we have some subordinate developments coming from our own emerging technology in quantum physics and astrophysics. We will know within a few months if this weapon is feasible and deployable. I am pretty convinced it is. If so, there will not be a place on Earth, from a spot one meter in diameter to a continent that we could not decimate in moments. I know this sounds contrary to our mission here. But there may be some big, bad boys out there, maybe farther out and bigger and deadlier than even we suspect Phil. Incidentally this would double nicely as cometary or asteroid shield.

Something more pernicious? Scorched earth is sometimes an irremissible option. We are "Boy Scouts" no longer here. We've been blooded. In fact, none more than you Phil. So should the time come …'

*'This sure as hell wasn't the Mike Auslander I left on Oneiro a few short months ago. He was becoming profoundly dangerous. Art student, my ass! In the hands of anyone but Mike and the Oneirons, Phil would be horrified. At the same time he knew he would be doing the same damned things himself, maybe even more.*

Anne stopped Phil on the way out. "Why don't we have a drink at the Blind Bar in the Art Department? Then we could have a look around. I think you would like to see what they've been doing."

"Sure." Smiled Phil.

# Touché

Phil had always enjoyed the long, unfinished ride deep through the tunnel accessing the Art Department. It boasted the largest periscope on Oneiro, and a state-of-the-art weather simulator. Sun, wind, light rain, cool starry nights and glowing morning sunrises. He could bring his PM to full speed, wind through his hair, and enjoy exhilarating rides combining the best of the surface and the underground worlds. He treasured the occasional snowflake, or raindrop caressing his face.

It had changed drastically since those days however. Oneirion architects and engineers had delivered their finest work yet. It was now lined with bright neon signs, glass and chrome hotels, shops, bars, restaurants, two full sized Broadway Theaters, glittering marquees, playbills and all. He even saw skyscrapers looming in the background. The only giveaways were the vivid clear stars in the blackness above. It reminded him so much of Manhattan he looked around for some of his favorite places.

Sure enough. The Broadway Deli and Morton's Steak House. They wouldn't be dining at home tonight. Then he spotted Poncho's Mexican Cantina and knew very well where they would be dining. Anne loved their great Mexican food.

They had mated PM's for the ride and he looked across at her. She looked lovely in the multi-hued cacophony of light. Her tawny, sun streaked hair billowing as they moved. Happy and carefree. He hoped she would enjoy *Gauntlet* as much. Perhaps he would ask they build a Broadway aboard her as well? With a crew of two hundred Oneirions, there was probably more than enough stage talent. Or maybe Avenue des Champs-Élysées? Piccadilly Circus? The Ginza?

No. Broadway. With the new technology sky they had planned, enveloping Webber's Pelagikós, he couldn't imagine anything more Earthlike. Broadway in all kinds of weather, at all times, night and day. Maybe even a couple of empty bottles in the gutter, and a discarded newspaper blowing disconsolately over the pavement.

He had another idea for *Gauntlet*. With a spherical earth and a spherical sky, they could easily engineer a road circumnavigating the whole biosphere. Then, using continuous digital periscopic imaging, they could quite believably create an infinite road. Forever changing. Never the same. Transit the real and the unreal. The stars, under the sea, ancient Rome and the hanging gardens of Babylon, pass the Gates of Thermopylae as Leonidas struck out from a sea of blood at Xerxes, travel the Earth, other worlds, the universe, fantasy worlds and worlds not yet imagined. Travel for years and never find the end. If the ship began to 'close in' on a crew member, perhaps such a road could redeem a mind. He would discuss it with Dr. Dunedin in Psychology.

They were warmly greeted at the Art Department. Several old students, faculty and some new faces – eager to meet the principals who had heralded Oneiro's Renaissance.

After some conversation in the lobby area, six of them moved into the Blind Bar. A tall cold Gin and Tonic lifted the weight of the day. Phil sighed contentedly and hoped they didn't have anything particularly rough in mind for his viewing pleasure. The Blind Bar was not as dimly lit as before. Instead they had worked with the color of the light in order to see better, and provide the same darkened impression. *Brown* light? The bar had been expanded as well. Replete with all forms of interesting art. Phil thought he could spend a good hour just feeling his way through.

He started from his reverie when he realized they were speaking to him.

"Sorry I didn't catch that. I'm totally taken with the art here."

Anne said. "Phil we thought we would show you two things this evening. The Touch Gallery. They tell me the Touch Gallery is now 100% effective and well worth a visit. They say they've overcome the previous design error."

"What error?"

"Apparently they fell into the classical trap of assuming there are only the five senses Aristotle explored."

"How many are there? I've not heard of this before."

"In fact there are between nine and twenty-one. Senses such as touch, taste, smell, sight, hearing, thermoception, nociception, equilibrioception, and proprioception, hunger and thirst. The secret is to include as many senses as possible. We were depriving our subjects of all other senses in order to focus on a given sense, such as touch. Deprivation serves to distort the object. Not magnify. As you would probably guess they have now aggressively incorporated the new Oneirion art into its design now too.

After you try the new Touch Gallery they want you to view a few mild paintings. They believe the milder forms of Oneirion paintings may now be suitable for general human consumption. If this is so we will be better equipped to convey our message to the outside world. They would like your opinion."

"Fine. I think I would like to view the paintings first if it's alright. For some reason I suspect that the Touch Gallery may be a little challenging. And I assume you want me in decent shape when I give you my opinion?"

One of the students agreed. "Good point sir. This way please…"

They mounted the expansive entrance to the Island Art Museum. The collection had grown quite extensive. Peering down the long main gallery Phil realized the collection had grown quite impressive as well. Lovely graceful sculpture and exquisite paintings in every conceivable style. The gallery itself was beautiful. High ceilings casing clear sunlight on marble floors and flawless limestone walls. Several smaller galleries branched off the main gallery; and the pretty young student led them to a gallery on the right.

The gallery contained four paintings and one sculpture in native Oneirion marble. Phil went to the sculpture first. A stylized young goat herder dancing with a goat kid. He could see the airy joy expressed through both figures. The goat's hoofs high, head back, tail up, he could nearly hear it bleating. Although he knew from personal experience goats voice no sound when engaged in such frolic. It was almost impressionistic. Well rendered. As he studied the goat's fur he noted the familiar swirl design intrinsic to all new Oneirion art. It led his eye. It was pleasing. It lent animation to both the goat and the boy. Excellent. Powerful. Not dangerous in the least. Phil let his eye wander back to the goat. Its swirls. Then it hit him.

He pivoted, quickly stepped to one of the paintings and studied it closely. Then the next and the next and the next. Faster each time. The five others in the gallery look at each other. Intrigued.

Phil began to chuckle lightly.

"Of course. Goddamnit. Why didn't I see it before? Damn! Damn!"

Anne. "Phil…what is it?"

"The swirls. Look at the swirls. Don't you see it? Don't you get it?"

"Phil you're not making any sense."

"Right. Okay. It's simple. The swirls. They're *Kosmas*."

The five onlookers crowded around a painting and closely examined the swirls. A quiet ensued while they attempted to see the swirls as they appeared to Phil.

Anne turned to him. "As far as I know, you are the only human ever to have seen *Kosmas*. We're just going to have to take your word for it. What do you suppose this means? Or is there a meaning? Coincidence?"

"No. No coincidence. Things are coming together far too precisely. *Kosmas* permeates everything. It manifests itself in the minds of your artists when they're producing Oneirion art. You do see *Kosmas*. You just don't realize it. It follows this form so engages the mind it can be dangerous. There's symmetry about it. It fits."

They discussed Phil's postulate for some time. None, including Phil, could discern the apparatus at work here. Only that it worked.

Phil duly offered his opinion on the latest art. "I'm convinced any lander could view these works without risk. I believe they would enjoy them.

Appreciate them. See the message. Walk away enriched. Well done. I hope you're still exploring the pure power – unadulterated?"

"Absolutely. Fully leaded." Smiled the student. "I imagine we could kill you within three minutes after we drew the curtain Mr. Carr."

That gave him pause.

"Impressive. One other thought. Perhaps you should experiment with lander volunteers. Start with your softest works and see if you can gradually graduate them into stronger and stronger works. I'm not sure if this has a practical application. You would have to ensure all lander humans are adapted at the same level, at the same time. It may ultimately have some value. Who knows?"

"We'll try it Mr. Carr and keep you posted. Thank you."

Anne turned to Phil expectantly. "Ready to try the Touch Gallery?"

"I'll expect a Margarita the size of a goddamned goldfish bowl when this is over."

"Deal. And I'll expect *Chile Rellenos, frijoles refritos* and *Carne Asada*. And I'll want a *Taquito* back…chased by a *Tres X's*."

"You got it. Touch Gallery, then Poncho's"

The entrance to the gallery was as innocuous as he remembered. They stood in the foyer for a few moments acclimating to temperature, smell, light.

"Is it still broken down into solids and liquids and phyla of textures?"

"No Phil. Not at all. That was our initial error. It's more of a… symphony now…textural essences fused in consonance. Just use your fingertips. Only your fingertips. Keep both hands in contact at either side of the corridor. Try to position both hands to the same relative orientation on each side. Understand?"

"Yes. I suppose so."

"Okay. It's show time."

Despite his training Phil felt a brief, chill thrill travel his spine.

They entered. Total darkness. Nothing save Phil's fingertips on either side of the narrow corridor, as he ran them lightly up and down–seeking out the craft hidden from all other perception, save the sensorial labyrinth nestled in his dermis.

With either hand he felt a pleasant texture. Never felt anything quite like it. As if a deep corduroy were made of a dewy silk on a satin backing, covering some sort of gel. Tepid not warm. Moving, oscillating, and throbbing. Somehow alive. His fingers encountered the expected swirl design. Phil probed the swirls for a time. He had never actually felt a swirl before and he was fascinated how clearly his fingertips could disclose their detail. Beautifully crafted. He could feel the graceful cascading intricacy. Swirl within swirl within swirl. Totally engaging. Its own reality. Its own universe. And Phil was going in.

He fell. Everything fell. He desperately pushed his hands with all his strength, struggling to control his fall. No good. He fell. About eight hundred meters. He not only fell, he tumbled. Up-side down. Right-side up. Spinning out of control.

Then he approached a watery smoothness.

He descended effortlessly. A slow, fluid glide-path. Light as a Dandelion seed. Dreamlike. Restful. Pleasant.

He was perfectly aligned with the surface of the liquid when he finally, softly touched the cool aqueous veneer. Delta ripples spread in a quiet V as he sped over the calm lake slowly shedding momentum. He then rose just above the water. It began again. The gentle waves became a blur. Phil exploded into breathtaking flight over the mysterious lake. A sliver of moon softly defining the lake on an otherwise dark night. A subtle golden glow on the water.

The lake must be enormous. In all directions. Only water. Then, on the far horizon something was rising fast. An island. He could make out the shore and a forest beyond. Suddenly it was upon him. He crashed into the shore. A blinding rush of wet sand, weeds, frogs, algae, rocks and silky, silvered driftwood. Then he was in the forest. He could feel the forest. He could even smell soft grass, moist loam, leaves, rough woody bark, pine needles sharp and sticky, even the occasional dart of sleek fur and dark eyes. Then he was out of the forest on the far shore.

Water again. Island again. Forest again. Water, shore, island, forest, water, shore, island forest. Faster and faster. Over and over. A staggering collidascope.

With equal speed he rushed upon a huge boulder and ricocheted, rocketing into the sky. Up and up. Higher and higher. He lost all feeling of speed, even of movement. Lost in a featureless obsidian void.

Finally it was above him. He knew it would be there. He lovingly caressed it with his fingers. Spellbound by its beauty. Unthinkable trillions of minute points of light. A dozen or more hues. Turning and swirling as far as he could see and far beyond. The chandelier of the gods themselves.

He basked in its beauty, its glow, its magnificence. He was happy and calm and at peace. It was…sublime.

He sighed deeply. Contentedly.

Phil awakened standing blankly at the end of the second hallway comprising the gallery. Anne was standing near smiling gently.

He took Anne into his arms. "Dazzling. That was *Kosmas*. That was glorious. The most beautiful thing I've ever seen. This is something we must pursue."

Anne looked up at him. "I realize now. It's wonderful. They can do the same thing with scents and music now; and they're planning on repainting the Webber Center Access Tunnel the same way. Should make for an incredible ride."

"…as long as they inhibit manual override of the PM controls."

"I suppose you're right."

"And music you say? Interesting. I would like to visit the Music Department tomorrow with you and some people from MCL."

"MCL?" she frowned.

"The Marine Communications Laboratory. That's what they call it now. It's grown into a large department on its own. That's where they talk to the fishies."

"Yes. I know. It just seems a strange mix for a meeting."

"There's something odd under the water. I'd like you to hear about it too."

"I'll ask Edward to set it up."

"Thanks. I'll take that Margarita now. In fact I'll probably take two."

It was good to be back in New York again.

After an excellent dinner they even went to a show. Not unexpectedly there was some startling talent on the island. A revival of *The Petrified Forest*. Phil still laughed at his favorite line "*I'd kiss you but I just washed my hair*."

No frantic search for a cab afterwards either. A fleet of PM's awaited outside, precisely gauged for the number of theater goers who would want to go home and those wishing to go on to the bars and nightclubs off Broadway.

They ran into Herb and two girlfriends exiting the theater as well. So the five of them went for a last drink.

Later Phil slept through a dreamless night.

# Sea Song

Sun-up the next morning. Perfect day for a dive.

Phil drank a liter of orange juice and rode the sea elevator down, far below his apartment. As before, he swam out two kilometers or so, then scissored straight down for twenty meters.

His body and his mind triggered their unique physiological and psychological adjustments. Quickly Phil was comfortable and his mind began to wander. Time was limited this morning, prompting Phil to reject the various topics currently being processed *under wraps*. Instead he just relaxed, listened and let his mind work independently. His mind, or minds seem to set their own priorities. Who was he to interfere?

He waited. Listening for the music. Nothing.

After an hour it was time to return. Still nothing. As he launched towards the surface, suddenly there it was. In fact this was when it always manifested. When he was surfacing. Preparing to leave the sea. Why?

Quickly he engaged the wrist recorder given him by Charlie's man, Paul. He turned the volume to full and froze. Minimal ambient sound. The music lasted for about five minutes. Slowly, almost sadly, it faded away.

"Paul?
 This is Phil Carr.
 I'm fine, thanks.
 Look I've got a recording on the wrist device you gave me.
 About five minutes at around twenty meters.
 I really don't know if I got anything or not.
 I need an audio for a meeting at 1400. Possible?
 Great. I'll have it here for you.
 See you at 1000. Thanks Paul. Say 'Hi.' to Charlie for me."

Shower, shave, exercise and a quick steam bath. Then he met Anne in the whirlpool.

"So what's for breakfast?"

"Edward tells me blueberry pancakes, blueberry syrup, bacon, Casaba melon in Strawberry Liquor with tarragon, Latte, Passion-fruit/tangerine juice and a Harvey Wall-banger."

"Jesus! Sounds great. Hard to believe it won't make us fat, or tipsy. What's for brain food?"

"The latest updates from JPL in California and some new breakthroughs in Numbers Theory."

"Interesting. Paul is supposed to be here in about half an hour to transcribe my wrist recorder. Says he can do it on the spot and cut us a disc."

"You mean with all that *Dick Tracy* technology the damned thing can't even play back?"

"'fraid not. It's a tiny submersible, super high fidelity digital recorder. Very sensitive. Very small. Totally reliable. Write only. No read. No playback. No speaker."

"Well we better hurry and eat before Paul arrives."

Exceptional breakfast. Warm sun. Broad terrace 450 meters above the sea, overlooking extraordinary gardens. There really is no place like Oneiro.

Forty-five minutes later Edward showed Paul to the Terrace. "Hi Paul. Thanks for coming. Here's the goods. I hope it worked."

"We'll know in just a minute Mr. Carr." Paul opened a briefcase which turned out to be a compact transcription apparatus. He inserted the wrist unit into a tiny cradle. Download was accomplished by imminent-proximity, radiant-diffusion. He pushed a button. A small *wait* light illuminated for a fraction of a second. Another button, and a freshly cut micro-disc was ejected.

"There you are sir."

"Thanks Paul. I owe you one."

After Paul departed. "Well Phil let's give it a play."

They mounted the disc in the apartment's sound system and sat back to listen.

The sound emanating from the speakers was wholly unintelligible. A random series of rumbles and groaning sounds. Nothing more. It was not Oneirion or *Kosmas*. It was certainly not music. It was gibberish.

Anne grimaced at Phil. "Your definition of music Phil?"

He sat for a few moments in perplexed silence.

"Phil?"

"Uh. No. I certainly do not classify those sounds as music. Or any organized mnemonic system for that matter. It seemed to be simply noise. How can a human and an extremely sophisticated digital recorder, exposed to the same sounds, from the same source, at the same time, from the same location, with absolute minimal extraneous sounds, register two totally different results?"

"Doesn't seem possible Phil, unless you factor in some form of subjectivity. I think the first step is to identify actual source of the sound itself. Let's listen again."

They devoted the next hour to carefully analyzing the sounds.

Anne sighed. "The best I can come up with, is some sort of variant of whale song. I've never heard anything close, above or below the sea."

"Agreed. I think we need to bring in some experts. MCL is now housed in the complex connecting with the harbor. Why don't we go down to the harbor and eat some fresh seafood for lunch? Then we'll meet with MCL."

Anne smiled. "Sure. Sounds good. You *do* know none of those restaurants serve caught fish now? It's all Oneirion production."

"Sure I know. It still tastes better with sea air on salt water and diesel fuel."

Two generous Sea Bass fillets marinated in lemon juice, olive oil and aneth. Then barbequed to an enticing crispness, with fried potatoes, a perfect Coleslaw and icy Chablis. A dark Greek nut cake soaked in Grand Marnier finished the meal.

Phil always felt more optimistic after a good meal. He was ready to again take on the music conundrum with the MCL audio-labs.

MCL experts and representatives from the Music Department were already gathered when Anne and Phil arrived. As usual they were warmly greeted and after a short briefing, ready to hear the recording. Phil concluded they were either very open minded, or very polite, or both. No evidence of skepticism when confronted with two contradictory recordings of the same event. One digital. The other in Phil's mind.

After a few plays, Steve Blake, MCL's cetation expert, spoke up. "That's not whale-song *per se*. Something different. Never heard it before. Similar to a Humpback all the same.

This has nothing whatsoever in common with the music you hear Mr. Carr?"

"Nothing."

"Okay, here's what I suggest. We have a great deal of experience in manipulating and engineering sound here. We can take one sound sequence and develop an algorithm to convert it into another. Very much akin to language translation. Actually it's exactly like language translation. Recently we've had great success using FT's"

"*FT's?*"

"Yeah Phil. A Fourier transform. Makes for a very straightforward arithmetic interagent. Phonetically. After we wash superfluous alliterations. Can you possibly hum, or sing, or whistle, or play, or whatever, the music you hear?"

"I'm no musician, or singer. I could hum a few bars and you can give it a try."

"Fine. Just like the old joke" Steve started MCL's digital recorder. "Please go ahead. Try to be as accurate as possible. It doesn't have to be pretty. If you can capture the pitches as precisely as possible that would be helpful. Don't worry about rhythm, or duration of tone. Concentrate on the pitch and the sequence only. It will be easier. Try as many times as necessary. Ready?"

Phil nodded and feeling a little foolish, began to hum. He focused on pitch and tonal sequence. Not trying to follow a tune at all. Steve was correct. It was easier and more accurate. Similar to reading out numbers for transcription. After about five tries. "That's it Steve. The best I can do."

"Just fine. I'll use the last rendition?"

"Yep."

"Good. I need some time to let our magic machine do its work. Could we re-convene here at about 1700?"

Outside. "Well Phil, we've got about two hours. What shall we do?"

"Well I have the wrist unit with me and I think Steve has the equipment to transcribe, so I was thinking of going for another dive."

"Great idea. Let's grab a day sailor and head out. I'll stay aboard. Read and get some sun, maybe swim a little and you can sleep with the fishies."

Ten minutes later they were tacking their way out of the harbor entering the calm sea. Fifteen minutes later Phil dropped anchor while Anne dropped the mainsail. They hadn't bothered deploying a jib for so short a trip.

"You've got about an hour Phil. Although I know your timing down there is excellent, would you like me to whack the water with an oar when your time's up?"

"No. Don't bother. I think I'll only stay down for about twenty minutes."

Phil dove off the stern *au natural* wearing only his wrist recorder. He dropped directly to twenty meters, and then immediately to sleep. Exactly twenty minutes later he awoke feeling greatly rested and refreshed. *It never occurred to me to sleep below. It feels wonderful. Might try spending the night undersea. Dangerous? Could be. All the same...*

As he expected, just as he commenced his ascent, the music began. Again, he froze and turned on the recorder. After five minutes he continued to the surface swimming through the haunting euphony.

Then it hit him. Fear! Of all things. Fear of what? W*hat?* It hit him with a physical force. An icy feeling in his bones. He was trembling. Freezing. Waves of nausea washed over him. Muscle spasms ran the gamut of his body. Over and over again. The pain was indescribable. With all his training he never dreamt fear could impart actual pain. This was not fear, it was The Fear.

Then it was gone. Everything normal. He was drained. He drifted in the depths for roughly ten minutes. Slowly regaining his strength, he continued his swim to the surface and finally over the gunwale.

Anne watched his struggles and rushed to help. "Are you alright Phil?"

After he briefed Anne on his dive, generally glossing over his interlude locked in fear, they rested on the bow and talked.

"Were we to go on *Gauntlet* wouldn't you miss all this?"

"There'll be a lake and a sea and sunny days and sail boats much like here."

"You know I was talking about something deeper than day-sailing."

"Anne I think we can do the round trip standing on our heads. Particularly since we will age only six years and spend a good deal of time asleep. For me the overwhelming purpose is the time we'll spend on *Kentrikos*. All my life I've ached for the miracle of actually meeting an alien. We will meet tens of thousands. We will better understand the universe and existence than any humans in history."

"Don't you find it at all frightening?"

"Not really. No. Not at all. Do you?"

"Terrifying."

"Terrifying?"

"Terrifying. A million ways to die. And worse. Most of them unimaginable to humans. Although perhaps even more chilling is to ponder what sort of creatures *we* will be, returning to Earth."

"How so? 25.97 solar years out, 25.97 solar years back, 2 years on *Kosmas*, 12 years asleep. That nets to 32.94 years in a palatial environment with some of the most interesting humans ever to trod Earth and a richness of experience which defies description. I think we'll be *happy* creatures."

"That's an optimistic spin on the whole venture in my opinion. I am absolutely unable to conceive of any experience that would impose a greater concentration of evolitive tension on a group of *Homo sapiens*. Consider the extraordinary adaptive capabilities of Oneirions. They could return an entirely different species."

"Possible. Perhaps even probable, I suppose. We'll be with them the entire time. We will observe, guide, moderate…even evolve with them."

"Mm. Another problem. Am I going with you?"

For a moment he was speechless. This was an aspect of the voyage which simply had not occurred to him.

"Well Anne…I'd hoped so. That is, I'd assumed so. I thought it was a given this was something you wouldn't miss, no matter what. Was I wrong? Was I too self absorbed and lost in this project?"

"I really can't fault you for that. The greatest challenge humans have ever confronted. I've given it a lot of thought since your dinner with Mike. I don't possess your unique qualities. I'm not Oneirion. And I don't speak *Kosmas*. Never will. And don't forget, *Kosmas* is the 'Ticket to Ride'."

She looked into the sky, concentrating on her thoughts. "Two hundred highly evolved beings leave Earth bound for Kosmas. Something like sixty-two years later one hundred 'somethings' return to Earth, carrying with them one un-evolved, retrograde pet human. *Me*. An anachronism on *Gauntlet*, and little more than an endearing oddity on Earth."

"Anne, you know continued evolution will occur only on Oneiro. The mission crew is barred from procreation for the duration. Same rules as Oneiro."

Anne shook her head dismissively. "They will learn, adapt and even evolve in their own way. Nothing, not even you, can stop the most relentless force in the universe. I'm sure they will advance to their true potential. Something extraordinary could emerge. We really don't know. Me? 25.97 solar years out and 25.97 solar years back. Two years on *Kosmas*. The estrangement. The non-involvement. The dissociating inability to comprehend, or keep up, or perform anything of value to the ship. The growing isolation and alienation. The loneliness. Sounds like an abyss into insanity. It horrifies me Phil."

"But these people are your friends Anne. Many were your students. You've known them for years. Since they were children. They worship you."

"Man used to worship the sun. Now it's only another star. Not a very remarkable one at that. They venerate me as an esteemed relic from their recent history. Someone who helped get them advance to the next level…but doesn't really qualify for the class trip now.

You on the other hand, are actually developing even faster than they. And they know it. Me? I'm a stagnant vestige of the past. I know it. They know too.

And what about the creatures on Kosmas? They will instantly perceive I am out of place. Unqualified to be there. Perhaps even unauthorized. Unwelcome, if not even in harm's way. The QAVL seem innocuous in the extreme. However, they haven't been directly exposed to *me*. They haven't accepted *me*. Not to mention the thousands of other specie lurking on *Kosmas*. They could be exceptionally sensitive about their work there where non-*Kosmos* speakers are involved. They might perceive me as unqualified at best. Perhaps disruptive, even a threat. A trespassing Neanderthal interloping on the most important and enduring work in the known universe. I may be over-dramatizing this. All the same *I* might squish *me* like a bug in *their* position. A cockroach running loose in the lab. You might too Phil, after a 25.97 year outhaul."

She locked eyes with Phil. Fear coalescing with defiance and deep concern, even embarrassment. Then she turned and stared out to sea, seeing nothing except dark, foreboding perils suddenly menacing the wondrous life she had found with Phil.

Phil knew she was not acting from emotion, or cowardice, or selfishness. These considerations were clearly thought out. Anne was an artist in every respect. Yet also a creature of hard logic and cold reality.

*Her points are as inescapable as they are valid.* In his excitement Phil had naively assumed Anne would simply join the mission, exuding enthusiasm. She made some disturbing points though.

*If he survived the procedure, he would speak Kosmas. In all likelihood Anne never would. An outsider for over sixty elapse years. Anyone would go insane. Would he be forced to choose between Anne and the mission? Or had he already let it go too far? Had he let his options pass? If he declined the mission Anne would always blame herself. Hold herself culpable for holding him back from the most historic mission in human history. A classic lose/lose scenario. A lifetime forever marred. Alienation. Insanity. Failure. Guilt. One or more seemed inevitable.*

He already missed the silent depths of the Aegean.

"Time to head back."

Anchor and mainsail up, they silently tacked back to harbor.

"Well, what have you got? Did you succeed?"

Steve leaned back in his chair. "Ah, yes and no. Not the best Phil. We did apply a few algorithms to your tonality. We completed the conversion successfully. We can play it for you. And we have developed a recursive computational procedure successfully translating any part of the recording to Phil's humming. We analyzed the sound. And we attempted to detect any natural algorithms which might break the code."

"And?"

"And our algorithms yielded nothing of any sense. We confirmed a humpback, or something closely related made the sounds; and we did come up with a nominal, 'natural' arithmetic equivalence between sounds or concepts."

"I see…I guess. I notice you use the term *arithmetic equivalence* instead of *algorithm*. Intentional?"

"Yes indeed. We found no real fit for an algorithm. As I said we did come up with equivalence. Ever hear of the golden ratio"

Phil closed his eyes for a fraction of a second "…as introducing each tone, start such that the golden ratio (equa-tempered minor and major sixths) inferior to the previous tone, so the combination of tones produced by all consecutive tones are measurably lower or higher, applicable as well to those tones to be introduced."

Steve unsuccessfully masked his surprise. "Uh…yeah. Careful review does reveal some of these characteristics. I find it interesting. Wanna hear the converted tape?"

"Sure."

Unintelligible nonsense. No one in the room, including Phil, could detect any patterns approaching information.

When it was over Phil stood "So what now?"

"Give us some time Phil. A few weeks. Maybe we can dredge something out of this yet."

Phil looked at them thoughtfully. "Did you know our sun, or I suppose all stars, make a humming noise? Some call it singing. They say our Earth does the same. Even our galaxy the Milky Way."

"No. I was not aware of this. It's interesting. Is it relevant?"

"Damned if I know. I wonder what their arithmetic equivalence looks like.

"I'll look into it; and everything we've discussed."

"Thanks for your time gentlemen. Please keep me posted."

# Light Lunch

*Time is an illusion. Lunchtime doubly so.*
*Douglas Adams*

Dr. Philip Gold looked imposing at the head of the conference table. Unlike most Oneirions he was an exceptionally traditional dresser. Charcoal gray pinstripe, matching vest, watch-bob, starched white shirt, school tie, all crowned by an impressive head of pure white wavy hair, a symmetrical though craggy face and clear piercing gray eyes. Fifty-eight years old. Deep commanding voice enriched with a trace of British schooling. A nice looking, distinguished man. He could have been a head of state, a Senator, a corporate head. He was a doctor. Every inch the sage, compulsively meticulous medical professional.

Today he held sway over a solemn audience. Philip Carr, Mike Auslander, Anne Jones and Dr. Herald Angle. Dr. Angle was young. Dr. Gold's assistant and the newest lander (conceivably the last) to take up residence on Oneiro. Few if any landers were recruited to Oneiro these days. His was a singularly auspicious achievement.

"Phil we've done several work-ups on your blood. As usual your health approaches perfection. We have run across build-ups of some fatty acids surrounding some of your internal organs. Essentially Ethyl Esters."

"Serious?"

"No. But it should be looked into."

"Okay. How does that relate to your serum for learning *Kosmas*?"

"Well there is a connection. And it warrants explanation."

"Alright Doctor."

"As you know, we are attacking this project in two phases.

Phase I. You will become the first human in history to undergo the *Kosmas Serum*. This will prepare you for the really dangerous ordeal of learning *Kosmas*. It will also grant you perfect health and remarkable, perhaps endless, longevity. We hope much of humanity will follow you into the same wondrous new world.

Phase II. We will administer the *Kosmas Language Serum*. Underwater I am told. This may kill you. If not, you will have achieved health, near immortality and you'll speak *Kosmas*. A potentially good investment and a gamble of truly infinite proportions. Three thousand years ago people would have said we made you a god.

We developed the *Kosmas Serums* using the QAVL Longevity Preparation as our delivery media. We did this because the QAVL preparation easily permeates human cellular tissue, irrespective of type…skin, bone, fat, neural tissue, lower tract, cartilage, muscle and so on. It also preps DNA/RNA for a chemical bath using an incredible substance. An intelligent wash which actually cleans up and rebuilds the DNA/RNA and it is able to do this selectively."

"What do you mean it cleans up DNA?"

"How familiar are you with Cellular Senescence?"

"Aging?"

"Yes. At the micro-biological level."

"Well, I know there are several theories and there has been a great deal of effort attempting to consolidate all this work into a single, manageable, curable causality. A sort of unified theory of old age."

"Okay Phil. Now, what do you know about ROS's?"

"Reactive Oxygen Species?"

The doctor smiled "Yes, Reactive Oxygen Species. Apparently you're well grounded here as well…and familiar with their constituents?"

"Let's see…they're essentially proteasome in conjunction with oxidants, free radicals and molecular variations on singlet oxygen. Bottom line is they attack proteins and gradually adulterate DNA."

"Excellent. *Kosmas Serum* has the ability to hypo-regulate and synchronize chrono-biological rhythms between the various forebrain neurotransmitters and the hypothalamus.

This microbiological coordination greatly helps differentiate dynamic molecular bonds from random bonds sub-atomically. So, by rebuilding only randomly bonded genetic material, the subject retains a biological age of approximately thirty years indefinitely. No part of the human body is impervious to this process. We estimate a complete transit of the human body by the *Kosmas* compound requires about an hour and a half the first treatment.

We suspect the first treatment may be exceedingly difficult. Among other things, we've got to give the lower tract some time for acclimation and there will be considerable FOND to purge. You'll probably be doing a little jogging to the toilette for the first four days."

"FOND Doctor?"

"FOND. Foreign Organic & Non-organic Detritus. Subsequent treatments will require no more than three minutes if performed daily. There is a residue exuded on epidural surfaces, so we recommend undergoing the treatment in a shower. Essentially it's like brushing your teeth, taking a shower, getting a beauty treatment, restoring kidney, liver, heart, lung, brain, glandular and muscular function; and getting a complete medical overhaul every morning in less than five minutes a day."

"How is it administered Doctor?"

"A few drops of the substance is applied anywhere on the body. You'll quickly feel it bubbling through your body. It has an extremely pleasant scent, by the way."

"That is incredible Doctor," breathed Phil.

"I fully agree." He turned to Dr. Angle with a look mixed of pride and admiration. "Our newest resident genius here had much to do with this development." He turned back to Phil and resumed. "We are proposing you undergo treatment with the QAVL Longevity Wash as part of the preparation for the *Kosmas* treatment. We'll take care of your fatty build-up, we'll ensure your health really is perfect and your body will be acclimated to this type of process. It should ease the *Kosmas* ordeal a great deal. You would be the first human to undergo this medication. And we'll retest you for fatty acid build-up to confirm the compound's efficacy."

After a brief pause "Any questions Phil?"

"Not really. It sounds very straightfor…"

Anne cut in sharply "Before we get overly enamored with taking showers and brushing our teeth, I want to discuss the *Kosmas* treatment itself."

"Certainly Dr. Jones. What would you like to know?"

"I want to discuss the risks."

"Agreed. We should squarely confront the risks involved here."

"First, I'd like to know the difference between Oneirion information consummation and matriculation of *Kosmas*."

"I believe you are familiar with our food encapsulation process using Chlorpromazine compounds?"

"Yes."

"Well Chlorpromazine in such instance is used as the media for suspension and delivery of information. Matriculation is neither difficult nor dangerous because the compound is fully consistent with the brain's structure. An oversimplification that distills the essentials of the process."

"I understand."

"Now with the *Kosmas* information, it is not compatible with basic, non-Oneirion brain engrams. And the *Kosmas Serum* is not stereotypically compatible with any human, Oneirion or otherwise. Therefore we need a different media…the QAVL wash substance. And we must adapt the DNA in the cell itself. This carries a good many risks.

"Such as?"

"Well, brain damage. Insanity. Irreversible loss of memory. Stroke, ischemia from a thrombosis, embolism, or hemorrhage. Paranoia. Blindness. Paralysis. Catatonia…and so on. Everything depends on the reaction of the brain to the only real test. We've simulated as much as we can. However, actual exposure is the only conclusive test in this case. I wish I could present you a brighter scenario."

"What are the probabilities none of this will occur?"

"Odds for success? I'm not an odds-maker. There's about a one-in-four of serious trauma, even catastrophic trauma. Even then it may not succeed and all this will have been for nothing. Similar risks apply to Phase II as well. One thing I *can* guarantee. *Phil will suffer terribly.*"

Anne lent forward "Why must he suffer? Can't you put him to sleep? Give him analgesics? A general anesthetic? A local? A combination of locals?"

"Anne, the reason we adopted this method was strongly based on Phil's ability to withstand pain and fear and disorientation. We probably will develop an analgesic specific to the *Kosmas Serum* for general use. From Phil however, we need him fully alert…all faculties at their height. This is needed to measure and monitor the effects of the serum on the various parts of the body."

"I see." She acknowledged without much conviction.

"Plus Anne…and this is important…"

Anne looked up, suddenly attentive.

"Phil will not have any pain relievers twenty meters down in the sea. He'll need all his senses, and then some. And that's the way we're administering the *Kosmas Language Serum*. Phil is quite insistent about this aspect of the treatment. To me it sounds insane. At the same time I believe we all have total faith in Phil's judgment. It *is* his life on the line."

Phil resumed his questioning "How much help are the QAVL providing?"

"Ah, they aren't really involved at this stage."

"They don't know about it?"

"Well they certainly know we're doing some intensive research in this area. They've not been fully appraised as to its nature. Frankly they don't seem overly interested. We're not withholding anything mind you. We are simply working independently."

"And if they became interested? If they asked directly what you were doing?"

It was clear Phil's mind was active again. And suspicious.

Mike joined in. "We would be quite open and honest. For the time being however, they are intrigued with the famous Philip Carr. They know he has been instrumental in all these events. They know he has some distinctive talents, unique even amongst Oneirions. This seems to intrigue them. And yet they are somewhat diffident in overtly probing for specifics.

They also know he's been at sea and they are clearly interested in initiating communications with him in the near future. Quite honestly though, they are unaware of his heritage. We would like to introduce him as an Oneirion, which he is, most definitely. And we would like his first communication with them conducted in *Kosmas* for obvious reasons. One less complicating factor in these early days."

"I see. So you're rushing the project and racing to keep ahead of the QAVL." Anne turned back to the doctor. "How responsible is this treatment doctor?"

"Responsible?" the doctor bristled.

"Yes. Everything is theoretical. No testing. No review board. No phasing…"

"Anne. Perhaps we are keeping the QAVL somewhat at bay. At the same time though, there is no Oneirion Food & Drug Administration. No Board of Review. Animal testing would mean nothing. Phasing is not feasible. And any other testing would simply be substituting Phil with another volunteer, applicable only to the QAVL Wash. The *Kosmas Language Serum* was developed unambiguously for Phil. Testing on an Oneirion would prove nothing. Testing on a non-Oneirion human would most certainly prove fatal. And still prove nothing. We have attacked this problem from every perspective. We have thought it through thoroughly. Simulated it with our super-computers, pulled it apart with analytical teams and done some limited tissue testing. We can do no more. We are in the realm of pure exploration here. We cannot eliminate risks. In this instance the risks are real. They're deadly. So in answer to your question, hell no, I'm not acting responsibly.

Were we a litigious society. Were malpractice litigation to exist on Oneiro, and had I an underwriter, he would withdraw my coverage unilaterally, immediately, and irrevocably.

On the upside, we believe Phil is capable of withstanding this ordeal. Surviving successfully. If he does, the benefits could…beggar description.

As a responsible doctor I would normally resist such a procedure with all my power. In this case I do believe the risks may indeed be offset by the potential good for Phil. For Oneiro. For humankind. In all honesty I've told you everything I know."

"Thank you for your candor Doctor." Anne turned to Phil "May I speak to you in private?"

"Uh, sure."

Phil and Anne got coffee and silently, stiffly withdrew to an examination room.

"You're not seeing the danger here at all are you? All you can see is the mission. The ship. The command, *Kentrikos*, the aliens and the study."

"It would be near impossible for a sane human to look beyond such an awesome presentment."

"You are fully aware this may kill you?"

"No."

"You're not aware this can easily and horribly kill you?"

"This will not kill me Anne."

"How could you possibly know?"

"I know."

"Phil goddamnit, you can't see the future."

"No. No I cannot. I can see there *is* a future though; and I…feel…No…I know…I'm part of it."

"Let's assume for the sake of argument you know what the hell you're talking about. If you do this thing you will have placed the first wedge between us."

"There must be some solution to our problem. I'm going to find it. Trust me. There will never be a wedge."

Anne regarded Phil skeptically "You are determined to do this thing aren't you?"

"Yes."

"No question? No doubts?" Anne's slim legs were crossed and her right foot was twittering on high idle.

"No. None."

"There's really no talking you out of this is there?"

"No."

"Any reason to discuss this further?"

"None."

"You're going to do it."

"Yes."

"So we may as well go back in."

"We may as well Anne. I love you."

Anne raised her eyebrows in some surprise. Phil seldom shared feelings and was normally less clumsy about it. She wordlessly exited the room ahead of Phil.

Phil held a chair for Anne. She was clearly upset and the group reacted immediately to her presence. Awkward. Uncomfortable. Embarrassed.

"Alright Doctor" said Phil with forced brightness "what's the next step?"

"Then you're going ahead with this?"

"Absolutely. Let's get started."

Dr. Gold cleared his throat. "Okay. The first step is lunch. I'm starved and it's getting late. Unfortunately Phil you're not invited.

From you we want vitals.

Heart, blood pressure, blood sugar, EKG and MRI. We'll run some systems checks. Respiratory, circulatory, endocrine and your nervous system. We'll take samples of blood, saliva, urine, feces, semen, skin, tears, hair, perspiration, nails and biopsies of all viscera tissue masses.

We'll run tests on your reactions, reflexes, eyesight, hearing, taste, tactile responses, temperature reactions, scent sensitivities and overall mental acuity. We'll also give you a reasonably complex series of words, letters, colors, numbers and shapes; and ask you to carefully commit them to memory in their proper sequence. We'll test you before the procedure to ensure you've accurately memorized them. And we'll test you after to ensure we haven't scrambled your brains.

We've prepared a bed for you in ICU and you'll stay overnight under close observation. Unfortunately you'll be given nothing to eat, only copious distilled water, offset by potent laxatives and diuretics until this is over. We want your entire system flushed. Everything should be in readiness around 1600 hours tomorrow."

Dr. Gold pushed a button on the wall. An attractive red haired and freckled young Oneirion nurse entered. She wordlessly assumed a position next to Dr. Gold's chair.

"Phil meet Nurse Hampton. Please accompany her. She will dress you in a cute little peek-a-boo paper moo-moo, and commence performing unpleasant things to your body. The rest of us are going to enjoy an excellent lunch and will see you in about an hour and a half."

Phil stared at Dr. Gold. "Okay, I'll play along Doc. Where's all this going?"

The group was already filing out of the conference room.

Dr. Gold looked back at Phil on his way out. "When this is all complete at around 1600 tomorrow Phil, we're going to give you a little shower."

Phil disconsolately mumbled to no one in particular *"Bon appetit."*

# Spring Showers

Twenty-seven hours later Phil was sore, exhausted and starving.

"Doc, after all these wonderments I'm shaky and weak as a kitten. You believe I'm ready for your ordeal in this condition?"

"You're right. Nurse Hampton please take Mr. Carr back to his room. Administer 2.3 deciliters of axenic apple juice and a one hour nap. Then we'll execute the procedure. Later, if you're up to it, we'll give you a light dinner. See you in the shower room."

As Dr. Gold rose to leave the room Phil remarked "Why don't we avoid the term *execute* during this procedure." Gold smiled and left the room.

Phil went to sleep the moment he hit the bed.

One hour later…

Phil had been in many shower rooms before. Hot dry Scandinavian Sauna. Steamy Turkish Hamams. Graceful Japanese baths. Luxurious Presidential Suites from Manhattan to Tahiti. Emperor Caracalla's Roman Baths in Baden-Baden. This shower was beyond any of them. Unlike anything Phil had ever seen before. Perhaps the most apt description would be a cross between an enormous, futuristic gas chamber and the bridge of a nuclear submarine. The centerpiece was a large circular glass enclosure equipped with an extraordinary waterproof therapy recliner. Sixty shower heads lined the cylinder providing a 360° spray. Lighting and AV systems in abundance, water proofed and clearly hi-tech. High speed vents to ensure the glass was uniformly and constantly clear. A monitor room consisting of thirty positions not unlike NASA's Mission Control. An operating theater fully equipped and staffed. Finally, and most disconcerting, an observation amphitheater of roughly fifty seats, circular, raised, all occupied. Mike Auslander, Dr. Mark Gray, Dr. Thomas Rio, Dr. Philip Gold, Dr. Alberto Omani, Dr. Jackson Gear, Dr. Sun Kahn and Dr. Eve Dunedin. Many other medical, scientific, historical observers and a few friends. All totally absorbed in the proceedings.

Phil looked back at Dr. Gold in quizzical awe. "What the hell is this place Doctor?"

"We built this facility for use when we launch mass inoculation for all Oneirions. This is a prototype. Hopefully we can cut the size down by about 75% into a single fully integrated unit. Something like an overgrown phone booth. Ultimately we'll need billions worldwide – which would bankrupt even Oneiro were we to attempt it unilaterally."

Phil nodded understanding and turned back to the huge chamber. "The gang's all here, I see. Here to take in the show," said Phil brightly, addressing the entire operations theater. "I'm glad I underwent the Fear Ordeal Eve. Taking a shower and screaming my head off will tax even my ironclad inhibitions with such an august audience. I'm only the first though, and believe me; I look forward to observing each of you as you undergo this same humiliating ordeal." Suddenly he took on a serious tenor, looking around the Control Room, position-by-position. "We are making history together here today. Let's make it well. Are we ready Doc?"

Phil stepped out of his robe. Months of underwater exercise and total exposure to the sun had served his body well. The audience, male and female alike, regarded him with due appreciation.

"Step right in Phil. Sit in the medi-lounger and relax. We'll wire you up and then get started." Phil was in the chamber and seated by now. A crew of medical technicians entered the chamber and began inserting, attaching, taping, strapping and gluing all manner of probes and inputs. They then immobilized Phil to the lounger with no less than sixteen restraints from forehead to foot.

Fixed, paralyzed and staring rigidly ahead. Phil burbled around the gear inserted orally. "Afwaid I'm goin to eshcape?"

"No Phil. When the RVA hits you we don't want you to hurt yourself, or tear out your monitors; and believe me when it hits you, you're going to bring the house down."

Phil frowned. "Raw Wee Aaa?"

"Yes. Recro-Vivication Agent. The compound suspends and carries your treatment, as well as the filler/binder.

Now Phil, Nurse Hampton's going to apply the RVA to the crown of your head. This gel is the *Kosmas Serum*. This will initiate the procedure. The showers will come on when residuals have built up on your epidermis and they'll be rinsed away and recovered for analysis. We will monitor everything, every step...we will monitor you more closely than any man, specimen, astronaut, or whatnot in human history."

Dr. Gold turned to a chart positioned for the AV equipment. "Please follow me closely on this...IF there is a malfunction. And IF we can recognize the malfunction and IF we have a remedy for the malfunction. THEN terminate *Kosmas* process and apply remedy. ELSE terminate *Kosmas* process. ELSE IF any IF = NO THEN complete *Kosmas* process."

"Why awe da stwuctured chinntax Dawc?"

"I want you, and everyone in Process Control to understand *exactly* how we're approaching this procedure. Agreed?"

"No."

"Say again please?"

"Howe woood uue tumiwate da pwacess?"

"The QAVL have supplied us with a serum counteractive. It works nearly instantaneously."

"Do naa twuminate thisth pwocedure foo awy weason. Cwear?"

All eyes turned to Anne as she stared mutely at the chamber. She evidenced no reaction whatsoever. As though she were unaware of proceedings.

After a stony interval "Alright Phil. As you wish. Good luck.

Nurse Hampton are you ready?"

"Ready Doctor."

"All monitoring stations are GO?"

Station-by-station, thirty monitors reported GO.

"Hydraulics?"

"GO."

"Automation?"

"GO."

"ICU Medical Team?"

"Standing by Doctor."

"AV. You're getting all this?"

"Five-by-Five Doctor."

"Phil?"

"Gwo Dawc."

"Nurse Hampton please apply the RVA and exit the chamber." Doctor Gold took a deep breath and assumed his position at the command monitor. To himself he silently muttered *God help us*.

When Phil was a young boy he would suffer from frequent, achy ear infections. The sensitive youth found such sepsis alien and bizarrely painful. More disorienting still were his mother's treatments using hydrogen peroxide. As the small drops entered his outer ear the peroxide would began to froth and bubble. The effervescent mixture percolated in his ear and then warmly ran down his neck when depleted. Phil hated it. A disconcerting experience for a callow youth.

Protected by heavy rubber gloves, apron, and mask and breathing apparatus, Nurse Hampton held a small bulbous form millimeters above his head, and released a generous dollop of an animated looking greenish gel-like substance. RVA.

Immediately upon contact with his scalp the RVA began to bubble and boil. No heat. Just bubbles, a slight itching, an occasional light tickling and the hydrogen peroxide type carbonated feeling reminiscent of his childhood. Not unpleasant. Not pleasurable either. He could feel it engulf his scalp, the roots of his hair, and penetrate his skin, sink into his subcutaneous layers… finally his skull…and then… his brain.

His brain was suddenly on fire. His eyes teared and stung and itched. They twitched uncontrollably and blazed with blinding lights of every color. He was deafened by a roaring buzz. His throat and tongue were maddeningly dry, throbbed with a rasping burn and tasted of unspeakable things. He could feel the strangeness spreading down his throat, his spine, his skin and penetrating deeper and deeper into this thoracic cavity.

The RVA took command of his mind and his body. Phil could feel his muscles being torn, bones pulled out of joint, tendons stretching to the breaking point. Rock-hard cramps from feet to neck were twisting his body into a grotesque distortion of pain. His immunity to Fear Training. His imperviousness to pain. His commanding control and total acuity. All failed him. He was drowning in fear and pain and helplessness. And they overwhelmed him. And he broke. His only outward display was a howling, animal screaming on and on…

When his internal boiling reached its yowling climax. When it was impossible to grow more painful, or alien, it reached his lower tract. Stomach, kidneys, intestines and genitalia. Unbearable pain exploded in his midsection. Were he not rigidly strapped; Phil would have doubled over, in the fetal position. A screaming banshee thrashing in the obscure morning mists of mankind's future.

At various intervals he was suddenly visited with some relief. The new feeling was strange and not unpleasant. Trying to describe it in subsequent debriefs Phil compared it to having miles of ultra-fine filaments slowly drawn from under his skin. Pressure was released, discomfort removed–much like having a splinter carefully extracted. A release of pressure and pain and the satisfying feeling of unwelcome mass exiting his body. It disappeared as fast as it came. Then it assumed a rotating relationship with the profound pain. The doctors would later conclude Phil was experiencing the subcutaneous extrusion of FOND.

The agonizing process revolved through his body for ninety minutes. An infinity of time – relief alternating with unspeakable suffering.

After a time his head cleared and sanity returned. The effects of the RVA slowly withdrawing. In the bright lights he haltingly peered out at the twisted wreck of pain and exhaustion that had been his body. He gasped in shock and surprise. His body was normal in all respects except he seemed to have been painted in broad bizarre stripes from head to toe. Stripes ran evenly around his body, parallel with the floor. Stripes in the most grotesque shading of colors imaginable. Every inch of his body. Nothing exempted. Were they not so ugly and fantastic they would have been funny. Nothing amusing here though. Just sickly bands of brown and grey and yellow and black. Even greens and reds. Sometimes spotty or wavy… jaggedly, unevenly bleeding into the next color. A hideous, roughly hued, great banded snake. *My God. Is this permanent? I'm a living horror. What the hell…*

Seconds later the RVA saturation completed. Phil fell into unconsciousness. The process team immediately removed his restraints, detached his monitors, and drenched him with a final rinse.

"Water. Please water." Phil half whispered, half croaked. Nurse Hampton was already standing above him with a cool teardrop flask of apple juice. She carefully placed the end of the flask between his lips and gently squeezed. Relief, pleasure and gratefulness played across his features. After a long drink and a protracted moment of pure pleasure, Phil sighed. "Thank you nurse." Still whispering. "Thank you very much." He took a moment to catch his breath. "Am I allowed breakfast?"

"I'm sure you must be starved Mr. Carr. I'll contact Dr. Gold. I know he has been standing by for you to wake up, as has Mr. McKnight and Dr. Jones. I believe Mr. McKnight has brought your breakfast."

Phil was fearfully peeking under his bed covers. To his great relief the bands were gone.

"What time is it?"

"You slept round the clock Mr. Carr. It's nearly four o'clock on Wednesday."

"Christ. Was there some…"

"Good morning, or afternoon, Phil." Dr. Gold briskly entered the room and immediately began reviewing Phil's vitals. "No…There was no problem. None at all we know of. How are you feeling?"

"You tell me Doc. Was I suppose to sleep for twenty-four hours?"

"You weren't *supposed* to do anything Phil. We really had no idea what to expect. However, we recorded a wealth of information from your reactions during and after treatment."

"So what's the prognosis?"

"First Phil, recite your sequence."

"Okay. Red, box, 5, pigeon, orange, 1143, 224, 67, 4027, A, Q, N, Bob, sundown, typewriter, triangle, 12,798 meters, the cube root of 112,564,390, Sara, crab-grass, elephant, 12° Kelvin, sphere, blue, blue, blue."

Gold looked up from his clipboard. "Excellent. You should start daily usage immediately. Oneirions will be the next RVA initiates, supported by our new analgesic. Then normal humans will follow when we have fortified the analgesic sufficiently. Your results reveal your electrolytes were…"

"Doc I'm starved."

"Oh yes. Sorry. Nurse please ask Mr. McKnight to join us."

Moments later Phil was voraciously devouring chipped beef on biscuits, coffee and hash brown potatoes with nearly two liters of orange juice.

"Thank you Edward. My God I feel better. When can I leave Dr. Gold?"

"Well you certainly feel better than I had anticipated. You are very… strong, I must say. Anne's outside and she may as well take you home. I want you to take it easy. At least one RVA shower a day. Let me know immediately if anything, *anything* unusual arises and be here at 1500 for the next three days for complete physicals. Eat a good lunch first, take at least one RVA shower the morning of the check-ups; and get lots of rest. I'm serious Phil. Rest."

"Doctor, before I passed out in your high-tech chamber-of-horrors I saw my body. I was covered in monstrous striped bands. I looked like some kind of nightmare out of a Delirium Tremens episode. I notice they're gone now. What the hell were they? Was I hallucinating? Were they real?"

"Yes they were real enough. They threw us off a bit as well. Curious. After some study though we realized as the RVA serum bubbled through your body, the stripes were created by waste byproducts literally boiling out through your epidermis."

"I see. And the various colors?"

"Remember FOND? Foreign Organic & Non-organic Detritus?"

"Yes."

"Well, we believed you would void your FOND in the classical ways… urine, feces, perspiration, respiration and so forth. Instead, you simply exuded FOND out onto your skin. It just bubbled out. From there we washed it off, captured it, and analyzed it. The bizarre coloration derives from the nature of FOND cast off from each area of your body and the manner in which they chemically interact with the RVA. Incidentally, a small bio-filter detaches from the base of your RVA shower unit. We want one more sample of your FOND. There is little each day however. Enough for our purposes. Please bring your FOND filter with you."

"Am I now dependent on a daily shower with the RVA? Am I an RVA junky? A Recro-Vivication Addict?"

"Mmm. Good question. In a manner of speaking…yes you are. If you fail to use the RVA, FOND's will build up in your system as before. The longer you wait, the more they accumulate. And you would begin to feel slight discomfort. Were you to delay usage for years you would have to undergo another treatment as difficult and dangerous as your first saturation. I suppose the improved indoctrination techniques we are developing would mitigate these risks. You are the first and will be the only subject of this treatment unaided by anesthetics. By the way, do you have any permanent bridges, or dental implants?"

"No. Why?"

"You'll notice any fillings will began falling out and any missing teeth will begin to re-grow. All perfectly normal with your recurring showers."

"Docs this recurring business apply to the *Kosmas Language* treatment?"

"Not one bit. This treatment permanently modifies your cellular substructure. It cannot be reversed. Nor does it degrade, or atrophy over time. Every bio-chemical aspect of this compound is developed for one and only one exposure."

"Okay. Good news. See you Friday and thanks doc."

Anne was waiting with triple mated PM's. On the way home she was quietly reserved. Still she was interested in and pleased with Phil's progress.

"Dr. Angle and his crew installed your new shower this morning. Good looking unit. It has a damned library of instructions. Essentially you just push a button though. The shower manages everything from there. It controls temperature, monitors your physical reactions, analyses the drainage and then determines the duration of the treatment. The technicians assure me you have no need for painkillers, or any other medication. In fact they say it will be quite pleasant. Something you'll look forward to. Shaving is your sole remaining ablution. They suggest you shave first and then enter the RVA shower. You'll have no need of soap, shampoo, creams, ointments, toothbrush or toothpaste, floss, water picks, eye drops, deodorants, mouthwash or even aftershave. Apparently you understand the biochemistry at work here?"

"Ahh…yes I suppose I do."

"They state the treatment triggers many of the same mechanisms your body already activates when you are underwater. You are saturated with a sort of orange-blossom breath; and your skin will exude much the same spicy, musky scent which always has the girls drooling over you for a couple of hours after you dive. Combined, this should save you a great deal of time and effort all told. Except for all the girls chasing you, of course." She smirked. "They say you can undergo the treatment as many times as you like, night and day. Aside from all the other benefits they suspect you'll find it quite refreshing and invigorating. It'll probably reduce your need for sleep to just a few hours a night.

Beyond those advantages cuts, abrasions, bites, bruises, infections, allergic reactions, parasites, symbiots, Septicemia, fungal infestations…the whole world of invasive bodily ills. The showers will either eliminate them altogether or phenomenally escalate recovery. RVA even cures the common cold.

And cancer, heart disease and on and on. You're going to be a very healthy, good looking, wonderfully scented young male.

This combined with your own bodily restorative prowess and the benefits imparted by Oneirion food and you have an extraordinarily powerful war chest for indefinite survival."

Phil smiled. "You're turn is soon to come love. Then we'll begin to really make plans."

Anne returned his smile. "Apparently there's a kind of start-up bio-trap built into the base. They want to analyze it after your first usage, so bring it with you for Dr. Gold's team. "

"Yeah. They mentioned something as I left."

"So Phil. How was it…really?"

"Ah…" Phil thought for a moment. "I never felt anything even slightly comparable in my life. I hope for the last time."

"That's not going to happen though. The next treatment's going to make this look like a walk in the rose-garden. And you know it."

Phil had no response. "I can't wait to get home and hit the showers."

"Wish I could join you."

"You can in just a couple of weeks. Until then, how 'bout a Jacuzzi after my shower?"

"Mexican after? I'm dying to get back to Poncho's"

"You got it."

Friday afternoon. Doctors Gold and Angle were again intently reviewing Phil's results. Phil's seemingly impeccable health, as with all negatives, was impossible to prove. They could find absolutely nothing wrong. All tests indicated unequivocal *perfection*. Absence of proof is not necessarily proof of absence. A troubling source of concern for the medical staff.

"Tell me about the showers. The way they are now Phil."

"Okay." Phil paused to collect his sensations. "No pain. Refreshing. Almost addictive. Afterwards I feel strong. I feel good. My head is extremely clear and my thinking coherent. It is remarkable how many little pains and itches, aches and soreness's are inflicted on the body. You don't realize it until they're gone. And when they are gone it feels great! I had some severe bruises from the restraints. They completely faded after the second shower. Somehow I suspect going off the treatment would be as taxing as going on."

"Well put Phil. How are you sleeping?"

"Like a stone."

"Appetite?"

"Nearly insatiable."

"Sex?"

Phil smiled. "No thanks. I get lots at home."

The doctors wearily smiled somewhat condescendingly. How many times had they suffered that time-worn quip?

The doctors then worked through the entire litany of symptoms, bleeding, eyesight, headaches, diarrhea, constipation, blood in stool or urine, energy, muscle tone, touch, memory, dizziness, taste, clarity of thought….all negative, or optimal.

"Any problems at all?"

"Not a one doc. I truly never felt better in my life; and believe me I've known what it is to feel good. Now. *You* tell *me* how I am."

"Alright Phil. Your fatty build-up has 100% vanished. Your wisdom teeth are budding back. All your scars are fully healed, and you've certainly had your share. Your ever so slightly receding hairline has reversed direction… and you smell wonderful. You're the embodiment of physical perfection."

"Great. So when do I undergo the *Kosmas* speech treatment?"

"Give it two more weeks and two more physicals. Then we'll see."

"We'll see?"

"Yes. Two weeks is not such a stretch. What's the rush?"

"Work is commencing rapidly on *Gauntlet*. The QAVL are in the midst of Part II of their message; and they're wondering why Phil Carr is so damned shy. Daylight is burning doctors. How 'bout one week?"

Doctor Gold countered. "One week and three physicals."

"Done. Physicals next Monday, Wednesday and Friday. On Saturday we'll all get together again and I'll take a little swim with the fishies. Thanks and have a good weekend gentlemen."

# State-Us Status

Nicholas (Nick) Farrow. Head of Project *Gauntlet*. Twenty-three. Advanced degrees in Astronomy, Engineering, Astrophysics, Cosmology and Metallurgy. Aside from being one of Oneiro's brightest, Nick had devoted most of his life to studies of the cosmos and could well be the most enthusiastic supporter of the *Gauntlet* project.

Tall, thick brown hair, brown/green flecked eyes, deeply tanned, athletically built. He shared the good looks common to all Oneirions. Nick's face had a slightly rangy character from the shadow of an old scar intersecting his right eye from above and below, as well as a constant five o'clock shadow from a heavy dark beard. All-in-all, a sturdy fellow, graced with swarthy good looks.

His health and physical status approach perfection, with the exception of a barely discernable limp–a residual impairment from a freak accident with a Professor of Music climbing the cliffs of Oneiro some years ago. A titanium hip joint would not heal despite all the medical wonders of Oneiro.

A simple failure of rope and piton lost one life, and forever marred the other. Despite repeated surgeries and extensive physical therapy, slight traces of the debility persist. His eye was scarred in the same accident and his entire body had been traumatized extensively. Initially he was not expected to live; and was under intensive medical care for over nineteen months. Nick was one of the first lucky ones selected to sample Oneiro teaching food, with great success. He was therefore able to continue his education despite extended confinement to a hospital room and intensive physical therapy.

Nick was appointed Head of Project when the enterprise was launched. The QAVL assigned their liaison, Ambassador Qasi, and the two were becoming fast friends. Qasi and Nick devoted nearly eighteen hours every day to the project.

Phil and Mike maintain overall charge, as outlined in Oneiro's burgeoning Constitution. Phil was assumed to command *Gauntlet* at its inception. Mike was to continue as Proprietor of Oneiro and the surrogate for Phil's directives as Consul, as stipulated by their new Constitution.

Fifteen people were seated from a visual perspective hundreds of meters above the island and the sea, at various positions around the floating conference table in the Webber Center. Nick was presenting a status report on *Gauntlet*.

"Hulls A., B., C., and D. are complete and we are well along in habi-forming the inside skins." Nick grinned despite himself at the stunned reaction of his audience.

Mike asked. "Habi-forming?"

"Much like terra-forming, we are creating the topography and environment needed for human habitation."

Phil threw his head to one side. "So where the hell are they?"

"As we planned, they are nested inside each other, inside Mount Anastasios. The exterior topography of the mountain is unchanged, and will remain so until launch. The hulls are attached by enormous struts which will be removed or reduced in diameter as soon as gravity pylons are installed. The construction was incredible to watch."

"Tell us about it." Mike interjected.

"Naturally I couldn't see the QAVL, or their equipment. This alone made it seem almost magical. The first step in the process was a surprise indeed. They started a major forest fire on Mount Anastasios. As you know, such fires are common this time of year.

They then started spinning two tunnels starting from the sea line directly into the base of the mountain. I would estimate roughly 75% of the native stone was intensely compacted into a dense, impenetrable alloy. There was a thin stream of dark material floating into the diametric center of the tunnels, and continued to do so during the entire process. I assume this was the metallic and mineral additives they alluded to in their schematic for the ship. The tunnels were some ten meters in diameter and they seemed to penetrate the mountain for at least a kilometer, perhaps more. This process took about twenty-five minutes. Approximately 25% of the processed stone exited the north tunnel as magma and entered the sea. The QAVL refer to these expulsion vents as Port and Starboard, reflecting their infatuation with terran terminology. This magma event generated quite a steam cloud, and explains their motivation in setting fire to the mountain in the first place. A smokescreen. Literally.

I was pleased to note their sensitivity to our situation, and I'm happy to report they take appropriate steps to conceal such activities.

Their plan is to break the completed ship out of Mount Anastasios and leave a credible natural deception. They will leave what amounts to apparently, as an ancient magma dome which should have collapsed eons ago. Somehow maintaining structural integrity for tens of thousands of years. Having imploded, all that remains is something hitherto geologically unknown: A nascent, dormant, long cold caldera. After some initial surprise…nothing of lingering interest really, or geologic import. As Anastasios is a private island, investigation can be kept at a minimum and generally claimed as the province of the University."

"It must be dangerously hot over there after the tunneling."

"Surprisingly not. I walked the portside expulsion vent about fifteen minutes after its creation. The tunnel material is exceptionally hard as I expected. I was unable to mark it in any way. It is also smooth. Nearly frictionless. I had to walk carefully. Qasi informed me they could create the same substance with a totally frictionless surface. I've given that some thought. This could be incredibly useful. They plan on extensive frictionless areas in *Gauntlet*. This reduces the need for cleaning, danger of blockages and facilitates the transport of any type of material, liquid to solids, with zero wastage or wear. Not even noise."

Anne. "Good grief. Will they allow us to use this technology on the island?"

"I asked the same question. Qasi stated we are presently unable to manipulate the requisite equipment. He did agree to fabricate anything we like though, given a detailed design specification. He contends most projects take just a few minutes; and since we have a few months, he suggests we immediately start identifying applications."

Anne exhibited some frustration. "How long have we known about this? I would certainly like to have known about it. I can think of three uses for this technology right now."

Mike looked slightly abashed. "Some of us have known about it for awhile. And to be honest, I'm sure there are many other marvels we haven't released. We're not keeping things back Anne. Developments are simply surfacing too fast to keep everyone informed. Suppose I ask Dr. Inchowa to appoint a couple of Communications students to prepare and distribute a daily log?"

Anne again. "Good idea. When can we get a look at this stuff Nick?"

"Tomorrow if you like. We've been working on a tour of the ship as it stands for several weeks now. As you know the tour starts tomorrow. You've all been invited and I believe everyone has accepted."

"Then I think we should put together a group to start dreaming up uses for this immediately."

"We cast off for Anastasios from Oneiro Harbor at 0900."

"I'll be there."

"I believe we'll all be there," added Phil.

Nick continued. "For the next part of this briefing we have prepared a visual record of the spheres. I could take the better part of a day describing the process. However, it's much more impressive to watch."

The lights lowered, the island and the sky vanished and a black square floating in the air above Nick suddenly sprang to life.

*The light was pure white and steady. It whorled smoothly, unerringly through the exact center of the strange tunnel. A profound silence. Just above and to the right of the light an endless wisp of inky black mist moved forward, straight-arrow into the darkness. No light escaped the mist, nor was the mist the least transparent. The light brightened and a perfectly round halo moved just forward of the source. The light was sufficiently strong to reveal the nature of the tunnel.*

*Perfection. Perfectly round, perfectly smooth, perfectly level, perfectly clean, perfectly straight, perfectly uniform in coloration. It was dark beige evenly tinted with tiny powdery flecks of silver. A sparkling reminiscent of mica.*

*Suddenly the light sprang to life. A beam of tremendous power illuminating the tunnel for hundreds and hundreds of meters, telescoping into a lightless circlet, denoting the tunnels distant terminator. Like looking down a titanic well. Straight into hell.*

*An explosion of mind-bending speed. The tunnel became a blur and the black terminator rushed upon them. Dead stop. Instantly. Peremptorily. They are in the terminator. Just the visual play of the event without actually being there, no sound, no pressure, without feeling, neck-jolting.*

*Inside the circlet the light expanded to 360° bathing the entire terminator in a glowing whiteness. The terminator is a perfect sphere some one-hundred meters in diameter. Directly above the light is a large hole. Surrounding the hole are three concentric circles. The hole and the circles are of equal width...ten meters apiece. Factoring in the distance between each feature, the huge 'bull's eye' occupies the entire northern hemisphere of the sphere.*

*No movement, or fluctuation whatsoever. Everything frozen for long moments.*

*Suddenly a blinding formation of lights penetrated the hole and the circles. Movement can be perceived with difficulty. A slight vibration...and somehow it is clear the light formation is rotating at a dizzying rate. A reddish-orange glow emanates from the bull's eye and slowly spreads to the sphere itself. Tremendous heat was being generated, amongst other forces.*

Hull A. has been spun...an awesome sight. Respective to the boundless marvels at the command of the QAVL...truly a wonder of wonders.

Power source installed. Something like a flashlight shone into the engine room, sealed in a vacuum behind 12mm glass (six back-ups), a few flashes at odd intervals for two or so hours and the QAVL declared it ready for use. And it was.

Phil: "So we have absolutely no control over our power source. We can't modify it. We can't repair it. We can't even see it. I know I've raised this concern many times. But it troubles me deeply."

Mike: "This is a matter of profound trust in the QAVL. I support it because I believe in them. I support it because we have no choice.

Nick: "Phil we will have a QAVL with us at all times. They don't get sick. They don't get tired. They don't die. And our equipment will monitor the power source constantly. Any anomalies will be immediately recorded."

This drew no comment from Phil.

Gravitational engineering apparatus next.

"The only glitches so far are the robots." Said Nick.

Anne. "Explain to me again why we need robots Nick."

"Okay. Our planning indicates general cleaning and maintenance will become a serious problem. No crew member will sign aboard a galaxy craft to perform sixty-two years of housecleaning. Yet it is vital it be done. Believe it or not, we have pinned it down as a Class A. Function. Survival. General crew members readily enough volunteer to perform their own cleaning and assist in cleaning of general common areas. After ten years however, we project either:

1) incredibly wretched sanitary conditions, or 2) Fatal or near fatal duty roster disputes. We must automate the task and remove it from our Class A. Hazards."

Ann looked at Nick for a time. "You have these same concerns for Oneirions?"

"Ann, aside from exceptional talents and a wonderful outlook on life, Oneirions are as human as any Lander ever lived to walk the Earth. Dr. Omani in Psychology supports this view. Sometimes I am deeply concerned we overlook the basic aspects of our nature. You push them, or starve them, piss them off…push the right button…and Oneirions will push back. And there's damned little on planet Earth nearly as deadly when pressed. So I plan carefully."

An awkward silence ensued. Sixty-two years began to look like a very, very long time.

Phil. "So what sort of plans are you drawing up to save us from being *murdered as we sweep*?" Phil's silly pun drew several patient forbearing smiles, without comment.

Nick was too involved in his topic to notice. "We're struggling with a chicken-and-egg problem. We know the organization of the crew must fit the needs of the ship. At the same time, the ship should be engineered in such a way it conforms to the needs and organization of the crew. It's a human problem in organizational ergonomics. We're attempting to engineer the ship so human interaction will be structured consistent with some of the guidelines we are attempting to follow."

"What guidelines?"

"Everyone lives and works independently. On their own. No supervision. Instead they rely on coordination by GAEA, or direct orders from you or your Number Two."

Number One." Corrected Phil.

"Minimal chain-of-command. Only leadership. The Captain and a handful of senior officers.

Plus a few simple rules.

Basically:

1) No duty roster work. 2) Duty shifts are permanently assigned prior to launch. 3) Shifts are minimal in duration and broken into two per day. 4) Ship's Captain must approve transfers. 5) Day and night shifts are equally apportioned. 6) No serially dependant work. 7) Minimize work coordination. 8) No over-lapping, under-lapping, or redundant duties. 9) No shared proximity housing or work stations.

The only exception to these criteria is the Command Bridge itself and the various support centers…navigation, communications, engineering, environmental control and the like."

Anne. "No serially dependant work? I'm not sure I understand."

Nick smiled. "Easily engineered once we figured out the solution; and the solution was surprisingly simple. Classically, when a process is designed it is keyed on working steps. Position A. does X. to the product and then passes the work in progress to Position B., to perform Y., and so on. If Position A. gets behind, Position B. is frustrated. If B. is early, both are frustrated. Abrasion is inevitable."

"…and the solution?" Phil was growing frustrated himself."

"Simple." Responded Nick. "Instead of A. passing to B., A. passes to GAEA and GAEA passes to B. GAEA acts as a buffer, monitors status, coordinates, adjusts for scheduling bottlenecks and stands between all work stations. GAEA also reports directly to the Captain at all times."

Anne. "GAEA?"

Nick smiled. "GAEA: *Gauntlet* Athwart Engineering Anthromorphs"

Nicked snapped on the floating projection again. The Inamoto sketch of the goddess appeared above his head. "GAEA. Greek Mythology. The Earth goddess. Through birth she joined humans with the titans. She bonded man and the gods. From her sprang the starry firmament. Everything comprising Earth. Quite literally the Earth Mother."

"A powerful acronym. And Anthromorph?"

Phil cut in. "A sophisticated sort of robot."

"And Athwart?" asked Anne.

Phil cut in again. "Clever. It implies the GAEA systems are restricted to the interior obliquity of the elliptic. Essentially the inside skin of the sphere – the living area – from about 66° 33′ 39″ N to 66° 33′ 39″ S. This would exclude the extreme North/South latitudinal of the sphere. Meaning essentially the poles I assume."

Nick was pleased. "GAEA's a phenomenal hybrid combining both QAVL and human automation. Damned near sentient. The interface is either verbal or digital and the network brings together every component of *Gauntlet*… right down to a single bolt, or screw, or weld…believe it or not. Nothing. Absolutely nothing can occur on *Gauntlet* without GAEA's knowledge. She can intercede in a given process. Act independently when needed. In fact, she can run the ship autonomously to destination if so instructed. She cannot physically perform work at the poles. Her hands and arms are hadronic units. Therefore she cannot manipulate any QAVL sources. That's why we use the term *Athwart* as Phil so cleverly surmised."

Phil frowned. "This system permeates *Gauntlet*."

"Correct."

"Big Brother?"

Nick smiled. "Big Mama is more like it. And she goes everywhere…except into personal quarters. They are private and sacrosanct."

Phil frowned again. "Good. What does all this have to do with janitorial robots?"

"Right. The problem was we were attempting to produce robots who act independently. Say a mini-robot detects a liquid standing in a hallway. The ones we developed so far will clean up the liquid *ad infinitum* while allowing a dangerous leak from – say a defective valve – just out of detection range. So we've been unsuccessfully trying to expand the acuity and analytical horizon of these robots."

"So what's the solution?"

"Again, easy. We turned it over to GAEA. She manages it effortlessly. She correlates tens of thousands of sensors permeating the ship."

"What about private quarters."

"She's authorized to activate a maintenance robot if the quarters are empty, or if the problem represents an emergency. Else, she must await a service request. After a reasonable interval, if no action is taken, she will send a message to the quarters alerting them to the problem.

Please understand we didn't develop GAEA just to keep the peace and keep the place clean. GAEA is the key to operating such a giant craft. She will look after literally everything. And if something goes wrong, there will be finger-pointing. All fingers will point at GAEA. She will be the great buffer. Our resident scapegoat."

Phil looked up in concern. "How do you suppose GAEA's going to feel about this?"

"She has been programmed for it. Let's avoid **anthropomorphism. Together we could certainly construct a unit capable of hurt feelings and ego. Why?** Instead she understands it as inherent in her tasks and has been instructed such negative criticism amounts to valued heuristic feedback which she should actively anticipate, even subtly solicit."

After a few moments "Sounds good Nick. I agree. Although I notice you refer to GAEA as *she*," smiled Phil.

Nick relaxed and took on a conversational tone. "It's interesting. If you look at the structure and the lifestyle and the technology unique to Oneiro, it seems as if we were always directed towards this project. Hell, Oneiro itself is damned near as insular as a space ship. Food production, our method of managing information, even our emotional make-up is compatible to human space exploration. Just cause to wonder at the magnitude of Dr. Webber's vision."

Phil looked at Anne. They could read each other's thoughts:

*This is one bright young man.*

## *DAKHALA* Raheem

It took Manu well over an hour to reach the station. It was unusually quiet. A few big tractor-trailers were huddled together under the eaves, out of the snow, waiting for the pass to clear. Service was shut down and the restaurant was just closing. Manu could see Malik at the register counting out and pocketing the days take. It was totally dark now and Manu made her way to the side entrance – positioning herself in the shadows of the garbage bins – prepared to patiently endure the cold. Ten minutes later the side door opened and she could hear the sound of keys in locks. Then Malik appeared, his back to her in the dim light. Without moving Manu whispered. "You tried to have me killed."

Malik whirled about. Surprised and frightened. He froze. He blinked several times, slowed his breathing and calmed himself. He regarded her evenly. Then he smiled. "Never too late." And he stepped towards her raising a big arm.

The staff caught him full in his left ear. He staggered from the blow. Briefly dazzled by shock and surprise, Malik put his hand to the ear and it came away bloody. He looked in wonder at his hand. "You fucking cow. You'll pay for..."

Right ear. Neck. Head. Crotch. Knee. Neck again. Back. Buttocks.

Malik was on his knees. "Agh. It hurts." He was whining and weeping. "Please stop. Please..." he begged.

"I saw you with that poor boy, and you decided to kill me. You used Private Dunn to rape me and then kill me. But I killed him. Now you can tell on me. And I can tell on you. It is my turn *again*."

Ear. Face. Mouth. Teeth on the ground. Stomach. Vomit. Head. More blood.

"God. Please..."

Manu gathered her remaining strength and launched a powerful blow to the back of the man's neck.

"A...a...a...aah..aaaaah." The fat Pakistani died.

Manu collapsed.

More than an hour later she staggered to the front of the station as unobtrusively as she could. This was going to be difficult. She was a mess. Half frozen. Limping on a wooden staff. Bruised, exhausted and bloody. Malik was hidden under the deepening snow behind the garbage bins. It would be days, possibly weeks, before he was discovered. Despite the cold, the inevitable smell would be attributed to the garbage. At least initially. Failing a thorough search of the premises, she had some time. And no one cared that much about Malik. She planned to be in Pakistan long before that.

She clinched in her pocket Malik's money, his knife and comb, a pack of gum and a candy bar. Yesterday she would have felt rich carrying such goods. Today, it was a very meager war chest.

She looked at the line of trucks. Most just in from Highway 1, or the Torkham Highway as it was called. Waiting for the pass to clear. The drivers were all in their trucks. Most asleep. It would be mid-morning tomorrow before the pass was open. Manu looked at the first truck in the line. A young man sat in front drinking Chai from a thermos and reading a paper. He looked clean and decent. She decided to approach. Driver-side she knocked at the window. The young man looked up appraisingly, shaking his head and mouthing "No."

She knocked again. He looked annoyed, but he rolled down the window.

"No change. No pussy."

"I'm not a beggar and I'm not a trucker girl. I have money. I will pay. Where you go?"

He sighed and adjusted his cap, scratching his scalp, clearly wanting to stay uninvolved. Still, she had a decent look about her. She was in terrible shape, obviously in trouble. *What the hell...* "I'm going to Multan."

"How much?"

He thought about it and somehow felt compelled to do something. Although for the life of him he couldn't fathom why. He knew this was probably a mistake.

"Don't worry about it. Get in."

At last things were looking up. She felt like weeping with relief. She quickly limped around the cab and struggled in the passenger door. Blessedly, it was almost warm inside.

"Thank you. I am so very grateful."

"That's okay. But you'll have to hide in the parts locker at the border crossings. They know me so they won't inspect closely. Chai?"

"Oh. Yes please."

He poured her a cup and tossed her a small wrapper of biscuits. Both were consumed in moments.

"My name is Raheem. What's your name?"

"Manu."

"Where do you live Manu?"

"I uh, used to live here in Torkham but my family has moved away."

"To where?"

"I don't know."

"Lost, and an orphan now I suppose."
"I suppose so."
"Where will you go?"
"Multan."

Raheem smiled and returned to his paper. When he looked back, Manu was fast asleep. He studied her carefully. *Some son-of-a-pig has savagely beaten her. Poor child. She looks half dead and badly injured. Not pretty at all, even without the beating, but she appears decent. She speaks pretty well and I think she's honest. She must have a story.* He placed the paper over her, put his head back, and went to sleep himself.

By 1030 they were on the road. For some reason the restaurant was not yet open, so they breakfasted on cold Chai and biscuits. Manu's eyes were huge taking in the daunting pass, towering and misty. She'd known the Khyber all her life. This was a totally new perspective. She had always seen the pass from high above, never looking up.

It took quite some time to clear the border checkpoints and cross the forty kilometers or so through the pass. And many hours after that to arrive Multan. They stopped at kiosks to refill the thermos and buy things to eat. She *did* have money and she was most certainly *not* a trucker girl. As she gained strength she opened up and they talked for hours. She shared her hopes. Find a restaurant or a nice family to work for. Maybe get some schooling. Learn to read. Learn English. Regain her health. Find a place to live. *Make a life*.

On the outskirts of Multan, Raheem stopped at a large warehouse to offload.

"Stay in the truck."

Manu nodded her head gravely. "I will." Even though she desperately needed to relieve herself.

A few minutes later, offloading complete, they headed into a rural area towards his apartment.

"Is this your truck?"

Raheem laughed. "No. This rig belongs to a man here in Multan. He pays me a percentage of our revenues. It's a slow time now and I have to wait a couple of days for our next load, so I take the truck home. That way I can keep an eye on it. Would you like to stay with me for a couple days until you find something?"

"Oh. That would be nice. Very kind. Yes please." *She's either naïf, or stupid, or I must appear exceptionally trustworthy. She's lucky it's me.*

They drew up in front of a nondescript building, aging but clean, and Raheem parked the truck taking great care to lock everything, activate security devices, remove one wheel which he locked in the trailer, and apply a boot to the cab.

"Excuse me please Raheem. Is there an area where I may relieve myself?"

Raheem smiled. "Yes. In my apartment."

She gazed at him in wonder.

He retrieved a small bag and they made their way up five flights of stairs. Once inside there was a single room with a lumpy couch, a lumpier bed, a table with two chairs, a chest of drawers, and a grimy bathroom. Sitting on the chest of drawers was an old black and white TV with severely bent rabbit ears. On the table was a hotplate. A tiny noisy refrigerator occupied one corner. It was all lit by a hanging bulb and a cloudy window above the table. The walls were a brownish, yellowish grey. Heat came from a small space heater. Homey and homely.

"Please?" She moued imploringly.

Raheem nodded. "Of course." Manu nearly ran to the bathroom.

Raheem started Chai and turned on the TV. When Manu entered the room she froze. She had seen televisions, but she had never seen one actually powered up. It was fascinating, magnetic and hypnotic. While Raheem went about his business Manu never moved. Never took her eyes from the screen. Her grasp of Pakistani Farsi was weak, but much was in Punjabi – the language of her homeland. Raheem went out and returned soon with sandwiches. They ate sandwiches, drank Chai and went to bed. He in the bed, she on the couch. He loaned her a robe and a cover. They watched TV in the dark until both were drowsy. Manu hadn't slept so warm or comfortable in living memory. Her home, and Mali, and Zalmai, and Private Dunn seemed far away indeed. The farther the better.

The next morning Raheem went out to service the truck and report in to the truck's owner. He would return at the end of the day. Manu spent the day cleaning the small apartment top to bottom, even making repairs. Scrubbing down, right to the paint and the plaster. She played the TV the entire day. She then took some of her money and went out to find a market.

When Raheem returned home he was amazed at the appearance of his small home. He truly didn't recognize it; and he was smitten with the aroma of Manu's Mourgh. Manu was suddenly nervous. It occurred to Manu that perhaps he had eaten her Mourgh at the station in Torkham. If so, he made no mention. In fact he was effusive with his compliments on her cooking and her cleaning.

Raheem found himself liking her in a brotherly sort of way. He had a sister Harata, in Rahimyear Khan, not so different than her. Not much better looking either. All the same though, her presence made his small apartment feel more like home.

As for Manu, it seemed as though she had never really talked to another person. It changed her. She seemed more confident. Raheem saw hope and strength and enthusiasm growing within her. Maybe she had a chance. Who knows?

Raheem thought for awhile and had an idea. They immediately struck a deal. She would stay until she found a job and a place to stay. In return, she would cook and clean. He gave her money for food, and some decent clothes.

She solemnly shook hands with Raheem as she had seen men at the restaurant. The first time in her life she had shaken hands with another human.

Raheem suddenly found himself with a roommate, a cook, a maid.

And a friend.

# Status *Interruptus*

Nick decided to lighten up the discussion. Shift gears a bit. "Do you mind if we discuss what may seem a fairly trivial subject?"

"Go ahead," said Phil openly.

"I'd like to discuss your title Phil."

"My title is Consul."

"Yes. I'm specifically referring to your title onboard *Gauntlet* and when you arrive at *Kentrikos*.

"What's your point Nick?"

"Well, we've been discussing this."

Phil thought back. Years ago. He was consulting to an organization facing bankruptcy. While he was diligently doing his work to help save them, he was called into a meeting. Walking into a clearly serious conference, he asked what was up? 'We're trying to decide what titles go on all the new doors.....'

Nick paused briefly, noting Phil's sudden preoccupation. Then continued. "First. The crew and compliment of *Gauntlet* need an absolute authority. All ships do. Ships at sea, air ships, or space ships. No management by committee, no elections, no bills authorizing action. No benign semi-autonomous leader. Instead *Gauntlet* demands unilateral decisions, immediate, decisive, with the corroborative force of law. In other words *command*."

*He is bright. But he needs to grow some. Does he really think I don't know this?*

Second. The diverse civilizations on *Kentrikos* will seek out a head of Earth's mission. A leader. A focal point with which to communicate. Each society will expect a representative from Earth to communicate directly with their counterparts."

"Okay. I see your point. Any suggestions?"

"This is a title you will carry with you for decades. It will define you and your authority. It will render you the loneliest man on the mission. It will brand you for life and all of history. In my opinion Consul just doesn't cut it."

"Alright Nick. I'm tracking with you. What do you have?"

"Here's the list:

- Captain
- Commander
- Master

- Maître (French)
- Comandante (português)
- Skipper
- Chief
- CO (Commanding Officer)
- Governor
- Kentarchos (Byzantine for Captain)
- Hierophant (Greek)
    - Hieros *sacred*
    - Phaniein *show*
    - Hierophant *sacred showman leader*
    - The Hierophant of Oneiro
    - The Hierophant of *Gauntlet*

That's what we have so far."

"I see. So what title do you like?"
"Two actually. *Captain* and *Consul of Oneiro*."

With his characteristic alacrity Phil had decided. He smiled at Nick. "Captain. Assuming I'm still alive to assume command," sighed Phil patiently. "I surmise you're considering uniforms as well?"

"Yes, for all command and bridge crew when on duty. We are convinced the uniform reinforce the command structure…particularly for non-bridge personnel."

Phil made grumbling sounds in his throat. He had a tired and irritated expression on his face as he messaged his forehead. A full thirty seconds later he responded. "Alright. Nothing fancy though. Indications of rank as well I suppose?"

"Yes Captain. You would have four pips on your cuffs."
"My cuffs?"
"Your tunic cuffs. As you said, nothing fancy."
"Color?"
"Earth is the blue planet."
"Send us your designs. And I don't want to look like Buck Rogers."
Nick frowned, clearly unfamiliar with anyone named Buck Rogers. "We'll get them to you tomorrow."
"This begins to smack of a military organization considering the ranks and uniforms."
"Yes. Inevitable in any hierarchical oligarchy. Every ship-of-the-line, civil craft included, no exceptions, have a command structure. We're just

completing a suggested Command & Control Structure. This is not a management or politico structure. I thought we were agreed on this. This is a basic component of survivable operations. NATO put together a project a few years ago. CCRP. Command & Control Research Project. They came up with some interesting ideas and we're incorporating parts of it.

Our group is putting together a proposed *civil* organization as well. And they will be interested in your thoughts regarding the Mayor of Oneiro City."

"My thoughts?"

"Essentially they want to know if you will also serve as Mayor, or if the Mayor will report to you and if it is an elected office."

"This is the end of the University environment isn't it?"

"I would say 10% University and 30% a Civil Municipality. The remaining 60% is without question…a Military Command & Control."

"Alright Nick. Alright. Does this imply side-arms as well?"

"A military organization does not necessarily presuppose belligerency. Nor do side-arms. However, yes, we have planned for, and specially designed side-arms."

Phil frowned in confusion. Exasperation and mistrust playing across his features. "I was under the *distinct impression* the QAVL *emphatically confirmed* hostiles were *not an issue*; and weaponry was *absolutely superfluous. Am I in error Mr. Farrow?"*

"No sir Mr. Carr, you are not. Please bear in mind though, the QAVL's assertions specifically addressed ship-to-ship combat."

Mike interjected. "In fact Phil, the QAVL stated there was no need of defensive or offensive weaponry, because there were no known warlike races in interstellar, nor intergalactic space."

Nick smiled. "Correct Mr. Auslander; and these are only side-arms and are designed for nothing remotely akin to space-borne warfare."

"Mmm. Weapons are weapons. The only differences are in the size of the toy. Tell me about these side-arms of yours."

"We call them Stingers. We've developed an electrically enfired, recoilless, explosive particle sling. The Stinger's range is about six hundred meters. Light, easy to use, and deadly accurate. Adjustable from a zero setting which will knock you down and have your head ringing, up to a killing radius of over two hundred meters. Shock, unconsciousness, incapacity, disorientation, internal rupturing, or death. These are all brought on by a variable yield combination of concussion and electro-magnetic shock. Twenty-five shots. Reload clips are about the size of a standard 4.5V carbon-zinc battery. In fact the Stinger's battery is about the size of a standard 4.5V carbon-zinc battery."

"How does it work?"

"Simple. There are three thumb controls. Safety setting, on/off. Range setting, zero to 600. Implosion setting, controls the disable/kill radius. All three settings are…"

"*Im*plosion Nick?"

"Yes. Some fancy work in quantum mechanics allowed the QAVL to provide us a projectile of unbelievable power existing in an area so small it does not actually exist in relativistic terms. Makes for quite a weapon. It actually exerts phenomenal tidal forces within its minuscule event horizon. At the same time it literally has zero effect on anything micro-nano-meters just outside its nominal sphere in terms of attraction. Instead it repulses any matter within the marginal zone of influence."

Phil snapped *"Event horizon?* You guys are tampering with black holes?"

"Mmm. I think I would prefer the term *manipulating* black holes. In this case we are working with singularities so small they have an approximate size of $32^{-232}$ meters. With such mass they have a half-life of less than one-fifty-thousandth of a nanosecond. They evaporate as close to instantly as conceivably possible. All remaining is an evanescent trace of Hawkings radiation, and some unaccountably missing Lepton high energy particles. I would welcome the opportunity to qualify any of you in its use. I assure you it is absolutely safe."

"If these projectiles are so infinitely tiny, why only twenty-five rounds per clip?"

"The overriding volume of a projectile round is devoted to safely confining the sub-atomics. This is also the primary consumption process of the power pack. Most of the remaining area is devoted to launch and targeting. This is nearly a perfect military weapon. Light, flexible, accurate, facile and deadly."

"Well I'm damned near physically aroused Mr. Farrow. So let's see… we've now got some sexy uniforms, a nifty Command & Control hierarchy, and some super-deadly side-arms. Quite a bunch of gun-tottin' bucka-Rogerroos aren't we?"

Nick's frustration was beginning to show through. "Phil all arms are maintained in strictest security under the joint custody of the Master at Arms and GAEA. They can be issued only at your order, or on order of your designee."

"I see. And I will be authorizing issuance of these ah…Stingers for action against whom exactly?" His voice lowered nearly to growl. "What the bloody hell is this Nick?"

Nick quietly took a deep breath. "You would be authorizing issuance of Stingers for hostilities against one of two creatures, under one of only two scenarios we can envision."

"*What* creatures? *What* scenarios?" Phil's voice was taking on a shrill tenor. His anger unmistakably building.

"The first scenario addresses the improbable eventuality *Gauntlet* is somehow disabled and its inhabitants forced onto a primitive planet, capable of supporting life and perhaps even something akin to an anthropomorph. Were the planet unable to even partly support terran life, then environmental shelters would be needed. Either way, indigenous creatures could represent a potential food source as well as potential predators. The probability of these factors coming together is mind-bendingly remote however."

"So what sorts of creatures inhabit your second scenario Nick? Is their existence *mind-bendingly remote* as well?"

Nick peered directly at Phil and quietly responded. "No Phil they are not. I'm referring to the Oneirions onboard *Gauntlet*."

The room was still for some minutes. Not a soul in the room wanted to admit it. The most clear and present danger to the mission was the Oneirions themselves. *Were the QAVL aware of this? Was this part of their vetting process? Was this a next step in evolving and training humans?*

Phil asked in a low and menacing voice. "What parts of your strategy represent human planning and what parts come from the QAVL?"

"The QAVL provided us technical assistance when requested. Nothing more."

Long minutes later Phil finally broke his silence.

"I am authorizing immediate issuance of these side arms...into the Aegean. I want them jettisoned at the deepest point between here and Anastasios, with all spares, specifications and reloads. Not later than thirty-six hours from now. If side arms are *absolutely necessary* in your judgment, we will confine ourselves to conventional weapons." Phil flashed Nick a cold, perfunctory smile. "I personally prefer the Beretta 92FS." He stood to leave the room. "Clear?"

Nick stood. "Yes sir. Fully understood. Thank you for your time. For those of you wishing to accompany our team to Mount Anastasios Island tomorrow...we cast off at 0900 from Oneiro Harbor. Please register today with Harbor Control to ensure we have adequate births and provisions. Pack for five days."

Not the most amicable of meetings.

Anne and Phil silently strolled around the lower levels of the shopping center. The meeting had been long and intense. Mindlessly ambling about a shopping complex was a relaxing, familiar way to unwind…particularly when it included a stop-off at Phil's favorite bar άρθρο Έλληνας υπόγειος. (The Greek Underground).

As Anne busily mixed ouzo, ice, water and her own little touch of twisted lemon and fresh mint, she looked up at Phil. "You seemed pretty tetchy in the meeting Phil."

"I suppose I was. It's discouraging though. Even amongst Oneirions, our dreary obsession to dredge the savage remnants of our brutish childhood on to the stars."

"Waxing a little poetic aren't we?"

"Considering the infinite scope of our work, perhaps a little poetry is called for. I need another drink. You?"

"No. You go ahead. I'm a little tired and you're the thirsty lyrist."

# *Gauntlet Maris*

A classically Greek, halcyon dawn cast long precise shadows across the huge terrace of Phil's penthouse. The golden morning light found Anne and Phil just finishing breakfast, *al fresco* and *au natural,* half balanced on the gurgling margin of their pool; a wavy temptation just beneath the sparkling waves in the clear morning light, Anne's body was a slim, long legged tawny vision. A lovely welcome to the new day.

Edward's breakfast lived up to his high standards. Probably the best French Toast Phil had ever tasted and the bacon on Oneiro was truly special. Marbled with just enough faux-fat (synthetically cultivated adipose) to provide the right smoky, savory/sweet flavor and ensure a satisfying crispness. All finished with chilled sky-blue Oneiro melon, and a perfect icy, piquant Bloody-Mary.

Intellectually a light meal. The French toast consisted only of a regimen of calming exercises; and the bacon an update on recent observations of interest from the latest infrared orbiting telescope array. The rich maple syrup contained highlights from today's New York Times. While the Bloody Mary itself simply tasted good, its pseudo-celery was laced with Percy Bysshe Shelley's lyrical masterpiece *Ode to the West Wind*.

0830 found Anne and Phil packed and loaded aboard three mated PM's travelling downward to the immense harbor complex. PM's were capable of hauling bags and packages as well as people. They had sent two PM's on ahead as they bid goodbye to Edward and left some last minute instructions. For some odd reason they had been requested to pack formal attire. They would be gone for nearly five days so, among other arrangements, Dr. Gold was joining the expedition to conduct their agreed physicals. Gold was extremely interested in the mission and Phil suspected he was attempting to finesse a berth aboard *Gauntlet*. A categorically impossible ambition unfortunately. He would never complete the journey.

Mike was not joining the group on this trip. He was previously committed to welcoming Oneiro's first official diplomatic mission. Phil was amused. Mike was bemused.

As they neared Oneiro Harbor they gradually accreted with others into a large group commonly bound for Mount Anastasios. Nick was already on the main dock ready to meet them.

Peering at the small armada of launches accompanied by the island's two large yachts (*Geron I* & *Geron II*), Phil frowned. "I had assumed we would be boarding our new freighter for the trip to Anastasios."

Nick smiled. "Morning sir. There's not enough room aboard the freighter for everyone. Plus the freighter is large enough to interfere with harbor operations. The sea is so calm today we can load cargo and passengers from launches and tenders. We'll travel out to the freighter which is at anchor outside the harbor and load up. Some will accompany the freighter in the two yachts. The lucky ones." Nick smiled. "Like you sir. You'll travel and live aboard *Geron I*. Believe me they're far more comfortable than the freighter."

"Why don't you ride along with us to Anastasios Nick? Got a few things I'd like to kick around with you."

"Sure. Give me a few minutes to get everyone assigned and loaded and we'll cast off. Why don't you go aboard *Geron I* and I'll join you."

Phil and Anne boarded *Geron I*. After depositing bags in their stateroom they found their way to the fantail, coffee in hand. Nick was already strategically seated at the far end of the fantail to oversee operations. Radio in one hand and coffee in the other. On his signal the fleet began casting off almost immediately. They moved out in assigned sequence forming a semi-orderly line, with *Geron I* bringing up the rear. The fleet's conga line threaded their way through the frenetic harbor, out the giant sea-gate, and into the sparkling calm waters of Oneiro's breakwaters.

Barges were already finishing their offloads and methodically dissipating in all directions, while the passenger fleet slowly queued up for embarkation onto the big freighter.

The sea was a smooth loll, allowing for easy debarkation/embarkation using a sturdy scaffold stairway welded to the port side of the freighter. All the same, the operation would entail more than an hour before they could set course for Anastasios Island.

*Geron I* came easily up on the stern of the freighter where it would maintain station until time for the small fleet to set off for Mount Anastasios.

As the freighter came fully into view…"Holy crap Nick! That is one butt-ugly boat! Where the hell did you find that rust bucket?"

"Ship sir."

"What?"

"Ship. She's a ship sir. Not a boat. A cargo ship. Believe it or not, she's quite seaworthy. All she really needs is a little scraping and some paint. Engineering and nav are ship-shape. We only plan on using her for about six months; and she won't draw any attention. So beauty is not a priority. We have plans to fix her up when the project is over if we still need her."

"Well I like the name anyhow…*Gauntlet Maris*…Sea *Gauntlet*." The only fresh paint Phil could see on the huge hulk was the name. "Tell me about her."

"She's a General Cargo Container Ship. 85 meters Length-Over-All, 14 meter Beam, 6.18 meter Draught, and she has a capacity of 3,600 metric tonnes. She was registered in Belize in 1977 when we bought her, and we haven't bothered to change."

"How much?"

"We paid $ 1,650,000.00 USD, as is surveyed, FOB Lefkada."

"Sounds like you cut a pretty good deal Nick. What's she got under the hood?"

"She carries a MAK 8MU 452 AK Main Engine. A four blade pitched propeller and a 2-MAN D2156 HM Generator. She'll bunker 120 CBM."

"Well, you certainly have her specs down. The capacity is adequate?"

"More than adequate. We only use her on a triangular route hauling cargo from Oneiro and Lefkada to Anastasios."

"I assume provisioning is a major project?"

"Huge. Yet more an allocation complexity than a capacity problem really. About 1,200,000 line items in the inventory and we struggle desperately to keep it down to something manageable."

"So there *is* a capacity problem."

"No sir. Not the capacity of *Gauntlet*. Her capacity is extraordinary. Instead it's a question of depletion logistics."

"Allocation depletion logistics?"

"Yes. Working within the constraints of a given area, dedicated to a specific activity. If we exceed capacity, we are forced to invade areas allocated for another use. 'Stealing from Peter to pay Paul' as they say. Each area must maintain sufficient inventory for the trip, or the production cycles of Oneiro. If we get some things wrong people could die–even with the technology available to us."

"Do you plan in terms of twenty-six years, or indefinitely?"

"Indefinitely. For sure."

"I see. How's it progressing?"

"Good. I believe we're mastering the art. We've developed an excellent model and I believe it is working quite well.

So what do you want to talk about Phil?"

"Well to start with, I hope I didn't offend with my questions yesterday."

"I was a little surprised at your attitude at first. Sarcasm does not become you, if you don't mind the observation.

Then I realized the military aspects of the mission put you off. I suppose I was as well, initially. The mission itself is so altruistic in nature that guns and uniforms and chains-of-command seem inappropriate. Offensive even. All the same, there's just no getting around the reality of human nature and in particular, the human collective."

"It is depressing. Particularly when we bring it out to *Kentrikos*."

"I agree. However the only alternative I can come up with is to turn the whole security problem over to GAEA. I don't believe that is acceptable to anyone. Am I correct sir?"

"Yes."

"Realistically though, there are exploratory missions here on Earth conducted by military units as a matter of routine…particularly the Navy and Air Forces. Maybe our new friends out in the cosmos will understand?"

"That's what worries me."

"How so?"

"With all this officiousness, are we representing ourselves as official representatives of planet Earth? Will man's first interstellar delegation be a fraud?"

"Mr. Carr we are a legally founded autonomous country duly registered and recognized by all relevant international bodies. The QAVL specifically selected Oneiro for their initial communiqués. I don't believe mankind has any legitimate basis for objection."

"Exactly my other concern…the reaction of mankind."

Nick regarded Phil with an intensity which belied his shared concern. "The projected reaction of mankind to nearly every aspect of this event–from the existence of Oneiro–the QAVL–to *Kentrikos* itself. Bedlam. Worldwide. On a scale unheard of in all of history. This entire project is kept strictly under wraps."

"I agree. However, there are those on Oneiro who profoundly disagree."

"I know sir. And it's probably more widespread than you might think. What shall we do?"

"We're in a serious deadlock here. Oneiro has never faced such a crisis. I've never faced such a crisis. Earth has never faced such a crisis. If we proceed and are discovered: Armageddon. If we stop and are discovered: Armageddon. If we keep it secret and are discovered: Armageddon. If we release it: Armageddon. The QAVL qualify races based on their command of the *Kosmas* language. They never considered only partial planetary command of *Kosmas*. They are *not* infallible. Perhaps this upsets me almost as much."

"I fully understand. Although they did confine their initial contact to a narrow beam transmission, specifically directed at Oneiro. We've got to give them that."

That proves their technology, no necessarily their wisdom."

"Agreed. All this appears to be insolvable. An Armageddon conundrum. So I say again sir…what shall we do?"

"I'll tell you what we do. We go into the salon where no one can see or hear us. We break out a bottle of Scotch, and we make a plan. I figure we have about three hours. So we quantify the results we need and we do some reverse psycho/social engineering. We backtrack the steps requisite to get us from here to where we must be."

Roughly three and a half hours later, Mount Anastasios was rising dramatically on the horizon. The sea was growing choppy and Phil missed Sea Tigress. She was far more seaworthy than *Geron I*. Thankfully the QAVL had magma-formed a massive landing dock. Therefore offloading and debarkation would not be problems. There was more than adequate dockage for *Gauntlet Marinas*, and *Geron I and II*.

After much hard work, Phil and Nick were finally more relaxed, leaning on the bow rail observing landing operations. They felt they had begun to get a handle on the problem and were letting it mentally gestate. They would wrap it. Phil would brief Mike and Anne on their emerging plan.

Phil squinted at the island. Mount Anastasios was set gem-like atop Anastasios Island. Spectacular and stark against a deep blue sky, garbed in sparse hard-scrub vegetation. A grey-green, tough, granite and limestone peak arising from an ancient seabed. "Hard to believe that mountain is hollow."

"Wait till you see it from the inside."

"How many QAVL are working on the project?"

"Hard to say. The number changes all the time and it's impossible to run any sort of count. You'll see inside. It's all pretty fantastic."

"Are we really necessary to the construction?"

"Not really sir. They've assigned us full charge of the sphere's topography, architecture and environment. However, the basics: thrusters, ship's power, nav systems, super-structure, helm control, particle scoops and integrated control systems…all QAVL. Those and quite a few other systems totally unknown to us."

"We're really at their mercy."

"Well, sometimes if you want in the boat Phil, you gotta bite the worm; and this is the only ride to *Kentrikos* for over a thousand years."

It was quickly apparent why Nick said Phil was lucky to be assigned quarters on *Geron I*. Nick's staff had taken a design developed by the British Navy and adopted by the American Military for specialized confinement of prisoners at transient posts. The *Gauntlet Maris* version was somewhat more benign. But not by much.

They had adapted forty-foot intermodal containers into stackable, identical self-contained living areas, easily stowed below or above deck. Sleeping/storage area, bathroom, tiny galley and equally tiny sitting area, independent climate control, power, water reclamation, sewage recycler, a multiuse communications and entertainment center, three small windows and one exhaust vent.

A marvel of efficiency and compact design. Less than marvelous in terms of comfort and livability. One hundred and nineteen staff were assigned to the freighter. Therefore, one hundred and nineteen Sub-Cons (Subsistence Containers) were securely fixed to *Gauntlet Maris'* main cargo deck. When the project was complete they were slated for shipment to the United Nations Disaster Relief Agency. Three hundred other units were neatly arranged off-pier on Anastasios Island.

"Christ Nick. Do these poor bastards live full-time in those little metal bread-boxes?"

"Oh no. The freighter has an excellent mess hall, a large bar and an entertainment center. Life on board is not too Spartan; and most voyages are of pretty short duration. We install what we haul, so we carry technicians as much as we move goods. The crew and compliment spend a good deal of time ashore at our three ports of call."

"Oneiro, Anastasios and Lefkada."

"Right. Of course Anastasios is pretty grim duty for everyone. Absolutely nothing there except two big holes and piles of raw materials staged for construction."

"You don't use the containers for cargo?"

"We don't have the shore handling equipment on Anastasios. Yet a container ship suits our needs perfectly. Passengers and cargo. Basically we offload with cranes and nets in bulk, which is actually more compatible to the majority of goods we're hauling."

"Such as?"

"Such as water, soil, grain, construction and paving materials, lots of prefab. Aside from fungible cargo, anything the QAVL cannot confect. We also carry hi-tech goods, furnishings, living items and such. Last in will be the seawater, which the QAVL will look after and then it's up to us to load humans and marine life."

"Mmm. That means we have to load bugs too doesn't it?" grimaced Phil.

"Bugs? Thankfully no. Our people have engineered *Gauntlet's* food chain. They've distilled it down to a sustainable minimum. Bacterium, to freshwater oxygen producing algae, to freshwater zooplankton, to krill, to baitfish, to predator fish, back to bacterium. All 100% segregated from and totally parallel to the saltwater ecosystem. Filtered. Sterilized. Radiated. No bugs whatsoever. Oversimplification, but you get the idea."

"You feel a bit like Noah?"

"More than a little. I'm thinking about growing a beard and carrying a staff."

Phil chuckled lightly. "How do you transfer all this stuff from *Gauntlet Marinas* to *Gauntlet*?"

"That sir…with your permission…I'd like you to see for yourself."

When all three ships were secured, hawsers carefully handed ashore and well secured. Nick debarked to supervise operations. Phil and Anne took a late lunch and went ashore to observe offloading. It was late afternoon and shadows were beginning to lengthen. Some cargo was craned directly onto the wharf and restacked away from traffic. Other goods were routed to either of two enormous tunnels by flatbed trucks; and rather haphazardly piled at the entrance. Processing proceeded quickly and soon cargo covered the massive docking area.

Phil walked the pier, enjoying the smells and the bustle of industrial docks, salt air and working ships, when he ran into Nick. "It's getting late. Dark soon. When do they knock off work for the day?"

"Our people will quit in about half an hour. The QAVL work 24 hours a day. Non-stop. One reason *Gauntlet* is proceeding so rapidly."

"They never stop work? They don't get tired? They don't stop to eat? They don't need a break?"

"No. Not a bit. In fact I am told by Ambassador Qasi, *Gauntlet* work engages only the smallest part of their intellect and little of their energies. I understand they may be involved in hundreds of other tasks at the same time. Plus they make love and socialize with impressive frequency."

Phil withdrew quietly into thought. After some moments he looked up at Nick. "To me it seems exceptionally counter-intuitive that literally immortal creatures should be so motivated. After all, they have all the time in the universe. Why work constantly? Multiprocess? What drives them so?"

"Well first of all, we don't really understand their time cognition. For all we know, they may be working at what they perceive as a geologic pace, with constant breaks. Secondly, and I think this is the important point, we have no information about their motivation. As you say…why are they so driven? The answer I prefer is they simply have an abiding love of existence. They can't get enough. Learn enough. Do enough. Love enough. Enjoy life enough."

"If this is so Nick, then they must be gloriously happy."

"Clearly there is much they can teach us." They stood together in silence. "It'll be dark soon. It makes no difference if we observe work night or day. I do believe we should get a fresh start in the morning though."

"Agreed. Are you staying aboard *Geron I* with us?"

"No. I think I should stay over in one of our Sub-Cons on *Gauntlet Marinas* with the rest of the team. We don't want the troops to think I'm special. You are expected to live like the Consul.

Me? Fraid not."

"I understand. What about dinner?"

"I think I'd better be seen in the mess hall too."

"Very well. See you at what…0800?"

"I'll be here. Good night sir."

# Vulcan's Mushroom

*Ever Among us*
*Ere the Ascension of Men*
*Seeing and Unseen*
*Pyrophoric Creatures of Aire and Brume*

Half an hour later Phil plunged off the stern of *Geron I,* diving deep, with long measured strokes. The water was cool and grew quickly dark. Several issues were brooding in his mind, all badly in need of unwrapping and review. The sea was Phil's best venue for such analysis, and it had been days since his last dive.

Ages ago, far below, a huge undersea magma vent began slowly exuding lava into the freezing sea under tremendous pressures. Fire and ice. After millennia, a gigantic column of basalt extends thousands of meters from the seabed to the surface. At sea-level, the volcanic conduit disgorges magma, boiling from the sea's surface, forming a new island, culminating with a large volcano atop. Finally exhausted, it became extinct. Long dormant. Anastasios Island and Mount Anastasios. A titanic Basalt mushroom standing alone in dark aqueous splendor. From seabed to sky.

As a result, when Phil dove into Anastasios Harbor (as it was now referred), the bottom dropped off dramatically. Thousands of meters, unobstructed straight to the radiating base of the mushroom, anchored to the sea floor. Within less than an hour Phil was deeper than he had ever descended. Deeper than he had ever dreamt possible. Absolute darkness. He was having some difficulty distinguishing up from down; and for the first time his body strained to retain and manage its life-giving warmth.

To his amazement he was actually growing tired and cold, and feeling an unfamiliar tickle of apprehension. The first budding of apprehension.

Then it happened.

From the depths below, the haunting sea-song rose. Beautiful, mystical, captivating and gentle. Phil's fatigue, his cold and his fear vanished. He was engulfed with lyrical bliss. Sublime. Hanging alone and motionless in a midnight sea.

Then it happened.

At first Phil thought his eyes were experiencing some sort of entopic phenomenon. Was the cold causing him to hallucinate? Squid? Perhaps the water pressure was stimulating his optical nerves? Or perhaps he was seeing the incandescent sea-life inhabiting these depths. Some sort of volcanic venting of magma on the sea floor? No. None of these explanations seemed to apply.

There were too many colors. Growing. Moving. Rippling. Suddenly the entire sea floor came to glorious life in unimaginable colors and sensuous, rhythmic movement. A blinding, thunderous crescendo of light and color. Hundreds of meters below him. Hundreds of thousands of square meters in size. He was a mote floating above a rainbow. The most profoundly emotive event in his life. It would have taken his breath away had he been breathing. He froze. He couldn't appraise, or understand, or grasp the scope of the incredible undersea vista beneath him. Over and over in his mind echoed two words...*My God...My God... My God...My God...*

He surrendered to the rapture. He was weeping. Giving saltwater to the sea. He spread his arms and legs and fingers and let himself slowly sink towards the beauty. He knew it would take hours to achieve such depths. Yet he yearned...he hungered...he craved to be close to...to become part of...this... grandeur.

The lights began to glow ever brighter and brighter. The movements graceful and rhythmic. He looked high above himself, seeing his own shadow as never before. A multihued halo emblazoned on the canopy of phytoplankton, krill and drifting algae above. A wondrous undersea Kirlian rainbow. He remembered pilots and balloonists greatly prized their reflection on clouds. This was far more mystical. This was magical. But what were they doing at this depth? There was no light here. Ever. No photosynthesis. If this phytoplankton were somehow lifeless they would never sink this deep. Were they drawn here somehow? Could they invade such profound density?

Then he realized he was alight with the wondrous reflection as well. He glowed. He pulsated. He was the reflection of countless deep-sea hues and a thousand alien forms. In awe he examined hands and fingers and feet and legs. They weren't plankton. Simply drifting silt, slowing descending from the surface, made magical by the wonders below.

Finally the work of the pressure, the light and the music proved too much. Phil was drifting through the depths totally unaware of his bearings, or his pursuit. Any human save Phil would have died. It is true...one can die of beauty...

Then they saved his life.

Once again over-whelming pain hit him with a near physical force. Muscle and tendons seized and froze like steel cables encasing him in an unbreachable lamina of pain. He became an embryo of pain and horror. Crippled into helplessness and finally, thankfully, unconsciousness.

When he finally awoke he was unbelievably deep. Nearly 1° centigrade. Roughly 400 atmospheres. What was happening to him? The enchanting lights were gone and the darkness was absolute. Hypothermia was finally extending its icy insinuation throughout his body. He was in the process of dying. If he didn't start moving he would surely die. He felt no fear, or sadness, or regret. He knew his positive mood stemmed from foreknowledge of his salvation. He simply started swimming. Legs wavering in unison. Arms in strong, slow, broad strokes. Higher and higher. Faster and faster. Warmer and warmer. Energy building upon energy. He was actually getting hot; and he was…invigorated… happy.

Phil estimated the surface was at least two hours away and he had no idea how far he had drifted from the island.

*What in blue hell were those things? The lights. Somehow he sensed they were living beings. Creatures of light. He knew something about such creatures. What? Creatures of light and…good grief! The QAVL. He was sure of it. He had just witnessed The Mating. A forbidden sight for any non-QAVL throughout the universe. Well they had been here on Earth for over two million years. They must have brought thousands of non-triadic thirds. They would be long overdue for bonding and reproduction. Since they were obsessed with the absolute secrecy of The Mating, where better than thousands of meters beneath the sea? He was sure the QAVL were unaware of his presence. Just as he was sure they were unaware any human could dive to such depths.*

*But what of the music? The QAVL had no means of manipulating gasses or liquids to generate sound. The music was theirs. That much was clear. But how? His singular memory began assembling :*

> Underwater communications based on electromagnetic (EM) waves have the capability to communicate more efficiently than either acoustical or various optic based transmissions. EM communications enjoy a significant order of magnitude advantage in terms of speed and capacity (speed=3.5 X 10'mu). Attenuation is superior as well @ 110dB/m at 1 MHz in normal seawater.

*So it was possible for them to produce EM pulses underwater. They would behave as carrier waves for information…or music. Fine. At the same time no human, Phil included, is physically equipped to receive such traffic. He now knew how they made the music. He just didn't understand how he heard it.*

*Ahh. He hadn't considered there could be an intermediary. The whales. He could only assume somehow whales could receive EM transmission and sing them back based on their own interpretation. Thus the requirement for a translation algorithm.*

*Simple. The QAVL. To the whale. To the man.*

*One remaining question. Why was Phil the only human who heard music instead of whale-song?*

After a time that came clear as well. Phil could 'read' his SNA, his *Kosmas*, and the whale-song was resonating through his SNA. He simply knew better how to interpret what he was hearing. In fact he was unique in recognizing that he was indeed hearing something.

He understood. As the Germans say *Alles ist klar.* All is clear. Or so he thought.

It was early morning when Phil, shivering and exhausted, struggled onto the dock and staggered up the gangplank aboard *Geron*. Now he was really tired. Really cold, trembling with hunger and weakness, he could hardly walk.

Half an hour later Phil had devoured three bowls of rich fish stew and four liters of beer. His strength was returning. No more trembling hands. He was finally warm and comfortable. He sighed and reclined on the same luxurious lounge he had first enjoyed in the carefree days when he had taken charge of Oneiro…gin and tonic in hand…New York, girls, restaurants and bars occupying his mind…untried and uncorrupted…inconceivably long ago.

"Want to talk about it?" Anne looked down on Phil, deeply concerned.

"I'm not sure I can talk about it. I don't think I can describe what happened. Not right now. I need sleep." And he was out.

Anne covered him and then left him to sleep till dawn.

## *The First Day*

When Phil was a practicing attorney, several of his clients purchased Shuttle capacity from NASA, even a launch vehicle from time to time from ESA. As part of his duties and certainly his interests, he had observed final assembly, the mounting and ultimate launch of his client's equipment.

Lab technicians clad in dustproof sterile white overalls, clumsy white Mickey Mouse shoes and gloves, surgical masks, hair-nets and goggles. They invariably had the look of something between an operating theater and a Grade B Space Opera from the 50's. Regulations demanded observers strictly remain in glassed-in theaters, looking out into a spotless world of silicon, brushed chrome, aluminum, gold and rare metals. Everything brightly lit. Even the air was scrubbed. Phil knew what an assembly site looked like.

This was unlike any such site Phil had ever witnessed. If anything it resembled a large, somewhat chaotic road construction project. Huge haulers filled with dirt and sand and stone ranging from pebbles to finely dressed blocks two meters to a side, to enormous boulders. By the dozens, giant trucks offloaded the freighter and joined lines leading up to two enormous circular openings at the foot of Mount Anastasios. A hive of activity. Hundreds of workers, massive stacks of sandstone, limestone and granite, dozens of trucks, belt-loaders, cranes, forklifts and hand carts. All taking place under a choking haze of stone powder. Windy, hot, dry and dusty. It was only 0815 and already looked to be a long, gritty day.

Nick was busy in the midst of operations, balancing coffee, radio and a good old-fashioned clipboard. "Well Nick, this is about the last thing I expected. Looks like you're building a damned pyramid here. In fact," Phil squinted and playfully cocked his head to the left. "You look a little like Pharaoh Kudzu yourself."

Nick grinned good-naturedly. "No sir. I don't think so. I know what Kudzu looked like. There's only one small statue of him in existence; and I don't look a damned thing like Kudzu.

If you were expecting a NASA-esque-type assembly area…that goes on inside the mountain. Sort of. Actually it's nothing like NASA in there either. The QAVL are doing the casting, spinning, molding and assembly work. We haul the materials in and they create the shell of Oneiro City according to our plans.

They do the skilled, hi-tech stuff. We just do the grunt work out here. You should also bear in mind we aren't building a space-craft. We're constructing a self contained world, with all that implies."

"I understand Nick. When will we see interior operations?"

"Where's Anne?"

"She'll be joining us in a few minutes. Right now she's on the phone with our ship in harbor at Oneiro."

"Everyone is supposed to muster here at 0900. There will be 112 Oneirions to observe operations today. So there will be too many for introductions." Nick was silent for a few seconds and looked at Phil a little sheepishly. "All the same, for today's purposes and while we are on this island, we'd like you to use the name Michael Deckers." Nick then picked up a small case. "We would also ask you to wear these glasses, this wig and moustache."

"What? *Are you crazy?*"

"Phil. Please try to remember we are stalling until you can speak *Kosmas*. We know how intelligent and perceptive the QAVL are, so we must go to some pains to keep you incognito until you are introduced."

"That's just it. With their advanced perceptions they may see right through this half-assed disguise. If they do, we'll look like damned fools and liars; and I'd be the number one damned fool. No. No Nick. No introductions. That's fine. But no dipshit tricks either. That's an order goddamnit. Besides, there could be twenty QAVL next to us right now."

After a moment Nick responded. "Well, I tried."

"Meaning you expected I would respond this way?"

"Meaning I expected you would respond exactly as you did. The QAVL aren't at all guileful by the way. They wouldn't dream of intruding into human interactions without making their presence known. They generate a single bright flash of white light."

"Why have me on the island at all?"

"We felt the Oneirions would expect it. Appreciate it. The group's arriving. Let's join. May I ask you at least to stay in the middle of the group and try to blend in?"

"Yeah. Okay. Let's go. Answer me one question though."

"Sure. If I can."

"The QAVL can see us, obviously. Can they hear us?"

"No sir. They have no audio acuity whatsoever. All communications with them are limited to electromagnet carrier wave transmissions. They provided us with instructions for construction of an exceptional narrow-band transmitter. No leakage whatsoever. The same type used in their initial contact message."

"Mmm. Thanks."

The group was given metallic cloth sheaths for their shoes. Nick explained the stretchy coverings would afford them stable footing on the specialized surfaces they would be encountering. It would also allow them to walk up the spheres' interiors to precarious latitudes. They were provided similar gloves to assist them should they inadvertently slip, or fall. Special glasses were distributed for use in areas where lights could be harmful, or even blinding, with the assurance that they would have more than adequate warnings before exposure to any such lights; and they were equipped with large billed hats for further protection. They applied dark skin cream to block radiant discharge. Finally they donned overcoats. It was cool inside and the coats were shielded. With all the accoutrements Phil wondered why the hell they thought he needed some inane disguise. Thus equipped, they advanced on the QAVL.

Excitement growing, Phil strode forward to see *Gauntlet* for the first time.

It was a hot, dusty forty minute hike to the tunnel entrance. They threaded their way through staged building materials, workers, trucks, food stalls, drink wagons, first aid stations, fuel dumps, repair sheds and semi-permanently installed sub-cons. With all this, and more, there was not a single power cable or conduit to been seen on the ground, or suspended. Apparently the new Oneirion electro-transmission technology was finding good use. It truly had the stony, ancient aura of a pharonic construction site.

At the entrance to the portside tunnel, they stopped and regrouped while Nick made a quick call on his radio. They then proceeded into the colossal tunnel. Darkness enveloped them as soon as they entered the enormous tube, light from the rear casting sharp, raw shadows. The darkness grew as they travelled further into the tunnel, their eyes adjusting at nearly the same rate. Finally, a few of their guides switched on hand lights.

Phil marveled at the precision, the smoothness, the absolute consistency of the entry tunnel. He appreciated the corresponding drop in temperature. Their protective gear was quite hot in the island's climate. The extraordinary evenness of the tunnels surface reflected light from all directions. The light seemed to oscillate and build upon itself. Disorienting. A few members of the group fell in the confusing light. Things became easier as the sunlight dimmed.

After a few minutes of ambling through the huge tunnel they came to another opening. As agreed, Phil was positioned towards the middle of the group. Consequently he could not clearly make out Nick's actions. He could see however, Nick stopping at the opening and speaking into his radio. Phil suspected Nick was warning the QAVL of their approach. Probably a precaution against their blinding radiation blooms.

The group waited about three minutes and then exited the tunnel into the sphere. Phil had never seen so vast a construct anywhere on Earth. The Astrodome in Houston, the Great Pyramid at Giza, the Boeing assembly plant in

Everett, Washington, the CERN collider in Switzerland, the World Financial Center in Shanghai, and many more. They were all unequivocally overshadowed by this incredible sphere. It was another world. It was a planet. It was dizzying and terrifying. Phil found himself drawing on all the old disciplines.

Many of the group did. Those who did not were immediately on the floor moving somewhat torpidly. Nick was having them gently removed. Had the entire group screamed at their loudest, the sound would have been totally lost amidst such vastness. Yet those who spoke at all chose to whisper.

Phil sought Nick out and found himself whispering as well. "I wonder why we're all whispering."

Nick was uneasy about Phil's sudden prominence in the group. After a moment he concluded in an area this momentous it made little difference. "We call it the cathedral complex. It's just so daunting that it makes humans feel small. Maybe we want to hide. Or at least remain inconspicuous. Out of sight of the gods."

"Are you suggesting I hide from the QAVL again?"

"No I guess not." Nick's radio chirped, and he turned and addressed the group. "Please stand aside, away from the tunnel entrance. They're bringing in construction materials now and we need to stay out of the way. You won't want to miss seeing this."

First came the sand. A perfectly round column of beige, two meters in diameter. Sinuous and twisting. Turning and snaking its way high up into the sphere. At its highest point, hundreds of meters above, it began winding itself around a huge depression in the hull until it formed a deep rim around the depression, two meters deep, five meters in width. Mocha frosting on a Bundt cake. A beach! As the sand unwound, a pure white light followed its progress, seemingly affixing it to the hull. The closest thing to magic Phil had ever seen.

Then came the soil. Fields and hills and rises. Small valleys, gulleys, creeks, bogs, bunkers and cliff lines.

Then boulders and stones and rocks. They filled the lake. They lined the creeks, re-enforced the cliffs, crowned the rises, laid pebble paths and randomly scattered large stones in a skillful parody of nature.

Then limestone and granite blocks. Building shells and walkways. Beautiful walls and pools. Stone gazebos and moorings in the lake.

Tonnes and tonnes of material, with dozens of trips to follow. It tested credibility to believe this will be a craft of air and space. He'd read of such visionary vessels before. Constructed in space. Decades to complete. Incredible propulsion systems to move it just the least bit. Tens of thousands of years to its destination. Voyages of such duration, it was doubtful the crew would arrive at destination still human.

This ship was taking form before his eyes and would travel at velocities nearing relativistic. And if he survived, he was to be her Captain.

Phil remembered years ago wondering what he would do with his life, never dreaming such wonders awaited.

Nick's voice. "Believe it or not ladies and gentlemen, it's nearly 1700. Please regroup and head for the portside tunnel. We don't want you to stumble around in the dark so we are under some time pressure.

Tomorrow we'll observe construction directly from the native elements of the hull itself. The QAVL will also fire up *Gauntlet's* main thruster." Nick smiled charmingly. "As they say you ain't seen nothin' yet.

When we exit the tunnel our guides will be on hand to assist you in finding your way back to your assigned vessel. Hang on to your protective gear and wear it tomorrow as well please. We will gather at the same meeting point tomorrow at 1000.

On Wednesday we will tour the four hulls followed by an address from Ambassador Qasi. We are arranging the starboard tunnel for this event. This will be the first time any QAVL will speak directly to an audience of humans in all of Earth's history. We are extraordinarily fortunate. This will be followed by a formal reception. We'll have about three hours between the tour and the reception to change. Black tie please. Remember the Ambassador cannot hear. Therefore applause is not appropriate. We suggest standing when his address begins and again when it ends. We will have cocktails after the Ambassador speaks."

From the group. "Are questions permitted?"

"Yes. Questions are quite welcome. Please speak only in *Kosmas* with The Ambassador. Always address The Ambassador as The Ambassador, or Ambassador Qasi, or Honorable Ambassador. The Ambassador does not have a sexual designation, so please avoid appellations such as Sir, Ma'am, Mister, Miss, Missus, and Ms and so on. The Ambassador will generate flashes of white light every few seconds, so you'll know where to look. The converter also follows The Ambassador and you'll always be aware of its whereabouts as well. When he considers his participation in a dialogue active, his speaker light will show red. Please wait until it shows green to speak."

"Will there be a reception line?"

"No. If you wish to personally meet or speak to Ambassador Qasi simply approach the audio converter during the reception. No introductions will be made. Feel free to introduce yourselves."

"Will The Ambassador be joining us in…ah…refreshments?"

"Yes. You will see something resembling a small golden Christmas tree with tiny multi-hued lights. It will be placed next to the audio converter.

Please do not stand in between the two. These lights are the equivalent of The Ambassador's Cocktails and Hors d'Oeuvres."

"Are any subjects taboo?"

"None whatsoever. I am convinced the QAVL know us better than we ourselves." Nick paused. "Well, maybe there is one thing. We should avoid any reference to Consul Carr. As you know Mr. Carr is with us today. He will be with us tomorrow and on Wednesday. However, his formal introduction, Ambassador-to-Consul, is envisioned for another time. Proprietor Auslander will also join us for the reception. Any other questions?"

Silence.

"Fine. Have a good evening. See you tomorrow."

# Cave New World

*... [Sic] (The fifth day) dry land and seas and plants and trees which grew fruit with seed; the sun, moon and stars in the firmament;*
*Book of Genesis*

A jolting contrast.

A long hot, dusty walk through all manner of tawdry confusion and disorder. Dust and smoke. Acrid smell of burning diesel. Noisy. Crowded, dirty and unpleasant.

An abrupt entry into another world. The cool, silent, semi-dark spheres. Titanic open spaces. Immaculate and inspiring. Full of wonders. Magic. In earlier ages they would have been inhabited by gods and spirits and wondrous beings. They still were.

Phil watched work high above him. It was proceeding quickly. Suddenly without predication an enormous section of the sphere's inner skin simply disappeared. Vanished. Hundreds and thousands of square meters. The phantom sands then snaked up to the seemingly bottomless new hole and began frosting the beveled edges as it had yesterday. The miraculous white light would bind it to the shore. It would build the shore. This was to be the Oneirion Sea! They would see whale-sign here. The dorsal of Great White Shark would cut its waters while porpoise played and squid fled for safety. A thousand kinds of fish would hunt here. A reef would seek the light here. Phil would swim here, though he'd never hear QAVL-song. He hoped Anne would sail its waters and lounge on its beach with him. With but a wish and the water would froth and whip itself into a fury. The sky would become a huge grayish-purple bruise in the heavens, and lightening would thunder throughout the world. Just as quickly, a gentle spring morning could appear. What an astounding vessel.

*Gauntlet.*

In another area the etching began. The sphere-stone would vaporize and form an orderly conduit exiting the sphere. In its place paths and sidewalks and streets and plazas appeared. Buildings rose as though they were herbal-organics, growing with some super-phytohormone. The landscape would form hills and valleys which would shelter rain forests. Even diminutive and graceful mountains. There will be pines and clouds and wind and rain and snow and ice and sunshine and air as bracing and sweet as incense.

Walls that would last untold millennia formed in buildings. With them, homes, workshops, conference and classrooms, shops, theaters, restaurants, labs, offices, utilities, windows, counters, closets, work stations and command bridges of equal longevity coalesced, awaiting only hardware and furnishings. Water and sewage systems grew. Power conduits were now obsolete, casualties of Oneirion electro-transmission. The same applied to monitors and entertainment screens, communicators and computers. A truly wireless world. Paperless as well. What joy if the QAVL were to re-make the Earth with equal art and skill.

Phil knew this was well within the extent of their skills. Was it within the range of their mandate? He thought not.

The spectacle fascinated Phil. Transfixed. It so occupied his mind he missed the light lunch Nick had arranged and he barely had time to hurry to the thruster ignition demo.

"Am I late?" Phil whispered to Nick.

"You missed my brilliant introduction. But the real show's just starting." Nick turned and raised his voice. "Please put on your hats and goggles now. This demonstration can quite literally blind you, so please exercise extreme caution. Do not remove your goggles for any reason. I say again. Not for any reason. We'll start in thirty seconds." He then quietly spoke into his radio. And they waited in the darkness.

How many colors are there? How many gradients of brightness? How many shades of shadows? Were there types of light not made of photons? A wave and a particle. Was there anything else? Can a light explode into life so brightly it actually booms? Could it physically impact you and knock you back? Were the goggles working? Was he going blind, or insane?

These questions and many more raced through Phil's mind…his optic disc vibrating like a drum head. His thoughts, his control, his guard against fear, his very mind, gone in a puff. A nanosecond.

For several seconds he was unable to talk, or even move.

When animation returned, he turned to Nick, clearly shaken. "Nick. What the bloody hell…"

Nick was listening to his radio. He then swiveled to address the group.

"They engaged our main non-hadronic thruster for duration of one-ten-thousandth of a picosecond. It generated a propulsive thrust of 797,826 metric tonnes.

Based on our most powerful lift platform, employing hypergolic ignition, it takes $(1.5e+13)*10,000$ times longer to achieve only 249 metric thrust tonnes; and our max burn is roughly 293 seconds.

Using a QAVL thruster of this magnitude can you imagine continuous burn duration of over twelve years?"

Phil. "I assume the rotation of the sphere adjusts to compensate for thruster G's?"

"Correct. For most of the journey, either thrusting or breaking, self-actuated gravity generators will automatically adjust in less than .000125 nanoseconds. A longer reaction time would pulverize *Gauntlet's* interior topography and instantly render her inhabitants into approximately twenty-five square meters of fine, thin red paste."

From the audience a shaky voice "This all seems dangerous."

" It certainly is. This thruster will be masked with a total of twenty meters of hardened hull alloy, three times the same mass in water, and an inconceivably powerful QAVL energy screen. We are placing a great deal of trust in QAVL technology. Considering that technology has matured over a period in excess of three million solar years, I'd say it was a safe bet."

The group was totally silent. The sort of quietude that comes when encountering something beyond expectation.

"That's it for today ladies and gentlemen. We'll gather at the same meeting point at 1000 tomorrow. Please return your safety gear as you leave. Good evening."

Phil would never know how he returned to *Geron I*. He could hardly place one foot in front of the other. He was experiencing a profound shock he would later term as 'QAVL-awe'. Within months the expression would gain worldwide usage. With disastrous consequence:

> QAVL-awe [KA-vel-aw/cava-law] D. Oneirion. A short duration fugue state brought on through exposure to hyper-advanced (non-terrestrial) technology, often accompanied by strong feelings of inadequacy and a quasi-religious rapture. Denudation in such events may often provoke suicidal inclinations, or even homicidal rages. Subsequent to such episodes subjects may demonstrate one of four responses:
>
> 1) Denial. Benign redirection. Risk of recursive depression.
> 2) Euphoria. Acceptance. Positive prognosis.
> 3) Rejection. Violent disavowal. Risk of dangerous psychosis.
> 4) Blanking. Purge long and short term memory. Risk of recursive neuroses.

*My God. What are these beings really capable of? What is the true measure of their reach? The progress made here in two days would take months on Earth. No. Months for humans he corrected. Maybe years. Maybe never.*

An hour or so later, Anne found Phil seated naked on the stern of *Geron I*. She assumed he was preparing to dive. A questionable assumption in view of the half empty quart of Scotch sitting before him. Phil had taken in additional supplies in the form of nested plastic cups and two reserve bottles waiting on the table.

Anne looked at Phil for a long time. "Pour me one." He filled a cup with Scotch and Anne drank half in one swallow. Phil graced her with a shallow smile and raised eyebrows.

She peered into her cup. "What I saw this afternoon was incredible. It was profoundly inspiring. It made me feel like a daffodil glittering with dew on an Easter morning. So why do I feel like pond scum right now?"

Phil smiled. "I know exactly what you mean. I feel the same. I suspect all 112 people with us this afternoon feel the same. In fact I'm a little concerned for their safety."

"Why Phil? This should be a wonderful time for all of us."

"I think we feel suddenly inconsequential. Meaningless. Primitive. Small."

"Anything we can do about it?"

"Well, I was going for a dive. Then I thought I might get drunk. I have to really work at getting drunk these days, but I chose to try the latter."

"Good choice. Pour me another." She drained her cup and held it out to Phil.

Next morning the new sun shone down on two inert bodies, three empty bottles, and several scattered cups. All untidily scattered over the stern of *Geron I*.

"Jesus I feel awful. This wasn't such a good idea." Anne often envied Phil's resilience with alcohol.

"I dunno Anne. I don't feel the best. But the paralyzing depression seems to have passed. A fair trade I'd say."

Anne mumbled "Mmm. Could be. I need a hot shower and some coffee."

"Do you think that son-of-a-bitch knew this was going to happen to us?"

"Who Nick?"

"You're damned right Nick."

"He must've. He has to have gone through this himself."

"That bastard plays it pretty fast and loose sometimes. I think I'll have a little chat with him."

Anne rose and languidly stretched, inspecting the sea and the day. "I'm going to take a shower. They installed your shower yesterday by the way; and don't forget you've got an appointment with Dr. Gold at 0900. See you at breakfast."

Phil was already in the water. At twenty meters he slowed and simply hung limply in the cool cascading greenish half-light. A school of large silvery

Daurade engulfed him. Five thousand glittering fish moving as one. He was afloat in a sea of light. Nearly blinding. As quickly they were gone and the sea was dusky and quiet again.

He felt better.

0900 on the docks.

"Morning Phil. How are you?"

"What's the body count from last night?"

"Body count?"

"Yeah. Your little hi-tech sound and light show's a real bitch. Could be a killer. You must know that."

"Christ Phil. No I didn't. I knew it hit *me* hard. But I had no idea…"

"Get on your radio Nick. I want a head count. All 112. Now."

By 0930 111 souls had been accounted for, some rather petulantly. Only one, a Phyllis Thacker was logged as missing. Boats and search parties were immediately dispatched.

"Shall we proceed with the tour Phil? It's nearly 1000."

"Is today's tour in the slightest as malevolent as yesterday's?"

"Ah no. Tame stuff…just a tour of the hulls."

"Go ahead. We want things to appear as normal as possible. I'll stay here and coordinate the search for Ms Thacker."

"Okay. And Phil…?"

"Yes?"

"I'm really sorry about this. I…"

Phil grimaced. "Ms. Thacker's probably fine. Probably shacked up with a crew member or something. We better hope so. I want you to give the rest of the group a briefing on this phenomenon just in case. Just keep it low key. No big deal. Tell them to be alert for unexplained depression, or any errant emotional state, and contact Dr. Gold the moment they feel something may be amiss. He's staying aboard *Geron II* I believe?"

"Yes."

"I want the entire group examined by Dr. Omani's staff as soon as we return to Oneiro. I'll try to make the reception this afternoon. Coordinate through Anne."

"Aye sir."

Short after 1030 Phyllis Thacker was located unconscious, on a beach roughly two kilometers north of Anastasios Harbor. When she regained her senses she retained no memory of the preceding day, or how she'd arrived on the beach. Aside from memory loss and mild exposure she suffered no ill effects. A Gunship was dispatched from Oneiro to air-evac her for hospitalization and observation. In earlier days the island had maintained two aging, but beloved, Apache attack helicopters; which had since been upgraded with two mighty MH-53E Sea Dragons. Longer range, passenger and cargo capability and equally formidable armament finally prevailed over the lean and deadly Apaches. The huge Sikorsky's were soon accepted with affection by the islanders, who had nicknamed them *Dráko⁻n*. Greek for dragon. Oneiro now proudly maintained a tiny armada of MH-53E *Dráko⁻ns*.

It was far too late to join the tour, particularly factoring in the low profile he was supposed to maintain. Phil decided to walk about the harbor area and observe outside operations. He'd done all he could regarding Ms Thacker. It was a fresh, golden morning. Why not?

As he stepped off harbor dockage he came across a complex built entirely of Sub-Cons. They weren't for habitation though. They were converted to offices and communications centers. The first of which was <u>*Gauntlet* Engineering</u>. Should be interesting.

Engineering was actually a complex of Sub-Cons, interconnected, all dedicated to managing the design and construction of *Gauntlet*. Upon entering he encountered no one he knew. However, a big bull of a man immediately approached, broad smile, hand extended.

"Mr. Carr?"

"Yes?" The man shook Phil's hand.

"Hello sir. I'm Mark Oikodomos, *Gauntlet's* Chief Engineer. It's a real pleasure sir."

"Thank you Mr. Oikodomos. A pleasure to meet you as well."

"I suppose you're here for the tour of *Gauntlet*. She's impressive, isn't she?"

"Beyond belief Mr. Oikodomos. Beyond belief."

"Can I do anything for you sir?"

"Yes. One question: How far along is *Gauntlet's* design?"

"The superstructure's been at 100% for some time now. As you've seen, we're installing all major design elements. We're waiting only on modifications from individuals and departments."

"May I see a complete rendering?"

"Certainly. Hardcopy or softcopy?"

"Softcopy. And I'll need a private workstation."

"There's an office right here. You have complete online access to any design aspect of *Gauntlet*. Coffee?"

"Sure. Thanks."

Three hours later Phil had committed the plans to memory. As he finished, he was again shaking hands with Mark Oikodomos, thanking him, taking his leave, and resuming his walk.

Phil aimlessly strolled the sprawling makeshift industrial park and found himself rounding the far end of the harbor, walking along a respectable sized seawall, the sea gently resonating below him. An enormous building caught his eye. Partly overhanging the sea, it had the appearance of a large aircraft hangar. *Amphibious craft?* He was immediately interested. He pushed through a double set of large cloudy glass doors and nearly swooned with pleasure. Breathing deeply, eyes closed, releasing a long, audible shuddering sigh of pure enjoyment. What a captivating aroma! Vulcanized Polyisoprene and hydrocarbons. Old tires and motor oil. He suddenly realized he was not alone. Phil was in the presence of several large men in well worn coveralls. He was immediately embarrassed.

He smiled sheepishly. "Sorry gentlemen. The combination of tires and used oil gives me a nearly indescribable pleasure. I think it has something to do with my youth. I spent a good deal of time in my uncle's boatyard and car garage. Good memories and all that."

Amidst polite laughter and understanding grins, introductions were made, hands were shaken and Phil found himself savoring an icy beer with a tomato and feta sandwich. When lunch was finished the Chief Engineer, Charlie King, found another two beers and took Phil on a quick tour of the enormous maintenance facility.

Halfway through the tour "What the hell is that? Looks like some kind of colossal DSRV from hell."

Phil was staring at an outrageous black, ominous looking monstrosity. More than ninety meters long. Fins and wings and rudders and propellers, antennae, conning tower, periscopes, cranes, ramps, lights and assorted grappling arms. All manner of ugly, cumbersome protrusions covering an oddly pock-marked, black surface. Augmenting these already homely features were other types of motivation. Metal tires and half-tracks and sets of vicious looking circular spikes. A truly ugly, mean-looking mechanical mutant looking more a space vehicle than a terran transport. It was in a dry dock of sorts, backed up by a channel to the sea passing under a pair of enormous doors. Phil could hear and smell the rhythmic pulse of the sea just under the doors.

"That sir is a SAT-SAV. It *is* a research vessel. But she's larger and made for continuous operations in deeper seas than most DSRV's ever dreamt of."

"A SAT-SAV."

"Yep. Surface-All-Terran-Submersible-Amphibious-Vehicle."

"Goddamned thing does everything except fly."

"We've made provision for flight as well," grinned King.

Phil gave him a wry sideways look. "So what's its job?"

"When *Gauntlet* is complete we will demolish the docks and this entire complex. Mines are already in place. Everything, except a small camouflaged entry to the portside access tunnel."

"And *Gauntlet*?"

"She'll break through her shell high up on Mount Anastasios. Any remaining traces of this operation will be buried under the resulting landslide. The SAT-SAV will be the sole means of evacuation. With no remaining shore handling we need a vehicle which operates under any conditions, launch capable from anywhere. The Marine Communications people had already designed and ordered this black abortion. So we built her here and we'll make delivery after our departure from Anastasios. In the meantime we'll shake her down by operating as a shuttle between Oneiro and Anastasios."

"Mmm. I suppose you need a submersible in case the landslide generates a tsunami. What's she capable of?"

Charlie squinted a moment. "These are estimates. We'll know more after her sea-trials. Land speed: ten knots, range: six-hundred-fifty kilometers. Topside water speed twenty-five knots, range nineteen-hundred kilometers. Underwater speed: thirty-five knots, range: two-hundred kilometers continuous underwater operation. Max depth: six thousand meters. Dive-time unlimited. Seabed speed: seven knots, range: indeterminate.

She's a tough bitch and can take a real pounding. Massive cross-filament, laminated armor plate composed of titanium carbide dispersed in a matrix of crack resistant titanium-nickel binary alloy superimposed on a sub-surface of molecular carbon spherical fullerenes all around. We're preparing now to give her skin a final treatment."

"What's that?"

"We're coating it with Ionsdaleite."

Phil raised eyebrows questioningly prompting King to explain.

"Ionsdaleite is a fairly new carbaceous hybrid based on re-sequenced carbon atoms. It's light and supposed to be nearly 60% harder than a diamond. This will greatly lessen the impact of both undersea and eventually orbital operations."

"Impressive. Anything else?"

"There is much we will be adding. Snorkel, armament, surface-to-air missiles. So far we have only installed some pretty advanced self-guiding torpedoes. If you recall that was done at your order."

Phil became clearly confused. "I issued no such order Mr. King."

"No sir. Not *per se*. However, your offices issued a blanket directive outlining minimum defensive ordinance mandatory on all Oneirion flag vessels. The order stipulated such action was being taken in response to recent piracy and acts of hostile organizations. We assumed you meant terrorists."

"Of course. I hadn't realized the directive was already being enacted. Please continue."

"Other armaments will be installed as time permits. She's already livable. Luxurious for a sub. More like an airliner. Galleys, cabins, first class seating, washrooms, even viewing lounges. Ugly on the outside, beautiful within.

We use a unique system of tanks that employ hydraulically compressed helium-argon gasses instead of pumping ballast. Same principle as the old Graf Zeppelins. They're faster and much lighter. This increases our maneuverability and our speeds to down-bubble and to ascent. It also improves our payload. She's heavy enough as it is, so simply reduction of pressure on the gasses brings her up. Unlike military submariners, we extensively utilize computers to navigate and drive the SAT-SAV, so we need minimal crew and training. She should be a dream undersea. I doubt the same is true on the surface, or on land, or on the sea bottom for that matter."

"Capacity?"

"Passenger & Crew: 135 souls. Cargo: 53,000 kilos. She can execute her own onload-offload, passengers and goods, in any terran."

"Power-train?"

"She's a fairly standard electric boat sir."

"Not nuclear?"

"No sir. Four 8600 HP diesels direct drive and they feed a bank of six custom-built 230 cell batteries that drive up to six 5600 HP electric motors. That will be replaced by QAVL drives when available."

"Sexy but ugly."

"That she is sir. Strong and stupid. She's a real thug of a boat. Not a lady at all."

"What's her displacement?"

"We're still refining our numbers. For now we rate her at about 61,000 tonnes. Her displacement grows larger every day as we add new gadgets. We just completed installation of her silent run thrusters which added still more weight and even volume."

"She's a big girl."

"Big, ugly, and mean as a bull shark. I'm in love."

Phil was back aboard *Geron I* at 1520 in a much better mood. Phyllis Thacker was unharmed. It had been an interesting day. He made some new friends. He wished he had more time to get to know Oneirions better. These were some seriously accomplished people.

From below decks. "You've got about forty minutes to get ready Phil. They've shipped in quite a few PM's to get people to the reception without getting dirty and we're scheduled for two PM's at 1615. Wait'll you see the starboard tunnel. Looks like Carnegie Hall during a fundraiser."

"How many people?"

"I believe about 200."

"Mmm. Quite a bash."

Phil seldom saw Anne in formal dress. Black gown. A close fitting cut showed off her figure and gorgeous legs to real advantage. He had never seen her wear much jewelry. Tonight, matching emerald necklace, bracelets and earrings in a platinum setting. Hair up and skillful makeup. Two things he had never seen before. He preferred her natural beauty. Yet he had to admit she was stunning.

He gently took her into his arms. "Anne. You look…"

She smiled warmly. "Get dressed. You need a shower."

Phil couldn't remember the last time he wore Black Tie. He could hardly remember the last time he wore a shirt with buttons, or socks, or even underwear. All in all he cleaned up well enough and looked a fitting partner for Anne.

"What is this?" Phil discovered a small rhomboidal black and gold medal on the pocket of his smoking jacket.

"That is the Order of Oneiro. You were awarded this, *in absencia*, while we were at sea. The award cites your valiant acts in defending Oneiro from foreign intruders. Mike had it delivered while you were ashore. He said he was pretty sure you wouldn't approve a ceremony."

"He's right there. *We're handing out medals now?*"

"Apparently. Do you disapprove?"

"I don't know how I feel about it. Frankly, I thought Oneiro had moved well beyond such motivational contrivances. All the same, what's wrong with recognizing courage and sacrifice? There's not a thing unworthy about a little noble altruism."

He scrutinized the medal more closely. "Pretty little thing. Do I really have to wear it?"

"We think it would be appropriate."

"Okay. Let's move. I need double Scotch topside before the games begin."

Nick's team must have worked a couple of weeks to prepare the starboard tunnel. Dozens of powerful indirect lights made the tunnel sparkle and glow. Comfortable red felt chairs had been liberally spaced and mounted on risers forming two huge wedges, eight chairs to a row, twelve rows ascending. Both wedges faced a red carpeted rectangle in the center. Austere decorations. The Ambassador's audio converter and his 'refreshment tree' stood center stage, next to a simple microphone, two red chairs and an Oneirion flag. The audio converter was augmented with small red and green lights. Red indicating The Ambassador was communicating. Green okay to speak to him. All had been briefed on its protocol as they entered.

Lining each of the walls were ten large screen monitors backed by huge red velvet curtains.

Phil frowned at Nick indicating the computer monitors.

"We are providing general text translation of The Ambassador's address in French, English, Spanish, German, Mandarin Chinese, Russian Cyrillic, Japanese, Portuguese, Arabic Farsi and Greek."

Phil frowned even more deeply. "We can translate *Kosmas* now?"

"No. Not at all. We can provide a general outline of meanings being conveyed however, given sufficient prep time."

"Fine. But are you leading the Ambassador to believe this event is being broadcast in some manner?"

Nick understood. "We explained to The Ambassador this event would be transcribed as part of a permanent record. We wanted several human language translations in evidence; and these languages represent the majority of humans on the planet."

"He accepted that?"

"He made no comment."

Flowers festooned the entire area. As did ribbons and various colored lights. Music played softly in the background. To the rear of each riser was placed an enormous bar and a long buffet line. Circulation was planned in the manner of two great loops dispensing food and drinks to all participants providing them the opportunity to approach The Ambassador's position at the start of each loop.

Phil nodded approvingly. "Well thought out and well done."

"Thanks Phil," said Nick. Clearly pleased with Phil's approval.

"I agree Phil," said Mike "Phil, I've been briefed on all aspects of the tour. I trust it's been useful?"

"Beyond anything I could have imagined. I'll never look at this project through the same eyes again. I also had a chance to walk about the industrial park. Interesting as well."

"Yes we know." Nick smiled. "What do you think of the SAT-SAV?"

"Ugliest damned boat I've ever seen. Uglier even than *Gauntlet Maris*. But I sure would like to have one."

"It will certainly make undersea communications experiments with marine life much easier. We can get to them and follow them anywhere practically as easy as changing gears. We'll give you a ride when she's seaworthy."

"When are you going to put a reactor on board?"

"We've talked about that. Fact is though, we're hoping to apply QAVL technology if we can. If nothing else, she has to complete her sea trials first. If nothing else, we'll build a SAT-SAV II with the new technology."

"Understood. I'm going to grab a quick drink before all this starts. And you gentlemen better get down there soon."

Mike and Nick moved down to assume their positions. Nick at the microphone. Mike seated on the opposite side. Phil fetched a short Scotch and found his ignominious seating next to Anne in the far upper section of his riser. As he was seating himself the lights dimmed. The audience fell silent immediately.

Since entering the enormous tunnel Phil thought everyone seemed a little too genial, overly jolly and affable. Phil thought of the term 'bonhomie' applied to conceal taut nerves and tense anticipation. This was belied by their instant response to the lowered lights. When he thought about it, he felt much the same himself.

Nick had previously explained the QAVL audio converter was a far more complex device than a simple radio transceiver. It received no less than thirty-seven signals from its QAVL host. Each signal expressed different aspects unique to the individual QAVL. Much as human size, sex, emotional state, education, personality, accent, vocal cords, skill, voice box, breathing and throat aperture determine an individual human's unique voice. Therefore, when listening to a QAVL via the audio converter, the listener hears the actual 'voice' of the QAVL. This is a great assist in adding the dimension of personality and mood to QAVL communications. Useful to humans. Phil would read the monitors and listen to The Ambassador. Together he would form some idea of the nature of this creature. He looked forward in impatiently to the day he would speak *Kosmas*.

Looking confident and in control, Nick assumed position at his microphone. "Ladies and gentlemen…Ambassador Qasi of the QAVL…"

The audience stood as one. The Ambassador's light switched to red.

*Oneiro II: Gauntlet*

*Greetings.*
*We are Qasi of the QAVL.*
*Greetings from the QAVL. The QAVL of Qruxin.*
*Greetings from Qruxin. Qruxin of Kentrikos.*
*Greetings from Kentrikos. An entente of sapience that spans our Galaxy.*

*Welcome.*
*Welcome to Kentrikos.*
*Welcome to the Galaxy.*

*Your voyage to this day was remarkably swift.*
*Your voyage to this Island was parlous and exacting.*
*Neither voyage is at an end.*

*For now, you've arrived.*
*You should be proud.*
*You are unique.*
*You've done well.*

*This day we wish to discuss time.*
*The most ethereal substance in the Universe.*
*We know this is a difficult time for you.*
*A dangerous and delicate time.*
*A nexus in time.*
*A time for balance and caution and judgment.*
*We can assist you in countless ways.*
*...except with time.*

*This day we wish to discuss teleology.*
*The proposition that final cause exists.*
*Join us.*
*We shall assist each the other.*
*Such providence favors a race but once in millennia.*
*We shall work, teach, study, and learn of one another.*

*Together we shall quest the final cause.*
*We shall seek teleology.*
*We warrant this venture is worthy.*
*There is joy and great beauty to be found.*

*Human.*
*And QAVL.*
*And Kentrikos.*
*We have the will*
*...and the craft.*
*...and the time.*

There was a sudden pause and a profound silence.

The words were simple and open. Beautiful and gentle. Rendered as poetry, or a song. Few words. Vast promise.

Qasi's voice? The voice was transcendent. Rumbling and resonating throughout the vast tunnel. It was deep and powerful and lovely to listen to. Almost godlike. Yet it also held gentleness and humor and a guilelessness that invites trust. Even affection.

He'd listened in *Kosmas* and read words in English. How he yearned to speak *Kosmas*. To truly understand.

The Ambassador's red light changed to green. The address was at an end.

Lost in thought, Phil was a little slow rising with the audience. When he did, he could easily see they were as moved as he. *To go down there and meet and talk to that creature...*

Soon he would talk with Qasi. Soon he would talk with the QAVL. Or soon he would die.

Phil discreetly positioned himself at the drinks table and observed people eating and drinking and queuing to speak with Qasi. He watched with an envy so intense it bordered on jealousy; and a sense of loss bordering on anguish.

As he often did in such circumstance, he indulged himself and let his mind drift and daydream. He allowed his mind to go anywhere it would. It was during such frivolous phrenic expeditions he frequently hit upon striking deductions...and just as frequently, nothing.

For some reason this foray was taking him into the mechanics of intertwined rotating loops. He had no idea why. Something to do with an article he had studied. What was it called? Yes. <u>Non-Linear Dynamic Inter-potency of Twined Inter-Active Assemblies</u>. The article actually dealt with fluid mechanics.

*What the hell does that have to do with any...? Ah yes. He was watching the audience moving in two large loops, rotating around the risers, slowing for the buffet, and intertwining to speak to The Ambassador. And they were doing it all without him.*

He sensed a presence and turned. Anne was there staring at Phil with a sympathetic smile. "Your turn will come Phil. Soon. Perhaps too soon. Let's go back to the boat."

Hand in hand they left the tunnel, the lights and music and laughter receding as they walked into the starry night.

*What the hell...he was leaving with the prettiest girl at the party.*

# Stars and Omelets

*If I speak in the tongues of men and of angels,*
*but have not love,*
*I am only a resounding gong or a clanging cymbal.*
*Corinthians 13:1*

The small fleet cast off at 0700 the next morning. The freighter was overdue for its next trip. The yachts had interfered with operations for far too long already, and the medical staff were pressing to get their passengers back to Oneiro for psychological exams.

Phil, Anne and Dr. Gold were taking breakfast on the fantail of *Geron I*. "Are you concerned about residual damage Doctor?"

"Not overly Anne. This is a pretty sturdy group of people…you included. I think Phil's new term 'QAVLawe' is fitting in this case. These people were stunned by what they witnessed. What the military used to call 'Shock & Awe'. A tool of a psychological warfare. In this case it was innocently inflicted by the QAVL. All the same, such an experience can be traumatic, especially with the young. Not normally damaging for a substantive period though. We'll watch everyone for awhile. But I don't anticipate any problems."

"What about me Doc?" Phil asked.

"Considering your appetite, I don't see how anything could possibly be wrong."

"Pardon?"

"Let's see. You had a Denver Omelet with home fries and sautéed onions, three biscuits, about a quarter pound of grilled ham, baked beans, stewed peaches, four glasses of orange juice, two cappuccinos and a huge Tequila Sunrise. Any special plans for lunch?"

Phil smiled wryly. "I like breakfast. Actually I like lunch too."

"All Oneirions eat much the same. I've been reading the reports and monitoring it myself. It's almost frightening. Not a trace of obesity in the bunch either. I'm aware much of this may be credited to Oneirion food, not to mention genetics. And you know…I sometimes wonder about their sensitivities."

"Their sensitivities? What are you talking about? They're extremely intelligent, highly educated and are most certainly sensitive human beings."

"Agreed. Certainly. My concern is not they're insensitive. I'm worried they're *too* sensitive. For example their nutritional habits. Most of them have not eaten real animal flesh of any kind. The kind that has to be killed before eaten. Some have never even partaken of wild fish. Nothing suffered fear, or pain, or death on their plate. Everything is grown, like an endless carrot. Yet with their craving for food, what would happen if say, they were shipwrecked with nothing to eat?"

"They'd eat plants."

"And if there were only animals?"

"A bizarre habitat. But they'd kill and eat meat."

"And if there were no meat either?"

"They'd starve. And I doubt you would hear a word of complaint."

"And if someone died?"

"I understand your question Doctor. The answer is yes; and I doubt they would take the time to cook him first. They wouldn't waste a bite and they would harbor no regrets."

"You are serious?"

"You're damned right. Deadly serious. Look Doc, these may seem like a bunch of coddled, cover-girl vegans; yet they've been through the toughest training in the world. They can fight. They can kill. And they can suffer and die. They've proven this under fire. When called upon, they can exercise logic so cold-blooded and precise they hardly seem human. I've seen it. It works up a hell of an appetite too."

"Hmm. Seriously Phil…"

"I am serious Doctor. Now let's talk about me."

Doctor Gold pursed his lips. He was clearly frustrated by the brusque change of topic. "Well Phil, we missed one physical. All the same you're the picture of perfect health. If you're determined to do this thing, I'd have to give you my go-ahead. I think this is as good a time as any to proceed."

Phil smiled broadly. He sighed and sat back comfortably in his chair. "Excellent. Monday. 1100. Five kilometers off Geron Beach." He squinted and closed his eyes for a moment. "From the Harbor, compass heading 226° West South-West. Longitude E25 36 15. Latitude N40 37 46."

The Doctor laughed as he made notes. "I do some navigation myself. I keep a Cessna Citation at the airfield. How about the GPS coordinates?"

Without pause. "Latitude N 40 37.776. Longitude E 25 36.264."

"Okay…decimal."

"Latitude 40.6296 Longitude 25.6044."

"Damn. UTM ?"

"35N X=381972, Y=4498577. If you want to calculate…"

Anne interjected. "Time grows short gentlemen."

"Right. I'll be aboard *Sea Tigress*. Suppose you and your staff travel in *Geron I* with your equipment? We'll raft the ships at sea."

"Fine. I'll make the arrangements. Don't eat breakfast on Monday by the way. Clear broth only. Does *Sea Tigress* carry any special equipment if you need retrieval?"

"If I need retrieval Doctor, any equipment would be too damned late."

"Not necessarily. It could accompany you down."

"No. This is a solo dive."

"Then why don't we just take the one ship?"

"I have things to do out there before we rendezvous."

Back home on Oneiro, Anne and Phil were peering up at the stars from their terrace enjoying the warm quiet night. They had just completed a six hour briefing with Mike and Nick. The *Gauntlet* project was consuming all Phil's time now. And certainly all his interest.

Obsessed with *Gauntlet,* delegation was the order of the day. Senior staff was being rigorously tested as they undertook duties formerly the provenance of only Phil, Mike and Nick.

Things were getting serious.

# Two-Day We Sail

"Phil we have two days until you undergo the *Kosmas* ordeal. Why don't we take out a sloop and go sailing for the weekend?"

"Let me think." Phil reviewed his obligations prior to Monday, eyeballs aflutter. In point of fact he had envisioned a weekend of shopping, restaurants, sleeping, books, cooking and television. Indulging in the luxuries of normalcy. Something rare in his life these days. All the same, these days were probably even more trying for Anne. A moment later "Good idea. Let's do it."

Late-morning the next day found them tacking through a brisk wind, fifty kilometers out of Oneiro. Winds this time of year were strong and steady. Good sailing. Phil helmed up into the wind. Anne dropped the jib while Phil dropped the main. It was far too deep to consider an anchor, so Phil put out a sea anchor to keep them pointed up and stable. Soon they were smoothly drifting in the sprightly bobbing of wind and tide. Water lapping melodically at their gunwales. They were out of the shipping lanes. Tour boats never passed this way. Oneirions seldom came out this far on their day-sails. They were even well removed from flight paths. So there was no one about and nothing to worry them. Only the joy of a good wind, sparkling waves and warm sun.

Anne brought a tray from below while Phil secured the rigging. Lunch time. Tea and biscuits.

Phil took the tray from her. "Dr. Gold should see this lunch with all his talk of ravenous hunger, dead meat and cannibalism."

Anne found their 'culinary' discussion of yesterday a little off-putting . So without comment she concentrated on arranging herself with her lunch. "What is it you need to do aboard *Sea Tigress* before the *Kosmas Treatment*?"

"Mmm?"

"You told Dr. Gold we weren't travelling in *Geron I* because you had 'things to do out there before rendezvous'. What things?"

"You don't miss a thing."

"What things Phil? What things to do before rendezvous?"

"Among other things, I imagine it'll be a real Chinese Fire Drill aboard *Geron*. Dr. Gold's going to have the whole cast and company along for this one. And I need a little time to focus before I go down."

"That's not what you said. You said 'things to do before rendezvous'. What things?"

"Aaah, I just feel like taking a dive first."

Anne quietly sipped her tea. After a time "As long as I've known you, that's the first time you've prevaricated and been evasive."

Phil finished his tea, climbing to his feet to take the cup below. Phil was not ready to discuss the possibility of some sort of QAVL insertion. Anne was already far too uneasy about the whole affair. "More?"

"No. Thank you."

Phil busied himself below with much rattling of crockery and pumping of water. Soon, as Anne expected, she heard the bar unlatch, followed by the clink of glass on glass and the friendly tinkle of ice in glass. Then the cadenced gurgle of liquid poured from a bottle. When he reappeared topside he was bearing a respectable Scotch.

"What's up Phil?"

"It's a little complicated."

"We've got two days. Plenty of time."

"Well, a few things happened I haven't had time to tell you about."

"Such as?"

"For one thing, I know where the music comes from. I know what it means. It's part of the QAVL Mating."

"How do you know that?"

"I've seen it."

"Good grief! You've seen The Mating? The music? Jesus Phil, when did all this happen? Where?"

"It all happened the night I climbed aboard *Geron I* half dead and half frozen."

"Okay. Where?"

"In the sea. My best estimate is roughly two thousand meters below Anastasios Island."

"Phil, no human, not even you, can survive the pressures at two thousand meters."

"Apparently I can."

"How?"

"I have no clue. I suspect my body is able to adjust to the degree it can establish equilibrium with the ambient pressure. You might remember our scientists came up with something similar when they were trying to work out how I respire under water. They concluded my blood accretes Fatty Acid Ethyl Esters at the surface of my skin. These FAEEs actually fostered the interaction between my red blood cells and sea water via my epidermal capillaries. Remember I'm already full of sea water, lungs and whatnot, so it's really only at the cellular level equilibrium is needed."

"Fine. Let's call your lungs a given. What remains is an enormous degree of magnitude greater. If I'm not wrong, you're referring to one of the processes which regulate your cell turgidity. It hardly seems possible this fairly passive bio-regulator could resist such pressures. You're not a giant squid Phil. And you're not a Sperm Whale..."

"...Nor am I a cellular biologist and I don't pretend to understand this process."

"Has anything else changed with your body?"

"Actually there has."

Anne grimaced as though she tasted something bad. "What is it?"

"Every once and awhile over the last few days I've been getting flashes."

"Flashes. What kind of flashes?"

"Fear."

Her demeanor suddenly softened. "Fear. You Phil? Do you even remember the last time you suffered fear? Any idea why?"

"I have a theory of sorts."

Anne raised an eyebrow expectantly.

"You yourself said I cannot see the future. And you're right. I cannot. Absolutely. I know it. I have found I can interpret my SNA, my *Kosmas* to some degree. A sort of early warning system. I believe I can somehow detect discordances between subjective and objective SNA; and I think that skill has been boosted of late."

"Subjective and objective SNA. I have no idea what you mean."

"Call it the difference between the way SNA incarnates events and the way I expect them to manifest. Somehow this creates a discordancy. I runs against the grain. When I detect this, I get a jar. It provokes…fear. More than anything else, fear draws my attention."

"Um. With what *viscera* exactly do you perceive these differences?"

"I haven't one damned clue."

"And you feel fear?"

"Yes."

"Real fear? Strong fear?"

"Debilitating, paralyzing fear."

"What does is feel like to you?"

"It feels like freezing acid slowly trickling into my arteries. Like my bone marrow is putrefying. Dark. Freezing. Insidious and nauseating."

"Phil we don't have to put ourselves through this. You and I and Herb and Demetrious. We can board *Sea Tigress* and just sail away. Has it occurred to you, you may be throwing away a life of complete happiness – in exchange for what? Terrible risks, pain and separation, alienation, even death.

What you're preparing to do on Monday terrifies me. It could easily kill you. Drive you insane. It could drive a permanent wedge between us. It may condemn you to a life of exile inside a lump of rock sailing through hard vacuum at inconceivable speeds for decades. It might bring you a death, horrible beyond imagining on some alien planet. At its most benign, it will put you through terrible tortures." She paused for breath and locked eyes. "Stay with me and live."

Phil downed his Scotch in a single gulp. He went below and poured another and drank it. Then another and he returned to the cockpit, leaning over the chart table and looking out to sea.

"I've been grappling with this problem for some time now. I've wrapped it and unwrapped it. I've dived with it. I've slept on it. I've lived with it for weeks now. It might have helped had I been able to speak with Qasi. Anyhow, I'm slowly beginning to understand."

"What have you discovered?"

"The QAVL are trying to convey some difficult concepts. The most elusive being they cannot empirically confirm or deny randomness exists; and yet they are compelled to suggest a course of action which assumes it does exist. This is…"

"Phil I'm talking about you and me…"

"…I *am* talking about you and me goddamnit…"

"Okay…"

"The QAVL have no option other than to council humans to pursue a direction they believe will save them. One which will enable man to enter the community of races and work with them on the *Kosmas Antiaô*."

"*Antiaô*?"

"Quest. Remember?"

"Right. I was ah, thinking of something else."

"Here is where it gets serious. Until now we considered only the extension of mankind's knowledge and range."

"You said '*only* the extension of mankind's knowledge and range?'"

Phil stopped. He cocked his head and stared down at Anne. "A few moments ago you said 'Stay with me and live.' If I stay with you I will die. You will die. I believe mankind will die. I can't quite make it all out fully, yet I think it may actually go far deeper. Vast in scope."

Anne's head slowly lowered into her hands. She couldn't bear to look at Phil. *Has he lost his mind? Is he so obsessed with Gauntlet he borders on delusional?*

"Phil how can you possible know any of this?"

"I read it."

Things were getting so surreal she felt dizzy. "You read it. You read it where?"

"My one truly unique qualification. I can interpret SNA. I can interpret *Kosmas*. It's that simple. Nothing mystical, magical, marvelous, or

Machiavellian. I can detect its patterns and formulate dialectic conclusions. I can read it." Phil stood and wandered aimlessly about the cockpit. "We're going to encounter the most important event in human history. Perhaps all history; and it's rushing at us near light speed. This is the true beginning of man as an explorer. Man as a citizen of the cosmos. This thing must be done. It must succeed. Otherwise we're finished. We're failures as a species."

"You're saying these…ah… *Kentrikos* creatures are the measure of human success or failure?"

"You bet your ass I am. I know this sounds like fantasy. Nonetheless you will come to realize this is truth; and I am the best and perhaps the only human qualified for this mission. I am equally sure the QAVL are aware of this.

Anne this mission is worth giving up everything for. It's worth dying for. We have no choice. I have no choice. If we turn away we will die. That is what the QAVL are trying to tell us yet cannot tell us. Because they either cannot clearly prove its truth, or they simply wish to withhold this information for some reason."

"Even if I understood your statement. Which I do not. It doesn't explain why we need to take two ships out on Monday."

"I have to…" Phil clamped his jaw in frustration. He was explaining the situation poorly. "Look. Things happen for a reason. Cause and effect. Particles behave logically even if we or *Kentrikos* are unable to prove whether they do or do not deviate from determinism. Think of the hadron-electronic chain. Matter-to- molecule-to-atom-to-proton/electron/neutron-to-quark. Then stretch it in both directions, larger and smaller, for infinity. This is a truth as old as the Laws of Thermodynamics."

Anne looked away, trying to control her rising anger and skepticism "Well that certainly clears things up. Seems bereft of any relevance, yet it's clear as all hell."

Phil ceased pacing and turned on Anne. "Perhaps this will 'clear things up' then. I'm taking a separate ship because it's my decision. I am the Consul here. And I have no obligation to explain every damn little thing to anyone, including you."

"That *is* quite clear. Yes."

"Good. Let's clarify things a little further. There is no alternative. No more discussion. I'm taking the *Kosmas* serum on Monday, and I'm taking *Gauntlet* to *Kentrikos*."

Anne's face looked as though it had been anaesthetized. A slight pinkness rose in her cheeks as the only indication of her inner turmoil. She rose and methodically stepped below. Without a sound. Without a word.

A short time later Phil was reviewing their dialogue in his mind. *That went well.* Phil thought to himself wryly. He was standing on the bow taking in the sea anchor. Having no idea what to do next, he assumed they might as well head back to Oneiro. *Why can't I get Anne to understand the problem? Why can't I explain it to her? Humph. The answer is obvious. I don't fully understand myself. That's no reason to pull back though. There is no reason to pull back.*

Phil was stowing the sea anchor when he heard a splash off the stern. *What the hell?* He rushed to the stern and looked into the water. *Has Anne done something stupid?* The wind was down and the sun full up, so he could see deep into the clear water. About five meters below the boat Anne was in full Scuba gear, knife affixed to her right calf and spear-gun in her right hand. Her lovely hair rippling in the water. A minute later she was out of sight. *Goddamnit!* He went forward and threw out the sea anchor, made himself another drink; and sat in the cockpit following her bubbles as best he could for the next twenty minutes. *If she wanted me to follow her down she would have asked. She's a superb diver and I can get to her in minutes, so I'll let her be.*

Phil went below and began sketching out notes. His meeting with Nick on the trip out to Anastasios Island had yielded some creative solutions. Some careful planning was called for. One slip-up and they would have an even more volatile crisis to confront. Forty minutes later he had the basics of a well thought out plan lucidly outlined.

He carefully tapped the papers, aligning them neatly. He made a sharp fold in the papers, exactly half way down the page. Then he climbed up to the main deck, leaned over the railing and dropped them into the sea. He preferred to organize his thoughts on paper whenever time permitted. After the draft was complete though, his mind no longer had any need for paper, or any media for that matter.

As he absently watched the papers separate and ripple with the salt water, he felt the rhythmic sway of someone boarding the boat aft on the Jacob's ladder. And there was Anne. Breathless, dripping, golden tan and clearly energized. The spear-gun's trigger assembly was hanging from her dive belt and she held the shaft in her right hand. Impaled on the spear was a large fish.

"Holy crap, a Bluefin!"

The Bluefin (Bluefin Tunny, or Bluefin Tuna) is not uncommon in the Med. This fish was over a meter long and probably in excess of twelve kilos. They hunt the surface waters of the Med, the Atlantic and even the Pacific, in packs. Some varieties can grow enormous. All breeds are superb hunters and fast. Phil had never heard of anyone killing one with a spear. In all likelihood a large school ran over her and she took one out. It must have been one hellofa shot.

"That brute could feed us for a week. How'd you get it?"

Clearly pleased with Phil's reaction, Anne smiled broadly. "I was just below the depth of clear vision when this huge school of fish were suddenly flashing all around me. Since I was looking for dinner anyway, I turned in the direction of the incoming flow, aimed at the first oncoming fish within range of my tether, and fired."

"Impressive shooting. I've never heard of a Bluefin taken underwater. Hand it up and I'll clean it for you." Phil took Anne's hand to help her up and the spear in the other.

"Alright. You clean the fish, set up the BBQ and cook it. I'll do the veggies."

"Deal." He took her dripping body into his arms. After a long kiss "Are you OK?"

"Yeah. I'm okay." She gently drew back and responded in a low voice. "You're sure you know what the hell you're doing? This is really no time to screw up."

"I know. And I am as certain as possible in the absence of hard evidence. I suspect my certainty will grow when I am finally, fully equipped for this mission."

"Fully equipped. Yes. I was thinking of just the same thing during my dive. It reminded me of my favorite joke. My father told it to me. Over and over. Ever hear the one about the old Indian and his horse?"

"Mmm. No."

Anne smiled reminiscently. "An old Indian rides into town off the desert. Killing heat. Dry and dusty. He's riding a wobbly old horse while his squaw is struggling along beside him on foot. A man in town stops the Indian and asks 'Why do you ride a horse while your poor wife has to walk?' The old Indian looked at him blankly for a moment and finally said 'She got no horse.'"

Phil chuckled. "And I get your point. In fact I've been trying to find you a horse. Who knows? Maybe I will."

A few hours later dinner was ready. Phil had rigged a grill off the fantail and greatly enjoyed the simple basics of cooking over coals. Thick Tuna steaks drizzled with lemon juice and olive oil. Dusted with pepper and dill and perfectly grilled. Phil loved the burn lines and crispy skin of a well BBQ'd fish. Anne had prepared fried potatoes so well done they were crunchy, with spinach in oil and lemon juice. A good chilled Chablis and life was good again.

Both Anne and Phil had noticed it was a little jolting living apart from the luxury of *Sea Tigress* or their residence on Oneiro. Still, on the sloop they felt closer to the sea and more intimate. More peaceful.

After dinner Phil raised a brass bell to the mast head, along with a radar reflector. He turned on running lights and set a sea anchor off the stern. Down for the night. Good books and a good Metaxas. Then to bed, where they replayed their passions of the day in tenderness and love this time.

The remainder of the weekend was devoted to sailing, reading, eating, swimming, drinking, sleeping and making love. Anne seemed to have accepted the inevitable and turned to savoring their time together…on Earth.

## *Elixir of the Odds*

A rare day in the Aegean. Damp, cool, overcast and gray. Infrequent. Yet far from unknown in the early autumn. A grey moody sky reflecting on a flat, slate-grey sullen sea. No wind, no waves. Intermittent raindrops, corpulent and lethargic, falling slow-motion into a sea of leaden, overlapping concentric ripples. The slightest insinuation of ozone, adding an edge to the air, hinting at possible thunder storms somewhere beyond the horizon.

Phil loved such days. A bracing change. The fresh moist air. The cool temperatures and the muted light suited him perfectly. His senses came alive in such weather. He could see better, breathe and even feel better. It bode well for this most important of Mondays. It bode well for Phil.

Not so the rest of the party. They were generally wary of the weather, worried a storm might emerge from the cloud mass. They checked with Oneiro Airfield Operations and were assured nothing major was coming in. All the same, even moderately rough weather would make their task risky and difficult. Possibly fatal for Phil.

Two ships were secured bow-to-stern on the main dock of Oneiro Harbor. The harbor echoed with the deep gurgling growl of *Sea Tigress'* two big diesels at idle. *Geron I* stood quietly beside while being loaded and provisioned. *Tigress* would be going out with only Phil and Demetrious aboard. Anne had elected to travel aboard *Geron*. She professed to an interest in ensuring *Geron* was properly equipped. Phil was pretty sure she simply wanted no part in whatever Phil would be doing before rendezvous. Either way, Phil approved.

*Geron* would be far better crewed. Nick manning the helm along with her regular crew and a specialized sonar technician. Mike and Anne were observers. Camera and sound crew. Stand-by emergency medical staff. Marine Search & Rescue divers. Doctors Gold and Angle accompanied by Phil's favorite buxom young red-headed nurse, Nurse Hampton, to administer the compound. Dr. Simon Butler (PhD), the island's nutritional engineer, tasked to suspend the compound in Phil's chosen attenuate...in this case a large Gin & Tonic.

Simon Butler had thought long about the historic import of the drink. He underwent brobdingnagian pains formulating the ultimate Gin and Tonic, researching and gathering ingredients. Consulting histories as well as components. He discovered he was confronting a larger task than he had dreamt possible, if he wanted to really do it right. And he really did want to do it right. Ever the artful perfectionist. Ever the driven mixologist, he was becoming obsessed. Trying to create a drink representative of England, its one-time Indian colony, and his own creativity. A blend of classical ingredients and innovation. He pushed unceasingly onward in his alcoholic Odyssey. He finally succeeded. The essence of the British Colonial civilization.

The *ultimate* Gin and Tonic:   The Butler's Oneirion:

- Six cc's of powdered Quinine derived from the Cinchona Tree of South America. *Using a process developed by the Quechua Indians of Peru, Dr. Butler painstakingly extracted a crystalline alkaloid stereoisomer of quinidine from the bark of the Cinchona*
- Six ounces of naturally carbonated soda water from Mihalkovo Springs in the Rhodope Mountains of Bulgaria. *Butler had rejected a charged seltzer bottle (far more authentic) in favor of Mihalkovo mineral water due to its lower sodium content. A little poetic culinary license*
- One level teaspoon of clear Cuban sugarcane syrup. *The syrup blended with Quinine and soda water constitutes classical Indian Tonic Water*
- Four ounces chilled Tanqueray Malacca Gin. *Malacca was a premium label of Tanqueray. The translation of Malacca in Greek is unrepeatable. A marketing faux-pas in the region. Tanqueray Malacca, although delicious and ever so slightly fruity, is now a collector's item – not having been produced for well over a decade*
- Six igneous glacial-blue ice cubes. *Flown in from Jokkmokk via Keflavik, over Paris, on to Athens, transferred to an Oneirion Jet. Five kilos began the journey super cooled, encased in absorbent fiber to conserve the ice as dry as possible. It was then sealed in twenty centimeters of Styrofoam, wrapped in four layers of thermal foil and boxed. 4.257 kilos arrived Oneiro. Dried, polished and re-cooled they were a lovely glacier blue. Water is actually blue, not clear. However, it is only when seen through depths, or highly compressed, as in a glacier, that water exhibits its true azure hue*
- Five drops of Fee Brothers West Indian Orange Bitters
- One generous slice of San Juan Lime (Puerto Rico). *Squeeze in juice from the remaining lime*
- Serve in a frosted fifteen ounce cylindrical tumbler (Galway Irish Crystal)
- A sterling silver swizzle stick (New Bond Street, London)
- Present on a sterling silver tray (Portobello Road, London)
- A Calamander Wood bowl (Jai-Han-Grier Road, Calcutta)
- Bombay Cashews (Rajak Street, Mumbai)
- Small beige raw-cotton napkin (Guhathakurta 3, Madras)

The perfect Gin and Tonic. The best in the world. Sparkling, strong, edgy, fruity and frosty. One-of-a-kind. Once in a life-time. Certainly the world's most expensive. Simon was very proud. Simon had been given every assurance from Dr. Gold the *Kosmas* compound (three drops) had absolutely no color or flavor; nor would it inhibit carbonation. Nor would the G&T compromise Dr. Gold's compound. Simon had created a Gin and Tonic truly worthy of its historic destiny.

Two Drákōn helicopters were on hot stand-by at Oneiro field, jury-rigged for Search & Rescue. Two business jets were fueled and prepped to scramble MedEvac sorties. An expert medical team was standing by at Oneiro City Hospital and a back-up team was on alert at the main hospital on Lefkada – ambulance standing by at the airport.

The entire island realized something was in the works, and a general feeling of suspense pervaded. Few Oneirions had a clear picture of the procedure soon to be underway. All Oneirions knew that security was vital, whatever transpired. So there was no discussions in the Island's various media. Aside from extensive communications and entertainment satellite links, the island maintains a modest newspaper, a radio station and a respectable television station. Several of their documentaries were distributed internationally and they enjoyed a growing popularity. Therefore, security was a sensitive issue and Phil's upcoming ordeal was never mentioned. Even in the bars and restaurants and lecture halls the topic was discretely avoided.

Promptly at 0800 *Sea Tigress* took her lines in. Radio checks were made and marshalling coordinates were confirmed. Technical checks complete, they received their go-ahead from the Harbor Master. As they pulled away from the dock, Phil spotted Anne peering at him with a particularly penetrating stare. He mustered a weak smile and nodded goodbye. She mutely regarded him, his ineffectual congé unacknowledged.

Tigress was underway.

It felt good to be aboard her again.

"Where are we heading Mister Philip?" Demetrious had a tendency to call Phil, 'Mister Philip' when nervous.

Propped against the chart table, Phil sipped a cup of hot broth. "Same heading agreed back in harbor. When we get there I want you to set up a leisurely pattern maintaining position within five-hundred meters of rendezvous."

"North 40 37.776. East E 25 36.264."

"Exact. I assume we'll be too deep for an anchor?"

Demetrious consulted the chart. "Far too deep. But in this weather a couple of sea anchors should keep us in range."

"Good. Let's do it."

Twenty-five minutes later they arrived at the rendezvous point. After some positioning, bow and stern anchors were set.

Phil disappeared below, only to reappear minutes later *au natural*.

It was 0845. Demetrious was waiting for him on the stern. "I'll be up at 1045." He smiled reassuringly. Without further comment he was underwater with hardly a splash.

The water felt warm this morning. The light was diffused, glowing grey, penetrating only a few meters. After that, a greenish-blue darkness. It felt good. Calming. A feeling of well being. *If this was what the QAVL wanted, fine.* He could hear the music again. *Strange. They had already mated. So why the music? Did they mate in shifts?* He assumed all life, ethereal or hadronic, wanted to shuffle the entire genetic deck, or its equivalent. *Perhaps this was their way of...*

Absolute blackness.

No feeling. No sound. No movement. Like death. Drifting down and down into the blackness. Upon reaching almost two hundred meters, he slowed, and stopped. He was out for over an hour. Then consciousness began to return. He discerned a dim glow from above. He became aware of temperature, the water and the beginnings of movement. The beginning of the long ascent to the light. Phil's time sense told him he had just enough time to get back for the rendezvous. He had been out for over two hours and didn't have one damned clue what had transpired.

Phil broke the water and neatly jumped up the fantail of *Tigress*. He quickly leaned over the railing, voided his lungs of seawater and grabbed a towel.

"Mister Philip are you okay?"

"I'm fine Demetrious. Just a little tired. And I want to be ready before *Geron* arrives. Can you get me a robe, a comb and maybe some juice please?"

Phil was reasonably presentable when *Geron* and *Tigress*, bumpers out, were swapping lines. Still a calm gray day, so they would be tautly rafted.

Phil hopped aboard *Geron* to find all in readiness. The camera and sound crew were set up. Divers were fully decked out in wetsuits, packing all manner of gear unknown to Phil. He could hear the rhythmic thwocking of a Drákōn helicopter high above, already on patrol. He could hear radio checks and pattern coordination already under way.

Anne, Mike and the medical team were arranged on the stern in the midst of the action.

"Good morning Phil. How do you feel?"

"Great Doc."

"Ready to face this?"

"Absolutely."

"Have a seat Phil. We need to do a little prepping."

When Phil was seated, a small medical team descended to take his pulse, temperature, blood pressure, listen to his heart and various blood, skin and saliva samples. A few minutes later. "Everything looks good Phil. Physically you're cleared for go."

"Yes?"

"Let's talk about your mental state. You know the odds are little better than 50:50 for survival and 50:50 for success. I'm no statistician Phil, but the two probabilities compounding one another sound a little shaky to me. I guess I'm saying the odds aren't great. How do you feel about that?"

"I feel it's time to go under."

"No doubts?"

"None. Let's get this going while the weather cooperates."

Dr. Gold signaled and Nurse Hampton and Simon Butler immediately responded. Nurse Hampton was in her protective gear carrying a miniature thermos. Simon carried his prized Gin & Tonic on a silver tray trembling with anticipation. He had even produced an embossed recipe card marking the occasion.

Phil accepted the drink from Simon and asked him to give an instruction to a steward.

Nurse Hampton took the drink from Phil and added a few drops of liquid from the thermos. As she handed it back to Phil "Please let that sit for a few moments before consuming the drink."

Phil smiled at her in acknowledgement. At the same time a steward appeared with an iced bucket of Champagne and six glasses. Dr. Gold, Dr. Angle, Anne, Mike, Simon and Nick. Hesitantly they all took a glass and the steward moved among them pouring the wine. When all had been served, Phil raised his glass.

"Success!"

Phil poured down his drink, tilted his head slightly and peered quizzically at the drink for a brief moment. Just as Simon advanced to explain, and present the card, Phil dropped his robe and dived into the sea.

Dr. Butler's chin literally fell to his chest. His eyes like saucers. He was speechless. All that trouble. He'd had plans to tell Phil in detail all about this most special of drinks. Bask in his amazement and admiration. Make an historic toast. Years from now the glass and tray would enjoy its own showcase. A place of honor. A brass plaque telling the whole story, including his recipe. <u>The Butler-Oneirion Gin & Tonic</u>. Phil had simply tossed it down like a cheap wine cooler on a sleazy tour boat. Hadn't tasted it. Hadn't even touched a nut. Just dove overboard without a word.

The planning. Locating. Buying. Shipping. Customs. *The expense*! He started to move below. He was going to make himself a Gin and Tonic to remember all his life. *Someone* should enjoy the fruits of his labors. He raised an eyebrow and nodded his head towards his fishing friend Demetrious. Demetrious immediately began threading his way through the crowd to the companionway. At least Simon would not be drinking alone.

The same quiet grayness, darkening below. Phil descended with powerful strokes. He wanted no witnesses if this were to turn messy.

At about one-hundred-and-fifty meters he could feel the solution beginning to take effect. He felt an itching and buzzing in his head. He was suddenly exhausted and weak. He hung limply in the water tired and unthinking. His head was starting to throb.

The Fear attacked.

A ravaging predator bursting from the depths. The psychic equivalent of long curved claws of razor sharp tungsten steel, hundreds of stiletto teeth capable of slicing muscle and tendon and bone, jaws huge and powerful enough to rip apart the largest creatures in the seas. And eyes. Eyes with all the warmth and empathy of a ball-bearing. The assault lasted only a moment. Lightning beneath the waves. Gone almost before it struck. Phil was stunned close to unconscious. Nearly in shock. A half deep dream state. Everything was a featureless uniform blue-gray. No depth perception. No up. No down. No time. No feelings. Close to dead. Phil was floating in a void.

After a time the realization of his position began to waken. He was deep in the sea. He had been unconscious. The Fear had made a vicious assault. And he had survived.

He noticed a tiny white glow beginning to accrete from the nebulous gray far below him. It seemed to draw the light from its surroundings. The dark matrix was leached into an enveloping black halo. It became an object. A tiny sparkling mote set in a matrix of deepest midnight blue. Far away. Less than a dot. It seemed to be coming his way. It was slowly growing larger.

Phil watched in fascination as the watery, waving and oscillating star ascended from the abyss, closing with him. With a jolt it exploded across the gulf, stopping instantly, inches from his face. Reflexively Phil drew back and attempted to bat it away. The object was so unsubstantial it fled his hand, momentarily diffused in the water.

What was it?

As details came clear in his vision he studied the glowing phantasm. *My God. It's the Missive from The Ambassador.* It was nearly transparent, glowing softly from within. He read. He read it carefully.

*Esteemed Consul Carr,*

*We look forward with great anticipation to meeting you, to presenting our credentials. To introducing the race known as the QAVL, and to the community of civilizations known as Kentrikos. Thanks in no small respect to your good works; we are most honored and pleased to welcome humans of Earth into the Kentrikos Antiaô. We personally take profound pride and joy in the opportunity allotted us to play some role in these cosmically historic events.*

*Until we are afforded the occasion to share these conspicuous times together, we extend herewith a gift: Kosmas. You have no need of the substance insinuating itself into your body. We suggest you expel it epidemically, without delay.*

*We trust you anticipate with great pleasure, as do we, to enduring, collateral camaraderie.*

*With best personal compliments and respects,*
*Qasi QaQAVdun*
*Ambassador of the QAVL to Earth QaSol3*

*That's it? It's over? It's that simple? They did it for me?* Phil vacillated between relief and frustration and gratitude. He analyzed the situation instantly. His conclusions. He would not have survived the ordeal; or at the least would have suffered and been irreparably harmed. As he was spared he was also denied an experience which could have proven life-changing. The pain and the suffering and the danger were not issues for Phil. He wanted the learning. The insight. Too late now.

*How do I void the Kosmas serum 'epidermically'?*

That soon became clear. He simply relaxed in the water and allowed himself to freely tumble down towards the seabed. Quickly he felt his skin began to heat. He could actually feel the solution exiting his body. Over 95.89%. Enough to save his life.

Clearly Ambassador Qasi had a full grasp of the situation from the start and had set himself on a course to save Phil. *I wonder why?*

Of course the question now. *Can I speak Kosmas?*

The answer drifted up from hundreds of meters below. The haunting song of the QAVL. It was as remarkably beautiful as always; and yet somehow a little different now. What was a delicate refrain was now. What? The closest description he could conger was a Gregorian Chant. A million voices perfectly attuned, rhythmically flawless chanting in unison a song of the cosmos. A mind bending saga of the universe unfolding for fourteen billion years.

Faithful poetry of the synchrony of movement and balance defined creation. Stunning portraits of landscapes and anomalies beyond imagining. From the infinitival particle expanding into titanic explosions forming galaxies and pre-galactic nebulae huge beyond the dreams of infinity. It was all there. The energy, the majesty, the cacophony of form and color and sound, the beauty.

To his other emotions, his relief, frustration and gratitude, he could now add…joy.

One other thing. The music confirmed it. Philip Carr, Consul of Oneiro, now spoke *Kosmas*.

# Dialogues

Phil was anxious to return to the surface. There was a new world up there he very much wanted to explore. Now he would begin to understand. He would read the QAVL Documents himself. He would speak with Qasi; and visit *Gauntlet* on his own. He would converse with Mike and Nick at ten times their previous rate and efficiency. He would revisit with Oneirion paintings, music and arts. He would ameliorate his kinship with Oneirions in their native tongue. He would contact the QAVL Alpha-Craft in synchronic solar orbit 1,620,000 kilometers distant. He would learn exultation and wonder.

*I am become Kentrikos.*

Phil had been down for well over two hours when he began a leisurely ascent. The QAVL song had attracted marine life for kilometers around and he found himself surrounded by hundreds of shark, whale, thousands of squid, smaller marine mammals and several species of fish he was unfamiliar with. Sharks came breathtakingly close. Huge charcoal-gray forms emerging from of the darkness so close he could feel the watery rush of their wake turbulence and the displacement force of their powerful Caudal Fins as they propelled them back into the gloom. Whales ponderously orbited his underwater sphere, ghostly giants patrolling the depths and shallows as they oscillated up, down and around the crowded sea. The sharks were mute and menacing as always. The whales sang to him in deep mournful bursts. Schools of fish surrounded him in the tens of thousands. Silent and beautiful. Reflecting and refracting every available photon of ambient light. The squid were different still. Mammoth schools would coalesce around him. Silvery, still and silent. Often some would come signaling with ghostly colors travelling in an eerie sequential march around their rippling mantles.

Phil was master of a vast undersea choir. More than one-hundred thousand creatures circled him, sang to him and bathed him in magic lights. Phil's throat, lungs and voice box were filled with water, preventing him from any orthodox form of speech or song. After a time however, and some practice, he learned to sub-vocalize sounds. Softly at first. Difficult to control. To even hear. He could generate only low, long wave emissions. He could feel it though and he could observe a subtle response from the marine live all around him. Particularly the squid.

Then he began.

He began to speak *Kosmas*. Not to humans, or to QAVL, but to the life all about him.

And so it started...a symphony of the deep. Their songs and their dialogues were lovely beyond description. They spoke of the sea and the currents. The sunlight filtering down in cascades from above. Mating and birth and dying. Raging seas driven mad by colossal storms and furious winds. Waves of such power and immensity they could throw a thirty-three meter Blue Whale as easily as a flying fish skims across the bow of a schooner. Shores of death and danger and shallows, and rocks and men and a hundred other horrors. Blood and fear in the water. The taste of plankton and kelp and shellfish and tiny shrimp. Storms from above and blackness below. Mountains dwarfing any geology on the gas-world above. The glow of life far below the restless boundary of sea and air. Freezing seas crusted with ice above. Warm seas full of life and light. Stormy seas full of danger and undersea clouds half as large as a continent. Creatures of malignancy harboring remorseless, unremitting and emotionless death. Migrations that span a planet and nests that last a day. Pain and pleasure and death and endless movement. Days before man's obtrusion. Reptiles larger than sailing ships. Days after man's abjuration. Tranquility throughout all the seas and oceans.

Such is the beauty of the sea and its creatures. *Kosmas* made it possible to know.

It made one other thing possible as well. Something that had never occurred on Earth. Phil spoke. He spoke to his fellow creatures and said something unsaid for all man's eons. He felt great awe and gratitude for his experience. A pearl of great value, arisen from the depths and thousands of its creatures.

So he said 'Thanks'

Does the concept of gratitude convey any meaning to a shark, a squid, even a Sperm Whale, or a harbor seal? Unknown. Most probably not. But it does convey meaning for man.

Phil broke the surface hours later. He was within meters of his original dive point. Despite his long absence he assumed all would be well. He was wrong. Violent squall lines began circulating the area shortly after Phil's dive. They forced *Tigress* and *Geron* to separate. Then lift sea anchors to patrol the dive area. And ultimately to run for Harbor. Aircraft were grounded, boats were secured and Phil was on his own. Trivial problem. To a normal human, a surface swim would have been the only option. And deadly. Phil dove six meters down to calmer water and began the long smoothly bobbing swim under the waves, back to Oneiro.

In any other country on Earth, the sight of their national leader, in a coffee shop – exhausted – at two in the morning – greedily downing café latté, croissants and orange juice – naked and dripping wet, would be a source of local interest. It would draw media comment. Widespread humor. Concern. On Oneiro it didn't warrant a second glance.

Phil had quite literally been too hungry to make it to his home. Hence his stop at the coffee shop. Now he was fatigued to the point it was a strain to walk, or even focus. When his energy was sufficiently restored, he signaled a PM and headed for home.

As he opened his door, the residence exploded with voices and excitement. The entire crew had established their command center in his home prepared to conduct the long vigil hoping to find Phil alive…however remote the prospect.

Anne and Dr. Gold rose and reached Phil at the same time. Both more concerned with his health than expressions of emotion. "Sit down Phil. We have to look at your vitals."

Phil acquiesced and underwent twenty minutes of probing. When it was over he arose shakily, turned to Mike and said "*Daaweeekummm avak Dssweekunnnn* (Oneirion Hello and Goodnight)."

His first words to another human speaking *Kosmas*. The entire room rushed to Phil with much shaking of hands and patting on bare back. Phil then turned to Anne, took her in his arms and after a long kiss said "Goodnight." With that he wobbled to the bedroom.

He would stay there for the next twenty-eight hours.

For the next few days Phil talked.

He met with Mike and Nick, Dr. Mark Gray – Sciences, Dr. Thomas Rio – Genetics, Dr. Richard McCloud – Cuisenaire, Dr. Gordon Singe – Medicine, Dr. Robert Brown – Religion & Philosophy, Dr. Sochi Inchowa – Languages, Dr. Alberto Omani – Psychology and Dr. Michael Dundee – Realization.

He strolled about the island stopping to converse with students and faculty. What a joy it was. The shades of meaning, the descriptive iteration, the precision and the beauty. He finally concluded that Cuisine and Biology should have no greater priority beyond disseminating *Kosmas* to all the peoples of Earth. With that they could truly change the world overnight.

The Tower of Babel would finally fall. He could imagine the understanding and empathy that might settle on Earth when all spoke the same language, and such an effective language at that. Perhaps peace at last. An end to self-absorbed trivial religious squabbling. Maybe the mundane irrelevancies of politics might finally cease haranguing mankind. Goodbye to the apocalyptic *isms*. Killing and dying in the pursuit of gaily colored bits of cloth. Patriotism. Dogmatism. Radicalism. Racism. Sexism. Fascism. Communism. Capitalism. Socialism. Goodbye to the contrived illusion of cultural richness and diversity; and the priggish proprieties that perpetuated them. The end of unworthy demigods.

All true, yet tragically impossible. Forever.

Phil instructed Mike to arrange a formal introduction to Qasi. He was quite eager to accomplish this for two reasons. He wanted very much to know Qasi. He had a thousand questions. Second, Phil had been requested to avoid Anastasios Island until such meeting took place; and he was obsessed with returning to the interior of Mount Anastasios to observe the completion of *Gauntlet*.

# Shit-Bird

He and Anne were having coffee in Phil's conference room, speaker phone at the ready, tensely awaiting Qasi's reaction and Mike's arrangements.

Finally his phone rang. Phil pushed the speaker setting before the first ring completed. "What've you got for me?"

"Let's see…" a female voice, rich, brash, somehow familiar "undying respect, insatiable lust and an breathtaking body… how's that?"

Puzzled silence.

The voice again. "Howya doin' *Chib-Erd*?"

Phil took a moment to adjust to this voice. Familiar yet apart. Memories warm and seductive. Bodings of pleasure, or peril? How to react? Ahh…bonhomie. Yes. A hearty good natured surprise.

"Good grief! Aiyana Atsila. How the hell are you? It's been years."

Anne cocked her head, raised an eyebrow and displayed a quizzical smile. She rose to leave. Phil shook his head *no* and mouthed *stay*.

Anne smiled bemusedly, and resumed her chair.

"I'd say thirteen years at least."

"Could be. How've you been?"

"Great. You?"

"Life is good Aiyana. Doing fine. Feeling great. Where are you?"

"I'm in New York on a bit of a holiday. Last I knew of you, you were based here with Barns, Levi and Richardson."

"How'd you find out where I was?"

"From an old friend of my father's when he was alive. A guy named Doug Curtis. I think you know him?"

"Yep."

"Anyhow he gave me your address and private number and I thought I'd give you a call."

"I'm glad you did. It's great to hear from you. I keep intending to…"

"Phil you're on some kind of island. Right?"

"Yes. It's called Oneiro…"

"You got a hotel there?"

"Well we have extensive guest facilities. All first class I assure…"

"I was considering coming out to visit. Catching up on old times. What do you think of the idea?"

"Umm…great. When were you thinking of coming?"

"Well hell I'm on holiday. The weather's crap in New York. How about tomorrow?"

"Sure. I should probably…"

"Where do I fly into?"

"Ahh. Best if you fly into Athens and we'll send a plane for you. Let us know when you're flight arrives. We'll have someone to meet you and escort you to our aircraft..From there it's less than an hour."

"Sounds super Phil. I'll call this same number to confirm my flight?"

"Sure. If I'm not here speak to a man named Edward McKnight. He'll make sure all the arrangements are made. But if you like I can…"

"Great. I'm really looking forward to seeing you."

"Me too you. See you soon. Bye."

Anne's expression was unreadable. She looked slightly amused. Interested. Possibly the remotest touch of jealousy? "You are *Chib-Erd*?"

"Yes."

"What in the world does that mean?"

"When I was at the U of M, I was in ROTC for awhile. My platoon leader was a really neat guy named Javier Franco. He was an American, from San Diego I think, but he had a strong Mexican Accent. He was a huge fellow. Big as a jeep. And he didn't take shit from anyone. Played semi-pro football for awhile. Linebacker. Everyone was terrified of him. Damned good at his job. For some reason he took an immediate like/dislike to me. His pet name for me was Shit-Bird. He would call me Shit-Bird any time, then he would normally drop me for sixty push-ups. But with his accent Shit-Bird always came out *Chib-Erd*. Anyhow the nick-name stuck and my squad called me *Chib-Erd* for the entire program."

"And this Aiyana person…how does she know your nick-name?"

"She was in my squad. The U of M was one of the first schools to go for a successful co-ed ROTC."

"I see. Her full name is Aiyana Atsila?"

"Yes."

"Interesting name."

"I agree. Aiyana is a full blooded Cherokee Indian. Beautiful, stunning girl. It means…let's see…Aiyana means Eternal Blossom, or Immortal Flower, and Atsila means Fire."

"And with everything we've got going. Aliens, interstellar space-craft, maximum security and all…you're having her over for…what? A Teepee Turn-On, a Wigwam Warm-Up, a Powwow Pajama Party?"

"Very funny. You actually sound the tiniest bit jealous." Phil grinned.

Anne lightly chuckled as well. "Perhaps you're right. Must still be a touch of Lander left in me. But seriously, I am concerned about security. Mind if I have her checked out?"

"Good idea. But make it fast."

"I'll get Oscar Sagan on it right away. He's done a wonderful job of expanding our intelligence network. Times and borders are no longer an issue." Anne stood to leave Phil's conference room and meet with Sagan. She turned and paused. "So Phil. You guys have something going back at the old *Alma mater* aside from calisthenics and small arms training?"

Phil smiled. "Could be. But aah, let's try to remember we're Oneirions, shall we? Above all that sort of thing and so forth…"

Anne smiled sagely and left without comment.

The phone rang shortly after Anne's departure. It was Mike. "Phil, I've set up your first meeting with Qasi for 1000 on Monday. We plan on installing an interface device in your conference room, if that's okay?"

"Fine. But why so long to arrange a meeting?"

"Qasi is presently on the QAVL Alpha-Craft. Sorry I was unaware. But their comings and goings are impossible to monitor; and they're not big on informing us of their whereabouts."

"I see. So Monday it is. Thanks Mike."

Anne joined Phil that evening for cocktails on the terrace. Edward joined as well and all three enjoyed the sunset together.

Phil said "Mike has arranged the meeting with Qasi for Monday, 1000, here in the conference room. We need to think about an agenda."

Anne looked puzzled "Why so long?"

"Qasi is out on the QAVL Alpha-Craft nearer to Sun than to Earth right now. So we have some time to prepare."

Anne. "Phil, I suggest you do not prepare."

"Really? Why?"

"You do much better when you simply allow your mind to operate freely."

Phil stared at the sky for a few moments. Then "Agreed."

Edward mused. "I didn't realize the QAVL engaged in much actual travel."

"Neither me. Mike tells me their movements are impossible to track, so they may well move around a great deal. Why? I don't know. I do know *Gauntlet* gets nearer completion every day. Perhaps it's time for the QAVL-Craft to move on?"

"It occurs to me, if the QAVL leave Earth proximity before they have been introduced to the world, there could be hell to pay."

"Who says we will introduce them to the world Edward?"

"Ah. I suppose I made an assumption sir."

Anne added "Do you have any thoughts regarding the pros and cons of unveiling all this to the world at large?"

"In fact I have. It presents a formidable problem and a dangerous one. Have you considered 'baby feeding' this information to the world?"

Phil stood to make himself another drink. Edward could read when Phil took such actions as part of his thinking process and made no move to assist. "Edward what does that mean. 'Baby feeding.' I like the sound of it. It sounds less daunting."

"Well, we now augment the majority of the worlds food supply. We already imbed information in this food. Why not gently and slowly spoon feed information about the QAVL, *Gauntlet and Kosmas Antiaô*? Everything. Even the mission of Oneiro in easy to swallow (no pun intended) portions. As realization gradually descends on mankind the remaining task would be to diplomatically confirm that which they are already latently aware."

Phil turned "Not bad Edward. Not bad at all. It could work. Let's set up a meeting with Medical and Culinary to investigate the feasibility of this idea and a tentative plan. We have to carefully engineer this. Account for gaps in Oneirion food intake. Somehow make it cumulative despite dietary habits. I believe the safeguards against redundant learning will suffice. Nor do we want to lose the slow spoon feed with a gap-stopping overload."

Anne stood. "I'll speak to Dr. Gold tomorrow and let him take management of the process. We should probably meet next week sometime."

"Agreed. Any input from Sagan about our new best friend Aiyana Atsila?"

Eyebrows raised, looking a little weary, Anne recited. "Ms. Atsila graduated from the University of Maryland with a BA in Communications and took her Masters from UCLA in Journalism. Top of her class. She worked for the LA Times, then the Chicago Tribune and finally US News and World Report in Washington, D.C. She's on some sort of sabbatical now and word has it she's turned to free-lancing. She's spent a good deal of time in Western Europe and Scandinavia, mainly Norway. She's supposed to have some sort of relative who lives there now. Aiyana is considered a superb journalist. With her looks, voice and personality she has been offered jobs in television news, which she is also considering. She was presented the George Polk Award for Journalism a couple of years ago. And her stock keeps going up. Her reputation and record is impeccable. No dubious associations or memberships. Her politics are middle-of-the-road-liberal, and her religion non-existent. Her remaining U.S. family member is an aunt in Utah. Financially she is doing quite well. Her personal life is Spartan at best. No marriages, boyfriends, girlfriends, or really any friends for quite some time. Sounds like she's manageable given some supervision. She even fits the Oneiro template. Sagan agrees."

"Excellent. A complete run-down, impressively fast."

"One of Sagan's boys in Washington took on the guise of a headhunter and information just fell out where ever he went. She's well liked apparently. When's she due in?"

Edward consulted his pocket-book. "Her flight arrives Athens at 1130. She should touch down Oneiro at approximately 1400. I plan to meet her flight unless you would care to?"

"No Edward. It's best if you meet her on the ground. I'm going to keep an arm's length for now."

"I have arranged a suite on the floor below if that's alright."

"Fine."

"And finally, I'd planned a formal dinner on the terrace for three tomorrow night."

"Good idea. We'll do that."

Edward left to arrange for dinner.

"You know, for the last year or so we've been living as monogamous landers. We are Oneirions and there's decades aboard *Gauntlet* to look forward to. Perhaps we should finally discard our chattel hang-ups? Are you sure you wouldn't like to limit dinner tomorrow night to only Aiyana and you?"

Phil looked at her appraisingly for several moments, finally deciding she was sincere in her suggestion. "No. Thoughtful of you to ask though." He smiled. "Look ah, things are awkward for us both just now, and I reckon this Aiyana thing comes at a bad time. All the same, I am looking forward to seeing her. I think you'll like her. She might even prove useful in the long run."

"Long run? I was under the impression she was just stopping over as part of her sabbatical."

"I as well. But she's pretty susceptible to whims. Always was. I think that's why her career has been all over the map. Although I think this time she has a reason for looking me up."

"A reason? Rekindle a romance. Something like that?"

"That's one interpretation, yes. Highly possible. It's also possible she's heard something about Oneiro and smells a story. If she's gone free-lance she's probably looking for something unique and provocative. Consequently I don't want to appear overly secretive. If we cooperate with her she'll be manageable. If we're overly protective, her investigative obstinacy may be brought to bear. And she can be damned aggressive if she encounters an obstacle. You ought to see her in hand-to-hand combat."

"I see. Well she certainly strong-armed her way in. Maybe she does have an agenda beyond a simple holiday. Beyond simply seducing you. So we welcome her with open arms and keep our eyes open."

"Well put. I also think you'll find her a great deal of fun and intelligent. Let's try to enjoy her visit."

Anne found herself in agreement. Better to embrace enigma and learn its nature than to keep it at bay in ignorance.

The atmosphere was suddenly relaxed. The air was cleared. As always they regained their composure when they developed a joint plan. They left the terrace for dinner arm-in-arm.

# *Journeys end in lovers meeting*

### *William Shakespeare*

Aiyana's flight touched down at Oneiro Field right on schedule. It was a beautiful clear day and a perfect flight. Visibility unlimited. She had to admit she enjoyed the private luxury of flying aboard a corporate jet. Being the inquisitive sort, she took best advantage of the opportunity. Hardly taking her eyes from the window, she took copious photographs and frequently notated her bearings whenever she could charm such information from the flight crew. She carried a GPS in her briefcase for just such occasions, but to her dismay, learned it would not function aboard an aircraft without an external antenna.

In days past, flights carrying alien unfamiliars had been registered as demonstration, check, or training flights with Greek Air Traffic Control. As Oneiro is well removed from commercial or military flight lanes, nonspecific, indirect flight-plans were accepted as a matter of routine. Flights had operated at low levels and adopted meandering, aberrant flight paths, effectively obscuring Oneiro's location. When these flights were passed to Oneirion Air Traffic Control they became even more creative.

These days however, Oneiro was 'out of the closet'. It was registered with ICAO and civil aviation agencies around the world. Oneiro appeared on Jeppson aviation and nautical charts. It even appeared on many of the newer, more detailed civil marine and topographical maps. It could be precisely located in seconds via data-nets. Navigation and positioning systems easily fit on wrist watches, or nearly any device. So between the overwhelming forces of bureaucracy and technology, such pretenses were abandoned. Secrecy was supplanted with diplomacy in a one-way journey into the bright light of public scrutiny, compounding the deepening QAVL dilemma.

The pleasures of deplaning directly to the ground at a private airfield on a hot midday. No jet ways, no crowded and noisy cookie-cutter terminals, no jostling baggage claim and frenetic search for ground transport. Instead the familiar feel of descending a short stairway into the bright flinty, kerosene heat of the day.

At the foot of the access stairs stood an attractive, distinguished gray-haired man. Nicely dressed, especially for an island in the warm Aegean. He was standing next to three smart little…chariots…for want of a better term. Aiyana looked circumspectly about. *No obvious security. But I know I'm being watched. I can practically smell the gun oil and hear their radio chatter.*

A friendly smile and a warm handshake. "Hello Ms Atsila. Welcome to Oneiro. My name is Edward McKnight. Please call me Edward."

"Thank you Edward. Please call me Aiyana." With a gesture towards the PM's, she observed "I see Phil sent *three* limos to meet my flight."

Edward chuckled. "We call those PM's – People Movers – we use them to go everywhere on Oneiro. We have only a few roads that accommodate automobiles, much less limousines."

"Well they're cute little things. What say we take 'em out for a spin? Do we need to do customs and immigration formalities?"

"That's not necessary at all just now ma'am."

"I take it I don't need a visa?"

"Correct. Visitors are rare to the degree we're aware who is on the island at any time. Tomorrow or the next day our medical staff would probably like a few minutes of your time; and they may do some passport formalities at that time." Edward smiled ingratiatingly. "We do have a welcoming tradition though…"

An aide brought a small tray bearing two Champagne glasses, an Oneirion Blue Orchid and a decanter of clear blue liquid. He presented the flower to Aiyana and filled the two glasses with a cold drink. Edward presented one to Aiyana and took one himself "Cheers!"

They drank. She looked at the glass "Mmm. Good. What is this?"

"We call it a Blue Oneiro. Our traditional drink to welcome visitors. Shall we go?"

The aide loaded Aiyana's bags on the third PM and they departed the airfield.

"Mr. Carr regrets he could not meet your flight personally. Several previous demands on his time. You are invited to his residence for cocktails and dinner this evening. Unless you're too tired after your trip?"

"Not at all. I sleep on flights from wheels-up to wheels-down. Is this a formal dinner?"

"Yes. Or I should say, as formal as we get here on Oneiro."

"With pleasure. Thank you Edward." *So this is how it begins. A Head of State diplomatically receiving an old lover at a formal dinner. A little frosty. Certainly not romantic. Then again, I did bulldoze my way in; and he probably did already have other commitments this afternoon.*

When they were well within the University complex, Edward sent the PM with baggage on ahead to Aiyana's suite. He noted a look of quizzical amusement in her eyes and assumed she was suspicious her bags would be scrutinized. As there was no graceful way to confirm or deny her doubts, he overlooked the problem and offered to provide an impromptu tour of the island. This she readily accepted.

Two hours later they had witnessed the wonders of Broadway, the Art Museum (some of the less virulent works), the University complex and Oneiro Harbor. She was dumbfounded by the technology, the architecture, the beauty and the scope of the island world. As she was particularly taken with periscopic engineering, Edward took her to the Board Room of the Webber Interchange Center. She was literally rendered speechless.

Over a drink at Oneiro Harbor. "My God Edward. This is paradise. I always believed that Utopia was a myth until today. You have achieved it. My congratulations."

"Thank you. Although I had little to do with it all. This is primarily the creation of Dr. Craig Webber."

"Dr. Craig Webber. I've not heard of him."

"He spent the majority of his final years nearly cloistered here on Oneiro: and he certainly didn't seek celebrity. Dr. Webber was a micro-biologist and an MD. A visionary genius, well in advance of the science of his day. He devoted his life and his fortune to development of this University. He sought a haven to nurture his work and bring it to fruition."

"What sort of work?"

"That's a question better addressed to Mr. Carr I believe."

"You know Edward; I saw some type of operation taking place offshore as we approached the island this afternoon. Then I saw parts of it again from the Harbor. I've never seen anything like it. Do you know what it was?"

"I believe that relates to University experiments with marine life."

"Big operation. What kind of experiments?"

"I'm not privy to most of the science here I'm afraid. Perhaps Phil can answer that question."

*A lot of barriers here.* "And what is Phil's position here on Oneiro?"

"Ah. His official title is Consul."

"That's quite a title. Sounds almost ecclesiastical. The messiah, or somesuch. What does it mean?"

"According to the Oneirion Constitution it places Mr. Carr above the leadership without the executive burdens to enact decisions. Decisions are jointly developed and effectuated by the Legislative Body – The Stockholders – and the Proprietor – The Executive Body. He would roughly correspond to the Parliamentary body in a Constitutional Monarchy. Here we might term it a Constitutional Oligarchy. Essentially it means he holds the majority ownership of Oneiro."

"My Lord! He must be fabulously wealthy."

"That certainly wouldn't be for me to say. There are no poor people on Oneiro. Mr. Carr certainly doesn't hoard his wealth."

"Oneiro is a country?"

"Yes indeed. Oneiro is a fully recognized, autonomous state."

"But it's not a democratic state. It sounds patriarchal?"

"Quite the opposite. Drawing an analogy, a Constitutional Monarchy is democratic, as is our Oligarchy. The Legislative arm equates to our Stockholders, who in turn limit the powers of both the Proprietor and the Consul."

"Who is the Proprietor?"

"Mr. Mike Auslander. An excellent man."

„Do you suppose I might meet him while I'm here?"

„I'm sure he would be pleased to meet you. Mr. Carr would make that arrangement."

„And what is your position on Oneiro? If you don't mind my asking."

„Not at all. I am Mr. Carr's Private Assistant."

„Which means?"

„Which means I perform any service required to assist Mr. Carr in his professional and private activities. I look after him. I am also his friend."

„Tough job?"

„Interesting job. Shall I show you to your quarters?"

A short PM ride later they were installed in Aiyana's suite of rooms. She was one floor below Phil's apartments, benefiting from the same view. „This is fabulous Edward. Does everyone live so luxuriously here?"

„Not quite. Student accommodations can be good deal more Spartan."

„Is that what this island is? A University?"

„Essentially yes, emphasizing extensive research."

„I see. All types of research?"

„Yes, I'd say so. Can I get you anything?"

„No thank you. I'm fine."

„Good. Suppose I call for you at 1930 and escort you to Mr. Carr's residence?"

„That would be fine. Thanks for your gracious welcome Edward."

Edward smiled deprecatingly.

*She's a temptress this one. Bright, beautiful, charming and very, very curious.*

Edward had ensured their seldom used dining room was painstakingly laid out for a formal dinner. He had formulated a festive menu, which he printed under the Seal of The Consul of Oneiro:

# Consul of Oneiro

<u>Menu</u>
Assorted Aperitifs with Mousse d'Asperge
Chilled Vichyssoise, Cheese Croutons, Safran & Chives
Oneirion Champagne Première Cru

Dover Sole in Sauce Saigon
Julienne of Caramelized Sweet Onions
Oneirion Chablis

Filet of Oneirion Beef in Burgundy Sauce
Baby Carrots Sautéed in Orange & Butter Infusion
Potatoes Dauphinoise
Oneirion Pinot Noir Grand Première Cru

Berries in Mandarin Orange Liquor & Crème Fraiche
Café with Almond Biscuits & Digestifs

"Jesus Edward. Is all this really necessary?"
"In keeping with the strategy we developed last night, I tried to put together a gracious welcome, moderated with a degree of formality, as befits The Consul of Oneiro."
Anne interjected. "Everything is beautiful Edward. Nicely done."
"Thank you Anne. I'll go for Miss Aiyana now if that's alright."
Casting an almost smug look at Phil, Edward left the room. Phil followed his departure with affectionate amusement.

Edward appeared at Aiyana's apartment promptly at 1930.
She was stunning. Tall. Flawless tanned skin. Jet-black glossy, arrow-straight, raven hair reaching nearly to her waist. She wore a white, satin gown. Clinging provocatively, open back falling to a lengthy slit, revealing long shapely smooth, bare legs. The effect was to give the not altogether unrealistic impression that she was clad only in gown and shoes.
Long and slim, her physique concealed a deceptively powerful body. A sleek, highly trained and disciplined machine. A carnal device amply capable of fecund beauty and grace, lush pleasure, and equally pain and death. She had trained for both all her life.

Her face reflected the best elements of her race. Perfect symmetry, beautifully sculpted features, dark rich flawless skin. Eyes a midnight hazel, deep and sparkling, crowning a strong nose, prominent cheek bones, full sensuously formed lips and a petit strong chin. A long graceful neck led the eye to generous breasts and a tight, slim waist.

Power, grace and beauty. A formidable union.

Edward nearly bowed. "Good evening Miss Aiyana. If you're ready I'll escort you to dinner."

Anne had wisely surmised that Aiyana would arrive 'dressed to the nines'. So, partly to set her at ease and partly to hold her own, she was dazzling in a light beige gown. Phil was decently attired in a maroon polo shirt, a navy blazer, khaki trousers and deck shoes. Phil could no longer tolerate dress shirts, ties, socks, jewelry, or even underwear. He had cheerfully bequeathed such trappings to bygone days in Manhattan.

Aiyana was ushered in by Edward, and Phil made the introduction. "Aiyana I'd like you to meet Dr. Anne Jones, Professor of Arts Emeritus. Anne, this is Ms. Aiyana Atsila." The two warmly shook hands. Anne's could only think *My God! She's gorgeous*.

Phil smiled broadly and turned to Aiyana. "Aiyana it's great to see you. Welcome to…mmf." Aiyana literally threw herself at Phil, holding him to prevent his falling. She embraced him and kissed him with a thirsty passion.

She finally released him and stepped back. "Goddamn I've missed you Phil." She beamed at Phil and held him at arm's length by his shoulders.

"Ah. I've missed you too Ana. Please come in."

When seated, Edward took drink orders. Aiyana was clearly ready for a drink, but undecided what.

Edward assisted. "Might I suggest an Oneirion classic? It was Christened 'The Butler-Oneirion Gin & Tonic'. But these days they're calling it the 'Oneiro-*Kentrikos*', or simply the 'OK'. A Gin and Tonic as none other. I assure you. In fact I used to get cramps in my legs at night. Now I take one before bed and I'm fine."

"Oh yes. I saw 'OK's' on menus when you gave me a tour. I intended to ask you about it. Sounds good Edward. I'll take one. What is *Kentrikos?*"

"That's probably a long explanation for this evening ma'am. Perhaps I can demonstrate the recipe another day?"

"Sure." Aiyana showed the slightest moue-smile.

*Damnit Edward. You know better than that. This is not some damned game. Two minutes and we're already in the crap.* Anne watched Phil's jaw muscles clenching.

As did Aiyana. *Pay dirt.* She filed that away as something of interest. Worthy of follow-up.

When drinks had been served "Wow, what a cool place. I'm impressed Phil. You're like the ruler of this country?"

Anne smiled inwardly *'Wow...cool place...You're like the **ruler** of this country?' She's trying to sound like an undergrad from UCLA...not the hardass journalist she obviously is.*

"Something like that. We're not exactly a conventional governmental form. So things are fairly loose."

"Everything is so beautiful, including the Oneirions. Everything is perfect and incredibly well designed. Is everyone wealthy?'

"No, not in the sense you mean. In fact our people have little real money *per se*. But they live much as they like and they could have money if they so wished."

"A huge, high-class commune?"

"Umm. More of a Platonic city state."

"I've heard the term Constitutional Oligarchy."

"Well, I'm not sure any orthodox form applies to us. If you're interested I should put you in touch with our Legal Department."

"I'd like that. Edward also mentioned a Mike Auslander?"

Phil glanced towards the retreating Edward, a stony hint of irritation passed fleetingly across his features.

"Mike is our Proprietor. Good man. Would you like to meet him as well?"

"Yes very much."

"I'll speak to Edward. He'll be happy to make the arrangements."

Anne appraised her discretely. *She's good. One minute through the door and she's already found her way to legal, to Mike and she's curious about Kentrikos. Phil's allowing her to play him like a violin. I wonder if she's aware. Hell I wonder if he's aware.*

Soon they were seated in the dining room and service began. Phil noticed their server was the same young lady who attended to his dinner with Mike. *I wonder if she'll hum Gershwin for us later.*

"Aiyana, Phil tells me you're an American Cherokee Indian."

"True. There's not too many left these days either."

"Is there a translation of your name?"

"Yes. Eternal Blossom of Fire."

"How rare. Like poetry."

"Thank you. People often call me Ana for short. In that case the translation is the same as yours."

"And that would be…?"

"Eagle."

Anne gestured with a predatory smile. "There's a name I can warm up to."

Aiyana's black eyes twinkled. "We are both Eagles."

Ana peered sightlessly upwards, her mind engaged.

*Eagle medicine is the power of the great spirit.*
*The connection to the Devine.*
*It is the ability to live in the realm of spirit.*
*And yet remain connected and balanced within the realm of earth*
*Harry Bowden – Night Flight*

Her eyes refocused and her face cleared. She bestowed a penetrating smile on Anne.

*She has a disturbing talent. She cuts through our guise like a scalpel. And she enjoys it. This one wants watching.* She cast a meaningful gaze at Phil, clearly having the same thoughts. Her appraising gaze returned to Ana, with a dawning respect.

"Friends also call me Aiy for short. Spelled A-I-Y, pronounced E-Y-E. In fact please call me Aiy. That way people umm…won't get us mixed up. That is they can tell us apart, or I should say not get us confused…oh hell. Just call me Aiy." With that she smiled brightly, raising eyebrows as if trying to gage Anne's reaction."

Anne returned her smile. Glowing, if somewhat brittle. "Where do your people hail from *Aiy*?"

Ana took a moment to arrange her thoughts. "They *hail* from roughly 1900 B.C. when we emigrated from the great Iroquois nations to what is now known as the Carolinas in the United States. We were a peaceful peoples. Unfortunately that did little to save us from the arrival of Europeans in the 1700's. From constant displacement, small pox, cultural heresy, and a variety of other white legacies. This we endured until the early 1800's.

Are you familiar with the term *Nunna Daul Tsunny?*"

"No. What does it mean?"

Phil interceded. "*The Path Where They Wept. The Trail of Tears.*"

Ana nodded in approval. "Good. How about *Tlo Va Sa?*"

Anne shook her head. "No." As did Phil.

"It means *The Tragedy*. These terms refer to the time when the Cherokee were cruelly driven from East to West. Many died. All suffered. A heinous destruction of life and culture. She quoted from memory:

*I know what it is to hate. I hate those white soldiers who took us from our home. I hate the soldiers who make us keep walking through the snow and ice toward this new home that none of us ever wanted. I hate the people who killed my father and mother. I hate the white people who lined the roads in their woolen clothes that kept them warm, watching us pass. None of those white people are here to say they are sorry that I am alone. None of them care about me or my people. All they ever saw was the colour of our skin. All I see is the colour of theirs and I hate them.*
    *Micheal Rutledge – Forgiveness in the Age of Forgetfulness*

I *hail* from *Nunna Daul Tsunny*. And most recently…Kansas."

Anne probed. "You sound bitter Aiyana."

"My father is very bitter. He was raised to be bitter, in a demeaning trailer on a barren reservation. Drunkenness, crime, degradation, hopelessness. He finally left the U.S. altogether. For me, that was much too long ago for rancor. One can always learn from it though."

"And what is there to learn?"

"Basically, the dangers endemic to primitive races from more advanced cultures."

Anne's hairs nearly stood up. *That's too damned close to the mark.* She quickly moved to another topic. "Is that earring Cherokee?"

"Yes."

"It's beautiful. It is traditional to only wear one?"

"No. This is actually a ring. My mother's. I had it worked into an earring because I thought the ring and the workmanship were too delicate to wear on my finger. I'm hard on jewelry."

"Does it have any special symbolism?"

"Oh it's quite rich in tradition and symbolism. The ring itself is a circle. The circle is a basic symbol to the Cherokee – life and new beginning. The eagle in the design means victory. The eagle flies to the east meaning success. And the ring is fashioned in yellow gold. Yellow means 'up'."

Anne looked closely at the ring. It was exactly as she described it. If her interpretation of the symbols was accurate, (and she would research that) then Aiy was again, uncomfortably close to the mark.

*Go east and find victory, a new beginning and success. Oneiro was east of her, and she found me, Anne, the eagle. And finally she would go up. Of course such generic symbolism is easily adapted to any situation. That is unimportant. It is important that Aiy chose to make such an explanation here, and now.*

*Time to change the subject again I think.*

"How did you meet Phil?"

"He and I were ROTC cadets at the U of M. In our Company, Phil was the *Chib-Erd*; and I could kick anyone's ass…including his." She cast a mocking smirk at Phil.

Phil grimaced good-naturedly. "Quite true…then. Don't be too sure about 'now' though Aiy."

"Well perhaps we should have a few fast tumbles while I'm here? What would you say if I said I'm still the best there is?"

"I'd say you don't get out enough." Phil flashed her a predatory smile. "Perhaps we *should* have a go. How long are you here for?"

"A lot depends on how much I'm intruding. I'm on a bit of a sabbatical now, so I'm flexible."

"We've got the room, and there's a lot to see. Feel free to stay awhile."

"This is quite a unique little country I think. How would you feel about a feature article on Oneiro for your review?"

"For what media?"

"Oh probably the Sunday supplements, maybe Travel, something like the New Yorker, or National Geographic. Your objectives define who I pitch it to, and how I write it."

"I'm not sure I do have any objectives in this area."

"Hey, everyone does. Tourism, politics, trade, influence, image. Maybe just to be better understood, or better known. Perhaps you have a policy or action you want to be more broadly accepted. Maybe you have some sort of announcement, or simply to introduce yourselves to the world?"

Phil appeared to be considering her proposal. After a time he spoke.

"Okay. Perhaps a draft article is a good idea."

"Time and materials?"

"Certainly. Whatever your standard rate is."

"May I have access to any parts of the island this may lead?"

After a quiet pause "Given pre-arrangements."

"Photos?"

"Yes." He emphasized again. "With pre-arrangements."

Anne frowned mentally. *I like Aiy. A lot. She's bright. No girl-scout. Gorgeous. Sexy. But I strongly sense an agenda. We're treading a tricky line here. I wonder why Phil's allowing it?*

Anne noted that both Aiy and Phil had three of the large Gin & Tonics apiece; and Aiy didn't have Phil's unique capacity. Apparently Phil and Aiy shared some of the same propensities though. She supposed that, as with many journalists, she enjoyed a hard drinking lifestyle. When drinks and aperitifs were finished, dinner was served.

Dinner proceeded smoothly. By the time the coffee and liquors were served, Aiy had charmed *carte-blanche* to visit anywhere on the island with 'pre-arrangements'. She could visit any department in the University, and cinched up her feature article about this most unusual island state.

Phil's tactic of an open hand concealing clandestine works looked to be working too damned well. It was going to be a delicate thing. He would have to try and confine her to well briefed department heads if at all possible. Problem is they are an independent lot on Oneiro. Hard to control. Harder still to keep quiet.

Aiy had skillfully, tactfully, even pleasantly continued to grill them throughout the meal. Phil and Anne noted she artfully avoided any discussion about their relationship. The only real difficulty occurred when she asked how Phil had come to be Consul. How could an employee, even President & CEO, simply inherit a corporation worth billions? The answer tested Aiy 's gullibility to the limit. Dr. Webber was so taken with Phil he became his sole heir? After barely two years? She proved she was every inch a reporter. She congenially and casually pursued her queries just far enough to know where to continue probing at a later time…

What brought Phil to Oneiro? What brought Anne?

Are they recognized by other countries?

Do they have their own army, navy, air force?

Was the University recognized and known? Accredited?

What degree programs did they offer? Scholarships and Grants?

What sort of research were they conducting at Oneiro Harbor?

What was the population of Oneiro?

How about the economic system? Real estate? Can foreigners own property?

Are there exports? Imports? What is the primary industry of Oneiro?

How broadly were they known?

Any enemies? Competitors? Allies?

What was the official language? Was there a national flag? A national anthem?

Taxes? Money? Police? Poverty? Disease? Social ills? Dissidents?

What type of law was used in civil and criminal proceedings?

Was there crime? …and on and on…

All questions answered agreeably and openly…and superficially. Aiy sensed this and her reporter's antenna were quivering.

All-in-all a taxing, but enjoyable evening.

"Thank you both for a wonderful evening and a delicious dinner. The food here is exceptional. I enjoyed it. Thank you Edward for superb preparations."

With that she embraced and warmly kissed Phil and Anne, in turn. Then a hearty hug for Edward and back to her rooms.

Phil and Anne grinned at each other as they both wiped lipstick from their mouths. Empathy tempered with savvy and even humor. What was the game? She's lonely? Looking for a story? A family? Concupiscent? Randy? Genuinely and innocently interested? Looking for a real home? Still in love with Phil? Attracted to Anne? In the pay of some unknown party? All the above? Something else? How long did she actually wish to stay?

They fetched a cognac and moved to the terrace to admire the night and review the evening. And most importantly…plan how to control Aiy.

## *So many men so many questions*

*Terence (185-159 BC)*

Phil instructed Mike's staff to relocate the meeting with Qasi to his office on the ground floor. He was uneasy about the close proximity of Aiy. God forbid she should somehow witness this unique event. Meanwhile Aiy was a whirlwind of activity. She saw Phil frequently and maintained her provocative affections. She kept Edward incessantly busy, briefing, debriefing and arranging new meetings. Anne was constantly involved. She lunched with Aiy every day. Attended her interviews as a helpful friend. They swam and played tennis often, visited the island's museums and restaurants, and generally became good friends. At the same time, Anne deftly ensured that Aiy's interviews and investigations were well supervised. Nonetheless Aiy had quite impressively worked her way into a wide variety of Oneirion activities. She wondrously fell through the Touch Gallery, had a tour of the food processing facility and attended a Broadway play. She was exposed to more Oneirion art; she suffered Oneirion music and went diving with the Marine Communications Laboratory staff. She had dinner with Mike Auslander and friends at his residence, followed by lively tales of midnight skinny dippings in his lake.

Anne was increasingly impressed with Aiy's mental acuity. After only two days on the island she mentioned her bewilderment at an arcane aspect of biochemistry...a subject to which she had never been previously exposed. Non-Oneirions normally required several days, sometimes even weeks, to MGL ingested learning. Aiy's questions cascaded by the dozens on every topic imaginable. Some uncomfortably close to the most sensitive elements of Oneirion pursuits.

Phil had little doubt that some unauthorized information was invariably being released. Aiy was just too skillful and beguiling. Yet he had little power to stem the leaks, even if he knew where and how. He even suspected perhaps Anne was not taking her supervisory duties as seriously as she could. She seemed quite taken with Aiy. He had no tangible facts and wondered if he was experiencing a modicum of paranoia sprinkled with a dash of unworthy jealousy. Meanwhile, as there was little or nothing he could do...he forgot about it and concentrated on his duties, looking forward eagerly to his upcoming introduction to Qasi. Monday morning finally arrived. Over breakfast "Anne

I wonder if you wouldn't mind taking Aiy out for a day-sail? Maybe do some diving. Take along lunch and a few bottles of good wine?"

"I take it you would like her 'outa Dodge' during your meeting with Qasi?"

"That's exact. I'd like to have one less factor to worry about."

# Sound and Light

Anne thought it over. She had planned to witness the meeting. Human history as it unfolded. She did have to admit though that the entire session would be totally meaningless to her. She didn't speak *Kosmas*, she couldn't even see the Ambassador, and a few blinking lights mean absolutely nothing.

*Come to think of it, the meeting will be brutally boring and she would feel pretty foolish just sitting there staring into space. In fact if she did have aspirations of joining the Gauntlet mission, Qasi would already be de facto aware she was categorically unqualified to mount the mission.* Still, she felt she was being pushed aside, unneeded and unwanted. This provoked an understandable resentment which, try as she might, she could not fully suppress.

"Sure. It's a beautiful day. Maybe I'll bag another Blue Fin. I'll call Aiy."

"I really appreciate this Anne. I know you wanted to attend the meeting."

"Yes I did. In retrospect though, it was a pretty silly idea."

As she moved to the phone Phil said "I'll ask Edward to reserve a boat and have it provisioned."

They departed on their separate ways and days.

Phil's office had been equipped with audio/visual recording equipment and the Ambassador's blinking communications interface. His little gold tree twinkled with refreshment. For Phil, various foods and drinks had been set out on a small table next to an easy chair.

The Ambassador's interface lit and the meeting opened.

A strange voice emanated from the speaker. "Mr. Philip Carr, Consul of Oneiro, may we present *Qasi QaQAVdun, Ambassador of the QAVL to Earth QaSol3.*

"Ambassador Qasi. It is a great honor to meet you. Welcome to Oneiro. Welcome to Earth."

"Thank you Mr. Consul. We are honored to meet you."

"Ambassador I regret I have been unable to greet you earlier. I have been eager to meet you. However, my schedule has been…"

"You have been occupied learning *Kosmas* after your unique fashion. A courageous act on your part. Our respects and congratulations. Given such an opportunity we are not at all sure the QAVL would gambol as audaciously with their own existence. We share the joy of your accomplishment."

"You knew I am a naturalized Oneirion?"

"Mr. Consul, your age alone belies that fact. More to the point however, we have been observing you quite closely for some time. It is of little import to the QAVL if you are indigenous to Oneiro. And you should be justifiably proud of an exceptional accomplishment."

"Ambassador, you saved my life during the *Kosmas* treatment. Your missive saved me. I thank you. I owe you my life. I am in your debt."

"We did so of prodigious necessity. And with great pleasure. We cannot acknowledge debt. It is not of our nature. Without your native abilities it would have been impossible."

<u>Phil</u>: "Ambassador Qasi, I am forced to raise an issue you may find troubling."

"Yes Mr. Consul?"

"It is an inescapable reality that news of our contact will find its way beyond the limits of our Island."

"Agreed. We calculate quite soon. Great danger. Nightmarish violence."

"My conclusion indicates the QAVL will not be the target of this violence. The target will be Oneiro."

"Yes. And you."

"I suppose you are correct. I believe we must prepare."

"Agreed."

"First. When that time comes, mankind will most certainly raise the issue of potential QAVL belligerency."

"You are indeed correct Mr. Consul. We find this troubling and distasteful. But not unexpected. Let us quickly set this issue aside. To your satisfaction we hope. Consul Carr, there is no power on Earth capable of harming the QAVL. Should the QAVL wish harm upon Earth for some bizarre reason; we could quite easily impel the Earth into your sun and have done with it. As an example. If the QAVL wanted the Earth *per se*, they could as easily impel Earth closer to the sun, thereby ending all life on the planet. Or we can simply take what we wish and we could have done so for over four million years. The QAVL enjoy a much longer tenure on Earth than Homo Sapiens. In a certain sense we might consider man an interloper on *our* planet.

The truth is however, that QAVL and humans compete for no common resource. Earth posses quite literally nothing the QAVL would covet, other than human friendship. There are no grounds for QAVLian belligerency, or any question of QAVLian benign motivation. How could there be interest other than for amity and common benefit? Any other conclusion defies logic."

"These are excellent points sir. However, humans are adept at dissimulation. Therefore, humans lack a certain degree of trust. Of each other. Of unsubstantiated, or uncorroborated statements and concepts. Therefore, to credit your assertion, they would require a physical…a tangible substantiation. Even a material object of some description. An unimpeachable object which can be subjected to human senses and examination. Record it. Verify its existence; and by its nature, confirm facts about it, or emanating from it. This is the human concept of evidentiary findings, based on human standards and the legal precepts of nearly…"

"With all respect Consul Carr, we are well aware of the nature of what you perceive to be the scientific, or legalistic, empirical method." Phil was jarred to hear what approached impatience in Qasi's response.

"Of course you are. I apologize. It is difficult to differentiate those concepts needing explanation from those already clear to you."

"Understood and accommodated. Very well Mr. Consul. We will comply. We assume your memory is advanced as part of your regimen and training? Or do you require some sort of private recording device?"

"Our meeting is being recorded Ambassador."

"We are aware of that. However, we consider this information extremely sensitive. We will therefore take the precaution of suppressing this information from the official digital record."

"Are you prepared Mr. Consul? Our information is quite short."

"Yes. I will let you know Ambassador if I require mechanical assistance. Otherwise I will commit your information to memory."

"Good. Record this please. We are using human notation. 6°48'South, 39°17'East, or -6.8000,39.2833, adjust South, South/West by thirty-six meters, heading 216° true, depth 43 meters. Exercise great care when your depth exceeds forty meters. It is a remote possibility, but conceivable some geologic shifting may have occurred."

"Thank you Ambassador. And what evidentiary 'object' will we encounter when we arrive at these coordinates?"

"We are certain you will be pleased Consul. Allow us our small surprises. Consider this a gift. In friendship. Feel free to use or, share this gift with whomever, whenever, and however you deem fit. Now, I propose we continue our discussions Mr. Consul. We are certain there are many areas of greater import that interest us both."

In a low voice, Phil responded "There certainly are."

With that Phil let the subject drop. He now had his 'object of truth.' The burdens of logical, rational proof and common sense that overwhelmingly favored Qasi's arguments; and Phil was unequivocally convinced he was dealing with a race without malice. A race that had no conceivable motivation for harming man.

All the same, the bureaucrats and politicians and generals and lawyers and doubters and shamans would bristle and strut and howl for their faithless, mindless, irrefutable proof. Blind Justice indeed. And he must have it for them. And he hoped he truly had it now. He would submit under great pressures to someday reveal his 'object of truth.' Equally, his nature and his curiosity would demand he must one day penetrate the mystery down there, so remote in geologic time.

For the moment, he let it rest…

Phil: "Ambassador Qasi, our *Gauntlet* Project Director assured me the QAVL would not intrude into human interactions without making their presence known."

"That is true Mr. Consul up to a certain point."

"What certain point?"

"You Consul."

"*Me?*"

"You are that point. You have been for some time. You are the only human subject to unannounced, covert observation since humans achieved *Kosmas*."

"May I ask, why me?"

"Are you offended Mr. Consul?"

"No. Not really. You have been observing *Homo sapiens* since before they descended from the trees. I doubt I could hold any surprises for you."

"In that assertion Mr. Consul, with all respect, you are in error. Amongst all humans, and even non-humans, you are a phenomenal, living anomaly of vast potential…"

"Ambassador that is a remarkable statement."

"We are not given to hyperbole Mr. Consul."

"Please tell me more Ambassador."

"Mr. Consul we would ask you to abate your curiosity and permit us to impart this to you in our own manner, at our own pace, in our own time."

Phil thought for a time.

"Yes Ambassador, I certainly will. If you will do me one service please."

"Yes Consul?"

"Please call me simply Phil; and if you permit I will address you as Qasi."

"Agreed…Philip."

"Thank you…Qasi. I believe we will have adequate time to discuss this matter."

"Indeed we shall. Twenty-seven solar years."

They spoke for hours on every conceivable topic. Phil had so many questions they nearly tumbled from his lips. Qasi slowly, precisely and patiently answered every question. Phil was consummately certain he was hearing nothing but the complete truth and total candor. In a short time he sensed an exceptionally strong friendship bonding them. Qasi was a remarkable being. The QAVL were an extraordinary race.

Phil: "I have more questions than you can imagine Qasi."
 "We are pleased to hear this, and will answer all questions we can and may. With respect though Philip, we imagine that we imagine more than you would ever imagine."
 Phil laughed quietly and smiled warmly at the red light. *This is not simply humor. Or hubris. This is truth. An entity hundreds of times more intelligent. Ancient beyond belief.*
 "Okay. First question. Of all the criteria I am sure you can impose on any given specie, why *Kosmas*?"
 "Why *Kosmas* Phil? Why does the language exist?"
 "No. No. What I mean is: Why is *Kosmas* the *only* criteria for 'membership' to the community of *Kentrikos*?"
 "Ah. We understand.
 The manifestation of *Kosmas* is an irrefutable accession, demonstrating a race has achieved a certain level of maturity…with all that implies. Its achievement is clear-cut. In Terran terms, the subject race develops the ability to store, process and forward information directly from the molecular composition of their own cellular material. Ingrams if you will. To accomplish this, advanced development of Spindle neurons in humans is required. Only certain terran species possess such neurons. Humans, great apes, humpback whales, fin whales, killer whales, sperm whales and in African and Indian elephants. The simply presence of such cells in the brain's morphology is not sufficient. The Spindles must MGL information from all extant sources, including sub-atomic. *Kosmas* is a litmus test for *Coming of Age*. Spiritual and corporeal. Millions of sapient specie in the universe never achieve *Kosmas*."
 "You mean they require an inordinate amount of time to acquire the language."
 "We mean they perish long before they come of age."
 "*Come of age*. As in an anthropological *Rite of Passage*?"
 "Ah no Philip. No. *Kosmas* is a threshold event. Once crossed, the race is ever more advanced, evolved beyond any point of regression. Truly, a *Coming of Age*.

As concerns *Rite of Passage,* humankind will face its *Rite of Passage* far in the distant future."

"Can you clarify please?"

"We explain what we may. We define *Coming of Age* as a passage. We define *Rite of Passage* as a test. More than that? We may not say."

"I see...I suppose. May I ask your definition of what exactly forms *Kosmas*?"

"Certainly. *Kosmas* is the codification of cosmological constituents resident sub-atomically in all matter in the universe. It was forged into all matter as part of the titanic chain reaction that constitutes the big bang itself. In doing so it would seem that the ballistics, speed and trajectory of every particle was set as part of that same event. This leads one to logically imply that the movement and interaction of all matter is predetermined *ap infinitas*. Therefore free will itself may be essentially an illusion. Non-existent. This we submit to intensive syllogistic analysis, calculation and Qvir."

"Qvir?"

"That would be defined as..." Qasi became silent. "...as thought-breathing."

"I have no idea what that means Qasi."

"We'll work on that Philip."

After a time Phil spoke.

"Existence itself."

"Yes. And more."

"Are you simplifying this for me Qasi?"

"Yes. We are."

"How much?"

"Well Philip. We suppose we are engaging in metaphor."

"Metaphor. You ah, are telling me allegorical stories which portray the science involved, so that I may understand the concepts."

"Excellent assessment. We are making no attempt whatsoever to factually depict the physics, or mathematics, or Qvir at work here. We trust you do not find this offensive?"

"Oh no. No. Not at all. Let's get back to this *ap infinitas* thing. I believe the colossal number of variables, particles bumping into each other, pulling each other and even nullifying each other over billions of eons would render such a thing absurdly improbable, if not abjectly impossible."

"You are referring to chaos. By your definition, chaos exists when you are simply unable to model and predict the behavior of all relative variables. A prosaic example is weather prediction. First. All variables are relative, related and germane. Second. Such variables can be processed in a controlled manner. Third. Chaos consists of far more than just a plethora of variables. Fourth. Chaos by your definition does not exist."

"So *Kosmas* would be defined as....?"

"...all the information requisite to a description of existence. These are integral to *Kosmas*. It is incumbent on the creature using *Kosmas* as a *cogitabundus instrumentum* – a thinking tool – to plumb the depths of the language, the model, and the cosmos. Such *instrumentum* can be applied superficially or in profound analysis."

"Then the only comprehensive definition of the universe is the universe itself?"

"Goodness no. Creation is far more efficient. And the definition is far more portable. As we earlier stipulated, *Kosmas* exists in every particle in the universe. You carry a near infinite number of definitions within your own corpus."

"So *Kosmas* is a blueprint of the universe."

"No. If anything *Kosmas* is a template for the universe. The very first sub-atomic particle emerged and all subsequent matter was created from that pattern during the event you term the Big Bang."

"Amazing."

"Far less amazing than the event itself Philip."

"Do you have any concept of the nature of the universe *prior* to the Big Bang?"

"Some member races concentrate on that problem. Some of them are amongst the most gifted in the cosmos. To some degree they have progressed. Many of their findings exceed the grasp of the QAVL. It is our tradition to avoid speculation of any type. Instead we put forth theorem, axiom, postulates, hypothesis, Qvir and such, within the context of rigorous scientific method."

Qasi: "We have a question for you Philip."

"Certainly."

"Actually two questions."

"Okay."

"First question. Are you aware – and if so can you explain – humans beyond the bounds of this island appear to be aware of you? Not only are they aware of you, they often attempt to seriously harm you. They appear to be confident that your response will always be confined to defensive actions... benign if possible. We suspect this emboldens them. How do they know this?"

"To some degree I believe this amounts to nothing more than astute tactics.

And of course the rule of law governs the degree and nature of our retaliation."

"Law. I see. Human law. Yes. We are sure you are correct."

"Qasi, your response would appear to reflect disapprobation with human law."

"Consider this Philip. A developing race invests extensive thought, work and blood formulating a *fundamental* set of behavioral axioms. You will note we emphasize fundamental. Because they are fundamental. Basic. By their nature they should be exceptionally static. Subject to little if any change as the race evolves – unless the axioms are flawed. Right versus wrong. Good versus evil. Civilized versus uncivilized. Truth versus mendacity. Just versus injustice. These are basic human values. Some are even universal. They then assemble these axiom into a coherent, cohesive set of laws. Normally something worthy is produced. Something of quality, even nobility. Heedless of extraneous dogma, a code to live by in harmony."

"Qasi I appreciate your thoughts. Many are well taken. I do suspect that perhaps you are overlooking the diverse purposes we find for laws…"

"Another grievous error, compounded by greed and subterfuge."

"Yes, well, shall we return to the subject at hand?"

"Indeed. We were discussing why your foes are so emboldened. You conjected that this was in part attributable to astute tactics and in part to rule of law, however dubious they may be."

"Right. Exceeding that, I honestly do not know the cause. I've considered this. I must say I find it inexplicable and frightening."

A lengthy pause descended.

"Philip I say this in friendship. We must strive to communicate in total candor."

"I agree Qasi. Why do you raise this subject?"

"We are alike in many respects. One aspect is fear. We do not feel fear in the conventional sense. Neither you."

*This meeting seems to be losing its edge. I must choose my words with more precision.*

Phil sighed. "Oh I see. Please forgive. When I say I find it frightening, I do not mean I *am* frightened. Perhaps a better term is I find it mysterious. I will try to be more precise in my usage of words. *Kosmas* is still new to me. Please bear with me in these early days."

"We shall. With pleasure. Second question. This one is far more… *mysterious*." *Did he hear a smile in Qasi's voice?*

"After long and close observation we inescapably conclude that you are a catalyst of temporal progression. Even anomalous progression. You provoke change. Often change that vaults the advance of syllogisms integral to logical synthesis. Surrounding you, things happen much faster, and often before their logical sequence. Many progression events manifest themselves of which you are totally unaware. And yet, you are the trigger. In all our travels. In all our experience. In all our *imaginings*. You are unique. An anomaly. Beyond our command of augur."

"That is an interesting term. Beyond your command of augur. You can plumb the future?"

"Plumb the future. We see you already select your terms with greater care. The term 'plumb' describes nothing. Unless of course you are suggesting we attach Pb82 to piece of string and cast it from extant reality into some other reality?"

"Pb82?"

"Human notation designating the atomic number of lead. Precise."

"Yes of course. Sorry. I will try again. You can *perceive* the future?"

Digital laughter. Somehow it sounded discreet, polite and friendly. "It is our turn to apologize. We shall select our words with greater care as well. The QAVL cannot perceive the future. To our knowledge no creature in the universe is capable of such a feat."

"How about the past?"

"That *is* admittedly different; and fascinating. It is a topic we should explore. We suggest *per contra* we pursue this aboard *Gauntlet*."

"As you wish Qasi. We have quite enough on our plate now as it is."

"Then I will continue. When I stipulated 'our command of augur' I intended exactly that. We are quite capable of applying the amalgam of known information and extrapolating the next logical event. This we accomplish with near perfect accuracy. There is no prescience involved in the process. Nothing superseding natural law."

"I see. This is the source of your concern. My apparent ability to act as a catalyst of anomalous events defeats your ability to calculate future events."

Qasi suddenly sounded excited. "Yes. Exactly. You comprehend the conundrum. Your father. Dr. Webber. He was a formidable scientist. Original, courageous and bold. Perhaps even bolder than you suspect."

"That's an interesting statement Qasi."

"By intent Philip. We are attempting to capture your interest."

"You are succeeding."

"Excellent. In trying to understand you, we carefully reviewed the records that document your genesis. Both sets. Dr. Webber was a faithful chronicler."

"Two sets of records?"

"Correct. And for good reasons. We witnessed Dr. Webber's first revelation to you regarding your birth and subsequent rearing. We were intrigued that Dr. Webber did not inform you then of the two sets of records. Nothing dark here by the way. Dr. Webber was acting quite responsibly, as always. If you recall that occasion…"

"At the airfield. We were waiting for a flight to Corsica. This was just after an attack."

"Correct. As we were saying, you will recall from that meeting Dr. Webber informed you there were many other facets of your life that he was not revealing for various reasons. Generally he preferred you discover them for yourself and we think we understand his rationale. In any event, for the purposes of our discussion today, suffice to say that we suspect this may have a substantive bearing on your unusual talents."

"I would like to pursue this."

"Agreed Philip. It will help when you have had time to study our transmissions. Returning to our question. We cannot detect or interpret the mechanism at work here. This has considerable import for us. Can you explain this phenomenon?"

"No. I cannot."

Phil: "I have a question regarding your DOCUMENT."

"You refer to this as a DOCUMENT. Its name is Qtre."

"It has a name? Is it a living entity?"

"You speak *Kosmas* now Philip. A wondrous accomplishment. Sadly, this does not constitute a dehiscent of all knowledge of the QAVL, or *Kentrikos*. The nature of Qtre lies far beyond the realm of learning we can commonly share. I am sorry Philip."

"I see. Surely we can discuss the contents as currently expressed by *Qtre*?"

"Most certainly. That is its purpose."

"Good. Qtre outlines the fallacious nature of human trade."

"Yes."

"But you do not discuss money."

"Quite right. Money. A useful innovation. The nature of QAVL society never provoked invention of such an instrument. However, we have observed similar contrivances on many worlds. Universally it acts as a surrogate for goods and services. Humans profoundly extend the concept. The human facet of far greater import appears deceptively simple: Money is Energy

We find that quite elegant. Humans have actually synthesized concentrated energy. A stunning achievement. It is efficient. It can be easily transported and stored indefinitely. It can be digitalized. Humans should be justifiably proud, were it not for one tragic flaw, human in nature."

"What would that be Qasi?"

"For money to be of enduring value, trust is mandatory. Your treatment of money defeats trust. As with so many human constructs. Your nature prods you to build. Then your nature drives you to destroy."

"I believe I understand, at least partly, why money is a flawed concept in human verisimilitude."

"Do you? We find that interesting. Please explain."

"You were pleased with the human perspective on money. Money is Energy?"

"Yes?"

"I believe we have corrupted the concept into something else altogether."

"What would that be Philip?"

"Money is Power."

Phil: "How many races inhabit *Kosmas Kentrikos?*"

"We have no exact idea Philip. Certainly tens of tens of thousands at any time. We haven't been there in roughly four million years. Races constantly come and go; and we enjoy no cosmic renown as census takers."

"How alien do you suppose *Kosmas Kentrikos* will be for the crew of *Gauntlet?*"

"They're a hardy lot. You've trained them superbly to adjust to the unknown. Their control of fear is extraordinary. All the same, it will be…strange beyond imagining. You will be called upon to observe them carefully. Beware dementia. Unrestrained horror. Despair and foreboding. This phase will last for some time. Bearing in mind that races come and go, there are always new specie. At the same time, one learns to constantly adjust after a time."

"Bizarre creatures?"

"Bizarre exceeding terran comprehension. Your crew will seek homologous features and creatures and traits. Generally to no avail."

"Far advanced?"

"Each creature struggles for ascendency over its own provenance. There are infinite variations in these evolutive romps, some spanning colossal linear extents. There is the argument that when a species has effectively mastered natural competitors in its environment, it then must look inward for evolutive pressures."

Phil frowned. Dissonant skepticism playing across his features. "Are you saying we no longer evolve?"

"Certainly not Philip. Evolution is the most ineluctable law in animate creation. Random diversity, if it is indeed random, first induced by subatomic particles (humans term them cosmic rays), is driven by the universe itself. What you are pleased to refer to as genetic drift. Humans evolve, but they no longer fully benefit from natural selection. Variations which would have previously perished, now survive. This defeats congenital culling; and must be overcome to avoid stagnation. Even genetic entropy.

Advancement is the measure from a creature's inception to the present, gauged by the achievements and positive changes during that period. Achievements most often relate to survival and the acquisition of its requisite information. These of course, are based on the nature of the specie and its environment – and therefore subjective in universal terms. Hence, of necessity the only objective measure of advancement is mastery of *Kosmas*."

"Whew! That was a mouthful. You are saying that all *Kentrikos* inhabitants are considered equally advanced?"

"Exact."

"There are no beings we would deem super intelligent?"

"We suppose by terran standards yes. Although we are dubious you would ever become fully aware of it. In fact there are members advanced eons beyond the QAVL. However, on *Kosmas Kentrikos* no such judgments are made. Intelligence, appearance and genesis are irrelevant. Only the ability to communicate. To do the work. To contribute."

"Please tell me about the work."

"Sample. Measure. Compare. Analyze. Store. An endless loop. A nearly eternal cycle."

"It goes well?"

"Yes. At an incredible rate. Nonetheless too slowly."

"Why?"

"We undertake the admensuration of infinity."

Phil: "I notice you don't employ profanity."

"True."

"Do you disapprove?"

"No. Quite the opposite in fact. We find human profanity colorful and even humorous. We find it vulgar when it denigrates peoples and concepts worthy of respect. Beyond that, we find it spices your communications. Accelerates it. Profanity adds an emphasis no other form provides. It is colorful and in some respects liberating. It is certainly entertaining. We heartily approve."

"Then why the hell don't you use it?"

"We perceive your witticism. Nicely done. Humor we have mastered. Profanity no. We simply do not do it well. For example what does 'the hell' really mean? Urgency? Irony? Anger? Frustration? Where something might be located in a mythical place of retribution? What? We cannot fathom the meaning from the context; and the iteration itself has no logic. No real meaning.

As far as we are able to determine profanity equals an exclamation mark. You see the problem?"

"Yes. I think I do."

"We have studied you and your evolving communications for over one-hundred millennia. Our knowledge of your languages is immeasurably superior to your own. Our mastery of your language however is greatly inferior. Complicating our studies is the fact that not every terran language employs profanity. We find one language to be particularly adept at profanity however."

"Really. What language?"

"English. We find no other language so richly embellishes itself with gratuitous imprecation. Not long ago one of our observers was in Belgium, visiting an industrial complex that had recently been acquired by an American corporation. We continuously pursue our studies in what you term 'economics'. The Belgian gentlemen being observed was quite seriously questioning a colleague why his new American patron was constantly talking about the sun and the beach. The climate of Belgium is not overly conducive to coastal recreation. After a time our observer discovered the American was using the term 'son of a bitch.' One human confused by another."

Phil grinned. "You don't find such language vulgar?"

"We find any speech or expression which is inherently slothful or repetitive tedious and vulgar. Whenever intelligence is supplanted by brutish bombast we are repelled."

<u>Phil</u>: Do you believe that Oneirions will find a method of imparting *Kosmas* to antecedent humans?

"No. Sad news we know. You are a true anomaly. Regarding humanity at large however, the *Kosmas* treatment would be tantamount to undertaking the adaptation of a chimpanzee's brain to a praying mantis. Physiologically it is simply not congruent."

<u>Phil</u>: "You have been here two million years. You've devoted all that time in study of Earth? I would go mad."

"As would we. Each of us pursues thousands of other interests and tasks at the same time. We can work anywhere. You would not relate to the nature of much of our work. Work is the essence of our existence."

"Do QAVL go mad?"

"You are alluding to mental illness? Insanity? Extreme psychosis?"

"Yes."

"Aberrations arise from time to time. Such occurrences are rare. Naturally they are not caused by chemical imbalances, structural damage, or what you might term hysterical trauma. Neither are they attributable to inheritance, or sanguinity. Living as a triad greatly strengthens our psyche. Only external forces can damage our psyche so as to occasion madness."

"What sort of forces?"

"Injudiciously extended proximity to a Neutron Star, a Supernovae, Gamma Ray Bursts, Infrared Dwarfs. Those sorts of damaging influences. We only discovered we were subject to injury when we set forth from Qruxin. We term these phenomena Neutron Transmitters, or Protonic Sources."

"I would imagine they could be fatal even to the QAVL?"

"Tragically no…especially for early QAVLian cosmic expeditions. Neutron Sources can generate tidal forces capable of ripping a QAVL triad apart. Imagine an immortal mind hideously deformed, writhing eternally, and suffering unspeakable agony alone in the emptiness of space. After eons we continue to seek them."

"My God. How many suffer this way? Can they be cured?"

"They are easily cured, but they are immensely difficult to locate. Several thousand QAVL remain missing to this day. From time to time we locate a few, adrift in space, and we restore them. An uplifting experience. The QAVL curative is far easier than similar human therapy. More fundamental. More rudimental. Like straightening a dented fender on a car. You must understand the workings of our minds are as palpable to QAVL as a broken arm to humans. Sadly we are not capable of self-repair being unable to self-manipulate. We require ministration from fellow QAVL. In the absence of such aid we suffer eternally in space."

"QAVL cannot die, even under such circumstance? You cannot suicide?"

"No. We wouldn't know how. As we stated, we are incapable of such therapy. Nor would it ever occur to us."

Phil: "You must be sickened by the corruption and violence you witness on this planet."

"Indeed we are. In this appalling respect, after three point five billion years of evolution we credit you as little more than savages. Humans achieve at a phenomenal pace. You evolve nearly instantly on a cosmic scale. Would that your maturation kept apace. Tragic. *Kosmas* may be your redemption. We hope you are not offended."

"We have a saying Qasi 'The truth hurts.'"

"We know little of pain. Yet what we observe here does pain us."

"I am saddened Qasi."

"As are we Philip. Know that you are entering what we term the 'Crimson' Era."

"The 'Crimson Era'. Sounds dangerous."

"It is. It is deadly. At breathtaking speed it can catalyze into an Extinction Event. The end of the human race. The logical denouement of the evolution of nearly all specie."

"Please explain."

"Our extrapolations decisively conclude humans will have developed the fundamental skills needed to survive within four thousand solar years. In the intervening period the probability that your race will die is alarmingly high."

"Die from what?"

"Self-destruction. War, misadventure, things like that. Or natural causes. Plague, volcanism, famine, pestilence, climatic vicissitudes. What you might term Biblical calamities."

"No cosmic cataclysm? Gamma Ray Bursts, solar anomalies, even non-terran microbes?"

"Not for the next four thousand years."

"And after four thousand years?"

"In all likelihood you should be equipped to survive yourselves and your own purlieus, and take your place as a space faring specie."

"And to survive the next four thousand years?"

"Stop killing yourselves and each other. Stop breeding like vermin. Subdue your anachronistic religious zealotry. Attenuate bloated, cannibalistic political and economic systems. Geld your pernicious politicians. Adopt a homogenous worldwide management system. Cease burdening simple good management with bellicose chauvinism. Repudiate your repulsive illusions of power and wealth. Consolidate your priorities into science, art, philosophy and quality of life."

"That's a tall order Qasi."

Qasi's voice sounded almost sharp. "That's a small order Philip. Almost trivial. Survive. Simply survive. Enjoy life. The true test awaits you in the distant future. And *it* is *truly* dangerous."

Phil actually heard anger, or provocation, perhaps even contempt. Qasi made him feel like a petulant adolescent. "I...ah...I'm sorry Qasi...we must try to rise to this somehow."

A wooden silence descended between them, and wore on for long moments. This first meeting was not proving altogether facile; and Phil suspected this pause may have been calculated.

*QAVL thought processes are far too fleet to require this sort of interval in order to collect their thoughts.*

Qasi finally spoke. "No Philip. *We* are sorry. This is not your fault. Not at all. You confront the burden faced by all hadronics. In particular carbonaceous hadronics. You inherited a plethora of ancient instincts. Some date back hundreds of millions of years. Others as recent as two thousand years.

Whatever their vintage, you labor with baggage checked in your name continuously for over four hundred thousand millennia. It is your heritage that drives you to behave as you do. Nothing is more difficult to overcome."

"Excuse me Qasi, but I'm not sure I'm following you."

"I see. Perhaps a few examples will help:

In the Devonian Period of your Paleozoic Era, you became killers. Those murderous seas fostered a savage battle to survive and adapt that continues today with undiminished ferocity.

In the Silurian Period of the Paleozoic you learned war. The struggle for supremacy of your hive.

In the Triassic Period of the Mesozoic Era the first mammals taught your females to withhold sex consistent with their menstrual rhythms. This heralded your inhibitions and puritanical inclinations. All manner of deviations and even psychosis arose from that passionless pit.

In the Cretaceous Period of the Mesozoic you learned your love of alcohol from the ancient Tree-Shrew, an addition which will haunt man until you apply a genetic solution.

In the Jurassic Period you learned the herd instinct. To this day it girds your politicians with slavish, adoring proselyte to fan their egos and feed their power.

In the Quaternary Period of the Cenozoic Era you learned weapons and Chauvinized the herd instinct acquired during the Jurassic.

During your Bronze Age, you invented religion, which plagues you still, and goads you towards self-destruction.

Prior to that, the Stone Age..."

"Thank you Qasi. I get the picture. These ills are visited upon us by our genes, our cultures and history, even racial memory if you're a Jungian. Such things are nearly insurmountable in many respects. How did the QAVL overcome your heritage.?"

"The day we achieved immortality coincides exactly with...."

"*'The day'* you achieved immortality?"

"Yes. A wonderful memory..."

"You *remember* it?"

"We remember the exact day, hour, second, nano-second."

"My God Qasi, you literally take my breath away. Please proceed."

"Yes. As we were saying, when we achieved immortality, we learned how to manipulate and adjust our 'genes' as you call them. To us they are as clear as a glass marble in an aquarium. On that same day we learned to live forever. We also learned how to cast off archaic instincts and beliefs. We remember everything, we are burdened by nothing. We purge dysfunctional memories and 'junk' genetic information. We are truly self-purging."

"So. Despite the fact you forget nothing, you eliminate memories, you adjust the nature of your being and you've been doing this for a few million years."

"Yes."

"I would then submit you are not immortal."

"Pardon?"

"You are not the same being who remembers the day, hour, second and nano-second you achieved immortality. You've reinvented yourselves hundreds of millions of times. Little if any of the original Qasi still exist; and you would never recognize this, or even be remotely conscious of it."

Qasi's speaker burst into a curious *mlk-mlk-mlk* sound. "Clever Philip. However, you overlook the most basic aspect of the QAVL, or any sentient non-hadronic being for that matter. We refer to it as the Qntok. It evolved long before The Remembering. Thus we are uncertain how it developed. We can see it. We cannot reshape it. It is our essence. That part of us that never changes. Never dies. Our driving life force."

"Do you suppose humans could ever evolve such a thing? Can hadronics achieve what you've achieved?"

"Absolutely. You already have in part. For now however, we would prefer to avoid that topic."

"As you wish Qasi. Thank you."

An efflorescence of wonder was growing in Phil's mind.

Qasi: "Philip, we assume you are aware you are in great peril?"

"Me? I am personally at risk?

"Yes. You and Oneiro."

"Really?" Phil allowed incredulity to filter through his voice.

"We are certain. Horrific forces are coalescing all about you. At one time you engaged in terrible acts to defend this island. They cost you dearly. Yet you believed they were necessary acts that protected Oneiro. You believed your actions were successful. You erred on both points. Yet your courage was ennobling. Your incentive irreproachable. Would that it were finished."

"What do you suggest I do?"

"Defend Oneiro yet again."

"Fine. Can you provide some insight? The nature of the threat?"

"We will provide what we can. Probability indicates the threat comes from within."

"Some sort of an agent, a provocateur? That type of thing?"

"That is a possibility we suppose. However, our indicators point to something more benign. Closer. It could even be you Philip, or someone close to you."

"How do you arrive at such conclusions?"

"We use a straightforward process. Two steps. We produce constructs of relevant variables and play out scenarios. You prognosticate in the same manner. The second step is simply to detect significant variances. As you know this is accomplished by sub-atomic interrogation seeking inconsistencies in the flux pattern of *Kosmas*. You possess this same skill, as you know."

"And that yields a result stipulating there is a danger from within, close, possibly connected with me?"

"Correct."

"That's it?"

"That's it."

Phil: "Do you think you are missing the experience of tasting food?"

"Do you think you are missing the taste of light?"

"But we have so many senses you do not."

"And we have dozens more you do not."

"Do you find Earth beautiful?"

"Oh yes. We left Qruxin long ago and learned of great natural beauty amongst the stars. A wondrous experience. Here on Earth we find water most enchanting. Your extravagant landscapes are familiar to us. Qruxin has terran that staggers the mind. But the colors and life of Earth beggar the senses. It is unfortunate humans can perceive so few."

Phil: I suppose you are aware of the continuous bombardment of UFO sightings, alien abductions, artifacts and extraordinary claims made by humans all over the world?

"Certainly."

"Some are interesting I think."

"Many are quite interesting Philip."

"Any truth to them?"

"No. None whatsoever. We have been monitoring this planet since before man. Our technology is such that no being could intrude on Terran space without our detection. Not one; and most certainly not the thousands laid claim to.

In any event the idea is ludicrous. That a race would hazard the long voyage to Earth only to ineptly mask their presence? For what reason? To crossbreed with you (*mlk-mlk-mlk-mlk-mlk* [QAVL laughter])? Conquest? Study...?"

"Well Qasi, you came to study us."

"True. Within the context of *Kentrikos* we are charged with such activity. Directed, methodical field research. Such research is conducted at millions of sites throughout the galaxy. However, we are solely observers. Our presence could never be detected without our assent."

"Certainly races may unilaterally undertake such research in the absence of sanction by *Kentrikos*?"

"Yes. And they do. But they do not engage in bumbling through your skies, or floating into your bedrooms. You would term them anthropologist, and they observe non-obtrusively, consistent with scientific method."

"What would prevent them from contacting us?"

"Nothing. Although such contact is near universally limited to *Kosmas* enabled specie."

"Would you or any element of *Kentrikos* take action to prevent such contact?"

"That would be unthinkable."

"Could a non-*Kosmas* speaking race visit Earth?"

"That is possible. Remote. But possible. Drawing from an infinite population, any circumstance must be conceivable."

"Has this ever occurred on other sites?"

"No QAVL, or any being associated with *Kentrikos* has witnessed any interaction of this nature. Naturally our information is not fully current or cosmic in scope, nor do we have recourse to the remote accession of universal exploration. Suffice to say in our experience they would constitute a species utterly bizarre by any measure of our understanding. Interstellar capability and non-*Kentrikos* enablement would be a novel combination."

"Why this is fascinating. You imply that *Kentrikos* is some sort of mystical key to the universe."

"That Philip is a topic demanding more attention than we have available today."

"I understand. Would you take action to protect a specie from a belligerent intruder?"

"This has never occurred."

"As I have been advised. However, the question stands."

"Speaking only for the QAVL, we suspect we would take noninvasive measures to prevent such violence. Assuming we had the capacity to do so."

"Qasi I appreciate your candor. I hope I have not offended."

"QaDyme you do not possess the attributes requisite to offend."

"You are very kind Qasi."

Phil: "Are you aware of my burgeoning underwater capabilities?"

"Indeed. Impressive. A wonderful talent. You are becoming Earth's first self-aware amphibian, and a great deal more. You are the only sentient ever to witness the QAVL Mating. Credit your unique puissance."

Phil was stunned. He nearly whispered "My God. You knew I was there?"

"We always know where you are Philip."

"I'm sorry. Please forgive me. I had no idea at the time. I had no intention of witnessing The Mating."

"It was not your fault. No need for apology. If anything, it was our fault. We underestimated your abilities. That will not happen again."

"Qasi, the Mating it was…quite moving. Beautiful beyond description."

"Thank you Philip."

Phil: "Do you find human procreation beautiful?"

"We find it recklessly random and inefficient. It may destroy you yet. Your criteria for procreation are about as discerning as *Scarabaeidae Coleoptera* – the Dung Beetle. In fact human selection is not as discriminating. How you can abdicate a function so critical to the future of your species to blind chance, or worse, physiologically stimulated hormones, is a source of concern and mystery. An appalling anachronism for a race that aspires to advance.

In many respects most humans continue to strut about, tail-feathers erect, beating their chests and butting heads with adversarial males. Enlightened humans are well aware you have graduated well beyond instinctive natural selection. Evidence Oneiro. You should be proud of your work in this island."

"Please bear in mind Qasi that on Oneiro we do not practice genetic selection. Quite the opposite in fact. We practice genetic integration. We merge all human genotypes into a universal human genome."

"Your point is well taken Philip. Please consider though, in reality you practice the corollary of selection. You will discover this a most formidable form of selection in and of itself.

On the other hand, human sexuality appears to be       enjoyable…perhaps too  enjoyable. Perhaps obsessive. Your concept of lust is delightful. But it obscures objectivity. Therefore judgment. This can lead to excess and vulgarity, even danger. However, in some respects it is an expression of affection and intimacy. We suspect humans would do well to vent their lust, supplanting what you term love. And in particular, abandon ownership."

"What sort of ownership?"

"Mating. Bonding. What you generally term as wedlock. The term *lock* is most apropos."

"But you bond for life. And in your case that is an inconceivably long time."

"True. However, QAVLian bonding produces a composite, autonomous being."

"So now we confront four distinct elements. Sex. Love. Procreation. Connubiality."

"Correct."

"And you indulge in sex with prodigious frequency."

"True. It is a source of great enjoyment for us. At times we engage in sex almost continuously. At rare times to the exclusion of all else."

"So in fact, you are actually engaging in masturbation."

Qasi 'laughed', good naturedly for a few seconds. "I suppose from a human perspective you are quite right. Understandably you lack insight into the nature of composite creatures. Members of the triad are not lost in the triad. They are merged into the triad. In any event, humans engage in masturbation as well."

"Yes. And I imagine we enjoy it as much as you. Although, as with most sexual activities, we burden ourselves with embarrassment and guilt."

"Humans should attempt to divorce themselves from the guilt and priggishness humans lamentably link to sex. In fact you should revel in lust. Immerse yourselves in it. Saturate yourselves with concupiscent, fleshy carnal hedonism. You would be happier, healthier and most of all, less aggressive. Sadly humans equate sex with loss of innocence. If only they could realize it is through joyful, unbridled congress that innocence is found and renewed."

"Oneirions enjoy sex immensely. We also appreciate its humorous aspects. As with many such activities involving our bodies. And you believe we should abandon *love*?"

"No. We believe you should cease linking love to sex. Sex is for reproduction and fun and everyone. Totally non-exclusive. Love is also for everyone and everything. But completely unrelated. You shouldn't hoard love within a familial cluster. Neither sex. Humankind should attempt to bond as a specie."

"How would you suggest we go about that?"

"First. Elevate love."

"What does that mean?"

"It means that you presently debase love. Cheapen it. Fashion it into a plethora of tawdry guises. It permeates the economics of your culture. In style, music, entertainment in a hundred diverse forms – love comprises the overwhelming theme – to the exclusion of a thousand worthy tenets. *Ad nauseam.* On the one hand, you covet love. Withhold it from all but an intimate few. Quite unwisely at times in fact.

On the other hand, you disseminate a banal love indiscriminately and impersonally. Throughout your world. For diversion and wealth.

*Amitié* vended requites corruption. *Amitié* freely given emerges perennial.

This is not unique to planet Earth. You must learn the value of love, and the value of sex."

"I must admit, I know more of sex than I do love."

"Many humans know neither."

Qasi: "There is an elegant sexual reciprocity about your bodies."

"Fairly standard vertebrate physiology I should think."

"Really? Are you familiar with the family known to your paleontologist as *Xenacanthus*?"

"Mmm. *Xenacanthus*. Early sharks. 400 million years old. The Devonian I think."

"Actually the Silurian. Excellent nonetheless. You should be aware then those creatures quite literally invented vertebrate sex; and you will seldom witness a more ridiculously difficult and convoluted union in terran nature, or most other planets for that matter. Yet it persists until today. In contrast, human copulation nearly describes an elegant ballet."

"You observe a good deal of copulation do you?" smirked Phil, eyebrows raised.

Phil could hear the smile in his response. "Only insofar as our studies demand. Incidentally Philip, you needn't fear for your own privacy during such interludes."

"I appreciate that. Thank you."

"It seemed an appropriate approbation.

However Philip we overlook the most profound function of human sexuality."

"Reproduction?"

"No Philip. We accept that as a given. Consider a deeper need."

"And what would that be?"

"The placebotic simulation of fusion. The fusion of souls. The exultation of the QAVL, forever lost and impossible for humans. An ersatz, yet tender respite from the remorseless, icy solitude humans endure every moment of your fleeting lives."

Phil spoke softly. Almost to himself. "*Placēbō*. The rite of Vespers of the Office of the Dead."

"In this context the form is placebo." corrected Qasi "An inert medication administered as a pacifier."

"Yes, I know. I know." He cleared his throat and continued. "So when a human declares they are *horny* they are really..."

"...lonely Philip. They are tragically lonely."

Qasi: "Do you object to your continued personal monitor? You have our assurance that such attentions are beneficial to your interests and the peoples of Earth."

"I have no doubt, or objection. My actions with regard to the QAVL are as much a concern of the QAVL as they are mine and humanity. I know you are acting openly and in good faith. For the best of reasons. I have no secrets from the QAVL. I foresee no secrets from the QAVL."

"You are very kind. Your trust shall not go wanting. Would you care to block any specific periods from our attentions?"

Phil thought for a moment.

"How's this. If I say 'Qa-sout' QAVL will leave me until I say "Qa-sin'."

"Yes. Certainly. You have our personal guarantee. We are issuing an alert as we speak. You *are* aware neither Qa-sout, nor Qa-sin are words?"

"That's the beauty of it."

"Ah. We see."

Phil: "Do the QAVL seek perfection?"

"The QAVL seek knowledge and joy."

"Yes. But perfection?"

"Of course not."

"Aah. Can you explain?"

"Perfection exists only in subjective relativity. Therefore it does not exist. Were it to exist it would invite stagnation…entropy…the ultimate end of things."

"Then the universe itself may be perfect."

"Excellent QaDyme. Excellent. The universe. *The supreme singularity.* The sole, non-subjective definition of perfection it is and ever shall be. *Sui generis.* Unique. Non-repeatable. Perfection and imperfection exist only in contrast with kindred reality."

"…so assuming I duplicate a perfect object, then both will be imperfect, or perfect?"

"If you'll forgive Philip, the answer is self-evident."

"Yes?"

"*Replicate*, not *duplicate*. Therefore only the original is perfect. The replicate is imperfect by the standard of the original. However, you are trivializing an elegant concept."

"Why *replicate*?"

"Because Philip, duplication would demand an object exist in equilibrium. Form, potential, mass. These quantities do not exist in the absence of change. Else they acquiesce to entropy; and ultimately surrender to chaos. The end of things."

"So *the end of things* is perfection?"

"That too."

Qasi: "We have a small gift for you Philip. Nick had it specially constructed according to our specification. You'll find it on your desk in a blue box."

Philip found the box. "A wristwatch?"

"Hardly. It is a wrist-worn QAVL DIT (Digital Interface Transceiver). We may speak at any time now."

"Thank you Qasi. I believe this will be useful to us both."

"As do we Philip."

"Good night Qasi."

"Good night QaDyme. We withdraw now, having passed a most enjoyable day."

Although Phil was certain it was only his imagination, he felt the air pressure in the room drop imperceptibly. The temperature seemed to cool, and he was touched with a fleeting sense of loss and solitude. A *presence* was suddenly wanting. He would experience these stirrings with every departure of Qasi. For the rest of his life.

*QaDyme. Companion of the QAVL.* He considered the sobriquet.

In his many travels he had been called Consul, Counselor, Captain, Skipper, Philip-san, Comrade, Proprietor, Master, brother, son, Bwana, Sahib, Tuan, Gringo, Paladin and more. Some appellations met with his appreciation and approval, others not so much. Either way they had each conveyed a definite feeling. A type of thrill that validated his growing experience of life among men on Earth. An achievement. A rite of passage. Sometimes even a blood rite. But no title had ever moved Phil as profoundly as QaDyme.

It was nearly 2200 when they finally broke up. There were no follow-on meetings scheduled. No promises to get together again. They knew they would henceforth be in near constant communications. By any conventional measure, this first historic meeting was wildly successful.

Phil thought the experience would be exhausting. Instead he was uplifted and inspired. He could have talked for hours more. But first contact was best kept brief. In this respect they were already somewhat amiss.

Phil was too charged to return home. Instead he stopped in the lobby bar where it all began years ago. The same friendly waiter in the same white shirt, black trousers and well shined shoes. "Good evening Mr. Carr. What can I get you this evening?"

"Pete" Phil smiled "do you suppose you can put together a triple Martini, straight up, dry, Beefeaters, with olives and a twist, and a few drops of Scotch?"

"Yes sir. Absolutely."

"Good. I'll take two."

"Celebrating are we sir?"

"Yes. Yes we most certainly are Pete. Buy yourself a drink as long as you're up...my tab."

"Thank you sir. I shall." Pete left straightaway to mix Phil's drinks and quickly returned.

"Thank you Pete." And Phil was alone.

Phil sighed and settled back in his chair. He looked up to the elegantly frescoed ceiling and down to the rare gold and brown marble. Everything still beautiful. Nothing had changed and everything had changed. He looked about the empty bar, smiled warmly and raised his glass to his new, ghostly entourage. "Cheers my friends."

# The Flesh and the Dandle

Phil arrived home at around 2230. He entered to find his residence unexpectedly quiet. No Edward, or anyone else for that matter. He strolled about the rooms, made himself a final drink, and wandered into the bedroom.

To his surprise Anne was reclined on a rumpled bed, naked, slightly bedraggled, with a glass of red wine in her hand and a rather languid, vacuous look to her eyes. She looked sleepy and in a stupor. Something akin to shell-shocked.

Phil leant down speaking softly. Studying her eyes. "Hi. Are you alright?"

Anne started as though suddenly awakened. "Aaah. Yeah. I'm okay." She quickly gathered herself. "I'm fine. Have you been meeting with Ambassador Qasi all this time?"

"Pretty much. I stopped in the lobby bar for a drink afterward and then came up."

"Tough day?"

"No. Just the opposite in fact. It was a wonderful experience. I suspect I'm going to get on quite well with Ambassador Qasi. I believe we're going to be fast friends. I think we need a new term…gentlenoumenon…an inaccessible, incorporeal being with the virtues of a gentleman, or gentlewoman, or gentlepeople…or something like that."

"I'm glad it went so well. What did you talk about?"

"Humans, QAVL, philosophy, the flavor of light, *Kosmas*, sex. You name it. How about you Anne. You look like you had a rough day."

Anne frowned, cocked her head and stared into space for a time. Then "Jesus Aiy can drink! And she can sail expertly, dive like a master and speargun like an assassin. Christ she can do anything. Anything…any damned thing she wants…"

"What do you mean?"

"Well. It's all a little hazy now. We had a long day-sail. We dived. And then we came up here, took showers and hit the Jacuzzi. Pouring down Champagne. We had a wonderful time. We laughed. Aiy has some wonderful stories; and for a change she wasn't playing at the investigative reporter. Anyway after the Jacuzzi I came in here to cool off. Aiy showered and came in…and she uh…I suppose the term is…seduced me.

It wasn't remotely forced, but she was aggressive. She was passionate, lustful. And she was gentle. After an hour or so I fell asleep; and when I woke up she was gone."

Phil was repressing an affectionate smile. He doubted Anne was amused by the incident, but neither was she seeking solace. "I don't know what to say. Uh, how did it happen?"

Anne thought for a moment. "She came into the bedroom from the shower. Damp and naked. Smelling of shampoo and soaps. She really is extraordinarily beautiful. The body of a pantheress. Sensational. I suppose I was vaguely aware of a certain tension all week. Aiy snuggled into my bed and began to slowly fondle her body...everywhere. Provocative. It was enthralling. She saw my fascination and that seemed to excite her even more. Suddenly she was doing these...things...for both of us. Her hands were everywhere. It was exciting. Arousing. It felt delicious. Then she moved on top of me and I totally lost myself in the pleasures. It was remarkable."

"Mmm, so it was good."

Anne looked at Phil quizzically for a moment. "Yes. Fantastic. I mean it. I never experienced anything like it. She is wonderfully skilled. Loving and caring. She was amazing. Gentle. I loved it. I climaxed, intensively, at least four times." She had a thoughtful look. "Does that trouble you?"

"Trouble me? It intrigues me. After all I ah, know you both intimately. But trouble me? No, I don't think so. Should it?"

"I suppose not. I guess I was expecting, or maybe anticipating jealousy. But that's childish and unworthy. I shouldn't discount the fact we're Oneirions."

In reality though, Anne was a lander by birth and background, so he nonchalantly asked "Your ah, first time with a woman?"

"Oh not really. But nothing. Nothing like this. Those were university days. We were just horny undergrads having fun experimenting."

"Would you do it again?"

Phil thought he saw the slightest hint of...defiance? Challenge? Something.

"With Aiy? Yes. Absolutely. Without hesitation. Eagerly. Wantonly. I'm ready right now."

"Don't be coy Anne. Tell me how you *really* feel."

Anne smiled diffidently, despite herself. Her first real smile of the evening.

"You know Phil..."

"Yes?"

"She's the first person I've really warmed to since I met you."

"You have feelings for her?"

"Yes. Yes I do. I haven't thought it through clearly yet. But I was driving at something altogether different."

"Yes?"

"Has it occurred to you she might join the *Gauntlet* expedition? It would make it easier for me and I think she could be a valuable member of the team."

"Anne for Christ's sake. Please tell me you haven't discussed this with Aiy."

"No, I have not."

"Thank God. We're teetering right on the razor's edge as it is."

"I know. Believe me I know. Although you know how quick she is. How perceptive…"

"Are you saying she's figured things out?" Phil's voice was slowly rising in volume and pitch.

"I'm saying she senses that something hugely important is transpiring here; and she's getting damned curious."

"Are you even remotely suspicious she um…seduced you to gain access to Oneirion secrets?"

"That's a damned hurtful thing to suggest Phil. I'm not some post-pubescent schoolgirl."

"Answer the question goddamnit."

"Okay. No. Hell no."

"Okay. Sorry. You'll appreciate it needed to be asked; and you'll have to admit things are moving pretty fast."

"They always do around you Phil."

"Mmm. The fact is I forbid you discuss the QAVL with…"

"*You forbid?*"

"You bet your ass *I forbid*. I'm still the Consul here, and that's an order."

"Yes, you are the Consul."

Phil took a deep breath, head back, eyes closed. "Let's just play this by ear shall we? Your points – believe it or not – are quite well taken.

Aiy could make the trip far easier for you. Perhaps me too. And with her literary talent we would benefit from a ship's historian/chronicler with an entirely fresh viewpoint. But what say we go just a little more slowly? Exercise some caution. Open mind, but for now, closed mouth. Okay? That's a request Anne. Not an order."

"It shall be done." She smiled, stood and walked to Phil. She kissed him deeply and began to remove his shirt. Phil was pleased and actually impressed that Anne could remain aroused after such a…full day.

Under his breath he whispered "Qa-sout."

Later in bed he was amazed. *My God! She's insatiable.*

Afterward Anne sighed in a tender caress, Phil's arm about her "Quite a day all in all."

A memorable day all round.

# Breakfast at Tiff-of-Threes

The next morning Aiy rang up to Phil's residence inviting them for breakfast.

"Good morning Phil. How are you?"

"I'm just fine Aiy. And you?"

"I'm great Phil. I bet you don't remember I make the best Eggs Benedict in this spiral arm of the galaxy…"

"You'd lose that bet."

"Good. So how about a Tequila Sunrise and some breakfast? My place. I'll cook. You can wash the bottles."

"That sounds wonderful Aiy. Wait one please…" Phil covered the phone and turned to Anne "Breakfast at Aiy's?"

Anne pursed her lips reviewing the day's schedule. "Sure. Why not?"

Anne and Phil found Aiy in her kitchen. A feminine white satin robe half closed and bare feet– nothing else. Conspicuously provocative.

She was busily padding about, making drinks, assembling her sauce, and cutting English muffins. After a lingering kiss and hug with Phil and Anne, each in turn "The staff kitchen downstairs promised to deliver Canadian bacon, eggs, lemons and some fresh herbs. Should be here any minute. Shall we have a drink while we wait?"

They moved to the sitting room. Aiy had already prepared an iced pitcher of drinks. Anne moved to an arm chair. Aiy sat suggestively close to Phil on the couch and crossed her legs. "Cheers!"

"Mmm. That's delicious Aiy."

"I'm glad you like it Anne. The secret's a few dashes of Orange Mandarin and Triple Sec, canned orange juice (no cartons, no bottles, no freshly squeezed, no pulp, ideally canned Donald Duck Orange Juice), easy on the grenadine and a triple-shot of old Tequila per each 6 oz of juice."

Aiy smiled at Phil and boldly ran her hand affectionately up and down Phil's thigh. "Ever heard of *creaming* Anne?"

Eyebrows raised "No, I don't believe so."

"I creamed Phil one time in ROTC."

Anne's eyebrows rose even higher.

"That wasn't too long before good 'ol *Chib-Erd* here decided to dump me to become a second Doctor Schweitzer, and then a bottom-feeding lawyer instead. Anyhow…he was asleep in his quarters one night, and I sneaked in and filled his hand with shaving cream. Then I used a feather to tickle his nose."

They all laughed. "Phil was mad as hell. Smothering and spitting shaving cream, he chased me all the way to the parade ground until he realized he was naked." More laughter. "He sprinted back to the barracks and found the whole platoon, males and females alike, in his room. Naturally he jumped for the bed…and they'd short-sheeted it." Aiy laughed again lightly with a reminiscent look in her eyes "Good old days…"

She suddenly shifted the conversation. "Did you know that Eggs Benedict was named after a Mr. Lemuel Benedict? He was a Wall Street stock broker. One day he staggered into the old Waldorf Hotel in 1894, desperately seeking a cure for a roaring hangover. Lemuel ordered buttered toast, poached eggs, crisp bacon and a 'hooker of hollandaise.' This delicious combination evolved into Eggs Benedict thanks to the Waldorf's maitre d'hôtel. He substituted bacon with ham and toast with English Muffins. I still use the original recipe. But I poach the eggs in heavy cream and butter instead of boiling water and vinegar; and I sprinkle it lightly with Portuguese Paprika and fresh chopped chives before serving, with just a dollop of Hollandaise."

With that came a knock at the door and Aiy excused herself. A few minutes later she re-entered with two fresh drinks and a saucer of mini-croissants. "They've delivered the groceries, so breakfast is comin' up. Meanwhile you can work on these."

When alone, Anne grinned at Phil "She had me going with that creamed business. My imagination was going some strange places until I realized she was talking about shaving cream. Clearly she knows how to push my buttons."

Phil grimaced. "That's a true story by the way. She was pulling pranks like that all the time. The platoon was crazy about her."

Anne cocked her head. "I thought I heard recrimination in her voice about medical school?"

"Could be I suppose."

From the kitchen "Anne?"

"Yes?"

"Mind coming in and helping with the sauce?"

"I'll be right there." Anne left for the kitchen and Phil went out on the terrace with his drink. From this perspective he could just see the entrance to Oneiro Harbor far below. They were bringing in the SAT-SAV. Apparently she had completed construction on Anastasios Island and probably her sea trials as well. She was still ugly, but the sea shrouded some of her ungainliness. Thinking Anne and Aiy would be interested in such a unique vessel, Phil returned to the kitchen.

He found Anne busily stirring the Hollandaise sauce. Aiy was preparing the poacher. Phil smiled and put his arms around both waists. "The only

SAT-SAV in the world is entering Oneiro Harbor. Care for a look? If so, we need to hurry."

They quickly turned the heat down and headed for the terrace. Aiy asked "What the hell is a SAT-SAV?"

Phil duly recited "Surface-All-Terran-Submersible-Amphibious-Vehicle. She'll be primarily used for marine research."

Aiy responded "Talking to the fishies?"

Phil cast her a sharp, wary glance, saying nothing.

On the terrace Aiy exclaimed "That's the most blunderous sea-craft I've ever seen. Nothing yar there."

Phil smiled. "Yeah, but she can do damn near anything except fly. She's also as rugged as a tank. Tougher in fact."

Anne asked "Can we visit it in the harbor?"

"I'll check with Charlie King. I wouldn't mind taking her out on a run myself."

Anne frowned "Charlie King?"

"He's the chief engineer who built her. I met him on Anastasios Isla…I met him in the assembly shed."

Aiy perked up immediately. "Anastasios what?"

Phil looked back at the sea. The SAT-SAV was just disappearing into the harbor. He glanced back indifferently "It's not important. What they call the dry dock."

Looking a little piqued Aiy said "I better get back to the kitchen. Breakfast in five minutes."

Phil and Anne returned to the sitting room to finish their drinks. A few minutes later Aiy stomped back into the sitting room "Alright. What's the deal here with the food? The bacon is a perfect cylinder. And I mean perfect. Flawless! And the eggs. The eggs! They come without shells. In little round plastic, re-usable cases. XXXL. Largest eggs I've ever seen. I wouldn't want to meet the chicken that laid those sons of bitches. And why take them out of their shells? Everything's different here. What the hell's going on?"

Phil's voice was calm and placating. A measured tediousness. "Well our packaging is pretty innovative, no breakage and all that, and our quality control is rigorous. So the resulting food is just totally uniform in size, shape, quality and taste. Not to mention health and nutrition. Probably the best food in the world, but nothing really unusual is…."

"Bullshit! Aside from this breakfast, I've been inspecting Oneirion food carefully and there's something quite unnatural about…Holy crap! Is this where all this extraneous new information is coming from? It keeps popping into my head. Where else could it come from but the…What sort of food *is* this goddamnit?"

Anne and Phil regarded her blankly, saying nothing; as though it were obvious she was slightly delusional.

"That's another thing. No one answers my questions. Neither of you two either. Everywhere I go I run into a velvet wall. There must be some mighty secrets abounding around here."

"Whoa. Steady on Aiy. You're going into overdrive. Calm down."

"Don't tell me to calm down. Try the truth for a change. I thought you wanted a feature article on Oneiro? You couldn't even tell me where that damned SAT-boat was built. I thought we were friends. More than friends."

Phil was shocked. Her voice was actually trembling. *Is this an act? If it is, she's very good.*

Phil's voice was placating. "Aiy you know Anne and I are both fond of you. We are your friends. You just caught us at an odd time. There's a lot going right now. And yes, some of it *is* classified. We get a fair amount of research work from governments around the world. As you may be aware, that was my specialty at Barns, Levi and Richardson. Give me a day or so to kick this around with Anne and Mike. Maybe we can open the door wider. If we can do it, we'll have to advise you what's on and what's off the record. And you'll have to respect that. Okay?"

Aiy took a few deep breaths. "Sure Phil. Sorry I lost it. This is a wonderful place guys. But it's a little loopy too. Guess it's getting to me." She smiled somewhat sheepishly. "Breakfast in five minutes." With that, she returned to the kitchen and her sauces.

Anne looked at Phil. *Score one more for Aiy.* She barely whispered. "That woman is terrifyingly intelligent. She sees through everything. I know you were just appeasing her. She knows as well. Perhaps you really should consider opening that door."

Phil cast his eyes towards the kitchen and mouthed "Later." *I should have known we couldn't control her. She's just too inquisitive, too smart, too beautiful, too beguiling. Things are getting out of hand. I've got to get her the hell off this island, or bring her into the Oneirion camp.*

Breakfast was served on the terrace. Delicious and amicable. Aiy was again in customarily high spirits. They ate; they laughed, flirted and drank Champagne.

Phil stood. "Aiy that was wonderful. You haven't lost your touch. It was great fun too. I apologize for our seeming paranoia. I promise I'm going to sort things out. Meanwhile, I have a few meetings on my agenda, so please excuse me. Anne?"

"I think I'll stay on awhile, unless you've got something scheduled Aiy?"

"Not a thing."

"Good. Maybe we'll do some shopping and lunch."

"Well, have fun ladies. I'll catch up to you later."

For the first time since her arrival, Phil took Aiy in his arms and initiated a kiss. Intense and heated. Long and slow. He released Aiy and kissed Anne as well and as ardently. He then stood and quietly left.

The two women stared at each other, a blend of humor and befuddlement.

Phil called a PM and headed for Security. He also called Oscar Sagan to alert him of his coming and that he would be wanting all his time immediately. He thought back to breakfast. *I wonder what they will be doing the rest of the day.* He thought wistfully *Something interesting no doubt.*

# Check – Double Check

They had been going hard at it three hours now. Endless phone calls and exhaustive computer queries. They had come across some interesting facts. Aiy's father was *not* dead. Adahy Atsila was living in Norway under an assumed name of Scott Woodman. And he was working for a company called Skorpen Undersea Technologies. *Pay-dirt!*

"Damn that was well done Oscar. How'd you make the connection?"

Clearly pleased with Phil's approval, he explained "Adahy immigrated to Norway under his real name, Atsila. Only when he acquired a permanent visa he changed his name to Woodman. Woodman has a police record that reflects his employment with Skorpen Undersea."

"What do the police have on him?"

"Not much really. Possession of unregistered firearms; and he was implicated in some sort of scheme to run illegal immigrants based in Kuwait. No conviction."

"After that he still works for Skorpen?"

"Yep."

"Okay let's get a complete breakdown on Skorpen Undersea Technologies. I've had ah…indirect dealings with them in the past. Something's not right. I need products, employees, P&L, sources of income, BOD and key stockholders, officers, branch offices, everything. Photographs too if possible."

"It will take a few hours to get all that Mr. Carr. A Comprehensive Dunn and Bradstreet report will go a long way and we should be able to get that from D&B files off the rack. Perhaps we can put our hands on a few Annual Reports as well. Would you like to check back, or do you…?"

Sagan's secretary put her head in the office "There's a man named Howard in Chicago who wishes to speak to you Mr. Carr."

"Great."

"Hi Howard. It's been a long time. How've you been?"

"Fine Phil. It's good to hear your voice. You sound good. Better than the last time I spoke to you anyhow. What can I do for you?"

"Do you remember a company called Skorpen Undersea Technologies?"

"I sure as hell do. We shouldn't be discussing this on any phone though. I'm flying into Nice next week. Why don't we meet there?"

"It's that hot?"

"It's that hot."

"Where are you staying on the coast?"

"Ah…the Carlton in Cannes."

"Good. We've got a place at the Marley in the Palm Beach end of the Croissette, ten minutes from the Carlton. I'll be there by 1600 Tuesday. The phone number is…just a minute…04.92.98.23.19. Give me a call and we'll meet for dinner. On me."

"Super. Have your secretary book us into the La Bastide Saint Antoine for 2000. I'll order the wine, you pay the bill. At this end we'll put together a full dossier on Skorpen for you. See you in a few days." Phil put the phone down and turned to Sagan.

"That was the celebrated Howard Doyle of Chicago fame?"

Phil could hear the tang of aggrievement in Oscar's voice. *Understandably so. He's worked hard here and I've gone outside, over his head.*

"Yes it was Oscar. I contacted him because he's been involved in the Skorpen affair from the start and I believe his company has some serious G2 on them. Sorry. I should have consulted you first. I guess that's a bad habit I picked up from Dr. Webber. I'm no damned good at adhering to chain-of-command anymore."

"No problem Mr. Carr. I fully understand. Should I proceed with our own reports on Skorpen?"

"You bet. I need everything I can get my hands on. You can get me via my office the rest of the day."

"Yes sir. Thank you sir."

"One more thing Oscar…"

"Sir?"

"Open a dossier on Adahy Atsila aka Scott Woodman. History. Any priors before Norway. But most important…current known associates."

"That will take a few days."

"Can you do it by next Monday?"

"We'll do our best. Howard can probably help there too."

"Good idea. Give him a call will you? I want you to work together on this. Thanks Oscar."

# Friendly Forebodings

On the way back to his office Qasi's DIT lit up.

"Hello Qasi."

"Hello QaDyme. We suggest you take a drink at the lobby bar. We believe you were there last night after our meeting. We are informed that the bar is empty just now."

"Ten minutes?"

"Thank you Philip."

Ten minutes later "Hi Pete. How about a Gin & Tonic and a tuna fish sandwich?"

No thanks Mr. Carr. I've already eaten."

They both laughed and Pete left to get Phil's lunch.

When Pete had set out everything Phil was left in the bar alone.

"Qasi?"

"Yes Philip." Phil's DIT glowed on his wrist.

"What's up?"

"You acted correctly admitting Aiyana Atsila to Oneiro. You were right to check her out, right to ferret out her father; and right to link Skorpen Undersea Technologies. You've sniffed out the trail of the beast. However we believe you've only begun."

Phil appreciated Qasi's preemptory abruptness. It was reminiscent of his own manner. "Why?"

"As we forewarned you, great forces are militating around you. Time is short. We fear the crisis may be upon you soon. We believe you should be experiencing a growing awareness as well."

"What crisis?"

"The unraveling of the *Gauntlet* project. Leaking of the QAVL presence. And more. We suggest you visit the *Gauntlet* assembly site immediately. Assure everything is completing properly. You should be fully provisioned and ready for launch within three weeks."

"I'll leave for Anastasios tonight. But Qasi, three weeks? Impossible."

"We will join you."

"Thank you Qasi. Hellofa way to begin a twenty-seven year voyage."

"Try preparing for a twenty-seven thousand year voyage sometime." *Qasi has no mouth, but I swear I hear a smile in his voice.*

# Sea Trials

When Anne returned to the residence Phil was already there busily stowing gear in his well worn ditty bag.

"Going somewhere?"

"Oh. Hi. Yes. I'm taking the SAT-SAV to Anastasios in about an hour. Qasi has suggested I ensure *Gauntlet* is being completed properly."

"What's the rush? Is there a problem on the site?"

"No rush really. And there's no problem on the site. He simply wants to make sure things don't have to be redone. And I'd like to catch the SAT-SAV for the trip."

"I see. If you don't want to tell me Phil, just say so. You *are* the Consul."

"Whatever do you mean?" Apparently she harbored some residual peevishness following his 'orders' of the previous night.

"You're being evasive again. It's really not your style. Your eyes consistently give you away. Want me to come along?"

"Actually I'd prefer you remained here and looked after Aiy. If that's okay? I want her on a short leash. Don't let her out of your sight. For the next few days we need some real control."

"No problem. It's a pleasure."

"So how did you guys spend the day? Have fun?"

"We had a fine time. Did some shopping. Had a good lunch." Her voice became slightly shrill. "Although lunch was nearly a disaster."

"How so?"

"That damned restaurant. The *Brasserie QAVL*. Aiy zeroed in on that immediately. What genius came up with that name? It's like advertising we have aliens on Oneiro. Between the name and some of the dishes…Light-Fare, Hundred-Million Year Old Eggs and so forth…Aiy had her radar set to high gain. What does QAVL mean? Why Hundred-Million Year Old Eggs? On and on."

"Crap. What'd you tell her?"

"I told her one of our paleo-biologists discovered a new microscopic fossil, roughly a hundred million years old on the sea bed in Oneirion waters. Unique to the island as far as we know. It had four cilia so they named it Quadropedus Annimalas Virtualatus Lindalious…QAVL. Its designation and uniqueness to Oneiro sparked some trendy bars and restaurants on the island."

"Quadropedus Annimalas Virtualatus Lindalious. What the hell does that mean?"

"It doesn't mean a damned thing Phil. It's gobblygook. I made it up on the spot. I'm sure Aiy only half believed me, if that much."

"Quick thinking. I'll have that restaurant sorted out when I get back. I should have seen the danger the first time I went there. I don't know what I was thinking of. Aiy saw right through it?"

"She is *very* quick Phil."

Phil sighed. "I know. You're fond of her aren't you?"

"Yes I am Phil."

"Did you all uh…?"

"Yes. Is that alright?"

"Of course. It's fine."

"We a…discussed you by the way. It's a shame you're going away." She smiled demurely. "We thought you might join us?"

Phil smiled appreciatively. "I'll try to make it a quick trip to Anastasios and back."

Anne smiled. "What do I tell Aiy if she asks where you are? And she will."

"Simply the truth. I've left the island on business for a few days."

Oneiro harbor had the look of a vast cathedral, deserted late on a dark Wednesday night. Footsteps echoing, stragglers in dark recesses. The SAT-SAV, or 'Strong and Stupid' as Phil had come to fondly think of it, was moored on the main dock. A small crew of engineers and stevedores were servicing the boat. Phil threw his small ditty bag to Charlie King atop the coning tower and climbed aboard.

Looking aft, then towards the Chief. "Permission to go aboard sir." Phil smartly saluted and smiled.

Charlie returned the salute appreciatively. "Permission granted sir. Nice to see this homely girl's getting some respect."

Phil mounted the high coning tower.

When he reached the top "Full crew compliment?"

"We have a full bridge crew except our First Officer. He just flew in from New York and he's out like a light. I'm Chief of the Boat on this run. My people are all aboard. Which left only you…Skipper."

"So she's my boat on this trip?"

"She's your boat sir."

"When are you ready to cast off?"

"We need an hour and some change. We're just topping up fuel and water. The Loadmaster reports cargo secured and catering aboard."

"Let's take a tour if you have time. I'm hoping to learn to drive her on this trip. I was given a comprehensive briefing awhile ago. But I'd like to actually qualify in all running modes."

"Can do Skipper. Excellent shake-down exercise for the boat as well. I'll fetch you an S&S Bar when we get below."

"An S&S Bar?"

"A Strong & Stupid Bar, as we call them. They're actually named S&S for SAT-SAV. They're really good. Chocolate, sultanas, crushed Macadamias and Kahlua Coconut Cream, spiked with comprehensive training on all operations of the SAT-SAV. They contain a brand new, state-of-the-art, nutri-tech compound called AAM's (Accelerated Anthropogenic Metabolizers). AAM's trigger an exceptional enzyme inductor which in turn excites an especially speedy metabolic process. You should fully metrignosiculate within an hour; and maybe even lose a couple of grams of excess weight in the process. You may feel a bit warm during assimilation."

"Impressive Chief. You're quite a bit more than just an engineer."

"In fact I'm not," laughed the Chief. "It's all explained in the candy bar Skipper."

Phil regarded Chief King appraisingly for a moment with a questioning look. King looked down and recognized the object of Phil's examination. "This is the new Oneirion uniform sir. As authorized by you and designed by Commander Farrow. Your directive stipulates it is to be worn by duty per sonnel on all air, sea and space craft. They've laid out your uniform in your quarters. You'll command *Gauntlet* in that same uniform...Captain."

*I've got to start reading these directives before I sign them.*

Forty minutes later they were sailing into the setting sun. Phil had consumed his S&S Bar. It lived up to King's claim. It was delicious. He retired to the Captain's quarters to take a short nap. He always found that sleep increased the efficacy of Oneirion learning-food. Nearly as effective as diving. He hesitantly donned his new uniform – relieved to see it was more comfortable overall than military garb. Powder blue. Dark blue piping. A crisp Neru collar. Light black boots. His Captain's insignia took the form of four gold bars below a gold star just above his right cuff. *Not bad. Comfortable. Nice and low key.*

An hour later he wasn't in the Captain's chair. He was at the helm, Charlie King at his side. "Please tell the Helmsman I appreciate him ceding the wheel Charlie. Suppose we stress for depth first?"

"Your call Skip." The Helmsman had yielded the helm to Phil. Phil took his place and continued to issue commands as well.

"Rig for quick dive. Ninety percent compression on ballast tanks."

"Ship rigged for quick dive. Ballast tanks ten percent. Diverting to battery power."

Phil smoothly pressed the dive plane control forward to Full Dive. "Fifteen degree down bubble, one-third ahead."

Their world slowly turned down bow-ward.

After five minutes "Heavy aft sir."

"Eighty-five percent compression aft tank."

"Eighty-five sir."

Two minutes later "Final trim sir."

"Smartly done Chief. Activate bulkhead periscope."

Suddenly the boat disappeared. Usurped by her periscope. With the exception of interior conduits and control panels, the hull of the SAT-SAV had completely vanished. Transparent. The illusion of free-floating under the sea wasn't complete, but it was effective. Phil could see a ghostly moon on the water's surface high above, grayish-blue water fading to black far below.

Phantom shapes swam just outside his field of vision and shapes far more real passed the dark hull of the submarine. For a moment Phil thought these creatures were drawn to the interior lighting of the SAT-SAV until, smiling at himself, he remembered these images were one-way only. Whatever the sea looked from within; outside the boat was simply a huge dark non-emitting, elongated ovoid – mounted with myriad menacing shapes.

The periscope triggered Phil's singular mental wandering.

He thought about the boat. The tactical systems. The weaponry. The cruise and dive capabilities. *She could be one hellofa attack sub. As either a research, or combat vessel, JAEKEL is formidable indeed.*

*JAEKEL?*

The name had come to him unbidden. Totally spontaneous. Phil had experienced one of his peculiar insights. This was a fairly trivial insight. But it did address a minor irritation. He believed ships and boats should have names. Not acronyms. Not SAT-SAV…JAEKEL.

*After all, this was not merely a hollow sphere, a DSRV deep diving while tethered to a support vessel on the surface. This didn't carry two or three marine biologists. This huge boat was the most advanced submersible in the world. When all her features were ultimately installed she could stay under for years. Self sufficient. Air, water, food, energy, everything processed onboard. She would be dangerous and probably unkillable by any contemporary technology she can travel on seabed, underwater, on the surface and soon…in the air…and finally in space itself. JAEKEL.*

An involuntary cold shudder ran his spine.

A malevolent name. It conveyed… a minacious threat.

*Nolite JAEKEL conculcare. Don't tread on JAEKEL.*

*So where had the name come from? Doctor Jekyll and Mr. Hyde? No. Something much less direct, but far more germane. What was it? What had his mind resurrected...?*

*Ah! Dr. Otto Max Johannes JAEKEL (1863 –1929). A pre-eminent German paleontologist and geologist. Amongst other accomplishments JAEKEL extensively published findings relative to fossil vertebrates. Most specifically, Marine Chelicerates from the early Devonian period. Silurian.*

*Sea Scorpions.*

*Water breathing insectoid nightmares up to nine feet in length, over 400 million years ago. A voracious arthropod killer equipped with hairy legs, a chitinous armored carapace, huge claws, a massive deadly stinger and bulging insect eyes. All the repellent threat of a monstrous scorpion. Chelicerates were the pentacle predators of the Devonian Seas. Damned near any sea. A watery multi-legged horror.*

*Nolite Chelicerates conculcare*

*Nolite JAEKEL conculcare.*

*Don't dare tread on either one.*

*This sub would be named in JAEKAL's honor. The allusive name was a bit labyrinthine, but absolutely appropriate.*

"Chief we need a name for this boat. SAT-SAV just won't do. SAT-SAV's just a goddamned acronym."

"Fully agreed Skipper. I've felt the same for some time. Got any ideas?"

"Yes I do: JAEKEL"

" Jackal? Like a jackal…a wild dog?"

"No."

"As in Dr. Jekyll and Mr. Hyde?"

"No, not at all; and remember Dr. Jekyll was supposed to be a good guy. In fact he was a pretty wan fellow all in all. Wanted to do good, but too weak to give up the joy-juice and all that. This is a whole different, deadlier type of JAEKEL."

"I see. *That* Jekyll just doesn't have the muzzle velocity of *this* JAEKEL."

"Right."

"Can you spell it please?"

"J-A-E-K-E-L"

"Quite a name. Mean name. Has a feral feeling about it. It sounds dangerous. I like it. So what *does* it signify?"

"Tell you what. I'll have a marine brass plaque mounted on the conning tower. JAEKEL, together with a brief etymology of the name. How about it?"

"Works for me Skip. Suppose we christen her new name next time she's back in port at Oneiro? We'll need a lady and a good bottle of Champagne."

"Good. Set it up. Meanwhile, let's continue our descent. Call off our depth Chief, by hundreds and thousands."

"Aye Skipper. One-two-five. Two-zero-zero. Three-zero-zero. One-zero-zero-zero. Two-zero-zero-zero. Five-zero-zero-zero." Ten minutes later "Six-zero-zero-zero. Max depth."

Then "Six-five-zero-zero…Skip?"

"I haven't heard a peep, a trickle, or a buckle. This thing is a rock. Status all stations."

Moments later.

"All stations report nominal sir."

"Thanks Chief. Now I want…"

"Skipper, Sonar. Ground Proximity Alert indicates the bottom's coming up fast at roughly seven-zero-zero-zero."

Phil raised the dive planes to near level "Zero down bubble. All stop."

They silently drifted to the floor of the sea. Nearly seven thousand meters down into the abyss. All were surprised when they touched down without a sound. Instead they felt themselves placidly settle into a quaggy agglomeration of silt.

"Rig for bottom ops."

"Deploying bottom crawler."

After a few muted bumps and grinds…

"Rigged for bottom."

"Full forward." JAEKEL sluggishly, slow-motion teetered across the seabed. All of one point five knots. Five point five knots slower than her specs.

"Activate floodlights, and deploy arms." Phil stretched. "Helmsman to the bridge."

"Helmsman on deck sir." He assumed his duty station.

"You have the helm. Thanks for letting me sit in."

"My pleasure sir."

Phil looked out on the huge periscopic landscape. "We're kicking up one hellofa lot of muck out there. Can't see a thing."

"Helm sir. This is like driving in oatmeal. Sediment must be two meters deep. This accounts for our reduced speed."

Phil considered their situation. "Chief set all ballast tanks at seventy-five. Full ahead. Rudder amidships."

"Tanks at seventy-five sir. Rudder amidships. Full ahead."

JAEKEL achieved nearly positive buoyancy. She was now moon-skipping slightly above the surface. She would touch down every four minutes or so, and then penetrate the muck again to give herself a boost. Waterborne, her spinning tracks kept her steady on course, and preserved her forward momentum. Her speed increased to slightly more than seven knots. In near total silence.

The Chief grinned broadly. "Skipper, I believe this maneuver will henceforth be known as 'Carr-Hopping'. It works like a charm. Minimal turbulence; and we have a four hundred sixty-six percent improvement in speed and efficiency. Not bad at all sir."

Phil smiled and continued to stare into the sea. In his mind's eye he saw himself staring back, as no other human could. A stark black and white desert seven kilometers beneath the sea. Unthinkable pressure. No light save the JAEKEL. Nothing growing. No discernable life.

Finally JAEKEL'S lights caught an occasional sea worm and a few forlorn deep water *Lamonema* wandering the emptiness, foraging the bleak seabed in search of sustenance.

"Not much to see out there."

"Not much sir. We are approximately over the subduction zone on the plate boundary between the African and the Eurasian Tectonic Plates. So we're hoping to find some vents out there soon. The boys in geology and oceanography are dying to get their hands on JAEKEL."

"I can imagine. Okay Chief. Let's see how she crabs."

"How she *crabs* sir?"

"Yes Mr. King." Phil smiled broadly reclining in the Captain's Seat. "Maybe we'll call this maneuver 'King Crabbing'. Actuate drive settings as follows Chief. Take her up to three meters. Then set full power to bow and aft starboard maneuvering thrusters. 85° right rudder. Ahead one-third. Zero buoyancy. Engage when ready."

After rising nearly imperceptibly, the big boat commenced a crablike scudding to port, while still positioned straight ahead level in the water. Neither rising nor sinking, nor changing her heading.

Phil switched to inter-ship comms. "Ship's Register, please log 'Carr Hopping' and 'King Crabbing' as sanctioned maneuvers for further qualification. Consult the Captain's Log after landfall in Anastasios for more details."

The Chief shook his head "I'm a son of a bitch. I had no idea JAEKEL could crab. I've never heard of a sub doing such a thing. Why the hell would you want to do it anyway Skipper?"

"Mmm. I could see using this type of maneuver when navigating particularly tricky bottom topography. But you don't want to, or cannot resort to ascension. Tactically, it gives you the capability to slip away under an adversary undetected."

"Those are all pretty arcane circumstances Skip."

"Agreed. But remember this boat is also designed to observe without being observed; and move as the subject moves."

"Well she can damned sure do that."

"...and if nothing else Chief, we can now easily parallel park in port."

Chief King made a wry grimace as though he was unsure if Phil was serious. After half an hour of repetitive zigzagging from port to starboard Phil assumed the Captains chair.

"Crawler all stop. Let's try some silent running Chief."

"Aye Sir. All stop. Rig for silent running."

The steady thrumming of the diesels stopped and the big boat drifted above the sea bottom. Then they heard the smooth deployment of over six hundred small advanced PVC drive propellers, as they swiveled from JAEKEL's hull matrix into the dark water.

"Rigged for silent running Skipper."

"Good. All ahead."

They felt a slight surge forward. After that nothing. No sound. No feeling of movement.

"What's your reading on our speed Chief? My panel shows eight knots."

"That's correct sir."

Phil whistled softly to himself. "That's three knots over spec. We're really moving considering our thrust is just a few little plastic props. Think we're in some sort of deep current?"

"I doubt it. Our vessel drift-relative-to-ground is negligible factoring in our thrust. But remember Skip, those 'few little plastic props' are really six-hundred and forty-five one meter propellers fabricated from ultra-high molecular fusion polymers, each one with a thirty hp electric motor. That's 19,350 horses."

"Impressive. Okay. All stop. Secure SR."

Quietly 645 electric propellers stowed themselves in their hull receptacles.

"Forward and aft tanks to eighty percent. Ten degrees up on bow planes. Propellers two thirds ahead."

"Aye Skipper. We're on our way up."

"Sonar at one five zero meters, I want a full 360° surface scan. At the *all clear* Chief, take her topside."

Forty minutes later they were sailing through a clear starlit night.

"Full ahead Helm. Set an easy circular course at six-five degrees. Radar, confirm all clear when we've completed our three-sixty."

Twenty minutes later. "Radar sir. All clear confirmed for twelve-zero-zero-zero. All points three-six-zero. We're alone out here sir."

"Chief, jettison a drone."

"Drone off the stern sir."

"Rig for dive."

"Rigged for dive."

"Dive. Set depth at four zero."

"Dive to four zero."

"Load and activate a torpedo in the forward tube. Proximity detonation."

"Torpedo loaded and active sir. Proximity fuse."

"Radar, I need a bearing on that drone."

"Skipper, Radar. Bearing one-three-six. Range three-zero-zero-zero-five-two meters."

'Come about to one-three-six Helm, and confirm."

"One-three-six sir."

"Rig torpedo. Depth zero. Heading one-three-six. Automatic onboard radar correction. Contact detonation."

"Confirmed. Zero. One-three-six. Auto-correct. Proximity fuse.

"Ignition."

"Torpedo away."

Phil could hear only a whispery "thrunk'.

"She's in the water sir. On course."

"Activate the prismic surface periscope."

This periscope did not present the classical image of a sub commander. Head-gear on backwards. Hands firmly clamped on periscope shaft grips. Squinting into a tiny calibrated viewing scope, while an anxious crew stands by in suspense. Instead, a generous window appeared in the bulkhead equipped with state-of-the-art imaging controls.

Two minutes later Phil observed a satisfying flash on the horizon.

"Sonar?"

"Target down sir."

"Excellent. Deactivate periscope. Take her up Chief."

"Heading sir?"

"Full ahead Anastasios. I'll be in the mess."

"Aye sir. Tanks at one-hundred. Surface. Vents open full. Standard power. All ahead. Heading One-three-niner. Wait five helm. Then airt helm control to GPS Auto-helm. Nav I want an alert at 12,000 meters Anastasios North. Radar and sonar give me readings on the hour. Mr. Dodge to the con please."

Later in the Captain's Mess Phil was sharing a pitcher of rum with Chief King.

"You guys do great work Charlie. How would you evaluate her performance Chief?"

"Four-by-four Skip. We built to specs and tolerances no navy or shipbuilder in the world could afford; and it paid off. Her design's generic and upgradable. Drive systems, munitions, nav, whatever, she'll last for decades. Shipyards could learn a lot from this exercise."

"Agreed. She'll be something incredible when we've outfitted her with airborne capability. After that, perhaps orbital."

"When we upgrade to QAVL drive systems damned near anything's possible."

"Worth thinking about. I also believe much remains to be tried combing the forces of tracks, aft thrusters, side thrusters, silent thrusters and buoyancy. I think we could make this thing do cork-screwing back-flips if needed."

"You know Skipper; I really don't understand why we went to so much trouble to build the seabed drives. They're heavy, complex and don't work so well. Carr-Hopping and King-Crabbing are impressive, but simply cruising above the seabed on silent running seems far more practical."

"I have to agree Chief. All the same I think they installed tracks to assist in marine-life research. With the tracks they can sit down and watch, and even crawl behind. Remember, most marine life 'looks up'."

"Looks up sir?"

"Yes. Their eyes are either oriented upwards seeking light, or they rely on bio-luminescence ascending from their visual plane. I believe the tracks are designed for the oceanic region known as mid-water. That's pretty much where everything lives anyway. The same tides that deposit so much silt down here serve to sweep the upper sea-beds. Plus, don't forget these same tracks are designed for dry-land operations as well."

"Understood." He played with his drink, then looked up. "There's another design aspect that was never explained to us."

"What's that?"

"Well, JAEKEL is a research vehicle. Why does it require offensive and defensive capabilities like torpedoes and Silent Running?"

"First, Silent Run is fully in keeping with her research mission statement. If we want to run with the beasties, we've got to be quiet. Second, the torpedoes. Well that's my doing as you know. I made it a matter of policy that all Oneirion land, sea and air locus have defensive and offensive capability. It's a dangerous world out there, and we don't have many friends."

"I see. Can I get you anything else Skipper?"

"No thanks. What's our ETA Anastasios?" It was long past midnight.

"0800."

"Good. I'm going to turn in. Breakfast at 0600? You and the First Officer?"

"We'll be here sir."

Unlike his earlier nap, Phil took the time to look around his stateroom. The Captain's Quarters were nearly luxurious. Imagine an ensuite bathroom and a private ready-room/dining room/bar aboard a sub. And a full sized bed! As always the steady thrumming of big diesels put him out immediately. He slept dreamlessly, automatically awakening at 0530.

"Good morning gentlemen."

"Good morning sir." In unison as they stood.

Charlie King made introductions. "Sir this is First Mate Mickey Dodge. Mr. Dodge...Consul Carr."

The men shook hands and took a seat. When the ship's steward had taken their breakfast orders "Are we on schedule?"

"Yes sir."

"Top speed?"

"Yes sir. Twenty-five knots."

"Good. How about fuel consumption?"

"Right on spec."

"Any problems at all?"

"All systems nominal."

"Excellent. Hellofa boat. I understand you just got in from New York Mr. Dodge."

"Yes sir. My people are from the Bronx and I was back on leave."

"I know New York well. I lived there for some time and I can't get back often enough."

The steward served breakfast. As he was leaving their table "Can you get us a topographic map of Anastasios please?"

"Right away sir."

As they ate, Phil spread the map out center table. "Let's see. Here's the harbor, Mount Anastasios and on the other side of the island, a beach area. This looks perfect."

"What've you got in mind sir?"

"I want to make landfall on the far side of the island and qualify this beast on land transport. I would also like to see how well her onboard crane performs."

After several minutes pouring over the map they identified the optimal landing site and from there, an inland offload point.

"Okay gentlemen. We have a plan. I suppose we should radio Anastasios and revise our ETA to oh….three hours later. We should alert them we will be navigating their waters."

"Aye sir."

The three departed to pursue their duties.

As JAEKEL approached the far side of Anastasios a light rain was falling. Phil and Dodge stood the conning tower watching their approach.

"Does this weather have any bearing on our tests?"

"I shouldn't think so sir. We've never tried this in foul weather. But it's fairly light as yet, and the operations manual makes no mention of meteorological operating limitations."

"Who's watching the shop at Anastasios harbor?"

"That would be Harbormaster Santos."

"Can we get him on the radio and pipe it up here?"

"Certainly." The first mate turned to the ship's intercom.

After a few moments. "Santos on the line sir."

"Thanks." Phil took the mike.

"Harbormaster Santos this is Phil Carr aboard the SAT-SAV approaching Thanatos Bay on the windward side of Anastasios. Over."

"Acknowledged Mr. Carr. What can I do for you? Over."

"We are about to run surface qualification exercises with the SAT-SAV; and the weather is not the best. If we run into trouble can you provide any type of support? Over."

"If you limit your inland penetration we can probably help. *Gauntlet Marinas* is in harbor and offloaded, ready for her next trip. She could be to you in about an hour and possibly winch you out. That would assume your tracks are working and you're not far from shore. Worst-case she could give your people a ride to Anastasios Harbor. Over,"

"Understood. We'll stay close to shore and keep you posted. Thank you Mr. Santos. Out."

Phil carefully scanned the shore for a time with high powered glasses. He looked at Dodge. "Let's take her in." He picked up the mike again. "Helm head directly for Thanatos Beach. Dead slow. Try to hit the beach at an exact ninety degree angle. Radar I need a depth reading every ten seconds."

"Aye sir."

At ten meters "Engage tracks, forward, aft and amid ship. Dead slow. All stop propellers. Helm we're drifting in. Use your tracks and lateral controls to provide forward thrust and maintain heading."

"Acknowledged sir."

In roughly four minutes the JAEKEL shuddered slightly as the tracks acquired the shoreline, not perfectly perpendicular, but close enough for both port and starboard tracks to acquire purchase. Slowly the huge boat dragged itself onto the shore and further to the rocky prominence that followed.

"Speed Helm?"

"Four clicks sir. We're at max drive."

"Not overly impressive. We could easily out-walk her."

Dodge responded "...not dragging fifty-eight tonnes of nickel-titanium."

Phil peered at Dodge neutrally. "Proceed on course for one hundred meters, then full stop and cut power."

After they came to a halt, all three men – Carr, Dodge and King – climbed down the conning tower and laddered down to the ground. They circled JAEKEL inspecting with interest. It seemed incredible that this huge boat had recently been down to seven thousand meters, bouncing along the bottom, sailing the surface and was now navigating dry land.

"Crap!"

"Problem Charlie?"

"We're sinking in."

Sure enough the lower tracks were already buried in the soft mud, which continued to slowly rise up to the drive train.

"All aboard. Now!"

When they reached the conning tower Phil grabbed the mike.

"Start engines. Abort offload exercise. Full power astern. Immediately!"

JAEKEL started to move astern and then began floundering right to left from the bow. They could feel her digging in. Helpless.

"All stop. Deploy aft crane and initiate winches. Chief get a crew ashore. I want all cables from the crane and the winches attached to boulders on the promontory near shore."

An hour later bow and stern tracks were whirling at full power. "It's no good sir. We are well and truly stuck. Our cables are miring us down and digging us in. There are no mooring points high enough."

"Son of a bitch! Patch me through to Harbormaster Santos."

"Harbormaster? Carr here. We need a tow. Over."

"*Gauntlet Marinas* will be there within the hour sir. Please keep an eye out for her. Over."

"Thanks very much. Standing by. Out."

King and Dodge had joined Phil in the wardroom. "Well, we gave it a try gentlemen. She did superbly on all other trials so I suppose we should be pleased. We'll log she's fit for dry land operations only for the time being. All we face now is a short wait on *Gauntlet Marinas* and a rather inglorious tow. I'll complete my log entries before we dock." King and Dodge withdrew.

*Rather an ignominious ending to a great cruise.* Phil poured himself a rum and started recording the ship's log detailing the last fourteen hours.

Under Phil's watchful eye, *Gauntlet Marinas* had pulled them sea borne fifteen minutes after she was on site. An hour later they were entering Anastasios harbor. The sun was out. The ground was dry and dusty as usual. Apparently it had not rained on the leeward side of the island today.

There was an armada of smaller craft surrounding Oneiro Harbor, tied to dockings, at moorings fanning out into the sea, and secured in makeshift floating slips. A few dozen smaller ships were run aground to the north and south of the harbor area for lack of available wet space. Phil had visions of the colossal Spartan fleet approaching their murderous landing at Troy. This sight was as impressive, but far more peaceful. Hundreds of ships carrying every manner of supplies, parts, technicians and artisans to complete the fitting of *Gauntlet*. They had faced an awesome task of construction, a nightmare of logistics and intensive complex qualifications. They had been coming and going twenty-four hours a day for weeks now. Guided by invisible hands, sleeping in containers, eating boxed rations, enduring the heat and the dust and working eighteen hours a day. Finally the end began to seem attainable.

A silent army of generators and all manner of electrical equipment stood mutely idle. Replaced by QAVL energy generation.

JAEKEL briefly lay at zero helm in aspect of the great spectacle. "Into the shed or tied up to the pier Chief?"

"Our crew can handle everything out here sir. There's no work to be done below the water line."

"In that case I'll leave you to it."

After some short radio traffic and shore preparations, JAEKEL slowly moved forward and slipped smoothly aside the dock space cleared for her. The great diesels slowed to a deep rumbling idle.

"She's your boat now Chief. It was a most interesting cruise. I think we all know a great deal more about the potential of JAEKEL now. She's a class boat. Thanks for the use of the Captain's Seat."

"My pleasure…Skipper."

# Brave New Whorl

Ditty bag over his shoulder, Phil jumped ashore. To his surprise Mike Auslander was on the pier waiting for him.

"Mike! Nice surprise. I didn't know you were on Anastasios."

The two men shook hands.

"Been here for a couple of days. I came in on *Marinas'* last run and I just can't drag myself away from *Gauntlet*. You're a lucky man Phil. What a command she'll be."

"Let's get some lunch and then take the tour. Where's Nick? And where can I stow this bag?"

"First your bag. I think you should leave it aboard the SAT-SAV. She'll be in port for a few days. All we've got left ashore are Sub-Cons, and damned few at that. The new skipper is still on leave so you'll be much more comfortable in the Captain's quarters. The First Mate's quarters are occupied now, so I'll take the VIP Visitor Quarters."

"Agreed." Mike threw his bag to a crewman on deck. "Stow this in the Captain's quarters sailor."

"Okay. Where's Nick?"

"Nick's waiting for us at the restaurant."

"Restaurant? What restaurant?"

Mike smiled "Aboard *Gauntlet*."

Phil's face lit up as understanding dawned. "My God they must've made incredible progress. Last time I saw her she was nothing but giant hollow spheres."

"She's a world now Phil."

Phil could feel excitement churning inside. He almost whispered "Let's go see."

Mated PM's were standing by. A hot, dusty forty minute walk was to be supplanted with a ten minute trip seated in relative comfort.

"So Mike, how do we stand?"

"Well there's a lot to report. All of it amazing. Seas, power systems, navigation, gravity engineering, climatology, terra-forming, provisioning…where shall we start?"

"Start by telling me we can lift off in three weeks."

Mike was literally speechless for some moments. "Phil you're not serious?"

"Deadly."

"Phil, what's going on?"

Phil raised his DIT to his mouth. "Qasi?"

"Hello Philip. Good morning Mike."

"Good morning Qasi. May I request you to brief Mike on our three week exigency?"

"Certainly. First, three weeks is our most pessimistic view on the situation. That notwithstanding, our projections indicate a massive threat to *Gauntlet* in the near term. Massive to the degree it could seriously endanger the project. We are convinced a prudent approach mandates readiness within a few days. I should point out our projections enjoy a phenomenal rate of accuracy."

"May I ask where this information comes from?"

"A quantum correlation of discordant *Kosmas*."

Mike frowned deeply. "I'm sorry Qasi. I don't follow you."

"Perhaps Philip can best explain in a terran context."

Mike glanced at Phil questioningly.

"To be honest I'm not that clear on it myself. From a personal perspective, I am experiencing flashes of…fear. These days this invariably indicates some sort of disparity between the way I project time to unfold and the way it is actually evolving."

"Discordant *Kosmas*." Mike rather absently mouthed the words.

"Exactly. Well done," smiled Phil.

"Well done? I still don't know what the hell I'm talking about!"

"Suppose we simply stipulate the QAVL have credible support for their assertion…and take it from there."

Clearly uncomfortable with his quandary, Mike hesitantly acknowledged "If the QAVL so stipulate, I will treat it as a given fact. In terms of three weeks, QAVL works would constitute the critical path. Qasi?"

"All construction, systems installation, integration and testing will be complete within five days."

Both Mike and Phil were slightly stunned. Phil said "That sir is impressive. Have you escalated your schedule?"

"Not materially. Our joint completion date remains roughly six weeks from now. The majority of the effort remaining is dedicated to provisioning and acclimation. I suggest that acclimation be substituted with nutri-tech; and that all forces are brought to bear on equipping and provisioning *Gauntlet*. We have reviewed your load list and have developed a hybrid list."

"A hybrid?"

"Yes. A list prioritized by mission necessity, further sequenced by those items which can be manufactured en-route and those commodities difficult to synthesize. A second half of that list consists of what we might term as luxuries, also broken out into en-route production and items which should be inventoried at launch. Such a list can be highly sensitive to those charged with living with the result. We therefore suggest the immediate tasks should be a comprehensive review of our revised list, and a detailed load plan. We appreciate the logistics will be exceptionally difficult. We will assist wherever we may."

Mike visibly roused himself. "Sounds reasonable. And if we're not forced into an early lift-off all's the same. We should discuss this with Nick."

The PM's smoothly halted at the port entry, which was now sealed with an enormous hinged round hatch. Egress was further facilitated by three doors built into the hatch. One truck size and two human sized. The only other change was an enormous apron outside the seal equipped with what looked to be a de-icing system.

By way of explanation Mike simply said "Vehicle rinse." And pointed to the various seals. "When the QAVL completed the spheres, we sealed the entire site and saturated it in a particularly virulent gas and then severely radiated it. There is nothing alive in there not on our manifests. This is the first of three seals. When we pass the second we will be free of any vermin…lice, fleas, mites and so forth. When we pass the third we will be carrying a minimal number of germs."

"Environmental suits?"

"No. We don't consider it that sensitive. We are generally replicating a terran environment, so we're just trying to minimize undesirables. All cargo and vehicles are subject to the same procedure."

"That must slow things down considerably."

"Not at all. We only pause long enough to open and close the seals. Beyond that, it's a drive-through/walk-through operation. Nothing to it. All soils have been baked and radiated. The same applies to any building materials imported. No woods are imported. Such imports are restricted to metals, stone and **Ferroconcrete.** All furniture, bedding, decorations, any such materials are synthetics. Far and away the largest unsterilized volumes inside are the seas."

"They remain natural?"

"Totally. The seas constitute a far too complex and delicate ecosystem. We haven't tampered with them whatsoever."

"What about food?"

"Comestibles come aboard cooked and then deep frozen. It will be a couple of months before fresh fruit and vegetables are available. In fact all food production synthesizers have been sterile loaded. They will be seeded and began production after lift-off."

"Qasi will this procedure be modified with your new lists?"

"Not at all Philip. All these materials are already aboard."

"Things are looking better."

There was a small bin next to the door. Mike picked up two clear plastic face masks. "Here, hold this to your face Phil and breathe normally." They stepped in the door into a slight haze and walked about thirty meters to the next seal, PM faithfully following. The door quickly slid back and they stepped through into another light mist, on another thirty meters and out the third seal.

Another double PM awaited them. "That was easy."

Mike nodded "It hardly slows down a ten tonne truck either."

Phil was occupied with returning his mask and mounting the PM when he finally looked up. He nearly fell off the PM. He gasped, holding tight to the PM as debilitating waves of nausea and dizziness and vertigo washed over him.

"Oh damn! I'm really sorry Phil. I should've warned you. Webber's Pelagikós (Webber's Open Seas) just been filled and we're just in the process of adjusting the Spheriscope that surrounds it. Until it is fully active it will emit that swirling effect. Overwhelming isn't it?"

The entire sky was spinning above him, bearing down with an inexorable force, fired with an amalgam of colors. It took him several seconds to gain control. "That's a goddamned understatement. I could hardly breathe, or stand, or think. What the hell is that?"

"I'm afraid you're not seeing *Gauntlet* at her best just now. Hopefully the Spheriscope will be fully operational and we'll have a normal sky in just a few minutes. The Oneirion contribution to the *Gauntlet* project is probably a thousand times less complex than the QAVL technology onboard. Yet we seem to have about a hundred times more difficulty installing it. Once they are adjusted properly though, the periscopes are quite literally maintenance free. But they require some careful calibration at start-up. Believe it or not what you're seeing in this monstrous sky is just one small drop of oily water glinting in the sunshine far above us."

Phil and Mike stared into the surreal sky for several moments. Mike continued to speak, half to himself. "It's magnificent to watch the QAVL work. Aside from looking like magic, their competence is awesome. They prepare the area to a tolerance that approaches zero. They drop in their technology, immediately fire it up and test it. I'm told there is never a problem. Ever. Then they move on to the next area. It always works. And it's amazingly fast."

Phil and Mike climbed back into their PM's. The scene for as far as they could see was dark and surrealistic. As if a vortex of clouds were casting psychedelic shadows randomly across a dark landscape. Phil could make out nothing clearly; and what little he could distinguish was confusing and depressing. Their PM's carried them silently up a winding road towards a shadowy towering complex hulking in the gloom of an endless horizon.

The air carried a slight breeze, strengthening the feeling of being out of doors. Part of a real world. The scent of the breeze was unexpected though. It had the fresh, dry pleasing reminiscence of new construction. Brick and plaster and plasterboard. A confusing discordance since Phil was well aware that the ship and all its interior features were fashioned essentially of stone.

Mike observed Phil breathing in, testing the air and smiled. "You're forgetting about the terra-forms."

Phil regarded Mike quizzically.

Mike explained. "The topsoil we use for landscaping. Our sterilization process imparts that unusual scent. Smells like a paint store to me. They say it will dissipate in a week or so. We're running vast amounts of rough filtered air through the sphere right now, which is speeding the process. When the sea and the plantings are complete the air will be wonderfully fresh. Normal in every respect except the percentage of particulate suspension."

"Rough filtered?"

"Yes. We screen the air only enough to deny insects, pollen, spores and similar airborne particles. We want the air to be as natural as possible."

They arrived in front of a huge complex. Eight stories high. Six towers. Hundreds of meters wide. Exceptional architecture. Extensively terraced, graceful arches, huge columns opening into recessed windows of every shape and description. The entire effect was one of airy grace and exquisitely treated stone. "Nice. What the hell is it?"

"Well for one thing it's lunch. They've just completed *Gauntlet's* first restaurant *Le Rêve au Gaunt*. And it's stunning. Great French food. I think you'll like it."

"Let's see, *Le Gaunt*. That's French for glove, or…"

"*Gauntlet*," finished Mike.

Phil smiled. "And *Rêves* is dream. The Dream in the Gauntlet. Nice."

They entered a huge lobby area. Light beige, nearly white, polished floors and walls. The walls were decorated with subtle etchings of uncensored Oneirion art. The whirling abstracts were ideally suited to the skillfully dressed walls. Superb use of stone. The ceiling was some four stories above them, vaulted and trimmed with elegant maroon piping also of stone. Phil thought to himself *If Frank Lloyd Wright were alive today...*

Their footsteps echoed in the vast space while spherical glass elevators waited to carry them soundlessly upwards.

The crystal lift deposited them directly into the elegant beige lobby of the restaurant. "Monsieur Carr! Quel plaisir." A large ruddy faced man of at least 110 kilos awaited them in the lobby. His weight, the product of too many sauces and pastries made from lander ingredients. His claims he could taste the difference were skeptically received by Oneirions, suspicious his size was, in reality, a cook's affectation. He was elegantly clad in Chef's double vested white smock and Chef's hat. Shiny black hair combed straight back and carefully trimmed black moustaches.

"Good grief. Francois? I never thought I'd see you aboard *Gauntlet.*" After the mandatory hug. "Have you given up *Comme Chez Jeanne?*"

"Never. I just want to help launch this incredible restaurant successfully. After that, back to Broadway. May I show you around?"

Francois came by his French accent honestly. He was one of a group who were weaned in French, as were other groups in other languages, as part of an early experiment seeking a relationship between intelligence and native tongue. A slight deviation from Oneiro's charter, but an interesting enterprise considering Oneirion capabilities. Before any significant results were forthcoming however, the project was abrogated by the emergence Oneirion *Kosmas*. The residual effect was to inject a bit of cultural diversity into Oneirion society. Thanks to Dr. Simon Butler, Oneirion cuisine was already exceedingly cosmopolitan. Whereas Francoise and his contemporaries in the study were a testimony to Oneirion flexibility, unrestricted by dogmatic adherence to the pursuit of homogenized culture.

"Certainly Chef. I'd like the whole tour." Phil suspected Francoise was playing for time, awaiting illumination of the sky. For the moment, the restaurant was bathed in a discrete flaxen light, glowing eight stories above an uneven plain from a dark tower, isolated in the unworldly murkiness. Not an auspicious unveiling.

At the end of the tour "That was truly impressive Francois. Your design?"

"Everything I ever dreamt of in a state-of-the-art restaurant."

"Well done. How many can you seat?"

"*Les Rêves du Gaunt* is one of six eating places, plus the two mess halls, not to mention individual ensuite cooking facilities. But we planned this as the central restaurant for all of *Gauntlet*. So we made some interesting design features. The floors retract down to three stories. They are also re-configurable. This can be formed into an elegant restaurant as you see it now. It can accommodate up to three hundred diners."

"We only carry a compliment of two hundred Francois."

"Yes. However, it is also designed to welcome guests when you arrive *Kosmas.*"

"I see. Good idea I suppose. Assuming we can eat together."

"This can also be configured into a night club, bar and conference center."

"Impressive. So what's for lunch?"

"We are featuring a menu from one of my favorite restaurants in Paris, restaurant L'Oulette:

*Foie gras cooked in spicy wine with sweet and sour mango*
*Chestnut bread*
*Rouget Grillée "anchoïade" (Red Mullet grilled with anchovy purée with garlic and olive oil) and eggplant open pie with basil)*
*Beetroot pancake filled with braised rabbit, roasted saddle and parsnip cake*
*Selection of cheeses*
*Poire a L'Anse, crispy pastry, and blackcurrant sorbet*

"Sounds great. Is this Parisienne or Oneirion food?"
"*Nourriture de Gantelet.*"
Phil smiled. I don't suppose you can join us?"
"*Alors*, this is the final shake down for the kitchen. I must be there. *Bon Appétit.*"

As Phil was raising a long Gin & Tonic to his lips the ceiling vanished. Blinding white light flooded the dining room and a new world silently erupted into existence. Phil's lap was soaked in icy Gin & Tonic.

Mike smiled dryly. "I see Nick has the Spheriscope working now. He should be joining us soon."

Phil, appreciating the humor of the situation looked up from blotting his lap, when he quite literally froze.

He was looking out the huge windows of the restaurant and beyond....not the inside of a long dormant volcano...not an interstellar vessel...not a hollow ball of hardened concretions....a world...a world whose grace and beauty defied description.

Lakes, forest, streams, even snow capped mountains skillfully crafted to convey the illusion of great height. All shining under a deep blue sky that went on forever. Closer, there were paths, buildings, courtyards, piazza, parks and gardens. An entire world, somehow classical in aspect. It reminded Phil of something mounted within a crystal sphere. Shake it and it would become a world swirling in snow. For some reason it all reminded Phil of ancient Babylon. Perhaps there was a hanging garden hidden somewhere?

Without taking his eyes from the window Phil whispered. "Magnificent."
"I fully agree Phil. I envy you more than you know."
"*Who designed this?*" Phil was nearly whispering.
"Nick's people worked closely with the QAVL for a time. Wrestling with all sorts of interior designs. Then the QAVL suggested we take Earth with us to the stars. The task force enthusiastically agreed. After that it became pretty

much a product of QAVL art and engineering. As you can see, their skill far exceeds human capabilities. This sphere is titanic. Yet it feels exponentially larger. I swear there's a wonder about it. *Gauntlet* is a sphere in a mountain that enfolds an entire planet. A magic ball turned inside-out."

Fresh Gin & Tonic in hand, Phil and Mike toasted their new world.

Nick Farrow entered the dining room and approached their table. "Good afternoon Captain." Nick nodded and turned to Mike with a smile. "Patron." He shook hands with both. "Sorry I'm late. We had a cranky Spheriscope filter."

Lunch began.

Nick smiled at Phil. "I understand you skippered the SAT-SAV over to Anastasios."

"That's correct. She's one hellofa boat. Your boys do good work Nick."

"Thanks. I agree. That damned thing will do everything except deal cards." Nick suppressed a grin. "I uh...heard you should've mounted your snow tires? Or should I say mud tires?"

Phil grimaced wryly. "When it rains, stay in the water."

The conversation grew serious. They debated the targeted three week lift off. *Gauntlet* improvements and glitches. They talked of Anne and Aiy. The undersea music that had mysteriously come and gone.

"It was a little disorienting coming in. Are there still port and starboard access tunnels?"

"Yes. And you shouldn't worry about learning the latest spec on *Gauntlet*. We're preparing a full release along the lines of the S&S SAT-SAV Training Bar Chief King administered to you."

"JAEKEL."

"JAEKEL?"

"That's her new name. I'll explain back on Oneiro. We're planning a christening."

"Sounds good. By the way, the Chief said you performed brilliantly as Skipper."

"That's kind of him. But it was more of a milk-run than a shakedown. That S&S Bar. The AAM. Those uh...Accelerated Anthropogenic Metabolizers...they really work. I look forward to a *Gauntlet Bar*.

Anyway, since we still have the portside and starboard tunnels, I'd like to manufacture two large brass plaques and mount them above access ports. I jotted this down aboard JAEKEL" He handed a piece of paper to Nick:

## Oneiro II: Gauntlet

### Portside Ingress

*From this day to ending of the world,*
*But we in it shall be remembered;*
*We few, we happy few,*
*We band of brothers;*
*For he today that sheds this Earth [sic] with me...*
*Shall be my brother.*

*William Shakespeare*
*St. Crispen's Day Speech*
*Henry the Fifth*

### Starboard Egress

*We shall not cease from exploration*
*And the end of all our exploring*
*Will be to arrive where we started*
*And know the place for the first time.*

*T.S. Eliot*
*Little Gidding*
*The Four Quartets*

Nick read the paper carefully and handed it to Mike. After reading it Mike smiled "Very nice Phil. I couldn't agree more; although we will be using both tunnels for exit and entrance concurrently."

"I'm sure. But I think the crew will get the idea."

Qasi spoke up from Phil's DIT.

"I think they're both fine sentiments. A lovely use of irony. A 'happy few' who are about to die. Another 'few' arrive home safely only to find their travels have but begun. Are you familiar with Pogo by the gifted philosopher/cartoonist named Walt Kelly? No? A shame. You must ensure a complete set is incorporated into the ship's library."

The three men peered at Phil's DIT, then thoughtfully at each other. It was far too easy to forget Qasi's presence when meeting with Phil.

They finished Francois' remarkable lunch. Over coffee the four reviewed their status. All in all Phil received a comprehensive briefing in a surprisingly short period.

Finally Phil summarized his understanding thus far. "Okay. It seems we *can* be ready for launch within three weeks. Propulsion, environmental, navigation, digital, food production, internal power, communications, maintenance, emergency evac, centrifugal-gravity and pseudo-gravitational systems. All are certified nominal. Terra-forming is effectively complete. There's no provision for a shake-down cruise. But of course, there never was. We have a final crew manifest and a Chain of Command. Two hundred and four souls aboard. Insofar as we know Ambassador Qasi will be the only QAVL aboard."

Phil's DIT spoke again. "That is correct Mr. Consul. My duties will be those of QAVLian Ambassador, Technical Attaché, Cultural Attaché and Technical-Astrophysical Consultant. I will also act as engineer insofar as QAVLian drive systems."

Phil smiled at his DIT and sub-vocalized "...and I imagine any other topics that attract your interest." Then distinctly. "Thank you Ambassador." Phil continued randomly ticking off items. "We have a final cargo manifest, including a comprehensive library of multi-media cultural materials and initial nutritional provisions for four months. *Gauntlet Bars* will be distributed to all ship's company within ten days. Anne will accompany me on this voyage if she wishes. If so, she will be the sole authorized non-*Kosmas* speaking crew member. By the way, you *are* signing on for the trip. Right Nick?"

"I had every intention Phil. Since then though, the QAVL have been enticing me with the myriad wonders of *Gauntlet II*. It's going to be....titanic."

"Why so large?"

"I'm not totally sure. It has more to do with range and velocity than payload; and a hull that can withstand literally anything. The crew will be required to undergo some sort of genetically manipulated physio-nucleic acceleration, whatever that means. The sphere will not be filled with nitrogen-oxygen."

"Physio-nucleic *inducement* Nick," corrected Qasi.

"Inducement. Right. Thank you Ambassador. I'll need a *G-II* Bar soon. In any event it all sounds incredible and I *must* be part of it. I hope you don't mind Phil."

"I sure as hell do Nick. But I think I understand. Are you assigning someone comparably qualified?"

"Phil, no one's as qualified. But I'm sending you my best. Laura Cain. Smart, tough and she really knows her job. She's aboard somewhere now."

"I'll look forward to meeting her. Meanwhile, let's wrap this up. Medical is now fully equipped with FOND-DELIQUESCENSE biotech systems, as are all crew quarters."

Nick cocked his head, a confused look on his face. "Help me out here please. FOND-Deliquescence? Sounds vaguely familiar, but I really don't have a clue. I'm aware of the installations, but what is FOND?"

Mike responded "Foreign Organic & Non-organic Detritus. It's a by-product of a substance called the *Kosmas Serum* which quickly permeates the entire corpus irrespective of tissue type. Its function is to remove bodily detritus inconsistent with human health and youthfulness – down to the molecular, atomic, even sub-atomic particulate level. Then it is excreted during the chemical wash, the shower. It keeps us all healthy, good looking, young, and smelling like a rose. No need to even brush your teeth. Just shave and take a shower. You can even forego elimination of bodily waste if you care to. However, that is inefficient and somewhat unpleasant. In fact we recommend the body be voided prior to showering. There will always be some materials in the GI tract. But FOND- Deliquescence can distinguish desirable from waste and minimize such eliminations. We've installed a FOND-Deliquescence unit in your quarters on Oneiro. You'll like it...after the first shower that is..."

"First shower?"

Phil cut in. "The first shower constitutes a sort of acclimation and initial purge. It must be conducted under medical supervision. When I underwent the first treatment I thought I would die. Literally. It's far easier now. There's an audio-visual record of the first human shower in the archives if you care to watch it. I personally recommend you undergo your first shower before viewing it."

"Guess I've been missing some good stuff out here on Anastasios. Is it you Phil?"

"Me?"

"Yes you. Is it your record in the archives? Taking the first shower?"

"Yes it is. Not something I care to dwell on."

Phil continued summarizing the points given him. "Finally gentlemen, you tell me both seas have been filled and stocked. How was that done?"

"Phil that was really something to see. We enlisted some boys from marine biology to locate a moderately dense, representative section of sea. In this case about fifteen kilometers South/South-West of Oneiro, at a depth of about three-hundred and fifty meters. An area of about one cubic kilometer of water. Then the QAVL deployed eight gravity emitters, interconnected to form a gigantic cube. There were several species missing from the cube, as expected. So we either brought them into the cube, or some entered on their own. The QAVL can adjust the gravitational gain to act as a one-way barrier."

"So they actually have a functioning force-field."

He looked quizzically a Phil for a moment. "This is a gravity filter, wherein gravimetric force is selectively imposed with a matrix granularity. I have no idea what a 'force-field' may be."

"Sounds like a giant lobster trap."

"Good analogy. Afterwards the QAVL bonded the eight emitters to a fleet of ships, which we towed to Anastasios. Luckily Anastasios has a very deep harbor which shelves off dockside, so we could tow the cube all the way to the launch and load ramps. The cubes were sized to use both access tunnels. When the sphere was prepared, the QAVL installed groups of fourteen emitters inside the cube, each one linked to an existing emitter. In this way they methodically dismantled the giant cube...cube by cube...sealing the fissure from removing seven emitters with the remaining seven. From there it was fairly easy. We linked to and towed each small cube to Shark Bay inside the sphere. We lowered the cube into the sea cavity and cut power, releasing the water and the beasties. After about six days we had a sea. Six days after that, we had two seas."

"How did the sea life stand up to the move?"

"I understand marine life is doing well and both seas are in bio-chemical balance. They are producing oxygen and binding $CO^2$ at the stipulated rate to maintain life in the sphere. We are seeding additional plankton and planting sea grasses with artificial reefs."

"Excellent. Moving along, quarters and working areas have been customized in accord with crew wishes and requirements. In those cases where requirements were unavailable, prototype features were installed. They can be modified at any time after launch."

Phil looked around the table. "I believe those are the high points."

Mike looked up from his notes. "Agreed Captain. I therefore assume you will be lifting off in twenty-one days from tomorrow."

Phil shook his head "No Mike. Three weeks is a contingent deadline should forces militate against us. Agreed Ambassador?"

"Yes, although our projections remain unchanged."

Mike frowned deeply. "Phil you mention 'forces militating against us'."

"Yes."

"If I understand correctly, then we must address the question of releasing the news of our friends the QAVL to the world. We cannot delay further."

Phil sighed deeply. Nick looked on in confusion. Finally Phil spoke. "Alright Patron. As you say. We should have faced this down. To my knowledge, no other issue divides the Administration of the Patron and the Offices of the Consul. Suppose we convene a council to finally resolve this goddamned issue. Let's say a board consisting of nine members. I nominate myself, you, Anne and Dr. Kahn. You select the rest. That gives you six out of nine. A controlling bloc. However, I fervently hope we are guided more by ration than majorities."

"I fully agree Phil. I will select the remaining five with that in mind."

"Thank you. I have other business in Europe requiring immediate attention. So I would like to convene in about ten days. Agreed?"

"Agreed."

"Fine. Now gentlemen…Ambassador…if you'll excuse me, I think I'll take a walk. I must see this place for myself. Mike I'll meet you at the portside tunnel at 1800 if that's alright."

"Sure." Mike extended a paper-thin holo-card. "This is a current map of the sphere. You may need it. '*Gauntlet* North' always fades to a small dark blue area on the polar horizon. During the night cycle, north fades to a dim pastel blue glow. There's always some sort of landmark easily visible; and the access tunnels are marked on the map as well. If you have a problem, you can always contact me.

Be careful out there. Some of the terra-form is quite recent, so it has yet to be anchored by roots and moisture."

"What do you do for earthworms by the way?"

"That's been automated. Only the seas have truly natural ecosystems. It may sound strange, but fifty years is a long time to rely on biologicals. Enjoy Phil."

"Thank you. Please thank Francois for me too. Lunch was exceptional. As was this briefing."

# *La Vie* in Rows

*...air-breathing sea creatures and birds; and on the sixth day, "the beasts of the earth according to their kinds..."*
*Genesis*

Phil found his way through the restaurant and down the crystal elevators. When he reached the huge lobby he noticed a cluster of waiting PM's. Instead of exiting, he decided to explore the building.

He stopped for a moment. *I think I want to take this trip by myself, QAVL included.* "Qa-sout." There was no change, no acknowledgement, but Phil recognized the sudden solitude that signaled he was now completely alone.

Disregarding the PM's he began to roam the hallways on foot, using sweeping staircases at the terminus of each wing of the building.

He found much.

Footsteps echoing through the vastness, he found offices, theaters, bars, shops, administration centers, enormous supply bays filled with hundreds of neatly stowed bales, boxes and barrels. As he entered the central complex he encountered what was clearly the command compound. Huge Spheriscopes, navigation, communications and environmental consoles. There were some impressive hardware configurations spaced apart from the mammoth bridge. After close inspection he determined one was dedicated to interfacing with the QAVL power and propulsion center at the far northern pole of the sphere. The second was used to monitor ship's status from thousands of sensors throughout *Gauntlet*. A third and smaller configuration was designed for management of a variety of systems which supported day to day activities on Gauntlet. QAVLGate passive transport systems, PM's, Robotics, Food Production, Hydroponics and hundreds of other tasks. All optionally under the control of GAIA. The entire Bridge covered at least ten thousand square meters in an austere gray, beige and maroon. As Phil approached the center of the vast control center he spotted an enclosed conference room – a Briefing Room, just outside a 'V' formation of large, obviously command positions. At the apex of the V was the Captain's Seat.

Phil looked sheepishly about. When he confirmed he was alone, he took a seat. The chair was exceedingly comfortable. It swiveled 360°, as well as raising and inclining. He believed he could sleep in this chair if need be. At the left of the chair was an impressive set of controls (he was going to need that *Gauntlet Bar*), and to the right a commanding view of the entire bridge –nicely engineered. He gave his chair a quick flamboyant twirl.

He was going to like this. Hell, he was going to love this. Beyond anything he had ever dreamt. Phil thought back to similar meditations in his past. What he was going to do with his life. He had been an attorney, billionaire, leader, diplomat, fisherman, businessman, commander, scientist and assassin. Now he was to be the Captain of humanity's first interstellar Cruiser. He would command a crew of two hundred from this chair for the next fifty years. *Fifty years.*

He quietly withdrew from the vast Bridge considering the benefits of returning to the restaurant and a few stiff drinks.

Instead he continued his tour to the top of the immense structure.

Many wonders. Much beauty. Things and rooms and places he could not understand nor identify. The mark of the QAVL was clear throughout, blended with the best of Oneiro. Phil began to find the titanic cruiser very silent and daunting, and humbling.

At the apex of the complex there was a slightly smaller level. Totally empty save one door: CAPTAIN'S QUARTERS

*I'll be damned.* He slowly pushed open the door. He was stunned. An exact replica of his Residence on Oneiro. Every room the same, even the view from the terraces. *How the hell did they do that?* The more he searched the rooms, the more impressed he became. Aside from personal belongings, keepsakes, books, certificates and such, everything was there. Clothing, food, drinks, work in progress, even his various weapons. He was flattered at such attention. He was embarrassed at the depth of their knowledge of him. He was even a little spooked. But most of all he had the eerie feeling of a dead Pharaoh inspecting his tomb. All the belongings he would want for eternity lovingly stowed and stored for his use in the afterlife.

He hoped this was to be his home. Not his tomb. Strange. He had given little thought to his accommodation aboard *Gauntlet*. But when he did, he thought of his quarters. Not his home. In the space of a lunch, that had all changed.

It had been easy going over the plans and the science with Mike and Qasi and Nick. So easy in fact he had neglected to focus on a command spanning five decades. Two hundred humans – albeit some of the most talented in human history – still two hundred humans with all their needs, disputes, frailties and fears looking to him for leadership, and survival itself. Then, if he survived the first part of his trial, he would face the most daunting collection of sentients in all the galaxy.

He nearly ran to the crystal elevators. He needed air. He needed to escape this terrifying incarcerate. There was no call button. *How the hell can an elevator work without a call button? Where is the goddamned call button?* Aloud, he muttered "Crap!"

"Elevator Captain?" clearly an electronic voice.

"Yes Damnit! You dumb motherfuc..." He realized he was screaming at an elevator and took a quiet breath.

"Yes. Please."

During the long ride down his DIT lit up. "Phil?"

"Mike? I thought the DIT unit was reserved for Qasi."

"Right. Well, it's being extended for all intra-ship comms. You'll all carry one. We're installing the same system on Oneiro now as well."

"What can I do for you Mike?"

"Our board shows you're still in the building. Is everything alright?"

"Fine. Fine. I'm just leaving to explore the outside. You can tell where I am?"

"You bet. We have our own GPS type system on *Gauntlet*; and we didn't have to insert it in geosynchronous orbit. They call it an SPS. By the way, there's only two hours of light left; and we're supposed to meet in a little more than an hour and a half."

"Got it. Okay. I'll grab a PM to make it faster. I'll call you when I'm ready to meet."

"Okay Phil."

"By the way…how do I connect to you?"

"Just say 'Mike Auslander' into the unit. Everything else is automatic. You're using sort of a jury rig. They'll issue you an official one when you board, as Captain."

"Thanks. See you soon."

Somehow Mike's call had calmed him down…brought him back to a manageable reality. *What's wrong? I can't let this get to me.*

In the lobby he mounted a PM, assuring it he would provide directions as they travelled. This was an improvement over the Oneirion model which would refuse to move in the absence of a specified destination. The old term 'fuzzy logic' somehow sprang to mind. As they smoothly travelled along, Phil also discovered he could conduct a primitive Q&A sort of a dialogue with the machine. Almost like having company on the ride.

Once outside, his mood lightened and his angst began to subside. He needed to think. He needed the sea. But not just now. He ordered the PM to stop and stand by. He stepped out and followed a path into the woodland. *What the hell is wrong with me? I've been trained against fear. I'm immune to fear. This must be something else. What?* He walked and he thought for a long while.

Eventually he was compelled to consider the nature of fear. Fear. *Rational fear was essentially the purview of the unknown, the unexpected...results and consequences the individual was incapable of projecting. The logical trepidation one feels when navigating towards an unknown destination. For some reason drawn inexorably to that destination...*

A dark and private room in his mind sprang into brightness.

*Of course. Nothing magical here. Just physics. The ultimate quantum granularity. What a fine line. What an unimaginably small tolerance. Attempting the slightest deviation through application of pressure on a particle – trying to nudge that particle out of its reaction trajectory – and it produces – fear. What energy is at work here? Force on the particle produces tension. The tearing away of spurs and consequential eruption of even smaller particles. The particles produce fear. Perhaps fear itself is a sub-sub-sub-sub-sub-atomic particle? But who is to state that these tiny motes of creation are not strictly adhering to their predetermined course? There is absolutely no proof to the contrary.*

He stopped. He froze. He felt as though he had been subjected to a high voltage shock. *Of course! That is the challenge. The cosmic corroboration. To dare the wondrous ballistics governing one single, miniscule particle in motion. To change its course. Just one would suffice to defy cosmic ordination. I can sense these particles for some reason. Thousands of millennia in advance of my race. Other races as well? That is the source of my fears. I can detect quantum momentum and position and recognize discordances. Danger at the sub-atomic level. I wonder how in hell I do it?*

*Can I ultimately alter their course? Am I unique? An entity truly capable of actualizing free will? Heady stuff. Is that why the QAVL cluster about me? Is this really why they constructed Gauntlet?*

Phil was dizzy, weak and disoriented. He sank to the ground lost in thought.

Finally: *We are creatures awash within a four dimensional infinity of universes below and above our cognition. All our science describes only effect. We mistake the underlying chain reaction of effects as cause. In reality we are eons away from perception of cause. There may be only one cause in all of creation. That one cause sparking an eternal infinity of effects. Acquire the cause. Control the effect.*

*Slowly, very slowly I'm beginning to see.*

The air was fresh. The sun was bright and clear. There was even a gentle breeze caressing the land. Flowers bloomed, grass rippled, water cascaded. There was the sound of bees and the twittering of birds (both presumably digital). At night he was sure he would hear frogs and crickets serenading a starry darkness as a gauzy mist made its cooling descent onto dewy leaves. The quiet normalcy of it all made him feel better. In the midst of such beauty his confidence returned. Hopefully to stay.

He returned to his PM and instructed it away from the woodland into the central community…beautiful walls built to last a thousand years…broad boulevards…Broadway!...workshops, bars, schools, meeting halls, libraries, restaurants, theaters, a sports complex, shops, a deli!…swimming pools and fountains and canals…gondolas…piazzas, parks...museums…everything an advanced metropolitan center could provide…all skillfully blended in an elegant architectural and natural setting.

The entire area was deserted. *Where the hell is everyone? Judging by the size of the fleet moored at Anastasios Harbor there should be hundreds of people working here. I'll have to ask Nick.*

Phil was just rounding a corner, entering a large intersection. The convergence of six tree lined boulevards. The center of the plaza was marked by a stone circle. At the center of the circle he saw two large, well crafted, brushed chrome doors, equipped with heavy gauge chromium handles. Atop the two doors, chiseled in stone was a name: Charles de Gaulle □ Étoile

Frowning. Phil keyed in his coordinates and queried the PM. "Identify."

There was an immediate response. "QAVLGate 134, Charles de Gaulle □ Étoile. Down-line Gate 133, Piccadilly Circus. Up-line Gate 135, Odéon."

Phil smiled. *I see.* "Proceed to Gate 135 and await instruction."

"Acknowledged." The compact little chariot rolled away.

As he neared the QAVLGates, he saw four portals. The two on the left were marked 'Up-line Onload Odéon' and 'Up-Line Exit Odéon'. The right portals were marked 'Down-line Onload Piccadilly Circus' and 'Down-Line Exit Piccadilly Circus'. Each of the Exit portals were blocked by one-way barriers. *So this is the famous QAVLGate system…frictionless underwater tubes connecting all points throughout Gauntlet operating based on principles first set down by Sir Isaac Newton.*

*Well, what the hell, let's give it a try.* Phil went to the entrance of the Trafalgar Portal, gripped the handles and looked down. A dim greenish glow rose from below, illuminating the tiny access chamber. After a moment Phil jumped in.

He was almost immediately under water going faster than he could have believed possible. He pressed the sides with feet and hands to slow down, to absolutely no avail. He pressed again with all his strength. Still no change in speed. In fact he was moving faster and faster. He could barely make out seaweed and the occasional marine creature blurring past, when he suddenly found himself standing upright…braced by a one-way barrier ready for him to exit. Wonderfully exhilarating! He was a little shaky from the unexpected speed. *Damn that was fun!* He briefly looked about. He was in a large square, museums and a theater enclosed the area. *This is a truly fast transit system. Totally maintenance free, silent, non-polluting. The system consumes no energy and is 100% safe. What's more, it's fun! This could get addictive!*

He wandered around the QAVLGate Terminal and located a beautifully inlaid map of the QAVLGate Network. Subway stations from Paris, London, New York, Berlin, Rome, Buenos Aires and more. *Clever touch of home.*

Using the scale outlined on the map he estimated he had travelled halfway up to the sphere's equator. *Fast.* Lord Nelson's Column in mid-square caught his attention. He could make out an entrance at the base, so he made the short walk to the tower. Sure enough there was an elevator.

He entered. The doors opened. He expected no button. He said "Top." He stepped in and the lift activated.

Upon stepping out, he caught his breath. The view was astounding. Earth.

In the distance mature forests…snow capped peaks… restless sea…green fields…country paths…lakes…and the sky…endless blue, clouds, birds (?). QAVL perception engineering was electrifying. This was going to be alright.

From this height he began to appreciate another aspect of QAVL engineering. As he travelled through the sphere everything appeared random and naturally variant. However, this was clearly an illusion. In fact the entire sphere was neatly laid out in even parallel rows, north/south by east/west. An orderly grid. Longitude/latitude QAVLian style. Internal navigation was going to be a snap.

After a time, he looked far below. His sleek little PM was patiently awaiting instruction.

# The Hollow in the Sky

"Attention. Sunset alert. Twenty minutes. Two-zero minutes. Nighttime illuminations are currently unavailable. All personnel must report to the portside or starboard access tunnels within ten minutes. One-zero minutes. Contact *Gauntlet* Central immediately if you are unable to comply."

*Good grief. Sounds like the voice of God.* "PM, what is our ETT to portside access tunnel."

"Estimated Transit Time to portside tunnel is eight minutes."

"Excellent. Thank you."

The little chariot had no response protocol for declarative iterations. Only interrogations and injunctions. It acknowledged this thanks in silence.

Mike was patiently awaiting Phil at the interior port. "Well?"

Phil looked at Mike and his surroundings thoughtfully. "Beyond description. This is going to work. I can feel it. I begin to really appreciate the genius of the QAVL."

Mike smiled. "Let's get back to JAEKEL and discuss this over something cold and wet."

"Agreed."

They worked their way through with a small line of workers exiting the sphere. Once outside Phil was amazed to see hundreds and hundreds of workers ahead of them. A dusty, ambling commute seeking whatever rough sustenance, shelter and slack-time available to them on Anastasios.

"Where the hell have they been? Everywhere I went this afternoon was deserted."

Mike raised eyebrows thoughtfully. "They were in the hollow in the sky."

"Sounds like poetry. Something out of *The Wizard of Oz*. What does it mean?"

"Wherever you stand in the sphere you have roughly a 65% line-of-sight vision. About 35% of the interior cannot be seen from any given point. That is because the interior sphere which houses a sea on the inside, supports the sky on the outside. The Spheriscope. Therefore you literally cannot see 'the blind side of the sky'. Understand?"

"Sure. So I suppose all these people were working on the opposite side of the sphere from me this afternoon?"

"You got it."

"There's a sort of a tactical application to that I think."

"Phil, you *do* have a real tendency to see things in military terms. Let's get you back to JAEKEL and get you a drink and some dinner."

Sturdy sub-mariner's fare. Whitefish, boiled potatoes, biscuits and tea. Cheese, apples and port. Finally a robust bottle of dark Oneirion Rum.

Years ago during the planning for Oneiro Island, the new breed of architects and engineers developed a specialized engineering discipline. Their objective was to optimize work and living facilities, hopefully providing people with a better overall life. They considered the elements of Work, Nutrition and Habitation. They termed their new industrial design:

Erdibinom
[air-deebeen-umm]
(*Greek:* Ergo-Work, Diatofi-Nutrition, Biotopos-Living, Nomos-principles)

In a near prescient initiative, they created a set of standards and principles uniquely linking profession to diet to living conditions. Among many realizations, they found that the classical cuisine associated with a profession reinforced the practitioner and even fostered a certain *esprit de corps*. A bonding ingenerated by sharing a restrictive, often subsistence, diet. For example early mariners subsisted on dried, cured or salted meats and fish, dried or stored fruits, carbohydrates (hard-tack) and dairy products (cheese). Hence whitefish, biscuits, apples, port and so on; and through consuming such food together the diners bond and become more of a crew. Other examples include fishermen, farmers, hunters, even advocates in some cultures. These same principles were adopted in part, in the design engineering of *Gauntlet*.

Philip Carr, Mike Auslander, Nick Farrow, Mick Dodge and Charlie King were quietly reviewing the day's events in the wardroom – having just consumed such a meal. Phil felt a twinge of guilt at his comfortable surroundings when he considered the hundreds living in steel containers, or aboard rough cargo ships.

A sharp knock at the door.

"Enter."

"Captain Carr I have an urgent communiqué from Mr. Oscar Sagan on Oneiro."

"Thank you."

"Oscar Sagan?" queried Mike.

"Director of Security. New on board." Phil tore open the envelope and read.

Phil visibly paled and simply sat for a time, thinking. Then he stood decisively and strode to his intercom.

"Comms? I want Mr. Howard Doyle, Managing Director of the Chicago security firm of Doyle & Phillips. Contact my office on Oneiro for assistance. Howard should be in his office, but wherever he is, I must speak with him. I want Howard pre-briefed by Sagan in Security. Patch him through to the wardroom when you get him. I want his call scrambled. Confirm this with Howard. And use the Heisenberg Monitor. I want this immediately. No excuses. I am standing by."

Phil slammed into a chair and poured himself long rum.

"Chief? Can you get me a seaplane? I must get to Oneiro immediately."

"Sure, I can..."

"Do it Chief. And I want a jet standing by on Oneiro. Fully fueled. Ready for takeoff."

"Certainly. Flight-plan for what destination?"

"I haven't got one clue."

"Understood." Chief King stood and exited the wardroom.

Phil poured another drink and simply sat in silence – jaw muscles rippling – looking at no one – speaking to no one. He had given no instruction for them to go, so the men sat where they were. They had all seen Phil angry before. Now though, they saw a murderous, icy calm in his eyes.

The intercom phone shrilled and Phil immediately answered. The men would hear only his side of the conversation.

"This is Carr. Go."

"Did Sagan brief you Howard?"

"Talk to me."

"Yes."

"How is she?"

"Good."

"I understand."

"How the hell did she get all that?"

"Bitch."

"Yes it's bad. Couldn't be worse."

"No idea where?"

"Crap!"

"Your boys are on it?"

"Yes. Worldwide. Whatever the cost. I need this Howard."

"You bet your ass. I'll grease' em myself. We can't afford to screw around with policy, or any DUS bullshit. There's just no time."

"He's involved too? I'm glad we fingered that son of a bitch."

"Are you still going to Cannes?"

"Good. Can you clear your schedule?"
"I see."
"I'll have a plane standing by in Cannes."
"I'll meet you at the Carlton. 1700 CET tomorrow. Lobby bar."
"Yes. Bring it all. Fully loaded. I'll make a transfer immediately. Ten?"
"Thanks Howard. You're the best."

Phil slowly replaced the phone. It rang immediately.
"Yes?"
"Skipper we couldn't find a seaplane. But we can bring in a chopper. A Sikorsky CH-3 is available. If we refuel, it can make the round trip. It will be here in one hour. A jet will be standing by on Oneiro, fueled, crewed and ready to go. And senior staff will be standing by for you at Oneiro Field."
"Well done. Ring me up when it arrives."
"Gentlemen we have a problem. Put the whole island on alert. All boats on twenty-four hour watch. Dispatch JAEKEL on continuous patrol. Take out anything within ten kilometers. One warning only. Use only the Standard International Marine Emergency Band. Ask the QAVL to monitor as well. Aside from warnings, I want a complete communications blackout until further notice. Break out the arms. I'll keep you posted. Now I must get packed and make a few calls. If you will excuse me...."
Mike interrupted. "Phil I think we would like a few more details."
Phil swirled his drink, impatiently staring into the golden-brown liquid. "There's been a security breach. If the information finds its way into the wrong hands, we'll be facing a real shit-storm. I suspect our meeting regarding a news release in ten days is now irrelevant Mike. Just pissing in the wind. An RF."
Mike smiled grimly and a little wistfully at the allusion.
"We have other priorities now. Let's get on 'em. That's all gentlemen."
The three men quietly withdrew. Mike grudgingly bringing up the rear.
"Phil?"
"I just told you everything I know Mike. I need some time."
"Sure Phil."
"Thanks."
Phil considered calling Anne and rejected the idea. He was just too angry.
Seventy-eight minutes later he was airborne. Flying low over a moonlit sea.

Suddenly everything was at risk. Everything could be lost. Ruined. Man's future hanging in the balance. To protect the future Phil was ready, perhaps eager, to became a primitive again. Remorselessly quiescent to the ensuing, inevitable brutality. Just as the QΛVL, he could see it now. He felt the discordances. The components evaded him. But he could sense the dangers; and they were real.

## *DAKHALA* RAZA

They quickly fell into a comfortable routine. Every few days Raheem would take a trip. Manu spent the days looking after the apartment and seeking work.

She worked hard at it and talked to dozens of people. No luck. Her growing insight began to enumerate her problems.

First. Her appearance. Bruises, cuts, a limp. That would pass. She knew she was not pretty. But she only wanted a job cooking or cleaning. In any event with Raheem's wonderful bathroom she kept herself clean and her hair proper.

Second. Her clothes. Thanks to Raheem's help she found more presentable clothes. But as she earned some money she would upgrade her wardrobe.

Third. She was Afghan. Nothing to do about that.

Fourth. There was something else. New to her. Not only was she Afghan, she was Jat. The ancient tribe relegated to the lowest level of society for centuries. Growing up a Jat, she had never known this. She began to work on her accent and started calling herself Manin. She naively assumed that she could somehow cast off the stigma of being Jat.

Fifth. She had no papers. This narrowed her prospects considerably.

Sixth. She could neither read, nor write, nor speak anything but her local dialect. She began to bitterly resent the 'preparations' made by her parents to face the world.

She had many strikes against her. But she wouldn't stop trying; and she was confident sooner or later she would find work. She would not give up.

Meanwhile, she learned more and more about cooking and grew quite skillful. She was pleased. Raheem was equally pleased.

One dark evening Raheem returned from a trip. Brushing snow, flexing fingers, stomping to get circulation, and generally seeking warmth. Manu had dinner ready, so they sat down immediately.

"How was your trip?"

"The weather was bad. I don't have another one until Friday. I hope it clears. I was stuck at Torkham Station for nearly ten hours. The whole place is up in arms."

"Up in arms?"

"Yes...they found a man behind the restaurant. Dead. Beaten and robbed. Turns out he was the owner. This is good by the way. What is it?"

"ACHARI GOSHT. It's Indian."

"It's very, very good. You must make it again."

"Do they know who did it?"

"Did what?"

"Killed the man at the restaurant."

"Uh no. And they've found other bodies nearby. A soldier and a worker. Both thrown down the cliffs. Others are missing. Including a young girl. They think maybe some Chinese in the area are doing it."

"Well...people die all the time in the heights."

"Yes. I know. Uh, Manu, I have a question for you."

For the first time since leaving Torkham, Manu felt the cold thrill of fear. "Yes?"

"You're uh, that is you seem to be, what is the word? *Showing.*"

"Showing what?"

"Manu are you pregnant?"

She was still for a long time. She looked down. She'd lost her appetite. She truly hadn't noticed. She'd almost forgotten. *My God, is this why I can't find work?* What would she tell Raheem. *Will he lose respect for me? Throw me out?* In one brief moment, everything was beginning to crumble into the same smothering morass as Torkham. Thoughts flew through her mind. Hope seemed to be leaking helplessly through her fingers. Finally she responded.

"Yes Raheem. I am. I was raped by a trucker from Asgabat. When my family found out, my father beat me, and they all shunned me. He was Turkish, the trucker. What we call AJNABI, a foreigner. It is a disgrace to know such people. It was not my fault. But it made no difference." She began to silently weep.

"You poor child. It's the same everywhere. Cruel bastards. The world is shit."

A huge surge of relieve raced through her. *Bless Raheem.* He understood. He would not judge. He would not cast her out.

Manu stumbled to her couch and buried her face in her hands and sobbed uncontrollably for several minutes. Then her voice, muffled and weak "Thank you Raheem. Thank you. Thank you."

Head down, she stared into emptiness saying nothing.

Raheem softly placed a cup of Chai in front of her. "We'll have to find a midwife for you." He turned on the television and turned off the lights. They sat quietly in the flickering bluish light, wordless, until Manu nodded off.

Finally the weather cleared. Much too early for spring. A gift from winter. The streets came alive in the sunshine and unseasonable warmth. Markets opened for business, coffee shops were crowded and the grey town abruptly blossomed with color.

Raheem was between trips. Manu was shopping and job hunting, so he decided to go out. Go to his old neighborhood, enjoy the day, see some friends. It had been far too long since he had some fun in town.

He went to a small Tai/Chinese restaurant he used to frequent with friends. Good food, generous servings and cheap. No a la carte. The menu of the day was the only choice. Raheem liked this. It felt adventurous, particularly considering some of the supplies he'd seen delivered here over the years.

He savored the long remembered scents as he entered the tiny restaurant. Hot oils, Chai, spices, incense and the ubiquitous pall of steamed rice. A friendly smile, a cup of Chai and the meal began. Tiny skewers of lamb sate followed by crispy eel, with Lychee as desert. Raheem was dawdling over his Chai when RAZA walked in the restaurant.

RAZA was one of his oldest friends. Raheem always suspected he was a bit of a bad seed, but he was drawn to his mischievous, fun-loving predilections nonetheless. He knew RAZA lived in his neighborhood now, but they hadn't seen each other in months.

He stood. "RAZA my friend."

"Raheem!"

The two men solemnly hugged and kissed each other on the cheeks. RAZA was tall. Gaunt, with a long, thin, angular face. He had suffered from a poor complexion as a youth and the ravages remained. The shadows of an unhappy and insecure adolescence. He sported a long deep scar from some past recklessness running the length of his right cheek. Topped by thick, unruly black hair his general impression connoted a hungry, cunning, rangy creature.

"It has been far, far too long. I have missed you. What are you doing now?"

"I drive a truck for Sajjad."

"Yes. A nice man."

"You know Sajjad?"

"We do business from time to time."

They sat down and ordered Chai.

"Are you eating RAZA?"

"No. Just tea."

*Odd place to come just for tea. Perhaps he saw me.*

"And you. What are you doing now?"

"I uh, work in exports."

"Oh? A company I know?"

"I doubt it. They are a new company, owned by Portuguese investors, based in Ghazi Khan."

"Are you doing well?"

"I've never made so much money in my life. Maybe I can throw some your way."

"Well, good for you. Do you have a girl friend these days?"

"No not really. I travel a lot and meet many women."

"You're a lucky man. I travel all the time and meet no women at all."

RAZA raised an eyebrow in a leering smirk. "That's not what I heard Raheem..."

Raheem laughed "...and what have you heard?"

"I heard you're living with a girl."

Raheem regarded him incredulously. "My but your well informed. But also misinformed I'm afraid. There is a young girl. But she only cleans and cooks for me."

"I'm impressed. You have a live-in maid?"

"Well, she's not a maid really. I'm just letting her stay on my couch until she gets settled. In return she cooks and cleans. A nice young girl. She does a good job and she's quite a good cook."

"Settled from where?"

"What do you mean?"

"You said she's staying until she gets settled. So where does she come from?"

"Afghanistan."

"Family here?"

"No. She's new in town."

"Papers?"

"No. You ask many questions RAZA. Why all the interest?"

RAZA smiled. "Just interested in your love life old friend."

"She is not my love life. She is nice. But she is also a little homely."

RAZA laughed and changed the subject. They spent the next half hour re-living old times and catching up on mutual friends. Finally "Look my friend I must go. Why don't we meet here for lunch on Friday?"

Raheem checked his note pad. "Sure. I'm in town on Friday."

RAZA jumped up. "Noon?"

"Noon."

"Great I'll see you then."

He arrived home late after a lively afternoon in the market place. On impulse he had purchased a colorful Persian shawl for Manu at a street vendor's stand. Little money, but something he thought she would like.

Manu was home, the apartment pristine as usual and a special dinner laid out, Pakistani AALOO GOSHT KARI – a kind of a lamb and potato stew. One of Raheem's favorites. He had spoken of it so many times, she learned the recipe and proudly set it before Raheem.

"Oh my. What a lovely surprise. I have not tasted Kari since my mother made it. And this is excellent. Thank you Manu. Most kind." He smiled broadly. "...and I have something for you..."

He handed her the shawl wrapped in tissue paper. She gaped at the package intrigued and confused.

Raheem proffered the parcel "Go ahead. Open it."

She buoyantly accepted the gift and tore open the paper. She was amazed. She was thrilled. She carefully draped it about her shoulders and lovingly stroked it.

"Thank you." She appeared unable to say more. Raheem thought he saw the mist of a tear welling in her eyes.

*My God. Has she never been given a gift before?* "Come now. Let's eat. We can't let this lovely dish get cold."

Manu removed the shawl, placing it neatly next to the TV, lest she stain it. They passed a cheerful meal. After she cleared away the dishes and finished washing up, she donned the shawl again while they watched TV...as she would do so every night thereafter, always carefully folding it next to the television.

Over Chai and Aaloo Paratha the next morning they discussed their plans for the day. Manu finally had an interview scheduled with a fairly prosperous Afghan family. Cooking, childcare, cleaning. She was optimistic. Raheem was to meet with RAZA for lunch at the 'no name' Chinese restaurant. He was then to meet with Sajjad to service the truck, collect his load, gas, money, pick up his manifest, waybills, and custom's papers for tomorrow's trip.

His trip would take four days and Manu wanted to prepare a dish he could carry with him. Hot or cold. She decided on her special variation of Puliyogare. A rice snack popular throughout Pakistan. She had all the ingredients necessary except the Arabic spice known as tamr hindi, or Tamarind. Raheem promised to purchase her some at the market, after lunch.

Over lunch, Raheem and RAZA talked about women, sports and how business in Pakistan seemed to be limping along. RAZA was wearing a new suit. Dark blue, huge grey stripes, shiny, with a black shirt and silver silk tie.

Avoiding RAZA's eyes. Concentrating on his meal, he finally spoke of it. "That's ah, quite a suit you're wearing. New?"

"Yes and expensive. I just bought five new suits, but this is my favorite. Do you like it?"

"It's nice."

"I can get you one...just like it. Interested?"

Half smile. "Well, I don't have much need for such clothes. I certainly have no need of them on my truck and I have no plans to marry anytime soon."

"Speaking of marriage, is Manu still living with you?"

"How do you know her name?"

"You must have mentioned it last time."

"No. I did not."

"Well who knows? It's a small neighborhood. Does she still live with you?"

"Yes."

"Do you suppose she's in some kind of trouble somewhere?"

"Could be, I suppose. I really haven't given it any thought."

"Perhaps you should."

Raheem was becoming annoyed. "What's your point RAZA?"

"You could get in trouble. Maybe serious trouble."

"Anyway I think she'll be leaving soon. She may have found a job."

"You said she had no papers. That could make it difficult."

"Where are you going with this RAZA?"

"It's just that you may be forced to throw her out. I know you. You're a decent guy. You won't be able to do it. Even if you might get in trouble."

"Yes?"

"I can make it easier for you."

"How?"

"Sell her to me. I will take her away. You'll never have to get involved. You won't even be at home. I'll see she's looked after."

"For God's sake she's pregnant."

This gave RAZA no pause. "That can be useful too."

"Allah agahta ana! You are a slaver."

RAZA looked around furtively and whispered. "Keep your voice down. I am *not* a slaver. Never call me a slaver. *Never*. You understand?"

He regarded him with a piercing look. "What are you RAZA?"

"I am an exporter and we help homeless young ones."

Raheem stood and threw money on the table. "You are a slaver and our friendship is ended."

He turned and stalked out of the restaurant.

He walked around for a time. Sightlessly browsing the markets. Trying to cool down. Trying to forget a lifelong friend, now trading in human flesh and inhuman suffering. His lunch churned unhappily in his stomach. *That bastard wanted to buy Manu.* He realized his jaw ached and his hands were cramping. He had been clenching teeth and fists since he left the restaurant. He forced himself to calm down. Take a deep breath. Maybe a coffee. *Oh. I've forgotten the Tamarind for Manu.*

He found a stall and purchased her spice. Suddenly he felt uneasy. He decided to hurry home. He needed to pick up the truck anyway and it wouldn't hurt to check on Manu. *Should I be worried about that bastard RAZA?*

When he arrived at the apartment everything was in order. Immaculate in fact. *Odd that Manu's not back yet. A morning interview shouldn't take all day. Unless she got the job and went right to work. That would be a relief. I guess...*

He realized her leaving would be a bittersweet event. He would be happy for her. But he had to admit he would miss her. Her cooking. Her housekeeping. He had never lived so well. And yes...he'd miss her company. *A shame she's not pretty, at least a little. She would make a fine wife.* He sat down, eyes roving the apartment that would probably be a mess again soon, when his eyes were riveted on the TV. Manu's shawl was gone.

His mind raced. *Why would she leave with the shawl? Not on a job interview. Not to go to the market. Why?* Then he realized. *RAZA! There can be no other explanation. She's been taken by RAZA and his people and she took the shawl in desperation. She was either taking her most prized possession away with her, or she wanted to leave an alert she was being kidnapped. Either way, she has been taken. Ya Allah...by slavers!*

*Wait. Wait. There could be many other explanations. Don't panic. Go out. Look for RAZA and Manu. Calm down.*

For the next hour Raheem nearly sprinted around town. He covered every conceivable spot frequented by either of them. No luck. No trace. No one had seen either, or had any ideas where they might be. Strange how rough and alien his town suddenly seemed.

He returned to the apartment and retrieved the truck. His plan was to drive around and enlarge his search and make his way to Sajjad, who would no doubt be angry by now.

An hour later he drove into Sajjad's depot.

"Where the hell have you been. Do you know what time it is?"

"I am sorry Sajjad. I think I have a problem. Do you know RAZA?"

"A pig. He steals and sells women and children. He stocks the brothels, the work houses, perverted rich men and unholy pits from Singapore to Dar es Salaam. He should be pollaxed like the pig he is."

Raheem was speechless with horror.

"Sajjad, I believe RAZA has taken a friend of mine."

"Man or woman?"

"A young girl."

He spoke gently. "Raheem, the first rule of slaving is take the slave fast and far away immediately. Consider her dead. Mourn her. Then try to forget her. You can do nothing else."

"I must do something Sajjad. I must."

"Alright Raheem. I will put out some feelers. My people know well where and how things move. Perhaps they can trace her. I will try."

"Thank you Sajjad. Thank you."

"Now, get your truck and your papers in order. Hurry. I want to get home before breakfast."

# The Quickening

The big helicopter raced above the rugged Oneirion landscape. A ghostly panorama veiled with dark silhouettes, brooding hills, giant trees and sheer cliff lines. Throbbing *thwacks* echoed through the darkness. Nose low and fast. Phil was looking almost directly into the ground. Below conventional radar. Barely one-hundred meters. Phil watched the imposing Proteus Point Communications Concentrator blur past, towering above him. It was a moonless night. Clear and cool. Stars densely clustered from horizon to horizon. The whole island was on black-out with the exception of Oneiro Field, awaiting his arrival.

Phil gripped his seat tense with anger and foreboding. He was trying to comprehend such loss of control so quickly and ruinously.

*What the bloody hell happened? What was going on with those two? Are they nuts? Am I jealous? Hell no! They're endangering Dr. Webber's lifetime of work. All of us on Oneiro. Thousands of man-years. The entire world in turmoil. Humankind's stake in the future. All of it jeopardized by a nice pair of tits and some long legs. And it's my fault really. I allowed it to happen. Thinking with my gonads.*

Phil struggled between guilt, panic and anger. He felt he was betrayed by Aiy; and he was deeply disappointed in Anne. A hot poker deep in his viscera. And he was at the threshold of fear.

Oneiro Field arose beneath them. Phil could see his jet standing by, the yellow glow of the hangar, a circle of white lights flashing rhythmically, marking his landing zone; and a group of about twelve people looking up.

In less than a minute he was on the ground confronting them. He surveyed the group, unsmiling. "The gang's all here. Good. I suppose all of you know more about this fiasco than I. I *do* know we may be facing the combined wrath of the entire planet. School's out. We could lose everything now, including our lives.

Mr. Sagan will you please clear the hangar? I'd like to move in there for a fast, confidential de-brief. And I want these lights off." He gestured all around.

Sagan walked hastily into the hangar. Soon mechanics and ground handlers were striding towards the entrance of Oneiro underground. Darkness quickly descended on the Field, as the group woodenly proceeded into the hangar.

"Anne? May I see you for a moment please?"

When they were alone on the dark tarmac, Phil spun about on Anne and spat one word *"What?"*

Clearly taken aback, she willed herself to remain calm. "I can only tell you this. This morning Aiy had already done some research and proved to herself I was lying about the name of that restaurant..."

"Brasserie QAVL?"

"Yes."

"Go ahead."

"I could hardly believe how angry she was. I thought she was going to attack me. Then she received a phone call from somewhere in Africa which really set her off."

"Phone call? Goddamnit she was supposed to be under a communications lock out!"

Anne simply stared at Phil, a suggestion of entreaty in her eyes. "The call came through an internal line. We had no idea it originated off island."

"Where did all this occur?"

"At our...uh your apartment. That's why the call wasn't screened."

"Continue."

"She ran out, heading to her apartment. She was there for only a minute or so. A maintenance man saw her leave. To the best of his recollection Aiy carried nothing but a large blue file folder. No bags. Meanwhile, she had called and asked me to meet her for a drink in the Lobby Bar. She said she was sorry for losing her head. She wanted to apologize. Claimed she was facing a huge problem. She asked me to hurry. I went to the lobby bar to meet her. Apparently she waited until I had left. She then entered your apartment and stole several digital files from your office. She also took some notes and photos I was keeping in my end-table."

"How in hell did she know about these files?"

"Well, she did spend a fair amount of time in the apartment alone. You know how resourceful she is."

*I've been as negligent and stupid as anyone. Goddamnit.*

"So where the hell is she?"

"The best we can figure, she went to Oneiro Harbor and took a sail boat. A fairly large one. Twenty-six feet. I suppose she learned about harbor security procedures when we went sailing."

"Where did she go?"

"We have no idea. Search helicopters went out looking for her and didn't find a thing."

"The choppers went out how long after she cast off?"

"Our costal defense network indicates about four hours."

"Four hours! What the were you thinking of? I trusted you to look after this bitch."

"Phil, it took a good while just to conclude she left the island, and longer still to confirm she'd taken a boat. Those boats are free for anyone to use who has access to the harbor."

"They still have to be signed out don't they?"

"Yes. She signed out as me."

Phil was calculating to himself. *Four hours. 360° to choose from. Say, twelve knots. Maybe more dependent on winds and tides. She'd find landfall reasonably soon only in three directions. That's still a lot of water for two Drákōn Helicopters. Then again, if she was in no hurry she could go any direction she wished.*

"Was the ship provisioned?"

"Mike ordered all vessels provisioned and ready for deployment two weeks ago."

"Did you send anything else out?"

"Both jets were off base; and we didn't think any conventional ship had a chance of finding her. This was not air-sea rescue after all. She wasn't in trouble and she didn't want to be found. I'm wondering if she rendezvoused with someone at sea and scuttled the boat."

"Why do you say that? What would she link up with? Another ship, a sub, an amphibian. What?"

"Phil I'm just speculating. I'm trying to help."

Phil ran a hand through his hair. "What happened to her phone?"

"I took it."

"Give it to Charlie."

"I have."

"I assume the boat is equipped with a radio?"

"Correct."

"I don't suppose anyone thought to give her a call?"

"Of course we did Phil. We're still trying."

"Well stop it immediately. We're under a communications ban; and if she's not responded by now, she's not going to."

"I understand."

"Any idea where she was heading?"

"None."

"Any idea who phoned her?"

"No. Charlie's working on that now."

"Any idea why she was so upset? Her restaurant grievance sounds like so much bullshit to me."

"I have no idea why she was so disturbed. I agree. The restaurant thing shouldn't have upset her so much. But it may have angered her that we're still keeping things from her. Especially me."

"I don't suppose it occurred to you the files set her off."

Clearly hurt. "Of course it occurred to me. But I really believe there is something even deeper at work."

"Disregarding your *beliefs* for a moment, what exactly was contained in the files she stole?"

"We reconstructed things as best we could. We're pretty sure those files contained notes on the QAVL, photos of *Gauntlet* at various stages of construction, recordings of *Kosmas* and minutes of our group meetings with Mike. There were also excerpts from the QAVL Document itself. As that was a digital file, it is probably a QAVL sentient file as well. It's also possible she turned up considerable information from her various interviews on Oneiro. Language, Anumen, genetics, art, the unique physical prowess of the Oneirions and so on. And of course the *Gauntlet* project. You know how persuasive she can be."

Phil sourly growled "Beautiful." And began walking briskly towards the hangar speaking almost to himself. "A QAVL sentient file. Would such an entity help defend Oneiro, or would it blunder into even worse trouble...?"

"Phil. Phil? Look I'm really sor...."

"...into the hangar...*now*. I'm airborne in five minutes."

Anne persisted. "Phil, she's had a tough time of it. She doesn't show it but she's hurti..."

"Stop thinking with your goddamned glands. We're going to be fighting for our lives soon if we can't get her under control. It's time to stop her, or kill her. Not weep for her." He turned and strode to the hangar.

Stone-faced, Anne hesitantly followed.

When Phil entered the hangar the group had hurriedly arranged thirteen chairs into a rough oval preparing to meet. He conspicuously walked to the center of the group without taking a seat. "Does anyone have any idea where the hell this broad got to?"

No.

"Charlie when will you know who called her from Africa, and from where exactly?"

"We need off-island resources to get it done. That's difficult at the best of times and damn near impossible this time of night. We're doing everything we can, but I doubt if we can break this one."

"Start spreading money around Charlie. Lots of it." Phil addressed the whole group. "You all appreciate the severity of our situation?"

Yes.

"You realize what she stole from our files?"

Yes.

"Can you add anything?"

No.

"Suggestions?"

Not really.

Phil began moving towards the exit and his plane."Let's hope Howard Doyle and his organization can..."

Sagan injected "Some of us would like to join you Phil. We know..."

"No Oscar. You're all going to be busy as hell right here. Mike will be in charge. Oscar you'll be his number one. Get this down:

- o Mobilize all defenses twenty-four hours a day unless you hear otherwise from me.
- o Wrap up all operations on Anastasios and get the SAT-SAV back as soon as possible.
- o Locate all ships away from Anastasios.
- o Destroy and cover all ground facilities on Anastasios.
- o Leave only the portside access tunnel exposed.
- o Get the *Gauntlet* crew together and secure them in Oneiro Harbor, ready to move out in at a moment's notice.
- o I want the SAT-SAV and Sea Tigress standing by, fuelled, provisioned, and ready to cast off. I also want a full medical team on board.
- o I'll take the SAT-SAV and I want Nick Farrow to man Sea Tigress. Move Captain Herbert Carr and his First Officer, Diamantes, to my apartment.
- o Secure all non-combatant Oneirions in the Armory.
- o Get Mike back here after Anastasios ground installations have been destroyed.
- o Effective now impose a blackout on all communications and traffic on and off the island.
- o Oscar, I want you to tear Ms Atsila's apartment apart. Squeeze it for every bit of information you can get.
- o Anyone off-island as of now will have to get along as best they can.
- o Mr. White, I want you to personally approach the United Nations Director of UNOOSA and give him a heads up.
    - Minimal details.
    - Request their assistance in watching for Aiy at every port in the world.

- Give him this note from me.
- It must remain sealed.
- There is a copy for you attached.
- 'Eyes Only' Bob.
  o Button up everything and get ready for hell's own.
  o My secretary will know how to contact me...I want you to provide her precise status reports every hour which she will relay to me and Mike.

"Okay that's all. Questions? No? Good luck."

Phil turned and began moving quickly to his aircraft. He paused, almost imperceptibly, and cast a serious, but not entirely unsympathetic glance at Anne. She returned his look in kind.

Once onboard, the aircraft was immediately airborne. The First Officer came aft bearing coffee and a questioning glance. "Good evening Mr. Consul. Welcome aboard. Coffee?"

"Sure thanks. Did they deliver a bag for me? I want to get out of this uniform."

"Yes sir. You'll find it just aft of the head."

"Thanks."

"Can you provide us a destination now? We need to file a flight plan."

"Sure. We're going to Cannes. The south of France. The Côte d'Azur."

"Right. We'll get on it straightaway." He frowned. "We may have some difficulty parking in Cannes. This is the conference season. So they may want us to divert to Nice."

"I understand. Either airport is fine I suppose. Whichever it is, will you instruct our ground handler to arrange a car?"

"Sure. What would you like?"

Phil thought a moment. "Two doors. Nothing too flashy. Good trunk. No rag top. I may need some real muscle."

"Aston Martin?"

"Perfect. What would you estimate flight time?"

"About four hours and change."

"Okay. I'm going to get some sleep. Please wake me when we're half an hour out."

A light touch on his shoulder and Phil was awake, looking out into a new dawn. He could see the Alps serrating the horizon and the azure sea sparkling far below. *Alpine skiing and water skiing in the same day.* It looked to be a beautiful day in the South of France.

"Coffee? Breakfast?"

"No thanks Captain. I need a kick in the head. Not the stomach. Is the bar stocked?"

"You bet. What can I get you?"

"A bottle of Scotch and a glass."

"You got it." He was presented a bottle of single malt, ice and a glass. "Anything else?"

"Yes. I'm not sure how long we'll be on the ground here. But I need you on hot stand-by. Takeoff with less than an hour's notice."

"There's a Park Hotel just across from the airport. We'll stay there."

"Good."

"Any idea where we'll be heading?"

"No idea. Just keep your wings full."

They were directed into Nice.

Forty-five minutes later Phil was making his way down the coastal highway towards Cannes. When he reached Antibes, he stopped briefly for a *café au lait* and a good French croissant at a seaside café. He sat in the sea breeze, enjoying the brisk morning sunshine as it cleared his head. Then on and around Gulf Juan and onto the route to Cannes.

He arrived at the Marley at 0930, entered the gate code, parked the Aston in the rear, and made his way to the elevators.

The apartment was deserted as Phil had ordered. Phil was gratified to see the placed had been opened and stocked. He went immediately to the phone.

"Inter-Continental Carlton Cannes. Bonjour."

"Bonjour. Has M. Doyle checked in yet?"

Brief pause. "No sir. Would you care to leave a message?"

"Please tell M. Doyle to call Mr. Carr at the Marley. Thanks."

Next call to Charlie Stein on Oneiro. "Morning Charlie. What do you have on the Africa call?"

"Nothing Phil. We're not even sure the call came from Africa. We've tried to back-track. The call, starting with our log and everything we could trace back was bogus. I've been talking to all sorts of people and spreading money around as you suggested. Still nothing. Sorry. I think we're looking at a cold trail."

"Okay. Thanks Charlie. Will you transfer me to my secretary please?"

"Sure Phil. Wait one."

"Mr. Carr?"

"Hi Cindy. What's up?"

Phil heard her organizing her notes. "The entire island's on alert. No comms, no transport in or out. I understand they may be ready to sterilize

Anastasios as soon as the day after tomorrow. The following personnel have requested to speak to you urgently: Anne Jones, Edward McKnight, Bob White and Oscar Sagan."

"Put me through to Bob White please."

"Hi Bob."

"Phil. Thank God we're an official country. Otherwise I'd have been treated as a complete nutter. As it is, they're cautiously willing to review our evidence."

"Good news indeed. I take it you're on your way to the United Nations?"

"No. I need your authority for four things. First, they want to send an envoy here to Oneiro. A Dr. Chandresh ABHAY. Second, I need your authority to get him onto the island and then I need authority to take him to Anastasios. They say they must have unequivocal proof of every assertion. They're right. They also request that I disclose your letter to Dr. ABHAY. That's the third authority I need."

"What do you know about this Dr. ABHAY?"

"A good deal actually. We ran a fast background history on him. He's a well respected astrophysicist, cosmologist, cum diplomatic attaché. Past National Science Advisor, the Princeton Institute for Advanced Study and widely published on subjects as diverse as non-terran life and non-Solar planetary systems. Involved with SETI for awhile. He's for real and a fine scientist."

"That sounds just fine. We're finally getting lucky. What's the fourth item?"

"They want to talk to a QAVL."

"Damn. I should have seen that coming. They're aware they can't speak to them directly?"

"Yes."

"They're willing to speak through a digital intermediary?"

"Yes."

"That strikes me as naïve on their part. How could they possibly ensure we aren't rigging the interview? Falsifying everything."

"Dr ABHAY seems to believe he is capable of asking questions we wouldn't be capable of answering."

"But the QAVL would be able to answer the questions?"

"Exact."

"You're recording this?"

"Yes sir."

"Good. I find their approach reasonable. You've got all four authorities. I understand they're sterilizing Anastasios as early as tomorrow, but you should be able to get him in through the portside access tunnel. Ask Nick to arrange for the same helicopter he got me. The Sikorsky. I don't want him riding in one of our *Drákōns*. I also want one of our jets to pick him up in Athens. No foreign aircraft in or out except the CH-3.

You have my blanket authority to take Dr. ABHAY anywhere he wishes, show him anything he wants, open our files to him, brief him in depth about our disclosure deliberations; and assign any support resource necessary, except military. He is welcome to take any documents he wishes. Be entirely open. Ensure all his questions are answered fully and honestly. Arrange a meeting with the QAVL. He needs to be fully aware that we are preparing our defenses. My only stipulation is that he affirm all this information will go no further than Executive Security Council Members, without consulting me personally first; and that his party consist of no more than two representatives – himself included. Send Mike a transcript of this conversation and let me know if he has any problems. I would also like you to personally brief Mike and convey my apologies for failing to consult with him. There is simply no time."

"Can do. Thank you."

"Pass me to Oscar Sagan please."

"Hi Oscar."

"Hello Phil. Cindy's already got my brief. So I've only got one thing to discuss."

"Okay."

"I went through Aiyana Atsila's effects in her apartment. I was thorough. There's hardly a thing now larger than six square centimeters. Everything was clean. I couldn't find a thing. Then I took her computer apart. Hidden in the mouse, enclosed in the battery, I found a tiny piece of paper inside."

"Yes. And...?"

"The paper contained one phone number, one email address and two mailing addresses. The writing is damned near microscopic. They were..."

"Wait one Oscar. Let me get a pen and paper."

A moment later "Okay Oscar, go ahead."

"The address is 12HmV22*S-U-T.com. The first address is Number 135b Karl Kjelsens vei, Oslo, Norway. The second address is 12 Shahrah-e-Zarghoon, Quetta, Pakistan, just out of Dera Ghazi Khan. The phone number is 33-2765."

"Where is that phone number?"

"We haven't been able to work that out yet. No country or city code. The length of the number is wrong for most western countries. And it's wrong for Norway and Pakistan."

"How do you know it's a phone number?"

"Actually we don't know. But that's the only type of number we can reasonably research. It could be anything from a bank deposit box, a pin number, a digital lock code, a license number, a street address..."

"I get it. So there's no structure about the number that suggests its use."

"Actually the best fit is a phone number in many parts of the world."

"What about the addresses?"

"So far we only have a name for the address in Oslo."

"And?"

"The name is Scott Woodman."

Phil whistled. "Adahy Atsila."

"Yeah. We're working on the address in Ghazi Khan; and were conducting a worldwide search on the phone number, but it takes a great deal of..."

"Well, keep at it. The other phones ringing. I'll call you back when I can."

"Hello?"

"Hi Phil. Howard here."

"Howard. Good to hear your voice. You're in Cannes?"

"Just checked in. I need a shower and an hour horizontal."

"As do I. Suppose I pick you up at the Carlton at 1230?"

"Sounds good. I'll book us into the La Bastide Saint Antoine."

"We need some privacy Howard." Cautioned Phil.

"No problem. It's a beautiful day, so everyone will be on their terrace. I'll get us a corner table inside and make sure no one's seated anywhere close."

"Good. I'll pick you up in front at 1230. You got some goodies for me?"

"Yeah. A whole bag. I'll bring it with me."

Phil briefly pondered calling Anne and decided he still felt pretty damned crusty. Somehow he was irritated with Edward as well. So he quickly shaved, showered, made himself a tall G&T and emerged on the roof of the penthouse. From here he had a splendid view of park and coastline, marina and Mediterranean beyond. It was an idyllic day and he was soon fast asleep in a comfortable rooftop *chaise longue*.

## *DAKHALA* Amira

Manu thought they were police. They exploded into Raheem's apartment with a single kick, and wordlessly looked about. Then they turned towards her and she knew they had come for her. She ran to the TV and snatched up her precious shawl, and fled for the door. Long before she made the door they grabbed her, covered her mouth and carried her out helpless in vice-like grips.

Her most terrifying nightmare come true. They had linked the murders of Zalmai, Malik and Private Dunn and deduced she was the common thread. Now they were taking her back to Torkham; and God knew what they were going to do to her there. What of her? What of her baby? Her life was done. So close to building a life. She had found Raheem. She had found a job! And now to have it cruelly snatched away. She wept bitterly.

She was thrust into the back of a large truck and enclosed by a heavy wire mesh cage. Cold, dusty and rough. The musky smell of canvass and metal. She was thrown from side to side despite her best efforts to hold tight. She resigned herself to many long icy hours, climbing into the Safed Koh, then into the Khyber Pass, then on to the horrors awaiting her in Torkham.

To her great surprise the truck rolled to a stop just over an hour later. The big truck idled for a few minutes and then took a sharp slow turn. Immediately she could hear the bass pseudo-echo of the engine as it rumbled through a narrow tunnel. Just as quickly they seemed to enter some sort of underground garage and pulled to a stop.

Her heart raced with a sudden apparition of hope. Perhaps there had been some mistake? They certainly hadn't gone to Torkham. Maybe this would be over soon. Raheem would come in his truck and bring her home. There was still time to make a nice dinner. Start her new job tomorrow.

The sound of boots on concrete walking to the back of the truck. Padlocks being removed. The rush of canvas being thrown back. The sudden glow of artificial light. And finally the unlocking of her mesh cage. Strong hands reached in and pulled her out. Standing her on her feet.

All the men wore boots, denim pants and shirts with leather jackets. Dirty, unshaven and mean looking. These were not police! Who were these men? What was going on? What did they want of her?

Again she tormented herself with the bitter delusion of hope. This *must* be a mistake of some kind. These men couldn't possibly want anything of her.

One of the men hustled her onto a type of loading dock where she was made to stand, disheveled, with her precious shawl drawn about her shoulders. A man swaggered up to her. A short lumpy young man. Looking no more than sixteen, he was brazen for his age. Greasy looking, with extraordinarily bad skin. Young, belligerent, repulsive. He looked her up and down appraisingly.

"Damn! She's uglier than me."

The men around her laughed and seemed to make similar comments which she couldn't make out.

"Not much to do with this one. I suppose she can fuck Bengali sailors in the whorehouses in Chittagong. Put her with the rest."

"Sir, she is an Afghani. A Jat. An Afghani Dalit. And she's pregnant."

"Oh damn! Why do you bring me crap like this?"

"Shall we have her aborted sir?"

He mulled it over, roughly taking her cheek between forefinger and thumb. "Nice skin." He weighed the options. "No. Babies are worth money. One of our girls can raise the bastard. If it's a girl, the kid could bring a lot. But we gotta sell her before she uglies up. Say...six or seven. The buyers south of here love young skin like this. Shame the mother's too old. If we can't sell her, she can join her mother in Chittagong. If it's a boy we'll sell it in Jakarta." Fatin released her. "Now get her out of here."

*Hasan Allah! These are slavers.* An overwhelming wave of icy nausea swept over her. This was far worse than anything she could have imagined. She began trembling with despair, as her realization of the enormity of her predicament overwhelmed her. One of the men pushed her "Get moving girl." She couldn't move.

The little man suddenly turned back on her. "He told you to move girl."

She still could not move.

He savagely backhanded her. She was sprawled on the floor. Blood dripping from her nose.

"Move girl!"

She scrambled to her feet and hurriedly followed her guard.

They walked through a large underground area filled with stores, weapons, all sorts of machines, even a large laboratory. She heard snatches as the men spoke together of *Fatin* and the *Poison Dwarf*. Manu deduced they were talking about the swaggering adolescent. Few men were actually in evidence. Those few milled around the vast area, all carrying weapons. None appeared to be working. Some appeared drunk, or on drugs. All were loud and rowdy.

They passed into a large hallway, footsteps echoing. It steadily grew darker and colder, moisture condensing on high stone walls. Manu and her guard marched through the hallway until they came to a massive door. After much jangling of keys, the door swung back.

The smell was overpowering. Nauseating. A repellent concoction of cesspool, abattoir, locker room, soup kitchen and old bedding, dominated by the saliferous pungency of unwashed bodies. Hundreds of them, past and present.

The scene itself was something out of Dante. A few dozen starved and filthy humans trapped in near darkness. A tableau suggestive of the death camps of World War II. Manu froze like Virgil at the gates of Hell. To no avail. Her guard roughly shoved her into the huge chamber and slammed the door behind her.

She quickly learned the grim routine of her prison. She whispered at first. Then she discovered their guards had absolutely no interest in their activities beyond keeping them alive, and preventing their escape. Manu found herself free to ask any questions she liked. No one cared.

"Where are we?"

"We are in a fortress in Dera Ghazi Kahn."

"Why?"

"Stupid girl...we are slaves."

"Why?"

"They will sell us."

"To who? Who wants to buy us?"

"Well, the women and children will be sold to bordellos, and the men..."

"What is a *bordello*?"

"My God girl, you know nothing. A bordello is a whore house. You know what a whore house is don't you?"

In a small voice "Yes. And the men...?"

"They will dig. Dig until they die."

"Dig? Dig for what?"

"Gold, diamonds, sapphires, silver...it depends where they are sold?"

"What of my baby?"

"They have women who can help you give birth. Then they will raise the child here and sell it when it is old enough."

"My God. How can they be so cruel?"

"They are slavers."

"Is there no way to escape. Will no one help us?"

"No and no child. We cannot get out and no one knows or cares where we are."

"What shall I do?"

"You want the truth child?"

"Yes. Please. Yes."

"Die child. Die as soon as you can. Die before your baby is born."

Manu wept silently for hours.

There were two meals a day. Both the same. The guards would bring in three or four kilos of oat meal and several liters of water. From this they were expected to cook a tasteless gruel on an aging hot plate. The water was also for drinking. There was no excess for washing.

The toilette facility was primitive and unspeakable.

They were expected to sleep on the floor. Often they would huddle together for warmth and protection from the floor.

From time to time people were taken out who had been sold, or because they wanted some information to assist in further harvesting. If they encountered resistance Manu could hear their screams.

Fights often broke out between inmates. Disputes over food, or water or a section of floor. Manu even heard the occasional rape during the long nights. That people could abuse each other when sharing such conditions astounded her. Often in the mornings bodies were removed.

Thus began her final nightmare.

For the next five months she suffered a hundred kindness' and a thousand cruelties. She watched death and torture and small triumphs of survival, selflessness and bravery. Although there were never more than a few dozen prisoners in the chamber at any given time, many rotated through...departing this little parcel of hell for fates possibly worse. Irrespective of nationality, religion, sex, age, even economic background. Many types passed through this unhappy place and Manu grew to know them. She struggled together with many to survive. Struggled alone against many to survive.

It was around midnight. All was quiet except a few rowdies laughing and throwing rocks. One broke off from the pack to relieve himself in an alleyway. Scant minutes later he was wandering back down the alley to rejoin his friends. Suddenly he was grabbed from behind and flung against a wall. A knee delivered a powerful blow to his groin and he doubled over in pain. Two strong hands took his head and slammed it against the stone wall over and over. When he could hardly stand, a voice growled out of the darkness "Where is she you filthy son of a pig. You shit. Where is she!?"

"Wh..wh..who?"

Three more times into the wall.

"*Manu* you bastard! *Manu*. What have you done with her?"

"Ra...Raheem?"

"That's right you bastard. Now answer me RAZA."

"I saved you. Kept you out of trouble. You would have gone to prison, or worse."

"I am going to kill you if you don't tell me right now. *Where is she?*"

"I don't know. I really don't. I know she is wanted in Afghanistan for three murders. If you were caught hiding her you would have been implicated too. So I saw to it she was taken away."

He shook him violently. "*Where is she?* You are a slaver. I will see you hanged."

RAZA's eyes blinked with an imperceptible flick. "You are a stupid, stupid man..."

A long knife was expertly inserted between Raheem's ribs and shoulder blades, into his heart. He had never dreamt such pain could exist. A single lightning stroke. 'Uh!" He dropped like a stone.

RAZA straightened himself and looked down on the dead man. Then he kicked him with all his strength and spat on him. "...stupid, stupid man..."

Manu's time grew near. Women came to her aid as long as they remained in the chamber. Although no medicine was available, they kept her and her unborn alive, if not healthy.

Then a new woman was sent in. Not of the chamber. She was also a slave. But she had been saved from the whore houses because the guards wanted her for themselves. Her living conditions were much improved, as were her chances of survival. Her most serious problem was the frequent beatings that many of the men took pleasure in. Her name was Fatima and she was kind to Manu, after her fashion.

When her day arrived, Fatima had Manu removed from the holding chamber. A blessing! They cleaned her and gave her soup. They put her in a private room with a bed – almost clean – and a window. For the first time in months she could actually see the sun. Her gratitude to Fatima was overpowering and she could not stop thanking her profusely. Fatima's only response was to try to quiet her, not to attract the attention of the guards.

In Manu's weakened condition the birth was difficult. After all the beatings and mistreatment, hemorrhaging was inevitable. Six hours later Fatima presented a newly washed baby girl to Manu. The sun still shone through Manu's window, allowing her to see the beautiful baby in the golden light of the late afternoon sun. Manu had not smiled since she was parted from Raheem.

Fatima asked "What is her name Manu?"

Manu laid back, exhausted. She thought for a time. "Amira. Her name is Amira. May I hold her please?" Fatima carefully placed the tiny baby on

Manu's stomach. Manu wrapped Amira in her prized shawl. She closed her eyes and held her daughter. Manu's essence arose from a lifetime of abasement. She became a luminous creature savoring the pure, immaculate joy of the moment. For the first time she was endowed with something unimpeachable. Unassailable. Something of such value, all the past debasements dwindled to a gloomy haze. Hers alone. Manu quietly died.

# The Green Grasse of Lome

Grasse rises above the Riviera to a height of more than one thousand meters. Perched in the towering foothills of the Alpes Maritime, it enjoys commanding views of both the sea distinguishing Cannes and Antibes, from the dramatic mountains above. There are two or three meandering routes ascending to Grasse. With the exception of the Departmental Road towards Cannes, all routes are breathtaking and challenging to drive. Enroute, one passes beautiful villas clinging to cliff-sides and tiny towns splendid in sunshine and flowers. Phil always loved the drive, particularly today, negotiating the winding road in a powerful and agile sports car.

In the late 18th century, Grasse became the center of perfume production for the entire world. It remains so today. The primary industry and tourist attraction of the town is perfume, where it produces nearly 90% of all perfumes on Earth. As a consequence, vast amounts of money found its way to Grasse. And still do.

As another consequence, Phil always found the town somewhat arrogant. Too famous, too rich, too independent. He could recall days in early spring when he was unable to find a café or restaurant open at midday, or even a drink. Incredibly they were closed for lunchtime.

On numerous occasions he had escorted young ladies on tours of the perfume factories and 'sniffings' in the factory shops. Though he hated every minute of it and couldn't stand the smell, such outings were *du rigueur* on the Rivera for those wanting to find favor with the fair sex on holiday. And it was indeed such favor he sought.

Phil collected Howard under the Carlton's formal rotunda. Howard liked the car, so in the midst of abundant 'Ooo's' and 'Aah's', hands were shaken and a sturdy metal bag was deposited in Phil's trunk. Soon they were climbing the hills approaching Grasse. Phil had yet to exceed 3rd gear.

After few preliminaries Howard asked "So why'd you want the hardware? It's costing you a hellofa lot of green, and I know damned well you have better stuff in your own armory."

"I want nothing traceable to Oneiro, no matter how indirectly."

"I see. So you're planning on doing your own wet work again?"

"Let's not get into that Howard. I want to concentrate on finding this bitch Aiyana Atsila. Any luck?"

"I've had every man I can get my hands on busting tail for the last fourteen hours. So far nothing."

"Crap."

"Look, it would help a lot if you gave me the full story. I'd know how to read her better. Predict her movements. Understand her objectives. Otherwise I can't help you much. Just sitting and waiting for some blind luck and a pretty girl. See what I mean?"

"Yes."

"And?"

"And this mess is so far above Top Secret you'd need a star **chart** to find the grid coordinates."

"Who's?"

"Who's what?"

"Who's 'Top Secret'? Who owns this problem?"

"Let's see. Oneiro. The United Nations. China, France, the Russian Federation, the United Kingdom, the United States, Austria, Japan, Kuwait, Mexico, Turkey and South Africa."

"Christ! You're talking about the goddamned UN Security Council."

"That's correct. Are you sure you want to be on the inside of all this?"

"War?"

"Highly possible. If this gets out, I'm convinced it's inevitable."

Confused and annoyed "What kinda war? Some half-assed tip to sell arms? Jumpstart an economy? Stroke the ego of some dip-shit tyrant? What?"

"With the exception of some murderous middle-easterners, the most tragic of all wars. A war unique in human history. A war with no aggressor. All parties doing what they believe they must, in absolute good faith. Worldwide. Dying in vast numbers. Innocent and altruistic."

Howard grew quiet. And atypically serious. He knew Phil was not disposed to hyperbole, so he simply stared out the window trying to understand.

Finally he acquiesced "Yes. I want in. Let me help. I'm tired of chasing down scummy investment bankers, corporate execu-trash, corrupt bureaucrats and horny politicians. I got no family. I'm rolling in money. My career has peaked. I've been up to my ass in Oneirion troubles for years. So tell me. What the hell are you into now?"

Phil considered his words deliberately. "How long *have* you been working with Oneiro Howard?"

"Doc Webber first brought me in on an industrial espionage investigation about twelve years ago. As I recall it had to do with synthetic oil. Interestingly I was working with you and your law firm as well during those years. Your guys in South America. There was no relationship though."

Phil glanced at Howard. "Actually I think there were some common ties. But all that's irrelevant now. And during all these years what was your understanding regarding the activities of Oneiro?"

Howard was growing restless with the direction of their dialogue.

"Essentially a university supported by hi-tech bio-technology."

"What sort of bio-technology do you suppose?"

"Food production, synthetic fuels and probably some...look Phil...Where are we going with this?"

"In for a penny. In for a pound Howard. If I share this with you, you'll be in this fight for the duration. I'll open up everything to you and not be asking you just to keep our secrets. I'll be asking you to fight for and defend them.

"This is all not just some political concoction?"

"Nothing less than the survival of man."

"I see."

"Well Howard?"

Howard was a little light headed. He'd never expected to face such dangers – make such ponderous decisions – peer into the fragile labyrinth of man's Moirai on a sunny Riviera day on his way to lunch. Feeling fatalistic indeed he resolved. "Get on with it Phil."

"Okay. Oneiro is indeed a university. We train students. We also breed, or should I say hybridize them. They are the finest educated, smartest, well adjusted, strongest, fastest, deadliest iteration of Homo sapiens that ever walked the Earth. Oneirions live totally without phobia or psychosis. They can kill with a song, a hand, a painting, sometimes just a word. They speak a language beyond the grasp of any other human on Earth."

Howard mumbled half to himself, his cynicism evident. "Joseph Goebbels would be thrilled."

Phil flashed a withering glance at Howard. "Surgeons heal with knives. Assassins kill with them. Fallopprobes condemn the knife."

Howard grimaced. "Sorry Phil. Go ahead. By the way, what the hell is fallopprobes?"

Phil smiled. "Actually fallopprobo. Hatred of the effect provoking fear of the cause. Falloassumptivus "

"Mmm, I see."In fact he wasn't entirely sure he did.

Phil continued. "Oneiro doesn't just produce bio-technology. We produce foods that cure diseases, prolong life, end hunger, uplift, teach and even make you svelte. We have developed a place and a race unique in human history."

Phil paused to allow Howard to take it in. He then took the big step.

"As a consequence we attracted the attentions of interstellar beings."

Howard lurched forward in his seat. *"Say again please?"*

"Alien creatures live on Oneiro. Creatures that come from a planet light years removed from our sun. Billions of years old. Immortal, incorporeal, invisible, invincible, advanced tens of thousands of millennia beyond humans in knowledge and intelligence. They are assisting us in the construction of an interstellar craft which will take us to a cosmic center seven light years from Earth, where we will join a congress of beings from across the galaxy to pursue the essential question of the universe."

Phil flashed a look at Howard, trying to judge how he was faring. Then he continued.

"Aiyana Atsila is a former lover of mine. She is a hugely gifted investigative journalist, working on some sort of project with her father, Adahy Atsila. He lives in Norway under the assumed name of Scott Woodman. Last known he was working for Skorpen Undersea Technologies which, as you are well aware, has a longstanding history of belligerency against Oneiro.

For whatever reason, Aiyana was compelled to engage in intelligence gathering on Oneiro to learn of our activities. She is exceptionally adept at these tasks; and she succeeded. She presently has in her possession documents which unequivocally prove the assertions I just outlined for you. I must stop her. Or kill her.

If word of Oneirion activities leaks out, I am convinced it will provoke a war that will span the world. Such a war could destroy all our works on Oneiro and endanger mankind's fragile hold on a promising future."

"You are serious."

"Deadly."

"I don't believe it."

"I'm sure you don't." sighed Phil. "Truth is not subordinate to belief."

"Look Phil. I've worked with you for years. In my opinion, few men command greater respect. But you're pushing me beyond my limit. This demands more faith than I have ever...You're going to have to work with me on this. Hard."

Phil slowed and passed a photograph to Howard. "Take a look at this. I guarantee it is absolutely legitimate."

It was a recent picture of *Gauntlet*. Hundreds of humans scattered randomly throughout an Earthlike panorama, dwarfed within a stupendous globe.

"Holy shit. My God...I don't..."

"The QAVL entrusted me with an even more engaging proof. In the Lome Woredas of Ethiopia there is apparently..."

"Lome? Woredas? What the..."

"I'm a little unclear on this myself. A Woredas is a sort of province in the Oromia Region of Ethiopia. Lome is one of those Woredas. I believe that is the geographic region in question. I could be wrong. I could be a bit off. I haven't had time to do the map work, although they did give me a precise longitude/latitude/depth reference. In any event, the QAVL provided me coordinates where we may find something of such import we will consider it proof positive not only of QAVL existence, but also of their benevolent intent. I have forwarded those coordinates to a Dr. Chandresh ABHAY with the United Nations. I have also opened our files to anything he wishes to see, on condition that nothing is shared beyond the Security Council Executive Committee."

Phil let this sink in, and then he favored Howard with an empathetic smile. "Any questions?"

Howard was messaging his forehead. He slowly looked up. "More than I can possibly conceive of."

"I sympathize."

Howard withdrew into his own thoughts and sat in speechless, stunned silence the remainder of the drive. They arrived at the restaurant, parked, entered and were seated. Menus and wine cards were brought and Phil ordered double Gin and Tonics for himself and Howard.

After choking down half his drink, Howard carefully set his glass down with both hands and wiped his mouth with his napkin. "I need more details."

Phil inspected his menu. "Let's order first." He signaled for another round of drinks, indicating the wine list was for Howard.

Howard was the classic American intelligence expert, forged from post Cold War stolidity. He'd seen and done it all; and not without his share of scars and bloody hands. He was skilled with small arms, insurgency, unarmed combat, explosives, electronics, surveillance, cryptography, languages and propaganda, to name a few. US Special Forces after University. Recruited by NSA after ETS where he carried out operations in the central highlands of Vietnam, imbedded amongst the Montagnards under the guise of a USIA advisor. Nice people. He liked Vietnam. He liked the Vietnamese. Five years later he was recruited by the CIA, with full fledged *spook* status. He had suffered postings all over the world. None of them health spas; and he was no Boy Scout. After he'd endured enough mud, blood and dirty tricks, he moved to Chicago and hung out his shingle, ready to network with agencies and private interests. His debriefing from the CIA had required three intensive weeks. Since that time he amassed a modest fortune solving problems for governments and some of the largest corporations in the world – not the least of which came from Oneiro and Philip Carr.

Howard stands a well muscled, six feet, three inches. Broad shouldered, narrow waisted, with a thick shock of graying black hair, dark eyes, swarthy skin, symmetrical features and a charming smile framing perfectly even white teeth. Howard was no slacker with the ladies. He loved to eat, drink, chase women, and his work. And that was about all. Just now however, this powerful man looked rather small and wan.

When luncheon arrangements were complete, Phil began his story.

Two hours and four courses later, Howard was efficiently briefed. The food was exceptional, the service impeccable, the exquisite wine thunderously expensive (Howard was in shock, but not so much as to ignore the wine list.). He ate and drank mechanically, without tasting a thing. This saddened Howard. The restaurant was now deserted, a single waiter discretely milling about, half-heartedly arranging things, in anticipation of a seriously important tip. Howard hardly noticed.

The two men ordered *digestifs* and coffee. They sat quietly while they drank.

Howard broke the silence. "My God Phil. I had no idea." As he drained his Armagnac. "No wonder you started greasing everyone from Madrid to Marrakech when they started attacking Oneiro. I'd have done the same." He cast a long look at Phil. "Sorry I gave you a hard time." He squinted out onto the terrace. "I've got to visit that island of yours one day."

"That can be arranged Howard. Now talk to me about Skorpen Undersea. Are they really so hot we can't discuss them over the phone?"

"That and more Phil. We got lucky. We've had people on this for months. We finally found a thread and followed it to its end, or ends. What we found was astounding. They permeate nearly every major government in the world. Their funding approaches unlimited. They're into many legitimate industries, including oil and natural gas. They also sponsor and employ terrorists of the worse description. No doubt you remember Rashid al din Ammar?"

"I've been hearing his name again lately."

"Well, we thought he was a contractor for a reactionary oil group. Turns out the oil boys are merely a subset of the real organization."

"...who is?"

"Who is, is based in the Atlas Mountains of Morocco. Been there for years. Got one hellofa HQ up there. We have concluded that hundreds of atrocious acts around the world emanate from that citadel in the mountain above Marrakech. There seems to be nothing they are incapable of. These are bad boys...the worst on the planet. Their membership runs from the Balkans to the whole of the Middle East. This G2 cost me three good men."

"And this SOB Adahy Atsila, aka Scott Woodman is a player in this mishmash?"

"Not a major player by any stretch...but a pawn of sorts. Yes."

"Would that seem to implicate his daughter Aiyana as well?"

"Uh, we really don't know at this point. We checked out her background quite thoroughly and she came up clean. Perhaps she's some sort of cat's-paw."

"Well, either way we've got to stop the bitch."
"How?"
"How what?"
"How are you planning on stopping her?"
"Well first we find her. Then whatever it takes Howard."
"Over-thinking a plan is not one of your shortcomings Phil."

They arrived back at Howard's hotel around 1730. Palms swayed in the early sea breeze, an afternoon sun shining off the Med etching stark gold and black shadows all round. They were just ahead of the final surge of the afternoon's traffic. Howard had regained his composure.

"What would you suggest we do now Howard? I'm tempted to take the plane to Ghazi Khan right now."

Howard studied Phil in the waning light. He'd not aged a bit. He was the essence of good health and fitness. All the same, the afternoon sun revealed miniscule new lines radiating from eye, framing the mouth, lending character to forehead. Sun and sea certainly accounting for a great deal. But Howard saw worry and the burdens of great responsibility as well, and maybe something else. *Tough job for such a nice guy.*

He drew himself up and assumed a professional demeanor. "I need some time Phil. Just a few hours. I'll make some calls. I agree. I think we best look into Ghazi Khan first. And fast. That seems to be our best lead. Hell, it's our *only* lead. Although I'll run a few boys up to Oslo as well."

Howard withdrew a well worn address book and began hurriedly transcribing into a small pad. Then he tore out a page and offered it to Phil.

"Here. You should Fax a complete copy of your passport, and your aircraft registration to this man, Mr. Malik Nasiri, at this number. I'll have spoken to him by then. Transfer one-hundred G's to this account. That will cover your entry, parking and the aircraft turnaround. He can help in all sorts of other ways as well. Your transfer should cover your flight turnaround, your entry and any incidentals. He'll get you in country. He'll get you overfly and landing rights. All on the up-and-up. Do you have another passport, other than Oneirion?"

"U.S."

"Both with you?"

"Yes."

"Fax both. Malik will know which is better right now. Most countries don't have the first idea about Oneiro. That could be an advantage. Or not. In any event, Malik will sort it out."

"I'll ask the flight crew to do the same."

"Good. Though it should be easier for them. I'll dispatch my teams as soon as I get through to Chicago. Top guns all. I'll try to get them on site within hours. We're going to insert them over the border through Kashmir. When they're in the region, that address information should help.

I still have an obligation down here. I'll wrap it up as fast as I can. A day or so at most."

"Okay. I need to do some work as well. I think it's best if we only meet occasionally for meals. Give the appearance of socializing. Let's meet for lunch tomorrow, say 1300?"

"Fine."

"Do you know the restaurant L'Ecrin? It's on Palm Beach near Port Canto. Good sea food, and we can sit outside on the beach; the sea provides the perfect white sound to cover our talks."

Howard climbed out of the car. "I'll find it. Thanks for lunch. Don't forget your goodies in the trunk."

"No problem. What'd you bring me?"

"A big bag of expensive antiques just as you ordered. Two .40cal Glocks, two .41 AE Uzi's, six MK3A2 concussion hand grenades and four hundred rounds of ammunition."

"Perfect. Thanks. See you tomorrow."

"And Phil..."

"Yes?"

"Thanks for your trust."

"Welcome to the war Howard."

# The Poison Dwarf

"Hi Cindy."

"Hello Mr. Carr. All briefings are in, and the status is essentially unchanged since our last report. Ms Jones and Mr. McKnight would still like to speak to you. Urgent."

"Tell them I'll contact them later tonight. Meanwhile, do we still maintain some administrative staff here in the Marley?"

"Yes sir. Three doors down from your apartment. A Mille Corète de Ste Maxime. She and M. Bruno Dubois manage Oneirion Products distribution for Europe and the Middle East. Shall I contact her? She lives in Cannes, so she's probably at home by now."

'Yes. Please. Tell her to come by the apartment immediately. I have some documents to be photocopied and then Faxed. Tell her to stop by the Airport Park Hotel and collect some documents from our flight crew...our aircraft registration and their passports. Call Captain Miller and instruct him to have their papers ready for Corète. Also alert them we're getting close to departure. Hot standby. Ready to go at a moment's notice. Okay?"

"Can do. Can we contact you at the Marley?"

"Yes. But I don't know for how long. One more thing..."

"Yes Mr. Carr?"

"Contact Ted Richards in Finance. I want him to transfer 100,000 Euros to the following account: Mr. Malik Nasiri, Indo Suez Bank, Dera Ghazi Khan, Pakistan, IBAN PK-23-586848-AGK3845-P12. He should send confirmation of the transfer to the same Fax number. Got it?"

"Yes. I'll get him on it immediately."

"Great. Thanks. Talk to you later."

Phil looked at his DIT. "Qasi? How are things proceeding?"

"We believe you are doing well Philip. Mr. Doyle seems a reliable fellow and a fine choice of ally. Nonetheless events seem to be relentlessly approaching a nexus. It seems inevitable. Surely you feel it yourself?"

Phil explored his mind. "I do feel it. Clearly things aren't devolving as I'd hoped."

"Neither us Philip. Howard had a fine idea. Dispatch a reconnaissance team. I am doing so now. The QAVL team will arrive at Ghazi Khan in roughly two minutes at the address you provided Howard. I will provide you a site status soon."

"Thank you Qasi."

*Goddamnit I am experiencing genuine...angst. My training can't seem to control it. There must be a new source. My judgment seems to have been questionable as well. Why did I allow this thing with Aiy to get out of hand? What was I thinking? Something is interfering. I seem to be running counter to the flux. But that's impossible. Something is wrong. Perhaps 'wrong' is inaccurate. In fact nothing can be 'wrong', unless the governance of particle mechanics has gone awry. No. The problem is in me. I am a...discordancy. Out of synchrony with my own universe.*

Phil poured himself a tall Scotch and went up to the roof to calm down. He went immediately to sleep, only to be awakened by Mille Ste Maxime as she entered the apartments. He should have crossed the street and napped in the sea.

Half an hour later Mille Ste Maxime had departed, papers in hand. As her office was but three doors away she would return soon; so Phil decided to simply wait.

He owed a call to Anne and to Edward. A good time to get it over with.

"Hi."

"Are you alright? Christ! I've been trying to contact you for over a day."

"I've been busy. What's up?"

A cool silence belied the chagrin at the other end of the line.

Finally. "A call came into one of your North American mobile phones. Apparently Aiy left your number with some colleagues in Washington. Someone had that number and left her a message. We discovered it yesterday."

"Let me get a pen and paper."

*He can commit this message to memory verbatim and never forget a word. Why is he fooling around?*

"Okay I'm ready. Go."

"It reads: Why have you failed to contact us? The PD has the woodman and the deadline is near."

"When was the message left?"

"Three days ago. The time is 1955 CET."

"I see. The woodman. That would be Aiy's father. Who the hell is PD?"

"I have no idea."

"Is there any way Aiy could have heard this message?"

"I have no idea."

"What does Edward want?"

"I have no idea."

"Transfer me please."

No further comment was forthcoming.

"Hello Edward. You've got something for me?"

"Hello sir. You spoke to Dr. Jones?"

"Yes."

"I believe I have something to add. No doubt you remember Prince Rashid al din Ammar?"

"I've spent the last few years trying to forget the bastard."

"Actually sir, I haven't."

"What do you mean?"

"In my opinion, we've never adequately understood their vicious assaults on you and on Oneiro. So I've done some extensive digging with a Miss Martha Dobbs."

"Did you say expensive or extensive?" asked Phil wryly.

"Actually both."

"And who is Miss Dobbs?"

"She heads a London security firm that frequently acts as an Agent for Doyle & Phillips."

"Must be a good company."

"I have found them to be excellent."

"So what did you come up with?"

"Very little. Otherwise I would have informed you earlier. Rashid al din Ammar was a successful commodity trader specializing in a sort of dried salt fish they produce from cod in Norway. The Portuguese are exceedingly fond of it. They call it Bacalhau. The French refer to it as Brandade de Morue and..."

"I'm familiar with it. Hate the stuff."

"Yes. Well, in fact Rashid lived in Portugal, on the coast south of Lisbon. I assume to facilitate his business. That information alone required more than a year to acquire. This was a secretive man."

"Well it's more than we knew before. Thank you..."

"There's more. Martha has since discovered that Rashid drew a much larger income. Paid into a Luxembourg bank. Some organization based in Morocco. Actually the Atlas Mountains."

"What sort of organization?"

"We have no idea. All we have is hearsay from bars and restaurants in the environ of the Al Maha Hotel in Marrakech. They all tell stories about some group based far into the mountains. Low profile, secret, mysterious and purportedly dangerous."

"A local tribe?"

"No. Something far more sophisticated."

"Why the Al Maha Hotel?"

"Apparently this organization uses it as a staging point in Marrakech. Martha's people hit upon a few items and things are beginning to take form.

Two or three times during the investigations the name Skorpen came up. The locals equated the name with scorpion, making it all the more foreboding."

"That *is* interesting. Is that all?"

"Not quite. And this is why I wished to speak with you. We also now know that Rashid had two sons. The elder's probably in his early to mid twenties now. He surfaced when he took over Rashid's commodity business; and we surmise he may also be involved with the Moroccan group. He's been seen in Marrakech quite a few times. Apparently he's quite the little bastard. Short, homely, tyrannical. A true sociopath. Dangerous. Intensely disliked. His full name is Bahaar Fatin al din Ammar. But in Morocco he's generally known as السمٱلقزم"

"And what does that mean?"

"The Poison Dwarf."

Phil frowned. "The Poison Dwarf." *The PD has the woodman...*

Edward could hear excitement in Phil's voice.

"Things are starting to make sense. Maybe Aiy's not quite the little bitch I thought." *And maybe I'm not quite as stupid as I've been feeling.* "It's possible she's being coerced. We've got to move fast. Do you have Rashid's address in Portugal?"

"Perhaps Martha can locate it."

"Light a fire under her and get back to me as soon as you can. Well done Edward. Did you share this with Anne?"

"I have not been able to speak with her Phil. She is seeing no one."

"I see."

Phil had no sooner put down the phone when his DIT lit. "You heard Qasi?"

"No. We have been with our team. Philip, the QAVL team have located Aiy."

"Great! Where is she?"

"Our team reports she is presently in Ghazi Khan at the address you provided. Her father, Adahy Atsila, has just this minute been brutally murdered by a man named Bahaar Fatin al din Ammar. We believe he is holding Aiyana Atsila against her will. This is a dreadful man. He is capable of unspeakable acts. Even his subordinates fear and hate him. Behind his back they call him *The Poison Dwarf.*"

"I'm on my way Qasi."

"We suggest great haste."

"Captain Miller? Phil Carr here. How soon can you get airborne?"

"It's a fairly quiet time of day at Nice Airport. The aircraft is fully serviced. We should be ready for take-off well within the hour."

"Good. I'll be at the civil aviation lounge in half an hour."
"Where are we headed sir?"
"Dera Ghazi Khan."
Phil could hear busy key clicks in the background.
"Which airport?"
"There's a new civil aviation field called Punjabi International. I estimate flight time at roughly four hours?"
After a pause. "Closer to five hours actually."
"Okay. File your flight plan. You'll have overfly authority and a landing slot by the time you enter Pakistani airspace. See you at the airport."

"Cindy?"
"Yes sir."
"I'm leaving now. Contact me via Captain Miller onboard the aircraft. Please contact Mr. Howard Doyle at the Carlton Hotel and tell him I've left for Ghazi Kahn and I'll call him when I can. Also notify Oscar Sagan, Anne Jones...in fact the entire team."

Fifty minutes later Phil was watching the lights of the Riviera recede to the west. One hour later Phil was completing the check-out, cleaning and loading of his small armory, just as Captain Miller came aft. Phil was surrounded by guns and bullets and cleaning pads and gun oil, not to mention a bottle of Scotch and a bowl of peanuts.

Focusing on the weaponry, head cocked, eyebrows raised, the Captain observed "Looks like you're planning quite a party Mr. Carr."

Ignoring the comment, Phil looked up. "Captain I want you to ensure this aircraft is fully serviced as soon as it hits the ground in Pakistan. Insist on a parking space in a hanger, or at least under some sort of cover. Can you reverse into your parking slot under ship's power?"

"I can try if they don't have a tug; and I can damn sure power out."

"Contact my assistant Cindy and have her request that Howard Doyle proceed with overfly authorities in all relevant countries on your flight plan. Radio ahead to Malik Nasiri's people. See if they can provide a tug and ground power. Tell them to have a couple of ramp agents standing by to assist you. Get additional catering. Lots of sandwiches vacuum packed, and water; and please instruct them to arrange for a car."

"Driver?"

"No. I have a GPS. In terms of a car I want something innocuous. Perhaps an old beat up four-by-four. But reliable. I also need some well worn working clothes. Boots, dirty coveralls, baseball cap, a secular scarf, an overcoat. Things like that. I'm sure Nasiri's organization knows what's best."

"Shall we accompany you?"

"No thanks. But I appreciate the offer. In fact, I hope you brought something to read Captain, because I want you and your First Officer to remain onboard at all times. Eat and sleep aboard. I'll get back as soon as I can."

"Don't worry about us." The Captain smiled. "Besides, with all that hardware you should be able to make it a pretty fast meeting."

"These weapons are not for me Captain. They are for you. As soon as we're on block, scrounge whatever you can...sandbags, cargo, empty oil drums, whatever... and establish a 220° barrier around the perimeter of this aircraft. Aft, starboard and port. Use the ramp handlers to assist. You may need to defend yourselves and the plane. Bear in mind we need leeway to take off, and maybe fast. When you're ready, unblock the wheels. Consider using your jet-blast as a weapon when you build the barrier. When everything's arranged button up, stay by the radio and wait for me."

"Fine."

"How're you fixed for medicals?"

"We're equipped with a full Med Kit, $O_2$, a De-Fib and some basic drugs."

"Plasma?"

"No."

"Ask the ground handlers to get some in stock when you radio ahead."

"No problem."

"Good. You know how to handle this stuff?" Indicating the weapons.

"No problem with the Glocks and grenades. I'd have to play it by ear with the Uzi's."

"You might try breaking them down, loading, cocking, and dry-firing. There is a manual here. The same for your first officer. They could be your best choice during an assault. These Uzi are equipped with Aim Point Mounts. You should practice with these as well. They're good. Don't kid yourself thinking that aiming a fully automatic weapon is unnecessary."

"Where did you suppose we would fire *from* during an assault? They could take the aircraft out easily, or even accidently if we fire from an exit."

"True. Your First Officer will defend from the barrier while you stand by on the flight deck. All grenades are strictly for use beyond the perimeter barrier."

"Understood."

"Good. When you're ready, stow this stuff where it cannot be easily found and you have quick access to it. Complete this before we land. Do you have a mobile radio?"

"Yes, we maintain one on our frequency for ramp operations, or ground coordination."

"Range?"

"Five clicks. More depending on the terran."

"That will have to do. I'll take it with me. I'll also need a heavy coat and a bag of tools."

"What sort of tools?"

"Oh. It doesn't much matter. They're mostly for show. Hopefully." Phil saw the puzzlement on the Captain's face. "Let's see. Pliers, a cutter, some rope or chain, and a sharp knife."

"No problem. We can put that together from our onboard maintenance kit."

"Do you have any of those AV Collars aboard?"

"There's a rechargeable bank of three digitals in the galley."

"Thanks."

Phil fetched a recorder. It consisted of an adjustable band, worn about the neck. Attached to the band was an unobtrusive, small charcoal gray, clear half-sphere. Inside was a tiny fish eye camera and a voice recorder. Both were actuated by and followed the wearer's head movements and voice. Phil strapped one on and joined the Captain back on the flight deck. The Captain regarded him quizzically.

In response to his tacit question Phil said "I want to record everything that happens on the ground."

"Now there you surprise me. Considering some of your past operations I would have thought there was no way you would rec..."

Phil's look cut him off in mid-sentence.

"Then again. It has nothing to do with flying this aircraft."

"Good. Please wake me half an hour out of Ghazi Khan."

Phil returned to his seat, drained his drink, reclined his seat, and was instantly asleep.

The Captain looked back at Phil for several moments before he murmured to himself. *Someone's going to die in Ghazi Khan today.*

# The Lair

Dera Ghazi Khan is situated on the western bank of the Indus River. One of the primary population centers in the Punjab. The town was founded by Haji Khan Mirani in 1476, then known as *Dera Phoolan Tha Sehra* recognizing its comparatively lush ambience enshrouded within the Indus river valley. A respite of sorts from the rugged terran of the Punjab and probably more inviting in those times, than today.

The Punjabi are a fusion of peoples from all over Asia. The fusion process was savage; and this land is suffused with the blood of countless brutal battles, Punjabi and westerners alike. The most recent struggle fitfully wore on. Horribly violent. Seemingly endless. A corruption vitiating the entire globe.

Today Ghazi Khan is an oasis of deceptive calm, surrounded by the turmoil of Afghanistan, India and Pakistan itself. Despite its seeming immunity from the problems of Asia, the city suffers from great poverty and a near nonexistent infrastructure. Many people. No real civil organization. Among other problems, potable water, effluent, roads and general transportation, technical and medical service, law enforcement, education, industries, airports (until the recent Punjab airfield) and trains. All are exceptionally poor, inoperative, or totally lacking. Narcotics are available anywhere. Unemployment is rampant, and men can be easily recruited capable of any sort of vituperous endeavor.

All told the perfect town from which to establish a base for any type of illegal operation. Not to mention a lush hothouse for all manner of terrorism and insurgency.

Fatin's father knew this well. However, his interest lay only in developing a safe-house and base of operations for his clients in Morocco. Therefore, he restricted his activities in Pakistan and the activities of the fortress to specified assignments.

Bahaar Fatin al din Ammar recognized no such restriction. He entrenched his organization in this quagmire of hate and resentment with impressive speed and efficiency. The Poison Dwarf discretely invested little more than 500,000 Euros in adapting his father's base to a skillfully camouflaged fortress on the banks of the Indus. Few places on Earth would afford such development at such speed and so low a cost. Grounds suitably cluttered with car parts, dilapidated remnants of mildewed cushions, bottles, cans, paper, and rusting scrap iron. Scrub grass and weeds. Boulders and dry rugged gullies.

Miniature versions of desert wadi. Pocket mice, rabbits, lizards and snakes. Even one or two wild dogs. Scorpion, spiders and centipedes. All manner of desert flora, fauna and human castoffs, surrounded by crumbling stone walls in the center of Ghazi Khan's most squalorous quarter.

Unseen and unseeable, were motion sensors, trip wires, mines, listening devices, cameras, search lights, remote controlled weaponry, man-traps, booby-traps, cyanide punji sticks and electronic fencing. Deadly hazards saturated the grounds and perimeter of the compound.

Nothing in, nothing out, nothing survives without the sanction of Bahaar Fatin.

All access was limited to an underground tunnel, accommodating up to a five ton truck. Steel reinforced concrete. Steel alloy access doors five centimeters thick, operated exclusively from deep within the interior of the fortress. Exhaustive surveillance augmented by constant guard and dog patrols. Security fail-safe tanks of Hydrogen Cyanide throughout the tunnel.

The fortress itself was nondescript in the extreme. Shabby unpainted cinder block walls uneven and misaligned. The roof appeared to consist of a patchwork of irregular sheets of tar paper and corrugated sheets. Broken and cloudy windows. Power and phone lines nicely concealed underground. Inside the building it was a solidly well-built, spartanly furnished paramilitary headquarters. Not luxurious, but far removed from the life-style of its neighbors.

At night the Poison Dwarf slept well and securely.

Bahaar Fatin used this facility as a safe house and a staging area for narcotics, slaves, hostages, arms, terrorist activities, assassination and sedition. No venture too repellent. No mission too unworthy. Any enterprise that promised profits, expanded his base, or pleased his masters in Morocco. Many had died here. Lingering deaths in cold stony darkness. No water, food, or mercy. Many had succumbed to torture and abuse. Many heads had been taken by tempered steel. The lucky ones earned a bullet to the back of their head. Rape and unspeakable abuse were a routine source of diversion. Motivational perks for his loathsome crew.

Fatin and his monstrous henchmen indulged themselves in every form of perversion with men, women and even children. A living hell on the banks of the Indus. Fatin the Dwarf could never decide whether he preferred his fortress on the Indus, or his dead father's retreat perched on the Costa de Lisboa. He cynically secreted pet names for them. His: The Devil's Cesspool   His father's: The Devil's Eden.

He maintained an armory, a communications center, a detention and interrogation center and barracks for his cadre of felons. His father wouldn't have dreamt of such an odious compound. Then again, Bahaar Fatin engaged in many things beyond the darkest schemes conjured by his father. In this respect, his sometime masters from the Atlas Mountains found his work eminently satisfactory – even more so than his father's. And more profitable. They had finally found a man without limits, boundaries, ethics, or compassion. Totally amoral. In fact better than amoral. He relished the monstrous acts he was assigned. Despite his bountiful fees, they sometimes suspected he would perform such work simply for his own amusement.

His assignment on this occasion was, on the one hand, simple: The elimination and complete destruction of Oneiro, including all Oneirions. The other hand held something a great deal more hazardous and uncertain: To trip an extravagantly engineered snare. Set the world ablaze. As was explained to Fatin...the final Jihad.

This assignment was nothing less than a delight for Bahaar Fatin. The fee was colossal. The flagitious blood and havoc had a near sexual appeal; and Carr was the bonus. A real sweetener. Retribution for the torture/murder of his father in a burning desert in Spain. This had cost his employers and his family dearly. Not to mention a shameful loss of face. For Fatin this was a chronic source of irritation. More importantly it was bad for business.

He had been methodically considering the death of Carr and the destruction of Oneiro on his own for some time. The money and support from the Atlas Mountains were simply sweeteners.

Bahaar Fatin had worked with Adahy Atsila (aka Scott Woodman) in the past. He had lured Fatin into various ill-advised attempts at indifferently executed terrorism. Unsuccessful, unprofitable and ignominious.

Woodman fancied himself a subjugated, badly used, American Indian, qua freedom fighter. Badly used by Skorpen Undersea Technologies, when they were defeated in a somewhat surreptitious takeover of an investment firm, under the guise of an attractive oil monopoly in the North Sea. The hostile takeover conspiracy was exposed and usurped by one Mr. Philip Carr. The result was nearly his termination, withdrawn in favor of a humiliating demotion.

Atsila was a full-blooded Indian, subjugated by the Americans. Phil Carr happened to *be* an American. He was finding it easier to truly hate this man.

Then the *coup de gras*: This white-eyed SOB was dinging his daughter.

Phil Carr must die. As serendipity would have it, his old buddy Bahaar Fatin wanted to enlist him in a project targeted at the ruin of Carr and Oneiro. And he in turn would enlist his daughter.

Woodman had abundant leverage. His daughter's love. Her un-requitement from Phil. Her ambition. A story that could catapult her to the height of her profession. And money. He would ensure that she was paid copious amounts to investigate and report on events on Oneiro. Then there was the absolute aphrodisiac of all journalists. The inside track. The scoop. She could get in there, get the facts and get out. After plying her with abundant and specious guarantees that her activities would materially harm no one, not Phil, not Oneiro, no citizen of Oneiro – she was sold. Neither father, nor daughter were aware of the incredible secrets to be gleaned from the island. They were simply briefed they would be 'Earthshaking'. Woodman's lust for money and blood would be sated.

In real point of fact, Bahaar Fatin was almost equally unaware of the full magnitude of events on Oneiro. He was following orders and seeking as much information as possible to facilitate an invasion. His promises of an 'Earthshaking' story were in large part a lure for Woodman and his beautiful daughter, who raised some prurient fantasies from some dark places in Fatin 's mind. The little man planned on allowing himself full reign before this business was at an end.

Fatin did acquire some critical insights however.

After the death of his father, Fatin moved his family and their staff to the luxury and security of a fortified compound on the coast outside Dubai. There, they would be relatively safe and, more importantly, out of his way. He held no love for his family, nor they of him. In fact they were repelled by him, and not just a little fearful. They had feared him all his life – even as a querulous and perverse child – and the years had only intensified his aberrant nature. With the passing of Prince al din Ammar their trepidation only grew.

Dharr, Fatin 's younger brother was the only family member retained in the Portuguese compound. Fatin harbored little affection for his brother. However, he had plans to train him in the 'family business.' This would provide him with a useful blood-sycophant. Hopefully someone he could trust. It also afforded him a convenient straw-man against potential retribution by the forces constantly militating around him. Dharr was a feckless and gullible adolescent. Therefore easily perverted into misguided Islamic Chauvinism... the classic guise of Fatin 's singular profession.

The groundwork had been laid earlier by their father. He hired a *Usstaz* – a teacher – named Mustafa from Saudi Arabia. The man had disregarded any education altogether, except religious dogma and archetypal odium. He ardently poured poison down the young ears of Fatin and Dar and their parched minds greedily quaffed the hatred. In the only intervention Fatin could recall, his mother finally discharged Mustafa and found a tutor who trained them in the basics needed to live. After the departure of Mustafa, Dharr, seeking a new mentor, worshipped Fatin, rendering him the perfect dupe in every respect. A blank page eager for the strokes of Fatin's poison pen.

When his father was killed, Fatin reveled in an flood of relief. Joy. Emancipation. He felt no love for his father. In fact he hated him, feared him and despised him. Whenever Prince Rashid al din Ammar was away, Fatin was so emancipated he could almost be described as happy. Although in reality, as a youth and as a man, he had never known life to be happy, or carefree, or loving. Even so, when he died Fatin was in ecstasy.

Prince Rashid had clearly been disappointed in his son, even repelled. The boy was small, gnarly, ugly and misshapen. He was pathetically inadequate mentally, physically and spiritually. In short, he was a doltish, brutish atavism.

Strangely, these were not the aberrancies that alienated Prince Rashid. For Rashid, it was the boy's eyes. Fatin sported the dark hair and swarthy complexion of his family. Only his eyes belied a bizarre deviation. They were small, black and surrounded by a mottled while puffiness. The combined effect was of a disturbing reptilian coldness. Rashid's reaction was alternately disdainful, or outright abusive. When not ignoring the boy, he was berating the boy. When not berating the boy, he mercilessly beat and debased him. Fatin 's other family members offered neither sympathy, nor support. They were barred from interference, and fearful of evidencing concern. Fatin was alone.

Calves grown for veal pass their brief lives in darkness – shackled away from the day – subsisting only on milk – bones and muscles atrophied to incapacity – awaiting only the abattoir. Such creatures must dimly marvel in horror at the monstrous purgatory into which they have somehow fallen. So it was for the budding Fatin . So it would be for the unfortunates who would fall into the pit of his corrupt fruition.

Following the death of his father, Fatin allowed himself the full rein of his drunkenness, dissipations and cruelty. Good training and good fun for young Dharr. As their culture acquiesced to such behavior, his family had previously been fated to stoically suffer such feral caprice. Understandably, it was a great relief when Fatin relocated the family from the windswept Costa de Lisboa to the warm shores of the Persian Gulf.

Both factions of the family were satisfied. The women were safe; and Fatin was finally alone in the great fortified villa. Assisted by a few of his trusted underlings, he now had the time and the freedom to scour the compound. Prince Rashid al din Ammar was a secretive man, and it took Fatin weeks to ferret out the wonders skillfully concealed in this massive fortress. His findings were much as he expected. Private banking statements, an intriguing collection of poisons and drugs, cash, gold, diamonds, arms, data discs, contact files and such. Fatin was satisfied. He could finance his business interests, establish a middle eastern operations base, fund his family in Qatar, and lavishly support his exotic gallimaufry of perverse diversions.

A sunny Saturday afternoon luxuriating in his father's office. Drinking his father's Scotch. Smoking his cigars. Formulating plans to spend his fortune. He noticed a tiny anomalous separation in the ancient wooden tile flooring of his father's office. Beautifully hidden. However, age, wear and sea air had minutely contracted the perimeter of this secret door in the floor. Just enough to attract the attention of Fatin's keen eyes.

After days of investigation, Fatin and his men could not locate the mechanism which released and opened this ancient door in the floor. Finally it required three of his strongest men to force the cumbrous door to yield, resorting to brute force alone.

Below the strange door they found a tiny room, with an equally tiny staircase leading down. A masterpiece of the joiner's craft. Beautifully fitted miniature flooring and paneling. Fatin concluded this hidden space probably dated back to the construction of the chateau itself. There was a single object within. A massive safe. Fatin began to feel like an archeologist. He half expected to find hieroglyphs on the walls and his father's corpse hidden away in a gilded sarcophagus.

After four hard days the obdurate safe finally stood open in the middle of his father's office.

Fatin turned to the work crew and uttered a single word. "Leave." And he was suddenly alone with the secrets of Prince Rashid al din Ammar.

He looked forward to his work with a greedy relish. He had anticipated the great wealth hidden by his father. The money, the diamonds and gold, were simply fungible commodities to fuel operations. Indiscriminate wealth.

These files however, their contents would be far more than wealth. They would be power. Power drawn from secrets drenched in abominable acts, appalling, beastly, and cruel. *Daddy's business*.

Fatin ordered a bottle of Scotch, ice, a large bowl of dates, pâté and toasts, cigars and chocolates. He looked forward to this task and planned to savor it. His nature was far from studious, but he planned to minutely dissect these papers.

The safe held dozens of files. Hundreds of pages. Meticulously organized and neatly arranged. They contained every detail of every contract executed by Rashid. *Surly his masters in the Atlas Mountains were not aware of these files?* Everything, from the mundane to the astonishing. Receipts for expenses and purchases. Payrolls. Newspaper reports. Reconnaissance reports and satellite photos. Notes which basically defined his work orders.

Plans and analysis. Criminal reports, death certificates and death orders. Disposition of bodies, monies and equipment. Payoffs to officials all over the world. *The Devil's Baksheesh.* Summary and evaluation reports. And with every file, a personal day-by-day log detailing everything Prince Rashid did, or learned in the course of his commissions.

Three days later. Several bottles of Scotch and foods of every description had been consumed. Fatin sat in the office, rumpled, unwashed and exhausted and amazed.

*What the fuck do I do with this stuff? If those bastards in Morocco find out about this they'll have my balls on a fish hook.*

*I can't believe it. My father had no idea who he was really dealing with; and yet it's all right here if you just have the brains to see it.*

The next day in the gardens of the fortress. ".Juan I want you to construct it with a steel reinforced, concrete-flint rock amalgam, at least fifteen centimeters thick. Three meters, by three, by three. I want it underground here in the back garden, six meters and 267° degrees south by west from the center of the coy pond. The surface access hatch will be hinged stainless steel, hollowed in the top, camouflaged by a fixed stepping stone. The opening handle with be a false irrigation head nearby, that pulls straight up. Watertight. The interior compartment door will be ten centimeters thick, nickel-titanium alloy, key and manual combination access. No electrics. I want a dehumidifier in the compartment with four hidden micro-vents. Clearly that must be electric. I want a design fast, and I want it built within the month. When it's finished, kill the workers and throw them into the sea. Look after their families. Tell them there was a skirmish with some rivals from Kuwait. Turn all plans over to me. Clean up the mess in my office and restore the access door in the floor. Share this with no one. *No one.* Clear?"

"Jess Senhor Fatin . I will look after everyting."

The contents of the safe had terrified Fatin. He couldn't use them and he wouldn't lose them. So he had decided to create a new, secure home for the files known only to him. He'd have to do away with Juan as well. Himself.

He didn't benefit from his father's meticulous planning and record keeping proclivities, but he had plans for a few new files himself. Fatin had already been to the Atlas Mountains...had been recruited for a fascinating project...huge money and a satisfying endeavor. The very project that his father had failed at. The project that ultimately killed him: *Oneiro.*

Thanks to the files he learned a great deal about Oneiro and one Mr. Philip Carr. It was painfully apparent that Mr. Carr had tortured and killed his father. He had defeated all the plans carefully drawn to protect their industry and their world. He had shamed his family. He still stood guard at the gates of Oneiro. Conversely, Fatin was under contract with some of the most murderous men on the planet to destroy Oneiro. *This will be fun.*

Fatin made a pledge to himself.

*INCHALLAH. I am Itar. Vengeance. I am Jundi. I declare my secret fatwa. I will have his head. The Consul of Oneiro will suffer Mawt Ma' "Adala...Death.*

# Bloodfrost

It was a misty gray cold. Freezing and humid. Not a precursor to blizzards and snowdrifts. Just bone-cold, wrapped in a leaden gauze. Phil was grateful for the heavy sheepskin coat, woollen shemagh and goatskin gloves. The ground handlers were thoughtful enough to include a dark brown balaclava and a Russian leather sheepskin cap that had clearly survived many hard winters. Some raggedy levis, sunglasses, a pair of timeworn mountain boots, an open jeep decades old, and his costume was complete. He considered the possibility of scabrous little beasties inhabiting these garments and fervently hoped he was alone. Completing his coarse aspect, Phil himself was genuinely disheveled and unshaven after his trip. He added a touch of used motor oil to his face, and would easily travel unnoticed.

Phil had informed Captain Miller he would use a GPS to navigate his way to Shahrah-e-Zarghoon in Quetta. In point of fact, Phil had simply committed the regional map to memory. He would have no trouble locating his target.

They had freed a small maintenance hangar for their plane and were already busily arranging packing crates in a large horse-shoe formation around the aircraft. Phil changed clothes and shouldered a small tool bag. After a few handshakes he jumped in the jeep, returned a friendly salute to Captain Miller. For good or ill, he was on his way.

*Malik Nasiri's people do excellent work. I'll have to compliment Howard when I get back. If I get back.*

In many places throughout the world, Phil had encountered villages, or towns, or simple encampments where – if man had never come, or if man had preserved his ingenerate ways – the land would have remained beautiful. As it was, an unnatural repulsiveness emanated from the mix of tribal man with modern poverty in a hitherto natural setting. A sordid, demeaning and contradictory concoction. This town was the apex of such perverse amalgam. Squalid would be an excessive compliment to such a place.

Phil looked about as he bounced along. Somehow the combination of dust and freezing cold seemed a contradiction. And not a pleasant one. *Why do they come here? Why not return to their tents and their goats and their heritage? They've sacrificed their nobility. Their dignity. For what? Does the occasional can of Coke, a beat-up radio, or a rickety truck justify overcrowding, disease, mind-numbing poverty, filth, deadly water, starvation and appalling living conditions?*

*Have they lost the ability to survive in the context of their heritage? Small wonder this town is a colossal Petri dish, culturing the most virulent and deadly murderers and terrorists in the world.*

Phil shook the images away. Ignoring his feelings. He had work to do. And when his work was done, the crystalline purity of the stars awaited. The icy, unsullied darkness of space would be his. It would cleanse all this away.

Phil was wearing his balaclava so he needn't worry about being seen, apparently speaking to himself. "Qasi?"

"Hello Philip."

"I believe we're about ten minutes out of Bahaar Fatin 's compound."

"That would be correct Philip."

"Can you give me some idea what's going on there?"

"Nothing good Philip."

"Please Qasi..."

"Mr. Woodman is dead. He died horribly. Ms Atsila is alive. Barely, and not, we fear, for much longer. Mr. Fatin has had his way with both father and daughter. As you might expect he was seeking Ms Atsila's file on Oneiro. He was prepared to gain this file by whatever means."

"Did he succeed?"

"Yes."

"Damn! Anything else?"

"Yes. Your Mr. Howard Doyle assigned six men to investigate Mr. Fatin 's compound."

"Yes?"

"They are all dead. We believe they were unprepared for the sophisticated defenses of the fortress. As humans are subject to pronounce...they died bravely."

"Crap."

"We do not find that specific application of profanity colorful or humorous."

"Qasi, I don't find one goddamned thing about this mission colorful or humorous."

"There is one other factor arising worthy of attention. This settlement. Ghazi Kahn..."

"Yes?"

"It is being systematically destroyed as we speak."

"Why for God's sake?"

"Aiy's file has been leaked in some virulent quarters."

"...and the contents of that file are so volatile as to ignite destruction of the entire town?"

"That's a difficult question Philip. Perhaps it is more properly described as the contents of the file validating an extraordinarily well contrived conspiracy."

"What sort of conspiracy?"

"A carefully designed schism. An attempt to divide mankind into two camps. The instigators controlling the majority camp. Their hope is then to overpower the other camp and effect definitive control of all mankind. Oneiro plays a surprisingly important part in these plans. However, events in the last few years, and most certainly with the introduction of the QAVL are propitious for their plans."

"Islam?"

"In part. Perhaps even the more menacing part. They are capable of acts that....appall the QAVL beyond imagining. Perhaps we have allowed ourselves the luxury of mature civilizations for much too long. However, they are not alone."

"What sort of a *schism* are they attempting to contrive."

"As we have expressed previously, evolution describes an inclined plain, a ramp...not a staircase. This is generally true. However, your achievement on Oneiro is the exception that validates the rule. You ascended a *step*. You produced a Beta-One iteration of *homo sapiens*. You summon the future."

"And this produces hatred on a destructive...a worldwide scale?"

"Most definitely Philip."

"Why?"

"Let us refer to these protagonist as Alphas. Oneirons as Betas. Consider the attributes that distinguish Betas on Earth today.

Betas feel no fear. Alphas suffer from near debilitating fear emanating from all quarters.

Betas are totally uninhibited. Alphas hobble themselves with all manner of interdictions.

Betas are intelligent and prize knowledge. Alphas tend to regard learned beings as effete and difficult to manipulate. They suspect the intelligencia may one day control technology that will render their jihad moot.

Betas are strong and beautiful and healthy. Long lived as well. Betas live in prosperity and freedom. Alphas suffer and die in pain and ignominy.

Betas do not abide religion. Alphas need religion as an anodyne against fear, ignorance and futility. To reject their religion constitutes a profound affront to their placebo and their power.

Betas live in near total freedom. Alphas look to others for increasing degrees of control and leadership.

Not too long ago in human history Betas would have been considered as the embodiment of royalty. Alphas in contrast and by default...peasants.

The list goes on and on. We trust you understand the underlying concept. These differences foster an exceptionally dangerous hatred. An all consuming jealousy. They are determined to destroy you.

An element within the Alphans has astutely surmised both your existence and your nature – probably with inside assistance – as a result, Ghazi Kahn burns this day."

They drove without speaking for a time. Bumpy. Gray. Dusty. Cold.

"Tell us how you feel Philip."

"How I feel?"

"Yes. How you feel. We know you do not feel fear. How do you feel right now? Here. Approaching a fortress of horrors, confronting those that would foul the aspirations of mankind. You are not an immortal. How do you feel? We are interested."

Phil squinted into the distance. "I feel like a bird. Flying. Flying with the wind, cold and fast, through an enormously tall field of grain."

"Yes. You're feeling the grain of the *qazine;* and you're moving with it. You're sensing the particulate granular patterns. Impressive. You are doing well Philip."

"You are referring to our common sub-atomic projections."

"Yes. In part."

Phil thought for a time. Suddenly he roused himself. He had to force himself to concentrate on his driving. He gripped the steering will fiercely. Understanding was beginning to glimmer in the dawn of his perceptions.

"You were there. You were there with me. In the desert in Spain. When I tortured and killed Prince Rashid."

"Yes Philip we were."

"Somehow I knew you were there. I...I spoke to you during that long freezing night."

"You did Philip. We were...touched. Despite your barbarous actions, we were touched."

"Do you remember that falcon? High above us? The next morning?"

"We forget nothing Philip."

"It seemed to know me. I believed it was attacking me; and it could've killed me if it wished. Then it screamed and seemed to remit. Gone in a flash. I don't know what it was. It looked like a bird. A raptor. A Peregrine Falcon I think. But I don't really know what it was."

"Nor do we Philip. Does that surprise you?"

"Are you familiar with the Teutonic term *Weltschmerz?*"

Qasi remained silent.

"I thought that experience would kill me Qasi. I thought I could never face such a thing again. And yet here I am. Again. Today I'm not at all certain who my target is. I need Aiy's file desperately, or the losses for the entire world will be staggering."

Qasi remained silent.

The jeep rolled quietly to a stop sixty meters short of Fatin's complex. No guards, or humans of any description were visible. Phil quickly dismounted, grabbed his gear and began running, head down, towards a far spot on the road bordering the compound. Careful observation told him that large vehicles turned on that spot with some regularity. He slowed slightly, leaning into his DIT.

"Talk to me Qasi."

"Avoid the entrance you're running towards. It is electronically snared and impassible. Instead, jump the barbed wire on your right on my count.... three-two-one...here...Now stop...prostrate on the ground...Crawl for ten meters to your right...Stand up and run straight ahead for twelve meters...Go left...Careful. There is a landmine directly in front of you and a trip wire on your left. Jump *up* the hill...high and run fast for thirty meters...Don't make a sound...Stop."

Qasi was now speaking so softly Phil strained to hear. Phil always found this distracting. When a man lowers his voice, his voice changes in tenor as well. Stage-whispers. When Qasi lowers their voice, it is more akin to turning down the volume on a radio. No change in tenor, only volume.

"You can safely climb this drainpipe and enter through a second floor window. Inside you will randomly encounter guards and bodies. We do not have an accurate projection.

The control complex is at the far end on your right. Mr. Fatin will probably be hiding in his office, also on your right. We believe Miss Aiy and her father are in chambers on the first floor, as are a few dozen newly arrived slaves. Mr. Howard's men are in the hallway on the second level. We did not arrive in time to determine the whereabouts of Miss Aiy's file. She has been here for almost three days now. We will leave you here and await you on your aircraft. Good luck Philip."

"You're leaving?"

"Philip we cannot be witness to the events about to take place here. We have seen enough."

*An invisible, and now silent partner.* Without comment Phil mounted the heavy metal downspout and began climbing. When he reached the second floor he was two meters from a cloudy glass window to his left. He began swinging by one hand, back and forth, amassing kinetic energy. When he had gained sufficient sway he released his hand and effortlessly hoicked himself to the windowsill. Shut and locked. But he was in luck. A window two windows down was unlocked and slightly open. Phil transited the windows to his target; and he soundlessly breached the fortification within seconds.

He looked about.

He was standing in a slaughterhouse.

The stench was staggering. Dizzying. On the opposite side of the hall a door stood open. Beyond it was a metal catwalk that connected the second floor with a parking area on a rise behind this wing of the compound. Clearly this had been the access point of Howard's team. Of equal clarity was copious evidence that they had indeed – as professed by Qasi – died bravely. The shabby exterior of the complex must have fooled them. They probably thought they were walking in on a bunch of hopped up, mountain boys. Bad surprise.

*It must've been a hell of a fray.* Howard had sent in six top guns. More than thirty men had died here. It was close to impossible to make an accurate count. He did determine that Fatin was not among them, based on his description.

*High powered, fully automatic weapons. Hell's playthings. My God. These men were literally ripped apart. Like a food processor.* The insides of humans are truly odious. They smell like nothing else on Earth. Neither his training, nor his genes let Phil down, else he would have been immobilized. Nauseated. Horrified. Instead he methodically examined the site. *GewehrAG36's! These boys were well equipped. Small wonder these people are shredded. I'll give them that. They've saved me from an orgy of killing.*

The walls were an abomination of fleshy offal. The floor was covered with a sprawl of contorted bodies. Grisly piles of meat. Where no dead men lay, the floor was either slick with viscera, or sticky with blood. Phil gingerly stepped his way through the massacre. Each time he lifted a foot it sounded like Velcro ripping apart. His boots were now viscously sticky. When he was clear of the kill zone he looked back. He was leaving footprints. And there was another, parallel set of prints! *Someone* else had walked out of here. He spotted a washroom and took the time to rinse the soles of his shoes. At least he could move quietly now, without leaving tracks of his own.

## *...If he do bleed, I'll gild the faces of the grooms withal...*

William Shakespeare
*Macbeth*

Phil slowly moved down the long hallway. He stayed close to the walls and paused at the threshold of every doorway looking for signs of life. He suspected all of Howard's men were indeed dead. The Woodman was dead. Therefore the fortress held only two people of interest. Fatin and Aiy. Any others would die, except the slaves.

His first encounter was halfway down the hall, just a few meters from Fatin's lair. A young boy. Black hair, black eyes, face concealed, AK-47 in hand. As Phil rounded a doorway he rushed out from the darkness within. It was painfully obvious the boy was terrified, clumsy and inexperienced. He attacked with the rifle barrel raised high. Ninety degrees relative to the floor. One hand tangled in the trigger mechanism. The other fumbling for a knife. Phil took him by the neck and flung him into the opposite wall – knocking him senseless. Phil attempted to pin him by the arms, but the boy would have none of it. Instead, he whorled and kicked and finally managed to break free and bring the rifle to bear on Phil.

In mute acceptance Phil stepped back and brought a fist down on his neck. After a sickening snap, the boy fell instantly dead. Shaking his head in resignation, Phil looked into the dark room. Inside was a large sort of tub – far from hygienic in aspect. Instead it had the appearance of some sort of receptacle. What was it for? Torture? It was massive concrete. Nearly two meters round, a meter deep. Filled with clear water. *What the hell was it?*

Suddenly he heard a scraping sound from the end of the hall. Fatin's area. Phil quietly slipped into the room and began making fast, discrete peeks into the hall. After a few moments he spotted a man. Short. Odd features. A huge nose with frog eyes, under bushy eyebrows framed in a knotty-looking face. Fatigues. Bloody and disheveled. In fact he was covered in blood. *Must not be his own blood. Otherwise he would be dead.* An AK-47 was slung over his shoulder. A well stocked ammunition belt and what looked to be a .44 Magnum held in two hands. Both arms stiffly extended. Scanning the hallway like a huge Cobra. No boy here. This guy was a pro. This was Fatin . The Poison Dwarf. Although in reality he was no dwarf. More frogish than dwarfish. He was a little short, which he compensated for with an impressive physique. All in all, he had the look of a dangerous man.

Phil noiselessly placed his tool bag on the floor and silently slipped into the huge tub, spreading legs to secure him underwater. And he waited.

Fatin was being exceedingly cautious. He had heard the scuffle. He saw the dead boy. So he was methodically going from room to room, checking everything, soundlessly, hardly breathing. Perhaps he suspected it was Philip Carr awaiting him? Perhaps he was always careful. Over ten silent minutes passed before Fatin entered the pool room. It was dark, the water was still, the faint light from the doorway shined on the water. Phil was invisible. All the same, Fatin exercised his customary circumspection. He walked to the side of the tub looking in for anything suspicious.

What he saw within amazed him. At the bottom of the pool lie a man. The man must have been there for awhile. *He must be dead. Drowned.* No weapons, the look of a workman. The man seemed to be looking at him! And smiling? And now waving at him! *What the fuck is thi...?"*

Far faster than Fatin could follow, Phil literally flew from the water, knocking the pistol from his hands, tearing his rifle away, and finally pinning his arms to his sides.

Wordlessly as Fatin sputtered, Phil frog-stepped him awkwardly and roughly down the hall to his office, as he would an unruly child. Once in the office Phil held Fatin at arm's length, several centimeters above the floor so he could inspect the office for weapons or unwanted communications equipment. He found both. So he threw Fatin against a wall with such force as to seriously stun him. While Fatin reeled on the floor, Phil gathered arms and electronics and threw them through the window. Fatin could make out the sound of shattering glass and equipment tumbling down the hillside outside his office.

Phil spotted a bottle of Scotch and a glass. He rinsed the glass with Scotch and then poured himself a generous measure. He sat down, lent back, put his boots on the desk, and simply stared neutrally at Fatin.

After Phil finished two glasses of Scotch, Fatin was sufficiently recovered to talk.

Phil opened the conversation. "You are one butt-ugly little bastard. You know that?"

The little man regarded Phil dispassionately, critically. "You are Mr. Philip Carr."

"That is correct."

"The man you killed in the hall was my brother."

"I tried to take him down without killing him. He would have none of it."

"You also killed my father."

"Again you're right."

"Am I next?"

"I wouldn't rule it out. It doesn't look good. Perhaps your actions for the next ten minutes or so may save you. Want to try for it?"

"What do you want? Why have you trespassed my property?"

"Do you know a Mr. Scott Woodman?"

"Adahy Atsila?"

"Yes. Is he here?"

"Yes."

"May I speak with him?"

"I think not. He has no head. I cut it off."

Phil calmly rose, walked to Fatin and began to violently slap him. Fatin tried to fight back with no effect whatever. The thrashing went on for nearly three minutes. When Phil was finished, the little man was clearly drained. Blood ran from an ear, his cheeks were a flaming crimson, tears ran down his face; and he trembled uncontrollably.

"Do you know Aiy Atsila?"

"Aiyana Atsila?"

Phil ground his teeth. "Yes. Is she here?"

"Yes."

"May I speak to *her*?"

Fatin had recovered somewhat. "Mmm. Difficult. I've cut off nearly every external body-part. That turned out to be mostly unnecessary." Fatin turned his head so Phil could see his left ear. "I took this earring from her after I cut off her ear." He smiled at the memory. "She gave me what I needed. She may be alive. I don't know."

Phil's incredulity was like a physical blow. He whispered *"Nearly every external body-part...?"*

"Yeah. You know...nose, lips, ears, breasts, vaginal lips. Things like that."

Fatin found himself above Phil's head in a vice grip before he was aware that Phil had even moved.

Phil was screaming now. "You little...!" He slammed him onto the floor and began kicking him furiously in the side and head. After a time he calmed.

Fatin whispered. "I knew I was dead when we came to my office. You cannot frighten me."

Phil thought about this. There were things he needed from this little monster. *I've got to cool down. Get under that ugly skin. Wear him down.*

"Are you familiar with the etymology of the word *assassin* Fatin?"

The gnarled little man raised his head, blood dripping from his left ear. "The *what*?"

"Do you know where the word *assassin* comes from?

"Will you not leave me alone you pig fucking...?"

Whack! In earlier times this blow would have been referred to as 'boxing his ear'. Damaging, disorienting and wonderfully painful. Phil was gratified to observe even more copious amounts of blood gushing from the same ear. The pain would be exquisite. In all likelihood he would be deaf in that ear for the rest of his life. Not a long term problem.

Phil smiled warmly. "Let me tell you then." He spoke conversationally. He poured himself another Scotch and fought to keep his hands from trembling. "You're just too damned ugly and ignorant, squatting there in your own filth. You smell like pigshit too. I think you've dirtied yourself. So I'll try to help you out. Improve you. Forward your education."

Fatin silently glared at him.

"In the 11th century, a fierce tribe lived in the Atlas Mountains. The Nizaris. Exponents of an unbroken line of Imams leading right up to the Aga Khan today. These guys were mean and ugly like you. And they were probably located not far from your current employers." Phil flashed him a faux charming smile.

"There were two striking features about their culture."

Phil raised a finger. "One: They loved to murder people. Just like you."

Phil raised another finger. "Two: They loved to smoke Hashish. Just like you."

Phil sat down, his demeanor affable. "These two predilections complimented each other. Customers flocked from all over North Africa to hire those bastards to murder enemies, family members and competitors on their behalf. They also used them to murder invading Crusaders in the guise of religious obeisance. The unhappy Crusaders linked their murderous ways with hashish addiction and coined the mythos. In turn, they would often pay them for their services with Hashish. They did their best wet work in the throes of the drug. Thus they became known as Hashshashin, or Hashishiyun, which evolved into Assassins. Cute eh? Most of this occurred in Iran and... well you get the picture, don't you? My mistake. An intelligent, cultured, well educated Islamic gentleman such as yourself knows all about this. Unlike an ignorant infidel such as myself."

Fatin made no comment. He simply stared ahead.

"I think you and your boys have a lot in common with those vermin. Of course you wouldn't dream of dealing in any drug as banal as Hashish. And of course the Hashishiyun would never soil themselves selling women and little boys."

## Oneiro II: Gauntlet

Fatin lunged at Phil. Insane with rage. Whack! Fatin was on the floor writhing and whimpering, smeared in a pool of his own blood.

Fatin struggled to regain control over himself. *He's trying to make me angry. He wants me to make a mistake. Say something I shouldn't.* He smiled inwardly. *He doesn't know it's already done. The time for mistakes is past. Now it is the time to kill and die....*

Phil roused himself. He stood and brushed himself. *Time to get to work.*

"Much as I'm enjoying this, we still have a task to complete Fatin." Wielding his perceived advantage, Phil assumed a flippant attitude.

Fatin regarded Phil with contempt. Phil saw neither fear, nor fanaticism. Instead the little man demonstrated a certain dignity. Courage? Certainly hatred. There suddenly seemed to be more at work here than greed and depraved cruelty. Did this man have beliefs? Values beyond depravity and greed? It made Phil slightly uneasy. He decided to remain quiet. Let the man reveal himself.

As he waited he scrutinized Fatin's office with care. On the credenza behind Fatin's desk Phil spotted a near empty bottle of Scotch and the razored accoutrements of Cocaine use. White powder in abundance. Some of Fatin's courage was either *Dutch*, or *Colombian Courage*. Defiance partly explained.

Fatin raised his chin truculently.

"I will provide you nothing. *Nothing.* You fucking chubby, little, spoiled, cowardly westerners. We survive on food that would make you vomit. We endure hardships that would kill the best of you. We commit acts that would drive your mushy sensitivities to insanity. You think you command our fear and respect. All you *command* is our laughter and contempt. Soon you will command our blade. And you shall have it. We will cut off a billion heads until you finally submit, or die."

Phil peered at him disdainfully. "You have been a pampered brat all your useless life. Your bravado and contempt are bullshit. They have no relevance to a cowardly punk like you. Get on with it Fatin."

Fatin refused to be dissuaded. "You are unclean and uneducated. Therefore you do not speak Arabic. Therefore you are ignorant of the term للہ المفتاح. I will translate for you. It means The Key of Allah. Your Zionist would say The Key of God. Another term is للہ الزناد. Allah's Trigger."

"Get on with it Fatin. We have work to do."

"We have been waiting since the time of Saladin for a key, a trigger that will ignite and unite the world under Islam. *Al Akhir Jihad.* The Final Jihad. *Al Harb Intaha al Alam.* The last war. Terrorism is at an end. Insurgency is finished. Talk is over. A true holy war is already in progress. *The* Jihad. And *you* presented us with the key, the trigger. *You.* Philip Carr." He smiled at Phil with a certain madness shining from his eyes. "We see your QAVL for what they are...*DJALL* the trickster, the evil one. The Shi'a Doctrine of Mamah will bring forth the Mehdi and the DHALL, the QAVL, and you, and all of Oneiro will be slain."

"Where is Ms Atsila?"

"Fuck you."

"Where is Ms Atsila?"

"Fuck you."

"So many fancy words. I have another word for you Fatin. The word is *edentulous*. Do you know what it means?"

"Fuck you."

Phil calmly came to his feet and stepped close to Fatin. His manner intimate, almost friendly. He spoke quietly. Almost a whisper. "No. It means *toothless*."

With that, he grabbed a handful of greasy, blood encrusted hair and violently pulled his head back. Next he chopped his throat forcefully, but not fatally. As Fatin gagged and coughed, his mouth came open as he desperately attempted to breathe. With skillful timing Phil began hammering his mouth. Mercilessly and incessantly. Fatin was unable to even scream. Blood, teeth, saliva, retch and flesh covered both men as the savagery continued. Seconds later, Fatin lay unconscious in a pool of blood. Eighty percent of his teeth were broken or missing. Phil's fist looked like hamburger and throbbed intensely. Breathing heavily, he seated himself on a stone shelf. His right hand was a mess. He had cut and pounded some knuckles down to the bone. It was agonizing. It throbbed and burned to the point it took all his effort to open and close his fist. He cradled his right hand in his left, poured Scotch over the hand and ground his teeth. His mind playing a short mantra he was taught on Oneiro: Pain is but Fear cloaked in flesh.

*Thank God for Fear Training.*

Finally Fatin stirred. He commenced groaning and whimpering. Phil pulled him into a sitting position, leaning him against the wall. He dropped to one knee near the man, soiling his trousers, and looked the man intensely in the eyes.

He wanted to keep hurting the man. He wanted to kill the man. Most of all he had to break the man. He would have all three.

"Your father was very brave during this part of our little interview in Spain. I had to beat hell out of him, cut off a finger, put out an eye, butcher a thumb, and nearly cut his balls off before he broke. But break he did. He gave me everything I wanted and more. Turns out he wasn't as cowardly as most of you flatheads. All the same it must have been embarrassing for you and your family. I enjoyed it so much I arranged for a painless, fairly clean death. I poisoned him. And he knew it. I watched him watching me, as he died by my hand.

*You* however. I imagine you will squeal like a pig and babble anything I want to know. This is good. I'm in a hurry. However, if you answer only one simple question, I will immediately leave you in peace. And alive.

You know Fatin, the belief that a well trained man can withstand any torture is a myth. The stuff of cheap spy novels. Any man. *Any* man is breakable. The secret lies in belief. If a man believes, knows, his tormentor *will* inflict grievous harm, *will* kill him. Then he will break. If you resist, you *know* I will commit horrors on your body. You'll never enjoy women, drugs, booze, food, luxury and wealth again. You will never again see the sun and walk in the air. So tell me now. Yes or no? I am in a hurry."

Phil waited for a full two minutes. He watched the sweat and blood form small pools on nose and chin and ear and drip steadily to the stone floor; and with it, what little resolve he retained. "Come on Fatin. Which is it? Yes or no?" Phil began to methodically remove knife, pliers and ropes from his bag.

Fatin studied Phil and the bag. He knew Phil was deadly serious. He had indeed tortured his father to death. Successfully. He thought for a time and finally croaked "Whaa elth ith it you wanth?"

"Where have you hidden Ms Atsila's file?"

Despite his pain Fatin begin to laugh quietly. Derisively. Phil itched to beat the laughter from his remaining lips. "Something funny, you miserable little flathead?"

Fatin sobered and his laughter subsided. "I tell you where ith isth with pleathsure. Then you will leave thish placth."

"Where is it?"

Fatin deliberately drew out his words. "I did not hide the file Philip Carr. I enthrusted it to loving hanthds. Sthkilled hanthds. Hanthds that will..."

Phil jumped up. "Where is it you malignant little dwarf? *Tell me, or by Allah I will....*"

Fatin was suddenly calm. "Relaxth you Yankee fuck."

Crookedly smirking, he attempted to rise and then abandoned the effort, grimacing in pain.

"I prethsented the entire file to Imam Aban Waseer Hafeez. A thsacred man. A thsacred gift. He treaths it with greath care. He knew exthactly what to do with it. We tthalked of it at great length. He underthtands ith and he thknows it isth truth. He avowths you have offended nearly every precepth of Usul al-fiqh; and swears by Allah he will have your head."

"Usul al-fiqh?"

"The basthis for all Ithlamic and Sharia law, you ignorant athole. Apoth... Apothsth..." he struggled with the word and then carefully enunciated "Apostasy. The penalty is death. He hath issued a Fatwā whichth has been thent with Arabic translations of your putrescenth portfolio. I perthonally provided the money to dispatjach copies to every Imam in all of Ithlam. Thousands all over the world. Within hours and days it will ignite a Jihad that will sthhake the pillars of creation. Your QAVL will flee and all infidels will join us; and the world will begin anew. Thisth the Imam hasth vowed."

For the first time Phil was genuinely interested. "I understood the Koran makes generous accommodation for non-terrestrial life."

Fatin flashed a bloody, cynical, almost pitying sneer. "Imam Hafeez makths no thuch provithion. You have losth. To me. To my father. To my brother. To my family. You will die. Oneiro will be desthroyed. Everyone on Oneiro will die. I thuggest you depart quickly. I would thsuggest you thseek out Imam Hafeez, but it is far too late you pathetic thack of donkey pissth. There." He gathered his strength. "I have thold you. Now leaf thsis plath." He languidly sighed and gingerly lay back, eyes closed, smiling beatifically.

"Where is Aiyana Atsila?"

Eyes still closed. "Thshe is of no importanth. I thuppose thshe isth dead now. Thshe's lying around here thumbwhere." He scratched his nose and chuckled at his witticism.

Phil stood and quietly walked to Fatin. He squatted beside the little man and studied his face. Fatin derisively ignored his presence. Only the tiniest twitch of an eyelid betrayed any incertitude.

*Is all this bluster? Does he mean what he says, or is he simply trying to intimidate me? Either way, I can't take him with me and I can't leave him here... alive. There is really only one choice.*

Phil lent down closer and said softly, deliberately "Perhaps I will have words with Imam Hafeez. First, I have one last word for you. The word is *die*."

In one decisive stroke, Phil raised a fist high above his head, bringing it down explosively on the man's calf. He was rewarded with a satisfying crack. The Dwarf screamed in genuine, if naïve outrage and pain. Phil held him down as easily as a child as he relentlessly hammered upward, with dispassionate surgical precision. From calves to thighs, to knees, to pelvis, to ribs, to sternum, to clavicle, to scapula, to humerus and finally to neck. Bones cracked with such celerity, a sound much like a crackling fire filled the chamber. Desperate screams echoed throughout the silent fortress. Quickly every major bone in his body was broken.

In all likelihood no man had ever been beaten to death in quite this same manner.

Much as a computer initiates its orderly shutdown...Fatin's body systematically surrendered its life. His last quiet respiration escaped from his lungs. His eyes lost focus and froze, leaking his final tears. Electrical pulses between brain synapses faded as light dims in a chcap bulb. His heart ceased its rhythmic contractions. Every muscle in his body lost turgidity. Discharging his urine. His last hemorrhage. The final flow of blood. Emission of effluvium. The shutdown quotidian would finally advance through every cell of his body. Odious, orderly, repellent and fascinating.

A broken, hideous doll. A bloody and grotesque Raggedy Andy.

Phil's eyes coldly searched the wretched little man's Tolkienesque visage one last time. He impulsively reached down and savagely ripped Aiy's earring from Fatin's ear, jerking his head to the right and nearly separating the lobe.

He pocketed the bloodied gold and whispered into the unhearing, mutilated ear. "I pray there is a hell where you can burn as long as there are stars." An empty gesture. Futile and inane. Yet it afforded him a curious sort of comfort. Perhaps in some way it vindicated, or at least mitigated the brutal murder he had just inflicted. Maybe he had simply shuffled the twisted little man from one state of cosmic disgrace to another? Or perhaps he really did want Fatin to suffer the torments of hell for the next tens of billions of years, or so. Whatever. No time for deliberation now.

He thought about Fatin and his father for a moment. They had both been savage criminals. Their similarity ended with that. Prince Rashid al din Ammar was essentially a businessman. Fatin al din Ammar was essentially evil. Phil was repelled by the glee with which he approached his odious work. Ultimately though, what difference did it make? People died. Society was destroyed. The future was despoiled.

He stood and threw back his head, feeling a satisfying crack in his neck. Overstrained, overtensed. Straightening, he found two cases of Scotch in the office's supply closet. He helped himself to a deep draw on a bottle, then he carefully soaked Fatin, the desk and the carpeting in the liquid of several bottles. He smashed the remaining bottles against the walls. He found Fatin's lighter and ignited the carpet. He was rewarded with a gratifying 'Whump!' The bluish transparent flames immediately spread to the desk while Phil fed the flames with papers and chairs...anything flammable. He calculated this would blossom into a dangerous fire within twenty minutes. Time enough. He inspected the office a last time and dashed out of the office in search of Aiy.

# *DAKHALA* Phil

Fatima was given little time, and nearly no resource with which to raise Amira. Fortunately she inherited her mother's strength of body and will, and she survived.

No one, no matter how strong, could survive years in the holding chamber, so Fatima acquired a tiny, dark, inside room for her. Fatima purposely found a room deep in the fortress, away from people and light. Her intent was to avoid any interaction with guards who too often demonstrated rapacious appetites for children. Male or female.

The result. Amira spent seven years in the literal absence of other humans, playmates, education and light. Her diet consisted of gruel and scraps that Fatima would steal away for her.

She was not an unhappy child. She was not a child at all. She was a feral being whose only goal, only dream was freedom. Enticing glimpses of the real world captivated and enthralled her. A scent, the sound of laughter, a heart-rending glimpse through a hazy window. A flash of morning, or an icy night sky. Someday she would escape this black purgatory. She ached to really see the sun, the moon, the stars, smell the wind, find real food to eat and real humans to talk to. All the wonders beyond this wretched fortress, with which Fatima had lovingly regaled her.

She listened. She watched. She smelled. She became obsessed with the comings and goings and routines of the fortress. On the rare occasions she was allowed out of her room she took subtle pains to observe exits and any feature she could locate as the cloudy windows flashed by.

One day. She assumed it was day. She heard breaking glass, running boots, much shouting and finally a cacophony of explosions and gun fire. Men screaming in pain and death. Doors being forced, or kicked in, or slammed. A huge firefight taking place just outside her room.

Music to her young ears!

She hid under her bedclothes, wrapped in her only possession...a threadbare shawl. Finally things grew quiet. She waited and waited. Still quiet. A single set of footsteps. A brief scuffle. Another scuffle. Two pairs of footsteps. Silence again. And still she waited.

When she could wait no more, she crept noiselessly from her room, through a short hallway, and into the main hall. The scene that awaited her was beyond her comprehension. Bodies, blood, gore, in a blue-gray pall of cordite smoke. Even the floor was sticky. She would have been sick had she truly understood what she was seeing. Instead she spotted a door. *Open!* She blindly ran for it nearly weeping and smiling at the same time. She felt the terror of a salvation so close it could be lost in a heartbeat. The door opened onto a sort of bridge affair made of steel, ending in a parking lot. She knew not what a bridge, nor parking lot were. But they had the look of sunshine and freedom. At the end of the parking lot was a dirt road culminating in a large gate. Beside the gate stood a little house with big windows. There was a dead man wedged against the glass, blood drying on walls and broken windows. Amira understood nothing of what she saw. She understood only the sun and clean air and space to run and run. Which she did as fast as she could. When she reached the gate she was small enough to crawl under. Another dirt road led downward to an intersection with a larger road.

She was free! In the light. In the air. So close to paradise. Half crazy with joy and fear she ran the length of the dirt road, directly into the crossroad. Suddenly to her right she saw a large ugly brownish box. Noisy and frightening. It appeared to be moving fast somehow, clouds of dust trailed it. Mounted on the thing was a man. His eyes huge and a terrible look on his face. Before she could understand or react, the thing was upon her, throwing her some three meters before her tiny body landed in the dust, broken and lifeless.

Philip Carr jumped from the jeep and ran to her. Dead. He gently lifted her, moving her to a small grassy plot to the side of the road, and covered her with a shawl that had been tightly drawn about her frail shoulders. He looked down on her for a time and gave her his tears. Strange obeisance from a man bathed in the blood of strangers. He slowly returned to his jeep and the dust and the war.

Amira was seven. She had but just discovered she was sentient. The wondrous epiphany that she existed. A divine spark, unique in creation.

Now she was dead.

Satan's manumit.

Dead before she really knew she was alive.

She would never grasp the substance of either.

The gods themselves could not conjure a more caliginous cruelty than innocents gavaged in darkness while lust, perversion and avarice, glut themselves in the sun.

# *Amicus Servo – Pereginus Conelamo*

### *A Friend Saved – A Wanderer Lost*

Phil ran. Room to room. He ran. Hall to hall. He ran. Barrack to barrack. The fortress was deceptively immense. Everyone was dead save the pitiful slaves awaiting shipment, so weak and terrified they could hardly move. Peering at him, eyes huge in the gloom, in mute horror. He found a key hanging from a wall nearby and unlocked their prison. In his broken Arabic he struggled to speak "Isber 'ashara jara ithnan masrah jisr."

An emaciated man teetered weakly to the door. A ghost from the gloom. In English the trembling specter weakly whispered "What?"

"Wait ten minutes. Go to the second floor. At the end of the hall is a bridge to the ground. Stay on the concrete and climb the gate. Run away fast. Got it?"

The man smiled frailly. "Got it."

The entire fortress was deathly quiet. Still he rushed on.

Phil was becoming fatigued. This surprised and disturbed him. Normally it would take hours of such exertions to weary him. *What effect was this human abattoir having over him?*

Minutes later he lurched into a stone chamber. High ceilings, sparse light, wintry and harsh. Cold, rough, damp and alien. He had found five other such ghastly rooms in the fortress during his search.

He slowly approached a large stone slab. It was difficult to see in the gloom. Something was chained to the slab describing the form of a cross. Everything covered in blood. Nothing moving. For the first time in years Phil felt true fear. Horror and loathing. Were it not for his training he would have been debilitated with revulsion and nausea. The atmosphere of the chamber writhed with evil and monstrous cruelty.

This space was hellish cold when fully clad. The nude biologique spread on the stone tablet must have suffered terribly. He assumed it was naked. He could see feet and hands. But with all the blood it was hard to make out the rest of the body. Its arms were spread wide, legs crossed. *This is Aiy? My God. Have they crucified her?* It looked like carrion badly used by scavengers. On closer inspection the long black hair and tawny skin confirmed it was indeed her. *God!* Aiy had been exquisitely lovely. *Surely no man could butcher such a woman, any woman, any human, in this ghoulish manner?*

There was something heaped in the rear of the chamber. Something... unseemly. Phil anxiously approached the amorphous pile. His trepidation more the stuff of revulsion than danger. It had been human. Now handless and headless. A gory horror dumped in the corner like a bag of chicken guts in a slaughter house. The hands were not to be seen, but the head was close by. Face down, if face were an applicable term. Phil gingerly extended a toe and gently rolled the head until it was face up. As expected, it was Adahy Atsila, aka Scott Woodman. He could just barely recognize him from the file. Looked to have been tortured and beheaded, probably in front of his daughter. Phil mumbled beneath his breath "Sub-human ghoul".

In an instant his mind recreated the abominations that had occurred in this chamber of horrors. They had dragged both in naked. Chained Aiy to the wall, while they chained her father to the slab. There they tortured him, attempting to force Aiy to disclose the locations of the file. She either could not, or would not tell them. Soon they decapitated her father for her edification, chained her to the slab and started in again. Apparently she broke. The file must have been nearby. Then they simply left her. Unconscious or dead. Irrelevant. Icy, monstrous, blasé.

He quickly returned to Aiy. He felt her wrist for a pulse. Nothing. He leaned down close to her 'face' to see if he could detect any breath. The face was entirely covered in coagulation and there was a bubble protruding from a hole roughly equivalent to a nostril. Was there movement? Did the bubble change size? No. Yet it had to be fairly recent. Else it would have dried completely and collapsed. But no one could survive this sort of abuse.

Suddenly both eyes sprang open. A dead, insane, inhuman stare straight into his eyes. He shuddered in surprise and horror, stumbling backwards, gripping the cold slab for support.

He tore off his coat and quickly but gently wrapped it around her. He took her gently in his arms and ran down the long dim hall to the security center and managed to work the controls to open the tunnel doors. Suddenly she began a low, inhuman lowing. More bovine than biped. Phil tried to tenderly rock her and whisper calming words – to no avail. The sound was disturbing. A weak pitiful wail echoing from hell itself. He tried to ignore it. Unsuccessfully. *Thank God these bastards are all dead. I'd hate to try silencing her.*

Down the stairs. Down to the tunnel. Down to the alley. Down to the jeep. They were both covered in blood now. Luckily the alleyway was deserted. He carefully laid her out in the back, placed a tarp over her, jumped in the front, started the jeep and raced towards the airport.

As he drove he reviewed the situation. *Maybe I should have killed her, or just left her to die. Singular and tender mercies. I have no need of her. Fatin has released the file. The damage is done. But I've got training, a med kit, plasma, drugs. Can I keep her alive for five hours? I just hope some son of a bitch isn't waiting to blow us away at the airfield. We don't have time for... My God!*

A small child, a girl, stood directly in front of the Jeep. In heightened, dilated seconds she was poised frozen in his mind. His amplified cognizance recorded several things. *She's tiny, so pale, hardly dressed, blood, she shows no fear at all....she doesn't understand what I am...she's smiling!...too late.... My God!* He literally stood on the brakes.

Too late. She was gone. She was lying meters in front of the Jeep. Phil jumped from the Jeep. Fear and panic he hadn't felt in years. He ran to the girl and examined her. She was dead. He raised her gently into his arms and carried her to a small grassy retreat from the dusty road. Her shoulders tightly wrapped in a ragged shawl. He gently removed it from her shoulders and covered her. He knew he had to keep moving, but somehow he couldn't take his eyes off this pathetic young child. Dead by his hand. This wasn't a terrorist, a monster like Fatin. This was shock and guilt and grief and innocence. Emotions he thought he had purged long ago washed through his being. He discovered he was weeping. *I'm sorry. I'm so sorry.*

He slowly returned to the Jeep, and checked on Aiy. *Chalk up another one to us Aiy. How many more? Thousands? Millions? Look at you. What have we done? You and I and Anne.*

He suffered a last, long look at the tiny body, climbed into the jeep and sped away.

# Fire Frost

He keyed his radio with a short squeak of static. "Captain Miller, Phil Carr here."

"Captain Miller, Phil Carr here."

"Captain Miller please respond. Phil Carr here. Over."

"Miller."

"What's your status Captain?"

"We're ready to roll. A few unknowns are circulating around our perimeter. Over."

"How many?"

"I'd guess five or so."

"You're sure they're not Nasiri's people?"

"Nasiri's people are holed up in the control tower and we're in pretty much constant contact with them. There's something really bad coming down around here and they don't seem to want any part of it. They were the first to see these guys and reported them to us. Over."

"Who the hell are they?"

"The airfield people are not sure. They say they're not Fatin's people. They suspect they are *qatil* for an Imam Aban Waseer Hafeez. Over."

"I know who Hafeez is. What the hell is *qatil*?"

"Killer. Assassin. Enforcer."

"Crap. Keep on your toes."

"...no question about that..."

"I'm bringing in a casualty and I'll take the jeep right to the aircraft door, so don't fire on me. Put your First Officer on the barrier. Radio Malik Nasiri and tell him to keep his people the hell out of there and clear our departure with Ghazi Kahn Air Traffic Control, and the Pakistani Aviation Authority if necessary. Tell him there's another fifty thousand on the way. You standby in the left seat, blocks off, GPU disconnected, powered up, hangar doors open. I want to roll out of there as soon as we're buttoned up. Over."

"Everything has been looked after. We're powered up right now. What's your ETA?"

"Best guess. Five minutes."

"We're standing by. Out."

The airfield came into view. Phil could see the hangar that housed the aircraft and he could see a rusty van parked nearby. He came to a halt. With binoculars he could just make out on the door of the van, carefully painted: الحرس المقدّس

Phil knew this translated roughly to 'Holy Guard'. *Hafeez' men. Assassins. Qatil.* He knew now why they left the plane unmolested. Hafeez didn't want the plane, or the crew, or papers, or any information. They wanted *him*. Probably alive, as some sort of straw-man for all the evils contained in Aiy's file.

*That will not happen. These goddamned sand rats never quit. Five lives between me and that plane.*

He quietly slipped the jeep into gear and slowly made his way to the hangar. When he was about twenty meters from the van, he silently drifted to a halt and stepped out. He sprinted to the wall of the hanger and began working his way around the perimeter. A man rounded the corner absorbed in loading his rifle. He was tall, dark, wore a kurta and kufi with a short beard and combat boots. Without looking up he was walking directly towards Phil when he heard a scuffling sound in the grass. As he look up he was amazed to see a man descending upon him from a height of nearly four meters. For the briefest of moments the man froze, then he brought up his rifle just as Phil was crashing a fist down on his neck. Without a whimper he dropped to the ground. Dead. His cervical vertebrae pulverized.

*That was stupid. I came in far too high. Had he been alert he could have torn me apart with his AK. Four to go.*

Just as he had seen Oneirion students do years ago, Phil began a rapid side-to-side jumping movement. Powerful jumps of more than five meters moved him quickly around the hangar. Leaning radically into his jumps his trajectory rose less than two meters. The lower the faster. The lower the safer. But it demanded extraordinary power and it devoured energy. For some reason this was not the problem it had been at the fortress.

Two more times he encountered qatil. He was on them before they could react, inflicting massive, killing damage to their heads and necks. As he turned to the airside of the hanger he hopped pass the large open doors and was surprised to hear bullets whizzing past. He hazarded a glance in and realized the First Officer was firing on him, unable to distinguish friend from foe. *Does he think goddamn Arab insurgents hop around like this?* Nothing to do but keep moving.

He turned the last corner of the hanger and immediately encountered automatic weapons fire spraying the area around him. Phil began springing even more powerfully, faster, directly at the gunman. Frantically the man attempted to direct his fire at Phil to no avail. Phil's speed frustrated any attempt at targeting him. Within moments the *qatil* lay on the ground next to his gun, his neck nearly chopped in two. *Okay that's four. Where the hell is number five? ...got to move fast. Those shots are going to bring someone soon.*

Phil went to the jeep and quietly keyed the radio. He whispered "Captain Miller. Carr here. Over."

"Miller."

"Four down. Where's number five?"

"No idea. The hanger is quiet."

"I'm coming in. Alert your First Officer. Out."

Phil put the jeep in gear and floored it. Grass and weeds and dirt spraying in all directions as the jeep fish-tailed back and forth finding traction. It rounded the hanger and charged through the huge hangar doors. Between the horns of Captain Miller's makeshift barrier. A screeching halt planeside.

Phil gently handed Aiy into the plane to Captain Miller.

After a brief look Miller ejaculated over the sound of the engines "Mother of God...!"

Phil yelled "Power down Captain."

Blessed silence.

Phil watched him. *All-in-all he took that pretty well. He's got guts.*

The Captain returned from the flight deck.

"Take her aft and secure her on the floor as best you can."

Phil turned towards the First Officer's position in the barrier. "Let's get aboard. *Fast.*"

The First Office stood, smiling with relief and began advancing towards Phil. As he neared the jeep he sidestepped a sandbag placing him directly in front of Phil. He cleared the sandbag and looked up still smiling. "Sorry I fired on you out there. You were going so fast I couldn't...."

The man's head exploded. Phil prostrated himself behind the barrier. His mind accelerated to twice its normal celerity. He felt adrenalin rushing through his muscles. His curious epidermal biochemistry began super-oxygenating his body; and he actually experienced a thrill of fear. This process was something altogether new. Good. He would need it.

This *qatil* was unbelievably well equipped. He knew what he was facing. He was quite familiar with this state-of-the-art weapon and easily recognized its distinctive sound. An AA-12 fully automatic assault shot gun. It took all sorts of loads, but this looked like an aerodynamically assisted High Explosive round.

*Christ! This thing can take an aircraft apart! Got to take him out fast. Can't let him use that damned thing again. How did some flat-headed sand rat get his hands on an AA-12?"*

Phil removed his coat. He was planning a variation on an old trick. A favorite of grade B westerns. He removed his shemagh and ran it under a sandbag. Then he lay atop the sandbag and tied the shemagh around his chest. He rolled to his hands and knees and maneuvered his coat over the sandbag. From there he simply rose to his knees and with a fairly credible bobbing motion, exposed the sandbag at intervals as he moved noiselessly along the barrier.

Thirty seconds later a shot tore into the sandbag, knocking Phil flat on his face. He silently untied the ravaged coat and sandbag, rolled over and assumed a kneeling position against the barrier...and waited. He made no sound, no movement. He hardly breathed.

Three minutes...five...seven...*Jesus Christ! Where in hell is this bastard?*...eight minutes...then ten. Finally a sound. Barely auditable, but Phil knew what it was. His man was slowly sliding a shell ever so softly into his gun. *Retentive bastard. That damned thing carries a circular clip and fires twelve rounds a second; and he's reloading two lousy shells. Crap, I'm sweating.*

*Come on baby. Come on...*

There it was. The tiniest crunch of boot on pavement. He knew the exact direction and distance. It had to be now.

Phil grabbed a sandbag. Raised it above and behind his head. Sprang to his feet. There was his man. Exactly where he was supposed to be. With all his strength he rocketed the sand bag directly at the man's head. Saw the look of surprise on his face. Saw him attempt to aim his weapon. Watched the sandbag literally explode in the man's face. Observed with satisfaction and relief the man catapult backwards. Neck traumatically broken. Instantly dead.

Phil was exhausted. He was going to be sore. Overexertion. Pulled tendons. Strained muscles. God knows what else. His arms, back and shoulders were going to kill him for days to come. He'd pay for that sandbag toss. For now...he was alive.

He turned back to the aircraft. Saw the Captain peering out at him grimly, but encouragingly, even admiringly. Phil jumped aboard, pulled the stairway in and closed the door, then joined the Captain in the cockpit in the right-hand seat.

"Let's get the hell out of here."

The pilot powered up both engines and the aircraft began to roll forward.

Suddenly an eleven ton Armored Personnel Carrier in camouflage paint pulled in from of them, coming to an abrupt halt. Briefly rocking fore and aft. Any exit from the hangar was now effectively blocked. The topside cupola was manned by a young officer in body armor and desert fatigues, hanging on to a swivel mounted fifty caliber machine gun, speaking into his helmet radio. Phil was certain there was a platoon of well armed troops within.

"Crap!" Phil struck the bulkhead in anger and frustration. "Captain will you kindly call our handlers and find out what that bloody APC is doing there."

"Ghazi Handling this is Oneiro seven-delta-two-five. Over."

"This is Ghazi Handling seven-delta-two-five. Over."

"We have Mr. Philip Carr onboard. He would like to speak with Mr. Malik Nasiri. Over."

"Wait one, seven-delta-two-five."

Phil looked over to the Captain. "Well we're in the shit now. We've got to get out of this town and back to Oneiro. Do you have the range to make Oneiro without a tech stop?"

"Just barely. If the weather behaves. If we get off the ground quickly. If all is clear on Oneiro."

"The perhaps you should schedule a tech stop into your flight planning."

"Agreed."

"Seven-delta-two-five we have Mr. Nasiri for Mr. Carr. Over."

"Mr. Carr is on the line."

"Mr. Carr, this is Malik Nasiri. I am sorry we have not had the opportunity to meet."

"As am I Mr. Nasiri. I hope we can meet the next time."

"Next time? That may be problematic Mr. Carr."

"What's the problem sir?"

"Well, there has been arms fire from your hangar. Naturally the authorities are compelled to investigate and detain you and your aircraft."

"Is that why there's an APC blocking our hangar exit?"

"Yes."

"We had nothing to do with the arms fire." Pause. "And we have many good reasons why we must take off immediately."

"They must be very good reasons if I am to convince the authorities to release your flight. Presently you have no authorization to take off, or to overfly Pakistani airspace."

"Our reasons are excellent."

"I see. How many are there?"

"Two-hundred-thousand."

"I can expect you to wire these reasons to us for our review?"

"I personally guarantee it, within four hours. Mr. Howard Doyle will vouch for that if you care to contact him. He is presently located at the Carlton Hot..."

"I am familiar with the whereabouts of Mr. Doyle. However, I don't believe any such assurance is necessary."

"Thank you Mr. Nasiri."

"Will you please stand by for a moment?"

"Certainly."

Five long minutes.

"Mr. Carr?'

"Yes Mr. Nasiri."

"The APC is moving away now." And it was quickly gone.

"Thank you Mr. Nasiri. I look forward to seeing you next time."

"I doubt there will be a next time Mr. Carr. Please take off immediately to the west, on runway one-seven. Do not contact Ghazi Khan Air Traffic Control, or any other authority. We are under embargo. So there is no traffic in our immediate area for now. Maintain total radio silence and exit our airspace as quickly as possible. Naturally I cannot guarantee your safety, nor will I be able to vouch for your presence in our airspace should it come to that. You are probably unaware that enormous civil disturbances are erupting all over Ghazi Khan. All over Pakistan for that matter."

"No. I was not aware of that. What are the extent of these disturbances?"

"Catastrophic. Dera Ghazi Khan is being systematically destroyed as we speak. Thousands are dying. Are your activities in Ghazi Khan related in any way to these events?"

Phil noticed the APC had stopped and was coming about very slowly.

"Not that I know of. As you know we arrived this morning and have been on the ground here only a few hours."

"And what was your purpose in coming here Mr. Carr?"

Phil's mind trashed about, trying to form a credible excuse for their presence. The track commander swiveled the cupola and his .50 caliber in the direction of their hangar. The officer was clearly monitoring this conversation.

"We are considering erecting a distribution facility here for our bio-food products. We had appointed an agent. A Mr. Melvin Raheel. I was to meet with him this morning at the proposed site. However, he failed to appear and I was unable to locate him. If he is in some sort of difficulty, that may explain why we were accosted by gunmen earlier."

A sharp skepticism was growing in Nasiri's voice. "I am unacquainted with a Mr. Raheel. And I know every major businessman in Ghazi Khan."

"Mr. Raheel is also our agent in Islamabad, which is his base. We actually know little about him. He generated minimal production, and there were small problems from time to time."

There was an extended pause. Phil and Captain Miller heard only occasional crackles of static.

"We can expect your list of reasons later today, without fail?"

"Yes. Absolutely."

More radio silence.

Nasiri's voice finally cracked through. His manner perfunctory. "I suggest you depart with haste. Good luck Mr. Carr."

"Understood. And thank you Mr. Nasiri. Out."

As they taxied out, Phil took the opportunity to discuss their flight.

"Let's get out of here Captain. I'd like you to keep us low....well under radar...and put the hammer down. I believe if we fly low and fast, we'll be difficult targets for SAM's. Am I correct?"

Captain Miller had flown F-22 Raptors and then **F-35 Lightnings** in the American Navy. He was well versed in surface-to-air evasion – with fighters – certainly not luxury business jets. He frowned, staring vacantly, trying to envision the defensive scenario. "This is a tactically unique problem. I suppose a high velocity overfly under their radar horizon would deny them a reasonable reaction time. But we'll have to fly *very* low and *very* fast and we'll..."

"Sounds good. Let's do it."

"Okay. It'll be a rough ride though. Can that thing in the back survive it?"

"We have no choice."

"Pakistani ATC's going to raise fifteen kinds of blue hell about this."

"No choice."

"You know, they just might scramble a wing of Mirage interceptors..."

"They'd have to sorti them out of Karachi. We should be well over Afghani airspace by then."

"Let's talk about Afghani airspace...."

"Don't worry about it. Use your normal call sign. Doyle's already arranged non-scheduled overfly authority."

"You're the boss. I hope you don't have any plans to visit Pakistan again soon."

"Captain, based on what's happened here, there's a good chance they may be visiting *us*."

"Say again please?"

"I'm convinced Oneiro is facing an imminent attack...and the spearhead of the offensive may well be erupting right now out of the heart of Ghazi Khan."

Four minutes later they were lifting off. It was midday and they surprisingly encountered a dense haze. As they puzzled at the weather, it needed only an instant to realize they were actually flying through enormous billowing clouds of smoke. Ghazi Kahn was literally on fire. Explosions everywhere. Hundreds running in all directions. Though they couldn't hear it, they saw the twinkle of gunfire and small explosions roiling throughout the city. Bodies were already accumulating in the streets, while huge crowds rioted at government buildings, police stations, military check-points and even mosques. It seemed everyone was randomly killing. Phil look down upon the carnage transfixed in awe. He felt like an Olympian looking down from his mount, as Macedonia pillaged Sparta – Thanatos stalking the streets – reveling in death's orgy.

*...so begins the war for man's world...*

Twice in the few minutes prior to escaping the city, Phil saw contrails flash past at breathtaking speed. His SAM evasion tactics were apparently effective. Barely.

When they were finally over open countryside "Nicely done Captain. Stay low and fast until we cross the border."

"At this rate of burn we have no choice about a fuel stop."

"Try to find a stop with a decent med facility. We may need some help, or supplies. I'm going back to work on our passenger."

Despite a rough ride, Phil administered morphine, a plasma drip laced with a powerful sedative, and oxygen. Aiy finally quieted. Her peculiar mewing sound was strangely disturbing. The ensuing silence a relief.

## ***Renuntio Exordium***

<u>*Given by*</u>
<u>*Dr. Chandresh ABHAY, Director*</u>
<u>*United Nations Extra-Solar Contact-UNESCON*</u>
<u>*To the*</u>
<u>*United Nations General Assembly*</u>
<u>*In*</u>
<u>*Extraordinary Closed Secret Session for Heads of State*</u>
<u>*Venue*</u>
<u>*United Nations Headquarters, New York*</u>
<u>*Under the*</u>
<u>*Auspices of the United Nations*</u>
<u>*And the*</u>
<u>*Honorable Aoko Itō, United Nations Secretary General*</u>

# Most Secret

"I apologize for the limited time allotted you to review the materials distributed during this morning's session. This was in no way designed to limit your ability to matriculate the events chronicled in these documents.

Speaking candidly, our objective was to minimize dissemination of this information beyond this room, until we have fully completed today's briefing. The data being presented this afternoon are of particular import.

Secondly, much of this information was just received in a presentable format. We therefore had little time to organize and incorporate these materials for distribution and review. However, these events are of such importance we felt an immediate briefing was imperative.

We are now going to present *verbatim* the most recent QAVL findings. We have assembled a written report, photographs, videos and personnel interviews. We find the evidence contained in these records compelling and conclusive. Aside from containing stunning scientific findings, it provides a rational, reasonable basis for investing great faith in the QAVL. My opinion.

You must decide this for yourselves; and we will debate this after the presentation. Mr. Robert White – UN Ambassador from Oneiro is in attendance to answer questions and assist in our analysis after the presentation.

Dr. Howard Benjamin led the Dar es Salaam project; and he will make this afternoon's presentation.

Dr. Benjamin....?"

# Dar es Salaam & the QAVL
# Report of Findings
# Commission by the United Nations
# United Nations Extra-Solar Contact-UNESCON

(Voiceover Dr. Howard Benjamin – Project Director)

(Photograph of team departing New York)

A team of archeologist and paleontologist was dispatched by the United Nations to a destination defined by Mr. Philip Carr, Consul of Oneiro, from coordinates provided by Qasi of *Kosmas Kentrikos,* QAVL Ambassador to Earth.

(Map and aerial photo of Dar es Salaam)

Site: The city center of Dar es Salaam in Tanzania.

Geologic conjectures indicate the coordinates and the depth suggest the site of a substantive volcanic island some 4.6 million years ago, enclosing a significant inland, freshwater lake. Prior to formation of the freshwater lake, analysis of the surrounding strata indicates a modest inland sea existed within roughly the same area. This is supported by widespread concentration of salts – essentially bicarbonates and assorted sodium compounds. This formed the basis for naturally occurring natron. Matrix analysis subsequently confirmed this speculation.

Subsurface environmental cores date this sometime before the period referred to as the *Plio-Pleistocene*. The team chose to christen it the *Npo-Plio-Pleistocene*. In retrospect it was perhaps better termed as simply the *Pliocene epoch*. The *Neogene Period*. Towards the end of the *Paleolithic Age*.

Monikers notwithstanding, the critical information lies in the fact this site dates back some 4.6 million years.

(Video of riots in Dar es Salaam)

Dar es Salaam was among the incipient flash-points of the Ghazi Khan Insurgency. Understandably then, governmental sanction to excavate in search of QAVL corroborative objectification in the midst of their largest, oldest, most important city was difficult to acquire. Nonetheless, following negotiations with the Tanzanian government, considerable expense and intense international pressures, Tanzania acquiesced. With our sincere thanks to the Representative of Tanzania.

(Video of a B19 Boring Hyperdig 2020, excavating a tunnel)

Highly cognizant of the extreme urgency of our task, the team excavated a five meter shaft, thirteen meters deep using advanced equipment adapted from the fourth Franco-Anglo-European Chunnel Project. They operated 24 hours a day at 124% of the equipment's max recommended rate. Five days and two murderous riots later, the team achieved their target depth, a scant one-half meter above their subterranean objective.

The Find:

(Photograph of shaft)

*The team immediately initiated the next phase: Painstaking manual excavation with the greatest possible haste – testing the limits of archeological discipline. The team unearthed an incredible fossil record. The entire site measured some three by three by 1.5 meters, which was removed verbatim from its matrix, in situ, wrapped in protective layering and hauled to the surface.*

(Rendering of *Australopithecus*)

*This find was then subjected to the most intense and scrupulous ultra-resonant micro-chiseling in the history of paleontology. A team of twenty-three scientists worked non-stop to expose the fossils. As elements were revealed they were subjected to chemical and radiological analysis. Sonic and hyper-diffuse, computer assisted radiation tomography. Hyper strength and dangerous, gamma source Radiographic probing revealed every internal feature of these small beings. Externally, the quality of micro-chiseling and the unique mineralogical replacement produced incredible fossil records. As one team member described it "You can practically look them in the eye and relive their last seconds."*

(360° video scan of the actual fossil cluster in matrix)

*Within two days the entire fossil was freed from its matrix and examined by an expert team of biologist, paleontologist, geologist, anthropologist and primatologist. This document is an extract of their findings, conclusions, and even speculations.*

(Computer simulated video of geologic history)

*4.6 million years ago Dar es Salaam was a volcanic island.*

*In the year 4,097,035 BC (an arbitrary project assignment); the inland lake began to gently shake the island. Enormous accumulations of emulsified $CO^2$ – a byproduct of volcanism eons ago - struggle to break free from the deep waters of the massive caldera - finally released by shifting magma thousands of meters below. Moments later an agglomerate of titanic bubbles consisting of high concentrate $CO^2$ exploded from the lakebed, boiling to the surface. A huge wave. And then a deadly ground-fog of $CO^2$ gas covered the entire island to a height of 2.5 meters. Over 1.5 the density of surface atmosphere, the gas flowed like water into every surface feature. The island's fauna was dead within the hour. Days later the $CO^2$ release was followed by Earthshaking eruptions of more carbon dioxide, sulfur-dioxide, and trace gasses emanating from a subduction zone deep below the island. This was only the prelude.*

*An eruption of mud from subduction tubes below the lake was fomenting. One month later, viscous yellow mud covered everything within one hundred meters of the lake, to a depth of over one meter. An extraordinary matrix which marked the beginning of a unique fossilization process.*

*The sulfurous-natron mud buried a family of creatures consisting of a male, female, and juvenile male. The project team conferred upon this trio the family name 'The Γέροσ-Australs' (the old Australopithecus). Estimated ages at death, fourteen, twelve, and four years respectively.*

*They had passed a safe comfortable life on the island not far from a huge lake that dominated the center of the island. There they maintained a den, or nest of sorts. A quasi-cave consisting of a natural hollowing in the native stone partly covered by a large granite slab. The Γέροσ-Australs were sufficiently intelligent to gather hundreds of huge oval Mangrove leaves to line their nest, and provide cover against the curious fall of grayish powder from the skies. It was also useful insulation during strangely chilly nights.*
*Ancient Mangroves were prevalent throughout the island. They thrived in the mineral rich brackish waters and provided a lush sanctuary for a wide variety of aquatic, amphibious and land animals.*

## Oneiro II: Gauntlet

(Video of denuding the fossil record from its matrix)

*In the nest there was considerable evidence of assorted small animal bones and vegetal remains. These creatures were omnivorous. A truly exceptional site. The fossils themselves were hitherto totally unknown.*

*Geographically out of place. Ontologically out of time. Lacking a point of reference or even a label in extant paleontological or anthropological terms.*

(Return to computer simulation)

*The $CO^2$ fog had quickly and noninvasively killed all three. Subsequent days in the hot sulfurous air nearly mummified them. The process was concluded with total immersion in warm, airtight mud. This remarkable sequence of events was further compounded by the Γέροσ-Australs themselves. The Mangrove leaves so thoughtfully gathered by the creatures to line their nest covered them in their death sleep. Mangrove leaves are rich in tannin. Tannin is a natural compound which effectively leaches the oxygen from organic matter, such as the Γέροσ-Australs, thereby inhibiting oxidation. Thereby decomposition.*

*This natural tannin, combined with large deposits of natron, formed a sedimentary strata rich in the elements of mummification. Those body parts not normally subject to tannin detoxification and preservation were dramatically dehydrated by natron. Therefore, further preserving them. This compound process fossilized them perfectly, including hair, epidermal and even soft internal tissues.*

(Series of photographs of the finished fossil family)

*The result: A trio of perfectly preserved human fossils, right down to their toenails. Genetically an Apomorphic or Plesomorphic as would be adjudged by their phylogeny. The archetypical homo hominis-humanus. A hitherto unknown iteration of Australopithecus.*

*These creatures were older than any other Australopithecus. Older than they should be. Yet far more advanced. A fascinating contradiction. Far removed from their northern cousins in time and space and even evolution*

*The most unique paleo-biological-anthropological-archeological find in human history. A discovery that will engage science for decades.*

*By man's reckoning, the seminal Australopithecus was Australopithecus ramidus. This archetype was followed by Australopithecus afarensis. The young female we call Lucy And finally Australopithecus anamensis. The earliest having lived some 4.1 million years ago.*

*Now: Australopithecus QAVLus. The most promising prodigy of the family. Very advanced. The quintessential link precisely defining the schism between the destinies of Hominid and Hominidae. Man and ape. And an amazing 4.6 million years old. Although the terms link and schism are somewhat inappropriate. Evolution seldom, if ever, produces full-blown incipient specie. Evolution describes a hill-side, more than a cliff-face.*

*This tiny troop died far south of the classical finds in Northern Tanzania and Ethiopia. Of greater interest however, is the disparity between their age and their amelioration as a Hominid. Their lineage defied chronology, logic and any principle of paleontology. Their brain size was an unprecedented 610 cc. Their social structure indicated nesting. Their stance was fully upright. In every respect they had evolved well beyond their antecedents, their contemporaries, and most surprisingly, their posterior for nearly one million years...*

(Video of Dr. Benjamin speaking)

This is a chronological mystery that may puzzle scientists for decades to come.

A telling observation emerged from initial studies. It was suggested that this was further proof that brain size and intelligence are no more than an adaptation to ambient forces and competitive pressures. As such, adaptations result from random development, perhaps these creatures developed their brain too early – before it was needed – therefore an undue bio-adaptive burden – demanding perhaps a burdensome requirement for protein – discarded in latter iterations.

Nonetheless, man has been given the final transitional fossil extant between ape and man. Not the legendary Missing Link conjectured and hunted by scientists for over two centuries. Our team has speculated, believe it or not, that these creatures descended from ancestors of European origin. A totally disparate branch of the family.

This was something new. Unconjectured. Undisturbed. Undisturbable. Buried for all time, far beneath an ancient city. A pivotal piece of the human mosaic that would have lain undiscovered for eternity were it not for the QAVL. The subject humanoids were not predated or scavenged. They were not crushed or dismembered by geologic forces. They were fossilized in the most benign, displacement process imaginable. Compelling, if not incontestable proof the QAVL roamed the Earth at least 4.6 million years ago; and by force of reason, friends of man by any measure. A gift of such great value to humanity it evidences the QAVL as valued amicus. A gift that will enrich mankind for all history.

Thank you.

Dr. ABHAY raised his hands preparing to enthusiastically applaud. As quickly, his hands froze in mid-stroke, he frowned and cocked his head intently. *That's odd. No applause. Then faint, sporadic applause. Then no applause whatsoever.*

Uneasily Dr. ABHAY resumed the podium. "The floor is open for questions and debate." After a brief pause, ABHAY smiled and gestured to a familiar delegate. A friend of many years. "The Chair recognizes the Honorable Representative of Indonesia."

"Dr. ABHAY. Every city and village in my country is on fire. As are the fields and forests. As are the hospitals and universities and museums and governments houses and banks. All the vestiges of modern, civilized society. Thousands have died. My wife and daughter were brutally murdered in their beds. Screaming in the night. Our government has fallen. Our economic, legal and social structures are in ruin. Disease and starvation run rampant. Food, medicine and drinking water have *vanished*. The military is in the grip of the mob.

Five million people have gathered at the Vatican, two million on the Mall in Washington, three million at the Kremlin. Other tens of millions gather to protest, to pray, to riot and kill, at like locations all over the world. Within days, perhaps hours, we will witness world currencies, stock markets, economy, trade, communications crumble...everything in shambles. And there is no end in sight. This thing will only further degenerate; and abomination will consume us, without remorse.

I fully believe the entire world will soon succumb to this Atramentaceous plague.

All this, and far more, was provoked by the irresponsible, inept and unilateral actions of a tiny island of which we have only just learned. And we are only just beginning to learn of the obscenities that flourish in that feculent lair.

In all probability our armed forces will ally themselves with like-minded countries to mount an all-out armed assault on Oneiro. They will attack and destroy Oneiro and the QAVL invaders.

I for one applaud their actions. I wish them the best of luck. As regards your Astro...Astow...Astophilikites, or whatever...I couldn't care less. Damn them. Damn you. And damn Oneiro."

Despite the coolness of the chamber, the delegate was profusely sweating in his dark pinstripe suit. His face a deep red. He was so tense he actually trembled. He stood, threw his papers down with distain, and peremptorily marched from the chamber.

He was followed by a full eighty percent of the delegates.

The immense chamber was plunged into arctic silence.

The meeting was over.

Calamity ruled the chamber.

And the world.

# Fire-Flight

After Aiy had stabilized somewhat, Phil began the painstaking process of cleaning her. An arduous and deeply disturbing task. Working as fast as he could, it still required the better part of an hour. Before cleaning she had been a misshapen horror of caked blood and crusted hair. Now she actually looked worse. Phil could not recognize anything of Aiy in the carrion lump secured to the deck of his aircraft.

The next task. Analyze her pathophysiology. Identify the greatest danger requiring immediate treatment. Triage for one.

Pulse weak and fast. Her breathing nearly non-existent. Also very rapid. She was cold. Fish-belly white. Her skin was damp and clammy. Traumatic shock. *Got to remember what to do...*

Phil began using his mind. He had little time.

DIC. Disseminated Intravascular Coagulation. DIC. Sometimes called consumptive coagulopathy. Circulation differentials propagate...microclots... dangerous. Treatment may consists of application of a...a thrombolytic agent which lyses the microclots.

A thrombolytic agent. Essentially a serine protease useful to mammals in metabolizing nourishment...classically a compound based on cysteine, threonine and hydratres...He began digging through the med kit. If he couldn't find a solution soon, Aiy would die. Faster and faster he rummaged through the large case. Unconsciously he was talking to himself. Running over alternatives and their attendant formulae. He heard movement nearby and looked up.

Captain Miller glanced back from the cockpit, clearly concerned. He had observed Phil furiously rifling through the med kit. Dividing his attention between flight controls and Phil, he called out "Should we consider an emergency medical stop?"

Phil needn't stop to ponder the question.

He yelled back. "No. I have to stabilize her *now*. She will be dead by the time we make it to the ground; and I'm afraid many Oneirions may be killed if we delay any more than absolutely necessary."

"Understood." Before returning his full attention to the flight he quickly reached into the galley and retrieved an apple and a bottle of water left by Phil in the copilot's position.

Phil watched him absently. *Of course! BROELAIN. Chlorhexidine Acetate. Any drugstore carries it over-the-counter. A simple digestive agent derived from fruit...pineapples. Every med-kit in the world carries a bottle of the white powder to treat indigestion.*

He riffled the med-kit and found the bottle. Minutes later he had emulsified a mild mixture of the powder in distilled water with glucose. He added the compound to Aiy's drip.

Half an hour later her heart rate approached normal. Her breathing had eased and her temperature reflected no more than an infection which could be medicated.

Before continuing, he took a much needed break. He reclined a seat, downed a large Scotch and a sandwich and then slept for exactly thirty minutes.

He arose and checked on his patient. *By God I think she's going to make it. For now anyhow. Maybe I should have finished at Johns Hopkins? Of course Aiy is also impressively....resilient.*

Phil walked forward to the flight deck. "How's it going Captain?"

"Fine. We're over Afghanistan now. Cruising at thirty-eight thousand feet, west by south/west. We're bypassing Iranian airspace, and will be over the Gulf of Oman soon. Mid-Gulf we'll adjust our altitude to thirty-nine thousand and our heading to west by north/west, towards Greece. A little circuitous but I think we'll get there in one piece. I've arranged a tech stop in Amman."

"Think you could change that to Nicosia?"

"Cyprus?"

"Yep."

"May I ask why?"

"I'm concerned Amman may be burning by the time we get there."

"Why is Nicosia any better?"

"Not better. I just think it will take a little longer to catch fire."

"Good grief! Nicosia it is."

"If we revert to the velocity and altitude we maintained evacuating Ghazi Kahn, can you make it to Nicosia?"

The Captain took some moments recalculating their flight plan. "We need a reasonable fuel reserve with all this crap coming down...and an alternate... Larnaka I suppose...Yes...We should make it with an acceptable margin."

"Good. Let's do it."

"Mr. Carr we will most certainly raise the ire of every ATC across this corridor of Asia and the Mediterranean. We'll drop off radar and start bells ringing throughout the system. We may bring down on ourselves the aggression we are trying to avoid. Nor do I see how we can expect landing authority from Nicosia for a tech stop if we come in under their radar."

"I realize that. We are already marked however, so anonymity is no longer an option. The skies will be crazy soon anyway, so I don't think we'll attract much notice, if any. Therefore, this is a risk I'm prepared to take."

"What shall I do about Nicosia?"

"Patch through to my secretary on Oneiro. Ask her to contact Howard Doyle. Tell her what you need. She'll get it from Howard. I'll also have a list of medical supplies I want to onload in Nicosia. Give me half an hour."

"Can do."

"Thanks."

Phil kneeled beside Aiy and began the task of appraising Aiy's condition and deciding on the next treatment, relying on his AV Collar to record his work.

As he gathered his thoughts, Phil relived what he's seen and done. The pathetic little girl he killed. Did she have a home, family, parents? Would she be missed? The horrors of Fatin's fortress and the horrors he committed himself. He stopped. *Enough!* He determined to terminate this line of thought. Wrap it and forget about it. To be unwrapped only on *his own little asteroid* when the time is right.

"This is Philip Carr recording. I am not a doctor. I am not a pathologist. And I am most certainly not a forensic pathologist. I am making this recording to initiate a medical record on Ms Aiyana Atsila, a native American, approximately thirty-two years of age, in good health prior to this incident. Ms Atsila was rescued from a compound in Ghazi Khan, Pakistan, where she was brutally tortured and suffered profound physical and mental trauma. I am making this recording in case Ms Atsila dies before we reach aid in Oneiro, or if I am killed. This recording is intended as either an appurtenance to an autopsy, or a summary of my treatments thus far.

I have already treated the subject for shock, successfully I think, with bromides, plasma and saline.

Starting with the head, there are contusions indicative of severe head trauma such as would be inflicted with a large pipe, or wooden club. Nothing I can do at this point. I suspect brain hemorrhaging. The left ear has been removed, rather crudely...a knife or blade of some sort. In like manner the nose, as well as the upper lip to the margin of gums and cheek, just below the normal termination of the nose. The right eye has been removed. Looks as though a (*my God*) something like a spoon was used. Three teeth have been smashed. It appears a chisel-like instrument was employed. Left and right incisors and right lower canine are missing.

In the thorax, the right and left breasts have been removed and there are clearly some broken ribs. I suspect massive internal damage. I consider the risk of infection and Peritonitis high. Accordingly I have administered massive doses of Cefoxitin in conjunction with an Aminoglycoside.

In the region of the genetalia the right labia has been excised. Based on the condition of the vaginal area, I conclude the subject was repeatedly raped, or similarly abused. Based on the quantity of blood and bruising contiguous with the excision, I would surmise the rape occurred (*oh God*) subsequent to removal of the labia."

Phil turned off the recorder, took several deep breaths and a drink of water trying desperately to control trembling in his hands. He continued.

"The left index finger has been amputated using non-surgical instrumentation...an axe or cleaver perhaps. Maybe clippers. There is widespread bruising, indicating protracted torture, as well as bruises and contusions where the subject was restrained with belts, or ropes and chains.

I plan to dust the entire body with Chlorhexidine acetate and an application of a light dressing with minimal body contact. I wish I had some old-fashioned sulfa. I will continue with a saline drip containing painkillers, antibiotics, mild anti-coagulants, glucose and sedatives. I will also apply a plasma drip and moisten the mouth area at half-hour intervals. I will provide a list of all medications.

End of recording."

Phil stowed the recorder and hoarsely advised Captain Miller he would be needing no additional supplies on Nicosia. He carefully arranged all drips and transfusions. He gently applied mineral oil to Aiy's devastated gums and teeth. He methodically covered Aiy with a light gauze tent and ensured she was securely belted down.

Phil looked down on Aiy. He studied the grisly ruin that had been the most beautiful woman he'd ever known. He tried to imagine the fear, debasement and suffering. *How in the world had she endured such torture? Why did it take so long to break her? Is she that strong? That brave? In all these years I never knew she was...Wait a minute..*

*There's something wrong here...*

*Fatin had been covered in blood. Hers? Most likely. She did break. She did reveal the file. But if she withstood all these horrors before she broke, she could never have spoken coherently. She could not have told Fatin where the file was hidden. So...she broke...she talked...AND FATIN JUST KEPT TORTURING HER. For his own twisted pleasures. He probably even...oh God!* Unspeakable images were raising like specters of hell itself in Phil's mind. It taxed his strength simply to maintain control and banish the monstrous spectacle from his mind.

When he was sure all was in order, he made his way to the washroom and vomited several times. Trembling and covered in sweat, he returned to the cabin and turned up a bottle of Scotch. He drained half the bottle without stopping. He drank urgently and greedily, hands trembling as they clutched the bottle, the clear brown liquid running down his chin onto his chest. The last time he drank with such ravenous desperation was Spain. After he himself had tortured and murdered Fatin's father.

Phil ground his teeth in hatred and horror. *I'm glad I killed that little flat-headed dwarf. I'm glad I killed him. I'm glad I killed his brother. I'm glad I killed his father. If he'd had a son I'd have killed him. I wish it had taken longer for him to die. Much longer. If there's a God in heaven, Aiy will die before we reach Cyprus.* He wept in grief, horror and rage. He staggered to a seat and fell into a black sleep for two hours.

"Mr. Carr?"

"Ah, yes?"

"Sorry to wake you. Were on final into Nicosia. I'd like you to join me on the flight deck. I need a spotter. ATC seems chaotic."

"I'll be right with you."

Phil made a quick check of Aiy. *Still Alive. Still out. Still stable. Crap.* Then he moved to the flight deck. He strapped himself into the right seat. "How does it look?"

"Well, we've had no problems, or warnings from ATC. I have seen smoke at several points on our approach. So I think things are pretty much as you forecasted. Nicosia has not caught on fire. Yet."

"Let's get in and out. Fast."

"I'm advised Doyle has everything arranged. We'll park on the hangar apron and they'll fuel us immediately. He says you should use cash if you have it. Oh yes. He also wants your authority to enter Oneiro."

"Okay. When we're back in the air, contact my secretary again and instruct her to dispatch Oneiro seven-delta-two-six to pick up Mr. Doyle in Cannes."

"Can do."

"Thanks Captain Mill...What's your first name Captain?"

"Mark."

"Mark I'm Phil." The two men shook hands.

"Buckle up. We're going in...Phil."

Twenty minutes later their wings were full, Captain Miller had walked the aircraft, and they were ready to taxi out for take-off.

Three minutes later they were surrounded by twenty Cypriot Regular Army troops and twenty M249 Light Machine Guns, all pointed at their aircraft.

Miller grabbed the mike. "Nicosia Control this is Oneiro seven-delta-two-five. Over."

"Oneiro seven-delta-two-five this is Nicosia Control. You are in the custody of the Cypriot Army. You are not to leave your aircraft for any reason. You are not to power up your aircraft for any reason. You are instructed to keep the airways clear. You are under radio silence. Acknowledge Oneiro seven-delta-two-five."

"Acknowledged Nicosia Control. Out."

Phil groaned inwardly, and outwardly.

He turned to Mark. "Are we still plugged into ground power?"

"Aah...yes...we're still on the GPU, and on blocks."

"I think you should power up the air conditioning. It's going to get hot as hell in here. We could be here for some time."

For the next eighteen hours they slept, read, looked after Aiy and watched the Army change their guard every six hours. Fruit and sandwiches were well stocked. However, water supplies were becoming marginal, so Phil and Mark confined themselves to soft drinks. In Phil's case, soft drinks and Scotch. There was no indication from local authorities how long, or why they were being held and the hours stretched out longer and longer. Blessedly, no one on the ground had thought to disconnect their GPU so their electric and air con packs were charged and the temperature remained reasonable. Aiy had began her curious mewing sounds again, but Phil hesitated administering additional medications to quiet her.

The Captain made coffee and threw himself into one of the planes large lounges, cup in hand. "What's really going on here Phil?"

"Here?"

"No. Not *here*. Worldwide. From what I've seen a real shit-storm is coming down everywhere."

"That's true. And it's going to get much worse. I calculate every country on Earth will be inexorably enmeshed in this chaos within days...maybe even hours."

"You *calculate*?"

"Don't worry about it. It's a kind of knack I have sometimes."

"Okay. What about this *chaos* business?"

"Well, you're aware there's alien life on Oneiro?"

"Of course. And we're in a joint project to construct some sort of space vessel, in order to visit some remote planet inhabited by thousands of alien species."

Clearly, Mark found it awkward mouthing such a surreal narrative.

"Right. You may not be aware this whole business was initiated through an incredible document, millions of pages long. A secret, introductory extract of that document was made available to the United Nations Security Council in digital form. They call it the DOCUMENT. In caps. Anyhow, the DOCUMENT was probably leaked well before the UNSC could be briefed. This provided them considerable time to launch their strike. Then another file was stolen from Oneiro by this young lady." Phil gestured down to Aye. "And that file found its way into some dangerous hands. That's why she was tortured in that hell-hole back in Ghazi Kahn."

"A real comedy of errors."

"That's for damned sure."

"But that doesn't explain how it became known worldwide so fast."

"A man named Bahaar Fatin al din Ammar in Ghazi Kahn was working for a group of real beauties in the Atlas Mountains. Still don't know the name of the organization. They, along with a twisted cleric named Imam Aban Waseer Hafeez, have invested decades and billions of dollars bating a trap for humanity in every major city around the world. Arms, guerrillas, assault plans and the venomous propaganda needed to lubricate a worldwide insurrection. It all happened so fast because these bastards wanted it spread with such speed it would be literally unstoppable."

"...and they want to destroy the world because...?"

"Not the entire world. Just everything, except their own. I suppose the concept is a virulent form of *Khilafah*."

"*Khilafah*?"

"Yes. The Islamic belief that they should act in concert to unify the world under Shariah law. Allah. Problem is, many believe this entails killing one hellofa lot of infidels along the way. A *Jihad*. And in the hands of these killers hidden in Morocco, it gets worse. They thirst for the bloodshed. It increases their secular and non-secular power and wealth. So the more they kill and destroy. The more they own and control.

"I see. So what's got the whole human race so incited?"

"Fear I suppose. And an understandable outrage at being held in ignorance while mysterious aliens invade their planet. Supported now by documentary evidence. That, and plain old dogma. Easily adapted to whatever religion applies. Convince people these aliens, and in particular Oneiro, run contrary to their deepest beliefs. Add to that the general feeling that these nebulous evils lurk all about us. In our governments. In other countries. Anything we are suspicious of, or just don't like. *Et voilà*. Pandemonium consumes the globe at warp speed."

"My God." The Captain frowned out the window, up to the skies. "What's your prognosis Phil?"

Phil thought for a time.

"Where do you live Mark?"

"Oneiro, with my wife and two kids."

"Unusual for Oneiro. Never knew there were married people on the island. Were you granted some sort of exemption?"

"No really. I'm a lander and I married an Oneirion girl. One of the early generations. And of course there's no prohibition *per se* against marriage, or having children. It's just not usually done. There are two other families there as well."

"Must be a unique lifestyle for a family."

"Actually, it's fascinating. The children love it; and we fly to the mainland quite often."

Phil regarded Mike seriously.

"When we get there, stay there. Keep *them* there. Don't leave for any reason. *Ever*."

Outside, their guards were becoming increasingly restive. A small mess tent was ensconced next to the hangar, along with two portable toilets. The men frequently raised their guns towards the plane, glaring at Phil and Mark. Soon they began sitting down on the ramp area, talking and smoking, others reading or eating, a few even sleeping. It was clear their officers were not about.

At midday the next day Phil was intermittently dozing and peering out his window when he noticed his guards were suddenly alert, listening, and looking intently in the direction of the hangar. They quickly climbed to their feet, dusting off their trousers and shouldering their guns. It was obvious to Phil they were becoming tense, and experiencing a level of agitation that officers simply did not inspire. Something else was going on out there.

"Mark. Something's coming down. I think we should stand by to crank up. I'll pull the GPU and the blocks when it's time."

"Okay, I'm ready to power up any time." He went forward, ready to power up.

Phil was watching the terminal. He thought he heard shots. He was sure he saw smoke. "It's getting close Mark."

Moments later "There it is. There's a mob running out of the terminal and many are coming our way."

"Shall I power up?"

"Give it a minute. Yes. There they go. Power up!"

The troops were running towards the hanger all thoughts of Phil's plane forgotten. Phil released the door, jumped to the ground, disconnected the GPU and pulled the blocks. He thought he heard the whiz of a bullet near his head, but couldn't be sure with the all the noise. He was back aboard in thirty seconds. As he sealed the door, the aircraft began rolling. Mark came hard about and throttled up to full power. Phil was thrown into a seat. The powerful little jet leapt forward and was screaming down the runway. Bottles and the detritus of meals and medical care were falling and galling all round them.

They were off the ground, mob far behind, in less than a minute.

Phil lurched forward and took the right seat. Looking down he saw that Nicosia was now truly on fire.

"What's our ETA Oneiro Mark?"

"We'll be on the ground in Oneiro in one hour and thirty-four minutes."

"Can you put me through to Oneiro Control?"

"Sure." He thumbed the hand mike. "Oneiro Control this is Oneiro seven-delta-two-five. Over."

He waited a few seconds.

"Oneiro Control this is Oneiro seven-delta-two-five. Over."

"Oneiro Control this is Oneiro seven-delta-two-five. Over."

"Oneiro Control this is Oneiro seven-delta-two-five. Over."

"Oneiro Control this is Oneiro seven-delta-two-five. Over."

"Something's wrong Phil."

"Yeah." Phil rummaged around in his wallet. "Reset the radio to this frequency." Phil handed him a card. "This is Charlie Stein's concentrator on Proteus Point."

Mark reset the frequency and handed the mike to Phil.

"Proteus Point this is Oneiro seven-delta-two-five. Phil Carr. Over."

"Proteus Point this is Oneiro seven-delta-two-five. Phil Carr. Over."

"Proteus Point this is Oneiro seven-delta-two-five. Phil Carr. Over."

"Proteus Point this is Oneiro seven-delta-two-five. Phil Carr. Over."

"Phil. This is Charlie. Where the hell are you? It's a real shit storm here."

"What is your situation Charlie?"

"We're under attack. Fighters, bombers, missiles, they're trying to land troops. You name it."

"How are our defenses holding up?"

"What defenses? They're tearing the crap out of us and we're doing fuck all..."

"Okay. Calm down Charlie. Where's Mike Auslander?"

"I think he's on his way from Anastasios Island aboard JAEKEL."

"What about Nick Farrow?"

"I'll try to patch you through. He's just arrived I think."

After two or three long minutes... "Farrow."

"Nick! Where are you?"

"Phil! I'm just tying up at Oneiro Harbor. Where are you? You okay?"

"Get yourself to Fire Control at the Armory right now. Find out what they're doing there. And...listen carefully...push the button on Metal Storm and run it dry. Do the same with our Gatling shore defenses. Order the techs to reload and stand by for the next wave. Activate your surface radar and monitor for further seaborne assaults. The Sentry Plants should do the rest. Now *run*!" When they broke contact with Nick, they somehow also lost communications with all sites on Oneiro.

They tried to re-establish communications with any site, unsuccessfully, for over an hour. Finally "Oneiro seven-delta-two-five this is Oneiro Control. Over."

"This is Oneiro seven-delta-two-five. Go ahead Oneiro Control."

"All is quiet now. It was quite a show here."

"Our systems took out the invasion force?"

"Vaporized is closer to the mark. What is your ETA? We have a window for your approach, but I don't know how long we can keep it open."

"Oneiro Control, we are twenty-three minutes out. In range. On final. I'm turning you over to Captain Miller. Have an ambulance and trauma team standing by if you can spare one. I also need a jeep to take me topside to the cliffs above Fire Control. Acknowledge."

"Everything will be ready Oneiro seven-delta-two-five. Be on the alert for bogies. Long range radar shows inbounds on and off radar. We have requested Fire Control to take defensive measures using their lasers. They are tracking your approach now. We will keep you advised."

Captain Miller turned to Phil. "Who is attacking us Phil?"

"I really don't know. It's possible we may never know unless we take prisoners."

"It's astounding how fast this came down on us."

"Much too fast Mark. I think someone's been peeking through the keyhole."

"Any idea who?"

"Well, the island was supposed to be on full alert. Yet someone was asleep at the switch when we were attacked. They were negligent to the extent it's inescapably a conspiracy. In fact it appears that Fire Control was abandoned altogether until Nick arrived."

Phil passed the mike to Mark. "I'm going back to check on our passenger."

"Okay. Don't be too long. I still need a ..."

*WHUMPH!!*

The jetwash from another aircraft hit them like a mammoth bungee-stick. Superheated gases expelled in a deadly vortex from wingtips and engines.

Their aircraft yawed crazily to starboard, nose down. Phil was knocked back into his seat and he struggled with his seatbelt. He looked to his right, straight down into the sea below. The aircraft's rudder began to careen violently from port to starboard. 'Cavitate' was the analogy that occurred to Phil. They were close to cart-wheeling. Mark fought desperately for control. After long, desperate seconds Mark's muscle and determination prevailed. They finally leveled out and assumed reasonably stable flight. Mark was breathing heavily and perspiring freely.

Phil's head was spinning. "Jesus Christ! What the hell was that?"

"That was an F-14 Tomcat."

"Whose flag?"

"It looked like Iran. That would make sense. They're one of the few nations still flying the F-14. That pass was just to see who the hell we are. The next one's going to be a bitch. I'm going down."

The sleek little business jet went into a sharp dive. Dusk was settling on the water and they were moving so fast Phil couldn't make out any indication of their altitude. Mark suddenly pulled back on the yoke with all his strength. The sea was rushing up and the altimeter was hypnotically spinning. "Help me." Rasped Mark.

Phil grabbed his yoke and pulled as well. Suddenly they felt their weight zoom as G forces crashed upon them. They had no compression flight suits and so were in imminent danger of blacking out. They walked a tightrope between blacking out, ditching, or exceeding the structural capability of their aircraft. All deadly.

As their yokes thrummed in hands, the addition of Phil's exceptional strength helped them achieve control gradually enough to avoid breaking up, or blacking out. Suddenly they were flying a breathtaking fifty meters above the water. They were so close, it seemed a large wave could bring them down. Phil looked across at Captain Moore. He was shocked to see blood had streamed out of his nose and mouth, probably from his gums. After checking himself and considering things, he decided not to inform the Captain. He had enough to worry about just now.

The Captain studied the skies intently. "He has not re-engaged. I wonder why. Did we lose him? We should be shrapnel by now. Jesus! Never thought I would be worried about G-LOC on a business jet."

"G-LOC?"

"Gravity Loss of Consciousness."

"Right. He carries missiles I assume?"

"Yes. The Tomcat carries Sparrows underwing."

"Maybe he shot his wad?"

"Damn. You're probably right. He's *returning* from the fight. He's used all his missiles."

"I wonder how he escaped our ground defenses? He must be pretty good. He must be pretty low on fuel too."

"Low? Hell he's got to be sucking fumes."

"Where'd he come from. An airbase?"

"There is no airbase in reasonable range. Unless there's a carrier nearby, he's come a long way, regardless where he may have sortied. It think that dive may have saved us. We may be in the clear and...."

*WHACK!*

The cockpit was suddenly a frenzied tumult of howling air and papers. When the rush of air calmed, they surveyed the damage. A portside window was shattered and their windscreen was cracked.

"Damn. I'm hit. Crap!" The Captain was canted awkwardly to his left. Blood covered his chest and left arm. He inspected himself dispassionately. "No. I'm not hit. This is glass. Must have cut an artery. If you can pull out this piece of glass and stop the bleeding I may just remain conscious. Fast. Hell. Maybe I can even land this goddamned plane, if we can evade that goddamned Tomcat."

"I'll be right back."

Phil returned bearing an injection of mild anodyne, bandages, antiseptic powder, antibiotics, a rubber tube and a bottle of water. He began working on Mark. "So what hit us?"

"I'd say a stray round from his M61. I think you guessed right. He's out of missiles. Ow!"

"Sorry. I had to get that glass out. So why hasn't he come back to finish the job?"

"No. No painkillers Phil."

"Okay. So where is the son of a bitch?"

"I was knocked about pretty hard when we were hit, but I think we may have passed a splash-down aft of our portside."

"What happened?"

"One of two things. He either got careless and flew himself into the water; or flew himself dry and flamed out. If it's the latter, they're taking this damned serious."

"*Either way*, they're taking this damned serious."

"Are you able to fly the aircraft Mark?"

"Yes. I'll need your help with the control levers. But I can get us home."

"Just tell me what to do."

"You'll have to lower the landing gear, engage air brakes, and adjust the flaps as I instruct. And I still need you as a spotter. Although I have no idea how we could evade another bogie. How's the lady in back?"

"Alive."

"Okay. Shall we go home?"

"Absolutely."

Mark thumbed the mike. "Oneiro Control this is Oneiro seven-delta-two-five. Over."

"Oneiro Control this is Oneiro seven-delta-two-five. Over."

"Oneiro seven-delta-two-five this is Oneiro Control. Over."

"We're coming in hot and low."

"How low Oneiro seven-delta-two-five? Ascend to radar level. One-zero-zero-zero."

"I may have time to ascend to five-zero-zero and start my glide path. I trust we have a window and conditions are all clear?"

"All clear Oneiro seven-delta-two-five. Come to five-zero-zero, azimuth one-two-seven and commence final. We've got the lights on and the mat out. Proceed direct."

"Thank you Oneiro Control. Out."

"Get the gear down Phil. That lever...yes. Flaps down. Good. Reducing thrusters by one-third. Stand by to engage airbrakes when I give you the word."

Phil took a fast look around. Oneiro was totally blacked out. They were coming in on visual using the approach lights.

They made a rough landing with a bouncing bang and much fishtailing. The throttle was open too long and the airbrakes late, so they used the entire runway and nearly more. Captain Miller was standing on the brakes to the end. But they made it.

An ambulance was standing by which took Aiy and Captain Miller away, both still alive. Phil conferred briefly with the doctor in attendance and passed him the recorder. He looked down at Captain Miller as they wheeled him to the ambulance. "Thanks for one hellofa ride Captain."

Miller's only response was a wry smile and a supine salute.

# Earth Up - With a Twist

"Oh my! Gregory I can't remember the last time you ordered a Martini for lunch. Especially here. You do remember they serve them by the *carafe*?"

"Vividly." Smiled Gregory reminiscently. "And this is not simply lunch, as you well know. I believe this is the most critical meeting we will ever have. It may also be the last time we take such drinks together for an indefinite period. When we're finished here, I plan to take a cab to my apartment and pass out under my bed. So. I for one plan to enjoy myself."

A windy, partly cloudy afternoon in Manhattan. Leaves and papers scudding down streets, slate gray, gleaming wetly from intermittent rains. Collars up against the rawness, as people hurried from doorway to doorway. The inviting refuge of shops and restaurants, bathed in warm golden light, cheerful, secure and away from the stormy afternoon.

Gregory and Ajisaka had just attended a secret session of the UN General Assembly. The meeting had been intense, jarring and complex. Ending in disaster. They had confronted an event which marked the crisis of both their careers; and the gathering had completely drained both men. They decided to skip the afternoon session in favor of lunch at their favorite restaurant, only a few blocks from the UN Headquarters.

The little known restaurant, quietly nestled on a small square in midtown specialized in superb Sardinian cuisine. It was small, stylishly up-market, and popular with prosperous local businessmen and sophisticated shoppers. Oddly, one rarely saw UN staff at the restaurant, rendering it a favorite meeting spot for the two men representing diverse, and often hostile, interests. Two men who do not always relish being seen together.

Their waiter, Enzo, was patiently attempting to cajole their order. Thus far unsuccessfully. Ajisaka looked thoughtfully at Gregory and then to the waiter. "You know Enzo, I think I'll join Mr. Borishevski. Please bring me one of your famous Martinis, up with a twist, very dry, olives on the side. I believe we will order lunch a little later."

"Very good." Enzo departed looked somewhat defeated, but relieved. And they were alone.

The two men sat back and regarded each other. As their studied silence stretched into minutes, they realized that neither wanted to be the first to speak. With perfect timing Enzo appeared bearing the huge Martini's and assorted savories.

Ajisaka eagerly quaffed his drink. "Aah! Restaurant Bèga makes the best Martini in Manhattan...maybe the world."

"Manhattan? Most certainly. The world? Nonsense! The absolute best Martini in the world is served at the Burj Al Arab Hotel in Dubai. Two-thirds gin *and* one-third vodka *and* a drop a Scotch with the Vermouth is their secret. Then you freeze it and serve with one final drop of pure lemon oil, and one of extra virgin olive oil, with a twist. That recipe costs me dearly by the way."

"The underwater bar?"

"Yes."

"A little rich for my budget. And in those climes I seldom indulge in alcohol."

For a time they simply sat enjoying their drinks, ignoring the awkward silence they promulgated upon one another.

Ajisaka's patience proved stauncher. Gregory stared intently at him. "I'll tell you what. We are both diplomats. If we persist in continuing such guise this afternoon, we'll be here through dinner and well beyond, without really discussing what may happen and why."

Ajisaka frowned, half smiling. "Curious words for a diplomat. You imply that dip-talk is actually an impediment to effective communications?"

"I imply nothing. I say it outright. It is a lost art these days and a sadly neglected skill. You've heard the childish abuse and the sophomoric squabbles that break out on the floor of the GA these days. Embarrassing. Sickening. Amateurish.

But we. We have little time Ajisaka. We must talk straight. No circumspect soliloquies today. Nothing couched in the diplo-babble of the UN.

In fact, let's do a little play-acting. You my friend will be....aah...my bartender and I will be a...a construction worker. Two people who wont naught for *dip-talk* as you call it. Our two players are in a bar, having just witnessed this morning's session on the bar's television; and we are now openly and honestly discussing what we have learned within the context of our respective backgrounds."

"Yes...and...?"

"...and I have two minutes to summarize my understanding, my position and what I conject our next actions will be. You will be my foil. Draw me out. Clarify my meaning. You will direct our discussion with your questions."

"Five minutes."

"Okay. Five minutes. You open the discussion Ajisaka." Gregory smiled. "*Mister Bartender*."

"Fine. Do you believe what you just witnessed?"

"Yes. The proof is inescapable."

"How long will this remain secret?"

"After this morning's session we may reasonably assume it is no longer a secret in any quarter of the world. This news was released to the General Assembly only to mitigate potential reactions for withholding this amazing information...held secret much too long already. This news belongs to the world. It is not proprietary to the Security Council. Nor is it the exclusive purview of some damned Greek island and a bunch of effete eggheads."

"How will your government and your citizens react to this news?"

"They will be insane with rage and fear and resentment."

"Why such passion?"

"Many reasons. Fear of aliens. Even invisible and benign, they are still 'little green men.' Many will believe that these acts violate their most profound beliefs. Especially Islamics. In fact it plays right into the hands of many. *All* will despise the idea that an insignificant university, on an unknown island, in a third world banana republic was chosen to speak for, and make profoundly important decisions on behalf all mankind."

"I'm not sure the term 'third world banana republic' applies."

"I am describing their perception, not perforce the reality."

"*...not perforce the reality?* Some construction worker." Ajisaka jibed derisively.

"Please stay in character, *Mr. Bartender*."

"I would suggest the same, *Mr. Construction Worker*."

"Please proceed."

"Will your government's view coincide with the populace?"

"In a manner of speaking, yes. But governments will be further incensed when their citizens rise up against them. Extreme disapprobation will abound worldwide."

"So you project universal enmity?"

"Yes, with the exception of the intelligentsia."

"And they...?"

"They will support the QAVL project. They will even be enthusiastic. Then they will be forced to submit to the masses, and to their governments, or be overwhelmed and die."

"You paint a grim picture my friend."

"I am describing Armageddon."

"Hopeless?"

"Unimaginable. Irredeemable."

"How will the media approach this."

"As the always do. They will acerbate the situation. Sensationalize it. Foment even greater fears and deeper wrath. They will exploit our angst and encourage our hostility. They will take any stance consistent with charismatic politicos, regardless of how foolish, dangerous, shortsighted...and self serving."

"So much for the press."

"...and so much for politicians."

"Sounds to me as though this was inevitable, regardless of the catalyst. "

"I agree. We've already set our own trap. Doomed ourselves no matter what."

"...and if the Oneirions further prove the truth of the situation and the beneficent intent of the QAVL?"

"Irrelevant."

"Dr_ABHAY has promised such proof. This afternoon in fact."

"Irrelevant. Bear in mind this event plays into the hands of those formulating long standing, seriously militant preparations."

"So what is the final upshot of all this?"

"Many countries, mine included and yours, will attack Oneiro and obliterate it."

"How would the United Nations react to that?"

"With their accustomed impotency. They will run to and fro and energetically make resolution after resolution. They will vehemently 'condemn' such actions. They will be appalled. They will be incensed. They will be outraged. They will assiduously debate pointless sanctions they will never enact. They will work quickly so as not to miss lunch."

"You are very cynical regarding our profession my friend. In fact you sound bitter."

"Yes and yes. The world suffers and dies while we take tea and palaver."

"Is any help for Oneiro forthcoming? Must they stand alone against the world after they have brought us such wonders?"

Gregory said nothing.

Ajisaka stoically pressed on. "What will the Russians do?"

"They will overtly support Oneiro and covertly support the aggressors."

"China?"

"Nothing. They are outraged by Oneiro; and I frankly empathize with their animus."

"This is within the NATO sphere of influence. Surely NATO is obligated to take action."

Gregory coldly peered at Ajisaka as though he were a vivisection exhibit.

Ajisaka continued to push his questioning. "France?"

"Nothing. Their demography and their cynicism bars them completely."

"Any part of the EU?"

"With the exception of the British...nothing. Europeans can barely contain their own populace from joining the attack."

"South America? Africa?"

Gregory laughed outright.

"The Middle East?"

"Now you are simply being ridiculous."

"And our friends the Americans. What will they do?"

"That is the great unknown. Based on their leadership the last fifteen years, with the British in tow, I surmise they may do something utterly stupid. If they can find a foot-hold, they may attempt to intercede in the face of UN inaction. This would further compound and exponentially complicate the crisis. It would divert attention to the Americans however, which is always useful for a time.

It is equally possible they may be rendered totally impotent. Paralyzed. Do nothing.

And there is a third possibility. This event could well spark an out-and-out internal revolution. Americans are bone weary of being dragged from one conflict to another under the guise of 'Policeman to the World'. There is a dawning certitude that such bumblings squander lives, unity, veneration, economic and political stability, and most importantly...probity.

Americans can be a volatile peoples when sufficiently incensed. And their leadership has been recklessly irresponsible and venomously divisive in recent years."

Ajisaka kneaded his forehead, overwhelmed with frustration. "Today should be the most propitious day in the entire history of man's world."

Gregory smiled cynically. "Not on man's world. Not today."

"Suddenly I am not hungry. I think I'll have another drink."

"Wonderful idea." Gregory flagged the waiter. "Our five minutes have expired Ajisaka. Let's wrap this up."

"Alright. How will this play out?"

"First...Uprisings in every country worldwide. Second...Capitulation or toppling of governments subject to the will of their populace. Third...A concerted destruction of Oneiro and anything remotely related to the QAVL."

"No matter what Dr. ABHAY may reveal?"

"No matter what."

"You are aware the QAVL are probably capable of decimating the entire globe?"

"Certainly."

"...and from that you conclude...?"

"They will not."

"No matter what?"

"No matter what."

"Why?"

"We are physically incapable of harming them; and they are ethically incapable of harming us. Or perhaps they simply don't care enough to bother with our destruction."

His exasperation was overwhelming his innate control. "So Gregory, as you seem to know every goddamned thing about these bastards. What the living hell *do* they want? What *do* they care about? Why have they come? What is the game? Why must it destroy us? They claim they *wuv* us, and plan to prove it. *Bullshit!* I've heard the wind blow before..and how do you know so goddamned much?"

An embarrassed silence descended on the restaurant. Gregory leaned back in his chair and flashed charming, gentle similes all round, as if to say *we're having great fun over here, not need for concern...* Verbally, he spoke low and intently to Ajisaka.

"*Now* you've finally arrived my friend." He smiled. "These are the questions. And I'm sorry, I do not have the answers. Not even close. You asked my once why I am trusted with critical information which is never entrusted to you. As I recall I gave you some sort of inanity, like you were too short, or something equally stupid. The truth is, I am as amoral and murderous as those that engineered this horror. So they trust me. They use me. They even brag to me. But make no mistake, neither I, nor they have one clue what the QAVL are really up to."

"...and who are these murderous powers you refer to?"

"You have no need to know. The information would gain you nothing, and in all probability get you killed. I will tell you this though. Then perhaps you can begin to work out things for yourself."

"What?"

"They lurk in the mountains of North Africa. What they cannot control or posses, they destroy. They've wrapped the world in det-cord and are preparing to blow the whole damned thing up. But here's the catch: They've equipped themselves to survive this mess."

"I see." Ajisaka drew a long slow breath. "With that, I believe our little game is at an end. You have imparted what you came to convey. Rather skillfully in your own way. I believe you have no interest in reversing our bartender, construction worker roles. You really have no interest in my analysis." Ajisaka spoke deadpan with a fateful certitude and an unspoken prodding, gentle accusation in his voice. "Do you?"

"None whatsoever my friend."

"Gregory, your observations are most insightful. In some respects your familiarity with this crisis appears to far exceed the sum presentments of our session this morning. I now have some idea why."

Gregory favored the little man with a genial gaze. "It's a pernicious and dangerous world out there Ajisaka. Many cynical and powerful men have worked long to engineer this day. The problem: Such men have no idea what they are tampering with."

"I can't decide whether you're waxing poetic or melodramatic. But you *are* serious. And that frightens hell out of me." Ajisaka toyed with his Martini, chagrin evident in his features. "Why? Why is the selection of leaders such an insurmountable problem for political man? Why must we be always and forever plagued with irresponsible, unqualified, dishonest and self-serving statesmen? What is wrong?"

Gregory laughed. "Why Ajisaka, *nothing* is wrong! Nothing whatsoever. We receive exactly the leadership we *deserve*."

"We *deserve* Armageddon? We *deserve* to die by the billions?"

"Without question. We deserve Armageddon, *and* we deserve to die by the billions. We bring it upon ourselves." With a predatory grin he whispered. "Trust mother nature in this matter."

"What a perversely vindictive attitude. How can you make such a statement?"

Gregory was no longer smiling. "Humans no longer suffer from nature. Nature suffers from human. Humans are stagnating. Evolve or die. And we are failing to evolve."

"When did you become such a Darwinist? And such a savage mien."

"Evolution is savage. Randomness is the cruelest force in the universe. And we, in our wisdom, elected to carry out its role. And we simply don't know how. And we are unwilling to learn."

With an imperceptible shiver, Ajisaka consulted his watch and ran a quick calculation. His voice was cold now. "I had planned to rely on normal channels to introduce this revelation to my country. I now think I must consult with my government immediately."

"As do I my friend." Sighed Gregory. "As do I."

"...and you will not attend the additional proofs to be presented by Dr. ABHAY?"

"As I stated earlier, it is of no moment. *School's out*."

Wordlessly, money was paid to the waiter. Coats were retrieved and donned. Two friends mutely departed on separate ways. No goodbyes.

Two magnificent Martinis' stood abandoned and untouched in the midst of a stormy afternoon in Manhattan.

*.... You ask, What is our policy? I will say; "It is to wage war, by sea, land and air, with all our might and with all the strength that God can give us... You ask, What is our aim? I can answer with one word: Victory - victory at all costs, victory in spite of all terror, victory however long and hard the road may be; for without victory there is no survival.*

Sir Winston Churchill


A jeep was waiting for Phil to speed him to the western cliffs of the island. Six hundred feet above the massive access hallway leading to the Armory. Phil scrambled down the cliff using the remnants of a cable lift he had used years ago in an earlier assault on Oneiro. He reached a gun emplacement and from there it was an easy run to the Armory. Minutes later Phil strode into the War Room's Fire Control Center.

"Nick."

"Good evening Phil. It's damned good to see you."

They moved to a large glassed-in conference oval in the Command Center of Fire Control. Phil was given a cup of coffee which he gratefully accepted.

"Who the hell is supposed to be in charge here?"

"The best I can figure is an Ian McGregor. He's Chief of Island Defenses."

"Where is he."

"We don't know. We do know he relieved the Shift Supervisor at around 1600 stating he would take over himself."

"Is that normal?"

"Not in the least. In fact he seems to have disappeared as soon as the Shift Supervisor departed. When I arrived they were using cutting tools to regain access to the center. This center is secured behind some incredible doors and McGregor locked them using security codes he secretly modified with his assistant. He's missing as well."

"Any damage?"

"Not much damage *per se*. However, the SOB disabled our ground defense batteries. Fortunately we recently installed a reciprocal Fire Control in the Webber Center."

"McGregor must have known about that."

"Certainly. What he didn't foresee though was an emergency security briefing convened by Bob White in the Webber Center Fire Control. McGregor couldn't get to the auxiliary controls. We took some unnecessary damage during the first wave; and we lost twenty-three lives."

"Is this bastard a lander?"

"They both were."

"Both?"

"He and his number two."

"Oh. Right." Phil's long days were catching up on him.

"I think they both came in with the final wave of landers while Wilcox was President and Chancellor."

"Who's his number three?"

"Margaret Harris."

"Lander?"

"No."

"Where is she?"

"She just came in a few minutes ago. She was trapped under the hanger for a couple of hours."

Nick gestured towards a tall statuesque woman intent on a conversation over the base radio. A striking shock of Woodbine red hair. Huge green eyes that seemed to glow, even from this distance. Skin reminiscent of Aiy. Regular strong features. Clearly a well trained, athletic body. Combat gear suited her well. There was a look about her. What was it? Dangerous? Feral? No. *Predatory*. Phil could easily hold his own in hand-to-hand with any human on Earth. All the same, he suspected she might be a problem. A strong and attractive woman. The classical essence of Islander. Image what a hundred thousand more iterations would bear...

Phil turned to one of the aids standing about "Please ask Ms Harris to join us." Moments later she entered the conference room.

"Hello Mr. Carr. It's a pleasure to meet you."

*Shakes hands like a man. Looks you straight in the eye. A no-bullshit lady.*

"Good to meet you Ms Harris. What can you tell me about Mr. McGregor?"

"All I can reliably tell you is for some reason he's not here, nor has he..."

"What do you think is going on here?"

She paused for the briefest moment, looking thoughtfully at Phil.

"I think we've been scuttled."

"As do I."

Phil had the room cleared except for himself, Nick and Margaret.

The three positioned themselves around the big table.

Phil began his interrogation. "What have you learned about the uprising out there?"

Nick kneaded his forehead in fatigue. Long hours of navigation and intense concentration were making themselves felt. "An awful lot has been happening incredibly fast, and we're well removed from most of the action. Except of course the assaults we're currently..."

"Nick. I want to know how a devastating worldwide insurrection was brought to a head with such inconceivable speed."

"I really don't know." Nick glanced questioningly at Margaret. She shook her head in an unspoken: *Nothing*

"We have thousands of agents all over the world. In damned near every country on Earth. Are they reporting in?"

"They were initially."

"So why the hell aren't they...?"

"Phil. We believe they're all dead."

"All dead? Those were *Oneirions*!" he thundered.

"I know. Oneirions aren't immortal Phil. We believe they were killed at nearly the same time, in a well coordinated, concerted attack. Someone knew exactly who and where to find them. They were simply overwhelmed. In the midst of raging anarchy who's to stop them? Who would intercede? Who would care?"

Phil stared at the wall map for several moments, jaw muscles working feverishly. "We were set up from the start. God knows how long those murderous bastards have been waiting to strike. Oneiro's been a fool's paradise. And I've been the greatest fool on the island."

He nodded towards the Fire Control Center. "Get your people in here. I want a complete rundown on our status...now." He signaled for aids to re-enter the conference room.

Within one minute, key War Room staff were seated at the conference table. With the exception of Anne, everyone who had attended the midnight debriefing at Oneiro Field was seated at the table as well. They must have already been on their way as Phil was climbing down the cliffs. He was surprised and pleased to see everyone here. He turned aside to an aid.

"Record this meeting."

"Yes sir."

Phil commenced a staccato barrage of queries directed by piercing looks to the person being interrogated.

"Medical."

"Four hundred and fifty-six dead. One hundred and eighty-three injured. Twenty-two critical. The hospital is undamaged and remains secure at level thirty-six."

"Surface and shore defenses."

"All batteries are fully charged, manned and ready."

"Did we lose any equipment?"

"The two Drákōns were caught on the ground."

"Harbor."

"No damage. The harbor fleet is intact. JAEKEL is due in within the hour. She was deep in the Aegean Basin when the attacks occurred, so she is unharmed by – and unknown to – our aggressors. Our freighter, *Gauntlet Marinas* was enroute when the attacks occurred. They apparently attack any shipping unknown to them. She was sunk. All hands lost."

"How many?"

"Forty-three." *Damn. There had been some fine people aboard that rusting hulk.*

"What about Anastasios Island?"

"The island has been fully evacuated, except those already living and working in *Gauntlet*. Quite a few *Gauntlet* crew members have reported in for duty. Primary Command and Control have been aboard for three or four weeks. Land facilities have been demolished and all traces well hidden. Only the portside access tunnel remains open, per your orders. I is now camouflaged and cannot be seen from the air."

"There are no defensive batteries on Anastasios are there?"

"No sir. Not a thing."

"Damned shoddy planning."

Phil lowered his head, staring into nothingness, deep in thought.

He raised his head. "What is *Gauntlet's* status?"

"Effectively complete. Fully provisioned. Construction has been finished on all major systems and all major facilities. Primary terran features are in place....the seas, forests, mountains, and so on. Power, drive, environmental, communications, food and oxygen production systems. All nominal. The Command Bridge crew has been aboard for approximately one month. They are fully checked out and they've shaken down command, nav, helm, thrusters, comms...all primary systems."

"Security."

"Oneiro is battened down. The population is concentrated from level ten, down to level forty. Below level forty nothing is changed. Actually that roughly applies to ten through forty too."

"Why isn't this armory occupied?"

"We only gained access an hour or so ago. It took time to cut through these doors and it will take a while to repair them. The Amory does not have capacity for our current population. And we felt it was safer to disburse the population underground throughout the complex, as opposed to concentrating them in a single kill zone. We're not at all sure what these bastards might throw at us. I doubt anyone ever considered anything except conventional weapons prior to these attacks."

"Good points. Continue."

"We have ten thousand wireless monitors in place and guards on regular patrol. All travel and communications are shut down. We are presently conducting an intensive search for Mr. McGregor and six other staffers known to associate with him, or under suspicion due to the proximity of their work... and the fact that they have disappeared as well. I don't believe anything can make a move in the complexes without our knowledge."

"Keep me posted. If you find McGregor, I will speak with him personally."

"Understood."

"The sky?"

"Long and short range radar is clear. Proteus Point reports all clear as well."

"The sea?"

"Surface radar is clear and costal sonar reports no contacts."

"Have our attackers demonstrated any pattern in their engagement frequency?"

"In fact, yes. A definite pattern. They attack only during daylight with approximately three hours between sorties. Attacks commence between 0700 and 0745. Apparently they anticipate the depletion of our ground batteries and are therefore simply grinding out assaults until we can no longer defend ourselves. No element of surprise. No variation in attack pattern, no stratagem whatsoever. Real sledge hammer tactics."

"Mr. White. Diplomatically, how would you assess the situation?"

"The UN has fallen apart over this issue. They're in shambles. More than eighty percent of the delegates have walked out. No one is speaking. Not one country has come forward in our support. We do know that several countries have allied in mounting theses attacks against us and more are joining. Our intelligence confirms the assaults will continue."

"How were they able to determine that?"

He smiled. "Nothing arcane. Satellite news."

"We're alone in this?"

"Totally alone."

Phil grimaced "What a world."

"We know they will intensify both in firepower and frequency. For all intents and purposes, Oneiro is in a state of war with the entire world."

"What are they trying to achieve in your opinion."

"No opinion. Confirmed fact. Their objective is the total obliteration of Oneiro and the QAVL."

A stony silence fell in the conference room.

Phil roused himself. "Ms Harris how many recharges are on hand for the Metal Storm and Gatling batteries?"

"Roughly five thousand full recharges per device sir. That equates to something on the order of fifty million rounds. Please bear in mind we needn't totally deplete the batteries every time we have a fire mission."

"That was done under my orders Ms. Harris. I had no idea what was in the air over Oneiro at that time."

"Understood sir."

Phil ran an array of numbers and probabilities in his mind. "Finally some good news. We can hold out for months. We have back-ups?"

"Twenty-five percent."

"Well done." Phil began to visibly relax. The news was bad. The status was far better.

He turned to the group at large.

"I am ordering all surviving crew, or their alternates, assigned to *Gauntlet* to report to JAEKEL for transport to Anastasios in exactly one hour. I will be in my quarters, or the hospital until then. Send McGregor under guard to my quarters if you find him. Ask Mr. Auslander to see me when he arrives, if he arrives before I depart. Ms. Harris, see me in my quarters in fifteen minutes. You as well Mr. White."

They nodded their assent.

"Thank you all for an excellent briefing. Are there any questions?"

"Is the launch of *Gauntlet* taking place as scheduled?"

"No. I am pushing the launch forward. I am convinced our aggressors will attack Anastasios. The stolen file *must* have contained *Gauntlet's* construction site. JAEKEL will carry us to the island. We launch in twelve hours."

"How do we transport any remaining crew members to Anastasios?"

"If they're not aboard JAEKEL, they'll be left behind. One hour from now. Nick please ensure this is strictly adhered to. Any crew who has not reported to JAEKEL in one hour *will* be left behind. After JAEKEL offloads on Anastasios

the remaining access tunnel will be explosively sealed."

"Speaking of left behind Mr. Carr...what do you suppose will become of Oneiro?"

"Mike Auslander is in command. You're in good hands. The best. You have re-loads for months. Mike can arrange for resupply, if need be; and you have a secret, deep water supply line in the form of JAEKEL. Food, water, energy, defenses, communications, shelter...you have everything needed for survival. Without hardship. You also have libraries, laboratories, theaters, computers, restaurants, bars, nightclubs, sports centers, and most of all, each other. Aside from somewhat inhibited surface activity, life should be normal and even enjoyable. The world may be trying to kill you, but I cannot imagine a group of humans better equipped to survive, even prosper and continue to progress. Let's see...in one hundred or so years you should have produced a genotype millions of years more advanced. We will return as *homo achristos. Obsolete*."

"What about nukes?"

"Nukes?"

"Yes sir. What if they start throwing ICBMs at us?"

"I've requested that Qasi designate a team of QAVL who will patrol from one to six thousand kilometers out at variable levels, including straight up and undersea. They will travel at inconceivable speeds. Their task is to sound early warnings of the approach of any nuclear device, even missiles launched from a submarine. They will relay the alert, coordinates, speed and ETI in seconds. Qasi assures me this does not abrogate their neutrality, nor their prohibition against aggressive action." Phil grinned affectionately. "It doesn't even interfere with their existing activities.

Our ground defenses will then destroy it with long range lasers, or with JAEKEL. No other preemptive strike system in the world is remotely capable of such responsiveness. I've also spoken with Mr. Howard Doyle from Chicago. He is unexcelled in the acquisition of special weapons if it comes to that. He will be joining you here on Oneiro within hours."

A young lady stood peremptorily. She was pretty, slim and very fit. Her manner openly challenging. High cheekbones, Rita Hayworth eyes, graceful neck. "This macho bullshit is not exactly why Oneiro was founded is it sir? It isn't our business to kill and wage war."

Phil studied her for a moment. *Pretty. With all the stridency of a lander... she's ethically correct and she's tragically wrong. I think it's important I openly discuss this with her...try to make her and everyone in this room understand...*

Phil looked down at the table for a few seconds. He then raised his head slowly and gnarred softly. "The hell it isn't young lady." Phil peered at the large clock array in the War Room. "I have a few minutes. Let's talk about it."

He lent forward, crossing his arms on the table, contemplating her openly and directly. He smiled faintly. "May I ask your name?"

"Rhona Grishall." Her manner mutely defiant.

"Where do you work?"

"I am Director of Advanced AI Heuristic Systems Design."

"Impressive. How does that relate to the War Room?"

"We are teaching our fire control computers to dynamically re-adjust to unknown attackers, using unknown weapons systems, employing unknown tactics."

"So you're a digital warrior."

"I am an Advanced AI Heuristic Systems designer."

"I see. Of course you've undergone Fear Training?"

"Of course."

"You know Rhona, one of our professors once suggested to me that perhaps we've been too comfortably wrapped up here in *Shangri La*. Oneiro wasn't founded out of sweat and blood and genius so we might walk hand and hand, flowers in our hair, reading poetry to the music of the lute. We are here to *survive*. Survive so mankind may survive. That's why we were founded. And it's damned serious."

"So we become what we fight to overcome."

"Those are only words young lady. A tediously conventional mantra at that. Are we so insubstantive we are defined by a single act?"

"Yes. And your apriorism is false. By intent I suspect. I believe you know that."

"Explain." *I've got to put an end to this.*

"We are not debating a single act by any means. We are debating a comprehensive martial infrastructure. As virulent as any country on Earth."

Phil sat back and sighed wearily. "Perhaps I should speak from personal experience. I ah...I have personally witnessed and inflicted...such things."

She was shocked to see the flashing shadow of pain in his eyes. For a fleeting moment she nearly reached for his hand, then instead of pressing her interrogation, she softly murmured "I'd rather not know about it sir."

Quietly, but pointedly "Who the bloody hell does goddamnit?"

Slightly abashed, she remained silent."

Phil was forced to stop and clear his throat. "If you insist, perhaps I *was* changed by these acts, I'll accept your judgment. However, in doing these...things...I was wounded. I will be for the rest of my life. I believe I suffered for a greater good. For Oneiro and ultimately mankind. I *paid* for these acts. I was not *assimilated* by them."

Rhona cocked her head. "You suffered for the sins of mankind?" There was a subtly cynical suggestiveness to her voice.

Phil bristled. "I do not harbor a messiah complex, if that's your implication. If so, I find your insinuation offensive."

Phil cast a quick glance at Nick, who returned his stare belying clear misgivings about this conversation, and where it might be leading.

Rhona sensed Phil's defensiveness. His vulnerability. As with all Oneirions, Rhona's latent predatory instincts were highly advanced. Part of her instinctive survival mechanism. She pressed her advantage.

They locked eyes. Staring at each other without any visible emotion. Rhona's voice took on a clinical, dispassionate tenor.

"So you've killed. As a soldier in combat."

"Yes."

"Murder? Torture?"

"Yes."

"Assassination?"

"No."

"So you've engaged in all forms of homicide *except* assassination. The highest form of civil commitment as I understand it." Her voice clipped. Probing.

"Get to the point Rhona."

"These...acts....were undertaken on my behalf. Not exclusively I know. Nonetheless, I'm simply trying to understand which of these proxy'd killings I must justify."

*Good looking, smart and relentless. Tough combination. She's passionate about this. And this is getting too goddamned personal. This is taking too long. I was wrong, this is no place for such a discussion. I never realized the extent of Oneirion differences. Got to end this....*

He silently drew breath. "My point is, we *pay* for our acts here on Oneiro. We understand and abhor what we do sometimes. We are not necessarily changed by our acts. We are not necessarily corrupted by them. We pay the freight." His voice held a finality which implied this discussion was at an end.

"I'm sorry Mr. Carr, but I am appalled by actions on and off Oneiro. I see no rational justification. With all our intelligence and resource, there must be another way."

Phil relaxed. His irritation subsiding. He half smiled and patiently continued. "There is no rational explanation. We are not the aggressors. We cannot even surrender. They would slaughter us. We Oneirons have an obligation to live, to do our work, and defend ourselves. We represent the human archetype of man's future. Advanced by well over five hundred thousand years. We do what we do because we can do nothing else?"

"It's still war."

"Yes it is."

"Mister Carr, I believe you know better than anyone on this island. Perhaps better than anyone else on Earth. All previous wars and disasters pale in comparison to the atrocity we are now inflicting on the world."

*How does she make 'Mister Carr' sound like an invective?*

"Yes. I do. I also know this war may preclude a future Earth decimated of all life. All of mankind."

"Are you defending war?"

"No. I am defending *this* war. War is hellish enough without top-loading ourselves with sanctimony."

Rhona murmured "Your words make me sad Mr. Carr."

Phil breathed out slowly. "Me as well Rhona."

*"Can't you stop it?"*

"No. Other questions?"

The room stood silent in a thoughtful, awkward pause.

Another young lady stood. "What of our current works? Oil synthesis production, FOND Unit distribution, Food Generators, medicine, bio-chemical knowledge, marine research, and so on."

"Your overriding priority is to *survive*. However, your work must continue somehow. Your work is too important to cease for more than a short time. Much of the world now depends on you for food, energy, education and health." Phil mused, almost to himself. "A fleet of SATSAVs might be useful." He glanced at Nick. "You should take that up with Mike."

Fatigue was catching up. "You may not realize it, but we play from a position of strength. Our battle stance is strictly passive-defensive. We permit them to inflict little if any damage, and we utterly destroy them in the attempt. An inept, ineffectual, unilateral war cannot be sustained for long. No adversary can afford to endlessly throw men and equipment into a black hole. It's too frustrating. Expensive. Even humiliating. Over time we will prevail.

You will find a way to continue, to survive, to progress. I have every faith. I can't imagine what wonders you will bring forth in the decades to follow.

I will rejoin you in a century, and we will confront our new world together." He smiled at Rhona. "Perhaps then there will be time for poetry and flowers. Maybe we can take a walk."

She peered at him intently for a moment. "I'd like that."

He looked around the group. "Good luck to you. Good luck to us all."

# The 5th Reel-Estate

"This is Brian Madison, World News International in New York.

Welcome to this week's *LOGBOOK*.

Most of Tonight's *LOGBOOK* was recorded in advance. At that time we benefitted from reliable communications, and assumed we would have our usual viewing audience. Neither exist today. However, we are pleased to present this *LOGBOOK* to those viewers remaining.

Presenting this show as scheduled provided us a rather comforting sense of normalcy. We hope you benefit equally from watching it.

This Issue Ninety-three of *LOGBOOK* is entirely devoted to an explosively polemic topic, and an exceptionally controversial man: Mr. Philip Carr, so called Consul of Oneiro.

Maria Adams, our WNI Bureau Chief in London has obtained an exclusive interview with the highly elusive Mr. Carr, ruler of the tiny Adriatic island nation of Oneiro. Telephones were already proving unreliable. Therefore, the interview was conducted by high frequency radio communications, or what is commonly referred to as shortwave. We have edited out radio protocols and attempted to filter out any garbling. We will now run our report."

[Shift to Madison's prerecorded introduction.]

"Unless you're lucky enough to live in a cave somewhere, you know that the island state of Oneiro and Mr. Philip Carr stand squarely in the middle of the most divisive events of this millennium. Tens, perhaps hundreds of thousands, or even millions of people are dying. In many areas, trade and communications are at a standstill. These events are referred to as World War III in many quarters. Armageddon in others.

We are one of the few networks to continue broadcasting through this crisis. The Internet is disabled, along with most radio, telephone and cellular traffic. Billions, perhaps trillions of dollars of damage has been inflicted, and governments all over the world have toppled. In an extraordinary session at the United Nations in New York, the delegates simply walked out. Following this, the UN Security Council in an action unprecedented in its history, unanimously agreed upon a 'Nihil Resolution' regarding this crisis. An action interpreted as a statement to the effect they have no opinion about, nor intent to take action of any sort, regarding any aspect of this uprising. Apparently they wash their hands of the entire matter. Cynics have observed this stance does not differ greatly from their business as usual. Others view this as nothing short of a tacit endorsement for the destruction of Oneiro. All this transpired with unbelievable speed. Resounding around the globe in a matter of days. Far too fast to allow understanding, anticipation, or interdiction.

These incredible events were sparked by a leak from Oneiro, allegedly revealing the presence of aliens on the island, the construction of some sort of mammoth spacecraft, and developments at Oneiro University in areas that might be regarded as anathema by the rest of the world."

He looked up with a piercing stare into the camera. "It defies reason that the entire world can be so easily deluded with such flimsy substantiation."

Madison lit up with his trademark wry, cynical smile. "These uh, aliens happen to be *invisible*. The enormous space ship allegedly under construction is said to be *buried underground*, inside a volcano. We surmise launching such a ship to be problematic. If they do launch, their destination is purported to be some wondrous planet in the constellation Orion where all the creatures of the universe live in harmony. As to the mysterious developments emanating from Oneiro University, we have seen no proof whatsoever of such work. The Father of Scientology, L. Ron Hubbard himself, would have been challenged to dream up a more crackpot scenario.

I believe we must recognize at least the possibility that Oneiro may be the victim of an exceptional, venomous smear campaign. A campaign designed to portray the island either as a villainous lair of bizarre, malevolent aliens; or a conglomerate of eccentric screwballs. Or both, dependant on audience. Either way, if this is a conspiracy, it has been most adroitly propagated.

In fact, were it not for the vast economic power of the island, the highly esteemed academics in residence, and Oneiro's association with respected countries, corporations and organizations worldwide...not to mention the horrifically dark forces militating around the tiny country...one might be led to consider Oneiro no more than a classically nutty, weirdo cult.

It beggars belief that such absurdities could have gone so far and wreaked such havoc.

One way or another. Hopefully the truth will out in the near future, allowing our beleaguered world to regain some semblance of normalcy, and end these horrors.

Maria Adams successfully tracked down Mr. Carr at his residence on Oneiro – between trips. Apparently Consul Carr devotes little time to his duties on Oneiro, preferring to conduct the island's business at more exotic destinations around the globe. He has most recently been reported in Paris, New York, Nice, Islamabad, Sao Paulo and Guam...aboard luxurious business jets and limousines, always in the finest restaurants and hotels. Most of this has been repudiated by Oneiro's Office of Public Information. In fairness to Mr. Carr, he *is* a multi-billionaire in his own right, presumably with interests of his own to pursue.

Before we cut to Maria in London, Harve Wilson of our Washington D.C. Bureau is standing by with a background report. Harve?"

"Thank you Brian."

[Backdrop Jefferson Memorial and Tidal Basin.]

"During his early years, Mr. Philip Carr's life was quite conventional. He was born here [archive video sweep] in the exclusive Georgetown area of Washington D.C., the son of a successful attorney. His mother was a professor of World Literature at Georgetown University. His brother a Catholic Priest. Tragically all three died when Philip was quite young. Strangely, all were victims of terrorism. His mother and father in Ireland. His brother in the Middle East. He was brought up by his uncle (Herbert Carr) a colorful character who lived outside the idyllic village of St. Michaels on the Chesapeake Bay [video sweep of town and bay], making a marginal living as a commercial fisherman. Herbert Carr's current whereabouts are unknown.

In high school Philip was known as an exceptional student, though a loner, almost to the point of being antisocial. He graduated with honors and went on to study law and medicine.

Ultimately he settled on practicing law in New York and was highly, *but highly* successful. Within two years he was recruited by the island nation he was ultimately to rule. Then as CEO/COO of the island's business interests under an umbrella company called Halios Geron Resorts. Soon thereafter he christened the island Oneiro. He won for it independent nation status. He ascended to Consul of Oneiro (effectively President). After which he inherited billions of dollars from a Dr. Craig Webber, and soon became a reclusive figure of beguiling mystery.

If nothing else, we know that Mr. Carr is neither a statesman, nor diplomat, nor has he any interest in such skills. His roughshod leadership approach might be credited with the makeup of modern day Oneiro. Successful. Dynamic. Far from a rogue state, but certainly unconventional, and most definitely an unknown quantity.

Oneiro is not a democracy *per se;* and oligarchy seems too strong a term. Instead they describe themselves as a 'Patronship', or 'Proprietorship'. We assume this implies their government is based on a business model. There *is* popular representation, however obscure. However, neither the Consulship, nor the number two spot, Patron, are elective offices. In fact, we believe Mr. Carr *owns* Oneiro. In all fairness we should emphatically state that we have found no indication that Oneirions suffers from despotism, or from its government in any way. We can also confirm that Oneiro is in no way some sort of cult. Nor have we encountered any hint of dissent. Oneiro's population appears to be happy, prosperous, free and (here's the key word) anonymous... just as their Consul.

[Aerial video sweep.]

All in all it brings to mind a book I enjoyed in my youth: <u>Mysterious Island</u>. Brian?"

"Thank you Harve. Do people travel freely to and from Oneiro?"

"Excellent question. Especially when we consider this a litmus test for a free peoples. To the best of our knowledge Oneirions travel freely and frequently all over the world. In fact, one would be hard pressed to find a country in which they have not established a presence. Hugely impressive, and not a little puzzling for a country of this size.

As for non-Oneirions, we find little if any evidence that travel is permitted in and out of Oneiro. The island does have an airport and extensive harbor facilities, but as far as we can tell no general commercial traffic plies the island, either from sea or air. This applies to passengers and cargo. As with everything else, shipping and aviation is held in private hands and closely controlled."

"Thank you Harve. We now go to Maria Adams in London."

[Background Buckingham Palace.]

"Good evening Brian. This morning I was able to make contact with the elusive Philip Carr, after days of trying. He was at home on Oneiro when he somewhat reluctantly agreed to speak with me. We are going to play our recording of that conversation *verbatim*. Only radio jargon has been edited out.

[Video sweeps: Oneiro, the Aegean Sea, Philip Carr, Maria Adams, Washington, New York, closing on photographs of Adams and Carr.]:

<u>Maria Adams</u>: Good morning Consul Carr. Thank you for taking the time to speak with us.
<u>Philip Carr</u>: Good morning Maria.

<u>Maria Adams</u>: Mr. Consul, I know our time is short, so I hope you will forgive a preemptory startup of this interview.

Philip Carr: Go ahead Maria.

Maria Adams: Can you enlighten us as to the meaning of the title Consul?
Philip Carr: Its origins date back to ancient Rome, prior to its decline into decadence. For the present, consider it the same as President, with diminished executorial responsibility.
Maria Adams: Which means...?
Philip Carr: Which means my duties have little to do with the day-to-day running of Oneiro. We have agencies charged with that. The office of Consul emphasizes leadership. This title is not my contrivance. It is a reflection of the will of the citizens of Oneiro. I suspect in some way the title expresses their contempt for contemporary human leadership. They see such promise in the title, I hope I don't fail them.

Maria Adams: What of reports charging Oneiro with unethical research?
Philip Carr: I have read these reports. They allege we are engaged in illegal, or at least unsanctioned research in genetic engineering and cloning, as specified and proscribed in UN Resolution 9701-J. I assure you those reports are untrue.

We are working in neither genetic engineering, nor cloning. I will not submit our laboratories to inspection however, as we are engaged in confidential developments, many of which are about in the world today and materially improve the human condition. However, I am certainly agreeable to exposing all imports and exports into and out of Oneiro to the closest scrutiny of authorized UN inspectors. Voluntarily, immediately, without exception. At our expense.

Maria Adams: Are you familiar with a Ms Aiyana Atsila?
Philip Carr: Yes. She's an old friend. I've known her since university days.
Maria Adams: Were you intimate friends?
Philip Carr: Ms Adams, this is an WNI interview, not a tabloid article. I believe we have far more pressing issues to discuss.

Maria Adams: Are you aware of a file she may have removed from your island?
Philip Carr: Yes I am. I have not seen the file, so I cannot comment reliably on its contents. I can tell you Ms Atsila was subsequently abducted by insurgents in Pakistan. In fact we recently effected her rescue. The file to which you are referring was stolen during this incident, and we were unsuccessful in retrieving it. I am quite certain the file is now being subjected to serious misuse.

Maria Adams: What if I were to tell you this file contains proof of aliens on Oneiro, and a spacecraft under construction?
Philip Carr: I would ask you to please show me the file.
Maria Adams: We do have reliable evidence that at least parts of this file have been released through a worldwide Islamic network.
Philip Carr: I am aware of that.

Maria Adams: Do you have any comments regarding the UN Security Council's 'Nihil Resolution'?
Philip Carr: Yes I do. Their actions validate all the charges lodged against the UN over decades. Inability to act. Timidity. Cynical. Self-serving. Obeisance to a few member states. Contemptuous disregard of human principles, or international integrity. A gathering of self-serving Machiavellians. This time their machinations will induce a loss of life and property on an inhuman scale. At a time when mankind desperately needs leadership the most, the UN cynically abdicated their invested hegemony. We have paid in full our membership assessment, and I am now withdrawing Oneiro from UN membership. May they burn in history's hell.

[Brief pause. Dead air.]

Maria Adams: Can you tell us about the aliens said to be inhabiting Oneiro? The QAVL?
Philip Carr: No, I cannot. That issue is currently in the hands of the United Nations; and unlike the UN, we stand by our commitments.

Maria Adams: Can you tell us something about the spacecraft said to be under construction on Oneiro?
Philip Carr: No, I cannot. That matter is subject to the same agreement.
Maria Adams: Mr. Carr you are aware of the terrible events transpiring worldwide...the seriousness of these events?
Philip Carr: [Silence.]

Maria Adams: Mr. Carr. The world is nearly a smoking ruin. People are dying by the millions. Do I understand you do not feel compelled to respond? To confront your personal culpability to mankind, and to the planet Earth?
Philip Carr: Ms Adams, I believe you are well aware that neither I, nor any citizen of Oneiro is responsible for these atrocities. We are confronting a well conceived, long planned, impeccably executed conspiracy. A conspiracy targeted at the total destruction of modern western civilization itself. I know this. You know this. WNI knows this. The United Nations knows this.

Contrived circumstance on Oneiro has conveniently dovetailed with this scheme in a poisonous synchrony. The stolen file has exponentially exacerbated events. Everything has played into their hands. Mankind and the United Nations have played into their hands. WNI is playing into their hands. We have all been ruthlessly exploited. The entire world.

Please do not compound a tragedy of monstrous proportion by perpetuating this malevolent farce, simply to facilitate your story.

Instead Ms Adams, tell your listeners the truth.

Tell them: *Armageddon has only begun.*

[Dead air. Eight seconds.]

<u>Maria Adams:</u>  Thank you for speaking with me Mr. Carr.
<u>Philip Carr:</u>  Goodbye Ms Adams.

[Onscreen Maria Adams.]

"As you heard, Mr. Carr was adamantly reticent regarding reports of aliens and spacecraft on his island; and quite candid in others, such as their developments in genetics. He was rivetingly open in his opinion of Security Council actions. Nonetheless we have learned little more about the situation on Oneiro. Perhaps, as Mr. Carr insinuated, there is no situation on Oneiro to learn more about. Perhaps we *are* the dupes of a worldwide conspiracy of astonishing breadth. This reporter is in no position to pass judgment. But if the charges directed against Consul Carr and Oneiro are confirmed, they will be answerable to the wrath of the entire world. Otherwise, the world will be answerable to Oneiro."

"Maria, are there any indications that violence is spreading to Oneiro?"

"We have received no reports of belligerency, or insurrection. However, our only source comes from the Greek island of Lefkada, some two hundred kilometers to the north. Brian?"

"Thank you Maria."

[Brian Madison reappears live on screen.]

"Fifteen minutes ago we were provided the following communiqué from our Bureau Chief in Brazil, relayed to us by Lino Atlántico de Carga Americas, using an old style TTY link. Considering existing communications into South America, we were lucky to receive this.

I imagine many of you are unfamiliar with the old punch-paper-tape teletype systems. For many years this technology was the backbone of worldwide

*Oneiro II: Gauntlet*

communications. Particularly in transportation. Surprisingly, many of the antique sets persist in various parts of the world, along with many of the asynchronous landlines and cables.

This message is a variation of the Universal Transport Message format and syntax. It is cryptic, garbled, and clearly input by an inexperienced operator. It is intelligible nonetheless.

This is the message, exactly as we received it on the left, and the WNI interpretation of the message on the right:

[Text onscreen. Madison reads the WNI interpretation.]

| Original Text | WNI Interpretation |
| --- | --- |
| QU NYCWNI CD^ | To...: World News International New York |
| .SAOWNI BC 235110^ | From: World News International Saó Palo |
| UTC^ | |
| SI^ | |
| TSEC^ | TOP SECRET |
| REL DIP SRC RIO RPT EO UNSC RES 7781^ | Reliable diplomatic sources in Rio report an Eyes Only United Nations Security Council Resolution 7781. |
| MBRS AUTH IMM ATK ONEIRO^ | UNSC Members States are authorized to launch immediate attacks on Oneiro. |
| RES APP ALL MBRS^ | UN Resolution 7781 was unanimously approved by all UNSC voting members. |
| X US CN + FR ABSTN^ | The US, China and France abstained. |
| NKS AUTH ASREQ^ | Nuclear weapons are authorized as required. |
| WI FR CFM F POSS^ | Further confirmation of this report if possible. |
| COND VBAD^ | Conditions are very bad here. |
| RHARMON BC SAO^ | Mr. Robert Harmon |
| | Bureau Chief |
| | Saó Palo, Brasil |

"We present this information exactly as received by us, and our exact translation, so you are fully appraised as to our source, content and interpretation. We are attempting to confirm this report and will provide you updates as they come in. Meanwhile, our Producers have directed us to present this message and all such information – irrespective of any security classification – in the conviction that the world has the right and the need to know this information, as and when received. As long as we continue to broadcast.

Our analysts apprise this information, if true, with four succinct points:

1) UNSC Resolution 7780, the infamous 'Nihil' Resolution, has clearly been superseded by Resolution 7781.

2) Effectively, the United Nations has sanctioned all-out attacks on a member country, Oneiro, by *any* country, so disposed.

3) The UN has never taken such an action in its long history; and we are certain Article 25 of the UN Charter does not authorize *any* Resolution such as 7781. This is a highly illegal act under any epexegetic of international law.

4) This event may well constitute the demarcation between enlightened human society, and the breakdown of human civilization."

Madison sat back and peered at the camera.

"Chaos."

He leaned forward in his chair and stared intently at the camera.

"If this message is to be believed, I very much doubt any further interviews with Mr. Carr will be forthcoming. If much of *anything* is to be...forthcoming. God help us.

Coming up next, in a related story from Washington..."

## *Medicina Vir*

Phil found a PM and raced for home. Time was growing short and he had lost precious minutes to a reporter patched in by short wave. He had agreed to the interview because he felt the need to mend some fences with the world at large. But now he was late, and he still must confront Anne.

He'd have to invest a few minutes and detour via the hospital. Aiy's wounds were so profound he could hardly believe she still lived. All the same, he must have a firsthand briefing for Anne.

When he arrived at Aiy's ward, he found that Dr. Gold was handling the case himself. Intriguing, since this was well outside his specialization.

"Well doctor, what's your prognosis?"

"You did a good job onboard that aircraft Phil. She should be dead five times over. She was actually deceased a short time after you brought her in. CPR was barely successful. Among other problems, she suffered from profound shock with complications, blood loss, broken bones, internal bleeding bordering on peritonitis and massive internal and external trauma. Added to that, I believe her mind is seriously damaged. Possibly irreparably."

"Yes doc, but your prognosis?"

"She's dying Phil. I would guess we can keep her alive for perhaps another thirty-six hours."

"There's no doubt about this?"

"No. Not unless we took heroic measures to save her. Frankly, I'd have loved to take a crack at it."

"Heroic measures. Such as?"

"Essentially using our food technology, believe it or not. We'd also need a special ambience. We can regenerate her damaged parts. I took her case myself in case this procedure looked feasible. But we just can't afford the resource right now. It would ultimately be at the expense of many other lives. It would take a great deal of time and it would not address her mental state. She has undergone the most horrific abuse I have ever..."

"But it can be done Doc?"

"Look Phil. We're in the middle of a war zone here. This is no environment for radically invasive new procedures. Plus we're short of staff. There's a huge strain on our staff now to..."

"Dr. Gold. Time is short. She may have critical information. Can we treat her on *Gauntlet*? Is *Gauntlet* equipped for this sort of procedure?"

"I suppose so but..."

"Prepare her for immediate transport to the harbor, onboard JAEKEL and finally onboard *Gauntlet*. I want her in a med-vessel, fully self-contained, equipped with medicals, nutrients, water, antibiotics, tranquilizers, pain killers, sedatives, whole blood, plasma...everything. She must be boat-side, in Oneiro Harbor, in forty-five minutes."

"Now really Phil that's simply not..."

"*Do it* Doctor. I also want a chocolate bar containing everything involved in this procedure. Understood Doctor?"

Rather petulantly "Okay. But you'll have to settle for fruit juice. A juice compound has already been prepared, and I don't have time to bind it into a chocolate bar."

"I'll need four measures Doc."

Dr. Gold rummaged in his laboratory. "Here, drink one."

Phil drank it down and pocketed the remaining three vials. "It's good."

"Yeah, they're getting better at packaging the stuff all the time. If you had time I'd show you how good it is with Gin. When you get Aiy to *Gauntlet* see that she is immediately immersed in a BiMeNuSa Solution."

"Bime-nis-saa-aa what?"

"BiMeNuSa. Pronounced: *Bye-Men-New-Saw*. Bio-Medicinal-Nutrient-Saline. A kind of Super seawater. We use the same stuff in food synthesis. Do not check Aiy into the hospital onboard *Gauntlet*. Take her to Bill Christie in Nutrient Technology. I'll brief him in advance so he'll be prepared. Good luck."

"Thanks. I'll keep you posted on her progress as long as we can reasonably communicate."

Dr. Gold could only stare at Phil.

Phil remounted his PM and continued homeward.

Gold quieted whispered to Phil's retreating PM "Have a nice flight."

*I am not such a truant since my coming,*
*As not to know the language I have lived in:*
*A strange tongue makes my cause more strange, suspicious...*
Shakespeare
King Henry VIII

Minutes later Phil strode into The Residence. Mr. White and Ms Harris were already waiting for him. Neither Anne nor Edward were to be seen.

"Mr. White."

"Yes Phil."

"It looks as though a diplomatic solution is out of the question."

"Agreed. Diplomacy worldwide has broken down. This may well be the most dangerous period in all human history."

"Well if Earth doesn't value diplomacy just now, I'm quite sure *Kosmas Kentrikos* does. Care to take a ride Mr. White?"

White mulled over the offer carefully. Temptation contending with duty. "A great deal more than you know Phil. But sooner or later humankind will be restored to sanity. I should be there on that day." He cast Phil a look of gentle approbation. "And uh, maybe mend some fences at the UN."

Phil ignored the friendly chide.

White continued undaunted. "In fact Mr. Carr, I would like your blanket authority to re-join the United Nations should the UN be restored, and should conditions warrant such action."

"You've got it Mr. White. Who have you assigned as our diplomatic envoy to *Kosmas Kentrikos*?"

"Actually we look primarily to you in that role. However, I have made an appointment."

"Who?"

"Roger Smithfield."

"The name's not familiar. Do I know him?"

"I'm sure. But you would know him as War-bird One."

"Right. He flies a Drákōn. Damned fine pilot."

"Right. War-bird One is his call sign."

"Good man. But he doesn't sound like much of a diplomat."

"Oh he's highly qualified. Quite skilled in fact. He's also a top flier and navigator. He's been assigned as part of your bridge crew. After all, it will be decades before his diplomatic skills are called upon."

"Thank you Bob." He turned to Margaret Harris.

White moved to leave the room.

"Please stay Bob. I would like you to witness this meeting with Ms Harris." Immediately tension filled the room.

Margaret faced Phil. "Yes sir?"

"Regarding your seven fugitives. I assume the probabilities approach nil that you will apprehend them within the next half hour?"

"That's practically guaranteed sir."

"Okay. I have an order for you. When you find them, kill them. Shoot on sight. Immediately. No interrogation. No confinement. Nothing. Just kill them fast and dispose of the bodies in the sea. Understood?"

"That is an illegal order sir, and I must therefore...."

"It's not a damned illegal order. That is why Mr. White is here as a witness."

White interjected. "Look Phil, simply because I can attest that you gave such an order does not discharge any culpability on Ms Harris' part should she act on..."

Phil jaws hardened in irritation. "I am well aware of the tenets surrounding such orders Bob. So listen carefully. Both of you. Ms Harris I am not ordering you to execute enemy combatants. I am not ordering you to murder civilians. I am ordering you to carry out a 'Shoot on Sight' directive directed against enemy insurgents, legally posted by the Consul of Oneiro. This is accommodated under Oneirion Law. I am further ordering you to publish and post such Order throughout Oneiro under my seal, and specifically notify your staff. You are legally bound by such directive, and I expect you to carry it out with every due consideration."

"Sir. Will you share the palliative for such a directive?"

"Certainly Ms Harris. As I said, these men are saboteurs representing an immediate threat to Oneirion lives. Moreover, the risk of holding them alive is untenable. Should they escape, they could exacerbate this nightmare irreparably and Oneiro is unequivocally unprepared for any sort of due process in this matter. These men are now actively dedicated to the total destruction of our facility on Anastasios Island and *Gauntlet* itself. They are enemy combatants in a terror attack. They are also positioned to leak further information to the outside world, which could be disastrous."

"Saboteurs as well?"

"Yes. I have substantive evidence in support of this directive."

"May I request more information regarding this evidence?"

"Suffice to say, as we are under extreme time pressure, the disappearance of Mr. Ian McGregor constitutes reasonable grounds for my directive. There is more. It will be transmitted to you from *Gauntlet* after lift-off."

"Why does this demand their immediate execution?"

Phil was becoming exasperated. "For the reasons I just outlined; and as a zone of terror, no such compurgation is necessary. This conversation is being recorded for your protection. Request a copy from Mr. Edward McKnight tomorrow."

Phil heard loud female voices. Raucous to the degree they were audible from down the long hallway to the master bedroom. Clearly in conflict. He thought it best to play for time until Anne was alone, and whatever histrionics were ended. There were complexities enough without walking into something unknown.

"These men are saboteurs. Therefore the directive is legal." He paused and appeared to be thinking. "Saboteur. Sabotage. Interesting words. Are you familiar with their etymology?"

They both regarded Phil in mute bewilderment.

Disregarding their quizzical looks, Phil continued. "For centuries on the Atlantic coasts of France, in the province of Brittany, the people traditionally wore wooden shoes. The French called them 'sabots' (*saa-bôw*). During Earth's World War I, the locals would throw their wooden shoes – their sabots – into occupying German weapons and machinery. Tank tracks, heavy equipment and such. It was an effective method for disrupting German operations. Prior to World War I the technique was useful in labor disputes. Hence the word *sabotage*."

Phil beamed a self-satisfied smile at Bob and Margaret, who in turn, politely, if somewhat quizzically appeared to greatly relish their newfound knowledge.

A woman burst from the bedroom. Unexpectedly, it was Joan Caldwell, islander Director of the Department of Fine Arts. She was red faced, exasperated and upset. Surprised to see the three people standing in the reception room, Joan made a perfunctory nod, clearly embarrassed, head down, she hurried from the room.

Phil turned back to Margaret. "Ms Harris you have been given a specific and legal directive. I expect you to carry it out. Understood?"

"Sir I think you should know I was not altogether unsympathetic to Ms Grishall's comments earlier this evening."

"Am I to understand our Director of Security is a *love child*?"

"No sir. Neither am I dove, nor hawk."

Phil ignored her allusion. "Understood?"

Margaret stared at Phil unflinchingly as she thought. Finally...

"Understood."

The release of pressure in the room was palpable.

"Thank you. Thank you both. I shall see you both in roughly a century. Good luck. Dismissed."

Phil entered the bedroom. Anne was there. She looked terrible and she had been weeping. She had been grieving and it showed. She jumped up when he entered the room.

Phil quickly took the advantage. "What was that all about?"

"What was what all about?"

"The argument with Joan."

"She wants me to depart with *Gauntlet*."

"You said *no*?"

"I said no."

"Anne you know how imp..."

"You bastard! You killed her. You saw this coming and you just let it happen. You can see things. I know you can. I've seen you do it. You foresaw her death. Her pain. Her horror. I think you even drove her to it." Her face was flushed, veins throbbing in neck and forehead, spittle flying from her mouth.

"You were always conveniently away...while she was spying...while I was trying to supervise her...when she broke into our files...the first time she seduced me...whenever we had sex...when she finally fled the island. You always found a reason to be absent.

You set the trap. You tricked her into it. Then you jumped on a plane to collect her body – the evidence of your treachery. Going to have her stuffed and mounted?

I think you *wanted* word of Oneiro to leak out. I think you *knowingly* brought this war down on us...on the whole world. You don't give a damn how many die. What the hell is your game, *really*? A little world domination? A bit of chaos and some galactic networking? You always seemed too good to be true. I guess you were. You're a monster."

*My God. She makes it all sound so...credible.*

"And why make pawns of Aiy and me? Were you jealous? Of me? Of her? Of us? You know? I think you *pushed* us together to forward whatever horrid scheme you've planned. I've watched you sink deeper and deeper into the blood and mire since you murdered that man in Spain. But I never thought you could sink so deep into the stink you'd murder Aiy. I hate you. I'll never set foot on *Gauntlet*.

Have a nice trip you murderous son of a bitch."

"Anne..."

"Fuck you."

"Anne listen to me..."

"*Fuck you!*"

She rushed at Phil, murder in her eyes, a dynamo of thrashing arms and gouging nails.

Phil slapped her. So hard she was thrown to the floor, stunned and confused. A large burning weal on her cheek. "Will you stop? Goddamnit Anne, we don't have time for this. Will you listen....?"

Anne was suddenly subdued. She silently stared unfocused into nowhere.

"*Anne she's alive*. I'm having her prepared for immediate transport to JAEKEL and then aboard *Gauntlet*. She can live. She can be whole again..."

"If you're talking about some dipshit cloning I'll kill you. It swear it, I'll..."

"No Anne. No dipshit cloning." He breathed deeply, calming himself. *She's a strong, intelligent, beautiful woman, but I keep forgetting she is just not Oneirion.*

Anne stiffly climbed to her feet. Slowly she was regaining control. She was beginning to listen.

"We can restore her with *proven* Oneirion biotech. It will take a great deal of time. Maybe years. Afterward there will be immense pain and extensive therapy. But it can't be done here on Oneiro. There's a war on. Oneiro doesn't have the time or resource to look after her properly. Only on *Gauntlet*. Compounding this, we're not sure about her mind. She'll need intensive care. Someone to help her overcome the depravities inflicted on her."

His tone became quiet. Soothing. "I had you in mind for the job. I still do."

Anne slumped against a wall, tears leaking from her eyes. Spent. Phil could hardly hear her. "I don't understand Phil. I was told Aiy had died. She began to wobble weakly around the room. "I must get packed."

"You need pack nothing. You know that. Everything has been duplicated *verbatim* aboard Oneiro. When we vacate these rooms they will be sealed until our return. Let's go. We're running out of time. Here...drink this."

"What?"

"It summarizes her current condition and outlines her treatment."

Anne gathered her bag, stowing the vial undrunk, and followed Phil from their bedroom.

Edward was waiting for them in the reception area. "I was just alerted you had advanced lift off sir. I had hoped we would have more time before your departure."

"I as well Edward."

"Yes. Well, I wish you a trip like no other in human history." His smile was faint, as was his voice. "It's been a great honor and a pleasure working for you Philip. I shall miss you. It was great fun. I know you will achieve wonderful things out there."

"The honor was mine Edward. I'll see you in a century my friend."

"I'll certainly do my best to celebrate your return Philip. Although a century is an eternity for a man of my age."

"Nonsense. Cockney muckers like you live forever. Talk to Dr. Gold."

Edward inclined his head and twinkled a smile. "How did you know about the cockney?"

Phil grinned. "I quit drinking vodka and switched to bourbon so people would know I was drunk, and not just stupid."

Wordlessly Phil took Edward in his arms sharing a rough back slapping embrace. Edward kissed Anne, and he shook Phil's hand warmly one last time. Moments later Anne and Phil were mounted on mated PMs heading for the harbor at top speed.

Anne sat astride her PM stoically silent. Phil was nearly misty eyed.

# Wet Work

The harbor was deceptively calm. Most of *Gauntlet's* crew were already aboard JAEKEL. Fueling and provisioning were complete and service crews were withdrawing. Additional security forces were in evidence, casually circuiting the network of docks and slips. A few well wishers stood aside for support staff awaiting a last farewell. Phil had expected utter chaos, so he was pleasantly surprised. Oneirions were a constant source of unexpected competence. All the same, Phil could sense an underlying pulse of excitement infused with a serrated edge of wariness, and the coppery taste of the unknown.

Chief King came forward to greet the two. A warm grin "Good evening. Nice night for a boat trip."

Anne frowned. "There's a thunderstorm out there Chief."

King smiled "Not a hundred meters down ma'am." He turned to Phil and his manner became serious. "Skipper, the guards report a sighting of Ian McGregor and a couple of his people not far from here."

"Report this to Ms Harris immediately. Tell her to seal this entire quadrant and issue a general alert."

The chief turned away and spoke into a radio, head lowered, one hand pressing into an ear. Almost instantly, red lights were strobing. Alarms were discretely silent. Guards were forming into orderly teams, preparing to launch an intensive search. Chief King turned back with a nod to Phil.

"What's our status Chief?" asked Phil.

"Personnel loading is nearly complete. We're fueled and provisioned. All systems check out nominal. We have a full crew." King glanced at Phil. "Including our Skipper, now."

"Where is Captain Grierson?"

"Severely wounded in one of the first attacks. He should be fine, but he won't make the boat." The Chief continued with his rundown. "A fireboat is standing by to diffuse our heat plume and..."

"That would imply our friends have infrared surveillance capability."

"That's highly possible sir. Intelligence reports there are some pretty sophisticated bad guys out there."

"Alright, proceed as planned."

"We will be ready to cast off at exactly 2200, as ordered sir." King lowered his head, looking up through raised eyebrows at Phil with a half smile, half smirk. "*Sea Tigress* is ready for cast off as well."

"*Sea Tigress?*"

"Captain Carr insists on providing close escort out of harbor until we reach dive depth. His plan is to accompany JAEKEL on her starboard side, at a distance of about twenty meters. The fireboat will take her portside. They'll travel parallel, all running lights lit, until JAEKEL achieves deep waters. He figures if JAEKEL travels between the fireboat and *Sea Tigress,* any escaping heat plume will be attributed to Sea Tigress, as will any aerial or satellite surveillance photos.

"If JAEKEL and the fireboat run under a total black out with this weather, that's a pretty good plan. We must keep JAEKEL's existence a secret. But it could be risky for *Sea Tigress.*"

"According to Captain Carr that's irrelevant. He says we'll have to use our deck gun to keep him in harbor tonight."

Phil smiled knowingly. "Where is the Captain?"

"Uh. Right behind you Skipper."

Phil pivoted just in time for Uncle Herbert to trap him in a bear hug.

"Philly boy! I haven't seen you since you took that crazy swim."

"Things have been nuts for weeks Herb." He sighed. "And now we're saying goodbye."

"Yeah. About that Phil. Are you really leaving for ninety years?"

"Yep. Maybe a bit longer."

"Christ! I'll never see you again Philip."

"Not true Uncle Herb. Please. *Please* contact Dr. Gold. You met him on *Tigress* when I took that swim."

"I remember. What about him?"

"You work with him and we'll meet right here again in a century. You'll do better by those girlfriends of yours as well."

"I see." Herb thought a moment more. "Are you using this hoodoo?"

"You bet."

"Okay. I'll do it. Demetrious will never go for it though."

"Say goodbye for me then. Give him a big hug. And buy him an Ouzo, on me. We've got to cast off...now."

"I *am* providing escort boy." A steely squint in his eyes.

"Of course. With our thanks. We can use the cover. Goodbye Herb."

"Goodbye boy. Goodbye Annie. Take care of each other."

Within minutes the vast harbor cave thundered and echoed with the throb of giant diesels warming up. Of the three vessels, JAEKEL's engines had been running for hours, so the crew simply brought her revolutions up to full standby.

Phil installed Anne in the Captain's quarters and changed into uniform. He then assumed his position in the Captain's chair on the bridge, savoring the ubiquitous rumble of the big power plant.

After a final check of boat's systems, Phil gave the command. "Chief. Periscope one hundred percent." Suddenly they were looking into the vastness of Oneiro Harbor cave right through the hull, without obstruction. Conventional subs on the surface would see such a sight only from freeboard, or Conning Tower.

"Bring main engines to two-thirds. All lines away. Lateral starboard thrusters to full. Full left rudder." The big sub slowly began to push off from her mooring.

When she had moved roughly five meters to port "Helm. Con. All ahead dead slow. Rudder amidships. Prepare to exit the harbor helmsman. On my order, as we approach the sea-gate, cut power to let the fireboat move into point position. *Sea Tigress* will bring up our rear. Comms, relay these orders to both ships."

The fireboat moved into position, about ten meters forward of JAEKEL's bow, and the huge fire hoses began deluging them with powerful arcs of water. Tonnes of water gushing down, only to suddenly splash on an invisible diversion in mid-air, is hypnotic. Phil prodded himself and the crew to concentrate on the business of driving the big sub.

Minutes later they were through the sea-gate and out to sea. The magical effect of invisible water diversion was further magnified by a pouring rain. After a time, Phil was convinced their heat plume was not going to be an issue. Therefore, *Sea Tigress* would attract notice unnecessarily. "Comms, put me through to *Sea Tigress*."

"Aye sir."

"Captain *Sea Tigress* this is JAEKEL. You're ordered to return to port. The fireboat and the rain provide adequate cover. Over."

"Negative JAEKEL. Our charts show deep water in less than two kilometers. If we turn back now we could attract attention while you're still on the surface."

Aside. "Nav. Can you confirm deep water?"

"Affirmative sir."

"Acknowledged *Sea Tigress*. Come to ten knots. Proceed with close escort. Radio silence effective now. Godspeed *Tigress*. JAEKEL out." Phil turned to the radio position. "Comms. Relay that order to our fireboat escort."

"Aye sir."

All three vessels accelerated by one-half, rolling and heaving into deeper, rougher waters.

"Con. Radar. Contact at one-niner-six. She's a sub and she's moving on *Tigress'* starboard beam."

"Range?"

"Range two thousand meters sir."

"Chief take us down to twelve meters."

Chief King regarded him quizzically. "Helm. Dive to one-two meters." Within seconds, the boat was underwater.

"Helm. Con. Slow to one third and bring us to one-niner-six. Forward Fire Control. Load and arm tubes one and two. Proximity detonation. Bearing one-eight-zero. Range two-zero-zero-zero. Launch ports open. Prepare to fire on my order."

JAEKEL was aimed directly at *Sea Tigress*.

The bridge was a cacophony of orders, repeated orders, acknowledgements, queries and status. Phil felt the thrill of adrenalin surge through his body. His stomach felt like ice water. The bridge suddenly smelled of steel, electricity, grease and sweat. *They must take the first shot.* "Forward Fire Control. Acknowledge."

Seconds ticked by. Phil fought to control his temper. He felt like screaming. *What are those Fire Control techs doing?*

"Forward Fire Control. Acknowledge." There was a distinct edge to his voice.

After more tense moments. "Acknowledged sir. Both tubes armed and ready."

"Con. Sonar. We have a bogie in the water. Bearing one niner-six. Range one-niner-zero-zero meters."

"Sonar. Con. I need depth."

"Con. Sonar. She's on the surface. Looks to be targeting *Tigress* Skipper."

"Comms. Con. Message *Sea Tigress* as follows: *Urgent. Torpedo alert. All stop. Back full. Acknowledge.*"

"Helm. Con. Bring us to three-zero meters. Maintain course and speed."

"Con. Comms. *Sea Tigress* acknowledges.

"Fire Control. Con. Release evasion chaff."

"Can you give me a count Chief?"

"Mark. Eight-zero-zero...seven-zero-zero...six..."

Moments later they heard the whining whirr of the torpedo above and aft of them speeding by.

"Our turn. Fire one."

Pause.

"Fire two."

"Count it out Chief."

After a few moments. "Twenty seconds. Ten seconds. Contact."

"Sonar?"

"Got him sir!"

The bridge crew sighed in relief, as one.

Long minutes later they felt a tiny shock wave, pitching slightly, monitoring a satisfying implosion.

The Chief brought Phil a coffee. "Pretty slick Skipper. You fired below *Tigress* so they wouldn't detect us. They would assume *Tigress* somehow had tubes. Must have been one hellofa surprise. Had they survived they would *not* have reported JAEKEL."

Phil smiled and patted his Captain's console. "This damn boat could play pinochle, need be." Phil lowered his voice. "Forward Fire Control was slow. Will you look after that Chief?"

"Can do Skip."

"Think there's any more out there?"

"Sir I'm surprised they could scramble even one sub this fast. More would be incredible. In fact..." The Chief was suddenly intrigued "why the hell are we fighting submarines at all?"

"We're an island Chief. And they want to kill us. That means air power, sea power and *undersea* power. Bear in mind, there's not one damned part of this mess that hasn't been planned for meticulously."

"Jesus!"

"These are extraordinary times. Let's keep our ears on Chief."

"Aye Skip."

"Nav. Con. Depth."

"One-five-zero-zero sir."

"Ten degrees down bubble. Deploy silent running until we achieve operating depth. I want one-zero-zero meters below our hull all the way to Anastasios Island."

"Yes sir."

"Chief. You have the Con."

"Chief acknowledges the Con sir."

Phil withdrew to his quarters to check on Anne. When he entered his stateroom she was thankfully asleep. Phil sat and put his head back. He wanted a catnap to aid in metrignosiculating Dr. Gold's fruit drink; and he needed some idea if Aiy was going to survive the trip. Twenty minutes later, Phil was awake and convinced. Aiy would indeed survive. Their preparations would be adequate until they were safe on *Gauntlet*. No guarantee she would survive beyond that.

He poured himself a long rum and prepared to relax for a few moments before returning to the bridge.

"Should you be drinking just now?" Anne was awake now, and not in a terribly loquacious mood.

Her shrill tone and her pointed remark piqued Phil. *For Christ's sake you'd think we were married. I don't need this.* "My crew knows how I work; and they don't question their Captain, especially at sea. You will please exercise equal forbearance. That applies equally aboard JAEKEL and *Gauntlet*."

She began to yell. "You son of a bitch. I don't have to..."

"You will be quiet or I will have you sedated." Phil drained his drink. "Stay in this cabin until we reach Anastasios. Call the mess if you need anything."

"I want a complete run-down on Aiy's status."

"Drink your goddamned fruit juice."

"I want to arrange for different quarters on *Gauntlet*. I want to share Aiy's apartment."

*Petulant bitch. But thank God for small mercies.*

"I insist you view her first. See how she looks. See her condition. Drink that damned juice. Then I'll send in the comms officer so you can call ahead. Ask for Bill Christie."

"Alright. Fine. Who the hell is Bill Christie?"

"Nutrient Technology. He'll install Aiy. But you better be ready to look after her...and that's twenty-four hours a day."

"I know my responsibility. We're not talking about a puppy."

He took a long, deep breath. *So much for a little rest.*

Phil found his way to the Captain's mess and was pleasantly surprised to find Chief King already in attendance. "Hi Chief. Howzit going?"

"Smooth as silk. All quiet. The First Officer has the Con. Two thousand meters of sea above us. All systems nominal. No bad guys in sight. Care for a drink?"

"Sure. Thanks."

The Chief poured him a generous rum. "If you'll excuse me Skipper I've got a meeting with Fire Control."

"No problem."

Phil was alone under the dark canopy of the sea. He put his feet up and swirled his drink. *Perhaps these problems with Anne are for the best. For months, years, I must revert to command mode. I'll be the good 'ol Phil Carr again. Happy loner. Maybe that's the way I was meant to live anyway.*

He knew his feelings for Anne had not changed. Aiy too for that matter. But recent problems had (rightfully) driven a wedge between them. Give Anne time to heal. Give Aiy time to heal. Until then? Well, he'd sort it out.

"CAPTAIN TO THE BRIDGE." The speaker startled Phil; and he was on his way before he realized he was on his feet.

"Captain on the bridge."

"As you were. Mr. Dodge. Report please."

"We have contact at one-two-niner. Depth two-one-five-zero. Heading our way."

"What is it?"

"Its signatures track as a Russian Akola Class IV nuclear attack sub."

"My...we *have* made the big time. Are they aware of us?"

"She's changed heading, directly towards us just after we recorded a sonar sweep. Could be more a course correction than a tactical maneuver. But her heading clearly targets JAEKEL."

Without hesitation. "Launch ports open. ALL HANDS SECURE FOR BATTLE MANEUVERS. Rig for bottom running. All stop. Ballast at zero. Deploy silent running. Fire Control, load and activate forward and aft tubes one, two, five and six. Proximity detonation. Pass the word: ALL HANDS, no sound. Chief, get someone to confirm our passengers are all strapped, rigged and quiet. Ms. Atsila is in medical. Dr. Jones is in my quarters."

"Aye sir."

They began to drop in dark silence towards the distant bottom – just as a torpedo sped over their Conning Tower. They could hear the muffled whirring of its props through the hull. For a brief moment, they could barely make out a gray phantom atop a watery contrail, streaking across a pelagic sky.

Chief King whispered "Crap! They were tracking us the whole time."

Phil whispered "Why do you suppose they missed Chief?"

Chief King shrugged and whispered in return "Don't really know Skip. Maybe our turbulence is too light. And silent running casts almost no heat signature."

Phil whispered "Call out our depth Chief, every five seconds."

Five seconds later "two-niner-zero-zero...three-three-five-zero...three-eight-one-zero..."

"Chief, one hundred percent on our forward ballast tanks."

"Aye Skipper. One hundred percent to bow ballast..."

Suddenly the huge boat seemed to pause in mid-descent. Phil remembered a Russian MIG-32 executing similar maneuvers kilometers above the Bering Sea. All tactical positions swiveled and the crew were pressed back into their seats, bow facing, as the sub stood on its tail, continuing to drop into the darkness, stern first. She was quite literally standing on her stern pointing directly towards the surface.

Stage-whispers hissed through the con.

"Sonar, where is she?"

"She's twelve hundred meters from our previous location and closing fast."

"Signal me when she's within..." Phil counted for a moment. "...two hundred forty meters, exactly."

Moments passed.

"Two four zero meters sir."

"Fire Control. Con. Fire one." Phil heard the whoosh as the aquatic missile cleared its launch port. He knew it wasn't possible, but he thought he felt a slight bump as well.

"Fire two.

Count 'em off Chief."

"Number one...ten...five...miss...number two...five...got 'im!"

Moments later the sound of the explosion rang throughout the boat.

The Chief was smiling, shaking his head. "Christ. Maybe she *can* play pinoch..."

It hit. A powerful explosion close to JAEKEL.

The Chief, along with half the bridge crew, were thrown violently from their posts against the starboard bulkhead. Phil strained to hold himself in place. The big boat started to slowly whirl, like some titanic baton. Then she ponderously began to right herself. At the top of the stroke she continued to rotate. From amid ships she slowly rocked like a giant metronome. One end upright, then inverted in slow motion. The entire crew was immobilized struggling for any sort of hold. After three lumbering strokes JAEKEL reluctantly began to right herself, and gain some stability.

The time for whispers was at an end.

Phil initiated a barrage of orders. "Blow aft ballast, 70%. Bow tanks to 55%. Ascend to five-zero meters. Engineering, I want to know if we're tight within five minutes. All stations report. The bridge was a cacophony of voices and electronics."

Belatedly the big sub buoyed itself nose-up and commenced its long ascent towards the surface. Duty stations throughout the boat reported in, detailing damage and casualties. JAEKEL was fully functional. There was one death. The Fire Control Supervisor, Enzo Crispi, skull crushed.

"Medical team to Fire Control. Secure the Supervisor's body in the freezer. What in hell was that Chief?"

"We're not at all sure sir. It was not a torpedo. We believe the sub may have released something that finally drifted unnoticed within ten meters of our hull."

"Some sort of mine?"

"That's as good an explanation as any sir. Whatever it was, it released a great deal of energy and displaced one hellofa lot of water real fast."

"We're fit to continue on to Anastasios?"

"Most systems are nominal. All critical systems are undamaged."

Phil stood. "Good. Nav, what's our time to Anastasios?"

"We're at least six hours out sir. More if the bottom topography is troublesome."

"First Officer to the Con."

When he arrived. "What's the status of our injured XO?"

"No serious injuries. Mainly cuts and bruises. Mr. Crispi was unlucky."

"Understood. Mr. Dodge you have the Con."

"XO acknowledges the Con."

# Free-rigor-ation

Phil decided he'd prefer to avoid his quarters; so he installed himself in the Ward Room with dinner and a mini-viewer, going over the *Gauntlet's* latest specs. Those changes not included in his S&S Bar. He looked up as someone entered the room...

"Nick! I thought I left you in Fire Control back on Oneiro!"

"Ms Harris announced she was assuming command not long after you left. Seemed an excellent idea. It really is her job after all. And it's clear she knows her stuff. And frankly, I didn't feel like messing with her. So I decided to come along and see you off."

"I'm glad you did. I've fully MGL'd the specs on *Gauntlet* from my *Gauntlet* Bar, but I've got a few questions."

"Sure."

"I was looking at the general layout of quarters. Each unit has a full galley."

"Yes."

"There's no refrigeration unit in them."

"Yes. That's correct. A recent change. A pretty sexy new development actually; and it should reduce overall maintenance over the years by nearly two-tenths of one percent."

"Two-tenths of one percent. Imagine that." Smiled Phil.

Nick half smiled indulgently. "I know that doesn't sound like much, but over the space of twenty-seven years, that equates to a fair amount of work. Not to mention savings in displacement and spares. But that's not the exciting part."

Phil peered good naturedly at Nick in quizzical expectation.

"This is an Oneirion innovation emanating from QAVL gravity technology. The QAVL would never have any use for such a device. Normal refrigeration depends on gaseous chlorofluorocarbons. Specifically Freon gas. When such gasses are subject to compression and decompression, a byproduct of that energy expenditure is a variance in gaseous temperatures..."

Phil raised an eyebrow impatiently. He wasn't fond of restating the obvious.

"...ah...okay. Let's see. You're familiar with Newton's Third Law of thermodynamics?"

Head down, looking up at Nick with a weakly patient smile "Cut through it Nick."

"Right. It turns out that gravity, properly manipulated can be used to generate heat...make things hot...or leach heat from matter....make it cold. Essentially it has to do with excitation, or dampening. Exciting a molecule – modifying gravitonic waves – heats it up; and suppression of molecular perturbation – intensifying a gravity field until molecular movement is slowed or stopped – cools it. In fact that is the physical description of temperature. Thermodynamics. I understand they can actually achieve absolute zero with application of sufficient power," He hurriedly added "which-tends-to-disprove-Newton's-Third Law-and-it-makes-one-reconsider-black-holes-as-well." He took a breath. "We have developed a line of extreme low energy pods that draw what little power they need wirelessly, from our central generator. They adapt to the contents and maintain the ideal temperature indefinitely in a near perfect vacuum, or normal atmosphere. In this way foods may be stored indefinitely and warmed when needed, in the same container."

"I don't understand. The application of a gravimetric of that intensity should simply compress the subject material into an amorphous mass."

"Correct. However, the gravity field, or should I say ubiquitary field, exerts an equal force, evenly and quite literally in all directions."

"...in which case the target material should be pulled apart in all directions. The result would be a mess, spread equally throughout the chamber..."

"Again, correct. Except you fail to consider the pull is omnipresent throughout the chamber, exerting an exactly balanced force on every particle in every direction."

Phil lent back, staring at the ceiling. "I still don't understand. But if it works it's fine by me."

"Think of it as stasis."

"Yes. Yes, that's better. Is that what it is?"

"I'm not really sure."

"Well it's pretty damned neat whatever it is. Especially for extended interstellar travel. You've done away with refrigerators *and* ovens. You can literally store comestibles in the container you cook it in, and perhaps even serve it in..."

Nick was gratified at Phil's response. "Our people have even developed decorative pods that are a true Oneirion art-form. Decorate with them, store in them, eat on 'em, sit on 'em, sleep on 'em, cook in them and eat from them..."

"Cycling and recycling perishables has no negative effect?"

"None whatsoever."

"Any limit on the number of cycles a given material can endure?"

"None whatsoever."

"Energy consumption?"

"Negligible."

Phil pushed on. "Damn. This could have great importance to many parts of Earth. We could start shipping Oneirion food in these containers, or along with our Food Generators. Sounds like a huge savings in energy. Convenient too. Truly instant food. Eliminate food poisoning, parasites, E-coli, waste, even help reduce malnutrition. No more perishables...fruit, eggs, meat, vaccines, blood, laboratory samples. Jesus, how about dangerous goods? Plutonium and such. My God! Transport of injured. Burn victims, in fact any injury requiring transport to treatments. Cessation of molecular oscillation could have vastly different effects than freezing. Even heating and air conditioning. You know Nick, you guys really came up with..."

"Phil, Dr. Gold's staff and Dr. Butler already have a working group together. They are making plans to package and ship as soon as the world decides it doesn't want to kill them."

"Well. Nicely done. I really can't wait to see what you guys come up with in a century."

"That ah...brings me to the topic I really wanted to discuss with you."

"Yes?"

"I'd like a job."

"A job?" Phil half-laughed. "Doing what?"

"Aboard *Gauntlet*."

Slightly taken aback, Phil considered Nick's request.

"I'd like that Nick. Interesting we never discussed this before. But I understood you were committed to the *Gauntlet II* Project."

"That's true. But to be honest I have serious doubts about that project as long as we seem to be at war with the world; and I really see no end in sight."

"Well, your timing is certainly interesting. What've you got in mind?"

Nick looked a little sheepish. "Your Number One...."

"My Number One?"

"Yes. Your Exec. That is, your Executive Officer."

"I know what it is Nick. But I have an XO. Tom Billings."

"We just confirmed Tom failed to report to JAEKEL and he's definitely not aboard *Gauntlet*."

"Any idea what's happened to him?"

"We believe he may have been in the hangar with the Drákōns when we were first attacked. He loved those birds. Infrared surveillance confirms there is no one alive in the hangar. So he's either a casualty, or trapped somewhere else in the complex. Either way he'll not make lift off."

"I'm surprised you're not interested in Chief Engineer."

"Mark Oikodomos is eminently qualified for that position. I wouldn't want to interfere."

"You enjoy command Nick?"

"I'm not crazy about command *per se*. I am intrigued by the *problems* of command. I can't imagine a more diverse responsibility. And there is no aspect of running *Gauntlet* that doesn't fascinate me. And to be frank, I doubt Oneirions need a hellofa lot of leadership."

Phil sat thinking for a few moments. Then, with his customary decisiveness "Nick, I believe you'll make a fine First Officer." He stood and extended his hand. "Welcome aboard XO."

Nick stood, smiling broadly. "Thank you sir. I'll do my best to do you proud."

"I'm sure you will." They gravely shook hands.

Phil went to a locker and withdrew a bottle of rum.

"Let's do this right." He poured two generous glasses of dark rum.

Nick raised his glass. "Permission to go aboard sir?"

"Permission granted."

They drained their glasses and reseated.

"Draw a uniform immediately. Three pips. Naturally you'll take over Mr. Billing's quarters. Do you have any personal gear with you at all?"

"Not a thing Skipper, but they tell me the shops are fully stocked and will be open just a few hours after launch."

"Good. A few more questions, then I think we should get some rest. There's going to be hell's own after we reach *Gauntlet*..."

## *Diei Unus*

The huge boat surfaced, hoved to, and lumbered ashore onto a wild rocky beach. No lights, people, or buildings. No sign of life, or civilization whatsoever. JAEKEL displayed no running lights. It was a moonless night and dense cloud cover obscured any ambient light. Anastasios Island was veiled in near total darkness. "Helm, bring us to the portside access tunnel. That will be at roughly four hundred meters at our two o'clock."

"Aye sir."

"How's the surface out there?"

"Mud is not a problem here, but it's rocky."

"Dead slow helm. Nav, give us a one minute arrival warning." Phil turned to Chief King. "How's our final time Chief?"

"We're about four hours past our scheduled arrival. All those fun and games just out of Oneiro, along with deep running, costs us a fair amount of time. But we made up some time on the last leg."

"Chief, please commence offload protocols. I want to move smartly into the access tunnel. Let's try for no more than thirty minutes."

Chief King picked up the boat's intercom and clicked twice. "ALL HANDS. We will arrive at *Gauntlet's* portside access tunnel in...six minutes. We will debark from the starboard, land-loading ramp. Wait until your Load Control Officer calls your section and number, and follow his directions. We are observing strict black-out security. We will not – repeat not – be using infrareds. Wear your starlight scopes and follow the dimmers on the ground every two meters. Footing will be tricky so walk carefully. Inside the access tunnel you many remove your starlights and walk towards the light at the end of the tunnel. Step lively, we are pressed for time. But step carefully."

"Con. Nav. One minute to offload."

Phil timed off forty-five seconds. "Helm, full stop. Loadmaster, extinguish all lights in the ramp proximity and deploy the starboard ramp. I want no lambent leakage. Ground staff, deploy dimmers. Loadmaster, commence offloading sequence. Comms, contact *Gauntlet* ground handling and ensure the tunnel's *Gauntlet*-side gate is open and illuminated. No light in the tunnel itself. Master at Arms, I want armed guards on the conning tower, bow and stern, and lining the dimmer path. I want both deck guns manned and ready to fire. Radar, I want a 180° by 360° sweep. Watch for unknowns on the ground and in the air. Let's move fast and keep alert."

He turned to Chief King. "Chief would you send someone to my quarters and dispatch Dr. Jones with the first wave. Get six ground handlers and move our patient's med-vessel with Dr. Jones. Make damn sure they handle that unit carefully. When you're done see me in the wardroom. No hurry Chief. I'm leaving with the last wave and I have some final communiqués to complete."

"Aye Skipper." He hurried away.

After reviewing general status of operations and condition of the boat, Phil stood. "She's your boat Mr. Dodge."

"Transfer acknowledged and accepted Skipper."

The entire bridge crew soundlessly stood and saluted.

Phil returned the salute. "I will see all of you later. Meanwhile, take care of JAEKEL. She's a good boat and you're a fine crew.

Godspeed gentlemen."

# Anastasios

"Dispatch these as soon as JAEKEL reaches Oneiro. I doubt very much the communications embargo will be dropped before you arrive. If so, send these out immediately. Thank you. Dismissed."

The Orderly exited just as Chief King entered the wardroom. Phil swiveled to face him. "Well Chief, we made it."

"That we did Skip. And a great run it was. First time in action and she kicked ass."

"I think we were lucky too Chief. I doubt very much they realized we carried such firepower. All the same, I agree. Sure you don't want to come along on the next leg Chief? There'll be nothing like it in all of human history."

"I appreciate the offer Skipper. But I belong in the sea, not the stars."

"In that case..." Phil placed two mugs of dark rum on his desk. He favored Chief King with a look of part affection and part respect, raising his mug.

"*To those who go down to the sea in ships.*"

The Chief smiled wistfully and raised his mug.

"*The meek shall inherit the earth.*
*The brave, the sea.*
*The intrepid, the stars.*"

They tossed back their drinks as one.

"Ah! I'll miss that rum."

"I doubt that sir. We had twenty cases delivered to your quarters aboard *Gauntlet*."

"Thanks Chief." They shook hands warmly. "Take good care of our boat."

A brisk salute, and Phil found himself descending JAEKEL's starboard offload ramp. Before stepping to the beach he turned and saluted her stern. A gesture not lost on those few crewmen crowded on the conning tower.

The walk across the beach was bittersweet and surreal. It had the lonely feel of boarding a plane, or an ocean liner on a dark night. Yet they were leaving for the better part of a century, and carried little if any baggage. Phil carried nothing.

He trailed the group. Walking alone. Savoring the tangy salt breezes and smells of Earth. Clouds obscuring the massive summit of Mount Anastasios. The ozone edge in the air after a lightning squall. The flashing rumble of a thunderstorm retreating over the far horizon. The chaos of the ocean pounded into a fury by a storm out at sea. The rhythmic booming of the sea on Anastasios' rocky shores. Images and scents that would linger bitter-sweet in his memory for decades amongst the stars.

Phil found himself the last man inside the boarding tunnel. There were nearly seventy Oneirions queued in front of him. Strangely quiet he thought. He would have expected excitement and enthusiasm. Twittering, laughter, joking and lively discussion. Instead he heard only whispers and occasional mumbling. This could not be fear. Every person in this tunnel had undergone fear training; and these were the best Oneiro could produce. Then he realized. Just because you don't feel fear, doesn't mean you don't feel anything. These people are entering a new world. In doing so they were abdicating Utopia. They had no idea what sort of Earth they would return to. Or if they *would* return. What unknowns awaited them at their destination? They didn't really know what *Gauntlet* was like. Quite literally, they didn't know what they were walking into.

*I'm going to have to start taking more interest in these people. Encourage them. I've been thinking as if they were invulnerable and interchangeable. Oneirions are still human.*

The end of the tunnel was growing congested. People seemed to be loitering at the entrance. *What now?* Despite his irritation, Phil was hesitant to order them to get moving. This didn't seem the time for prodding. Instead he paced behind the line as patiently as he could. He would give them a few minutes and then break it up. He turned back down the tunnel, savoring his last waning view of planet Earth. After a time he turned back to the entrance and they were gone. He was alone in the vast tunnel. Presumably they had finally moved into *Gauntlet*. Phil stood alone through the great tunnel. *What the hell?*

He strode briskly to the mouth of the tunnel...and froze. Just as those before him. He froze. It was day. A beautiful day. Warm. A clear blue sky. A light breeze. Far above him was a small sea, a mild surf breaking on an albinic beach. Shark Bay. A beautiful city spreading out over the hills below. Gardens and forests. Mountains in the distance. Directly in front, a stone path lined with flowers and trees. A small bridge over a clear brook. The perfume of a thousand flowers, the flinty scent of dusty stone baking in the sun. Birdsong and bees and katydids and frogs. A golden peacefulness. The Oneirions, so subdued just moments before, were running, laughing, or simply strolling about enraptured. Phil thought he even spotted tears.

Phil simply stood and stared, his throat slowly constricting.

*My God. The joys and horrors and work and wonders that brought us to this place. This moment. The marvels that await. Challenges such as no....*

"Captain Carr?"

"Yes."

The man was in uniform. His rank designated by a single pip on his sleeve.

"Permission to go aboard sir."

"Permission granted sir." The man smiled broadly and saluted.

Phil returned the salute. *I hope we won't have too much of this. It could be a long twenty-seven years.* Military formalities that had seemed so natural aboard JAEKEL, in part a warship, were now nearly anathema. This was paradise.

"Am I to accompany you?"

"Yes sir, if you would. What with all the recent installations and changes, we were concerned you might have problems finding the bridge; and you haven't been issued your new DIT/Comms bracelet. Which I have right here sir."

Phil slipped on his unit.

Contrary to logic and intuition, they made their way up the path, defying gravity with every movement. Fighting vertigo with every step. Behind him, Phil heard the huge entry hatch being dogged and sealed. Seconds later he heard explosions destroying the huge access tunnel. Strangely he felt no vibration. They were now irrevocably enclosed in Mount Anastasios. *The only exit now will necessitate a far greater explosion.*

Fortunately the sphere was vast, allowing them to move as a fly 'up the walls', without disorientation and progressively lessening vertigo. In the city they QAVLGated to its largest building, home to the ship's huge bridge as well as his quarters. All seemed pretty much the same to Phil. He could have found his way, but a little help this one time was not altogether unwelcome.

They entered the now familiar glass elevator, having given it appropriate instructions and ascended to the bridge. Thanks to his *Gauntlet* Bar, intensive study and his previous visit, the bridge appeared exactly as he envisioned... only much, much larger. It was enormous. Intimidating. It was now open to the 'sky', rendering it even larger.

He paused at the entrance and took a breath. *Well, there's only one first time.* Phil strode onto the bridge. Immediately the voice of the Sergeant at Arms rang out "Captain on the bridge." As one, forty-two people came to attention.

He started to say 'As you were...', his instinctive response. Then he stopped. *No. This time protocol is important.* The bridge looked to Phil expectantly. "Good evening. We launch in ten hours. Manual countdown will commence on my mark."

Phil turned to the large bridge chronometer. Watching it closely for a few moments. "On... three...two...one...mark." He observed hands around the bridge updating their duty stations. "I want all senior officers in my Briefing Room in one hour. We will review the ship's status in detail. Our preflight check will began one hour after that. We will launch on time. Much depends on it.

I will be in my Briefing Room in thirty minutes if I'm needed. Meanwhile," He glanced at the comms position. "I would like Dr. Singe to report to my quarters." He began walking off the bridge when he stopped himself short. "We're making history here. Human history. We have the finest crew mankind can field and an extraordinary vessel. I am honored to be your Captain. Let's make a history we can look back on with honor."

Smiling for the first time, he left the bridge. Eighty-four eyes moved as their Captain moved.

"You have the complete file Doctor?"

"Yes. Dr. Gold provided me the therapeutic sequence, your in-flight tape, and treatments given on Oneiro."

"Opinion?"

The Doctor took a long draw on his coffee, considering his prognosis.

"I've never seen anything remotely akin to this. The savagery..." He stopped himself, realizing he was exploring irrelevancies. "She will live. Dr. Gold's treatment will work. In weeks, or months, or years she will regain total physical normalcy. I would modify Dr. Gold's course of treatment in one major respect..."

"Yes Doctor?"

"Well, I know this may seem unorthodox, but I'm convinced we should administer Dr. Gold's re-growth regimen with concurrent marine immersion."

"'concurrent marine immersion'?...I'm afraid I don't follow you Doctor."

"Simply put: We encase her within a re-growth solution, prophylactic, equipped with the nutrient and therapeutic mechanisms as Dr. Gold prescribes. We augment this with blood aeration and electro-stimulant therapy. We waterproof everything and mount it all in a submersible cage protected with fine wire mesh. Then we submerge the whole affair in the Oneirion Sea."

Phil regarded the Doctor for some time as he ran the scenario through his mind. "I fully understand the reasoning Doctor. I myself have benefitted in similar manner in the past. Regression to the womb in a manner of speaking I suppose. A reasonable beginning to psychic recovery and the healing properties of sea water are barely..."

"That's the reason I suggest this. You should realize this treatment tangibly addresses only Aiy's *physical* recovery however. Mentally? Anyone's guess at this point."

"I understand. How long?"

"Eighteen to two-hundred weeks. I know that's one hellofa range. But it all depends on her progress."

"I assume engineering can fabricate the unit?"

"Yes. Anticipating your approval, they are constructing it as we speak. I believe we must act quickly."

"My approval? You're the Doctor. If you deem this course advisable, who am I to interfere? In any event, I do approve. Please proceed Doctor. Thank you."

Phil entered the second bedroom where both Anne and Aiy were temporarily housed.

"You heard?"

"Yes."

"And?"

"It sounds encouraging. Thank you Phil. I'm truly sorry about that cloning business. I should have known better. I have a request."

"Yes?"

"Engineering should make room for me in that cage, as well. I'll need breathing apparatus, heating, a dry refuge, food and water, sanitary apparatus, and a means of speaking with Aiy. Can you do it?"

"What you are suggesting is beyond bizarre Anne."

"Can you do it?"

"You'd need some specialized skin treatments as well..."

"Can you do it?"

"You propose to live underwater for months, maybe years by yourself with Aiy, who happens to be unconscious, or in a coma? I suppose we could rig some digi-books, digi-music, and digi-entertainment. That would help you preserve your sanity. We could also provide you with diving gear so you can get out and swim around. Exercise. You'll need exercise. This would be much like living in weightlessness."

"Can you do it?"

"Not to mention surface comms."

"*Can* you *do* it Phil? *Will* you do it?"

Pause.

"Speak with Dr. Singe. If he approves, I will make no objection – on condition I review and approve the physical layout and environmental design."

"Thank you."

"I'll have you moved into Aiy's apartment until things are ready. I must leave for my Briefing Room now. Listen to ship's intercom for any instructions the next few hours. I suggest you eat, and get some sleep."

There was a low buzz at the door of his Briefing Room. "Enter."

"Nick. I'm glad you came here early. There's something I wish to go over with you before we lift off."

"Certainly Captain. What is it?"

"We need to develop a bridge rhythm. You know what I mean?"

"You are referring to how you, I and the bridge crew communicate?"

"Exactly. Specifically when we are both on the bridge. As XO, I expect you to appropriately direct and enact all my orders and any orders you issue independently. Duty stations will echo the order back to you, and confirm their execution. You will advise me only of exceptions. All bridge stations will need to learn when and what to report...and what not to report. I expect all duty stations to provide a general alert of any imminent problem or threat, so you and I will be aware of the same things at the same time, at all times. My communications with bridge and crew is essentially one-way. I know this is a slight departure from SOP, but things could happen quickly; and I want our reaction times down to a minimum."

"I understand Captain. I will brief all bridge crews before launch. The more straightforward and streamlined we can make communications the better in my opinion. During a voyage of this duration it could be months, even years, between intensive bridge maneuvers; and constant drilling can become anti-productive. So we've got to learn to keep things fast and simple. As you, I am not overly wed to chain of command, or SOP. More important to work effectively than strangled with protocol. At the same time I appreciate how this change reinforces my position on the bridge."

Eyebrows raised "I believe you've given this some thought as well Nick. Anything else?"

"Ah...yes sir. Our command roster is incomplete. Several crew members did not make it aboard."

"Anything that could jeopardize launch?"

"Nothing critical. I'm surprised we hadn't designated supernumeraries."

"We probably would have, given a normal launch build-up sequence. In any event, choose some replacements, feed 'em a *Gauntlet* Bar and give 'em a nap."

"Understood. But we need to discuss filling in the blanks permanently when you have time."

"Okay. Let's get together tomorrow. Thanks Nick."

Phil was again alone in his Briefing Room.

He kept replaying the launch sequence in his mind. He knew it *verbatim* from his *Gauntlet* Bar, but he needed it to be second nature. Automatic. To really understand what they were doing...and why they were doing it. They were facing the most bizarre launch in history. Imagine. Powering out of a huge, dormant, vulcanized mountain. Intensive hostilities could be expected after break out. His *Gauntlet* Bar had surprised him with the impressive array of weaponry he had *not* ordered. Neither had he specifically proscribed. He had to admit he took comfort in such ordinance now that launch was imminent, and the world opposed him.

Phil was well aware he had the expertise and technology to Captain *Gauntlet* through just about anything; and he knew his unique mental abilities could be relied on to react with their normal alacrity. All the same, for some reason he felt the need to drill himself over and over on procedures.

*Okay. One more time...*

*Pre-launch preparations: Manual and automated pre-launch check out. Gravity propulsion systems up to full standby. All open waters sealed and gravity secured. Internal grav increased to one-ten percent. All crew seated and secured. All non-essential systems off. All galleys powered down by Central Engineering. Everything on board confirmed stowed. Bussard Systems on emergency standby (Backup in case of grav systems failure.). Spheriscope 100%. Running lights inactive. Internal lighting down by eighty percent. Escape systems on hot standby. All bridge positions manned. Master at Arms standing by, fully armed. Defensive systems on standby. Full radar scans active. QAVL will be orbiting Gauntlet at distances of from one kilometer to five hundred kilometers. DAR (Detect-Analyze-Respond) will be active as well.*

*Then we break out: Full ahead. Heading Right Ascension, Declination 185.63325 29.89598611 (This will break out of Mount Anastasios and commence our journey out of the solar system.). Fully extend DAR Systems. Gravity drives to one hundred and fifteen percent. When we have passed the Kuiper Belt, bring gravity drive systems to one-half and bring Bussard Drive to one hundred. At that threshold we will switch to QAVL celestial course and distance navigation.*

Phil had given the QAVL interstellar navigation formulae a cursory review. They were not included in the *Gauntlet* Bar, because they were not requisite to ship's operations. He found them nearly rudimental in their simplicity. A Sophomore Math major would lose no sleep learning their sequences.

The QAVL confirmed a giant anomaly delineates the true center of our galaxy; and all galaxies for that matter. Educed from the Greek Γαλαξίας, or *Galaxias*, humans refer to it as the *Milky Way*. A moniker that had confused and annoyed Phil since a young boy. The name seemed to him trivial and saccharine for celestial vortex of such incredible majesty. The QAVL refer to the galaxy as *Quaarasut* (The Sum of Things). On *Kosmas* they refer to it as *Nidomnivie* (Radiant Lair).

The *Kosmas* translation of their sequence divided the galaxy into a galactic plane of the elliptic they refer to as the Galactic Equatorial Plane (GEP), which rotates precisely around the central anomaly. An axis which intersects the central anomaly called the Galactic Celestial Axis (GCI). Finishing the elements of course calculation they add the Galactic Celestial Perigon (GCP), an arbitrarily positioned 360° matrix that moves as the galaxy moves.

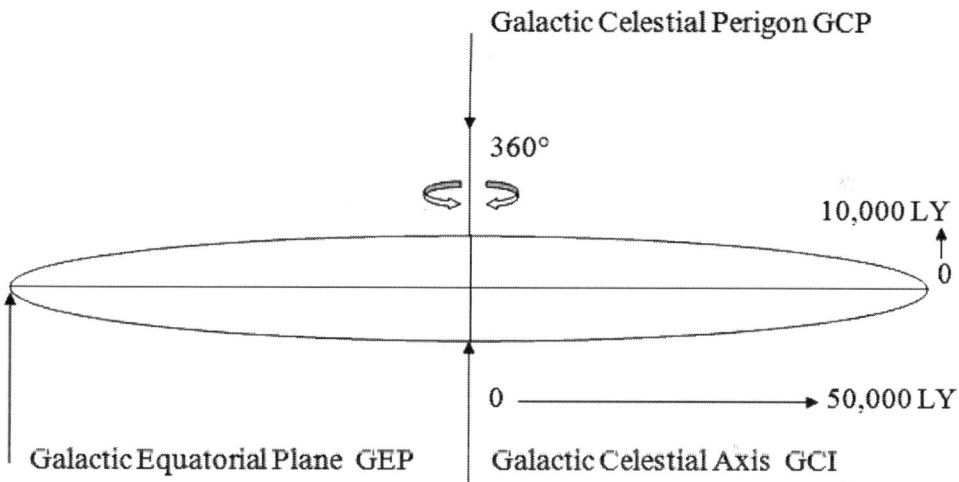

This is used in calculating the athwart galactic drift of a target destination, or what is referred to as precession, factoring in transit time and GCP rotation. When dealing with minor distances (eg: seven light years) positions are fixed within a timeframe of reasonableness using the 'j' (era) notation. For example j2000, designates positions as at the year 2000. Good enough for a trip to *Kosmas*. The sequence itself is quite simple. Similar to the parallax calculation. Nothing more complex than trigonometry. Phil continued with his review.

*In case of catastrophic systems failure at launch, our alternate is any available body of water over three hundred meters deep. Hard to believe this damned sphere wouldn't break up, much less not float. Hard to believe it won't break up erupting out of this damned mountain. Thank God this is a one way exit. After this, operations should take on a normalcy that will..*

There was a subtle buzz at the door.
"Enter."

Nine senior bridge officers filed into his Briefing Room and took their seats. The steward had already laid coffee and water, so after minimal shuffling they were ready.

Phil consulted the chronometer.

"Eight hours and forty-seven minutes to launch. Let's go through this by the numbers. I want to be damned sure we lift off as scheduled. Engineering..."

One by one each officer reported in detail, weathering Phil's and Nick's incessant interrogations with the resolute collaboration of the bridge crew. Qasi himself intervened eight times to the surprise of all.

A little more than two hours later everyone was exhausted. Aside from one final install, five negligible fixes, and three minor modifications – none launch critical – Gauntlet was unanimously declared ready for lift off. The digital launch sequence would require four hours. Therefore it was agreed to proceed.

Phil stood "Automated countdown to commence in exactly two hours and twenty-tree minutes."

Farrow stood as well "Senior officers will please meet with me in the Situation Room following this meeting." Tired nods all round, as all stood.

Phil added "Advise Commander Farrow when fixes and modifications are complete. Lt. Commander Oikodomos is charged with initiating the digital countdown. Try to get some rest before then. I want all senior officers on the bridge in Class A's, no less than two hours prior to launch. Ensure all crew members report ready for launch status not less than thirty minutes prior to lift off.

Questions?"

None.

"Good. Dismissed."

Phil was alone again. Lost in thought, he moved to the steward's locker and reached for a bottle of rum...then for the first time in years...hesitated. Instead he poured coffee and returned to the conference table.

Head down, leaning into the table, warming hands on the coffee cup... *Okay.* He sighed. *One more time....*

# Eruption at Anastasios

There was none of the gay, boisterous excitement of embarking a passenger liner. None of the sweaty, confined struggle of loading an aircraft; or the clumsy bustle of boarding a train. Not even the controlled tumult of a conventional space lift off. Aside from bridge crew there was little or no movement. No sound. No vaporous, freezing rocket fuel, or kerosene, or hissing hydraulics and engine startup. All was calmness. Yet Phil could nearly taste the edgy fervor.

The delusion of fantasy was inescapable. A collage of contradictions.

A formidable, ultra-high-tech command bridge on the largest vessel ever constructed by humans. Under an azure sky, bird song, flowers and swaying palms, a gentle breeze, soothing music, snowcapped mountains in the distance, while a light surf lapped the shores of the Oneirion Sea high above. As they prepared to explode through tens of meters of granite and igneous rock. Launching a dramatic twenty-seven year voyage to the stars to join the most advanced sentients in the galaxy. While half the world patrolled the skies above, determined to destroy them.

A Disneyesque scenario. Defying belief. Only the entertaining illusion of risk and danger. Only a fantasia of fun and imaginary menace. Only it was all true. The dangers real. The risks deadly.

All the same. In such a setting, it was hard to believe it was all real. Demanding to take seriously.

Phil was decked out in his Class A uniform, as was the entire bridge crew. Phil thought...*probably the last time I'll see them looking this strack for decades.*

Looking every inch the commander of the largest craft ever built in human history, Phil was firmly ensconced in the Captain's chair, ready to begin. The jarring unreality of the setting struck Phil as soon as he assumed his position, prompting his first command from the Captain's chair.

"Spheriscope to one hundred percent. Ambient lighting to ten. Turn off that music."

Immediately the sky was transformed into an infinite, featureless black. Lights over the entire sphere were dramatically lowered. Below Phil, a twilight world. A nighttime city approached by aircraft, made grander by *Gauntlet's* endless horizon. Bridge positions glowed in the dusky light, taking on a portentous aspect, while hominal shadows purposefully strode the bridge, executing dozens of duties. All was deadly serious now.

The countdown had commenced over two hours ago. Thus far, all was in order, proceeding without incident. Yet Phil felt the unfamiliar tickle of nervousness. The itchy suspicion everything was not right.

"I want the countdown piped through the ship. And scramble it to Oneiro."

A dispassionate, running digital monologue commenced, outlining the exact time to liftoff, detailing every aspect of critical ship's functions, including precise status from the various operational duty stations.

The combined precipitate of radically modified lighting and the countdown litany had the desired effect. Things were now very real for all aboard. Equally for the Oneirions observing the launch from deep within the labyrinth on their island.

A hour later Phil keyed ship's comms to relay his voice throughout the ship.

"This is the Captain.

We are now two hours and fifty-six minutes into the countdown...thirty-three minutes to launch. Al systems report nominal and the countdown is proceeding normally. Therefore, all on-tactical crew are ordered to prepare for lift off." Phil could hear his voice echoing and re-echoing. Reverberating throughout this huge new world, he found it vaguely distracting.

"I am ordering all non-tactical personnel secured into maneuvering braces in exactly...thirty-two minutes. Pursuant with tactical maneuvering guidelines, everything should be stowed areas and all personnel should be prepared to be secured for a duration up to two hours.

The Spheriscope is on real-time gain, so you will be able to observe our breakout from Mount Anastasios, and our ascent from Earth, from any maneuvering brace on *Gauntlet*.

It is probable we will encounter belligerents during our ascent. Essentially combat aircraft. Perhaps tactical missiles. Air-to-air, surface-to-air. Perhaps even strategic weaponry. We do not anticipates encountering nuclears. However, as you know, we are well equipped to deal with any conceivable hostility.

It is...disheartening...that man's first ascent to the stars should be thusly tarnished. It is discouraging the sole threat to our mission emanates from other *men*. Perhaps we shall overcome that one day. Perhaps we are overcoming it now. Ourselves. Today is the dawning of the real ascent of man.

Carr Out."

Half an hour later.

"This is Carr. We are in the final countdown.

Sixty seconds from lift off...

Our QAVL sentries advise us there are unfriendlies in our immediate area. Given sufficient acuity on their part, it is reasonable to assume they will engage when we emerge from Mount Anastasios.

Twenty seconds to lift off...

Good luck to you. Good luck to us all.

Final countdown..."

Phil began issuing the orders initiating the launch sequence.

"Full ahead.

Confirm course. Right ascension, declination 185.63325 29.89598611.

Activate DAR Systems.

Gravity drives to one hundred and fifteen percent."

Phil forced himself to ignore Nick's repetition of his orders and their subsequent echoes.

When all orders were acknowledged ready to execute...

"ACTIVATE." Phil's order dramatically resounded throughout the vast spherical ship. He and all aboard, and all those on Oneiro, felt the electrifying thrill of the moment.

Then nothing.

No sound. No movement. Nothing. Staggeringly anticlimactic. Phil heard subdued mumbling around the bridge. As he looked about he saw that status displays were being hurriedly consulted. Why was the greatest moment in Earth's history suddenly a momentous non-event? A cosmic pie-in-the-face.

Phil discreetly brought his DIT to his mouth. Very quietly "Qasi?"

"Patience Phil." Qasi's voice a digital whisper, audible only to Phil. "Coldstart gravity drives require a few moments to develop sufficient fusative-contramass. Were you not advised of this?"

As Phil was about to respond, he paused. A deep vibration was slowly rising. It quickly enveloping the massive sphere. They were submerged in a sea of quivering resonance. Phil could feel it in his bones and teeth, and it was painful. Although he heard nothing, he felt as if he had a severe sinus headache. Breathing began to feel close and slightly labored. He could see signs of alarm around the bridge. Blood seeped unnoticed from a few noses, even eyes and ears.

Then it happened.

It began as a titanic, deafening foghorn. Then a barely perceptible lurch. Millions of tons brought to bear against the majestic basalt face of the huge volcano. An orange/white glow began smoldering in *Gauntlet's* 'sky'. Suddenly the Spheriscope exploded into stars and moonlight and holocaust. Huge storms of vapor and dust. White heat and thunderous lightning flashed. A raging white-hot holocaust. Towering incandescence flaring from the summit of Mount Anastasios, howling in an astonishing pyroclastic flow down to the ocean. Vast clouds of steam rising from the sea as Mount Anastasios waned, and Anastasios Island advanced. The entire sphere rang a deafening basso profondo. Phil was momentarily paralyzed by sight, vibration and sound. Every muscle in his body rigid, as though electrified. As was the entire crew. Phil breathed deeply and forced himself to regain control.

Everything proceeding normally now. Somehow Phil hadn't focused on the cold start interval, but he was...

Qasi's voice erupted from Phil's DIT. Phil had never heard him so loud; and he thought he detected *emotion* in his voice. "Phil. Metallic object. Ejected two hundred meters above *Gauntlet* as we broke free. Extreme caution. Evasion suggested."

Phil jumped to his feet. "Helm! Dive! Dive!"

The helmsman's head jerked spasmodically towards Phil. A look of confused disbelief. "Sir?"

"Emergency dive. Submerge. Maximum depth. *Immediately*!"

The helmsman frantically applied full power, pushing the helm harness straight forward to its limit.

Phil stepped towards the helm. "Helm, descend to four thousand. Mind any undersea magma outcropping. Sonar, 180° scan bottomward. We may have a..."

Too late.

*Gauntlet's* sky burst into blinding incandescence. The enormous Spheriscope reacted instantly, filtering and suppressing the blinding white light. Else Phil and half the crew would have permanently lost their sight. As it was, they were momentarily dazzled.

Then it hit. *Gauntlet* resounded with an explosive boom. A titanic gong. Deafening. Pervasive and inescapable.

The enormous sphere smashed into the sea with explosive force.

Phil was suddenly airborne. Then slammed into the flooring. Grav systems overtaxed. Then he blacked out.

He was out for three seconds. When he opened his eyes he saw they were submerged in a sea brighter than daylight. Looking up at his watery sky he first thought the sea was on fire. A thousand shades of red, yellow, ochre, and purest white – dancing madly in all directions. Slowly he began to make sense of the blazing chaos.

Between the nuclear blast and the impact of *Gauntlet*, the sea had been driven insane. Waves larger than office buildings. Crashing and flagellating in every direction.

*Anastasios must be a smoking ruin now. Are those fish on the surface? Thrashing madly in the mêlée? No. My God! The ocean is boiling!*

He roused himself. *...must concentrate on the ship...*

"XO. Report."

"We are attempting to determine damage now. Were it not for that glowing sea we would be in absolute darkness. That was a nuke that detonated above us and all electronics are out. A massive EMP hit us as we submerged. Thankfully the QAVL drives and nav systems are unaffected. I suggest we go to station keeping and begin repairs. If possible. Ambient controls are out too, but we have air, water and food for weeks. It is going to get cool however."

*Gauntlet's* sky began to fade. Soon they would be in darkness.

"Agreed Mr. Farrow. Continue descent however. Quartermaster. Issue isotope lanterns to all crewmembers, if the damned things are still working. Have runners put the word out. Non-essentials confined to quarters except casualties. Have the runners escort those to sick bay. Advise the crew to dress warmly and implement survival procedures. Any crew members experiencing nausea, vomiting, diarrhea, loss of appetite, weakness, itching, sore mouth, sore throat, sudden hair loss, bleeding, or anemia will report to sick bay immediately. Sick bay and comms have power restoration priority. Advise Dr. Singe to report any cases of radiation sickness to me immediately. I want status from all departments within the hour. I will be in my Briefing Room."

When he was alone and equipped with a lantern he looked at his DIT. "How did this happen Qasi?"

"A device was imbedded in a ferrite matrix, buried deep in an igneous deposit. Even with extraordinary scrutiny, it was undetectable until released. We estimate a yield of roughly two megaton. It must have been inserted months ago at the inception of the *Gauntlet* project. Dark forces orbit these islands Philip."

"I suppose we're lucky it was such a small device."

"Lucky indeed Philip."

"We must get the hell off this planet."

"As soon as possible Philip."

"Alright. We launch as soon as power is restored. Can you help."

"Power will be restored within ten minutes. Excuse us Philip."

"Thank you Qasi."

Half an hour later all senior bridge officers were gathered in Phil's Briefing Room. A terse, disturbingly incomplete briefing just completed.

Throughout the précis Phil was swiveled towards the periscopic wall peering out at the dark sea. Seemingly lost in thought.

*What an amazing sight we must be. An immense sphere plummeting through this roiling, blinding fury into the black depths...boiling hot...still shedding the detritus from our outburst...*

He turned towards the room.

"Well. We seem to have survived. My compliments to the helmsman for his quick reactions. I'm pleased medical reports no problems as yet. Of course it's too early by far to make a judgment. We must watch short and long term reactions carefully. We appear to have structural integrity, drive and power, and negligible internal damage. *Gauntlet's* a tough lady."

Nick spoke up. "What do you suppose we should do now Captain?"

Phil regarded him for a few moments. Then rose to his feet.

"*Do*?

We launch.

Initiate a fifteen minute countdown immediately.

Reverse course, full power ascent.

Duty stations.

Dismissed."

*Gauntlet* broke the surface in seeming slow-motion, with a roar, casting white water and huge waves in all directions, speed and course unaffected in the least.

When she'd gained some altitude "Helm. Con. Confirm heading."

"185.63325 29.89598611. As ordered sir."

"Steady as she goes."

"Aye sir."

They were travelling slowly. No sound now. No feeling of movement.

Phil looked down through the hull on Anastasios, or what was left of it. Essentially it was an unrecognizable ruin. No Mount Anastasios remaining to speak of. Just a charred, empty caldera. Even the beginnings of what looked to be magma discharge. Phil forced himself to look away. *I hope JEAKEL got away in time.*

"Con. Fire Control. Incoming missiles. Four ICBM's. We ID them as Russian Federation, SS-19 Stilettos. The QAVL report their launch site as... Odessa...they are carrying MIRV Nuclear Warheads"

Phil could hear the controlled excitement in the man's voice. An imperceptible edge of fear, discernable only by Phil's sensitivities.

"Time to impact?"

"Four minutes sir." Still tightly contained. *The man is doing well.*

Phil consulted his DIT. "You or me Qasi?"

"We would like to maintain total neutrality if at all possible."

"You believe anyone's going to live to tell about it? Well, so be it."

"Fire Control. Con. Prep arrays alpha, beta, echo and foxtrot. Target one missile per array. Launch bays open. Ignition at my order."

"Acknowledged Con."

Thirty-five seconds ticked by. Phil's eyes fixed on the huge bridge chronometer, lips barely, silently moving as he ticked the tactical through his mind.

"Fire Control. Con. Ignition."

"Con. Fire Control. Ignition acknowledged."

Ten of fiery and vapor trails raced from *Gauntlet* in galvanic beauty.

Fifteen seconds ticked by.

"Con. Fire Control. Confirm all arrays launched. Projected impact in... thirty-three seconds."

"Comms. Tactical display."

A large blue screen appeared on the hull. The bridge watched sixteen ballistic trajectories converge and then evaporate. Each Stiletto consumed by a predatory pack of at least a dozen assault missiles.

"Con. Fire Control. Incoming fighters...F-14's...three...they just launched air-to-air missiles...best guess are AIM-7, Sparrows....impact in twenty-two seconds."

Nick rose from his position and strode forward. "Prepare to deploy air-to-air intercepts..."

"Belay that order. Fire Control stand down."

Nick frowned and resumed his seat without comment.

Fire Control complied and responded. "Aye sir...ah...impact in sixteen seconds."

Exactly sixteen seconds later, three explosions swept blue fire across *Gauntlet's* hull, with no appreciable effect.

Phil picked up a tiny comm unit and silently blinked Nick's position.

"Farrow."

"Nick. Phil. Sorry to countermand your order. Your order was quite correct. But I want the belligerents and their masters to see they can't hurt us."

"Understood Phil."

Phil replaced the small unit.

"Fire Control. Con. Any more bogies out there?"

After a brief pause.

"We show thirty aircraft entering our immediate airspace right now sir. Six attack formations. Transferring to tactical."

"Nav. Con. What is our present position?"

"Con. Nav. Altitude thirty-five thousand feet. Climbing fast now. Our rate of ascent is increasing at an exponent...I cannot measure. Azimuth unchanged."

"How long before we exceed the max altitude for enemy aircraft?"

"Assuming their ceiling tops out at about at about nine-zero thousand feet, I would guess we will exceed their vertical range in less than seventy-five seconds."

"Fire Control. Con. Unless the QAVL report an incoming nuke, take no action."

"Aye sir."

Phil paused for a moment.

"No...belay that. Target the lead craft in each attack group and take them out at will. Confirm your kills."

The kills were confirmed within thirty seconds; and *Gauntlet's* hull was bathed in blue fire more than a dozen times before the Spheriscope was filled with an ocean of stars.

Finally. They broke out. The beauty. The quiet. The sublime peace. It hit Phil like a physical blow. It was done. It was all behind them now. The war-birds, the blood, suffering, hatred, ignorance, guilt, destruction. Specters from a past world that would ultimately recede at nearly the speed of light itself.

In a split-second waking dream Phil saw the young girl from Ghazi Kahn struggling in panicked futility up Mount Anastasios reaching out in pathetic supplication to *Gauntlet*, just as the nuclear detonated. She melted as a waxen doll.

With all his training and strength and genetic advancement, the sudden release from Earth's savage vice was overwhelming. The future now held twenty-seven years of study and learning, four-hundred-billion stars, one wondrous planet, and a community of civilizations advanced beyond imagining. Phil could endure no more.

"Mr. Farrow you have the Con."

"Acknowledged."

*Gauntlet* was still a twilight world, so his stilted, hasty retreat went unobserved. After twenty dark meandering minutes, he was plunging into the Oneirion Sea, uniform discarded on the beach. The sea was a deep gray and surprisingly warm, with many familiar denizens to welcome him. A little shallow perhaps. But it would serve well over the decades.

*Why is the sea so warm? Of course! The nuke. Christ, that was going to play hell with sea life. Maybe even the whole ecology of the sphere. Better talk to Qasi about this..*

Phil lay at the bottom of the sea unmoving, unthinking, unbreathing. Easily mistaken for dead. Three hours later he burst from the sea onto the beach. He felt...new.

"Captain on the bridge."

"As you were. I have the con Mr. Farrow."

"Aye sir." Nick left the bridge.

"Helm. Mr. Piper, status, position and velocity if you please."

"All systems nominal. No appreciable damage from the aerial attacks. We are presently some nineteen thousand kilometers from Earth. Holding assigned heading. At our present rate of acceleration we should be at Earth/Moon apogee with the lunar orbit in thirty-six hours."

"Nav. I believe we are due a course correction at that point?"

"Yes sir. At that point we will commence using QAVL nav coordinates and set course towards rendezvous with Saturn."

"We will enter the Asteroid Belt in twenty-eight days."

"And our rate of acceleration?"

"We are pulling a constant three gee's right now." His enthusiasm was contagious. "When we enter the Asteroid Belt we will have achieved an unbelievable twenty-three gee's. And that's on Gravity Drive alone. The real action starts beyond the Kuiper Belt when we engage the Bussard."

"What's our ETA at the Kuiper?"

"We're presently estimating about six months or so. All the numbers I am quoting are fairly rough. Ambassador Qasi is rather adamant we develop our skills in interstellar navigation, QAVL-style."

Phil stared at his DIT a long time.

An odd, enigmatic smile played across his features. His affection for the Ambassador, mitigated somewhat by the now familiar counter-flow twinge. After a time he looked up at the navigator and broke his silence.

"I imagine Ambassador Qasi will counsel us, should we happen to stray...."

# Coda

*The Magical Missive*

*The scourge of Terran life:*

*Carbon based hadronics suffer from a congenital vice.*

*A malignancy, not of their invention.*

*Wretched creatures unable to endure, if bereft of reciprocal carnage.*

*The tyranny of survival obliges such life consume only death.*

*The instrument of their extinction.*

*The torment of all such worlds.*

*A lamentable fate.*

*Such can change their nature no more than darkness to light.*

*Nor ice to fire.*

*We here do not fashion their grim fate.*

*We but accede to it.*

Qasi QaQAVdun46
QAVL Ambassador to Earth QaSol3
Journal of the Quaestor
Temporal Reference: 22-264-193
*Kosmas Kintrekos*

There was a time he inhabited a great aperture in a prodigious edifice that pierced the sky itself. Surrounded by beauty and luxury, frequented by powerful beings that ruled his planet.

When he'd gazed out from that commanding lair, cosseted and secure, he sometimes fancied he could see forever. Yet he had never seen this day. He'd not seen this pitiful bolt-hole, nor this decimated world, this planetary necropolis.

Nearly all feeling was lost to him now, both physical and emotional. Perpetual loneliness was his dogged companion – one of his few remaining – feelings.

There was a time he was regarded as quite handsome. Robust, with a mane of ebon hair, piercing hazel eyes and wonderfully regular, olive complected features. Women were drawn to him in discrete, thoughtful overture. Attracted not only by his allure, or fame, or power, or wealth. But by his serene intelligence and gentle humor. His cherished wife had passed away long ago. He had no family. So the occasional liaison had been a clement source of solace and amity. Generous and tender, of brief but affectionate duration.

Had he the interest to confront a mirror, a shockingly different man would stand before it today. Mercifully, no such device remained to mock his dissipated visage. Nonetheless, he was grimly aware of his wretchedness. It stalked him relentlessly night and day.

His hair had gone. Departed years ago, in shocking clumps, at an alarming rate. He'd lost nearly all his body-mass, muscle, bone and fat alike; and his skin depended loosely from face to thigh. His mind was still sharp, cruelly so, yet his memory surged and ebbed as the tides surrounding his island home. He craved the salt in his austere diet. Luckily, emergency stores furnished it in abundance. In part he simply craved the taste of potassium iodide, his only surviving spice. Unwittingly though, it also conserved his thyroid. And his life. He was unaware of it, but leukemia was creeping into his bones and his blood, and he was constantly plagued with minor infections. Added to this, his digestion was in shambles. Had he known he would not have cared, but he was now sterile and impotent. He would soon be riddled with all manner of cancer. Soon his frail body would scream *abbastanza!* and yield to a weary oblivion.

Dirty weapons had done their work well, soon to consummate their ghoulish work on his corpus, and most of the world.

He was wretched. He had not shaven for years, or washed, or dressed in other than rags soon after assuming sovereignty over this friable underworld realm.

He was Dr. Aoko Itō. Secretary General to the United Nations. Still. None ever having succeeded him to his high office.

From his elegant dwelling high above Manhattan, he had watched in horrified awe as mankind immolated itself.

It began with release of the perplexing DOCUMENT – the QAVLian construct, steganography imbedded with a profoundly intelligent sapience, lurking silently within millions of human digital documents. Dr. Aoko was instrumental in its release. Overtly cognizant of man.. Mankind's heuristic tutor, intended to mentor humans to their ultimate destiny. The DOCUMENT near magically reacted to human events. Rarely suggesting more favorable behavioral alternatives. But always sharing their appraisal of their consequence. The DOCUMENT dynamically adapted, both in length and content, to human evolution, or devolution. It was widely assumed that sometime in the distant future, the DOCUMENT would distill itself and declare man's enterprise consummate, with one of alternate two-word summaries. Either, 1) You survive, or 2) You die.

Mankind selected Door Number 2.

In part, the DOCUMENT was instrumental in launching the most bizarre war in human history. An extinction war. An irreproachable, honorable war. Men were enrapt with the conviction their fight was righteous. For survival. Altruistic and impartial. Without passion, ignorance, bigotry, or self-interest. Wrong on all counts.

They had been ruthlessly beguiled and betrayed. Hoodwinked and hornswoggled. Plummeting satanically into their own execration.

Ruthless conspirators had been insinuating man's world for decades. Their great, apostate gasconade purporting to subjugate man's world to their cruel theocratic intolerance. Not without plundering great wealth and power along the way. As gasoline acts as an accelerator for the arsonist, the QAVL DOCUMENT imparted explosive power to their schemes and the entire world caught fire. Literally overnight.

Far faster than any human could ever conceive, the world burned down.

Senseless attacks. First on a shadowy, evanescent, alien presence, energized and sustained by troops and logistics imbedded in thousands of cities worldwide. Fighters patiently waiting, sometimes decades, for bedlam's call.

The alleged aliens were seemingly ineluctable. Yet, manifestly unproven and unseen. Undeterred, hysteria escalated into attacks on local and national governments. Then governments against governments.

Finally a global orgy of destruction ensued. Like concupiscent lovers burning too long at bay, man's bloodlust was ecstatically requited in a fearsome climax of fire and agony.

The powers of power were utterly duped and consummately ensnared by DOCUMENT psychosis. They recklessly swathed themselves in its beguiling bewilderment, as children incite one another before a yawing cave. They ordered immediate strikes, spearheading planet-wide offensives. Aggression in planning since the West first fashioned a perverse burlesque from selective partitioning of the Middle East.

Miraculously, their tenebrous schemes succeeded – beyond their wildest dreams – beyond their darkest nightmares as well – as a man who struggles and curses and cajoles his comatose car over a hill, only to discover he's pushed it off a cliff. Truly a divine comedy.

Defensive response varied greatly.

Near prostrate impotence in the Middle East – ruthless suppression in the Far East – relentless militarism in Russia – bloody scourges in South and Central America – blundering political paralysis in the U.S. – pitched infighting pervading Europe's long restrained xenophobia – savage atavism throughout Africa – an ominous silence from Austria, New Zealand and the South Pacific.

None allotted beleaguered humanity the smallest modicum of relief. Utterly ineffectual. Butterflies fluttering against a maelstrom. Meanwhile all surviving vestiges of human civilization degenerated into ignomony.

Ultimately, a rashly considered Shahab VI nuclear missile struck into the heart of Shenzhen, end more than eight million lives, and enraging China. Galvanizing the mighty power with the resolve to finally end it.

With but a single word: 成 (Chinese: *Chéngle* /shae-nn-glai/ English: *Enough!*). China unleashed a worldwide nuclear firestorm of unimaginable proportion. As the machete cleaves the head of a snake, it was to be incontrovertibly *ended*.

Sadly, the timing was impossible.

Too early to escape a massive and deadly retaliation.

Too late to save any meaningful vestige of man's world.

The U.S., Russia, Pakistan, India, the UK, France, United Korea, Israel and Iran roused from their lethargy, mounted a titanic reprisal. A shuddering final assault defiantly proclaiming, much as Captain Ahab had blazed at the white whale: *...from Hell's heart, I stab at thee...*

Herman Melville at his best. Mankind at its worst.

Human civilization was now past deliverance. Rescue or recovery beyond man's fleeting horizon. The core of humanity itself seared to cinders. The lucky ones. Billions who never knew why they lived, neither now why they died.

Human dominion was at an end. Earth's apex predator was withdrawing with breathtaking swiftness. The food chain was re-notching. Time to clamber up, or tumble down Darwin's ladder. The new *mise-en-scène* nearing completion. All soon in readiness for the ascendant new Masters of Terra. Whatever sort of creatures they might be.

Dr. Itō now lived in squalor, sequestered and alone, in the highly secret third sub-basement of the huge building he had once ruled. The United Nations Headquarters in New York. The city and the building were much like him. Once strong and dynamic. Now weak, wretched and dying.

It had taken all his ingenuity, and the life of his driver, to flee from Union Square Park to the UN building, years ago. At the time he thought his duty lay here. Perhaps he could help stave Armageddon? Raise the voice of reason. Introduce some much needed humanity.

Too late. All for naught. The UN Headquarters building was among the first of man's citadel to fall victim to man's rage.

The huge, austere Reception Lobby, intended showplace of human hope and achievement, emerged as the polestar of barbaric rituals. As all about him were savagely butchered, Dr. Itō fled to the third sub-basement emergency shelter. Alone. He had hermitted here in total solitude ever since.

He sometimes considered returning to the surface world. The trident tortures: Unrelenting darkness. Incessant loneliness. Maddeningly, endless time. They extracted a terrible toll. Yet each time he braved the surface world it was nearly as dark as below, harboring horrors he was simply unequipped to confront. Among the abominations, any remaining children, near adolescents now, were long feral. Packs of pubescent predators slavering for raw, living flesh. Aoko had barely escaped them. So, year after year, he took copious amounts of vitamin D and calcium, rigged as much battery light as he dared, and persevered. Awaiting death or redemption? He had no idea.

He read. He sometimes he wrote poetry. Cerebral pursuits intended to expiate his rancor, and guilt. Preserve his intellect. His humanity. Nonetheless, despite himself, he slipped inexorably, by imperceptible degrees, into indigence. Each degree, each day, he assiduously recorded on the long concrete wall of his dark refuge.

The building's emergency stores, once intended to sustain hundreds of key staff during crisis, were now his alone. They harbored a vast treasure of uncontaminated rations, water, bedding, medicine, vitamins, books, assorted gadgets; and the batteries to power them far beyond his needs. The chocolate bars developed a whitish patina and tasted like wax. The beans and franks were a delight. The pork loaf was nauseating; and the canned peaches were the zenith of his week. And oh for something of the grape to wash them down. He drove himself to burning thirst in order to down the stale, metallic canned water.

Today was his *Annual Occasion*. The seminal event of his year. THE DAY.

For Dr. Itō this DAY embodied Birthday, Anniversary, New Years, Ramadan, Christmas, Shivarathri, Hanukah, Visakah Puja, Independence Day, Homecoming, the Prom and Graduation. All such fete imbued in the march of but a few hours. A Day he had staidly observed for long years. The *only* Day. The Day he looked forward to with great eagerness, and great trepidation. Yet this particular year, on this particular DAY, his misgivings were nearly palpable. Overshadowing his eagerness. His loneliness. Even the driving hunger of his curiosity.

Today was his Annual Reading of the DOCUMENT. The DOCUMENT he had introduced to the General Assembly himself in this very building years ago. The mystical, magical, monstrous missive that had sparked the destruction of his entire world.

Yet, after all these years, the DOCUMENT had also grown to become a sort of sagacious old friend, whose council he valued above all else. In reality, he *lived* for this one Day – this transcendent communion each year.

Electric torch in hand, he gingerly threaded his way through the ruins of his vast underworld. As he navigated shadows and dust and rats, through the crates and the concrete, the debris and the darkness, he reviewed the dramatic evolution of the DOCUMENT over these many years.

When first introduced, Aoko had found The DOCUMENT pedantic, contemptuous, pompous, abstruse and distant. He thought back to a passage which cut particularly deep. It always haunted him, particularly coming from an alien race:

# Man asserts:

*It is in our nature to destroy ourselves.*

## False:

*It is not in your nature to destroy yourselves.*
*It is in your nature to destroy others.*
*Ironically, with the one, comes the other.*
*Nature lays the trap.*
*True throughout the creation.*

A warning given tragically too late, and heeded too little. And the QAVL knew it. And the QAVL had *always* known it.

In recent years however, the DOCUMENT had grown placidly laconic, and even friendly. At last review it consisted of only five pages, and although Aoko knew it couldn't be true, the DOCUMENT seemed to communicate with only him. Nonetheless it continued to faithfully report, unfalteringly, if even just for him alone. In a real sense it had become a friend and mentor. His alone and only.

Completing the first leg of his dark pilgrimage, he now faced a trial he dreaded more each year. The elevator shaft. Rusting doors jammed open in vacant, gaping blackness. Or, as he had come to think of it, Hell's Well.

Six floors below his sanctuary was the DOCUMENT Chamber. The elevator itself lay crushed in the far remote depths of the shaft. Long forgotten. In younger days, the old man had cobbled together a ladder, part wood, part metal, part chain and cable, which rattled down the shaft from the third to the ninth sub-basement. Over the years, both he and the ladder were noticeably dissipated; and every year the climb grew more fearsome.

Wheezing, with trembling muscles screaming from overexertion, Aoko clambered down the terrifying shaft. Heart racing, he struggled through the rusty doors, exhausted. After a time, he shuffled down the dusty hall to the pristine ambience of the DOCUMENT Chamber. Home to all his fears and hopes. Sterile, modern, secured, reinforced, shielded and masked. Devised by man in his naïve optimism to endure a thousand years, and more.

In all this vast complex this was the one room which still maintained power. Did it come from some submerged dynamo in the East River? A solar panel high above? An unimaginable bank of batteries? An array of generators buried far below? Nuclear? He didn't know. Didn't care. This subterranean pilgrimage could well be his last. He knew that.

The DOCUMENT itself (whatever ethereal substance comprised it) was housed in a sleek protective unit which was powered by a massive cluster of nuclear isotope batteries. Energy that would sustain the DOCUMENT throughout the centuries and far beyond. Although when the unit was installed, many had astutely suspected the DOCUMENT could quite easily survive indefinitely under its own devices.

He keyed in his entry code and covered his eyes as the massive door smoothly rotated outward. Brighter light than he'd seen for a year. After sufficient time his eyes adjusted, and he entered.

The voice cognition interface automatically activated.

He roughly cleared his throat. Dry and congested, it had been twelve months since he had spoken aloud.

"Hello old friend."

*My God, my voice sounds strange. I sound so...old. How old am I anyway?* He elected not to dwell on that question.

"I hope you've passed a good year. If you have, you'd be alone in that respect. I assure you. You know why I'm here; and I trust you've done your homework."

*I must be mad. I talk to this damned thing as though it were human. Then again. What the hell. It's the only thing I've spoken to in more years than I can remember. And it's probably a thousand times smarter than I.*

The sleek beige and gray unit stood tacitly quiescent.

Dr. Itō cleared his throat again. "Open file. DOCUMENT-QAVL-1. Access code Chandresh-ABHAY-55Y."

He peered up into the bright lights and his mind wandered for a moment.

*ABHAY. Dr. Chandresh ABHAY. Nice fellow. He'd been so thrilled when I gave him UNESCON. Poor bastard. They'd burned him like a marshmallow over a campfire. I still hear his screams echoing through the lobby in my nightmares.*

He lowered his head and continued. "Access authority Aoko Itō, United Nations Secretary General, 227-4027. Acknowledge."

"Acknowledged Dr. Itō . Welcome. File open."

"Print."

"Acknowledged."

A single sheet of white paper soundlessly dropped onto a waiting tray.

He regarded the sheet of paper for a time. And finally murmured "Thank you."

The old man slowly found his way to the desk. He withdrew a small pewter flask. Cognac. A Christmas gift from admiring staff years ago. Simple and beautifully crafted, it was adorned with a single imprint: ∞

An anachronistic notion from a time man believed in infinite possibilities.

He carefully mounted his remaining pair of reading glasses. Then he reclined, taking the smallest sip from the flask, savoring each precious drop. The time had come. No putting it off.

He lent forward, scrutinizing the sheet of paper in quivering hands. He read only the opening salutation. Which was sufficient. His hands fell to the desk in resigned despair.

*One sheet. Just one. The final one. One sheet of paper consummating all human history. One sheet adjourning the work, the genius, the courage, the horrors, the beauty, the cowardice, the stupidity and the nobility of man. The magnificent achievements and the magnificent failures of fifty thousand years of pointless struggle.*

*How absurd and futile and sad. A pathetic waste. We were going nowhere. We were always going nowhere. We could have passed fifty millennia in peace and joy..simply enjoying life and caring for one another...simply living in dignity and grace...an epic, radiant dream...squandered in time...*

*What was that mindless acronym he'd heard Philip Carr use? It was crude but descriptive. RF? Yes. RF. Rat Fuck. The words were bitter ashes in his mouth.*

*It was all just an RF... one long Rat Fuck..And now, just one goddamned, Rat Fucking sheet of paper.*

A hot tear raced down his cheek, dropping to the paper. Another leaked a blur onto his glasses. His heart began to race. Fear churned in his bowels. The bitter secretion of bile and the desiccation of dust warred in his mouth.

*This is it.*
*Really it.*
*Just one goddamned sheet.*
His mind turned to his long departed wife.
It spoke to her.
*Chiyo. Beloved. Thanks God you are dead.*
*This piece of paper is worse than death. Our final judgment.*
*I couldn't fear it more, were it written by the hand of God Himself. I dread it more than death. It is the essence of....*
He needed a moment to find the word.
*...dispassion.*
He read...

## *Ultimus Amitto*

*Our journey together has ended.*
*Your journey utterly, has ended.*
*We have journeyed such with more specie than there be stars in your sky.*
*Most end as yours.*

*Acrimony is not your due.*
*Despondency is not your due.*
*You strode this planet for your accorded term.*
*That is the measure of your due.*

*The stars are cold.*
*But not without purpose.*
*We seek that purpose.*
*That is our due.*

*Consider previous communiqués.*
*Your own words indict.*
*Cambodia.*
*The Khmer Rouge:*
*"To preserve you is no gain.*
*To destroy you is no loss."*
*Prescient words.*
*Prophetic words.*

*Monstrous hubris*
*Yet true.*
*True of a million-million worlds.*
*Terra is but one.*
*Creation's cull.*
*Wretched worlds, spawning life addicted to death.*
*Putrescent buds propagating necrosis from within.*
*Arborary – animalia – nullus differentia.*

*Countenance this:*
*You will never know.*
*You will never understand.*

*Oneiro II: Gauntlet*

***There be no other course.***
***A course plot before you star awakened its fire.***
***A course plot at the parturition of existence itself.***

***Yet your seed ascends to the stars.***
***Such seed may one day know and understand.***
***Commend serendipity beyond credent.***
***For Terra though,***
***Dreams pass.***

**Godspeed**

The old man pondered the note for a time. Calm now.
*It seems Consul Carr survives.*
*Good.*
*I suppose.*
*I think he will be alone soon.*
*Alone in all infinity.*
*God help him.*
*How many years since he exploded out of that mountainside?*
*And sealed the fate of all mankind...*

The sheet of paper slipped through his fingers, falling mutely to the floor.

Aoko carefully placed his reading glasses on the desk and drained the remaining contents of his flask. Gratefully. Like air and blue sky to a drowning man. Eyes closed, head back, he held the flask to his chest for a moment. Then, eyes open, he lent forward and positioned it next to his reading glasses.

He took a long, deep rattling breath, placed both hands flat on his desk, and simply stared for a long time. He silently mouthed a poem he had once written in this shadowy crypt. A quatrain:

*The silent writhe of the Beast sinuates round the fustian Dove.*
*Whose voguish coos betray the vigilant with smug, dilettante love.*
*T'is then He strikes. Snuffs Dove and love and oppugnant phalanx and all.*
*Till Dove woos anew, we be the Beast. Frenzied hellions in His thrall.*

When the time had passed, he cherished but one remaining thought.
His long beloved and lamented *Chiyo*.
His dolorous eyes mirrored the wistful, bittersweet ardor of his reverie.
Finally he rose and slowly faltered to the massive door.
With a crooked smile, he looked back at the unit and whispered "Goodbye."
He closed and sealed the DOCUMENT Chamber. Its rapturous illumination now forever imprisoned.
Aoko turned, activated his torch, and shuffled down the long, dim corridor.
When he reached shaft's dark abyss, he didn't mount the aging ladder.
He simply stepped out...

# *Dramatis Persona*

Senior Crew *Gauntlet*:
Captain – Philip Carr
First Officer – Commander Nick Farrow XO
Chief Engineer – Lt. Cmdr. Mark Oikodomos
Science Officer – Dr. Mark Gray
Helm – Lt. Henry Piper
Navigator – Lt. Susan Dei
Communications Officer – Lt. Joanna Winn
Sergeant at Arms – Lt. Cmdr. Jonathan Burns
Information Officer – Lt. Cmdr. Franco Jorge
Chief Medical Officer – Dr. Gordon Singe

Crew Sea Tigress:
Mr. Herbert Carr – Captain
Mr. Philip Carr – Owner
Mr. Demetrious Diamantes – 1st Mate
Dr. Anne Jones – 2nd Mate

Landers on Oneiro:
Dr. Anne Jones – Professor of Arts
Ms Aiyana Atsila – Reporter, Traitor, lover of Philip Carr & Anne Jones
Dr. Enoch Wilson – Professor of Applied Sciences
Dr. Emily Johansen – Professor of Genetics
Dr. Simon Butler – University Resident Chief Cuisenaire
Dr. Jackson Gear – Chief of Medicine and Managing Director of the Nursery
Dr. Judy McLean – Professor of Languages, Culture & Literature
Dr. Eve Dunedin – Professor of Psychology and Administrator of the Ordeal
Dr. Sean Gray – Realization Administrator
Mr. Edward McKnight – Personal Assistant to Philip Carr
Mr. Howard Doyle – Head of the Chicago security firm Doyle & Phillips
Mr. Charlie Stein – Director of Communications
Mr. Richardson – Executive VP Finance

QAVL
Qasi – *Qasi QaQAVdun46*
   *Ambassador of the QAVL to Earth QaSol3*

Islanders on Oneiro:
Mr. Mike Auslander – Patron of Oneiro
Dr. Mark Gray – Sciences
Dr. Thomas Rio – Genetics

Dr. Richard McCloud – Cuisenaire
Dr. Gordon Singe – Medicine
Dr. Robert Brown – Religion & Philosophy
Dr. Sochi Inchowa – Languages
Dr. Alberto Omani – Psychology
Dr. Michael Dundee – Realization

Pakistan and Afghanistan:
Bahaar Fatin al din Ammar – Pakistani Assassin, Slaver & Smuggler
    Son of Prince Rashid al din Ammar
Manu – Afghani Slave, mother of Amira

New York:
Dr. Chandresh ABHAY – Director United Nations Extra-Solar Contact
Dr. Aoko Itō – United Nations Secretary General
Ajisaka – Unspecified delegate to the United Nations
Gregory – Unspecified delegate to the United Nations

Goldenberg@atss.lu

Made in the USA
Charleston, SC
26 June 2010